THE CONTEMPORARY ESSAY

BOOKS BY DONALD HALL

Books of Poetry

Exiles and Marriages, 1955
The Dark Houses, 1958
A Roof of Tiger Lilies, 1964
The Alligator Bride: Poems New and Selected, 1969
The Yellow Room: Love Poems, 1971
The Town of Hill, 1975
Kicking the Leaves, 1978

Books of Prose

String Too Short to Be Saved, 1961
Henry Moore, 1966
Writing Well, 1973, 1976, 1979, 1982
Playing Around (with G. McCauley et al.), 1974
Dock Ellis in the Country of Baseball, 1976
Goatfoot Milktongue Twinbird, 1978
Remembering Poets, 1978
Ox-Cart Man, 1979
To Keep Moving, 1981
The Weather for Poetry, 1982

Edited Works

New Poets of England and America (with R. Pack and L. Simpson),
    1957
The Poetry Sampler, 1961
New Poets of England and America (Second Selection) (with R. Pack),
    1962
Contemporary American Poets, 1962, 1971
A Concise Encyclopedia of English and American Poetry and Poets
    (with Stephen Spender), 1963
Poetry in English, 1963, 1970 (with Warren Taylor)
The Faber Book of Modern Verse (New Edition with Supplement),
    1965
The Modern Stylists, 1968
A Choice of Whitman's Verse, 1968
Man and Boy, 1968
American Poetry, 1970
A Writer's Reader (with D. L. Emblen), 1976, 1979, 1982
Oxford Book of American Literary Anecdotes, 1981
To Read Literature, 1981, 1982
Claims for Poetry, 1982

THE
CONTEMPORARY
ESSAY

EDITED BY

Donald Hall

A Bedford Book

ST. MARTIN'S PRESS · NEW YORK

For Nan and Dick Smart

Library of Congress Catalog Card Number: 83–61620
Copyright © 1984 by St. Martin's Press, Inc.
All Rights Reserved.
Manufactured in the United States of America
8 7 6 5 4
f e d c b a
For information, write St. Martin's Press, Inc.,
175 Fifth Avenue, New York, N.Y. 10010
Editorial Offices: Bedford Books of St. Martin's Press
165 Marlborough Street, Boston, MA 02116

ISBN: 0–312–16667–2

Typography: Anna Post
Cover Design: Richard S. Emery

ACKNOWLEDGMENTS

Edward Abbey, "The Most Beautiful Place on Earth." Reprinted from *Desert Solitaire* by permission of Don Congdon Associates, Inc. Copyright © 1968 by Edward Abbey.

Roger Angell, "Sharing the Beat." From *Late Innings*, copyright © 1982 by Roger Angell. Reprinted by permission of Simon & Schuster, Inc.

Michael J. Arlen, "The Cold Bright Charms of Immortality." From *The View From Highway 1* by Michael J. Arlen. Copyright © 1974, 1975, 1976 by Michael J. Arlen. Reprinted by permission of Farrar, Straus and Giroux, Inc.

James Baldwin, "Notes of a Native Son." From *Notes of a Native Son* by James Baldwin. Copyright © 1955 by James Baldwin. Reprinted by permission of Beacon Press.

Jeremy Bernstein, "Calculators: Self-Replications." Originally titled "When the Computer Procreates" in *The New York Times Magazine* February 15, 1976. © 1976 by The New York Times Company. Reprinted by permission.

Wendell Berry, "The Making of a Marginal Farm." Excerpted from *Recollected Essays 1965–1980*. © 1981 by Wendell Berry. Published by North Point Press. All rights reserved.

(Continued on page 483)

Preface
for Instructors

The Contemporary Essay is intended for composition instructors who believe, as I do, that much of the best recent writing in America is nonfiction — and who regret that more of this excellent writing does not appear in composition anthologies because it defies rhetorical or thematic classification. Instructors who use this book will demand from their students sustained attention to essays that are longer and more challenging than usual. But good prose and good thinking require each other; a composition course that demands more attentive and thoughtful reading will encourage attentive and thoughtful writing.

The Introduction that follows speaks to the diversity of the writers assembled here. This anthology could have been three times as long without lowering its standards; my final selection of thirty-four essays was necessarily arbitrary. I arrived at the mix by seeking diversity in tone, in level of difficulty, in strategy, and in subject matter: *The Contemporary Essay* entertains matters of economics and fashion, dinosaurs and hamburgers, surgery and the marginal farm.

The chronological arrangement of the essays makes for arbitrary juxtaposition. But any rhetorical or thematic organization would belie the actual range and variety of these essays. Very few could easily associate under one topic heading; no essay exemplifies only one rhetorical device.

In both its choice of selections and its editorial apparatus, *The Contemporary Essay* tries to avoid the condescension to students endemic to so many composition anthologies. I assume that students have dictionaries; I assume that the class uses a rhetoric or a handbook. Therefore, I do not footnote words easily available in dictionaries or gloss common rhetorical terms. The Introduction gives advice about reading in general, and the headnotes supply help toward reading each essay. After each selection, I provide questions under a variety of headings — questions about content and about strategies or style, explorations further afield, comparisons between essays, and topics for writing. These questions should be useful not only in class discussion but also for students reviewing the essays before rereading. At the back of the book is an index to passages that illustrate the rhetorical modes. An instructor's manual continues the discussion initiated by the questions.

My debts in assembling this collection are many. I am indebted to writers and editors, to my old teachers and to colleagues at the University of Michigan where I taught for many years. I am indebted to students. In recent years, I have talked about teaching exposition with composition staffs at many colleges and universities, from Lynchburg College in Virginia to the University of Utah in Salt Lake, from the University of New Hampshire to Pacific Lutheran in Tacoma, Washington. I wish to express my gratitude to more people than I can name.

More locally, I am indebted to Jane Kenyon who proofread, to Lois Fierro who typed (and re-typed, and re-re-typed). At Bedford Books, I am always indebted to Charles Christensen, who approached me about this book remembering my wistful notion of years ago. I am grateful as well to Joan Feinberg, who helped early, and to Sue Warne, who helped late. I am grateful to Tim Evans for help with the questions after the essays, and to Margaret Holmes for her answers in the Instructor's Manual. I am grateful to Nancy Lyman and to Ann Packer for many specific chores. I am grateful to Barbara Flanagan, who copy-edited this immense manuscript, and to Helen LaFleur who saved me from many errors. Donald McQuade gave excellent and useful advice, especially when I was planning this book.

D. H.
Wilmot, New Hampshire

Contents

A man of letters reflects on the particularities of turning eighty: vanity, stinginess, pain, weariness — and the dignity of refusing to give up.

Watching a young woman perform on a circus horse, this master of the modern essay reflects on eternal things — and on the passion and injustice of the day.

CONTENTS

CONTENTS

CONTENTS

CONTENTS

Introduction for Students

On These Writers and Their Work

Often one literary form dominates an era. In Shakespeare's time the play was the thing, and lyric poets and pamphleteers wrote for the stage when they turned aside from their primary work. A few decades ago, American novelists wrote novels when they could afford to, but paid their bills by writing short stories for *Colliers* and the *Saturday Evening Post*. Today the same novelists under different names — Norman Mailer, Joan Didion, John Updike, James Baldwin — become masters of the essay, for we live in an age of exposition.

We live in a time bewildered by the multiplicity of information; we cherish the selection and organization of information by our best writers. We live in a time that allows writers freedom to choose what they investigate, to follow their thoughts wherever they lead, and to use a variety of styles and strategies. Therefore the essay thrives, and many of our best essayists are writers for whom, as Annie Dillard puts it, the essay is "the real work." Obviously it was always the real work for E. B. White. In our age, we are also fortunate to read essayists whose real work is science — the exposition of technology is a major necessity — and who write brilliant prose in the service of medicine, economics, and paleontology. We are fortunate also in an extraordinary group of women now writing on diverse matters: Alison Lurie, Frances FitzGerald, Diane Johnson, Annie Dillard. The editor's burden, in this age of exposition, is to choose wisely and representatively among the dazzling variety of the best. We have tried for diversity of author, style, and subject.

Contemporary factual writing explores the universe. This book begins with an account of old age written by an octogenarian; then an essay describes a circus scene — only to leap sideways and engage the subject of racism; next an economist analyzes the structure of American corporations. Our writers explain, describe, narrate, argue, and reminisce about childhood, men and women, the Arizona desert, bad habits of the civilized mind, fast food, dinosaurs, education, rape, a marginal farm in Kentucky, surgery, the fourteenth century, baseball, astronauts, the history of medicine, snobbishness, a Republican political convention, clothing, computers, television, oranges, murder, mothers, and nuclear holocaust. Nothing human is alien to the essay.

As subjects of these essays vary, so do their length and difficulty. Walker Percy's philosophical ideas and John Kenneth Galbraith's observations on corporate structure both make difficult work for the reader, but the difficulty is appropriate and necessary: If such paragraphs were not hard to read, they would oversimplify their subjects and misrepresent them. At the other extreme, Calvin Trillin's reminiscences of Kansas City hamburgers and Eudora Welty's of a neighborhood store do not tax our attention; here, difficulty would be inappropriate.

These essays also vary in their strategies. Alison Lurie speaks of clothing by constructing a long and ingenious analogy to language. Richard Rodriguez describes his growing up, using personal narrative for purposes of persuasion, as he discusses ethnicity and bilingualism. Mounting an argument about medicine and scientific research, Lewis Thomas establishes his premises by a narrative of medical history. These differences in strategy derive partly from subject matter, but also from the diverse abilities and interests of their authors. Even if Lurie wrote about medicine, and Thomas about fashions and clothing — an improbability we might enjoy imagining — their strategies would differ.

These diversities show in voice and tone. It pleases John McPhee to use his skill partly in self-effacement; this author's talent renders the author invisible behind his subject matter. On the other hand, no one will accuse Norman Mailer of invisibility; his essays often feature a character called ''Norman Mailer,'' sometimes under a pseudonym like ''Aquarius.'' Even when he writes scientific exposition, with a studious clarity, his own personality remains visible and becomes a part of his strategy of exposition. Other writers like Annie Dillard (and, in a different way, Jeremy Bernstein) include themselves in their stories. Some like Tom Wolfe leave themselves out but fly the flag of an idiosyncratic style. Frances FitzGerald and Jonathan Schell, more like John McPhee, cultivate an art by which the story tells itself.

In subjects and strategies, this book offers a diversity for study. Yet when we look at the prose of these writers from a distance — for instance, from the vantage point of another century's style — we realize that certain agreements about writing unite the distinct minds of Truman Capote and Roger Angell, E. B. White and Frances FitzGerald. These writers agree, by and large, to use the concrete detail in place of the abstraction; to employ the active not the passive mood; to withhold the adjective and search for the verb. They agree to pursue clarity and vigor. And most would agree with Robert Graves (English poet, novelist, and essayist), who said some years ago: "The writing of good English is . . . a moral matter."

Graves wrote these words in the late 1930s, shortly before George Orwell (novelist and pamphleteer, author of *Animal Farm* and *1984*) wrote "Politics and the English Language," an essay which introduced or codified many assumptions about modern prose style. Orwell noted that the vices of vagueness, triteness, jargon, and pomposity are often not merely errors; often they serve the purposes of deceit. A clear prose style will not deceive others, and will help the writer to avoid self-deceit. Even earlier, the American poet Ezra Pound had talked about closing the "gap between one's real and one's declared meaning." Bad writers are vague ones. The novelist Ernest Hemingway said: "If a man writes clearly, anyone can see if he fakes." These writers reached a consensus which emphasized, in Pound's words, that "good writers are those who keep the language efficient . . . accurate . . . clear."

Much good nonfiction works the way an efficient machine works, by directness that matches energy to production. A sentence is good the way an ax handle is good. Order and organization move from writer's mind to reader's by the ethics of clarity in sentence structure and transition. For good prose to aid us, both socially and psychologically, it need not speak of society nor psyche; for good style, all by itself, *is* good politics and good mental hygiene. Thus John McPhee, who writes without revealing his values, contributes to ethics by the lucidity, clarity, and vigor of his exposition.

But efficiency and clarity are not the only values we derive from good style. It is true that sentences show us around the surface of the globe, lead us from one place to another; but sentences also dig beneath the earth's surface. The subjectivity of much contemporary writing — private feelings publicly exposed — provides a model for self-examination. Thus we find room not only for John McPhee but also for Annie Dillard, with whom we explore underworlds of feeling. If she did not write with the efficiency and clarity of a John McPhee, her self-exploration would reveal nothing. But because she writes with intense clarity about matters seldom regarded as clear, the light of the imagination blazes in a dark place.

On Reading Essays

We read to become more human. When we read *Gilgamesh* — the oldest surviving narrative, a Babylonian epic from two thousand B.C. — we connect with other human beings. We raise a glass across four thousand years of time and drink with our ancestors the old wine of friendship, courage, loss, and the will to survive. And in *The Contemporary Essay*, when we read Jeremy Bernstein on scientific history or Alice Walker on her mother, we find another kind of linkage. We connect, not across chasms of millenia, but across contemporary gaps of knowledge and experience. We read for information and pleasure together. We read to understand, to investigate, to provide background for decision, to find confirmation, to find contradiction.

We also read in order to learn how to write. If we study architecture, we learn in part by studying structures already designed and built. If we study basketball, we learn in part by watching other players dribble, drive to the left, and shoot. Although in learning anything we add our own flourishes, develop our talents and overcome our drawbacks, we build on things that others did before us. For the writer of essays today, the things done are the essays written yesterday. We build on others' work and add our own uniqueness. Many professional writers, not only students in composition classes, prepare for the day's work by reading an admirable example of the kind of prose they undertake — for the example of excellence, the encouragement of brilliance, the stimulation of achievement.

APPROPRIATE READING

Reading is as various as writing is. If we read well we read differently according to what we read. Suppose when we eat breakfast we look at a daily paper; later in the day we take on a philosophical essay, a poem, a chemistry assignment, *People* magazine, and the instructions in a box of film. If we try reading the newspaper as we should read the poem, nightfall will find us halfway through the first section. If we try reading the philosophy essay as we read *People*, the essay passes us by. Every piece of print requires a different level of attention; good readers adjust their speed automatically when they read the first words of anything. Something tells them: "Slow down or you'll miss out!" or "Speed up or you'll bore yourself to death!"

In our education, in the culture that shapes us, we acquire unconscious habits of reading. Some habits are good, some bad. It helps to become conscious of how we read; it helps to learn appropriate reading.

ACTIVE READING

A century ago, even sixty years ago, silent reading was noisier to the mental ear, because people were used to hearing books read aloud. Long church services included much reading of scripture. Home entertainment was reading aloud from novels, scripture, or poetry. Public entertainment — before radio, films, or television — was lectures, debates, and dramatic recitation. In school students memorized pieces for speaking and read aloud to their classmates. Because students practiced recitation themselves, they could not read a text in silence without considering how they would say it out loud. Unconsciously, as they read alone, they decided in what tone or with what feeling they would enunciate each word.

Mental mimickry makes for *active* reading. We cannot supply the tone of a word unless we understand its meaning. Nowadays, most of us grow up passive readers. Our passivity is encouraged by television, which provides everything for us, even a laughtrack to tell us when to laugh. This collection of essays is intended for students who want more than printed television. These essays require active reading.

A few years ago I taught a composition class in which I assigned an article by Richard Rhodes called "Packaged Sentiment." This essay about greeting cards came out in *Harper's*, addressed to an audience which would expect to find that magazine contemptuous of prefabricated emotions. But the sophisticated author took pains to explore the opposite of the preconception; he made a limited, reasonable defense of the greeting card industry. At the end of his argument, he quoted an English novelist's qualified praise of a political institution: "I celebrate [greeting] cards as E. M. Forster celebrated democracy, with a hearty two cheers." When my students came to class that morning I wrote on the blackboard: "Five minutes. Why *two* cheers?" I expected them to tell me why Rhodes's praise was incomplete. They told me something different: They told me what Rhodes found to praise about greeting cards, as if I had asked, "Why two *cheers*?"

My students were victims of passive reading. They read Rhodes's essay, and accepted "two cheers" without asking themselves, "Why two rather than twelve, or one, or ten million?" When I said this much at the next meeting of the class, three or four students slapped their palms on their foreheads — the classic gesture: "How *could* I have missed that one?" These students learned a lesson; they had neglected to read actively, and to note that Richard Rhodes withheld one third of the normal tribute: "Three Cheers! Hip Hip Hooray! Hip Hip Hooray! Hip Hip Hooray!"

Those students who got the point should never again forget that three is the normal number for cheers. But how would they keep from making the same kind of mistake in further reading? How would they learn to read actively, engaging the text, requiring the text to make sense? Here is a series of answers to these questions.

1. *Learn the model for active reading.* Put the author on the witness stand and make him tell not only the truth, but the whole truth. Give the author the benefit of the doubt — expect him to reveal himself if you work hard at it — but be prepared on occasion to discover that the author, rather than the reader, is at fault (illogic, missed step in an argument, unfairness, lack of support).

2. *Adjust the speed of your reading.* Learn to adjust your reading to an appropriate speed. Most of these essays ought to be read slowly, but their demands will vary. It should take twice as long to read a page of Annie Dillard as it does to read a page by Joan Didion. (I refer to the essays by these writers in this book. Joan Didion is sometimes, appropriately, slower reading, and Annie Dillard faster.) If you tend to read quickly, learn to slow down when it is appropriate. If you tend to read slowly, make sure that your slowness results from close attention to the text, and not from a wandering mind. But be neither a slow reader nor a fast one: Be an appropriate reader, adjusting your speed to the text you are reading.

3. *Take notes as you read.* Everyone should take reading notes; they help to make sure that you understand *as* you read. Pause regularly, perhaps at the end of each paragraph, at least at the end of every page or two, to inspect yourself and your text. Underline the most crucial sentences, passages with which you tentatively disagree, and phrases you need to return to. Ask yourself: Do I know where we are and how we got there? Why are we entertaining *this* subject, in *this* essay? Try to answer yourself, in a note. Write in a notebook or on the margin of the page. When you commit yourself by writing a note, often you recognize that your understanding is less secure than you had considered it.

4. *Look up what you need to know.* Learn what it is appropriate to know exactly, and what you can understand approximately. If an essayist on medicine refers to "the etiology of disease," we need to understand the word "etiology" in order to follow the sense. We turn to the dictionary. On the other hand, the essayist may refer to a particular disease by a long Latinate name, in a context where we understand that the word is an example and that the exact nature of the disease (which we could discover scurrying from definition to definition in a dictionary) is irrelevant to our understanding of the sentence. Learn what to look up, and learn what not to look up; this knowledge resembles social tact. If you are in doubt, look it up, but mature readers when they read Lewis Thomas need not trace down "subacute bacterial endocarditis" in a dictionary. They can figure out the first two words and they need not know the third: They know a "for instance" when they see one.

5. *Read and re-read.* Most important: Read, re-read, and re-read again. When your teacher assigns an essay, read it through the first time as soon as you can. Read the headnote first; read the essay at an appropriate speed,

pausing to interrogate it; take notes and underline; use a dictionary. Then read the questions that follow the essay. Using the questions as a guide, think the essay over. Consult your notes, look back at the text for difficult points, think about the whole essay — and then sleep on it. It is useful to come back to *anything* a second time after an interval, especially after sleep-work. Never write a paper or read an essay once only, at one sitting, even if it is a long sitting.

When you return to the essay a day later, re-read the questions first, and keep them in mind as you re-read the essay. Re-read the headnote, which should be more useful the second time. Re-read the essay more slowly, now that you know its plot, and take further notes. Take notes on the questions. Take notes on your notes.

6. *Make your own list.* Finally, there are problems that vary from reader to reader. Think about your *own* problems in reading, before you begin to read each essay assigned. Study your own reading to identify mistakes made in the past. ("How did I manage *not* to notice that 'two cheers' is a diminution of 'three cheers'?") When a neighbor in class finds more in an essay than you found, interrogate yourself. What in your reading prevented you from getting it all?

Keep a list, at the front of a reading notebook, of injunctions that you need to remember. "Pause after every page to summarize." "Watch for transitions." "Look up words." Toward the end of term, maybe you can cross some injunctions out.

Everyone assigned this textbook knows how to read. Everyone can improve as a reader.

When we improve as readers we improve as writers. By observing Malcolm Cowley or John McPhee or Annie Dillard solve a problem in writing, be it as small as a transition or as large as an essay's whole shape, we add to our own equipment for solving problems of style and construction. By reading we also improve as human beings; we increase our ability to absorb the history of our species, preserved in the language of the tribe through time, and in the language of our contemporaries in an age of the essay.

THE
CONTEMPORARY
ESSAY

MALCOLM
COWLEY

*M*AYBE MALCOLM COWLEY (b. 1898) *looks back on "The View from 80"
as youthful work. Five years after he wrote the piece, vigorous essays continue to emerge from his Connecticut house, often in commemoration of younger
writers, now dead, whom Cowley befriended at the beginnings of their careers. His
affectionate, acute reminiscence of the novelist and short-story writer John Cheever
appeared in the* Sewanee Review *in 1983.*

*Cowley has much to look back on. He drove an ambulance during World War I,
interrupting his studies at Harvard, and when he graduated in 1920 he returned to
France, where literary Americans lived as expatriates in those days. Cowley published his first book of poems,* Blue Juniata, *in 1929 — and almost forty years later
he used the same title for his collected poems. Back in the United States he became an
editor at the* New Republic *and a free-lance writer, professions he has combined ever
since. He has been literary adviser for the Viking Press since 1948 and has written
many books about writers and writing.* Exile's Return *is best known, chronicling
the expatriate generation Cowley belonged to. It appeared first in 1934 and, extensively revised, in 1951.*

*Age has not slowed him down. Who's Who lists five books published by Cowley
after the age of seventy, almost as many as he published before the age of seventy. His*

1

most recent books, criticism and literary reminiscence, include A Second Flowering *(1973),* And I Worked at the Writer's Trade *(1978), and* The Dream of the Golden Mountains *(1980). In 1981 he received the Gold Medal of the American Academy of Arts and Letters.*

It made good sense for the editors of Life *magazine to ask him in 1978 to write about turning eighty — a commission that prompted "The View from 80." Later the essay became the first chapter of a book with the same title, which makes a metaphor of age as vantage point. Cowley writes as a traveler reporting on a landscape many of us will not live to visit. As a writer he knows how to gather and assemble varied material. In this essay Cowley includes research on the literature and scholarship of old age as well as his personal experience of the phenomenon. Notice how he integrates different kinds of material and how his attitude toward old age shows itself both in direct statement and, by implication, in the mountaintop he writes from.*

The View from 80

They gave me a party on my 80th birthday in August 1978. First there were cards, letters, telegrams, even a cable of congratulation or condolence; then there were gifts, mostly bottles; there was catered food and finally a big cake with, for some reason, two candles (had I gone back to very early childhood?). I blew the candles out a little unsteadily. Amid the applause and clatter I thought about a former custom of the Northern Ojibwas when they lived on the shores of Lake Winnipeg. They were kind to their old people, who remembered and enforced the ancient customs of the tribe, but when an old person became decrepit, it was time for him to go. Sometimes he was simply abandoned, with a little food, on an island in the lake. If he deserved special honor, they held a tribal feast for him. The old man sang a death song and danced, if he could. While he was still singing, his son came from behind and brained him with a tomahawk.

That was quick, it was dignified, and I wonder whether it was any more cruel, essentially, than some of our civilized customs or inadvertences in disposing of the aged. I believe in rites and ceremonies. I believe in big parties for special occasions such as an 80th birthday. It is a sort of belated bar mitzvah, since the 80-year-old, like a Jewish adolescent, is entering a new stage of life; let him (or her) undergo a *rite de passage*, with toasts and a cantor. Seventy-year-olds, or septuas, have the illusion of being middle-aged, even if they have been pushed back on a shelf. The 80-year-old, the octo, looks at the double-dumpling figure and admits that he is old. The last act has begun, and it will be the test of the play.

He has joined a select minority that numbers, in this country, 4,842,000   3
persons (according to Census Bureau estimates for 1977), or about two percent of the American population. Two-thirds of the octos are women, who
have retained the good habit of living longer than men. Someday you, the
reader, will join that minority, if you escape hypertension and cancer, the
two killers, and if you survive the dangerous years from 75 to 79, when half
the survivors till then are lost. With advances in medicine, the living space
taken over by octos is growing larger year by year.

To enter the country of age is a new experience, different from what you   4
supposed it to be. Nobody, man or woman, knows the country until he has
lived in it and has taken out his citizenship papers. Here is my own report,
submitted as a road map and guide to some of the principal monuments.

The new octogenarian feels as strong as ever when he is sitting back in a   5
comfortable chair. He ruminates, he dreams, he remembers. He doesn't
want to be disturbed by others. It seems to him that old age is only a costume assumed for those others; the true, the essential self is ageless. In a
moment he will rise and go for a ramble in the woods, taking a gun along, or
a fishing rod, if it is spring. Then he creaks to his feet, bending forward to
keep his balance, and realizes that he will do nothing of the sort. The body
and its surroundings have their messages for him, or only one message:
"You are old." Here are some of the occasions on which he receives the
message:

- when it becomes an achievement to do thoughtfully, step by step, what
  he once did instinctively
- when his bones ache
- when there are more and more little bottles in the medicine cabinet, with
  instructions for taking four times a day
- when he fumbles and drops his toothbrush (butterfingers)
- when his face has bumps and wrinkles, so that he cuts himself while
  shaving (blood on the towel)
- when year by year his feet seem farther from his hands
- when he can't stand on one leg and has trouble pulling on his pants
- when he hesitates on the landing before walking down a flight of stairs
- when he spends more time looking for things misplaced than he spends
  using them after he (or more often his wife) has found them
- when he falls asleep in the afternoon
- when it becomes harder to bear in mind two things at once
- when a pretty girl passes him in the street and he doesn't turn his head
- when he forgets names, even of people he saw last month ("Now I'm beginning to forget nouns," the poet Conrad Aiken said at 80)
- when he listens hard to jokes and catches everything but the snapper

- when he decides not to drive at night anymore
- when everything takes longer to do — bathing, shaving, getting dressed or undressed — but when time passes quickly, as if he were gathering speed while coasting downhill. The year from 79 to 80 is like a week when he was a boy.

Those are some of the intimate messages. "Put cotton in your ears and pebbles in your shoes," said a gerontologist, a member of that new profession dedicated to alleviating all maladies of old people except the passage of years. "Pull on rubber gloves. Smear Vaseline over your glasses, and there you have it: instant aging." Not quite. His formula omits the messages from the social world, which are louder, in most cases, than those from within. We start by growing old in other people's eyes, then slowly we come to share their judgment.

I remember a morning many years ago when I was backing out of the parking lot near the railroad station in Brewster, New York. There was a near collision. The driver of the other car jumped out and started to abuse me; he had his fists ready. Then he looked hard at me and said, "Why, you're an old man." He got back into his car, slammed the door, and drove away, while I stood there fuming. "I'm only 65," I thought. "He wasn't driving carefully. I can still take care of myself in a car, or in a fight, for that matter."

My hair was whiter — it may have been in 1974 — when a young woman rose and offered me her seat in a Madison Avenue bus. That message was kind and also devastating. "Can't I even stand up?" I thought as I thanked her and declined the seat. But the same thing happened twice the following year, and the second time I gratefully accepted the offer, though with a sense of having diminished myself. "People are right about me," I thought while wondering why all those kind gestures were made by women. Do men now regard themselves as the weaker sex, not called upon to show consideration? All the same it was a relief to sit down and relax.

A few days later I wrote a poem, "The Red Wagon," that belongs in the record of aging:

> For his birthday they gave him a red express wagon
> with a driver's high seat and a handle that steered.
> His mother pulled him around the yard.
> "Giddyap," he said, but she laughed and went off
> to wash the breakfast dishes.
>
> "I wanta ride too," his sister said,
> and he pulled her to the edge of a hill.
> "Now, sister, go home and wait for me,
> but first give a push to the wagon."

He climbed again to the high seat,
this time grasping that handle-that-steered.
The red wagon rolled slowly down the slope,
then faster as it passed the schoolhouse
and faster as it passed the store,
the road still dropping away.
Oh, it was fun.

But would it ever stop?
Would the road always go downhill?

The red wagon rolled faster.
Now it was in strange country.
It passed a white house he must have dreamed about,
deep woods he had never seen,
a graveyard where, something told him, his sister was buried.

Far below
the sun was sinking into a broad plain.

The red wagon rolled faster.
Now he was clutching the seat, not even trying to steer.
Sweat clouded his heavy spectacles.
His white hair streamed in the wind.

Even before he or she is 80, the aging person may undergo another iden- 10
tity crisis like that of adolescence. Perhaps there had also been a middle-
aged crisis, the male or the female menopause, but the rest of adult life he
had taken himself for granted, with his capabilities and failings. Now, when
he looks in the mirror, he asks himself, "Is this really me?" — or he avoids
the mirror out of distress at what it reveals, those bags and wrinkles. In his
new makeup he is called upon to play a new role in a play that must be im-
provised. André Gide, that long-lived man of letters, wrote in his journal,
"My heart has remained so young that I have the continual feeling of playing a part, the part of the 70-year-old that I certainly am; and the infirmities
and weaknesses that remind me of my age act like a prompter, reminding
me of my lines when I tend to stray. Then, like the good actor I want to be, I
go back into my role, and I pride myself on playing it well."

In his new role the old person will find that he is tempted by new vices, 11
that he receives new compensations (not so widely known), and that he may
possibly achieve new virtues. Chief among these is the heroic or merely ob-
stinate refusal to surrender in the face of time. One admires the ships that go
down with all flags flying and the captain on the bridge.

Among the vices of age are avarice, untidiness, and vanity, which last 12
takes the form of a craving to be loved or simply admired. Avarice is the

worst of those three. Why do so many old persons, men and women alike, insist on hoarding money when they have no prospect of using it and even when they have no heirs? They eat the cheapest food, buy no clothes, and live in a single room when they could afford better lodging. It may be that they regard money as a form of power; there is a comfort in watching it accumulate while other powers are dwindling away. How often we read of an old person found dead in a hovel, on a mattress partly stuffed with bankbooks and stock certificates! The bankbook syndrome, we call it in our family, which has never succumbed.

Untidiness we call the Langley Collyer syndrome. To explain, Langley Collyer was a former concert pianist who lived alone with his 70-year-old brother in a brownstone house on upper Fifth Avenue. The once fashionable neighborhood had become part of Harlem. Homer, the brother, had been an admiralty lawyer, but was now blind and partly paralyzed; Langley played for him and fed him on buns and oranges, which he thought would restore Homer's sight. He never threw away a daily paper because Homer, he said, might want to read them all. He saved other things as well and the house became filled with rubbish from roof to basement. The halls were lined on both sides with bundled newspapers, leaving narrow passageways in which Langley had devised booby traps to catch intruders.

On March 21, 1947, some unnamed person telephoned the police to report that there was a dead body in the Collyer house. The police broke down the front door and found the hall impassable; then they hoisted a ladder to a second-story window. Behind it Homer was lying on the floor in a bathrobe; he had starved to death. Langley had disappeared. After some delay, the police broke into the basement, chopped a hole in the roof, and began throwing junk out of the house, top and bottom. It was 18 days before they found Langley's body, gnawed by rats. Caught in one of his own booby traps, he had died in a hallway just outside Homer's door. By that time the police had collected, and the Department of Sanitation had hauled away, 120 tons of rubbish, including, besides the newspapers, 14 grand pianos and the parts of a dismantled Model T Ford.

Why do so many old people accumulate junk, not on the scale of Langley Collyer, but still in a dismaying fashion? Their tables are piled high with it, their bureau drawers are stuffed with it, their closet rods bend with the weight of clothes not worn for years. I suppose that the piling up is partly from lethargy and partly from the feeling that everything once useful, including their own bodies, should be preserved. Others, though not so many, have such a fear of becoming Langley Collyers that they strive to be painfully neat. Every tool they own is in its place, though it will never be used again; every scrap of paper is filed away in alphabetical order. At last their immoderate neatness becomes another vice of age, if a milder one.

The vanity of older people is an easier weakness to explain, and to con- 16
done. With less to look forward to, they yearn for recognition of what they
have been: the reigning beauty, the athlete, the soldier, the scholar. It is the
beauties who have the hardest time. A portrait of themselves at twenty
hangs on the wall, and they try to resemble it by making an extravagant use
of creams, powders, and dyes. Being young at heart, they think they are
merely revealing their essential persons. The athletes find shelves for their
silver trophies, which are polished once a year. Perhaps a letter sweater lies
wrapped in a bureau drawer. I remember one evening when a no-longer
athlete had guests for dinner and tried to find his sweater. "Oh, that old
thing," his wife said. "The moths got into it and I threw it away." The athlete sulked and his guests went home early.

Often the yearning to be recognized appears in conversation as an inno- 17
cent boast. Thus, a distinguished physician, retired at 94, remarks casually
that a disease was named after him. A former judge bursts into chuckles as
he repeats bright things that he said on the bench. Aging scholars complain
in letters (or one of them does), "As I approach 70 I'm becoming avid of
honors, and such things — medals, honorary degrees, etc. — are only
passed around among academics on a *quid pro quo*° basis (one hood capping
another)." Or they say querulously, "Bill Underwood has ten honorary doc-
torates and I have only three. Why didn't they elect me to . . .?" and they
mention the name of some learned society. That search for honors is a harmless passion, though it may lead to jealousies and deformations of character,
as with Robert Frost in his later years. Still, honors cost little. Why shouldn't
the very old have more than their share of them?

To be admired and praised, especially by the young, is an autumnal plea- 18
sure enjoyed by the lucky ones (who are not always the most deserving).
"What is more charming," Cicero° observes in his famous essay *De Senec-
tute,* "than an old age surrounded by the enthusiasm of youth! . . . Atten-
tions which seem trivial and conventional are marks of honors — the morning call, being sought after, precedence, having people rise for you, being
escorted to and from the forum. . . . What pleasures of the body can be compared to the prerogatives of influence?" But there are also pleasures of the
body, or the mind, that are enjoyed by a greater number of older persons.

Those pleasures include some that younger people find hard to appreci- 19
ate. One of them is simply sitting still, like a snake on a sun-warmed stone,
with a delicious feeling of indolence that was seldom attained in earlier
years. A leaf flutters down; a cloud moves by inches across the horizon. At
such moments the older person, completely relaxed, has become a part of

---

Quid pro quo Something given for something received.
Cicero Roman orator and philosopher, 106–43 B.C.

nature — and a living part, with blood coursing through his veins. The future does not exist for him. He thinks, if he thinks at all, that life for younger persons is still a battle royal of each against each, but that now he has nothing more to win or lose. He is not so much above as outside the battle, as if he had assumed the uniform of some small neutral country, perhaps Liechtenstein or Andorra. From a distance he notes that some of the combatants, men or women, are jostling ahead — but why do they fight so hard when the most they can hope for is a longer obituary? He can watch the scrounging and gouging, he can hear the shouts of exultation, the moans of the gravely wounded, and meanwhile he feels secure; nobody will attack him from ambush.

Age has other physical compensations besides the nirvana of dozing in the sun. A few of the simplest needs become a pleasure to satisfy. When an old woman in a nursing home was asked what she really liked to do, she answered in one word: "Eat." She might have been speaking for many of her fellows. Meals in a nursing home, however badly cooked, serve as climactic moments of the day. The physical essence of the pensioners is being renewed at an appointed hour; now they can go back to meditating or to watching TV while looking forward to the next meal. They can also look forward to sleep, which has become a definite pleasure, not the mere interruption it once had been.

Here I am thinking of old persons under nursing care. Others ferociously guard their independence, and some of them suffer less than one might expect from being lonely and impoverished. They can be rejoiced by visits and meetings, but they also have company inside their heads. Some of them are busiest when their hands are still. What passes through the minds of many is a stream of persons, images, phrases, and familiar tunes. For some that stream has continued since childhood, but now it is deeper; it is their present and their past combined. At times they conduct silent dialogues with a vanished friend, and these are less tiring — often more rewarding — than spoken conversations. If inner resources are lacking, old persons living alone may seek comfort and a kind of companionship in the bottle. I should judge from the gossip of various neighborhoods that the outer suburbs from Boston to San Diego are full of secretly alcoholic widows. One of those widows, an old friend, was moved from her apartment into a retirement home. She left behind her a closet in which the floor was covered wall to wall with whiskey bottles. "Oh, those empty bottles!" she explained. "They were left by a former tenant."

Not whiskey or cooking sherry but simply giving up is the greatest temptation of age. It is something different from a stoical acceptance of infirmities, which is something to be admired. At 63, when he first recognized that his powers were failing, Emerson wrote one of his best poems, "Terminus":

It is time to be old,
To take in sail: —
The god of bounds,
Who sets to seas a shore,
Came to me in his fatal rounds,
And said: ''No more!
No farther shoot
Thy broad ambitious branches, and thy root.
Fancy departs: no more invent;
Contract thy firmament
To compass of a tent.''

Emerson lived in good health to the age of 79. Within his narrowed firmament, he continued working until his memory failed; then he consented to having younger editors and collaborators. The givers-up see no reason for working. Sometimes they lie in bed all day when moving about would still be possible, if difficult. I had a friend, a distinguished poet, who surrendered in that fashion. The doctors tried to stir him to action, but he refused to leave his room. Another friend, once a successful artist, stopped painting when his eyes began to fail. His doctor made the mistake of telling him that he suffered from a fatal disease. He then lost interest in everything except the splendid Rolls-Royce, acquired in his prosperous days, that stood in the garage. Daily he wiped the dust from its hood. He couldn't drive it on the road any longer, but he used to sit in the driver's seat, start the motor, then back the Rolls out of the garage and drive it in again, back twenty feet and forward twenty feet; that was his only distraction. 23

I haven't the right to blame those who surrender, not being able to put myself inside their minds or bodies. Often they must have compelling reasons, physical or moral. Not only do they suffer from a variety of ailments, but also they are made to feel that they no longer have a function in the community. Their families and neighbors don't ask them for advice, don't really listen when they speak, don't call on them for efforts. One notes that there are not a few recoveries from apparent senility when that situation changes. If it doesn't change, old persons may decide that efforts are useless. I sympathize with their problems, but the men and women I envy are those who accept old age as a series of challenges. 24

For such persons, every new infirmity is an enemy to be outwitted, an obstacle to be overcome by force of will. They enjoy each little victory over themselves, and sometimes they win a major success. Renoir was one of them. He continued painting, and magnificently, for years after he was crippled by arthritis; the brush had to be strapped to his arm. ''You don't need your hand to paint,'' he said. Goya was another of the unvanquished. At 72 he retired as an official painter of the Spanish court and decided to work 25 only for himself. His later years were those of the famous "black paintings" in which he let his imagination run (and also of the lithographs, then a new technique). At 78 he escaped a reign of terror in Spain by fleeing to Bordeaux. He was deaf and his eyes were failing; in order to work he had to wear several pairs of spectacles, one over another, and then use a magnifying glass; but he was producing splendid work in a totally new style. At 80 he drew an ancient man propped on two sticks, with a mass of white hair and beard hiding his face and with the inscription "I am still learning."

Giovanni Papini said when he was nearly blind, "I prefer martyrdom to imbecility." After writing sixty books, including his famous *Life of Christ*, he was at work on two huge projects when he was stricken with a form of muscular atrophy. He lost the use of his left leg, then of his fingers, so that he couldn't hold a pen. The two big books, though never to be finished, moved forward slowly by dictation; that in itself was a triumph. Toward the end, when his voice had become incomprehensible, he spelled out a word, tapping on the table to indicate letters of the alphabet. One hopes never to be faced with the need for such heroic measures.

"Eighty years old!" the great Catholic poet Paul Claudel wrote in his journal. "No eyes left, no ears, no teeth, no legs, no wind! And when all is said and done, how astonishingly well one does without them!"

Yeats is the great modern poet of age, though he died — I am now tempted to say — as a mere stripling of 73. His reaction to growing old was not that of a stoic like Emerson or Cicero, bent on obeying nature's laws and the edicts of Terminus, the god "Who sets to seas a shore"; it was that of a romantic rebel, the Faustian° man. He was only 61 when he wrote (in "The Tower"):

> What shall I do with this absurdity —
> O heart, O troubled heart — this caricature,
> Decrepit age that has been tied to me
> As to a dog's tail?

At 68 he began to be worried because he wasn't producing many new poems. Could it be, he must have wondered, that his libido had lost its force and that it was somehow connected with his imagination? He had the Faustian desire for renewed youth, felt almost universally, but in Yeats's case with a stronger excuse, since his imagination was the center of his life. A friend told him, with gestures, about Dr. Steinach's then famous operation designed to rejuvenate men by implanting new sex glands. The operation

---

Faustian In German legend, Faust sells his soul to the devil in return for ultimate knowledge and eternal youth.

has since fallen into such medical disfavor that Steinach's name is nowhere mentioned in the latest edition of *The Encyclopaedia Britannica*. But Yeats read a pamphlet about it in the Trinity College library, in Dublin, and was favorably impressed. After consulting a physician, who wouldn't say yes or no, he arranged to have the operation performed in a London clinic; that was in May 1934.

Back in Dublin he felt himself to be a different man. Oliver St. John Gogarty, himself a physician, reports a conversation with Yeats that took place the following summer. "I was horrified," he says, "to hear when it was too late that he had undergone such an operation. 'On both sides?' I asked. 30

" 'Yes,' he acknowledged. 31
" 'But why on earth did you not consult anyone?' 32
" 'I read a pamphlet.' 33
" 'What was wrong with you?' 34
" 'I used to fall asleep after lunch.' " 35

It was no use making a serious answer to Gogarty the jester. He tells us in his memoir of Yeats that the poet claimed to have been greatly benefitted by the operation, but adds, "I have reason to believe that this was not so. He had reached the age when he would not take 'Yes' for an answer." Gogarty's judgment as a physician was probably right; the poet's physical health did not improve and in fact deteriorated. One conjectures that the operation may have put an added strain on his heart and thus may have shortened his life by years. Psychologically, however, Yeats was transformed. He began to think of himself as "the wild old wicked man," and in that character he wrote dozens of poems in a new style, direct, earthy, and passionate. One of them reads: 36

> You think it horrible that lust and rage
> Should dance attention upon my old age;
> They were not such a plague when I was young;
> What else have I to spur me into song?

False remedies are sometimes beneficial in their own fashion. What artists would not sacrifice a few years of life in order to produce work on a level with Yeats's *Last Poems*? Early in January 1939, he wrote to his friend Lady Elizabeth Pelham: 37

> I know for certain that my time will not be long. . . . I am happy, and I think full of energy, of an energy I had despaired of. It seems to me that I have found what I wanted. When I try to put all into a phrase I say, "Man can embody truth but he cannot know it." I must embody it in the completion of my life.

His very last poem, and one of the best, is "The Black Tower," dated the 21st of that month. Yeats died a week after writing it. 38

QUESTIONS ON MEANING

1. Cowley's essay presents so much information about the psychology of aging and takes so open-minded a view of the subject that we may have to remind ourselves that Cowley is, after all, a particular individual with a personal point of view. What *is* his point of view? How does he himself approach the problems of getting older?

2. Much of "The View from 80" is concerned with the morals of aging. What are some of the virtues and vices, the temptations and pleasures of old people that Cowley emphasizes? Is he critical of or sympathetic toward old people's vices? He refuses to judge those who "surrender" (paragraph 24), but he envies those who do not. How does his discussion of Yeats bring out both of those feelings?

3. In the book from which this essay is taken, Cowley quotes the English novelist John Cowper Powys: "The one supreme advantage that Old Age possesses over Middle Age and Youth is its nearness to Death. The very thing that makes it seem pitiable to those less threatened and therefore less enlightened ages of man is the thing that deepens, heightens, and thickens out its felicity." How does this sense of things come out in what Cowley says about aging here?

4. Do Cowley's remarks about old age reveal anything about how to live when we are younger? What attitude is implicit in his ruminations?

5. Cowley ends with a series of heroic examples of the very old — all of them artists. Is this mere egotism, because Cowley is himself a writer? Are there reasons why artists remain more active than nonartists in extreme old age?

QUESTIONS ON STRATEGY

1. Loose and flexible in structure, "The View from 80" uses a variety of expository techniques. Look at Cowley's introduction alone (paragraphs 1 through 4): the first paragraph moves from personal experience to anecdote; paragraph 2 presents a fundamental organizing metaphor of the rite of passage; paragraph 3 provides statistical exposition; and paragraph 4 introduces a second metaphor, of age as an unfamiliar country. These varied paragraphs set the scene for Cowley's development of his themes. When and how does he refer back to each of these different elements?

2. Cowley ends his first paragraph with a shocking anecdote. What effect does the placement of this anecdote have on the essay? How does Cowley develop the image and implications of this anecdote?

3. In paragraph 5 Cowley catalogues the ways in which old people receive the "message" of age from their bodies and surroundings. How does he organize this catalogue? What gives it unity? Why is this an effective tactic?

4. Consider the anecdote in paragraphs 13 and 14. How does the story contribute to Cowley's point about old people's habits? Is it an appropriate story? Effective? How does it fit with the rest of Cowley's anecdotes?

EXPLORATIONS

1. In paragraph 18 Cowley mentions Cicero's essay on old age. In the book *The View from 80* he refers to books by contemporary authors: Simone de Beauvoir (*The Coming of Age*), Alex Comfort (*A Good Age*), and Ronald Blythe (*The View from Winter*). Not all of these writers are as optimistic about old age as Cowley or as sympathetic about the foibles of the elderly. Compare and contrast a chapter from one of these books and Cowley's essay.

WRITING TOPICS

1. Cowley uses a variety of methods in "The View from 80," but he brings the essay to a close with a powerful anecdote. Everything he has said about aging as a challenge is reinforced and illuminated by this story about Yeats. Write an essay in which you develop your argument in several ways as Cowley does, and conclude with a telling anecdote — something you've read, heard about, or experienced yourself that brings your subject into a conclusive light. Possible subjects include the transition from living at home to living away or growing up in the eighties.
2. "The View from 80" describes the many messages the aged receive from their bodies and their environment, all of which add up to "only one message: 'You are old.'" Write an essay on the messages your body and environment used to send you when you were a child about the fact that you were young.
3. Write a descriptive or narrative essay from the point of view of an old person. Using "The View from 80" as a stimulus to your imagination, put yourself in the place of an elderly member of our society, perhaps someone you know well. How does the world look and feel to this person? What is special about his or her position in the world? How does he or she feel about being one of the aged?

BOOKS AVAILABLE IN PAPERBACK

And I Worked at the Writer's Trade: Chapters of Literary History, 1918–1978. New York: Penguin. *Nonfiction: Literary history.*

The Dream of the Golden Mountains: Remembering the 1930s. New York: Penguin. *Nonfiction: Personal history.*

Exile's Return: A Literary Odyssey of the 1920s. New York: Penguin. *Nonfiction: Literary history.*

A Second Flowering: Works and Days of the Lost Generation. New York: Penguin. *Nonfiction: Literary history.*

Think Back on Us: A Contemporary Chronicle of the 1930s. 2 vols. Carbondale: Southern Illinois University Press. *Essays.*

The View from 80. New York: Penguin. *Essay on aging.*

E. B. WHITE

*T*HE ESSAYIST," writes E. B. White, "is a self-liberated man, sustained by the childish belief that everything he thinks about, everything that happens to him, is of general interest." White ought to know. An editor of The New Yorker magazine, author of some of our best books for children (Stuart Little, 1945; Charlotte's Web, 1952), White is first of all an essayist, prime instigator of the contemporary essay, and a master of modern American prose style. Despite his comment about the childishness of essayists' egotism, White writes so well that in fact "everything that happens to him" becomes "of general interest."

Born in 1899 in Mount Vernon, New York, White graduated from Cornell University and worked in advertising before he joined the year-old New Yorker in 1927. As an editor he was especially responsible for the opening columns of commentary, "Talk of the Town." He started at a salary of thirty dollars a week, with five dollars extra for each "Talk" item printed. His five-dollar bonuses must have added up. The New Yorker's characteristic manner — deft, ironic, amusing, wise — is largely E. B. White's creation. When the Letters of E. B. White appeared in 1976, readers discovered paragraphs that sound like The New Yorker, written before there was a New Yorker.

White's example influenced humorist and cartoonist James Thurber and count-less other writers. When he gathered his thoughts on prose into The Elements of Style *(1959) — a revision of an English manual by the late William Strunk, Jr., his Cornell instructor — generations of students in composition classes took advice on their writing from E. B. White and his old teacher.*

One of White's handyman tasks on The New Yorker *was to handle "news-breaks" — short excerpts of garbled prose and misprints from newspapers, maga-zines, and other writing with which the magazine fills out its columns. White wrote the witty comments that accompanied the short blunders and invented many of the categories, such as "Letters We Never Finished Reading," "Neatest Trick of the Week," and "Raised Eyebrows Department." In 1959 James Thurber estimated that White had written thirty thousand such comments.*

By that time, White was dreaming up one-liners at his home in Maine, where he first retreated late in the 1930s and where he wrote a column for Harper's *magazine called "One Man's Meat," later collected into a book of that title. Other books as-sembled* New Yorker *pieces and articles commissioned by other magazines. His wife, who died in 1977, was Katharine Angell White, formerly fiction editor of* The New Yorker *and author of articles about gardening, collected in* Onward and Upward in the Garden *(1979). His stepson is Roger Angell, present fiction editor at* The New Yorker *(see pp. 92–123). In recent years, Harper & Row has collected not only White's* Letters *but also selections called* Essays of E. B. White *(1977) and* Poems and Sketches *(1981).*

White wrote "The Ring of Time" in 1956, two years after the Supreme Court, in Brown v. Topeka, *struck down "separate but equal" segregation. "The essayist," he wrote in his foreword to* Essays of E. B. White, *can "be any sort of person, ac-cording to his mood or subject matter." Often E. B. White takes a while before he lets us understand his mood and subject matter. In the following essay he describes a scene directly in front of him — with scrupulous attention, brilliance, intimacy, and affection — while at the periphery of his thought another subject, bothering him, struggles for his attention. By delivering himself to this problem at the mind's edge, he delivers his readers also.*

The Ring of Time

Fiddler Bayou, March 22, 1956

After the lions had returned to their cages, creeping angrily through the chutes, a little bunch of us drifted away and into an open doorway nearby, where we stood for a while in semidarkness, watching a big brown circus horse go harumphing around the practice ring. His trainer was a woman of about forty, and the two of them, horse and woman, seemed caught up in one of those desultory treadmills of afternoon from which there is no apparent escape. The day was hot, and we kibitzers were grateful to be briefly out of the sun's glare. The long rein, or tape, by which the woman guided her charge counterclockwise in his dull career formed the radius of their private circle, of which she was the resolving center; and she, too, stepped a tiny circumference of her own, in order to accommodate the horse and allow him his maximum scope. She had on a short-skirted costume and a conical straw hat. Her legs were bare and she wore high heels, which probed deep into the loose tanbark and kept her ankles in a state of constant turmoil. The great size and meekness of the horse, the repetitious exercise, the heat of the afternoon, all exerted a hypnotic charm that invited boredom; we spectators were experiencing a languor — we neither expected relief nor felt entitled to any. We had paid a dollar to get into the grounds, to be sure, but we had got our dollar's worth a few minutes before, when the lion trainer's whiplash had got caught around a toe of one of the lions. What more did we want for a dollar?

Behind me I heard someone say, "Excuse me, please," in a low voice. She was halfway into the building when I turned and saw her — a girl of sixteen or seventeen, politely threading her way through us onlookers who blocked the entrance. As she emerged in front of us, I saw that she was barefoot, her dirty little feet fighting the uneven ground. In most respects she was like any of two or three dozen showgirls you encounter if you wander about the winter quarters of Mr. John Ringling North's circus, in Sarasota — cleverly proportioned, deeply browned by the sun, dusty, eager, and almost naked. But her grave face and the naturalness of her manner gave her a sort of quick distinction and brought a new note into the gloomy octagonal building where we had all cast our lot for a few moments. As soon as she had squeezed through the crowd, she spoke a word or two to the older woman, whom I took to be her mother, stepped to the ring, and waited while the horse coasted to a stop in front of her. She gave the animal a couple of affectionate swipes on his enormous neck and then swung herself aboard. The horse immediately resumed his rocking canter, the woman goading him on, chanting something that sounded like "Hop! Hop!"

In attempting to recapture this mild spectacle, I am merely acting as recording secretary for one of the oldest of societies — the society of those who, at one time or another, have surrendered, without even a show of resistance, to the bedazzlement of a circus rider. As a writing man, or secretary, I have always felt charged with the safekeeping of all unexpected items of worldly or unworldly enchantment, as though I might be held personally responsible if even a small one were to be lost. But it is not easy to communicate anything of this nature. The circus comes as close to being the world in microcosm as anything I know; in a way, it puts all the rest of show business in the shade. Its magic is universal and complex. Out of its wild disorder comes order; from its rank smell rises the good aroma of courage and daring; out of its preliminary shabbiness comes the final splendor. And buried in the familiar boasts of its advance agents lies the modesty of most of its people. For me the circus is at its best before it has been put together. It is at its best at certain moments when it comes to a point, as through a burning glass, in the activity and destiny of a single performer out of so many. One ring is always bigger than three. One rider, one aerialist, is always greater than six. In short, a man has to catch the circus unawares to experience its full impact and share its gaudy dream.

The ten-minute ride the girl took achieved — as far as I was concerned, 4
who wasn't looking for it, and quite unbeknownst to her, who wasn't even striving for it — the thing that is sought by performers everywhere, on whatever stage, whether struggling in the tidal currents of Shakespeare or bucking the difficult motion of a horse. I somehow got the idea she was just cadging a ride, improving a shining ten minutes in the diligent way all serious artists seize free moments to hone the blade of their talent and keep themselves in trim. Her brief tour included only elementary postures and tricks, perhaps because they were all she was capable of, perhaps because her warmup at this hour was unscheduled and the ring was not rigged for a real practice session. She swung herself off and on the horse several times, gripping his mane. She did a few knee-stands — or whatever they are called — dropping to her knees and quickly bouncing back up on her feet again. Most of the time she simply rode in a standing position, well aft on the beast, her hands hanging easily at her sides, her head erect, her straw-colored ponytail lightly brushing her shoulders, the blood of exertion showing faintly through the tan of her skin. Twice she managed a one-foot stance — a sort of ballet pose, with arms outstretched. At one point the neck strap of her bathing suit broke and she went twice around the ring in the classic attitude of a woman making minor repairs to a garment. The fact that she was standing on the back of a moving horse while doing this invested the matter with a clownish significance that perfectly fitted the spirit of the circus — jocund, yet charming. She just rolled the strap into a neat ball and stowed it inside her bodice while the horse rocked and rolled beneath her in dutiful innocence. The bathing suit proved as self-reliant as its owner and stood up well enough without benefit of strap.

The richness of the scene was in its plainness, its natural condition — of 5
horse, of ring, of girl, even to the girl's bare feet that gripped the bare back of her proud and ridiculous mount. The enchantment grew not out of anything that happened or was performed but out of something that seemed to go round and around and around with the girl, attending her, a steady

gleam in the shape of a circle — a ring of ambition, of happiness, of youth. (And the positive pleasures of equilibrium under difficulties.) In a week or two, all would be changed, all (or almost all) lost: the girl would wear makeup, the horse would wear gold, the ring would be painted, the bark would be clean for the feet of the horse, the girl's feet would be clean for the slippers that she'd wear. All, all would be lost.

As I watched with the others, our jaws adroop, our eyes alight, I became painfully conscious of the element of time. Everything in the hideous old building seemed to take the shape of a circle, conforming to the course of the horse. The rider's gaze, as she peered straight ahead, seemed to be circular, as though bent by force of circumstance; then time itself began running in circles, and so the beginning was where the end was, and the two were the same, and one thing ran into the next and time went round and around and got nowhere. The girl wasn't so young that she did not know the delicious satisfaction of having a perfectly behaved body and the fun of using it to do a trick most people can't do, but she was too young to know that time does not really move in a circle at all. I thought: "She will never be as beautiful as this again" — a thought that made me acutely unhappy — and in a flash my mind (which is too much of a busybody to suit me) had projected her twenty-five years ahead, and she was now in the center of the ring, on foot, wearing a conical hat and high-heeled shoes, the image of the older woman, holding the long rein, caught in the treadmill of an afternoon long in the future. "She is at that enviable moment in life [I thought] when she believes she can go once around the ring, make one complete circuit, and at the end be exactly the same age as at the start." Everything in her movements, her expression, told you that for her the ring of time was perfectly formed, changeless, predictable, without beginning or end, like the ring in which she was traveling at this moment with the horse that wallowed under her. And then I slipped back into my trance, and time was circular again — time, pausing quietly with the rest of us, so as not to disturb the balance of a performer.

Her ride ended as casually as it had begun. The older woman stopped the horse, and the girl slid to the ground. As she walked toward us to leave, there was a quick, small burst of applause. She smiled broadly, in surprise and pleasure; then her face suddenly regained its gravity and she disappeared through the door.

It has been ambitious and plucky of me to attempt to describe what is indescribable, and I have failed, as I knew I would. But I have discharged my duty to my society; and besides, a writer, like an acrobat, must occasionally try a stunt that is too much for him. At any rate, it is worth reporting that long before the circus comes to town, its most notable performances have already been given. Under the bright lights of the finished show, a performer need only reflect the electric candle power that is directed upon him; but in the dark and dirty old training rings and in the makeshift cages, whatever light is generated, whatever excitement, whatever beauty, must come from original sources — from internal fires of professional hunger and delight, from the exuberance and gravity of youth. It is the difference between planetary light and the combustion of stars.

The South is the land of the sustained sibilant. Everywhere, for the appreciative visitor, the letter "s" insinuates itself in the scene: in the sound of sea and sand, in the singing shell, in the heat of sun and sky, in the sultriness of the gentle hours, in the siesta, in the stir of birds and insects. In contrast to the softness of its music, the South is also cruel and hard and prickly. A little striped lizard, flattened along the sharp green bayonet of a yucca, wears in its tiny face and watchful eye the pure look of death and violence. And all over the place, hidden at the bottom of their small sandy craters, the ant lions lie in wait for the ant that will stumble into their trap. (There are three kinds of lions in this region: the lions of the circus, the ant lions, and the Lions of the Tampa Lions Club, who roared their approval of segregation at a meeting the other day — all except one, a Lion named Monty Gurwit, who declined to roar and thereby got his picture in the paper.)

The day starts on a note of despair: the sorrowing dove, alone on its telephone wire, mourns the loss of night, weeps at the bright perils of the unfolding day. But soon the mockingbird wakes and begins an early rehearsal, setting the dove down by force of character, running through a few slick imitations, and trying a couple of original numbers into the bargain. The redbird takes it from there. Despair gives way to good humor. The Southern dawn is a pale affair, usually, quite different from our northern daybreak. It is a triumph of gradualism, night turns to day imperceptibly, softly, with no theatrics. It is subtle and undisturbing. As the first light seeps in through the blinds I lie in bed half awake, despairing with the dove, sounding the A for the brothers Alsop.° All seems lost, all seems sorrowful. Then a mullet jumps in the bayou outside the bedroom window. It falls back into the water with a smart smack. I have asked several people why the mullet incessantly jump and I have received a variety of answers. Some say the mullet jump to shake off a parasite that annoys them. Some say they jump for the love of jumping — as the girl on the horse seemed to ride for the love of riding (although she, too, like all artists, may have been shaking off some parasite that fastens itself to the creative spirit and can be got rid of only by fifty turns around a ring while standing on a horse).

9

10

---

brothers Alsop   Joseph and Stuart Alsop, authors of a syndicated political column for newspapers.

In Florida at this time of year, the sun does not take command of the day
until a couple of hours after it has appeared in the east. It seems to carry no
authority at first. The sun and the lizard keep the same schedule; they bide
their time until the morning has advanced a good long way before they
come fully forth and strike. The cold lizard waits astride his warming leaf for
the perfect moment; the cold sun waits in his nest of clouds for the crucial
time.

On many days, the dampness of the air pervades all life, all living.
Matches refuse to strike. The towel, hung to dry, grows wetter by the hour.
The newspaper, with its headlines about integration, wilts in your hand and
falls limply into the coffee and the egg. Envelopes seal themselves. Postage
stamps mate with one another as shamelessly as grasshoppers. But most of
the time the days are models of beauty and wonder and comfort, with the
kind sea stroking the back of the warm sand. At evening there are great
flights of birds over the sea, where the light lingers; the gulls, the pelicans,
the terns, the herons stay aloft for half an hour after land birds have gone to
roost. They hold their ancient formations, wheel and fish over the Pass, enjoying the last of day like children playing outdoors after suppertime.

To a beachcomber from the North, which is my present status, the race
problem has no pertinence, no immediacy. Here in Florida I am a guest in
two houses — the house of the sun, the house of the State of Florida. As a
guest, I mind my manners and do not criticize the customs of my hosts. It
gives me a queer feeling, though, to be at the center of the greatest social crisis of my time and see hardly a sign of it. Yet the very absence of signs seems
to increase one's awareness. Colored people do not come to the public beach
to bathe, because they would not be made welcome there; and they don't
fritter away their time visiting the circus, because they have other things to
do. A few of them turn up at the ballpark, where they occupy a separate but
equal section of the left-field bleachers and watch Negro players on the visiting Braves team using the same bases as the white players, instead of separate (but equal) bases. I have had only two small encounters with "color." A
colored woman named Viola, who had been a friend of my wife's sister
years ago, showed up one day with some laundry of ours that she had consented to do for us, and with the bundle she brought a bunch of nastur-
tiums, as a sort of natural accompaniment to the delivery of clean clothes.
The flowers seemed a very acceptable thing and I was touched by them. We
asked Viola about her daughter, and she said she was at Kentucky State College, studying voice.

The other encounter was when I was explaining to our cook, who is from
Finland, the mysteries of bus travel in the American Southland. I showed
her the bus stop, armed her with a timetable, and then, as a matter of duty,
mentioned the customs of the Romans. "When you get on the bus," I said,

"I think you'd better sit in one of the front seats — the seats in back are for colored people." A look of great weariness came into her face, as it does when we use too many dishes, and she replied, "Oh, I know — isn't it silly!"

Her remark, coming as it did all the way from Finland and landing on 15 this sandbar with a plunk, impressed me. The Supreme Court said nothing about silliness, but I suspect it may play more of a role than one might suppose. People are, if anything, more touchy about being thought silly than they are about being thought unjust. I note that one of the arguments in the recent manifesto of Southern Congressmen in support of the doctrine of "separate but equal" was that it had been founded on "common sense." The sense that is common to one generation is uncommon to the next. Probably the first slave ship, with Negroes lying in chains on its decks, seemed commonsensical to the owners who operated it and to the planters who patronized it. But such a vessel would not be in the realm of common sense today. The only sense that is common, in the long run, is the sense of change — and we all instinctively avoid it, and object to the passage of time, and would rather have none of it.

The Supreme Court decision is like the Southern sun, laggard in its early 16 stages, biding its time. It has been the law in Florida for two years now, and the years have been like the hours of the morning before the sun has gathered its strength. I think the decision is as incontrovertible and warming as the sun, and, like the sun, will eventually take charge.

But there is certainly a great temptation in Florida to duck the passage of 17 time. Lying in warm comfort by the sea, you receive gratefully the gift of the sun, the gift of the South. This is true seduction. The day is a circle — morning, afternoon, and night. After a few days I was clearly enjoying the same delusion as the girl on the horse — that I could ride clear around the ring of day, guarded by wind and sun and sea and sand, and be not a moment older.

P.S. (April 1962). When I first laid eyes on Fiddler Bayou, it was wild land, 18 populated chiefly by the little crabs that gave it its name, visited by wading birds and by an occasional fisherman. Today, houses ring the bayou, and part of the mangrove shore has been bulkheaded with a concrete wall. Green lawns stretch from patio to water's edge, and sprinklers make rainbows in the light. But despite man's encroachment, Nature manages to hold her own and assert her authority: high tides and high winds in the gulf sometimes send the sea crashing across the sand barrier, depositing its wrack on lawns and ringing everyone's front door bell. The birds and the crabs accommodate themselves quite readily to the changes that have taken place; every day brings herons to hunt around among the roots of the mangroves, and I have discovered that I can approach to within about eight feet of a Little Blue Heron simply by entering the water and swimming slowly toward him. Apparently he has decided that when I'm in the water, I am without guile — possibly even desirable, like a fish.

The Ringling circus has quit Sarasota and gone elsewhere for its hiberna-   1
tion. A few circus families still own homes in the town, and every spring the students at the high school put on a circus, to let off steam, work off physical requirements, and provide a promotional spectacle for Sarasota. At the drugstore you can buy a postcard showing the bed John Ringling slept in. Time has not stood still for anybody but the dead, and even the dead must be able to hear the acceleration of little sports cars and know that things have changed.

From the all-wise *New York Times*, which has the animal kingdom ever in   2
mind, I have learned that one of the creatures most acutely aware of the passing of time is the fiddler crab himself. Tiny spots on his body enlarge during daytime hours, giving him the same color as the mudbank he explores and thus protecting him from his enemies. At night the spots shrink, his color fades, and he is almost invisible in the light of the moon. These changes are synchronized with the tides, so that each day they occur at a different hour. A scientist who experimented with the crabs to learn more about the phenomenon discovered that even when they are removed from their natural environment and held in confinement, the rhythm of their bodily change continues uninterrupted, and they mark the passage of time in their laboratory prison, faithful to the tides in their fashion.

QUESTIONS ON MEANING

1. White shows us three distinct and seemingly unrelated images or ideas: the circus performer, the natural life of the bayou, and the segregation of blacks in the South at the time of the Supreme Court's desegregation decision. In paragraphs 16 and 17 White ties all three images together. What is his theme in this essay and how does each image contribute to it? Where else does he tie two or more of the images together?

2. Paragraph 15 concludes with an observation about common sense and change. How does White's observation relate to the issue of racial integration? Does White's observation relate in the same way to his description of the girl on the horse?

QUESTIONS ON STRATEGY

1. Paragraph 10 contains a long description of dawn in the bayou. How does White's use of language evoke the circus even before he explicitly mentions the circus performer?

2. We find out only after many paragraphs that White's essay is not really about the circus or about nature in the bayou. How do White's exposition and description prepare us for the points he wants to make about racial integration and about change? Cite specific sentences and images that White uses to prepare us.

WRITING TOPICS

1. White gives several examples of circular motion, the ring of time. He describes each in vivid detail and at points gives his own response to the examples. Eventually, he ties the examples together to illustrate his notions about change and our resistance to it. Write an essay about change using White's methods as a model.

BOOKS AVAILABLE IN PAPERBACK

Charlotte's Web. New York: Harper & Row, Trophy Books. *Children's novel.*

Essays of E. B. White. New York: Harper Colophon.

Letters of E. B. White. Collected and edited by Dorothy Lobrano Guth. New York: Harper Colophon.

Poems and Sketches of E. B. White. New York: Harper Colophon.

The Points of My Compass. New York: Harper & Row, Perennial Library. *Essays.*

The Second Tree from the Corner. New York: Harper & Row, Perennial Library. *Essays.*

Stuart Little. New York: Harper & Row, Trophy Books. *Children's novel.*

The Trumpet of the Swan. New York: Harper & Row, Trophy Books. *Children's novel.*

With Will Strunk. *The Elements of Style.* 3rd ed. New York: Macmillan. *Nonfiction: Guidebook for writers.*

With James Thurber. *Is Sex Necessary? Or Why You Feel the Way You Do.* New York: Harper & Row, Perennial Library. *Nonfiction: Humor.*

JOHN KENNETH
GALBRAITH

JOHN KENNETH GALBRAITH was born in 1908 at Iona Station in Ontario, Canada. He took his B.S. at the University of Toronto, then began graduate work by studying agricultural economics and received an M.S. at the University of California. Enlarging his studies into general economics, he took his Ph.D. at the University of California, taught at Harvard late in the 1930s and then at Princeton, until he left the academic world to work for the United States government during World War II. He served as economic adviser to the National Defense Advisory Committee and as deputy head of the Office of Price Administration. His experience in government during the war years was crucial to his development as an economics thinker. After a few years at Fortune *magazine, he returned to the faculty of Harvard, where he was Paul M. Warburg Professor of Economics when he retired in 1975. On leave from Harvard from 1961 to 1963, he was ambassador to India under President John F. Kennedy.*

Galbraith's vision as an economist has been consistently political and historical, developed especially in a core of four books. The Affluent Society *(1958) criticized the conventional wisdom of classical economics.* American Capitalism *(1972) set forth the ideas that other volumes elucidated in detail.* The New Industrial State *(1967), from which we reprint "The Technostructure," analyzed things as they are.*

Economics and the Public Purpose *(1973) set forth Galbraith's notions for an economics adequate for the future.*

His many books have contributed not only to the study of economics but to our understanding of ourselves and our culture. His other economics works include The Great Crash *(1955), which analyzes the 1929 stock market crash that precipitated the Great Depression;* The Liberal Hour *(1960); and* The Nature of Mass Poverty *(1979). Although he is most eminent as an economist, Galbraith does not limit himself to economics: Among his other books are a novel* The Triumph *(1968), published pseudonymously; and the nonfiction works* The Scotch, *a memoir (1964);* Indian Painting *(1968);* Ambassador's Journal *(1969); and* A China Passage *(1973).* The Galbraith Reader *(1977) is a collection of Galbraith's prose, and most recently he has published an autobiography,* A Life in Our Times *(1981).*

Whether Galbraith writes about painting or Scotch ancestry or politics, his general intelligence and his wit bring economics to bear on his subject. This author could wear on his crest the Latin motto from Terence, humani nihil alienum, *which translates "nothing human is alien." The same qualities of wit and intelligence illuminate his prose when he writes directly on economics. The editors of* The Galbraith Reader *quote him as believing and exemplifying that "there is no mystery in the science of economics that cannot be phrased in good English prose." "The Technostructure," with its innovative analysis of contemporary managerial structure, lies at the center of Galbraith's economic thought.*

The Technostructure

". . . the prevalence of group, instead of individual, action is a striking characteristic of management organization in the large corporations."

– R. A. GORDON
BUSINESS LEADERSHIP IN THE LARGE CORPORATION

The individual has far more standing in our culture than the group. An 1 individual has a presumption of accomplishment; a committee has a presumption of inaction. We react sympathetically to the individual who seeks to safeguard his personality from engulfment by the mass. We call for proof, at least in principle, before curbing his aggressions. Individuals have souls; corporations are notably soulless. The entrepreneur — individualistic, restless, with vision, guile and courage — has been the economists' only hero. The great business organization arouses no similar admiration. Admission to heaven is individually and by families; the top management even of an enterprise with an excellent corporate image cannot yet go in as a group. To have, in pursuit of truth, to assert the superiority of the organization over the individual for important social tasks is a taxing prospect.

Yet it is a necessary task. It is not to individuals but to organizations that power in the business enterprise and power in the society has passed. And modern economic society can only be understood as an effort, wholly successful, to synthesize by organization a group personality far superior *for its purposes* to a natural person and with the added advantage of immortality.

The need for such a group personality begins with the circumstance that in modern industry a large number of decisions, and *all* that are important, draw on information possessed by more than one man. Typically they draw on the specialized scientific and technical knowledge, the accumulated information or experience and the artistic or intuitive sense of many persons. And this is guided by further information which is assembled, analyzed and interpreted by professionals using highly technical equipment. The final decision will be informed only as it draws systematically on all those whose information is relevant. Nor, human beings what they are, can it take all of the information that is offered at face value. There must, additionally, be a mechanism for testing each person's contribution for its relevance and reliability as it is brought to bear on the decision.

II

The need to draw on, and appraise, the information of numerous individuals in modern industrial decision-making has three principal points of origin. It derives, first, from the technological requirements of modern industry. It is not that these are always inordinately sophisticated; a man of moderate genius could, quite conceivably, provide himself with the knowledge of the various branches of metallurgy and chemistry, and of engineering, procurement, production management, quality control, labor relations, styling and merchandising which are involved in the development of a modern motorcar. But even moderate genius is in unpredictable supply, and to keep abreast of all these branches of science, engineering and art would be time-consuming even for a genius. The elementary solution, which allows of the use of far more common talent and with far greater predictability of result, is to have men who are appropriately qualified or experienced in each limited area of specialized knowledge or art. Their information is then combined for carrying out the design and production of the vehicle. It is a common public impression, not discouraged by scientists, engineers and industrialists, that modern scientific, engineering and industrial achievements are the work of a new and quite remarkable race of men. This is pure vanity; were it so, there would be few such achievements. The real accomplishment of modern science and technology consists in taking ordinary men, informing them narrowly and deeply and then, through appropriate organization, arranging to have their knowledge combined with that of other specialized but equally ordinary men. This dispenses with the need for genius. The resulting performance, though less inspiring, is far more predictable. No individual genius arranged the flights to the moon. It was the work of organization — bureaucracy. And the men walking on the moon and contemplating their return could be glad it was so.

The second factor requiring the combination of specialized talent derives 5 from advanced technology, the associated use of capital and the resulting need for planning with its accompanying control of environment. The market is, in remarkable degree, an intellectually undemanding institution. The Wisconsin farmer need not anticipate his requirements for fertilizers, pesticides or even machine parts; the market stocks and supplies them. The cost of these is substantially the same for the man of intelligence and for his neighbor who, under medical examination, shows daylight in either ear. And the farmer need have no price or selling strategy; the market takes all his milk at the ruling price. Much of the appeal of the market, to economists at least, has been from the way it seems to simplify life. Better orderly error than complex truth.

For complexity enters with planning and is endemic thereto. The manu- 6 facturer of missiles, space vehicles or modern aircraft must foresee the requirements for specialized plant, specialized manpower, exotic materials and intricate components and take steps to ensure their availability when they are needed. For procuring such things, we have seen, the market is either unreliable or unavailable. And there is no open market for the finished product. Everything here depends on the care and skill with which contracts are sought and nurtured in Washington or in Whitehall or Paris.

The same foresight and responding action are required, in lesser degree, 7 from manufacturers of automobiles, processed foods and detergents. They too must foresee requirements and manage markets. Planning, in short, requires a great variety of information. It requires variously informed men and men who are suitably specialized in obtaining the requisite information. There must be men whose knowledge allows them to foresee need and to ensure a supply of labor, materials and other production requirements; those who have knowledge to plan price strategies and see that customers are suitably persuaded to buy at these prices; those who, at higher levels of technology, are informed that they can work effectively with the state to see that it is suitably guided; and those who can organize the flow of information that the above tasks and many others require. Thus, to the requirements of technology for specialized technical and scientific talent are added the very large further requirements of the planning that technology makes necessary.

Finally, following from the need for this variety of specialized talent, is 8 the need for its coordination. Talent must be brought to bear on the common purpose. More specifically, on large and small matters, information must be extracted from the various specialists, tested for its reliability and revelance, and made to yield a decision. This process, which is much misunderstood, requires a special word.

III

The modern business organization, or that part which has to do with guidance and direction, consists of numerous individuals who are engaged, at any given time, in obtaining, digesting or exchanging and testing information. A very large part of the exchange and testing of information is by word of mouth — a discussion in an office, at lunch or over the telephone. But the most typical procedure is through the committee and the committee meeting. One can do worse than think of a business organization as a hierarchy of committees. Coordination, in turn, consists in assigning the appropriate talent to committees, intervening on occasion to force a decision, and, as the case may be, announcing the decision or carrying it as information for a yet further decision by a yet higher committee.

Nor should it be supposed that this is an inefficient procedure. On the contrary it is, normally, the only efficient procedure. Association in a committee enables each member to come to know the intellectual resources and the reliability of his colleagues. Committee discussion enables members to pool information under circumstances which allow, also, of immediate probing to assess the relevance and reliability of the information offered. Uncertainty about one's information or error is revealed as in no other way. There is also, no doubt, considerable stimulus to mental effort from such association. One may enjoy torpor in private but not so comfortably in public, at least during working hours. Men who believe themselves deeply engaged in private thought are usually doing nothing. Committees are condemned by those who have been captured by the cliché that individual effort is somehow superior to group effort; by those who guiltily suspect that since group effort is more congenial, it must be less productive; and by those who do not see that the process of extracting, and especially of testing, information has necessarily a somewhat undirected quality — briskly conducted meetings invariably decide matters previously decided; and by those who fail to realize that highly paid men, when sitting around a table as a committee, are not necessarily wasting more time than, in the aggregate, they would each waste in private by themselves. Forthright and determined administrators frequently react to belief in the superior capacity of individuals for decision by abolishing all committees. They then constitute working parties, task forces or executive groups in order to avoid the one truly disastrous consequence of their action which would be that they should make the decisions themselves.

Thus decision in the modern business enterprise is the product not of in- 11
dividuals but of groups. The groups are numerous, as often informal as formal and subject to constant change in composition. Each contains the men
possessed of the information, or with access to the information, that bears
on the particular decision together with those whose skill consists in extracting and testing this information and obtaining a conclusion. This is how
men act successfully on matters where no single one, however exalted or intelligent, has more than a fraction of the necessary knowledge. It is what
makes modern business possible, and in other contexts it is what makes
modern government possible. It is fortunate that men of limited knowledge
are so constituted that they can work together in this way. Were it otherwise, business and government, at any given moment, would be at a stand-
still awaiting the appearance of a man with the requisite breadth of knowledge to resolve the problem presently at hand. Some further characteristics
of group decision-making must now be noticed.

I V

Group decision-making extends deeply into the business enterprise. Ef- 12
fective participation is not closely related to rank in the formal hierarchy of
the organization. This takes an effort of mind to grasp. Everyone is influenced by the stereotyped organization chart of the business enterprise. At
its top is the Board of Directors and the Board Chairman; next comes the
President; next comes the Executive Vice President; thereafter come the Department or Divisional heads — those who preside over the Chevrolet division, the large-generators division, the computer division. Power is assumed to pass down from the pinnacle. Those at the top give orders; those
below relay them on or respond.

This happens, but only in very simple organizations — the peacetime 13
drill of the National Guard or a troop of Boy Scouts moving out on Saturday
maneuvers. Elsewhere the decision will require information. Some power
will then pass to the person or persons who have this information. If this
knowledge is highly particular to themselves, then their power becomes
very great. In Los Alamos, during the development of the atomic bomb,
Enrico Fermi° rode a bicycle up the hill to work; Major General Leslie R.
Groves presided in grandeur over the entire Manhattan District.° In association with a handful of others Fermi could, at various early stages, have

---

Enrico Fermi   Italian physicist (1901–1954) involved in the development of the atomic
bomb.
Manhattan District   The group of scientists at Oak Ridge, Tenn., who developed the
atomic bomb in 1942. The code name for the project was the Manhattan Project.

brought the entire enterprise to an end. No such power resided with Groves. At any moment he could have been replaced without loss.

When power is exercised by a group, not only does it pass into the orga- 14 nization but it passes irrevocably. If an individual has taken a decision, he can be called before another individual, who is his superior in the hierarchy, his information can be examined and his decision reversed by the greater wisdom or experience of the superior. But if the decision required the combined information of a group, it cannot be safely reversed by an individual. He will have to get the judgment of other specialists. This returns the power once more to organization.

No one should insist, in these matters, on pure cases. There will often be 15 instances when an individual has the knowledge to modify or change the finding of a group. But the broad rule holds: If a decision requires the specialized knowledge of a group of men, it is subject to safe review only by the similar knowledge of a similar group. Group decision, unless acted upon by another group, tends to be absolute.

V

Next, it must not be supposed that group decision is important only in 16 such evident instances as nuclear technology or space mechanics. Simple products are made and packaged by sophisticated processes. And the most massive programs of market control, together with the most specialized marketing talent, are used on behalf of soap, detergents, cigarettes, aspirin, packaged cereals and gasoline. These, beyond others, are the valued advertising accounts. The simplicity and uniformity of these products require the investment of compensatingly elaborate science and art to suppress market influences and make prices and amounts sold subject to the largest possible measure of control. For these products too, decision passes to a group which combines specialized and esoteric knowledge. Here too power goes deeply and more or less irrevocably into the organization.

For purposes of pedagogy, I have sometimes illustrated these tendencies 17 by reference to a technically uncomplicated product, which, unaccountably, neither General Electric nor Westinghouse has yet placed on the market. It is a toaster of standard performance, the pop-up kind, except that it etches on the surface of the toast, in darker carbon, one of a selection of standard messages or designs. For the elegant, an attractive monogram would be available or a coat of arms; for the devout, at breakfast there would be an appropriate devotional message from the Reverend Billy Graham; for the patriotic or worried, there would be an aphorism urging vigilance from Mr. J. Edgar Hoover; for modern painters and economists, there would be a purely abstract design. A restaurant version would sell advertising.

Conceivably this is a vision that could come from the head of General 18 Electric. But the systematic proliferation of such ideas is the designated function of much more lowly men who are charged with product development. At an early stage in the development of the toaster the participation of specialists in engineering, production, styling and design and possibly philosophy, art and spelling would have to be sought. No one in position to authorize the product would do so without a judgment on how the problems of inscription were to be solved and at what cost. Nor, ordinarily, would an adverse finding on technical and economic feasibility be overridden. At some stage, further development would become contingent on the findings of market researchers and merchandise experts on whether the toaster could be sold and at what price. Nor would an adverse decision by this group be overruled. In the end there would be a comprehensive finding on the feasibility of the innovation. If unfavorable this would not be overruled. Nor, given the notoriety that attaches to lost opportunity, would be the more plausible contingency of a favorable recommendation. It will be evident that nearly all powers — initiation, character of development, rejection or acceptance — are exercised deep in the company. It is not the managers who decide. Effective power of decision is lodged deeply in the technical, planning and other specialized staff.

V I

We must notice next that this exercise of group power can be rendered 19 unreliable or ineffective by external interference. Not only does power pass into the organization but the quality of decision can easily be impaired by efforts of an individual to retain control over the decision-making process.

Specifically the group reaches decision by receiving and evaluating the 20 specialized information of its members. If it is to act responsibly, it must be accorded responsibility. It cannot be arbitrarily or capriciously overruled. If it is, it will develop the same tendencies to irresponsibility as an individual similarly treated.

But the tendency will be far more damaging. The efficiency of the group 21 and the quality of its decisions depend on the quality of the information provided and the precision with which it is tested. The last increases greatly as men work together. It comes to be known that some are reliable and that some, though useful, are at a tacit discount. All information offered must be so weighed. The sudden intervention of a superior introduces information, often of dubious quality, that is not subject to this testing. His reliability, as a newcomer, is unknown; his information, since he is boss, may be automatically exempt from the proper discount; or his intervention may take the form of an instruction and thus be outside the process of group decision in a matter where only group decision incorporating the required specialized judgments is reliable. In all cases the intrusion is damaging.

It follows both from the tendency for decision-making to pass down into 22 organization and the need to protect the autonomy of the group that those who hold high formal rank in an organization — the President of General Motors or General Electric — exercise only modest powers of substantive decision. This power is certainly less than conventional obeisance, professional public relations or, on occasion, personal vanity insist. Decision and ratification are often confused. The first is important; the second is not. There is a tendency to associate power with any decision, however routine, that involves a good deal of money. Business protocol requires that money be treated with solemnity and respect and likewise the man who passes on its use. The nominal head of a large corporation, though with slight power, and perhaps in the first stages of retirement, is visible, tangible and comprehensible. It is tempting and perhaps valuable for the corporate personality to attribute to him power of decision that, in fact, belongs to a dull and not easily comprehended collectivity. Nor is it a valid explanation that the boss, though impotent on specific questions, acts on broad issues of policy. Such issues of policy, if genuine, are pre-eminently the ones that require the specialized information of the group.

Leadership assigns tasks to committees from which decisions emerge. In doing so, it breaks usefully with the routine into which organization tends to fall. And it selects the men who comprise the groups that make the decisions, and it constitutes and reconstitutes these groups in accordance with changing need. This is, perhaps, its most important function. In an economy where organized intelligence is the decisive factor of production, the selection of the intelligence so organized is of central importance. But it cannot be supposed that a boss can replace or even second-guess organized intelligence on substantive decisions.

VII

In the past, leadership in business organizations was identified with the entrepreneur — the individual who united ownership or control of capital with capacity for organizing the other factors of production and, in most contexts, with a further capacity for innovation. With the rise of the modern corporation, the emergence of the organization required by modern technology and planning and the divorce of the owner of the capital from control of the enterprise, the entrepreneur no longer exists as an individual person in the mature industrial enterprise. Everyday discourse, except in the economics textbooks, recognizes this change. It replaces the entrepreneur, as the directing force of the enterprise, with management. This is a collective and imperfectly defined entity; in the large corporation it embraces chairman, president, those vice presidents with important staff or departmental responsibility, occupants of other major staff positions and, perhaps, division or department heads not included above. It includes, however, only a small proportion of those who, as participants, contribute information to group decisions. This latter group is very large; it extends from the most senior officials of the corporation to where it meets, at the outer perimeter, the white- and blue-collar workers whose function is to conform more or less mechanically to instruction or routine. It embraces all who bring specialized knowledge, talent or experience to group decision-making. This, not the management, is the guiding intelligence — the brain — of the enterprise. There is no name for all who participate in group decision-making or the organization which they form. I propose to call this organization the Technostructure.

QUESTIONS ON MEANING

1. Galbraith's primary purpose in this essay is to define the term he coins in the title. Why is it necessary for him to invent this word? When does he actually introduce the term *technostructure*? Why does he wait until this point?
2. Galbraith argues for a better understanding and appreciation of the way in which decisions are reached in modern business organizations. What are the essential points in his argument? How does the epigraph, the introductory quotation from Gordon, prepare us for Galbraith's argument?
3. One of the tasks Galbraith takes on in "The Technostructure" is to correct or refute some misconceptions about how decisions are made in business organizations. What common assumption does he address in paragraph 1? What others do you find in this essay? How does Galbraith use these false assumptions to further his argument?

QUESTIONS ON STRATEGY

1. In the first sentence of paragraph 4, Galbraith indicates a three-part structure to his argument in section II. How does he follow through on this plan?
2. What is Galbraith's subject in section III? How does this material follow from the first two sections? How does it relate to the "further characteristics of group decision-making" described in sections IV through VII?
3. In section V, Galbraith introduces a product he has conceived of — a special toaster. Does it seem that he is straying from his point here? What points does his toaster allow him to make about his main subject?

EXPLORATIONS

1. Galbraith, like Lewis Thomas, defends large corporate structures in fields marked by a high degree of specialization and the use of advanced technologies. Both authors take the position that fundamental misunderstandings determine people's view of the large corporation or the medical establishment. Review both essays and list several points in each one's arguments.

Do they convince you that "the public" is really out of touch with the conditions of life in a corporate society? Are Thomas and Galbraith elitists?

2. Do writers like Walker Percy (pages 74–91) and Wendell Berry (pages 349–359) offer convincing alternatives to such advocates of the status quo as Galbraith and Thomas? Explain.

WRITING TOPICS

1. Construct an argument along Galbraith's lines about the decision-making process in an organization with which you are familiar — a sports team, a club, a student government, any formally constituted group with a specific purpose. You may not find it appropriate to coin your own descriptive term, but use at least some of Galbraith's leading methods — the refutation of common errors, argument by description, example, analogy, and so on.

BOOKS AVAILABLE IN PAPERBACK

The Affluent Society. 3rd ed., rev. New York: New American Library. *Nonfiction: Economics.*

The Age of Uncertainty. Boston: Houghton Mifflin. *Nonfiction: Companion volume to BBC television series on modern economic history.*

American Capitalism. Boston: Houghton Mifflin. *Nonfiction: Economics.*

Economics and the Public Purpose. New York: New American Library. *Nonfiction: Economics.*

The Great Crash of 1929. New York: Avon. *Nonfiction: Economic history.*

A Life in Our Times. New York: Ballantine. *Nonfiction: Autobiography.*

Money: Whence It Came, Where It Went. New York: Bantam. *Nonfiction: Economic history.*

The Nature of Mass Poverty. Cambridge: Harvard University Press. *Nonfiction: Economics.*

The New Industrial State. 3rd ed., rev. New York: New American Library. *Nonfiction: Economics.*

EUDORA
WELTY

E UDORA WELTY *(b. 1909) published her* Collected Stories *in 1980, bringing together 576 pages of the short fiction for which she is celebrated. Her short stories first appeared in magazines, often the literary quarterlies, and became regular features of annual collections of the best fiction from periodicals. Two of her most enduring stories are "Why I Live at the P.O.," which shows her comic genius, and "The Worn Path," which recounts the courage and perseverance of an old black woman.*

Among her novels are Delta Wedding *(1946),* Losing Battles *(1970), and* The Optimist's Daughter *(1972), which won the Pulitzer Prize. "The Little Store" comes from* The Eye of the Story *(1978), which is a collection of her essays, most on the art of fiction. She has won the Gold Medal of the National Institute of Arts and Letters, the National Medal for Literature, and the Presidential Medal of Freedom.*

Born in Jackson, Mississippi, she still resides in Jackson, Mississippi. In this small town, her observation and imagination have found all the material they require. When she writes an essay out of memory, as she does in "The Little Store," she brings to reminiscence the storyteller's skills of narration and use of significant detail. Maybe more important, she also brings the stylist's ear for rhythms of word and sentence that compel attention. Her gifts for evoking intimacy and cherished detail lead in the end to hints of the darker vision that underlies her best work.

The Little Store

Two blocks away from the Mississippi State Capitol, and on the same street with it, where our house was when I was a child growing up in Jackson, it was possible to have a little pasture behind your backyard where you could keep a Jersey cow, which we did. My mother herself milked her. A thrifty homemaker, wife, mother of three, she also did all her own cooking. And as far as I can recall, she never set foot inside a grocery store. It wasn't necessary.

For her regular needs, she stood at the telephone in our front hall and consulted with Mr. Lemly, of Lemly's Market and Grocery downtown, who took her order and sent it out on his next delivery. And since Jackson at the heart of it was still within very near reach of the open country, the blackberry lady clanged on her bucket with a quart measure at your front door in June without fail, the watermelon man rolled up to your house exactly on time for the Fourth of July, and down through the summer, the quiet of the early-morning streets was pierced by the calls of farmers driving in with their plenty. One brought his with a song, so plaintive we would sing it with him:

> "Milk, milk,
> Buttermilk,
> Snap beans — butterbeans —
> Tender okra — fresh greens . . .
> And buttermilk."

My mother considered herself pretty well prepared in her kitchen and pantry for any emergency that, in her words, might choose to present itself. But if she should, all of a sudden, need another lemon or find she was out of bread, all she had to do was call out, "Quick! Who'd like to run to the Little Store for me?"

I would.

She'd count out the change into my hand, and I was away. I'll bet the nickel that would be left over that all over the country, for those of my day, the neighborhood grocery played a similar part in our growing up.

Our store had its name — it was that of the grocer who owned it, whom I'll call Mr. Sessions — but "the Little Store" is what we called it at home. It was a block down our street toward the capitol and a half a block further, around the corner, toward the cemetery. I knew even the sidewalk to it as well as I knew my own skin. I'd skipped my jumping-rope up and down it, hopped its length through mazes of hopscotch, played jacks in its islands of shade, serpentined along it on my Princess bicycle, skated it backward and forward. In the twilight I had dragged my steamboat by its string (this was homemade out of every new shoebox, with candle in the bottom lighted and shining through colored tissue paper pasted over windows scissored out in the shapes of the sun, moon and stars) across every crack of the walk without letting it bump or catch fire. I'd "played out" on that street after supper with my brothers and friends as long as "first-dark" lasted; I'd caught its lightning bugs. On the first Armistice Day° (and this will set the time I'm speaking of) we made our own parade down that walk on a single velocipede — my brother pedaling, our little brother riding the handlebars, and myself standing on the back, all with arms wide, flying flags in each hand. (My father snapped that picture as we raced by. It came out blurred.)

As I set forth for the Little Store, a tune would float toward me from the 7
house where there lived three sisters, girls in their teens, who ratted their hair over their ears, wore headbands like gladiators, and were considered to be very popular. They practiced for this in the daytime; they'd wind up the Victrola, leave the same record on they'd played before, and you'd see them bobbing past their dining-room windows while they danced with each other. Being three, they could go all day, cutting in:

> "Everybody ought to know-oh
> How to do the Tickle-Toe
> (how to do the Tickle-Toe)" —

they sang it and danced to it, and as I went by to the same song, I believed it.

A little further on, across the street, was the house where the principal of 8
our grade school lived — lived on, even while we were having vacation. What if she would come out? She would halt me in my tracks — she had a very carrying and well-known voice in Jackson, where she'd taught almost everybody — saying "Eudora Alice Welty, spell OBLIGE." OBLIGE was the word that she of course knew had kept me from making 100 on my spelling exam. She'd make me miss it again now, by boring her eyes through me from across the street. This was my vacation fantasy, one good way to scare myself on the way to the store.

Down near the corner waited the house of a little boy named Lindsey. 9
The sidewalk here was old brick, which the roots of a giant chinaberry tree had humped up and tilted this way and that. On skates, you took it fast, in a

---

the first Armistice Day November 11, 1918, marked the end of World War I. Now celebrated as Veterans Day.

series of skittering hops, trying not to touch ground anywhere. If the china-berries had fallen and rolled in the cracks, it was like skating through a whole shooting match of marbles. I crossed my fingers that Lindsey wouldn't be looking.

During the big flu epidemic he and I, as it happened, were being nursed through our sieges at the same time. I'd hear my father and mother mur-muring to each other, at the end of a long day, "And I wonder how poor lit-tle *Lindsey* got along today?" Just as, down the street, he no doubt would have to hear his family saying, "And I wonder how is poor *Eudora* by now?" I got the idea that a choice was going to be made soon between poor little Lindsey and poor Eudora, and I came up with a funny poem. I wasn't pre-pared for it when my father told me it wasn't funny and my mother cried that if I couldn't be ashamed for myself, she'd have to be ashamed for me:

> There was a little boy and his name was Lindsey.
> He went to heaven with the influinzy.

He didn't, he survived it, poem and all, the same as I did. But his chinaber-ries could have brought me down in my skates in a flying act of contrition before his eyes, looking pretty funny myself, right in front of his house.

Setting out in this world, a child feels so indelible. He only comes to find out later that it's all the others along his way who are making themselves in-delible to him.

Our Little Store rose right up from the sidewalk; standing in a street of family houses, it alone hadn't any yard in front, any tree or flowerbed. It was a plain frame building covered over with brick. Above the door, a little railed porch ran across on an upstairs level and four windows with shades were looking out. But I didn't catch on to those.

Running in out of the sun, you met what seemed total obscurity inside. There were almost tangible smells — licorice recently sucked in a child's cheek, dill-pickle brine that had leaked through a paper sack in a fresh trail across the wooden floor, ammonia-loaded ice that had been hoisted from wet croker sacks and slammed into the icebox with its sweet butter at the door, and perhaps the smell of still-untrapped mice.

Then through the motes of cracker dust, cornmeal dust, the Gold Dust of the Gold Dust Twins that the floor had been swept out with, the realities emerged. Shelves climbed to high reach all the way around, set out with not too much of any one thing but a lot of things — lard, molasses, vinegar, starch, matches, kerosene, Octagon soap (about a year's worth of octagon-shaped coupons cut out and saved brought a signet ring addressed to you in the mail. Furthermore, when the postman arrived at your door, he blew a whistle). It was up to you to remember what you came for, while your eye traveled from cans of sardines to ice cream salt to harmonicas to flypaper (over your head, batting around on a thread beneath the blades of the ceiling fan, stuck with its testimonial catch).

Its confusion may have been in the eye of its beholder. Enchantment is 15 cast upon you by all those things you weren't supposed to have need for, it lures you close to wooden tops you'd outgrown, boy's marbles and agates in little net pouches, small rubber balls that wouldn't bounce straight, frazzly kite-string, clay bubble-pipes that would snap off in your teeth, the stiffest scissors. You could contemplate those long narrow boxes of sparklers gathering dust while you waited for it to be the Fourth of July or Christmas, and noisemakers in the shape of tin frogs for somebody's birthday party you hadn't been invited to yet, and see that they were all marvelous.

You might not have even looked for Mr. Sessions when he came around 16 his store cheese (as big as a doll's house) and in front of the counter looking for you. When you'd finally asked him for, and received from him in its paper bag, whatever single thing it was that you had been sent for, the nickel that was left over was yours to spend.

Down at a child's eye level, inside those glass jars with mouths in their 17 sides through which the grocer could run his scoop or a child's hand might be invited to reach for a choice, were wineballs, all-day suckers, gumdrops, peppermints. Making a row under the glass of a counter were the Tootsie Rolls, Hershey Bars, Goo-Goo Clusters, Baby Ruths. And whatever was the name of those pastilles that came stacked in a cardboard cylinder with a cardboard lid? They were thin and dry, about the size of tiddlywinks, and in the shape of twisted rosettes. A kind of chocolate dust came out with them when you shook them out in your hand. Were they chocolate? I'd say rather they were brown. They didn't taste of anything at all, unless it was wood. Their attraction was the number you got for a nickel.

Making up your mind, you circled the store around and around, around 18 the pickle barrel, around the tower of Cracker Jack boxes; Mr. Sessions had built it for us himself on top of a packing case, like a house of cards.

If it seemed too hot for Cracker Jacks, I might get a cold drink. Mr. Ses- 19 sions might have already stationed himself by the cold-drinks barrel, like a mind reader. Deep in ice water that looked black as ink, murky shapes that would come up as Coca-Colas, Orange Crushes, and various flavors of pop, were all swimming around together. When you gave the word, Mr. Sessions plunged his bare arm in to the elbow and fished out your choice, first try. I favored a locally bottled concoction called Lake's Celery. (What else could it be called? It was made by a Mr. Lake out of celery. It was a popular drink here for years but was not known universally, as I found out when I arrived in New York and ordered one in the Astor bar.) You drank on the premises, with feet set wide apart to miss the drip, and gave him back his bottle.

But he didn't hurry you off. A standing scales was by the door, with a 20 stack of iron weights and a brass slide on the balance arm, that would weigh you up to three hundred pounds. Mr. Sessions, whose hands were gentle and smelled of carbolic, would lift you up and set your feet on the platform, hold your loaf of bread for you, and taking his time while you stood still for him, he would make certain of what you weighed today. He could even remember what you weighed the last time, so you could subtract and announce how much you'd gained. That was goodbye.

Is there always a hard way to go home? From the Little Store, you could go partway through the sewer. If your brothers had called you a scarecat, then across the next street beyond the Little Store, it was possible to enter this sewer by passing through a privet hedge, climbing down into the bed of a creek, and going into its mouth on your knees. The sewer — it might have been no more than a "storm sewer" — came out and emptied here, where Town Creek, a sandy, most often shallow little stream that ambled through Jackson on its way to the Pearl River, ran along the edge of the cemetery. You could go in darkness through this tunnel to where you next saw light (if you ever did) and climb out through the culvert at your own street corner.

I was a scarecat, all right, but I was a reader with my own refuge in storybooks. Making my way under the sidewalk, under the street and the streetcar track, under the Little Store, down there in the wet dark by myself, I could be Persephone° entering into my six-month sojourn underground — though I didn't suppose Persephone had to crawl, hanging onto a loaf of bread, and come out through the teeth of an iron grating. Mother Ceres° would indeed be wondering where she could find me, and mad when she knew. "Now am I going to have to start marching to the Little Store for *myself?*"

I couldn't picture it. Indeed I'm unable today to picture the Little Store with a grown person in it, except for Mr. Sessions and the lady who helped him, who belonged there. We children thought it was ours. The happiness of errands was in part that of running for the moment away from home, a free spirit. I believed the Little Store to be a center of the outside world, and hence of happiness — as I believed what I found in the Cracker Jack box to be a genuine prize, which was as simply as I believed in the Golden Fleece.°

But a day came when I ran to the store to discover, sitting on the front step, a grown person, after all — more than a grown person. It was the Monkey Man, together with his monkey. His grinding-organ was lowered to the step beside him. In my whole life so far, I must have laid eyes on the Monkey Man no more than five or six times. An itinerant of rare and wayward

---

Persephone In Greek mythology, the daughter of Zeus and Demeter. She is abducted by Pluto to reign with him in the underworld for six months of every year.

Ceres The Roman name for Demeter, mother of Persephone.

Golden Fleece In Greek mythology, the fleece of the golden ram, stolen by Jason and the Argonauts.

appearances, he was not punctual like the Gipsies, who every year with the
first cool days of fall showed up in the aisles of Woolworth's. You never
knew when the Monkey Man might decide to favor Jackson, or which way
he'd go. Sometimes you heard him as close as the next street, and then he
didn't come up yours.

But now I saw the Monkey Man at the Little Store, where I'd never seen   25
him before. I'd never seen him sitting down. Low on that familiar doorstep,
he was not the same any longer, and neither was his monkey. They looked
just like an old man and an old friend of his that wore a fez, meeting quietly
together, tired, and resting with their eyes fixed on some place far away, and
not the same place. Yet their romance for me didn't have it in its power to
waver. I wavered. I simply didn't know how to step around them, to proceed on into the Little Store for my mother's emergency as if nothing had
happened. If I could have gone in there after it, whatever it was, I would
have given it to them — putting it into the monkey's cool little fingers. I
would have given them the Little Store itself.

In my memory they are still attached to the store — so are all the others.   26
Everyone I saw on my way seemed to me then part of my errand, and in a
way they were. As I myself, the free spirit, was part of it too.

All the years we lived in that house where we children were born, the   27
same people lived in the other houses on our street too. People changed
through the arithmetic of birth, marriage and death, but not by going away.
So families just accrued stories, which through the fullness of time, in those
times, their own lives made. And I grew up in those.

But I didn't know there'd ever been a story at the Little Store, one that   28
was going on while I was there. Of course, all the time the Sessions family
had been living right overhead there, in the upstairs rooms behind the little
railed porch and the shaded windows; but I think we children never thought
of that. Did I fail to see them as a family because they weren't living in an
ordinary house? Because I so seldom saw them close together, or having
anything to say to each other? She sat in the back of the store, her pencil
over a ledger, while he stood and waited on children to make up their
minds. They worked in twin black eyeshades, held on their gray heads by
elastic bands. It may be harder to recognize kindness — or unkindness either
— in a face whose eyes are in shadow. His face underneath his shade was as
round as the little wooden wheels in the Tinker Toy box. So was her face. I
didn't know, perhaps didn't even wonder: were they husband and wife or
brother and sister? Were they father and mother? There were a few other
persons, of various ages, wandering singly in by the back door and out. But
none of their relationships could I imagine, when I'd never seen them sitting
down together around their own table.

The possibility that they had any other life at all, anything beyond what   29
we could see within the four walls of the Little Store, occurred to me only

when tragedy struck their family. There was some act of violence. The shock to the neighborhood traveled to the children, of course; but I couldn't find out from my parents what had happened. They held it back from me, as they'd already held back many things, "until the time comes for you to know."

You could find out some of these things by looking in the unabridged dictionary and the encyclopedia — kept to hand in our dining room — but you couldn't find out there what had happened to the family who for all the years of your life had lived upstairs over the Little Store, who had never been anything but patient and kind to you, who never once had sent you away. All I ever knew was its aftermath: they were the only people ever known to me who simply vanished. At the point where their life overlapped into ours, the story broke off.

We weren't being sent to the neighborhood grocery for facts of life, or death. But of course those are what we were on the track of, anyway. With the loaf of bread and the Cracker Jack prize, I was bringing home the intimations of pride and disgrace, and rumors and early news of people coming to hurt one another, while others practiced for joy — storing up a portion for myself of the human mystery.

QUESTIONS ON MEANING

1. Welty writes as an adult recounting childhood experiences. Give some examples of the perspectives of the adult and of the child. At what points does the adult voice intrude explicitly? How does the presence of that adult voice affect the ending?

2. In paragraph 2, we hear of a Mr. Lemly. Why does Welty use the proper name here? Later in paragraph 2, we hear of other food vendors. Why does she omit their names?

3. How does the author mean *indelible* in paragraph 11?

4. What effect does the Monkey Man (introduced in paragraphs 24 and 25) have on the young Welty? What effect does he have on the adult Welty's story? Why does Welty introduce this figure in a paragraph beginning with *but*? When she repeats this device later, does it have the same purpose?

5. Welty does not reveal "the mystery" of the Sessions family. Why is this an effective strategy? How does this flavor the rest of the essay?

QUESTIONS ON STRATEGY

1. Many writers prefer to provide readers with necessary background information — called "exposition" — as subtly as possible. In her first paragraph, Welty supplies information with a skill that hides itself. Look again at this

paragraph in the light of the essay as a whole. What essential facts do we learn from this paragraph? Why do we need to know these facts?

2. In the fourth sentence of paragraph 6, Welty uses a long sentence to tell us how she became acquainted with a particular sidewalk. Aside from informing us, how does this sentence add to the atmosphere?

3. Paragraphs 7 through 10 relate anecdotes of Welty's childhood in Jackson, Mississippi. How are these built into the essay? Assuming that "The Little Store" is not simply a random series of recollections but a deliberate organizing of details, how are these details arranged?

4. When we write description, most of us appeal almost exclusively to the sense of sight. How many senses does Welty appeal to in this descriptive and narrative essay? Mark in the margin every detail that relates to one particular sense (sight, touch, taste, smell, hearing).

5. When we talk about poetry, we commonly examine its rhythms; less so, when we talk about prose. As poets control the sound of their verses by breaking their sentences into lines, prose writers create rhythms through paragraphing, sentence structure, and punctuation. Look at the first two sentences of this essay. The first one is a complex sentence with many modifying phrases and clauses. The second sentence is a simple sentence. What is the rhythmic effect of the contrast between the two sentences? Find two other examples of Welty's use of sentence structure to create a purposeful rhythm.

6. In a scientific paper or an essay in modern philosophy, writers cultivate an impersonal tone. Their object is not to communicate their personalities but to convey specialized information. But in a personal reminiscence, the sound of everyday speech is appropriate and effective. How does Welty achieve a personal voice in her language and sentence structure? Give specific examples.

EXPLORATIONS

1. "The Little Store" is very much a storyteller's essay. Analyze the balance Welty strikes between narrative and exposition. Read one of her short stories — "Petrified Man" or "Why I Live at the P.O." — and determine how it resembles this essay and how it differs from it. Consider setting, mood, pace, development, language, and sentence structure.

WRITING TOPICS

1. Pick one small detail of your childhood, maybe your own Little Store, and write an essay that brings it alive for the reader, following Welty's model. Vary the rhythms of your sentences. Make your details appeal to a variety of senses. Try to interweave the adult perspective and the child's perspective.

2. Part of Welty's point is that she was "protected" by her parents and her environment from the perils of life, but she also describes how reality manifested itself anyway. Consider how your parents or other adults attempted

to protect you from real life when you were a child. Write an essay describing one incident when their protection failed.

BOOKS AVAILABLE IN PAPERBACK

The Bride of Innisfallen and Other Stories. New York: Harcourt Brace Jovanovich, Harvest Books.

The Collected Stories of Eudora Welty. New York: Harcourt Brace Jovanovich, Harvest Books.

A Curtain of Green and Other Stories. New York: Harcourt Brace Jovanovich, Harvest Books.

Delta Wedding. New York: Harcourt Brace Jovanovich, Harvest Books. *Novel.*

The Eye of the Story: Selected Essays and Reviews. New York: Vintage.

The Golden Apples. New York: Harcourt Brace Jovanovich, Harvest Books. *Short novel and stories.*

Losing Battles. New York: Vintage. *Novel.*

The Optimist's Daughter. New York: Vintage. *Novel.*

The Ponder Heart. New York: Harcourt Brace Jovanovich, Harvest Books. *Novel.*

The Robber Bridegroom. New York: Harcourt Brace Jovanovich, Harvest Books. *Novel.*

Thirteen Stories. Selected and with an introduction by Ruth M. Vande Kieft. New York: Harcourt Brace Jovanovich, Harvest Books.

The Wide Net and Other Stories. New York: Harcourt Brace Jovanovich.

BARBARA
TUCHMAN

*W*HEN WE CALL SOMEONE *a historian, these days, we usually mean a professor who teaches courses in a history department. Barbara Tuchman is a
historian in an older sense: She studies the past, makes her own sense of things, and
writes books to proclaim and defend her understanding. To work, she must study,
consulting the documents assembled in archives and libraries. ("To an historian,"
she writes, "libraries are food, shelter, and even Muse.") She must take notes, follow clues, organize, make judgments, and write narrative that allows room for ideas
and moral argument. By selection and organization of detail, she emphasizes particular themes and shows her interpretations.*

*Born in New York in 1912, she graduated from Radcliffe College in 1933. Her
early interests turned her Eastward, and she worked as a research assistant at the Institute of Pacific Relations. (Much later this interest found expression in her* Stilwell
and the American Experience in China, *which won a Pulitzer Prize in 1971.)
Later in the 1930s she wrote on politics for* The Nation, *the political magazine
which her father owned. Then she worked as a journalist in London and wrote about
the Spanish Civil War. After Pearl Harbor she took a job with the Office of War Information in Washington.*

Perhaps because she matured in the 1930s as the world was heading toward World War II, she has always attended to the origins of war. Her first publishing success was The Guns of August *(1961), about the beginnings of World War I; subsequently* The Proud Tower *(1966) described that war's antecedents in European and in American history.*

When Tuchman writes about the fourteenth century in Europe, as she does in A Distant Mirror *(1978), she seems to leave modern history behind, but her theme is a six-hundred-year-old reflection. It is a commonplace that history repeats itself; Tuchman analyzing the fourteenth century writes by analogy about the twentieth. Her pursuit of this analogy is addressed to readers of her own time; she published it in 1973, during the Watergate scandal. Her argument depends on her acute selection and organization of detail.*

History as Mirror

At a time when everyone's mind is on the explosions of the moment, it might seem obtuse of me to discuss the fourteenth century. But I think a backward look at that disordered, violent, bewildered, disintegrating, and calamity-prone age can be consoling and possibly instructive in a time of similar disarray. Reflected in a six-hundred-year-old mirror, a more revealing image of ourselves and our species might be seen than is visible in the clutter of circumstances under our noses. The value of historical comparison was made keenly apparent to the French medievalist, Edouard Perroy, when he was writing his book on the Hundred Years' War while dodging the Gestapo in World War II. "Certain ways of behaving," he wrote, "certain reactions against fate, throw mutual light upon each other."

Besides, if one suspects that the twentieth century's record of inhumanity and folly represents a phase of mankind at its worst, and that our last decade of collapsing assumptions has been one of unprecedented discomfort, it is reassuring to discover that the human race has been in this box before — and emerged. The historian has the comfort of knowing that man (meaning, here and hereafter, the species, not the sex) is always capable of his worst; has indulged in it, painfully struggled up from it, slid back, and gone on again.

In what follows, the parallels are not always in physical events but rather in the effect on society, and sometimes in both.

The afflictions of the fourteenth century were the classic riders of the Apocalypse — famine, plague, war, and death, this time on a black horse. These combined to produce an epidemic of violence, depopulation, bad government, oppressive taxes, an accelerated breakdown of feudal bonds, working class insurrection, monetary crisis, decline of morals and rise in crime, decay of chivalry, the governing idea of the governing class, and above all, corruption of society's central institution, the Church, whose loss of authority and prestige deprived man of his accustomed guide in a darkening world.

Yet amidst the disintegration were sprouting, invisible to contempo- 5
raries, the green shoots of the Renaissance to come. In human affairs as in nature, decay is compost for new growth.

Some medievalists reject the title of decline for the fourteenth century, 6
asserting instead that it was the dawn of a new age. Since the processes obviously overlap, I am not sure that the question is worth arguing, but it becomes poignantly interesting when applied to ourselves. Do *we* walk amidst trends of a new world without knowing it? How far ahead is the dividing line? Or are we on it? What designation will our age earn from historians six hundred years hence? One wishes one could make a pact with the devil like Enoch Soames, the neglected poet in Max Beerbohm's story, allowing us to return and look ourselves up in the library catalogue. In that future history book, shall we find the chapter title for the twentieth century reading Decline and Fall, or Eve of Revival?

The fourteenth century opened with a series of famines brought on when 7
population growth outstripped the techniques of food production. The precarious balance was tipped by a series of heavy rains and floods and by a chilling of the climate in what has been called the Little Ice Age. Upon a people thus weakened fell the century's central disaster, the Black Death, an eruption of bubonic plague which swept the known world in the years 1347–1349 and carried off an estimated one-third of the population in two and a half years. This makes it the most lethal episode known to history, which is of some interest to an age equipped with the tools of overkill.

The plague raged at terrifying speed, increasing the impression of hor- 8
ror. In a given locality it accomplished its kill within four to six months, except in larger cities, where it struck again in spring after lying dormant in winter. The death rate in Avignon was said to have claimed half the population, of whom ten thousand were buried in the first six weeks in a single mass grave. The mortality was in fact erratic. Some communities whose last survivors fled in despair were simply wiped out and disappeared from the map forever, leaving only a grassed-over hump as their mortal trace.

Whole families died, leaving empty houses and property a prey to 9
looters. Wolves came down from the mountains to attack plague-stricken villages, crops went unharvested, dikes crumbled, salt water reinvaded and soured the lowlands, the forest crept back, and second growth, with the awful energy of nature unchecked, reconverted cleared land to waste. For lack

of hands to cultivate, it was thought impossible that the world could ever regain its former prosperity.

Once the dark bubonic swellings appeared in armpit and groin, death followed rapidly within one to three days, often overnight. For lack of gravediggers, corpses piled up in the streets or were buried so hastily that dogs dug them up and ate them. Doctors were helpless, and priests lacking to administer that final sacrament so that people died believing they must go to hell. No bells tolled, the dead were buried without prayers or funeral rites or tears; families did not weep for the loss of loved ones, for everyone expected death. Matteo Villani, taking up the chronicle of Florence from the hands of his dead brother, believed he was recording the "extermination of mankind."

People reacted variously, as they always do: some prayed, some robbed, some tried to help, most fled if they could, others abandoned themselves to debauchery on the theory that there would be no tomorrow. On balance, the dominant reaction was fear and a desire to save one's own skin regardless of the closest ties. "A father did not visit his son, nor the son his father; charity was dead," wrote one physician, and that was not an isolated observation. Boccaccio in his famous account reports that "kinsfolk held aloof, brother was forsaken by brother . . . often times husband by wife; nay what is more, and scarcely to be believed, fathers and mothers were found to abandon their own children to their fate, untended, unvisited as if they had been strangers."

"Men grew bold," wrote another chronicler, "in their indulgence in pleasure. . . . No fear of God or law of man deterred a criminal. Seeing that all perished alike, they reflected that offenses against human or Divine law would bring no punishment for no one would live long enough to be held to account." This is an accurate summary, but it was written by Thucydides about the Plague of Athens in the fifth century B.C. — which indicates a certain permanence of human behavior.

The nightmare of the plague was compounded for the fourteenth century by the awful mystery of its cause. The idea of disease carried by insect bite was undreamed of. Fleas and rats, which were in fact the carriers, are not mentioned in the plague writings. Contagion could be observed but not explained and thus seemed doubly sinister. The medical faculty of the University of Paris favored a theory of poisonous air spread by a conjunction of the planets, but the general and fundamental belief, made official by a papal bull, was that the pestilence was divine punishment for man's sins. Such horror could only be caused by the wrath of God. "In the year of our Lord, 1348," sadly wrote a professor of law at the University of Pisa, "the hostility of God was greater than the hostility of men."

That belief enhanced the sense of guilt, or rather the consciousness of sin (guilt, I suspect, is modern; sin is medieval), which was always so close to the surface throughout the Middle Ages. Out of the effort to appease divine wrath came the flagellants, a morbid frenzy of self-punishment that almost at once found a better object in the Jews.

A storm of pogroms followed in the track of the Black Death, widely   15 stimulated by the flagellants, who often rushed straight for the Jewish quarter, even in towns which had not yet suffered the plague. As outsiders within the unity of Christendom the Jews were natural persons to suspect of evil design on the Christian world. They were accused of poisoning the wells. Although the Pope condemned the attacks as inspired by "that liar the devil," pointing out that Jews died of plague like everyone else, the populace wanted victims, and fell upon them in three hundred communities throughout Europe. Slaughtered and burned alive, the entire colonies of Frankfurt, Cologne, Mainz, and other towns of Germany and the Lowlands were exterminated, despite the restraining efforts of town authorities. Elsewhere the Jews were expelled by judicial process after confession of well-poisoning was extracted by torture. In every case their goods and property, whether looted or confiscated, ended in the hands of the persecutors. The process was lucrative, as it was to be again in our time under the Nazis, although the fourteenth century had no gold teeth to rob from the corpses. Where survivors slowly returned and the communities revived, it was on worse terms than before and in walled isolation. This was the beginning of the ghetto.

Men of the fourteenth century were particularly vulnerable because of   16 the loss of credibility by the Church, which alone could absolve sin and offer salvation from hell. When the papal schism dating from 1378 divided the Church under two popes, it brought the highest authority in society into disrepute, a situation with which we are familiar. The schism was the second great calamity of the time, displaying before all the world the unedifying spectacle of twin vicars of God, each trying to bump the other off the chair of St. Peter, each appointing his own college of cardinals, each collecting tithes and revenues and excommunicating the partisans of his rival. No conflict of ideology was involved; the split arose from a simple squabble for the office of the papacy and remained no more than that for the fifty years the schism lasted. Plunged in this scandal, the Church lost moral authority, the more so as its two halves scrambled in the political arena for support. Kingdoms, principalities, even towns, took sides, finding new cause for the endless wars that scourged the times.

The Church's corruption by worldliness long antedated the schism. By   17 the fourteenth century the papal court at Avignon was called Babylon and rivaled temporal courts in luxury and magnificence. Its bureaucracy was enormous and its upkeep mired in a commercial traffic in spiritual things. Pardons, indulgences, prayers, every benefice and bishopric, everything the Church had or was, from cardinal's hat to pilgrim's relic, everything that represented man's relation to God, was for sale. Today it is the processes of government that are for sale, especially the electoral process, which is as vital to our political security as salvation was to the emotional security of the fourteenth century.

Men still craved God and spun off from the Church in sects and heresies, seeking to purify the realm of the spirit. They too yearned for a greening of the system. The yearning, and disgust with the Establishment, produced freak orders of mystics who lived in coeducational communes, rejected marriage, and glorified sexual indulgence. Passionate reformers ranged from St. Catherine of Siena, who scolded everyone in the hierarchy from the popes down, to John Wycliffe, who plowed the soil of Protestant revolt. Both strove to renew the Church, which for so long had been the only institution to give order and meaning to the untidy business of living on earth. When in the last quarter of the century the schism brought the Church into scorn and ridicule and fratricidal war, serious men took alarm. The University of Paris made strenuous and ceaseless efforts to find a remedy, finally demanding submission of the conflict to a supreme Council of the Church whose object should be not only reunification but reform.

Without reform, said the University's theologians in their letter to the popes, the damaging effect of the current scandal could be irreversible. In words that could have been addressed to our own secular potentate although he is — happily — not double, they wrote, "The Church will suffer for your overconfidence if you repent too late of having neglected reform. If you postpone it longer the harm will be incurable. Do you think people will suffer forever from your bad government? Who do you think can endure, amid so many abuses . . . your elevation of men without literacy or virtue to the most eminent positions?" The echo sounds over the gulf of six hundred years with a timeliness almost supernatural.

When the twin popes failed to respond, pressure at last brought about a series of Church councils which endeavored to limit and constitutionalize the powers of the papacy. After a thirty-year struggle, the councils succeeded in ending the schism but the papacy resisted reform. The decades of debate only served to prove that the institution could not be reformed from within. Eighty years of mounting protest were to pass before pressure produced Luther and the great crack.

Despite the parallel with the present struggle between Congress and the presidency, there is no historical law that says the outcome must necessarily be the same. The American presidency at age two hundred is not a massive rock of ages embedded in a thousand years of acceptance as was the medieval Church, and should be easier to reform. One can wish for Congress a better result than the councils had in the effort to curb the executive — or at least one can hope.

The more important parallel lies in the decay of public confidence in our 22
governing institutions, as the fourteenth-century public lost confidence in
the Church. Who believes today in the integrity of government? — or of
business, or of law or justice or labor unions or the military or the police?
Even physicians, the last of the admired, are now in disfavor. I have a theory
that the credibility vacuum owes something to our nurture in that conspiracy of fables called advertising, which we daily absorb without believing.
Since public affairs and ideas and candidates are now presented to us as a
form of advertising, we automatically suspend belief or suspect fraud as
soon as we recognize the familiar slickness. I realize, of course, that the roots
of disbelief go down to deeper ground. Meanwhile the effect is a loss of trust
in all authority which leaves us guideless and dismayed and cynical — even
as in the fourteenth century.

Over that whole century hung the smoke of war — dominated by the An- 23
glo-French conflict known to us, though fortunately not to them, as the
Hundred Years' War. (With the clock still ticking in Indochina, one wonders
how many years there are still to go in that conflict.) Fought on French soil
and extending into Flanders and Spain, the Hundred Years' War actually
lasted for more than a century, from 1337 to 1453. In addition, the English
fought the Scots; the French fought incessant civil wars against Gascons,
Bretons, Normans, and Navarrese; the Italian republics fought each other —
Florence against Pisa, Venice against Genoa, Milan against everybody; the
kingdom of Naples and Sicily was fought over by claimants from Hungary
to Aragon; the papacy fought a war that included unbridled massacre to re-
conquer the Papal States; the Savoyards fought the Lombards; the Swiss
fought the Austrians; the tangled wars of Bohemia, Poland, and the German
Empire defy listing; crusades were launched against the Saracens, and to fill
up any pauses the Teutonic Knights conducted annual campaigns against
pagan Lithuania which other knights could join for extra practice. Fighting
was the function of the Second Estate, that is, of the landed nobles and
knights. A knight without a war or tournament to go to felt as restless as a
man who cannot go to the office.

Every one of these conflicts threw off Free Companies of mercenaries, or- 24
ganized for brigandage under a professional captain, which became an evil
of the period as malignant as the plague. In the money economy of the fourteenth century, armed forces were no longer feudal levies serving under a
vassal's obligation who went home after forty days, but were recruited
bodies who served for pay. Since this was at great cost to the sovereign, he
cut off the payroll as soon as he safely could during halts of truce or negotiation. Thrown on their own resources and having acquired a taste for plun-
der, the men-at-arms banded together in the Free Companies, whose savage

success swelled their ranks with landless knights and squires and roving ad-
venturers.

The companies contracted their services to whatever ruler was in need of
troops, and between contracts held up towns for huge ransom, ravaged the
countryside, and burned, pillaged, raped, and slaughtered their way back
and forth across Europe. No one was safe, no town or village knew when it
might be attacked. The leaders, prototypes of the *condottieri* in Italy, became
powers and made fortunes and even became respectable like Sir John
Hawkwood, commander of the famous White Company. Smaller bands,
called in France the *tards-venus* (latecomers), scavenged like jackals, living off
the land, plundering, killing, carrying off women, torturing peasants for
their small horde of grain or townsmen for their hidden goods, and burning,
always burning. They set fire to whatever they left behind, farmhouses,
vineyards, abbeys, in a kind of madness to destroy the very sources off
which they lived, or would live tomorrow. Destruction and cruelty became
self-engendering, not merely for loot but almost one might say for sport.
The phenomenon is not peculiar to any one time or people, as we know
from the experience of our own century, but in the fourteenth century it
seems to have reached a degree and extent beyond explanation.

It must be added that in practice and often personnel the Free Companies were hardly distinguishable from the troops of organized official wars.
About 80 percent of the activity of a declared war consisted of raids of plun-
der and burning through enemy territory. That paragon of chivalry, the
Black Prince, could well have earned his name from the blackened ruins he
left across France. His baggage train and men-at-arms were often so heavily
laden with loot that they moved as slowly as a woman's litter.

The saddest aspect of the Hundred Years' War was the persistent but
vain efforts of the belligerents themselves to stop it. As in our case, it spread
political damage at home, and the cost was appalling. Moreover it harmed
the relations of all the powers at a time when they were anxious to unite to
repel the infidel at the gates. For Christendom was now on the defensive
against the encroaching Turks. For that reason the Church, too, tried to end
the war that was keeping Europe at odds. On the very morning of the fatal
battle of Poitiers, two cardinals hurried with offers and counter-offers between the two armed camps, trying in vain to prevent the clash. During periods of truce the parties held long parleys lasting months and sometimes
years in the effort to negotiate a definitive peace. It always eluded them, failing over questions of prestige, or put off by the feeling of whichever side
held a slight advantage that one more push would bring the desired gains.

All this took place under a code of chivalry whose creed was honor, loyalty, and courtesy and whose purpose, like that of every social code evolved
by man in his long search for order, was to civilize and supply a pattern of
rules. A knight's task under the code was to uphold the Church, defend his

land and vassals, maintain the peace of his province, protect the weak and guard the poor from injustice, shed his blood for his comrade, and lay down his life if needs must. For the land-owning warrior class, chivalry was their ideology, their politics, their system — what democracy is to us or Marxism to the Communists.

Originating out of feudal needs, it was already slipping into anachronism 29 by the fourteenth century because the development of monarchy and a royal bureaucracy was taking away the knight's functions, economic facts were forcing him to commute labor dues for money, and a rival element was appearing in the urban magnates. Even his military prowess was being nullified by trained bodies of English longbowmen and Swiss pikemen, nonmembers of the warrior class who in feudal theory had no business in battle at all.

Yet in decadence chivalry threw its brightest light; never were its cere- 30 monies more brilliant, its jousts and tournaments so brave, its apparel so splendid, its manners so gay and amorous, its entertainments so festive, its self-glorification more eloquent. The gentry elaborated the forms of chivalry just *because* institutions around them were crumbling. They clung to what gave their status meaning in a desperate embrace of the past. This is the time when the Order of the Garter was founded by the King of England, the Order of the Star by the King of France, the Golden Fleece by the Duke of Burgundy — in deliberate imitation of King Arthur's Knights of the Round Table.

The rules still worked well enough among themselves, with occasional 31 notorious exceptions such as Charles of Navarre, a bad man appropriately known as Charles the Bad. Whenever necessity required him to swear loyal reconciliation and fealty to the King of France, his mortal enemy, he promptly engaged in treacherous intrigues with the King of England, leaving his knightly oaths to become, in the White House word, inoperative. On the whole, however, the nobility laid great stress on high standards of honor. It was vis-à-vis the Third Estate that chivalry fell so far short of the theory. Yet it remained an ideal of human relations, as Christianity remained an ideal of faith, that kept men reaching for the unattainable. The effort of society is always toward order, away from anarchy. Sometimes it moves forward, sometimes it slips back. Which is the direction of one's own time may be obscure.

The fourteenth century was further afflicted by a series of convulsions 32 and upheavals in the working class, both urban and rural. Causes were various: the cost of constant war was thrown upon the people in hearth taxes, salt taxes, sales taxes, and debasement of coinage. In France the failure of the knights to protect the populace from incessant ravaging was a factor. It exacerbated the peasants' misery, giving it the energy of anger which erupted in the ferocious mid-century rising called the *Jacquerie*. Shortage of labor caused by the plague had temporarily brought higher wages and rising expectations. When these were met, especially in England, by statutes clamping wages at pre-plague levels, the result was the historic Peasants' Revolt of 1381. In the towns, capitalism was widening the gap between masters and artisans, producing the sustained weavers' revolts in the cloth towns of Flanders and major outbreaks in Florence and Paris. In Paris, too, the merchant class rose against the royal councillors, whom they despised as both corrupt and incompetent. To frighten the regent into submission, they murdered his two chief councillors in his presence.

All these struggles had one thing in common: they were doomed. United against a common threat, the ruling class could summon greater strength than its antagonists and acted to suppress insurrection with savagery equal to the fury from below. Yet discontent had found its voice; dissent and rejection of authority for the first time in the Middle Ages became a social force. Demagogues and determined leaders, reformers and agitators came to the surface. Though all were killed, several by mobs of their own followers, the uprisings they led were the beginning of modern, conscious, class war.

Meanwhile, over the second half-century, the plague returned with lesser virulence at intervals of every twelve to fifteen years. It is hardly to be wondered that people of the time saw man's fate as an endless succession of evils. He must indeed be wicked and his enemy Satan finally triumphant. According to a popular belief at the end of the century, no one since the beginning of the schism had entered Paradise.

Pessimism was a mark of the age and the *Danse Macabre* or Dance of Death its most vivid expression. Performed at occasions of popular drama and public sermons, it was an actual dance or pantomime in which a figure from every walk of life — king, clerk, lawyer, friar, goldsmith, bailiff, and so on — confronts the loathsome corpse he must become. In the accompanying verses and illustrations which have survived, the theme repeats itself over and over: the end of all life is putrefaction and the grave; no one escapes; no matter what beauty or kingly power or poor man's misery has been the lot in life, all end alike as food for worms. Death is not treated poetically as the soul's flight to reunion with God; it is a skeleton grinning at the vanity of life.

Life as well as death was viewed with disgust. The vices and corruptions of the age, a low opinion of one's fellowmen, and nostalgia for the well-ordered past were the favorite themes of literary men. Even Boccaccio in his later works became ill-tempered. "All good customs fail," laments Christine de Pisan of France, "and virtues are held at little worth." Eustache Deschamps complains that "the child of today has become a ruffian. . . . People are gluttons and drunkards, haughty of heart, caring for nought, not honor nor goodness nor kindness . . ." and he ends each verse with the refrain,

"Time past had virtue and righteousness but today reigns only vice." In England John Gower denounces Rome for simony, Lollards for heresy, clergy and monks for idleness and lust, kings, nobles, and knights for self-indulgence and rapine, the law for bribery, merchants for usury and fraud, the commons for ignorance, and in general the sins of perjury, lechery, avarice, and pride as displayed in extravagant fashions.

These last did indeed, as in all distracted times, reflect a reaching for the 37 absurd, especially in the long pointed shoes which kept getting longer until the points had to be tied up around the knee, and the young men's doublets which kept getting shorter until they revealed the buttocks, to the censure of moralists and snickers of the crowd. Leaving miniskirts to the males, the ladies inexplicably adopted a fashion of gowns and posture designed to make them look pregnant.

Self-disgust, it seems to me, has reappeared in our time, not without 38 cause. The succession of events since 1914 has disqualified belief in moral progress, and pollution of the physical world is our bubonic plague. Like the fourteenth century, we have lost confidence in man's capacity to control his fate and even in his capacity to be good. So we have a literature of the anti-hero aimlessly wandering among the perverse, absurd, and depraved; we have porn and pop and blank canvases and anti-music designed to deafen. I am not sure whether in all this the artists are expressing contempt for their fellowman or the loud laugh that bespeaks emptiness of feeling, but whatever the message, it has a faint ring of the *Danse Macabre*.

Historians until recently have hurried over the fourteenth century be- 39 cause like most people they prefer not to deal with failure. But it would be a mistake to imply that it was solid gloom. Seen from inside, especially from a position of privilege, it had beauties and wonders, and the ferment itself was exciting. "In these fifty years," said the renowned Comte de Foix to the chronicler Froissart in the year 1389, "there have been more feats of arms and more marvels in the world than in the three hundred years before." The Count himself, a famous huntsman, was known as Phoebus for his personal beauty and splendid court.

The streets of cities were bright with colored clothes: crimson fur-lined 40 gowns of merchants, parti-colored velvets and silks of a nobleman's retinue, in sky blue and fawn or two shades of scarlet or it might be the all-emerald liveries of the Green Count of Savoy. Street sounds were those of human voices: criers of news and official announcements, shopkeepers in their doorways and itinerant vendors crying fresh eggs, charcoal at a penny a sack, candlewicks "brighter than the stars," cakes and waffles, mushrooms, hot baths. Mountebanks entertained the public in the town square or village green with tricks and magic and trained animals. Jongleurs sang ballads of adventure in Saracen lands. After church on Sundays, laborers gathered in cookshops and taverns; burghers promenaded in their gardens or visited their vineyards outside the city walls. Church bells marked the eight times of day from Matins through Vespers, when shops closed, work ceased, silence succeeded bustle, and the darkness of unlit night descended.

The gaudy extravagance of noble life was awesome. Now and then its patronage brought forth works of eternal beauty like the exquisite illuminated Books of Hours commissioned by the Duc de Berry. More often it was pure ostentation and conspicuous consumption. Charles V of France owned forty-seven jeweled and golden crowns and sixty-three complete sets of chapel furnishings, including vestments, gold crucifixes, altarpieces, reliquaries, and prayer books. Jewels and cloth of gold marked every occasion and every occasion was pretext for a spectacle — a grand procession, or ceremonial welcome to a visiting prince, a tournament or entertainment with music, and dancing by the light of great torches. When Gian Galeazzo Visconti, ruler of Milan, gave a wedding banquet for his daughter, eighteen double courses were served, each of fish and meat, including trout, quail, herons, eels, sturgeon, and suckling pig spouting fire. The gifts presented after *each* course to several hundred guests included greyhounds in gem-studded velvet collars, hawks in tinkling silver bells, suits of armor, rolls of silk and brocade, garments trimmed with pearls and ermine, fully caparisoned warhorses, and twelve fat oxen. For the entry into Paris of the new Queen, Isabel of Bavaria, the entire length of the Rue St. Denis was hung with a canopy representing the firmament twinkling with stars from which sweetly singing angels descended bearing a crown, and fountains ran with wine, distributed to the people in golden cups by lovely maidens wearing caps of solid gold.

One wonders where all the money came from for such luxury and festivity in a time of devastation. What taxes could burned-out and destitute people pay? This is a puzzle until one remembers that the Aga Khan got to be the richest man in the world on the backs of the poorest people, and that disaster is never as pervasive as it seems from recorded accounts. It is one of the pitfalls for historians that the very fact of being on the record makes a happening appear to have been continuous and all-inclusive, whereas in reality it is more likely to have been sporadic both in time and place. Besides, persistence of the normal is usually greater than the effect of disturbance, as we know from our own times. After absorbing the daily paper and weekly magazine, one expects to face a world consisting entirely of strikes, crimes, power shortages, broken water mains, stalled trains, school shutdowns, Black Panthers, addicts, transvestites, rapists, and militant lesbians. The fact is that one can come home in the evening — on a lucky day — without having encountered more than two or three of these phenomena. This has led me to formulate Tuchman's Law, as follows: "The fact of being reported increases the *apparent* extent of a deplorable development by a factor of ten." (I snatch the figure from the air and will leave it to the quantifiers to justify.)

The astonishing fact is that except for Boccaccio, to whom we owe the 43 most vivid account, the Black Death was virtually ignored by the great writers of the time. Petrarch, who was forty-four when it happened, mentions it only as the occasion for the death of Laura; Chaucer, from what I have read, passes it over in silence; Jean Froissart, the Herodotus of his time, gives it no more than one casual paragraph, and even that second Isaiah, the author of *Piers Plowman*, who might have been expected to make it central to his theme of woe, uses it only incidentally. One could argue that in 1348 Chaucer was only eight or nine years old and Froissart ten or eleven and the unknown Langland probably of the same vintage, but that is old enough to absorb and remember a great catastrophe, especially when they lived through several returns of the plague as grown men.

Perhaps this tells us that disaster, once survived, leaves less track than 44 one supposed, or that man's instinct for living pushes it down below the surface, or simply that his recuperative powers are remarkable. Or was it just an accident of personality? Is it significant or just chance that Chaucer, the greatest writer of his age, was so uncharacteristic of it in sanguine temperament and good-humored view of his fellow creatures?

As for Froissart, never was a man more in love with his age. To him it ap- 45 peared as a marvelous pageant of glittering armor and the beauty of emblazoned banners fluttering in the breeze and the clear shrill call of the trumpet. Still believing, still enraptured by the chivalric ideal, he reports savagery, treachery, limitless greed, and the pitiless slaughter of the poor when driven to revolt as minor stumbles in the grand adventure of valor and honor. Yet near the end, even Froissart could not hide from himself the decay made plain by a dissolute court, venality in high places, and a knighthood that kept losing battles. In 1397, the year he turned sixty, the defeat and massacre of the flower of chivalry at the hands of the Turks in the battle of Nicopolis set the seal on the incompetence of his heroes. Lastly, the murder of a King in England shocked him deeply, not for any love of Richard II but because the act was subversive of the whole order that sustained his world. As in Watergate, the underside had rolled to the surface all too visibly. Froissart had not the heart to continue and brought his chronicle to an end.

The sad century closed with a meeting between King Charles VI of 46 France and the Emperor Wenceslaus, the one intermittently mad and the other regularly drunk. They met at Reims in 1397 to consult on means of ending the papal schism, but whenever Charles had a lucid interval, Wenceslaus was in a stupor and so the conference, proving fruitless, was called off.

It makes an artistic ending. Yet in that same year Johann Gutenberg, 47 who was to change the world, was born. In the next century appeared Joan of Arc, embodying the new spirit of nationalism, still pure like mountain water before it runs downhill; and Columbus, who opened a new hemisphere; and Copernicus, who revolutionized the concept of the earth's relation to the universe; and Michelangelo, whose sculptured visions gave man a new status; in those proud, superb, unconquered figures, the human being, not God, was captain.

As our century enters its final quarter, I am not persuaded, despite the signs, that the end is necessarily doom. The doomsayers work by extrapolation; they take a trend and extend it, forgetting that the doom factor sooner or later generates a coping mechanism. I have a rule for this situation too, which is absolute: you cannot extrapolate any series in which the human element intrudes; history, that is, the human narrative, never follows, and will always fool, the scientific curve. I cannot tell you what twists it will take, but I expect, that like our ancestors, we, too, will muddle through.

QUESTIONS ON MEANING

1. Tuchman's essay sets out the similarities between the present time and the fourteenth century: What are these similarities? What are some important differences? Do the differences weaken or support her argument?
2. "History as Mirror" confirms the fourteenth century's reputation as an age of darkness; the general description of paragraph 4 is systematically filled out as the essay proceeds. But what are Tuchman's points in paragraphs 5 and 6? Where else in her essay does she explicitly move from gloom to glory? How does this important organizing device aid in her argument that "the direction of one's own time may be obscure" (paragraph 31)?
3. In paragraph 2 Tuchman refers to "man," and then adds a parenthesis: "(meaning, here and hereafter, the species, not the sex)." Does this parenthetical clarification dispel the controversy over the use of *man* to mean "men and women"?
4. In the second sentence in paragraph 16, Tuchman refers to "a situation with which we are familiar," the Watergate scandal. In paragraph 22 she gives reasons for our lack of faith in government and other authority. Have things improved since Tuchman published this essay in 1973?

QUESTIONS ON STRATEGY

1. Consider Tuchman's use of argument in paragraph 22, where she urges us to accept one particular parallel between recent history and the fourteenth century. How does she situate this paragraph in the essay as a whole? What precedes it, and what follows?
2. Tuchman's style has been called aphoristic. (An aphorism is a short, often clever statement of a truth or sentiment — such as "the clothes make the man.") Find some examples of aphorisms in this essay. Are they supported

by the essay as a whole or are they merely superficial statements? In what ways are they a useful device?

3. "When it comes to language," Tuchman has observed, "nothing is more satisfying than to write a good sentence. . . . It is a pleasure to achieve, if one can, a clear running prose that is simple yet full of surprises." Paragraphs 30 and 31 form a sequence that exhibits these qualities. Notice how much Tuchman accomplishes in these paragraphs — how broad an overview they provide and how pointed are the details of the picture. Part of the effectiveness of this sequence derives from the speed and grace of the prose. Notice how the sentences relate to one another. What sets off the middle two sentences of paragraph 30? How do the first and fourth sentences work together? How does Tuchman set up the final three sentences of paragraph 31? How do they differ from what precedes them? How do they follow from what she has been saying?

EXPLORATIONS

1. In a book of essays called *Practicing History* (1981), Tuchman talks about the research and writing techniques of the historian's discipline. Show how Tuchman had to use the equipment and methods she describes in this book to write "History as Mirror."
2. Does Tuchman's concluding emphasis on "muddling through" have any practical application to the nuclear "extermination of mankind" she alludes to throughout? Is it possible to "muddle through," given our technological capabilities?

WRITING TOPICS

1. Tuchman sets forth Tuchman's Law in paragraph 42: "The fact of being reported increases the *apparent* extent of a deplorable development by a factor of ten." Choose a recent issue of a weekly magazine. Support or reject Tuchman's Law by considering the contents of the magazine as well as your own experience during the time covered by the magazine.
2. Do some research on the contemporary crises Tuchman refers to as parallels to the troubles of the fourteenth century. Is the Watergate scandal equivalent to the papal schism? Is the nuclear threat approximately as dreadful as the plague? Write an essay in which your conclusions about these questions form the basis of a judgment on the effectiveness of "History as Mirror."

BOOKS AVAILABLE IN PAPERBACK

A Distant Mirror: The Calamitous Fourteenth Century. New York: Ballantine. *Nonfiction: History.*

The Guns of August. New York: Bantam. *Nonfiction: History of the early days of World War I.*

Practicing History: Selected Essays. New York: Ballantine.

The Proud Tower: A Portrait of the World Before the War, 1890–1914. New York: Bantam. *Nonfiction: History.*

Stilwell and the American Experience in China, 1911–1945. New York: Bantam. *Nonfiction: History, including biography of American General Joseph W. Stilwell (1883–1946).*

LEWIS
THOMAS

*L*EWIS THOMAS *(b. 1913) grew up a doctor's son on Long Island, attended Princeton University, and took his M.D. at Harvard.* For most of his life, he *has practiced research in laboratories, more scientist than clinician, and served as administrator for medical schools and great hospitals. At present he is chancellor of Memorial Sloan-Kettering Cancer Center in New York City.*

For many years his publications labored under titles like "The Physiological Disturbances Produced by Endotoxins" (Annual Review of Physiology, 1954) *and "Reversible Collapse of Rabbit Ears after Intravenous Papain and Prevention of Recovery by Cortisone"* (Journal of Experimental Medicine, 1956). *Then, in 1975, he received not only a distinguished achievement award from* Modern Medicine *but also a National Book Award in Arts and Letters; the National Book Award is not awarded for papers on the collapse of rabbit ears.*

Lewis Thomas's career as a prose stylist began with a series of columns written for The New England Journal of Medicine; *he now writes a column for* Discovery, *a popular science magazine. He has assembled two collections of essays:* The Lives of a Cell *(1974) was subtitled "Notes of a Biology Watcher." "Medical Lessons from History" comes from* The Medusa and the Snail *(1979). In 1983 he published an autobiography called* The Youngest Science, *subtitled "Notes of a Medicine Watcher," and in 1984 a book of essays called* Late Night Thoughts on Listening to Mahler's Ninth Symphony.

Reading the autobiography, Thomas's admirers were amused and unsurprised to discover a literary past. While he was intern and resident during the Depression in the 1930s, Thomas picked up pocket money by selling poems to the Atlantic Monthly, Harper's Bazaar, and the old Saturday Evening Post. *"Millennium"* appeared in the Atlantic *long before the atomic bomb fell on Hiroshima:*

> It will be soft, the sound that we will hear
> When we have reached the end of time and light.
> A quiet, final noise within the air
> Before we are returned into the night.
>
> A sound for each to recognize and fear
> In one enormous moment, as he grieves —
> A sound of rustling, dry and very near,
> A sudden fluttering of all the leaves.
>
> It will be heard in all the open air
> Above the fading rumble of the guns,
> And we shall stand uneasily and stare,
> The finally forsaken, lonely ones.
>
> From all the distant secret places then
> A little breeze will shift across the sky,
> When all the earth at last is free of men
> And settles with a vast and easy sigh.

Readers of The Youngest Science *learn how Thomas's enthusiasm for modern medicine and his scientific optimism take energy from recollecting his father's medical practice, at a time when doctors had little to offer patients except morphine and sympathy. His columns and essays usually report on medical and biological science, often making necessary use of technical language, so they are far from personal essays. But Thomas allows his personal enthusiasm and gusto to show forth, qualities attractive to the unscientific but curious reader. Reading this scientist talking about science, we hear the sound of one human voice.*

Medical Lessons
from History

It is customary to place the date for the beginnings of modern medicine somewhere in the mid-1930s, with the entry of sulfonamides and penicillin into the pharmacopoeia, and it is usual to ascribe to these events the force of a revolution in medical practice. This is what things seemed like at the time. 1

Medicine was upheaved, revolutionized indeed. Therapy had been discovered for great numbers of patients whose illnesses had previously been untreatable. Cures were now available. As we saw it then, it seemed a totally new world. Doctors could now *cure* disease, and this was astonishing, most of all to the doctors themselves.

It was, no doubt about it, a major occurrence in medicine, and a triumph 2 for biological science applied to medicine but perhaps not a revolution after all, looking back from this distance. For the real revolution in medicine, which set the stage for antibiotics and whatever else we have in the way of effective therapy today, had already occurred one hundred years before penicillin. It did not begin with the introduction of science into medicine. That came years later. Like a good many revolutions, this one began with the destruction of dogma. It was discovered, sometime in the 1830s, that the greater part of medicine was nonsense.

The history of medicine has never been a particularly attractive subject to 3 medical education, and one reason for this is that it is so unrelievedly deplorable a story. For century after century, all the way into the remote millennia of its origins, medicine got along by sheer guesswork and the crudest sort of empiricism. It is hard to conceive of a less scientific enterprise among human endeavors. Virtually anything that could be thought up for the treatment of disease was tried out at one time or another, and, once tried, lasted decades or even centuries before being given up. It was, in retrospect, the most frivolous and irresponsible kind of human experimentation, based on nothing but trial and error, and usually resulting in precisely that sequence. Bleeding, purging, cupping, the administration of infusions of every known plant, solutions of every known metal, every conceivable diet including total fasting, most of these based on the weirdest imaginings about the cause of disease, concocted out of nothing but thin air — this was the heritage of medicine up until a little over a century ago. It is astounding that the profession survived so long, and got away with so much with so little outcry. Almost everyone seems to have been taken in. Evidently one had to be a born skeptic, like Montaigne, to see through the old nonsense; but even Montaigne, who wrote scathingly about the illnesses caused by doctoring centuries before Ivan Illich, had little effect. Most people were convinced of the magical powers of medicine and put up with it.

Then, sometime in the early nineteenth century, it was realized by a few 4 of the leading figures in medicine that almost all of the complicated treatments then available for disease did not really work, and the suggestion was made by several courageous physicians, here and abroad, that most of them actually did more harm than good. Simultaneously, the surprising discovery was made that certain diseases were self-limited, got better by themselves, possessed, so to speak, a "natural history." It is hard for us now to imagine the magnitude of this discovery and its effect on the practice of medicine.

The long habit of medicine, extending back into the distant past, had been to treat everything with something, and it was taken for granted that every disease demanded treatment and might in fact end fatally if not treated. In a sober essay written on this topic in 1876, Professor Edward H. Clarke of Harvard reviewed what he regarded as the major scientific accomplishment of medicine in the preceding fifty years, which consisted of studies proving that patients with typhoid and typhus fever could recover all by themselves, without medical intervention, and often did better for being untreated than when they received the bizarre herbs, heavy metals, and fomentations that were popular at that time. Delirium tremens, a disorder long believed to be fatal in all cases unless subjected to constant and aggressive medical intervention, was observed to subside by itself more readily in patients left untreated, with a substantially improved rate of survival.

Gradually, over the succeeding decades, the traditional therapeutic ritual of medicine was given up, and what came to be called the "art of medicine" emerged to take its place. In retrospect, this art was really the beginning of the science of medicine. It was based on meticulous, objective, even cool observations of sick people. From this endeavor we learned the details of the natural history of illness, so that, for example, it came to be understood that typhoid and typhus were really two entirely separate, unrelated disorders, with quite different causes. Accurate diagnosis became the central purpose and justification for medicine, and as the methods for diagnosis improved, accurate prognosis also became possible, so that patients and their families could be told not only the name of the illness but also, with some reliability, how it was most likely to turn out. By the time this century had begun, these were becoming generally accepted as the principal responsibilities of the physician. In addition, a new kind of much less ambitious and flamboyant therapy began to emerge, termed "supportive treatment" and consisting in large part of plain common sense: good nursing care, appropriate bed rest, a sensible diet, avoidance of traditional nostrums and patent medicine, and a measured degree of trust that nature, in taking its course, would very often bring things to a satisfactory conclusion.

The doctor became a considerably more useful and respected professional. For all his limitations, and despite his inability to do much in the way of preventing or terminating illness, he could be depended on to explain things, to relieve anxieties, and to be on hand. He was trusted as an adviser and guide in difficult times, including the time of dying.

Meanwhile, starting in the last decade of the nineteenth century, the basic science needed for a future science of medicine got under way. The role of bacteria and viruses in illness was discerned, and research on the details of this connection began in earnest. The major pathogenic organisms, most notably the tubercle bacillus and the syphilis spirochete, were recognized for what they were and did. By the late 1930s this research had already paid off;

the techniques of active and passive immunization had been worked out for diphtheria, tetanus, lobar pneumonia, and a few other bacterial infections; the taxonomy of infectious disease had become an orderly discipline; and the time was ready for sulfanilamide, penicillin, streptomycin, and all the rest. But it needs emphasizing that it took about fifty years of concentrated effort in basic research to reach this level; if this research had not been done we could not have guessed that streptococci and pneumococci exist, and the search for antibiotics would have made no sense at all. Without the long, painstaking research on the tubercle bacillus, we would still be thinking that tuberculosis was due to night air and we would still be trying to cure it by sunlight.

At that time, after almost a century of modified skepticism about therapy amounting finally to near nihilism, we abruptly entered a new era in which, almost overnight, it became possible with antibiotics to cure outright some of the most common and lethal illnesses of human beings — lobar pneumonia, meningitis, typhoid, typhus, tuberculosis, septicemias of various types. Only the virus diseases lay beyond reach, and even some of these were shortly to come under control — as in poliomyelitis and measles — by new techniques for making vaccines. 8

These events were simply overwhelming when they occurred. I was a medical student at the time of sulfanilamide and penicillin, and I remember the earliest reaction of flat disbelief concerning such things. We had given up on therapy, a century earlier. With a few exceptions which we regarded as anomalies, such as vitamin B for pellagra, liver extract for pernicious anemia, and insulin for diabetes, we were educated to be skeptical about the treatment of disease. Miliary tuberculosis and subacute bacterial endocarditis were fatal in 100 percent of cases, and we were convinced that the course of master diseases like these could never be changed, not in our lifetime or in any other. 9

Overnight, we became optimists, enthusiasts. The realization that disease could be turned around by treatment, provided that one knew enough about the underlying mechanism, was a totally new idea just forty years ago. 10

Most people have forgotten about that time, or are too young to remember it, and tend now to take such things for granted. They were born knowing about antibiotics, or the drugs simply fell by luck into their laps. We need reminding, now more than ever, that the capacity of medicine to deal with infectious disease was not a lucky fluke, nor was it something that happened simply as the result of the passage of time. It was the direct outcome of many years of hard work, done by imaginative and skilled scientists, none of whom had the faintest idea that penicillin and streptomycin lay somewhere in the decades ahead. It was basic science of a very high order, storing up a great mass of interesting knowledge for its own sake, creating, 11 so to speak, a bank of information, ready for drawing on when the time for intelligent use arrived.

For example, it took a great deal of time, and work, before it could be understood that there were such things as hemolytic streptococci, that there were more than forty different serological types of the principal streptococcal species responsible for human disease, and that some of these were responsible for rheumatic fever and valvular heart disease. The bacteriology and immunology had to be done first, over decades, and by the early 1930s the work had progressed just far enough so that the connection between streptococcal infection and rheumatic fever could be perceived.

Not until this information was at hand did it become a certainty that rheumatic fever could be prevented, and with it a large amount of the chief heart disease affecting young people, if only a way could be found to prevent streptococcal infection. Similarly, the identification of the role of pneumococci in lobar pneumonia, of brucellae in undulant fever, typhoid bacilli in typhoid fever, the meningococci in epidemic meningitis, required the sorting out and analysis of what seemed at the time an immensely complicated body of information. Most of the labor in infectious-disease laboratories went into work of this kind in the first third of this century. When it was finished, the scene was ready for antibiotics.

What was not realized then and is not fully realized even now was how difficult it would be to accomplish the same end for the other diseases of man. We still have heart disease, cancer, stroke, schizophrenia, arthritis, kidney failure, cirrhosis, and the degenerative diseases associated with aging. All told, there is a list of around twenty-five major afflictions of man in this country, and a still more formidable list of parasitic, viral, and nutritional diseases in the less developed countries of the world, which make up the unfinished agenda of modern biomedical science.

How does one make plans for science policy with such a list? The quick and easy way is to conclude that these diseases, not yet mastered, are simply beyond our grasp. The thing to do is to settle down with today's versions of science and technology, and make sure that our health-care system is equipped to do the best it can in an imperfect world. The trouble with this approach is that we cannot afford it. The costs are already too high, and they escalate higher each year. Moreover, the measures available are simply not good enough. We cannot go on indefinitely trying to cope with heart disease by open-heart surgery, carried out at formidable expense after the disease has run its destructive course. Nor can we postpone such issues by oversimplifying the problems, which is what we do, in my opinion, by attributing so much of today's chronic and disabling disease to the environment, or to wrong ways of living. The plain fact of the matter is that we do not know enough about the facts of the matter, and we should be more open about our ignorance.

At the same time, and this will have a paradoxical sound, there has never 16
been a period in medicine when the future has looked so bright. There is
within medicine, somewhere beneath the pessimism and discouragement
resulting from the disarray of the health-care system and its stupendous
cost, an undercurrent of almost outrageous optimism about what may lie
ahead for the treatment of human disease if we can only keep learning. The
scientists who do research on the cardiovascular system are entirely confident that they will soon be working close to the center of things, and they no
longer regard the mechanisms of heart disease as impenetrable mysteries.
The cancer scientists, for all their public disagreements about how best to organize their research, are in possession of insights into the intimate functioning of normal and neoplastic cells that were unimaginable a few years
back. The eukaryotic cell, the cell with a true nucleus, has itself become a
laboratory instrument almost as neat and handy as the bacterial cell became
in the early 1950s, ready now to be used for elucidating the mechanisms by
which genes are switched on or off as developing cells differentiate or, as in
the case of cancer cells, dedifferentiate. The ways in which carcinogenic sub-
stances, or viruses, or other factors still unrecognized intervene in the regulation of cell behavior represent problems still unsolved, but the problems
themselves now appear to be approachable; with what has been learned in
the past decade, they can now be worked on.

The neurobiologists can do all sorts of things in their investigation, and 17
the brain is an organ different from what it seemed twenty-five years ago.
Far from being an intricate but ultimately simplifiable mass of electronic circuitry governed by wiring diagrams, it now has the aspect of a fundamentally endocrine tissue, in which the essential reactions, the internal traffic of
nerve impulses, are determined by biochemical activators and their suppres-
sors. The technologies available for quantitative study of individual nerve
cells are powerful and precise, and the work is now turning toward the functioning of collections of cells, the centers for visual and auditory perception
and the like, because work at this level can now be done. It is difficult to
think of problems that cannot be studied, ever. The matter of consciousness
is argued over, naturally, as a candidate for perpetual unapproachability,
but this has more the sound of a philosophical discussion. Nobody has the
feeling any longer, as we used to believe, that we can never find out how the
brain works.

The immunologists, the molecular biochemists, and the new generation 18
of investigators obsessed with the structure and function of cell membranes
have all discovered that they are really working together, along with the ge-
neticists, on a common set of problems: how do cells and tissues become
labeled for what they are, what are the forces that govern the orderly development and differentiation of tissues and organs, and how are errors in the
process controlled?

There has never been a time like it, and I find it difficult to imagine that this tremendous surge of new information will terminate with nothing more than an understanding of how normal cells and tissues, and organisms, function. I regard it as a certainty that there will be uncovered, at the same time, detailed information concerning the mechanisms of disease.

The record of the past half century has established, I think, two general principles about human disease. First, it is necessary to know a great deal about underlying mechanisms before one can really act effectively; one had to know that the pneumococcus causes lobar pneumonia before one could begin thinking about antibiotics. One did not have to know all the details, not even how the pneumococcus does its damage to the lungs, but one had to know that it was there, and in charge.

Second, for every disease there is a single key mechanism that dominates all others. If one can find it, and then think one's way around it, one can control the disorder. This generalization is harder to prove, and arguable — it is more like a strong hunch than a scientific assertion — but I believe that the record thus far tends to support it. The most complicated, multicell, multitissue, and multiorgan diseases I know of are tertiary syphilis, chronic tuberculosis, and pernicious anemia. In each, there are at least five major organs and tissues involved, and each appears to be affected by a variety of environmental influences. Before they came under scientific appraisal each was thought to be what we now call a "multifactorial" disease, far too complex to allow for any single causative mechanism. And yet, when all the necessary facts were in, it was clear that by simply switching off one thing — the spirochete, the tubercle bacillus, or a single vitamin deficiency — the whole array of disordered and seemingly unrelated pathologic mechanisms could be switched off, at once.

I believe that a prospect something like this is the likelihood for the future of medicine. I have no doubt that there will turn out to be dozens of separate influences that can launch cancer, including all sorts of environmental carcinogens and very likely many sorts of virus, but I think there will turn out to be a single switch at the center of things, there for the finding. I think that schizophrenia will turn out to be a neurochemical disorder, with some central, single chemical event gone wrong. I think there is a single causative agent responsible for rheumatoid arthritis, which has not yet been found. I think that the central vascular abnormalities that launch coronary occlusion and stroke have not yet been glimpsed, but they are there, waiting to be switched on or off.

In short, I believe that the major diseases of human beings have become approachable biological puzzles, ultimately solvable. It follows from this that it is now possible to begin thinking about a human society relatively free of disease. This would surely have been an unthinkable notion a half century ago, and oddly enough it has a rather apocalyptic sound today. What will we do about dying, and about all that population, if such things were to come about? What can we die of, if not disease?

My response is that it would not make all that much difference. We 24 would still age away and wear out, on about the same schedule as today, with the terminal event being more like a sudden disintegration and collapse all at once of Oliver Wendell Holmes's well-known one-hoss shay. The main effect, almost pure benefit it seems to me, would be that we would not be beset and raddled by disease in the last decades of life, as most of us are today. We could become a healthy species, not all that different from the healthy stocks of domestic plants and animals that we already take for granted. Strokes, and senile dementia, and cancer, and arthritis are not natural aspects of the human condition, and we ought to rid ourselves of such impediments as quickly as we can.

There is another argument against this view of the future which needs 25 comment. It is said that we are fundamentally fallible as organisms, prone to failure, and if we succeed in getting rid of one set of ailments there will always be other new diseases, now waiting out in the forest, ready to take their places. I do not know why this is said, for I can see no evidence that such a thing has ever happened. To be sure, we have a higher incidence of chronic illness among older people than we had in the early years of this century, but that is because more of us have survived to become older people. No new disease, so far as I know, has come in to take the place of diphtheria, or smallpox, or whooping cough, or poliomyelitis. Nature being inventive, we will probably always have the odd new illness turning up, but not in order to fill out some ordained, predestined quota of human maladies.

Indeed, the official public-health tables of morbidity and morality seem 26 to be telling us this sort of thing already, even though, in all our anxiety, we seem unwilling to accept the news. We have already become in the Western world, on the record, the healthiest society in the history of humankind. Compared with a century ago, when every family was obliged to count on losing members throughout the early years of life, we are in a new world. A death in a young family has become a rare and dreadful catastrophe, no longer a commonplace event. Our estimated life expectancy, collectively, is longer this year than ever before in history. Part of this general and gradual improvement in health and survival is thanks to sanitary engineering, better housing, and, probably, more affluence, but a substantial part is also attributable, in recent years, to biomedical science. We have not done badly at all, and having begun so well, I see no reason why we should not do even better in the future.

My argument about how to do this will come as no surprise. I say that we 27 must continue doing biomedical research, on about the same scale and scope as in the past twenty years, with expansion and growth of the enterprise being dependent on where new leads seem to be taking us. It is an expensive undertaking, but still it is less than 3 percent of the total annual cost of today's health industry, which at last count was over $140 billion, and it is nothing like as expensive as trying to live with the halfway technologies we are obliged to depend on in medicine today; if we try to stay with these for the rest of the century the costs will go through the ionosphere.

But I should like to insert a qualification in this argument, which may be somewhat more of a surprise, coming from a doctor. I believe that the major research effort, and far and away the greatest investment for the future, must be in the broad area of basic biological science. Here and there, to be sure, there will be opportunities for productive applied science, comparable, say, to the making of polio vaccine or the devising of multidrug therapy for childhood leukemia, but these opportunities will not come often, nor can they be forced into existence before their time. The great need now, for the medicine of the future, is for more information at the most fundamental levels of the living process. We are nowhere near ready for large-scale programs of applied science in medicine, for we do not yet know enough.

Good applied science in medicine, as in physics, requires a high degree of certainty about the basic facts at hand, and especially about their meaning, and we have not yet reached this point for most of medicine. Nor can we predict at this stage, with much confidence, which particular items of new information, from which fields, are the likeliest to be relevant to particular disease problems. In this circumstance there has to be a certain amount of guessing, even gambling, and my own view is that the highest yield for the future will come from whatever fields are generating the most interesting, exciting, and surprising sorts of information, most of all, surprising.

It seems to me that the safest and most prudent of bets to lay money on is surprise. There is a very high probability that whatever astonishes us in biology today will turn out to be usable, and useful, tomorrow. This, I think, is the established record of science itself, over the past two hundred years, and we ought to have more confidence in the process. It worked this way for the beginnings of chemistry; we obtained electricity in this manner; using surprise as a guide, we progressed from Newtonian physics to electromagnetism, to quantum mechanics and contemporary geophysics and cosmology. In biology, evolution and genetics were the earliest big astonishments, but what has been going on in the past quarter century is simply flabbergasting. For medicine, the greater surprises lie still ahead of us, but they are there, waiting to be discovered or stumbled over, sooner or later.

I am arguing this way from the most practical, down-to-earth, pragmatic point of view. This kind of science is most likely, in the real world, to lead to significant improvements in human health, and at low cost. This is a point worth further emphasis, by the way. When medicine has really succeeded brilliantly in technology, as in immunization, for example, or antibiotics, or nutrition, or endocrine-replacement therapy, so that the therapeutic measures can be directed straight at the underlying disease mechanism and are decisively effective, the cost is likely to be very low indeed. It is when our technologies have to be applied halfway along against the progress of disease, or must be brought in after the fact to shore up the loss of destroyed tissue, that health care becomes enormously expensive. The deeper our understanding of a disease mechanism, the greater are our chances of devising direct and decisive measures to prevent disease, or to turn it around before it is too late.

So much for the practical side of the argument. We need much more basic science for the future of human health, and I will leave the matter there. 32

But I have one last thing to say about biological science. Even if I should 33 be wrong about some of these predictions, and it turns out that we can blunder our way into treating or preventing one disease or another without understanding the process (which I will not believe until it happens), and if we continue to invest in biological science anyway, we cannot lose. The Congress, in its wisdom, cannot lose. The public cannot lose.

Here is what I have in mind. 34

These ought to be the best of times for the human mind, but it is not so. 35 All sorts of things seem to be turning out wrong, and the century seems to be slipping through our fingers here at the end, with almost all promises unfulfilled. I cannot begin to guess at all the causes of our cultural sadness, not even the most important ones, but I can think of one thing that is wrong with us and eats away at us: we do not know enough about ourselves. We are ignorant about how we work, about where we fit in, and most of all about the enormous, imponderable system of life in which we are embedded as working parts. We do not really understand nature, at all. We have come a long way indeed, but just enough to become conscious of our ignorance. It is not so bad a thing to be totally ignorant; the hard thing is to be partway along toward real knowledge, far enough to be aware of being ignorant. It is embarrassing and depressing, and it is one of our troubles today.

It is a new experience for all of us. Only two centuries ago we could ex- 36 plain everything about everything, out of pure reason, and now most of that elaborate and harmonious structure has come apart before our eyes. We are *dumb*.

This is, in a certain sense, a health problem after all. For as long as we are 37 bewildered by the mystery of ourselves, and confused by the strangeness of our uncomfortable connection to all the rest of life, and dumbfounded by the inscrutability of our own minds, we cannot be said to be healthy animals in today's world.

We need to know more. To come to realize this is what this seemingly in- 38 conclusive century has been all about. We have discovered how to ask important questions, and now we really do need, as an urgent matter, for the sake of our civilization, to obtain some answers. We now know that we cannot do this any longer by searching our minds, for there is not enough there to search, nor can we find the truth by guessing at it or by making up stories for ourselves. We cannot stop where we are, stuck with today's level of understanding, nor can we go back. I do not see that we have a real choice in this, for I can see only the one way ahead. We need science, more and better science, not for its technology, not for leisure, not even for health or longevity, but for the hope of wisdom which our kind of culture must acquire for its survival.

QUESTIONS ON MEANING

1. Thomas gives us a history of medical science, mostly the last hundred and forty years, in the paragraphs at the beginning of his essay. At first it seems that he is presenting a narrative, pure and simple. Then in paragraphs 7 through 11, his real subject emerges: the "lessons" derived from "history." What are these lessons? What do they tell us about the public policy we should follow toward science, toward medicine in particular?
2. Can you follow the thought of paragraph 21? What makes it harder to grasp than most of the other paragraphs? Look ahead to the startling prediction Thomas makes in paragraph 22. Does his argument need paragraph 21 for support?
3. In paragraph 24 Thomas says, "We could become a healthy species, not all that different from the healthy stocks of domestic plants and animals that we already take for granted." What does Thomas mean by this sentence? Taken out of context, the sentence has some frightening connotations — of selective breeding to improve a species, of manipulating genetic material to produce "desirable" traits. Do you think Thomas intends to include these connotations in his meaning?

QUESTIONS ON STRATEGY

1. There are 38 paragraphs in this essay. Choose any sequence of ten paragraphs, and write a one-sentence summary of each paragraph. This exercise will allow you to trace the development of a part of Thomas's argument. Pay close attention to his transitions from one subject to the next. Be prepared to discuss in class how Thomas moves the reader from topic to topic.
2. The original audience for Thomas's essays was the medical profession, but the collections of those essays have been published for a general audience. In paragraph 7 and afterward, this essay uses words and technical terms unfamiliar to most laypeople. How many of these do you need to know? Does the dictionary definition of pellagra (paragraph 9) help you to understand this essay? Try to decide, as you read, which words need exact definition and which need only a general understanding.

3. Look at paragraphs 11 and 12, which contain a definition of *basic science*. Use your own words to define *basic science* according to Thomas. Why didn't he begin with the definition, instead of deriving it from example?
4. Notice how the tone of Thomas's essay changes from point to point. In the early paragraphs (1 through 6) what is the tone? Where does it begin to change, and how would you characterize it at the end of the essay? What is the effect of the increasing use of the first-person pronoun *we*?

EXPLORATIONS

1. Seat Barbara Tuchman and Lewis Thomas facing each other and have them discuss humankind's present troubles in light of Tuchman's statement (paragraph 48) that "the human narrative never follows, and will always fool, the scientific curve." How does her position compare with Thomas's argument about surprise in paragraph 30?

WRITING TOPICS

1. Thomas's approach to the persuasive essay relies on a combination of narrative and argument. Study his essay as a model, and adapt his methods to your own persuasive ends in an essay arguing a point of contemporary controversy by appeal to a historical narrative. Topics suitable to Thomas's methods might involve issues related to technical progress, such as the U.S. space program, the widespread use of computers, or the nuclear power industry.
2. Consider paragraph 25. Does Legionnaire's Disease or the recent emergence of AIDS (acquired immune deficiency syndrome) weaken this part of Thomas's argument? Write an essay illustrating how Thomas's optimism might deal with such current problems.

BOOKS AVAILABLE IN PAPERBACK

The Lives of a Cell: Notes of a Biology Watcher. New York: Penguin. *Essays.*

The Medusa and the Snail: More Notes of a Biology Watcher. New York: Bantam. *Essays.*

The Youngest Science: Notes of a Medicine Watcher. New York: Bantam. *Essays.*

WALKER
PERCY

*W*ALKER PERCY *(b. 1916) was educated as a physician and completed his internship, but became a novelist. (Maybe medical training is more useful than Writers' Workshops; the playwright and story writer Anton Chekhov studied to be a doctor; John Keats and William Carlos Williams were two doctors turned poets.) Born in Alabama, Percy took his B.A. at the University of North Carolina, then attended medical school at Columbia University, in New York City, where he also interned. He returned to reside in the South, where he lives in Covington, Louisiana, near New Orleans, the site of much of his fiction. The most important biographical information about Walker Percy is his religion: He is a convert to Roman Catholicism, and his religious sensibility informs his imagination and his thought.*

He was middle-aged before he published his first novel, The Moviegoer, *in 1961; It won the National Book Award, and Percy was immediately recognized as a major contemporary novelist. Subsequent novels include* The Last Gentleman *(1966) and* The Second Coming *(1980). In 1975 he published a book of essays,* The Message in the Bottle, *from which ''The Loss of the Creature'' is taken. The articles in that book appeared over twenty years, in literary quarterlies (*The Southern Review, Sewanee Review, Partisan Review*) and in philosophical journals (*Thought, The Journal of Philosophy, Philosophy and Phenomenological

Research.*) Few philosophers publish in literary quarterlies; few novelists publish in philosophical quarterlies.* In 1983 Percy published Lost in the Cosmos, *a collection of parodies and essays critical of contemporary society.*

In his author's note to The Message in the Bottle, *Percy refers to his "recurring interest" in "the nature of human communication." "The Loss of the Creature" begins with people naming something and continues by examining the relation of experience to the language by which we communicate experience. The loss that Percy describes is a psychic distance that civilization, or its development in our time, puts between reality and our mind's connection to reality. Before you read it, tuck away in your mind the author's subtitle for* The Message in the Bottle: *"How Queer Man Is, How Queer Language Is, and What One Has to Do with the Other."*

The Loss of
the Creature

Every explorer names his island Formosa, beautiful. To him it is beautiful   1
because, being first, he has access to it and can see it for what it is. But to no
one else is it ever as beautiful — except the rare man who manages to recover
it, who knows that it has to be recovered.

Garcia López de Cárdenas discovered the Grand Canyon and was   2
amazed at the sight. It can be imagined: One crosses miles of desert, breaks
through the mesquite, and there it is at one's feet. Later the government set
the place aside as a national park, hoping to pass along to millions the experience of Cárdenas. Does not one see the same sight from the Bright Angel
Lodge that Cárdenas saw?

The assumption is that the Grand Canyon is a remarkably interesting   3
and beautiful place and that if it had a certain value P for Cárdenas, the same
value P may be transmitted to any number of sightseers — just as Banting's
discovery of insulin can be transmitted to any number of diabetics. A coun-
terinfluence is at work, however, and it would be nearer the truth to say that
if the place is seen by a million sightseers, a single sightseer does not receive
value P but a millionth part of value P.

It is assumed that since the Grand Canyon has the fixed interest value   4
P, tours can be organized for any number of people. A man in Boston decides to spend his vacation at the Grand Canyon. He visits his travel bureau,
looks at the folder, signs up for a two-week tour. He and his family take the
tour, see the Grand Canyon, and return to Boston. May we say that this

man has seen the Grand Canyon? Possibly he has. But it is more likely that what he has done is the one sure way not to see the canyon.

Why is it almost impossible to gaze directly at the Grand Canyon under these circumstances and see it for what it is — as one picks up a strange object from one's back yard and gazes directly at it? It is almost impossible because the Grand Canyon, the thing as it is, has been appropriated by the symbolic complex which has already been formed in the sightseer's mind. Seeing the canyon under approved circumstances is seeing the symbolic complex head on. The thing is no longer the thing as it confronted the Spaniard; it is rather that which has already been formulated — by picture postcard, geography book, tourist folders, and the words *Grand Canyon*. As a result of this preformulation, the source of the sightseer's pleasure undergoes a shift. Where the wonder and delight of the Spaniard arose from his penetration of the thing itself, from a progressive discovery of depths, patterns, colors, shadows, etc., now the sightseer measures his satisfaction *by the degree to which the canyon conforms to the preformed complex*. If it does so, if it looks just like the postcard, he is pleased; he might even say, "Why it is every bit as beautiful as a picture postcard!" He feels he has not been cheated. But if it does not conform, if the colors are somber, he will not be able to see it directly; he will only be conscious of the disparity between what it is and what it is supposed to be. He will say later that he was unlucky in not being there at the right time. The highest point, the term of the sightseer's satisfaction, is not the sovereign discovery of the thing before him; it is rather the measuring up of the thing to the criterion of the preformed symbolic complex.

Seeing the canyon is made even more difficult by what the sightseer does when the moment arrives, when sovereign knower confronts the thing to be known. Instead of looking at it, he photographs it. There is no confrontation at all. At the end of forty years of preformulation and with the Grand Canyon yawning at his feet, what does he do? He waives his right of seeing and knowing and records symbols for the next forty years. For him there is no present; there is only the past of what has been formulated and seen and the future of what has been formulated and not seen. The present is surrendered to the past and the future.

The sightseer may be aware that something is wrong. He may simply be bored; or he may be conscious of the difficulty: that the great thing yawning at his feet somehow eludes him. The harder he looks at it, the less he can see. It eludes everybody. The tourist cannot see it; the bellboy at the Angel Lodge cannot see it: for him it is only one side of the space he lives in, like one wall of a room; to the ranger it is a tissue of everyday signs relevant to his own prospects — the blue haze down there means that he will probably get rained on during the donkey ride.

How can the sightseer recover the Grand Canyon? He can recover it in 8
any number of ways, all sharing in common the stratagem of avoiding the
approved confrontation of the tour and the Park Service.

It may be recovered by leaving the beaten track. The tourist leaves the 9
tour, camps in the back country. He arises before dawn and approaches the
South Rim through a wild terrain where there are no trails and no railed-in
lookout points. In other words, he sees the canyon by avoiding all the facilities for seeing the canyon. If the benevolent Park Service hears about this
fellow and thinks he has a good idea and places the following notice in the
Bright Angel Lodge: *Consult ranger for information on getting off the beaten track*
— the end result will only be the closing of another access to the canyon.

It may be recovered by a dialectical movement which brings one back to 10
the beaten track but at a level above it. For example, after a lifetime of avoiding the beaten track and guided tours, a man may deliberately seek out the
most beaten track of all, the most commonplace tour imaginable: he may
visit the canyon by a Greyhound tour in the company of a party from Terre
Haute — just as a man who has lived in New York all his life may visit the
Statue of Liberty. (Such dialectical savorings of the familiar as the familiar
are, of course, a favorite stratagem of *The New Yorker* magazine.) The thing is
recovered from familiarity by means of an exercise in familiarity. Our complex friend stands behind the fellow tourists at the Bright Angel Lodge and
sees the canyon through them and their predicament, their picture taking
and busy disregard. In a sense, he exploits his fellow tourists; he stands on
their shoulders to see the canyon.

Such a man is far more advanced in the dialectic than the sightseer who 11
is trying to get off the beaten track — getting up at dawn and approaching
the canyon through the mesquite. This stratagem is, in fact, for our complex
man the weariest, most beaten track of all.

It may be recovered as a consequence of a breakdown of the symbolic 12
machinery by which the experts present the experience to the consumer. A
family visits the canyon in the usual way. But shortly after their arrival, the
park is closed by an outbreak of typhus in the south. They have the canyon
to themselves. What do they mean when they tell the home folks of their
good luck: ''We had the whole place to ourselves''? How does one see the
thing better when the others are absent? Is looking like sucking: the more
lookers, the less there is to see? They could hardly answer, but by saying
this they testify to a state of affairs which is considerably more complex than
the simple statement of the schoolbook about the Spaniard and the millions
who followed him. It is a state in which there is a complex distribution of
sovereignty, of zoning.

It may be recovered in a time of national disaster. The Bright Angel 13
Lodge is converted into a rest home, a function that has nothing to do with

the canyon a few yards away. A wounded man is brought in. He regains consciousness; there outside his window is the canyon.

The most extreme case of access by privilege conferred by disaster is the Huxleyan° novel of the adventures of the surviving remnant after the great wars of the twentieth century. An expedition from Australia lands in Southern California and heads east. They stumble across the Bright Angel Lodge, now fallen into ruins. The trails are grown over, the guard rails fallen away, the dime telescope at Battleship Point rusted. But there is the canyon, exposed at last. Exposed by what? By the decay of those facilities which were designed to help the sightseer.

This dialectic of sightseeing cannot be taken into account by planners, for the object of the dialectic is nothing other than the subversion of the efforts of the planners.

The dialectic is not known to objective theorists, psychologists, and the like. Yet it is quite well known in the fantasy-consciousness of the popular arts. The devices by which the museum exhibit, the Grand Canyon, the ordinary thing, is recovered have long since been stumbled upon. A movie shows a man visiting the Grand Canyon. But the moviemaker knows something the planner does not know. He knows that one cannot take the sight frontally. The canyon must be approached by the stratagems we have mentioned: the Inside Track, the Familiar Revisited, the Accidental Encounter. Who is the stranger at the Bright Angel Lodge? Is he the ordinary tourist from Terre Haute that he makes himself out to be? He is not. He has another objective in mind, to revenge his wronged brother, counterespionage, etc. By virtue of the fact that he has other fish to fry, he may take a stroll along the rim after supper and then we can see the canyon through him. The movie accomplishes its purpose by concealing it. Overtly the characters (the American family marooned by typhus) and we the onlookers experience pity for the sufferers, and the family experience anxiety for themselves; covertly and in truth they are the happiest of people and we are happy through them, for we have the canyon to ourselves. The movie cashes in on the recovery of sovereignty through disaster. Not only is the canyon now accessible to the remnant: the members of the remnant are now accessible to each other; a whole new ensemble of relations becomes possible — friendship, love, hatred, clandestine sexual adventures. In a movie when a man sits next to a woman on a bus, it is necessary either that the bus break down or that the woman lose her memory. (The question occurs to one: Do you imagine there are sightseers who see sights just as they are supposed to? a family who live in Terre Haute, who decide to take the canyon tour, who go

---

Huxleyan   Aldous Huxley (1894–1963), English writer, best known for his novel *Brave New World* (1932), which depicts a scientific, mechanized utopia.

there, see it, enjoy it immensely, and go home content? a family who are entirely innocent of all the barriers, zones, losses of sovereignty I have been talking about? Wouldn't most people be sorry if Battleship Point fell into the canyon, carrying all one's fellow passengers to their death, leaving one alone on the South Rim? I cannot answer this. Perhaps there are such people. Certainly a great many American families would swear they had no such problems, that they came, saw, and went away happy. Yet it is just these families who would be happiest if they had gotten the Inside Track and been among the surviving remnant.)

It is now apparent that as between the many measures which may be taken to overcome the opacity, the boredom, of the direct confrontation of the thing or creature in its citadel of symbolic investiture, some are less authentic than others. That is to say, some stratagems obviously serve other purposes than that of providing access to being — for example, various unconscious motivations which it is not necessary to go into here. **17**

Let us take an example in which the recovery of being is ambiguous, where it may under the same circumstances contain both authentic and unauthentic components. An American couple, we will say, drives down into Mexico. They see the usual sights and have a fair time of it. Yet they are never without the sense of missing something. Although Taxco and Cuernavaca are interesting and picturesque as advertised, they fall short of "it." What do the couple have in mind by "it"? What do they really hope for? What sort of experience could they have in Mexico so that upon their return, they would feel that "it" had happened? We have a clue: Their hope has something to do with their own role as tourists in a foreign country and the way in which they conceive this role. It has something to do with other American tourists. Certainly they feel that they are very far from "it" when, after traveling five thousand miles, they arrive at the plaza in Guanajuato only to find themselves surrounded by a dozen other couples from the Midwest. **18**

Already we may distinguish authentic and unauthentic elements. First, we see the problem the couple faces and we understand their efforts to surmount it. The problem is to find an "unspoiled" place. "Unspoiled" does not mean only that a place is left physically intact; it means also that it is not encrusted by renown and by the familiar (as in Taxco), that it has not been discovered by others. We understand that the couple really want to get at the place and enjoy it. Yet at the same time we wonder if there is not something wrong in their dislike of their compatriots. Does access to the place require the exclusion of others? **19**

Let us see what happens. **20**

The couple decide to drive from Guanajuato to Mexico City. On the way they get lost. After hours on a rocky mountain road, they find themselves in a tiny valley not even marked on the map. There they discover an Indian vil- **21** lage. Some sort of religious festival is going on. It is apparently a corn dance in supplication of the rain god.

The couple know at once that this is "it." They are entranced. They spend several days in the village, observing the Indians and being themselves observed with friendly curiosity.

Now may we not say that the sightseers have at last come face to face with an authentic sight, a sight which is charming, quaint, picturesque, unspoiled, and that they see the sight and come away rewarded? Possibly this may occur. Yet it is more likely that what happens is a far cry indeed from an immediate encounter with being, that the experience, while masquerading as such, is in truth a rather desperate impersonation. I use the word *desperate* advisedly to signify an actual loss of hope.

The clue to the spuriousness of their enjoyment of the village and the festival is a certain restiveness in the sightseers themselves. It is given expression by their repeated exclamations that "this is too good to be true," and by their anxiety that it may not prove to be so perfect, and finally by their downright relief at leaving the valley and having the experience in the bag, so to speak — that is, safely embalmed in memory and movie film.

What is the source of their anxiety during the visit? Does it not mean that the couple are looking at the place with a certain standard of performance in mind? Are they like Fabre,° who gazed at the world about him with wonder, letting it be what it is; or are they not like the overanxious mother who sees her child as one performing, now doing badly, now doing well? The village is their child and their love for it is an anxious love because they are afraid that at any moment it might fail them.

We have another clue in their subsequent remark to an ethnologist friend. "How we wished you had been there with us! What a perfect goldmine of folkways! Every minute we would say to each other, if only you were here! You must return with us." This surely testifies to a generosity of spirit, a willingness to share their experience with others, not at all like their feelings toward their fellow Iowans on the plaza at Guanajuato!

I am afraid this is not the case at all. It is true that they longed for their ethnologist friend, but it was for an entirely different reason. They wanted him, not to share their experience, but to certify their experience as genuine.

"This is it" and "Now we are really living" do not necessarily refer to the sovereign encounter of the person with the sight that enlivens the mind and gladdens the heart. It means that now at last we are having the acceptable experience. The present experience is always measured by a prototype, the "it" of their dreams. "Now I am really living" means that now I am filling the role of sightseer and the sight is living up to the prototype of sights.

Fabre Jean-Henri Fabre (1823–1915), French entomologist (a scientist who studies insects).

This quaint and picturesque village is measured by a Platonic ideal of the Quaint and the Picturesque.

Hence their anxiety during the encounter. For at any minute something 29 could go wrong. A fellow Iowan might emerge from a 'dobe hut; the chief might show them his Sears catalogue. (If the failures are "wrong" enough, as these are, they might still be turned to account as rueful conversation pieces: "There we were expecting the chief to bring us a churinga and he shows up with a Sears catalogue!") They have snatched victory from disaster, but their experience always runs the danger of failure.

They need the ethnologist to certify their experience as genuine. This is 30 borne out by their behavior when the three of them return for the next corn dance. During the dance, the couple do not watch the goings-on; instead they watch the ethnologist! Their highest hope is that their friend should find the dance interesting. And if he should show signs of true absorption, an interest in the goings-on so powerful that he becomes oblivious of his friends — then their cup is full. "Didn't we tell you?" they say at last. What they want from him is not ethnological explanations; all they want is his approval.

What has taken place is a radical loss of sovereignty over that which is as 31 much theirs as it is the ethnologist's. The fault does not lie with the ethnologist. He has no wish to stake a claim to the village; in fact, he desires the opposite: he will bore his friends to death by telling them about the village and the meaning of the folkways. A degree of sovereignty has been surrendered by the couple. It is the nature of the loss, moreover, that they are not aware of the loss, beyond a certain uneasiness. (Even if they read this and admitted it, it would be very difficult for them to bridge the gap in their confrontation of the world. Their consciousness of the corn dance cannot escape their consciousness of their consciousness, so that with the onset of the first direct enjoyment, their higher consciousness pounces and certifies: "Now you are doing it! Now you are really living!" and, in certifying the experience, sets it at nought.)

Their basic placement in the world is such that they recognize a priority 32 of title of the expert over his particular department of being. The whole horizon of being is staked out by "them," the experts. The highest satisfaction of the sightseer (not merely the tourist but any layman seer of sights) is that his sight should be certified as genuine. The worst of this impoverishment is that there is no sense of impoverishment. The surrender of title is so complete that it never even occurs to one to reassert title. A poor man may envy the rich man, but the sightseer does not envy the expert. When a caste system becomes absolute, envy disappears. Yet the caste of layman-expert is not the fault of the expert. It is due altogether to the eager surrender of sovereignty by the layman so that he may take up the role not of the person but of the consumer.

I do not refer only to the special relation of layman to theorist. I refer to the general situation in which sovereignty is surrendered to a class of privileged knowers, whether these be theorists or artists. A reader may surrender sovereignty over that which has been written about, just as a consumer may surrender sovereignty over a thing which has been theorized about. The consumer is content to receive an experience just as it has been presented to him by theorists and planners. The reader may also be content to judge life by whether it has or has not been formulated by those who know and write about life. A young man goes to France. He too has a fair time of it, sees the sights, enjoys the food. On his last day, in fact as he sits in a restaurant in Le Havre waiting for his boat, something happens. A group of French students in the restaurant get into an impassioned argument over a recent play. A riot takes place. Madame la concierge joins in, swinging her mop at the rioters. Our young American is transported. This is "it." And he had almost left France without seeing "it"!

But the young man's delight is ambiguous. On the one hand, it is a pleasure for him to encounter the same Gallic temperament he had heard about from Puccini° and Rolland.° But on the other hand, the source of his pleasure testifies to a certain alienation. For the young man is actually barred from a direct encounter with anything French excepting only that which has been set forth, authenticated by Puccini and Rolland — those who know. If he had encountered the restaurant scene without reading Hemingway, without knowing that the performance was so typically, charmingly French, he would not have been delighted. He would only have been anxious at seeing things get so out of hand. The source of his delight is the sanction of those who know.

This loss of sovereignty is not a marginal process, as might appear from my example of estranged sightseers. It is a generalized surrender of the horizon to those experts within whose competence a particular segment of the horizon is thought to lie. Kwakiutls are surrendered to Franz Boas°; decaying Southern mansions are surrendered to Faulkner and Tennessee Williams. So that, although it is by no means the intention of the expert to expropriate sovereignty — in fact he would not even know what sovereignty meant in this context — the danger of theory and consumption is a seduction and deprivation of the consumer.

Puccini Giacomo Puccini (1853–1924), Italian composer of emotional, somewhat melancholic operas.

Rolland Romain Rolland (1866–1944), French author and playwright whose works depicted the contemporary French character.

Franz Boas German-born American anthropologist and ethnologist (1858–1942) whose fieldwork took place primarily in North America, Mexico, and Puerto Rico.

In the New Mexican desert, natives occasionally come across strange- 36
looking artifacts which have fallen from the skies and which are stenciled:
Return to U.S. Experimental Project, Alamogordo. Reward. The finder returns the
object and is rewarded. He knows nothing of the nature of the object he has
found and does not care to know. The sole role of the native, the highest role
he can play, is that of finder and returner of the mysterious equipment.

The same is true of the layman's relation to *natural* objects in a modern 37
technical society. No matter what the object or event is, whether it is a star, a
swallow, a Kwakiutl, a "psychological phenomenon," the layman who confronts it does not confront it as a sovereign person, as Crusoe confronts a
seashell he finds on the beach. The highest role he can conceive himself as
playing is to be able to recognize the title of the object, to return it to the appropriate expert and have it certified as a genuine find. He does not even
permit himself to see the thing — as Gerard Hopkins° could see a rock or a
cloud or a field. If anyone asks him why he doesn't look, he may reply that
he didn't take that subject in college (or he hasn't read Faulkner).

This loss of sovereignty extends even to oneself. There is the neurotic 38
who asks nothing more of his doctor than that his symptoms should prove
interesting. When all else fails, the poor fellow has nothing to offer but his
own neurosis. But even this is sufficient if only the doctor will show interest
when he says, "Last night I had a curious sort of dream; perhaps it will be
significant to one who knows about such things. It seems I was standing in a
sort of alley — " (I have nothing else to offer you but my own unhappiness.
Please say that it, at least, measures up, that it is a *proper* sort of unhappiness.)

I I

A young Falkland Islander walking along a beach and spying a dead dog- 39
fish and going to work on it with his jackknife has, in a fashion wholly un-
provided in modern educational theory, a great advantage over the Scarsdale high-school pupil who finds the dogfish on his laboratory desk.
Similarly the citizen of Huxley's *Brave New World* who stumbles across a volume of Shakespeare in some vine-grown ruins and squats on a potsherd to
read it is in a fairer way of getting at a sonnet than the Harvard sophomore
taking English Poetry II.

The educator whose business it is to teach students biology or poetry is 40
unaware of a whole ensemble of relations which exist between the student
and the dogfish and between the student and the Shakespeare sonnet. To

---

Gerard Hopkins Gerard Manley Hopkins (1844–1889), English poet noted for his innovative rhythms and his keen observation of the details of nature.

83

put it bluntly: A student who has the desire to get at a dogfish or a Shakespeare sonnet may have the greatest difficulty in salvaging the creature itself from the educational package in which it is presented. The great difficulty is that he is not aware that there is a difficulty; surely, he thinks, in such a fine classroom, with such a fine textbook, the sonnet must come across! What's wrong with me?

The sonnet and the dogfish are obscured by two different processes. The sonnet is obscured by the symbolic package which is formulated not by the sonnet itself but by the *media* through which the sonnet is transmitted, the media which the educators believe for some reason to be transparent. The new textbook, the type, the smell of the page, the classroom, the aluminum windows and the winter sky, the personality of Miss Hawkins — these media which are supposed to transmit the sonnet may only succeed in transmitting themselves. It is only the hardiest and cleverest of students who can salvage the sonnet from this many-tissued package. It is only the rarest student who knows that the sonnet must be salvaged from the package. (The educator is well aware that something is wrong, that there is a fatal gap between the student's learning and the student's life: The student reads the poem, appears to understand it, and gives all the answers. But what does he recall if he should happen to read a Shakespeare sonnet twenty years later? Does he recall the poem or does he recall the smell of the page and the smell of Miss Hawkins?)

One might object, pointing out that Huxley's citizen reading his sonnet in the ruins and the Falkland Islander looking at his dogfish on the beach also receive them in a certain package. Yes, but the difference lies in the fundamental placement of the student in the world, a placement which makes it possible to extract the thing from the package. The pupil at Scarsdale High sees himself placed as a consumer receiving an experience-package; but the Falkland Islander exploring his dogfish is a person exercising the sovereign right of a person in his lordship and mastery of creation. He too could use an instructor and a book and a technique, but he would use them as his subordinates, just as he uses his jackknife. The biology student does not use his scalpel as an instrument; he uses it as a magic wand! Since it is a "scientific instrument," it should do "scientific things."

The dogfish is concealed in the same symbolic package as the sonnet. But the dogfish suffers an additional loss. As a consequence of this double deprivation, the Sarah Lawrence student who scores A in zoology is apt to know very little about a dogfish. She is twice removed from the dogfish, once by the symbolic complex by which the dogfish is concealed, once again by the spoliation of the dogfish by theory which renders it invisible. Through no fault of zoology instructors, it is nevertheless a fact that the zoology laboratory at Sarah Lawrence College is one of the few places in the world where it is all but impossible to see a dogfish.

The dogfish, the tree, the seashell, the American Negro, the dream, are 44
rendered invisible by a shift of reality from concrete thing to theory which
Whitehead° has called the fallacy of misplaced concreteness. It is the mistaking of an idea, a principle, an abstraction, for the real. As a consequence of
the shift, the "specimen" is seen as less real than the theory of the specimen. As Kierkegaard° said, once a person is seen as a specimen of a race or a
species, at that very moment he ceases to be an individual. Then there are no
more individuals but only specimens.

To illustrate: A student enters a laboratory which, in the pragmatic view, 45
offers the student the optimum conditions under which an educational experience may be had. In the existential view, however — that view of the
student in which he is regarded not as a receptacle of experience but as a
knowing being whose peculiar property it is to see himself as being in a certain situation — the modern laboratory could not have been more effectively
designed to conceal the dogfish forever.

The student comes to his desk. On it, neatly arranged by his instructor, 46
he finds his laboratory manual, a dissecting board, instruments, and a mim-
eographed list:

Exercise 22: Materials

1 dissecting board
1 scalpel
1 forceps
1 probe
1 bottle india ink and syringe
1 specimen of *Squalus acanthias*

The clue to the situation in which the student finds himself is to be found 47
in the last item: 1 specimen of *Squalus acanthias*.

The phrase *specimen of* expresses in the most succinct way imaginable the 48
radical character of the loss of being which has occurred under his very nose.
To refer to the dogfish, the unique concrete existent before him, as a "specimen of *Squalus acanthias*" reveals by its grammar the spoliation of the dogfish by the theoretical method. This phrase, *specimen of*, example of, instance
of, indicates the ontological status of the individual creature in the eyes of
the theorist. The dogfish itself is seen as a rather shabby expression of an
ideal reality, the species *Squalus acanthias*. The result is the radical devalua-

---

Whitehead   Alfred North Whitehead (1861–1947), English mathematician and philosopher.

Kierkegaard   Sören Aabye Kierkegaard (1813–1855), Danish philosopher and theolo-
gian whose philosophy was based on faith and knowledge, thought and reality.

tion of the individual dogfish. (The *reductio ad absurdum*° of Whitehead's shift is Toynbee's° employment of it in his historical method. If a gram of NaCl is referred to by the chemist as a "sample of" NaCl, one may think of it as such and not much is missed by the oversight of the act of being of this particular pinch of salt, but when the Jews and the Jewish religion are understood as — in Toynbee's favorite phrase — a "classical example of" such and such a kind of *Voelkerwanderung,*° we begin to suspect that something is being left out.)

If we look into the ways in which the student can recover the dogfish (or the sonnet), we will see that they have in common the stratagem of avoiding the educator's direct presentation of the object as a lesson to be learned and restoring access to sonnet and dogfish as beings to be known, reasserting the sovereignty of knower over known.

In truth, the biography of scientists and poets is usually the story of the discovery of the indirect approach, the circumvention of the educator's presentation — the young man who was sent to the *Technikum*° and on his way fell into the habit of loitering in book stores and reading poetry; or the young man dutifully attending law school who on the way became curious about the comings and goings of ants. One remembers the scene in *The Heart Is a Lonely Hunter*° where the girl hides in the bushes to hear the Capehart in the big house play Beethoven. Perhaps she was the lucky one after all. Think of the unhappy souls inside, who see the record, worry about scratches, and most of all worry about whether they are *getting it,* whether they are bona fide music lovers. What is the best way to hear Beethoven: sitting in a proper silence around the Capehart or eavesdropping from an azalea bush?

However it may come about, we notice two traits of the second situation: (1) an openness of the thing before one — instead of being an exercise to be learned according to an approved mode, it is a garden of delights which beckons to one; (2) a sovereignty of the knower — instead of being a consumer of a prepared experience, I am a sovereign wayfarer, a wanderer in the neighborhood of being who stumbles into the garden.

One can think of two sorts of circumstances through which the thing may be restored to the person. (There is always, of course, the direct recovery: A student may simply be strong enough, brave enough, clever enough

---

reductio ad absurdum   A method of disproving a proposition by showing that it leads to an absurdity when carried to its logical conclusion.

Toynbee   Arnold Toynbee (1889–1975), English historian, who believed that history is shaped by spiritual rather than economic forces.

Voelkerwanderung   Barbarian invasions.

Technikum   Technical school.

The Heart Is a Lonely Hunter   Novel (1940) by Carson McCullers (1917–1967).

to take the dogfish and the sonnet by storm, to wrest control of it from the educators and the educational package.) First by ordeal: The Bomb falls; when the young man recovers consciousness in the shambles of the biology laboratory, there not ten inches from his nose lies the dogfish. Now all at once he can see it, directly and without let, just as the exile or the prisoner or the sick man sees the sparrow at his window in all its inexhaustibility; just as the commuter who has had a heart attack sees his own hand for the first time. In these cases, the simulacrum of everydayness and of consumption has been destroyed by disaster; in the case of the bomb, literally destroyed. Secondly, by apprenticeship to a great man: One day a great biologist walks into the laboratory; he stops in front of our student's desk; he leans over, picks up the dogfish, and, ignoring instruments and procedure, probes with a broken fingernail into the little carcass. ''Now here is a curious business,'' he says, ignoring also the proper jargon of the specialty. ''Look here how this little duct reverses its direction and drops into the pelvis. Now if you would look into a coelacanth, you would see that it — '' And all at once the student can see. The technician and the sophomore who loves his textbooks are always offended by the genuine research man because the latter is usually a little vague and always humble before the thing; he doesn't have much use for the equipment or the jargon. Whereas the technician is never vague and never humble before the thing; he holds the thing disposed of by the principle, the formula, the textbook outline; and he thinks a great deal of equipment and jargon.

But since neither of these methods of recovering the dogfish is pedagogi- 53 cally feasible — perhaps the great man even less so than the Bomb — I wish to propose the following educational technique which should prove equally effective for Harvard and Shreveport High School. I propose that English poetry and biology should be taught as usual, but that at irregular intervals, poetry students should find dogfishes on their desks and biology students should find Shakespeare sonnets on their dissecting boards. I am serious in declaring that a Sarah Lawrence English major who began poking about in a dogfish with a bobby pin would learn more in thirty minutes than a biology major in a whole semester; and that the latter upon reading on her dissecting board

> That time of year Thou may'st in me behold
> When yellow leaves, or none, or few, do hang
> Upon those boughs which shake against the cold —
> Bare ruin'd choirs where late the sweet birds sang.

might catch fire at the beauty of it.

The situation of the tourist at the Grand Canyon and the biology student 54 are special cases of a predicament in which everyone finds himself in a modern technical society — a society, that is, in which there is a division between expert and layman, planner and consumer, in which experts and planners take special measures to teach and edify the consumer. The measures taken are measures appropriate to the consumer: The expert and the planner *know* and *plan*, but the consumer *needs* and *experiences*.

There is a double deprivation. First, the thing is lost through its packaging. The very means by which the thing is presented for consumption, the very techniques by which the thing is made available as an item of need-satisfaction, these very means operate to remove the thing from the sovereignty of the knower. A loss of title occurs. The measures which the museum curator takes to present the thing to the public are self-liquidating. The upshot of the curator's efforts are not that everyone can see the exhibit but that no one can see it. The curator protests: Why are they so indifferent? Why do they even deface the exhibit? Don't they know it is theirs? But it is not theirs. It is his, the curator's. By the most exclusive sort of zoning, the museum exhibit, the park oak tree, is part of an ensemble, a package, which is almost impenetrable to them. The archaeologist who puts his find in a museum so that everyone can see it accomplishes the reverse of his expectations. The result of his action is that no one can see it now but the archaeologist. He would have done better to keep it in his pocket and show it now and then to strangers.

The tourist who carves his initials in a public place, which is theoretically "his" in the first place, has good reasons for doing so, reasons which the exhibitor and planner know nothing about. He does so because in his role of consumer of an experience (a "recreational experience" to satisfy a "recreational need") he knows that he is disinherited. He is deprived of his title over being. He knows very well that he is in a very special sort of zone in which his only rights are the rights of a consumer. He moves like a ghost through schoolroom, city streets, trains, parks, movies. He carves his initials as a last desperate measure to escape his ghostly role of consumer. He is saying in effect: I am not a ghost after all; I am a sovereign person. And he establishes title the only way remaining to him, by staking his claim over one square inch of wood or stone.

Does this mean that we should get rid of museums? No, but it means that the sightseer should be prepared to enter into a struggle to recover a sight from a museum.

The second loss is the spoliation of the thing, the tree, the rock, the swallow, by the layman's misunderstanding of scientific theory. He believes that the thing is *disposed of* by theory, that it stands in the Platonic relation of being a *specimen of* such and such an underlying principle. In the transmission of scientific theory from theorist to layman, the expectation of the theorist is reversed. Instead of the marvels of the universe being made available to the public, the universe is disposed of by theory. The loss of sovereignty takes this form: As a result of the science of botany, trees are not made available to every man. On the contrary. The tree loses its proper density and mystery as a concrete existent and, as merely another *specimen of* a species, becomes itself nugatory.

Does this mean that there is no use taking biology at Harvard and Shreveport High? No, but it means that the student should know what a fight he has on his hands to rescue the specimen from the educational package. The educator is only partly to blame. For there is nothing the educator can do to provide for this need of the student. Everything the educator does only succeeds in becoming, for the student, part of the educational package. The highest role of the educator is the maieutic role of Socrates: to help the student come to himself not as a consumer of experience but as a sovereign individual.

The thing is twice lost to the consumer. First, sovereignty is lost: It is theirs, not his. Second, it is radically devalued by theory. This is a loss which has been brought about by science but through no fault of the scientist and through no fault of scientific theory. The loss has come about as a consequence of the seduction of the layman by science. The layman will be seduced as long as he regards beings as consumer items to be experienced rather than prizes to be won, and as long as he waives his sovereign rights as a person and accepts his role of consumer as the highest estate to which the layman can aspire.

As Mounier said, the person is not something one can study and provide for; he is something one struggles for. But unless he also struggles for himself, unless he knows that there is a struggle, he is going to be just what the planners think he is.

QUESTIONS ON MEANING

1. The ideas in Percy's essay come in two separate sections. In the first part of the essay, what does Percy tell us about our ability to see, to experience? How does he say our ability to see and to experience may be impaired?
2. Paragraph 44 reads in part: ''once a person is seen as a specimen of a race or a species, at that very moment he ceases to be an individual.'' What does the second part of Percy's essay say about our inability to see as it relates to our educational system? What does this section of the essay suggest about how we might rejuvenate our educational system? About how you personally should approach learning?
3. Percy repeatedly brings up the idea of disaster as an aid to the renewal of our capacity for experience. What does this imply about his view of the contemporary predicament?

4. What is "subversive" about Percy's argument? How does his citation of Socrates in paragraph 59 fit in with this subversiveness?

QUESTIONS ON STRATEGY

1. Consider the progress of Percy's argument in the first part of this essay. Paragraphs 1 through 7 set out the problem — that direct experience is often made impossible by "preformulation." Paragraphs 8 through 17 catalogue strategies for recovering experience. In paragraphs 18 through 31, Percy describes the danger of "ambiguous recovery." This leads him to conclude that "expertise" is a bad influence. How does this sequence prepare us for the subject of part two?

2. Notice the many techniques Perry uses to make his argument — definition, narration, description, argument, analogy. Look at paragraphs 8 through 16, for example, where he uses classification to sketch strategies for recovering the purity of individual experience. How do "the Inside Track, the Familiar Revisited, the Accidental Encounter" help Percy's argument? What ideas do they support? Or look at the introductory paragraphs of part two, 39 through 43, which are organized by comparison and contrast. How do the examples of the dogfish and the sonnet bring out the distinction Percy is making here? How does the difference between Scarsdale and the Falkland Islands relate to the argument in part one? How does this contrast make the transition to the new phase of his argument in part two?

3. "The Loss of the Creature" begins very strongly, with an effective opening sentence. Look through the essays you have read and compare their beginnings with Percy's. Try to determine what makes a good first sentence.

4. In paragraph 3, Percy uses a capital letter, as in a mathematical equation. What purpose does this have in the essay? How does it affect his argument and the tone of this paragraph?

5. Look up *dialectical*. How does Percy use the word? Is it appropriate in paragraph 10?

6. Percy attempts to persuade us that we are not as conscious of ourselves and our environment as we may think. He does this primarily by making us think critically about a series of hypothetical situations. He proposes, for example, that we imagine the response of the first explorer of the Grand Canyon as a way of criticizing the response of the average tourist. Why is this use of hypothesis, as opposed to concrete evidence, appropriate in an essay like "The Loss of the Creature"? How do Percy's hypotheses support and advance his argument?

EXPLORATIONS

1. "The Loss of the Creature" argues that we need a recovery of our control over experience and outlines an array of techniques for accomplishing this. How serious is Percy in taking this how-to approach? Read Percy's *Lost in the Cosmos*, and compare his how-to approach there and in this essay.

2. How does Percy's point about "packaging" (paragraph 55) relate to Tuchman's point about advertising (see paragraph 22).

WRITING TOPICS

1. Choose among the following devalued experiences and explain how they might be recovered (short of blowing up the world): true love, one's roots, an encounter with the devil, the sense of a city as a community.

BOOKS AVAILABLE IN PAPERBACK

Lancelot. New York: Avon. *Novel.*

The Last Gentlemen. New York: Avon. *Novel.*

Love in the Ruins. New York: Avon. *Novel.*

The Message in the Bottle: How Queer Man Is, How Queer Language Is, and What One Has to Do with the Other. New York: Farrar, Straus & Giroux, Noonday Press. *Essays.*

The Moviegoer. New York: Avon. *Novel.*

The Second Coming. New York: Washington Square Press. *Novel.*

ROGER
ANGELL

*I*F GENETICS PERMITTED *the inheritance of acquired characteristics, we might believe that a good prose style was born to Roger Angell (b. 1920). His mother was Katharine Angell White, longtime editor at* The New Yorker *magazine and author of* Onward and Upward in the Garden. *But if style is made, not born, we may admit the influence of his environment, which included not only his mother but E. B. White, the great essayist, who early on became Angell's stepfather (see pp. 14–23).*

After serving in the Air Force during World War II, Angell became editor for a travel magazine called Holiday. *He wrote short stories which he published in* The New Yorker *and then joined the rest of his family as a fiction editor at* The New Yorker *in 1956. He has published a book of short stories and another of satires and parodies, but his best writing is about baseball. Usually he supplies three large reports a year to* The New Yorker, *essays later collected into books:* The Summer Game *(1972),* Five Seasons *(1977), and* Late Innings *(1982).*

Angell brings to baseball faculties of attention, affection, devotion, moral outrage, metaphoric invention, and humor. Watching Luis Tiant pitch for Boston in the 1975

World Series against Cincinnati, Angell described the great Cuban's eccentric manner on the mound:

> *Stands on hill like sunstruck archaeologist at Knossos. Regards ruins.*
> *Studies sun. Studies landscape. Looks at artifact in hand. Wonders:*
> *Keep this potsherd or throw it away? Does Smithsonian want it?*
> *Hmm. Prepares to throw it away. Pauses. Sudd. discovers writing*
> *on object. Hmm. Possible Linear B inscript? Sighs. Throws. Wipes*
> *face. Repeats whole thing.*

But Angell does not attend only to the excellence and oddity of exemplary professionals. He also turns his scrupulous and generous attention to fans, to a semipro ballplayer who lacks skill at the game he loves, to the ninety-one-year-old former pitcher Smokey Joe Wood. It is often said that if you tend your own garden, and look closely enough, you can find everything there. Angell's mother took the expression literally in her essays on the garden. With Roger Angell the figure becomes metaphorical; for in the limited, pastoral world of a sport he discovers an entire moral world.

In this chapter from Late Innings, *Angell's essay, written in March 1979, uses baseball not as foreground but as background. Behind his sentences we hear the sounds of cleats on cement and the noises of shock, for the foreground is the attempt of women sportswriters — in a minor skirmish of the women's movement — to invade the chauvinist priesthood of the press box and the male sanctum of the locker room.*

Sharing the Beat

Early this month, a few weeks before the beginning of the new baseball   1
season, Commissioner Bowie Kuhn sent an advisory memorandum to the
twenty-six major-league clubs suggesting new regulations to govern the admission of female reporters to the teams' clubhouses this year. He said that
the matter would be largely left to the discretion of the individual teams (as it
is in professional basketball, hockey, and football), and urged all the clubs to
do what they could to "minimize problems in this area" and to take steps
"to afford identical access, in one way or another, to all reporters, regardless
of sex." The initial response from the clubs suggests that in about half of the
twenty-six ballparks women reporters will now have some form of
postgame access to the clubhouses, at least for a time. The practical effects of
Mr. Kuhn's dictum remain to be seen — specifically, whether male and female reporters will be able to talk to the players on a truly equal basis, and
whether access to the clubhouses for all reporters will be more restricted

than it has been in the past. On the surface, however, the new plan does seem to represent a change of direction for the Commissioner, who was taken to court last year in a celebrated case for his refusal to allow women reporters to enter the home-team and visitors clubhouses at Yankee Stadium. The plaintiffs — Melissa Ludtke, a young reporter for *Sports Illustrated*, and her employer, Time, Inc. — said that Miss Ludtke had been excluded from the clubhouse during the 1977 World Series (between the Yankees and the Dodgers), and claimed that the exclusion had been based solely on her sex, thus violating Miss Ludtke's right to pursue her profession under the equal-protection and due-process clauses of the Fourteenth Amendment. Mr. Kuhn, speaking for his sport and his co-defendants (the Yankees, the president of the American League, and the Mayor and other officials of the City of New York, which owns Yankee Stadium), responded in an affidavit that he had ordered women reporters kept out of all major-league clubhouses in order to protect the "sexual privacy" of players who were undressing and showering, to protect the image of baseball as a family sport, and to preserve traditional notions of decency and propriety. His tone suggested that the suit posed a threat to the game almost equal to the Black Sox° scandal. He stated that the American public accepts baseball as "emblematic of the highest standards of integrity and morality in professional sports," and that the "standards of conduct and the attitudes and behavior of people in the 'big leagues' often serve as role models for millions of children." He said that "to permit members of the opposite sex into this place of privacy, where players, who are, of course, men, are in a state of undress, would be to undermine the basic dignity of the game."

The case was first heard last April before Judge Constance Baker Motley, in Federal District Court in New York, who found for the plaintiffs. She enjoined the Yankees from further exclusion of women from the Stadium clubhouses unless men were also excluded, and said that the privacy of the players could be adequately assured by installing a curtain or a swinging door in front of each player's dressing cubicle, or simply by instructing the players to wear towels. The Stadium locker rooms became officially heterosexual on September 26th, during the last week of the 1978 regular season. Because the Commissioner had said that the court's edict would not apply to any other major-league clubhouses, women reporters were still barred from the players' quarters at Veterans Stadium, in Philadelphia, and at Dodger Stadium, in Los Angeles, during the National League playoffs, and also at the Kansas City Royals' stadium during the American League playoff games there, between the Royals and the Yankees. During the World Series, no

---

Black Sox Name given to the eight Chicago White Sox players who, after losing the 1919 World Series to Cincinnati, were accused of throwing the series and were suspended for life from baseball.

women reporters were admitted to either clubhouse in Dodger Stadium, but they did come into both clubhouses at Yankee Stadium during the three Series games there.

Bowie Kuhn did not have a very happy time of it in the courts last fall. 3 His concern for the privacy of his players and for the protection of baseball as a family sport was dismissed by Judge Motley as being ''clearly too insubstantial to merit serious consideration.'' The Commissioner then requested Judge Motley to stay her order while his attorneys prepared an appeal, but was denied. Persisting, he did win a clarifying order from Judge Motley, in which she explained that the Yankees' options included the right to ban all reporters, male and female, from their clubhouses for a period long enough to permit the players to dress, and to ban them altogether if a separate interview room were provided. During the World Series, Mr. Kuhn moved along to the Second Circuit Court of Appeals in search of a stay of action while baseball's official appeal was polished up. *This* motion was denied almost immediately by a three-judge panel. The presiding jurist, Judge Walter Mansfield, commenting on the ''baseball is a family game'' argument, said, ''The last I heard, the family includes women as well as men.'' On February 8th of this year, Mr. Kuhn and his attorneys dropped their appeal. The matter is out of the courts, at least for the present.

In recent weeks, Mr. Kuhn seems to have moved away from his obdu- 4 rate, arms-akimbo stance at the clubhouse door. He consulted at length with editors and lawyers at Time, Inc., before issuing his memorandum to the clubs. This is commendable, I guess, but no memorandum can wipe out the injuries and strong feelings that have arisen from this conflict, whose meanings may go deeper into American sport and the American unconscious than most of us would admit.

Women in the clubhouse is an emotional issue — almost a parade float of 5 classical postures in which noble-visaged representations of Propriety, Wholesome Sports, and the Innocence of the American Family are seen to be under attack by similarly admirable figures representing Social Mobility, Equal Opportunity, and Freedom of the Press. Evaluating public response to this crowded tableau is extremely difficult, and even among professional journalists there appears to be a wide swing between public and private attitudes, between conscious scruples and unconscious fears and wishes. Many male reporters I have talked to support their female colleagues' claim that any ban or limitation on their admission to the clubhouse is discriminatory and places them at an impossible disadvantage in their trade. Other male reporters admit all this but still oppose the change, because it offends their sense of propriety or chivalry, or because it seems to violate the players' right to privacy within their den, or simply because it shatters tradition. All the male sportswriters, however, are concerned about the evident possibility that Commissioner Kuhn's recent ruling will lead to severe limitations on their own rights and long habits of access to the ballplayers — specifically, on their being able to talk to them in the clubhouse immediately after the last out, when the sweaty, beergulping young participants are fresh in their memories of the game, and their reactions (exultant or despondent, bitter or comical, or evasive) may be taken down or taped and translated at once into the heart of the next edition's story or column or sidebar on the game. Women sportswriters, who as yet make up a very small percentage of the total, have the same concern about any limitation of access, but they have sharper and more personal feelings of anxiety. Almost all of them have encountered the closed locker-room door, in baseball and in other sports, and the professional leagues that have reversed themselves and opened some of their clubhouses — notably the National Basketball Association and the National Hockey League — have done so only after prolonged skirmishing with a few vehement pioneering women writers and their editors. For the most part, women reporters have had to cajole individual players into emerging, half-dressed or clutching a towel, for a fragmentary interview in a corridor or an equipment room, or have had to wait outside the door interminably, dying by inches as a deadline crept closer, until the players emerged — combed and dressed, homeward- or hotelward-bound, and often sucked dry of news by multiple interviews — and then have had to beg them to summon up again the now receding contest. One alternative to the open locker room is a separate, formal interview room, to which the rival managers and a few individual stars or goats may be summoned, to testify into a battery of microphones, like some visiting rock star or foreign minister. Interview rooms are now customary at championship games or all-star games in most major sports, for they offer an alternative to the noise and crush of the locker rooms, where several hundred newspaper and magazine and TV and radio reporters are trying to get at a handful of bewildered athletes. The interview room, however, usually yields a guarded, statesmanlike form of sports news, or a succession of wrenching one-liners by athletes and coaches who secretly envision themselves as television personalities. Other variations suggested in the wake of the Motley decision — the closing of the locker rooms until all the players are dressed, or a fifteen- or twenty-minute interview period inside the clubhouse, followed by the departure of all media people — seem inadequate or stifling in comparison with an open clubhouse, in which a quick and questing sportswriter can search out conflicting game stories, rumors, whispers of team feuds, hidden injuries, managerial pomposities, salary discontents, or incipient trades, all in a day's or a night's work. Reporters are endlessly harassed by bureaucratic obstacles to their labors, and the smallest hint of some fresh restraint to their freedom elicits instant outrage and cries for redress. Women sportswriters find a clanging irony in all this, for the real or threatened limitations to the male reporters' working customs in baseball as a result of Ludtke v. Kuhn are exactly the same handicaps that women on the sports beat have had to put up with all along. These women, who have never received much public support from their colleagues, are concerned now that any rules imposed by the various clubs in response to their presence on the baseball scene will cause fresh bitterness among their male adversaries, and will even turn their supporters against them in the end. The women sportswriters — and many of the men, too — suspect that this may be the secret hope of not a few sports executives.

Notoriety pursues the Yankees everywhere, and vice versa, and the arrival of the first female reporters in the Yankee clubhouse last September had perfectly predictable results. On the night that Judge Motley's order took effect, the Yankee clubhouse was suddenly crowded with strangers, male and female, who had come to report on the new socio-journalistic phenomenon. Most of the women, I have been told (I was not there), were local television reporters, and they smilingly asked the players what they thought about the presence of women in the locker room, while the cameras caught it all. This, by the way, was the last Tuesday of the regular season, and the Yankees, who were playing the Toronto Blue Jays that night, were then leading the Boston Red Sox by a single game. Reggie Jackson, after delivering his opinion about the admission of women to the clubhouse (for, with reservations) to Carol Jenkins, of WNBC News, finally said, "Aren't you going to ask about this pennant race we're in?" An Associated Press photographer snapped a picture of Willie Randolph, who was naked, talking to a female reporter; Randolph was furious — not about the interview but about the photo. Clyde King, a Yankee coach, came out of the shower room with no clothes on and jumped back in. Goose Gossage pulled off a towel worn by Coach Art Fowler. Still another coach, Gene Michael, delivered an angry harangue about women reporters and their motives. So did some of the players, the two loudest being reserve outfielder Jay Johnstone and backup catcher Cliff Johnson. Most of the other players seemed calm. A day or two later, Johnstone tacked up an obscene message about Judge Motley over his cubicle, and relief pitcher Sparky Lyle brought in a cake in the shape of a phallus with the message "For Women Sportswriters Only" on it. 6

After the first night, however, the clubhouse was a much quieter place, and the players, caught up in their excruciating race, talked mostly baseball. On Friday night, the Yankees, now in possession of Judge Motley's clarifying order, announced that the clubhouse would be closed to all reporters for forty-five minutes after the game, to permit the players to shower and dress. The reporters — most of them regulars who had been covering the club all summer — were badly upset. There was some angry shouting in the press elevator between writers and club executives; during the game, Yankee owner George Steinbrenner conferred with several local newspapermen at 7 the back of the press box, and a compromise was worked out: the clubhouse would remain open for fifteen minutes immediately after the game, to accommodate writers for the morning papers and late-news TV reporters, and then would close for thirty minutes. A week later, when the Royals came to town for the playoff games at the Stadium, the clubhouse remained open for an initial forty-five minutes, and this period was extended to an hour during the subsequent World Series games in New York. Several women reporters and photographers came into the clubhouse during the Series games, but no one seemed to pay any special attention to them.

I had begun to pay attention, however. I missed the first-night sideshow at the Stadium — fortunately, I thought — and my subsequent visits (I was there as a reporter) indicated only that scandal and innovation were giving way to acceptance and custom, which was all right with me. It was not all right, I had begun to notice, with a lot of other people. Sports columnists across the country took up the Ludtke decision, and a great many of them suggested that women sportwriters had fought and struggled and finally gone to the courts to get into the clubhouse mostly because they wanted to ogle naked athletes. This was generally put in the form of a joke. "Folks, I'm all for equal rights for gals," it went, "but what about *my* equal rights? When do I get into a locker room to interview Chrissie Evert with her clothes off?" A lot of my friends — male friends — got off this same joke, and I think I may have smiled at it the first eight or ten times I heard it. (The question it poses, although the question is not its point, is easily answered: in women's professional tennis — and in most other women's sports — the athletes are interviewed immediately after the match is over, at courtside or in some neutral area; the locker rooms are closed to all reporters.) I was not much startled by the columns I read, but the names of some of the columnists did surprise me — surprised me both ways. Dick Young, the conservative, enormously popular sports columnist for the [New York *Daily*] *News* (he is also its sports editor), accepted the arrival of women reporters in the clubhouse as being no less than their due; he suggested that all professional teams might do well to follow the example set three or four years ago by the New York Cosmos, of the North American Soccer League, who had issued bathrobes to their players and then welcomed all reporters. (More recently, during an appearance on "The Dick Cavett Show," Mr. Young revived the women-tennis-players joke and then went on to suggest by innuendo that women sportswriters give sexual favors to athletes as a means of getting news.) Red Smith, in a column that appeared in the [New York] *Times* shortly after the Ludtke suit was instituted, came out on the side of player privacy and the interview room — thus allying himself, almost for the first time ever, with Bowie Kuhn. Writing with his customary lightness and civility, he said that Melissa Ludtke would be much better off in an interview room than she would be being "buffeted, elbowed, and trampled" in the winning locker room after the last game of the World Series. "Had she been thus occupied," he concluded, "she would have missed the gathering in another room [the interview room, that is] down the hall, where managers of both teams and key players on both sides were present to answer all her questions." This was the last line of Mr. Smith's column in the *Times*, but when the syndicated piece appeared in many out-of-town papers it terminated with one more sentence: "Still, she might have got to see Reggie in the buff."

Other things happened in the lively and familiar settings of autumn baseball that began to make me owlish. In the crowded pressrooms and hospitality rooms of the playoffs and the World Series, where hundreds of reporters — almost all of them men, of course — gathered, as usual, to talk shop and to drink and pass the time of day, the Ludtke case and its rulings were frequently discussed, and in the course of the conversations I often heard Melissa Ludtke defamed by people in her own profession. Her reportorial abilities, her seriousness, her motives for bringing the suit, her appearance, and her private life were snickered at and vilified. Only some of the writers talked this way, and none of the remarks came from members of the New York press corps, who know Melissa Ludtke, as I do, as a hardworking young professional and as a friend. (Her name, by the way, is now Melissa Ludtke Lincoln. She was married last year to Eric Lincoln, who is an editor and reporter with the sports department of the *Times*.) I was startled by the slanders, not just because I know Miss Ludtke but because the worst of them were delivered with a perceptible, barely concealed rage — verbal hate mail. Something was going on here.

After the last out of the first game of the World Series, which the Dodgers won, 11–5, in their home park (they won the next game, too, it will be recalled, and then dropped four straight games and the Series to the Yankees), I took an elevator down to the clubhouse level of Dodger Stadium and hurried to the interview room, where, in company with scores of other reporters, I heard Ron Cey and Tommy John and Dodger manager Tom Lasorda and others describe their cheerful recent adventures. I left before the interviews were over, heading for the locker rooms, and on the way I nodded to another woman sportswriter I know, B. J. Phillips, who was taking notes for her story; she is an associate editor of *Time* and is its chief writer on sports. Thirty or forty minutes later, emerging from the Yankee dressing rooms, I came into a sort of rotunda that lies between the two locker rooms and is open to the public, and there I saw B. J. Phillips again. She was leaning against a railing and was bent over in an odd posture and clutching her notebook. She was still wearing her press credentials — a large printed blue ticket, which was fastened by its string to her blouse. I went over and asked rather casually if something was wrong (she was a recent acquaintance, whom I had met for the first time the previous week, at the National League

9

10

playoffs in Philadelphia), and when she looked up I saw that her eyes were swimming. She glared at me, and in a strangled voice she said, "I won't cry! I *won't!* I won't let the bastards make me cry!"

She told me that when she had left the interview room, in company with many other writers, she had started down the corridor leading to the rotunda and had been met there by two public-relations men, representing the Commissioner, who barred her path, even though she told them that she was not heading for the Dodger locker room, which she knew was closed to women. One of the men politely explained that she had been issued the wrong credentials; he proffered her a yellow credential card, on which someone's name had been crossed out and hers written in. "There's been a mistake," the P.R. man said. "*These* are your credentials." B. J. Phillips — aware, of course, that a yellow credential card did not entitle its bearer to enter the clubhouses — said that she was keeping the credentials she had been mailed. Again she said to the men that she had no intention of going into the locker room. She told them that lawyers for Time, Inc., had undertaken negotiations with the Commissioner's office, before the World Series, to have her admitted there, but had failed. She told the men that she did not believe in confrontation. She said, however, that she would not give up her blue credential card. "I treated that yellow card like a dead rat," she told me. The men still would not allow her to go down the corridor and ordered her to leave via a tunnel leading to the Dodger dugout and then out onto the field. "You even have a servants' entrance for us, don't you?" she said, giving up at last. When she reached the field, she discovered that the only way she could return to the rotunda and the elevators to the parking lot was through the lower grandstands. There were loiterers and drunks still in the stands, who saw her credential card and offered loud suggestions about why she had been in the Dodger clubhouse and what she had seen there.

B. J. Phillips had stopped crying by the time she told me all this, but then she looked up and noticed several TV reporters and camera crews approaching, and again she looked stricken. "I'm the wrong person for this," she murmured. "I *hate* this. I want anonymity. It's the only way for a reporter to work." (She and her story did subsequently appear on national television, though.) I said something encouraging to her, and then I left, promising that I would bring her any interesting comments I could pick up in the Dodger locker room, where I was now headed. She thanked me, but I never did take her the quotes. While I was listening to the players, I kept thinking about her, and then, uneasily, I remembered making the same kind of promise to Melissa Ludtke in previous years, at previous important games or Series games in New York and Boston and Philadelphia and Cincinnati and other cities, when I had glimpsed her outside the doors of different clubhouses, standing among the pushing, jammed-together fans and hangers-on and guards and kids and policemen while she waited for some ballplayer to come out and answer her questions. Sometimes I remembered my promise to Melissa, and sometimes I forgot it, because the truth is that I hardly thought about the matter. I was always sure I was doing her a favor, or was about to.

Since last October, I have tried to think about this a little more, and I have asked a lot of people about women in the clubhouse. I have talked to athletes and sports executives and male sportswriters, but most of all I have tried to listen to the women sportswriters themselves. Their voices seemed to be charged with a special resonance. They spoke as if they represented some foreign constituency within us all that has been waiting and wondering if it would ever be remembered or dealt with. Sports, I keep reminding myself, mean a lot in this country.   13

Women sports reporters and announcers have been turning up in increasing numbers on television screens and on the radio; some of the TV reporters, like their male counterparts, seem to have been hired mostly for their looks. It is extremely difficult to find out how many women are now employed as working sportswriters on newspapers. I talked about this not long ago with Le Anne Schreiber, who is the sports editor of the [New York] *Times* and at the moment is the only woman journalist on its sports staff. "Women sportswriters are still a very small minority," she told me. "Newspaper sports departments all around the country are beginning to hire women, but in a pretty gingerly way. I lost an experienced reporter, Robin Herman, to our Metropolitan Desk this year, and I'm looking for qualified women right now — and qualified men, too. The Washington *Post* just hired its third woman for sports. Any paper that has taken on a second or third woman in its sports department has probably moved beyond tokenism."   14

Women sportswriters are not a perfectly new phenomenon. Some years ago, I remember, the *Times* had a former champion golfer named Maureen Orcutt on its staff, who covered women's golf. Another woman, Jeane Hoffman, used to write about baseball and other sports for the [New York] *Journal-American* — stories about Edna Stengel and that sort of thing. Mary Garber, who is in her sixties, has been covering tennis, track, football, and basketball — Atlantic Coast Conference college games, for the most part — for the Winston-Salem *Journal* ever since 1944. But these have been rarities, like women surgeons or women railroad conductors, and only in the past seven or eight years have greater numbers of young women who were starting careers in journalism begun to give serious consideration to the sports beat. In many newspaper sports departments, they are still looked upon as oddities. Several male sportswriters I know have told me that they have never met or worked with a woman who seemed to know anything about sports, and   15 others were dubious about women's motives or sports experience. Speculating on this subject in the Boston *Globe* last fall, Leigh Montville ("Leigh," in this case, is a man's name) wrote,

> I have only a few questions. . . . I ask them because I am serious and I wonder if the lady is serious. . . . That is all I would want to know about anyone in this business. . . . Did she grow up on sports? Was her life absolutely dominated by sports when she was a kid? . . . Has she ever held a hockey stick in her hands? Has she ever shot a basketball from behind a pick? Has she ever set a pick? Was she ever given a subscription to the *Sporting News* for Christmas? Did she ever spit in a baseball glove?

And so on. Some of the women in sports I have talked to would pass Mr. Montville's test, and others might not. There doesn't seem to be any pattern to it.

B. J. Phillips: *(She is of medium height, with pale, wide-set eyes and a humorous, combative expression. She attended the University of Georgia in the mid-sixties and then dropped out. There is a faint trace of Georgia in her speech. She has been a news reporter with the Atlanta* Constitution *and the Washington* Post. *She joined the staff of* Time *in 1970, and wrote national news. She won an Alicia Patterson Fellowship in 1973, and went to Vietnam and Ireland and the Middle East. When she returned to* Time, *she began to cover sports. What "B. J." stands for is a secret; no one except her family knows. Thirty-five years old.)*

"I think if I'd been a guy I'd have been a sportswriter from the start. I've always thought sports was a poorly reported and misunderstood phenomenon. I took the chance when it came. I think I was tired of writing about dead people. I like sports. I like to get into things. I played short center on the *Time* softball team two years ago, when we won our championship. I won a Gold Glove for my fielding, and I batted over .400 for the season.

"I think I have a reputation as being a pretty tough lady. I've been around. I was a marcher in the sixties. When I was with the *Post*, I covered Woodstock, the Apollo 13 space shot, Capitol Hill — everything. I've picked up a severed leg outside a blown-out pub in Northern Ireland, I've interviewed women terrorists, I've heard a President of the United States lie at a press conference. But the first time in twelve years I've been forced to tears in public was there in Dodger Stadium. I think it was the World Series that did it — it's ludicrous. It's like that line 'It's so sad it makes you want to laugh; it's so sad it makes you want to cry.' I've been treated worse in sports than anywhere else. I've never felt that resentment anywhere else. I covered a series of games between the Royals and the White Sox in Chicago three years ago, and nobody in the press box spoke to me for three days. Nobody. I'm bitter about what happens to women sportswriters. I can't accept it.

"You know, after I was on television that time, I heard a lot of people 20
say, 'Some people will do anything for publicity.' Jesus Christ! I can get all
the publicity I want, from my own work. I wrote the first cover story *Time*
ever ran on Jimmy Carter. Last year, I wrote four cover stories and won a
Page One Award for a sports piece. But that doesn't matter to some people.
What hurts is that so much of this comes from my professional colleagues,
who know why access is essential in our business. It *kills* me that my peers
treat women writers with an attitude that says they're something between a
pariah and a sex-crazed thrill seeker. It hurts privately. I don't think anybody knows the price we're paying.

"It confuses me when I realize that there are men who really can't see 21
that what we care about in the locker room is not the naked bodies but our
work. They can't seem to grasp that. I'm treated like a pervert for trying to
do my work. It's clear that something has these people terrified. I don't understand what's behind it. I don't understand the social dynamic. Maybe
I'm dense. I just don't get it."

Robin Herman: *(She is tall, with dark hair. She graduated summa cum laude* 22
from Princeton in 1973 — the first Princeton class to admit women as freshmen. In
college, she joined the Daily Princetonian, *the undergraduate newspaper, and even-*
tually became its sports co-editor. She was a member of Phi Beta Kappa. She joined
the [New York] Times *in 1973, and was quickly assigned to cover the New York Is-*
landers, in the National Hockey League. Later, she became the Times *writer cover-*
ing the New York Rangers. She has also covered professional basketball. She is now
on general assignment for the Metropolitan Desk. Twenty-seven years old.)
"I didn't get deeply interested in sports until I was sent to the Islanders. 23
A professional curiosity sets in, and you realize that if you're going to do it
right you have to learn everything. You've got to be right. I was sent to the
Islanders because they were an expansion team, way out in the boonies, and
nobody else wanted to cover them.

"I was one of the first women to get into a National Hockey League 24
locker room, but now all the teams except five — Chicago, Buffalo, Toronto,
Detroit, and St. Louis — let women in. Each of them has an old-line ownership or an old hockey figure who has stood in the way. Bob Pulford, in Chicago, is a decent man, but he's adamant about this. There was a lot of trouble with the Atlanta Flames. Their coach, Fred Creighton, told me that he
was against it, but that he didn't know about the players. I asked if he'd poll
them, and when he did they voted unanimously to let us in. So Fred said it
was O.K. It always seems easy when it finally happens.

"I was covering the N.H.L. All-Star Game back in 1975, in Montreal, and 25
at a press conference before the game Leo Monahan, of the Boston *Herald*
American, asked the two coaches, 'When are you going to let accredited
women reporters into your clubhouses?' The coaches were Fred Shero and

Bep Guidolin, and they sort of looked at each other and shrugged and said it would be O.K. that night. That was how it all began. It was treated like a joke. Marcelle St. Cyr, who'd been broadcasting Canadiens games for Station CKLM, in Montreal, and I were the first women in. I had no plans to make it happen, or anything. I couldn't believe it. All-star games are sort of boring, and Marcelle and I were the story that night, not the players. There were a lot of jokes and pranks.

"The Rangers didn't let any women in that year. Emile Francis was the general manager, and he said that the players' wives would object. Somebody always says that, but I don't believe it anymore. Once the players get used to you, it never comes up again. When John Ferguson took over at the Rangers in the middle of the 1975–76 season, I asked him if I could get in. Ferguson is a macho, no-nonsense sort of guy, but he has a real sense of fairness. He just waved his arm toward the locker room. I said 'You mean? . . .' and he nodded. Later on, when Lawrie Mifflin had started writing hockey for the [New York *Daily*] *News*, he even offered to try to ban *all* reporters from the visiting-team locker room at Madison Square Garden if a visiting team wouldn't let women in, but we said no, we didn't want that. Can you imagine how that would have gone over with the other writers? Wow!

"Hockey players are friendly and polite, but basketball players are a lot looser. Most of them are black, of course, and they seem able to treat you like an individual — like a woman as well as like a reporter. They're cooler dudes, or something. They're big-city people, most of them, and almost all of them went to college. They've been around. I think they may be more at ease with their own sexuality. Basketball players are treated like men by their coaches. Nobody watches them or keeps a curfew on the road. Hockey players are treated more like boys.

"It's been tough. It was awful at the beginning. I remember a playoff game in Toronto — I think Philadelphia was playing the Maple Leafs. I'd been through it all so many times, and we were still having trouble with the Flyers then. It was late at night, my time was running out, and I had to write. I was outside the door of the Flyers' dressing room, and there were a lot of people there looking at me and making remarks. Finally, one player came out — I think it was Bob Dailey. I asked him some questions about the game, and when I was finished I had to hurry down a long corridor and then up a flight of stairs to get to the pressroom. I stopped in a stairwell, because I realized I was so angry I couldn't speak. I was like Billy Budd — I was *silenced*. I thought, What am I doing here? Why am I putting up with this? I got my crying out — nobody saw me — and then I went up and wrote my story.

"Getting into the locker room seems like such a foolish thing to waste your energies on. Sixty percent of my time and effort used to be spent on just trying to get to the players, instead of on what I was writing. It's emotionally draining. It uses you up. Before I left sports, I sometimes wondered about writing baseball someday, but I wouldn't try it now. I just couldn't go through that clubhouse thing all over again, now that I know it doesn't mean anything.''

Diane K. Shah: *(She is an associate editor of* Newsweek, *where today she* 30 *writes mostly for the ''Life/Style'' department. She grew up in Chicago, and graduated from Indiana University in 1967. She worked as a reporter for the* National Observer *and for the Chicago bureau of United Press International before joining* Newsweek *in 1977. She has published a novel,* The Mackin Cover — *a thriller, with a professional-football setting. She is married but is separated from her husband. She is very tall, with striking, faintly Oriental-looking eyes. Thirty-three years old.)*

''Sports has changed in its attitude toward women, but baseball still has 31 a pretty long way to go. Back in September of 1972, I persuaded my editor at the *Observer* to send me up to Boston to cover some Red Sox games at Fenway Park. The team was in a close pennant race with the Tigers and Orioles and Yankees, and everybody was very excited and involved. It looked like a great story. I got in touch with the Red Sox public-relations man, Bill Crowley, and he said, 'We don't let women on the field, and the Baseball Writers Association runs the press box.' When I called up the man who was running the Baseball Writers in Boston that year, he sort of stuttered and put me on hold for a long time, and then he said I couldn't do it. My editor, Henry Gemmill, and one of the company attorneys talked with the Red Sox people, but when I got up there all I'd heard was 'Well, that girl can come in if she behaves herself,' and I didn't know what that meant. Bill Crowley had told me he'd get me a box seat and said he'd bring players there for me to interview. I said, 'You mean you'll bring Carl Yastrzemski to see me in the stands right after a game?' and he said, 'Well, I'll *try.*' Finally, I got my pass to go out on the field, but when I went out there during batting practice I found that none of the players would talk to me. They simply wouldn't answer when I asked them questions. Then I discovered that there had just been a team meeting, where they'd been told I was coming and warned to watch their language. Only two of them talked to me in the end — Carlton Fisk and that left-handed pitcher John Curtis. The rest thought they'd been told not to say anything at all.

''Before the game, Dick Bresciani, the assistant public-relations man, 32 took me up on the roof, where the press box and the pressroom are. I could see he was terribly uncomfortable about something, and when we got there he explained that I could come into the press box but that the pressroom was a social place, for eating and drinking, and no women were allowed in there. I saw that they'd set up a little ice-cream table outside the pressroom, with one chair and one place setting, and there was a little folder on it with

'Ladies' Pavilion' written across it. I didn't eat at all that night. I just ignored it.

"During the game, Dick Bresciani sat between me and Bill Crowley in the press box. I think he thought I'd make a terrible scene, or something. Finally, after about four innings, I introduced myself to Mr. Crowley and I said, 'See? Nothing terrible has happened.' He said, 'Well, it will,' and I asked him what could happen. He said, 'Tomorrow, there'll be fifty girls like you here.' I said I didn't think there were fifty women sportswriters in the whole country, and he said, 'Maybe not, but they'll say they are, just so they can get at my players.'

"The next night, I was allowed in the pressroom. Tom Yawkey, the team owner, had told everybody that if I was accredited I was to be let in. I sat all alone. Nobody came near me. But then Mr. Yawkey sent word over to me to come and join him at his table. When I wrote the story, I sort of made it a point of honor not to put any of this stuff in. The strangest thing of all, when I look back on it, is that none of this seemed to have been done with any malice. They were all polite, in a distant sort of way. They just didn't know what to do about me.

"The leadership on a team makes a big difference in how you're treated. Earl Weaver, of the Orioles, is very accommodating and easy, and so are his players. So is Chuck Tanner, of the Pirates. The Red Sox always make you feel sort of uncomfortable, but I think they're an uncomfortable kind of team, even among themselves. The Yankees — well, I rode on a team bus with them in Kansas City a couple of times last year, while I was working on a story, and there was a lot of bad language in the back of the bus. I mean a *lot*. You could tell that most of it was for my benefit. Billy Martin, who was still manager then, was very nervous about it, and Elston Howard was so embarrassed that he offered to take me with him in a cab next time. The Yankees aren't exactly a mature team, to put it mildly.

"I get the feeling that baseball players have always been a pretty special sort of athlete. From an early age, their whole lives have been tied up with the locker room and its intensely male feelings. They usually get married very young, when they're still in the minors, and they talk a lot about protecting their wives. Some of them have never met a woman as an equal — maybe most of them. They have no women as friends. They live together more of the time than other athletes do. It's a long season, with a lot of travelling. They hang out together a lot.

"I always try to meet their wives and talk to them, so I can show them that I'm serious. Hardly any of them have ever met a woman reporter. The players and their wives both seem to think that you're some kind of groupie who's been clever enough to get her hands on a press pass.

"There's nothing I love more than baseball, but every time I walk out onto a baseball field I feel a dread about being there. It upsets me, because I started in with baseball exactly the same way most kids did. My father was a secret Yankee fan in Chicago — an exile — and he began taking me to a lot of games when I was about twelve. He taught me how to keep score. I used to keep Yankee scrapbooks — I cut out all the Yankee stories and Yankee box scores I could find and pasted them up. I was very self-conscious about this, because I knew other girls didn't do it. I used to buy *Sport* magazine, and I'd bring it home inside an envelope, so people couldn't tell. When I grew up, one of the very first stories I got to write for the *Observer* was about an old Yankee hero of mine, who was still in baseball as a coach. I went and talked with him, and when we went out to dinner he got drunk and fell down in the street. He said he was wearing new shoes, or something, but that wasn't it. It was sad. I didn't write that, either."

Betty Cuniberti: *(She covers the University of Maryland football and basketball* 39 *teams for the Washington* Post, *and fills in on the paper's coverage of the Washington Redskins and Bullets. Previously, she was a sports reporter for the San Bernardino, California,* Sun-Telegram *and then for the San Francisco* Chronicle. *She is twenty-seven years old, with curly brown hair and a quick smile.)*

"Most women in this business don't cover games. Ninety percent of us 40 don't — not a good balance. The standard idea of a woman sportswriter's story is doing Steve Garvey's wife or writing a feature about Nancy Lopez. The men on the beat are always aware of that. This is why locker-room access is the heart of it all. Access is the key to covering games, and you aren't a sportswriter — you haven't paid your dues — unless you cover games.

"Pro football is just about the last bastion. The N.F.L. leaves it up to the 41 individual teams, but only the Eagles and the Vikings let women into their locker rooms. Tom Landry, of the Cowboys, closed his locker rooms to everybody last fall rather than let women in. Pro football is the prestige beat, the biggest of them all, and sports editors almost never let a woman near it. They think we haven't earned the assignment, or else it just doesn't occur to them. They think it's like sending a dog to do your income-tax return, or something.

"When I was with the *Chronicle* in 1976, I went on a game trip to Kansas 42 City with the Oakland Raiders, and I heard that Al Davis, the Oakland owner, was upset about my presence on the charter flight. I had a feeling that I was being watched, to see if anything would happen. Davis told people that he was also afraid I might be bad luck — like a woman on a ship. The stewardesses didn't count, of course. I used to have real trouble with some of the Raider players. They'd hassle me — hide my typewriter, or hide my car in the parking lot. One of them grabbed me in a hallway. None of that ever happened with the 49ers. I finally spoke up to John Madden, the Raider coach, and it stopped right away. But those were rocky times.

"I hate to say it, but I think it's going to take more court action to change 43 all this. There aren't enough of us, and there aren't enough editors or newspapers like mine, who will make an issue of women. I think more editors and more reporters in the business have to see that this is a writers' issue, not a women's issue. And then, even if you do get some support, at the end of it all you just get bombarded with bad mail. You know, sportswriters aren't very popular anyway. People just don't understand deadlines. The players are always blaming us for what we report — for real quotes or for criticisms of them — and they blame us when they lose. No matter what you do, the image that the public holds on to is of a ravening, fire-eating woman coming in and taking advantage of some poor, shy, tired boys. My name is synonymous with nudity — I think it's the first thing most people think about me.

"I never saw any of this coming when I was growing up. When I was a kid in San Francisco, I always knew I was going to be a writer — I asked Santa Claus for a typewriter when I was five years old — but I thought I was going to be a professional athlete, too. I was a tomboy. I was always the fastest runner on my block. My family had season tickets for the 49ers, and in the summer we went to a lot of the Giants' games. I thought I was going to grow up and pitch for the Giants. I was sure of it. My hero was Mike McCormick, who had won the Cy Young Award. The only thing that worried me about my future was that he was left-handed and I wasn't. I thought that was all there was that stood in my way."

Melissa Ludtke Lincoln: *(She became a reporter on* Sports Illustrated *in 1974, shortly after her graduation from Wellesley. Her byline has appeared occasionally in the magazine, but for the most part she has done legwork and research for writers who are senior to her. She has covered baseball and professional basketball. She has an oval face and brownish-blond hair, which falls to her shoulders. She speaks in a flat, quiet voice. Twenty-seven years old.)*

"I'm politically naïve. I never thought much about discrimination until I saw how women were treated over the locker-room thing. When I tried to get into the locker room back at the 1977 World Series, it was for obvious professional reasons. I went through all the proper steps, asked all the right people, explained my reasons. Then the door was slammed in my face. Literally, I mean: It was Pete Carry, my editor — the baseball editor — who took it up from there and made it all happen. He was the hero. It took a long time, and it was worth it, of course, but things haven't exactly turned around. If I'm sent on a story to Detroit, let's say, this summer, I still won't be able to get into the locker room there. I'm still only one bus stop down the road.

"This crusade has worn me down. I'm a little discouraged by my own situation. I think I was a symbol for Time, Inc. More than fifty per cent of the employees there are women, and some of them filed a complaint about discrimination with the New York Division of Human Rights a few years ago. It was settled by agreement, and my suit was the most convenient way for

Time, Inc., to show its support for women. But the basic workings of my magazine haven't changed much.

"I'm tired of the difference between public and private attitudes. When I 48 first tried to get into the clubhouses in 1977, the Dodgers voted to let me in. Billy Martin said I could come into his office. Then the Commissioner stepped in and began collecting affidavits, and suddenly everything was different. Last summer, one of the Yankee executives introduced me to his wife and two daughters, and they congratulated me on what I had done. He looked at me and winked, because he and I knew that his official stand had been one of absolute opposition to me.

"Some of the Yankees were terrific with me last fall. Roy White was su- 49 per. So was Fred Stanley. Reggie apologized to me for some of the bad scenes in the clubhouse. I think I got that open hostility from players like Jay Johnstone and Cliff Johnson because they hadn't been much involved in the pennant race or the playoffs. They were having trouble with their careers and their egos. It was a way for them to be a star at something — to get the writers around them.

"I hope I'll begin to feel at ease in the Yankee clubhouse, the way I do in 50 the basketball locker rooms. I'm still not anxious to go in there. If I'm afraid, it may be because people there don't know my face yet. If people know me, I'm all right. I can't tell if what I feel is a human nervousness or if it's because I'm a woman. I can't separate them."

There are many hundreds of men who write regularly about sports in this 51 country — most of them for the daily papers. No survey of their opinions about women sportswriters or the admission of those women to the athletes' locker rooms has ever been undertaken. The three sportswriters quoted here were selected not in any attempt to present a balance but because each is a friend of mine and because each, it turned out, was willing to speak his mind in a remarkably candid fashion.

Murray Chass: (*After graduating from the University of Pittsburgh, he* 52 *worked for ten years as a sportswriter with the Associated Press. He has been with the* [New York] Times *since 1969, and is the current chairman of the New York chapter of the Baseball Writers of America. He covers the Yankees, and he has become widely known for his reporting on the financial, legal, and labor aspects of big-time sports. He is married, and has two sons, a daughter, a stepson, and a stepdaughter. He has reddish-brown hair and a small beard. Forty years old.*)

"The only thing that bothers me about women sportswriters is when 53 they're dumb or don't know what they're doing. But I feel exactly the same way about male sportswriters. I would guess that some of the women are going to have to work a little harder at it than the men do, because they may not know quite so much in advance. There's a pressure on them to be very good. I think it's the same as it was when Jackie Robinson first came up.° He knew he had to excel. I don't like to make the comparison, but it's there.

"There's no question in my mind but that the Yankees tried to turn the male writers against the women after the Ludtke ruling last fall. You could see it happening, and they did it on purpose. If the Commissioner and everyone else had just left the issue alone, it all would have been resolved in three days. It just would have gone away.

"Being kept out of the clubhouse for any reason or taking players into another area for interviews is unacceptable, and I'll scream about it. The issue is perfectly plain. It's freedom of access for all writers. Wherever I have a right to go, a woman has a right to go, as long as she's there to do a job.

"The players' right to privacy is a tricky issue, though. Last spring, in Fort Lauderdale, a woman photographer was allowed into the clubhouse, and some of the Yankee players were genuinely shocked. One of the pitchers was talking to me about it, and I pointed out to him that most of the players — easily ninety percent of them, married or unmarried — fooled around when they were on the road, so they couldn't be too shy. He said sure, but when he was in bed with a woman they *both* had their clothes off, and he had been — well, consulted about it. I had to think about that. Later on, I asked my daughter Debbie, who is fourteen, what she thought about this business of the players' privacy and the reporters. She said, 'Are men allowed in there to see them?' I said yes, and she said, 'Well, then women should be in, too.' She was right, of course."

Jerome Holtzman: *(He is the senior baseball writer for the Chicago* Sun-Times. *He has been on the baseball beat for twenty-two years, covering the Cubs for half of each season and the White Sox for the other half. He writes a lengthy summary of each baseball year for the* Official Baseball Guide. *He owns a notable collection of baseball books and memorabilia, and he has written three books about baseball. One of them,* No Cheering in the Press Box, *is a series of interviews with old-time titans of the press box — men like Richards Vidmer, John Kieran, John Drebinger, and Ford Frick. He is of medium height, with broad shoulders, gray hair, and bushy eyebrows. He smokes cigars. He is married, with four daughters. Fifty-two years old.)*

"The liberal in me says that women reporters are entitled to be in the clubhouse and to get all the courtesies I get. The chauvinist and the realist in me say they don't belong. I feel that by getting their rights — all that they're entitled to — they're abrogating the players' right to privacy. Anyhow, I

Jackie Robinson first came up Jackie Robinson (1919–1972) was the first Black baseball player in the major leagues. He came up from the Negro leagues to the Brooklyn Dodgers in 1947.

think clubhouse reporting is overrated. Editors are impressed by it, but players don't always tell the truth in that kind of interview. Clubhouse reporting results in a pretty sloppy kind of work. You can come to the park in the seventh inning and skip the game altogether. I think there's going to be a swing back to the other kind of sportswriting — to game writing. And that macho feeling of the clubhouse isn't a very important part of a team.

"Listen, I know it's a problem. I know women are entitled to be sports- 59 writers. But I feel there's something unwholesome about it all. There's something unwholesome about a woman having to scramble at a World Series or at a big game — having to run after the players. I don't mind men running, the way you and I do, but why should women have to do it? I think I still have something of a romantic attitude toward women.

"Women reporters have certain advantages over men. I've seen it. Ath- 60 letes open up to women more in a one-on-one situation. Most of the women also have the advantage of their age, and that applies to younger male reporters, of course. I used to be a lot closer to the players than I am today. One of the worst aspects of being a sportswriter is that you get older and the athletes get younger. Jimmy Cannon once said that sportswriters are entombed in a prolonged boyhood. And the Midwest sports editor of the A.P. [Associated Press], Jerry Liska — he's retired now — always said that after you got to be thirty-five or forty you shouldn't be a sportswriter anymore.

"The assignment has changed. There's more behind-the-scenes crap. 61 Nobody wants to know who went from first to third. Sports is getting to be just entertainment. I suppose the fact that this was an all-male world was what made it so exciting to me at first. And now that it's being invaded and eroded it's much less attractive. Maybe I am a chauvinist — I don't know. The press box used to be a male preserve — that was its charm. I'd rather not have a woman as a seatmate at a World Series game. It wouldn't be as much fun. I've never met a woman who knew as much baseball as a man. But there was a woman once who was an official scorer. I remember reading about it. It was in some minor league — maybe the Texas League. Isn't that interesting? You could look it up."

Maury Allen: *(He has been a sportswriter with the [New York] Post for eigh-* 62
teen years, mostly covering the Yankees and the Mets, and is now a columnist. He
was one of the original "Chipmunks" — a group of young, iconoclastic sportswriters
who became celebrated in the early nineteen-sixties for their questioning, irreverent
attitude toward athletes and sports institutions. He has written fifteen baseball
books, including a biography of Joe DiMaggio. He is married, with a son and a
daughter. He has prematurely white hair and a black mustache. His manner is cheer-
ful. Forty-six years old.)

"I have a gut feeling that letting women into the clubhouse violates the 63
traditions of baseball. The idea of a girl romping through a clubhouse filled

111

with naked athletes is not going to be good for the game. I am also very concerned that the baseball establishment is going to use the arrival of women as an excuse to cut off the clubhouse altogether. Professional athletes make so much money now that they only just tolerate the press, and Bowie thinks that we only come into the clubhouse to agitate the players and to snoop. But you have to report the clubhouse — the inside environment of baseball. Ever since television began covering the game, the clubhouse has been the writer's beat. The players and the general managers and the Commissioner are agreed on one thing — we are the enemy.

"What will happen to the women reporters on the road? Most of the women writers I've seen are girls I wouldn't cross the street to ask for a date. But there will be some attractive girls among them, and they'll be thrown into compromising situations. There will be a scandal, and it will be bad for all reporters.

"Sex is a very significant aspect of athletes' lives. If you think about it, you realize right away that athletic performance and sexual performance always go hand in hand. Why did Joe Namath become such a national hero? Because he was macho. Because deep down in our hearts *we* wanted all those broads. I think sexual performance is even more important to baseball players, because they have so much time on their hands, being on the road so much. They have all that hotel time. The peer pressure to drink and chase girls and commit adultery is almost impossible for the younger players to resist. This is what's behind the macho, kidding-around atmosphere of the clubhouse — the cursing and that male coquettishness. The players are wary of any mention of the on-the-road part of their lives. It's never written about, and they all cover up for each other. The writers are sworn to secrecy, and they know it. That's why there was such a stink about Jim Bouton's book *Ball Four* — it broke the unwritten rule. Any reporter who wrote about all this might just as well turn in his baseball card. He'd be as good as dead. I don't know if a woman would understand any of that.

"I think most male sportswriters are failed athletes. I was a high-school baseball player at James Madison High, in Brooklyn. But I was never much more than a fringe player, so I could see it wasn't going to happen. I did the next-best thing, which was to become a baseball writer. But what is the psychology of a woman in this business? Is it a misplaced role for her? I'm in terrible conflict about this. I consider myself a political liberal. I have an eleven-year-old daughter, and she wants to be a sportswriter. I want women to be brain surgeons and Supreme Court justices. If Barbara Jordan° ran for President, I'd vote for her. But I think that just as I can't become pregnant,

---

Barbara Jordan (b. 1936) Democratic state senator in Texas (1967–1972), first Black woman in Texas legislature in the twentieth century; U.S. representative (1972–1978); became nationally well known as the keynote speaker to the 1976 Democratic national convention.

women shouldn't become sportswriters. When I was ten years old, my father began taking me to ballgames, and this relationship was very significant to me. It was male. It was something that separated me from my mother. Baseball is our most traditional game, and on an emotional level I don't want to break away from those traditions. I have disagreements with other writers about this. But I think the coverage of baseball is as traditional as the game itself. I see the erosion of all our deepest sports feelings coming. I feel that the romance of the game will be damaged.

"Maybe I don't want this changed because I want to think of sports as being unchanged, still juvenile. I want to go on thinking about baseball as being a part of our life that doesn't have the same values as the rest of it. Something about the joy of the game is going. I trouble in my mind about all this. I wish I weren't presented with it."

Three more women:

Jane Gross: *(She is the daughter of the late Milton Gross, who was a well-known sportswriter and columnist on the [New York] Post. After graduating from Skidmore, she became a researcher at Sports Illustrated, and in 1975 she joined the sports staff of Newsday. That year, she started covering the New York Nets, and she has also covered the Knicks. She has been to Wimbledon for Newsday, and she will soon travel to North Korea to cover an international table-tennis tournament. She is small and slight, and she speaks in a precise, confident manner. She is thirty-one years old.)*

"I'm an accidental sports reporter. I planned on being a different sort of writer. I didn't play sports as a kid, and I don't much like sports. I never watch sports on TV on my day off. I think I was hired by *S.I.* out of college because they were sure I knew all about sports — on account of my father. All I had was a network of sports connections, and I had to learn a lot of things that Stephanie Salter and Melissa Ludtke knew already. My father almost hysterically discouraged me from going into sports. He wanted me to be in an easier side of journalism, like magazines or TV, where there would be rugs on the floor. I've heard that because of my father some old-time sportswriters get upset at the thought of me in the locker room with a lot of naked athletes. But I'm loyal enough to his intelligence to think that I could convince him it was right. Maybe not, though.

"I was perfectly sure that Melissa was going to win her lawsuit, and I was perfectly sure that the Yankees would respond to it by closing the locker room in some way. They would fulfill the obligation to be equal, but 'equal' would take something away from the men. That's a very worrisome trend, because we women writers have to live in this world and we're so outnumbered. The men are going to be justifiably furious if their prerogatives are taken away from them, and a lot of them are going to take it out on us.

"I think women reporters have a lot of advantages, starting with the advantage of the players' natural chivalry. We women are interested in different things from the men writers, so we ask different questions. When Bob McAdoo gets traded from the Knicks, my first thought is, How is his wife, Brenda, going to finish law school this year? And that may be what's most on *his* mind. I'm very close to the players' wives. Julius Erving's wife, Turquoise, is a good friend of mine. I don't think the wives worry about me or other women writers when the team is on the road. Athletes' wives have very anxious lives. They have a lot to be nervous about, but the only complaint I've ever had from them is that I get to spend more time with their husbands than they do.

''The other advantage of being a woman is that you're perpetually forced to be an outsider. As a rule, you're not invited to come along to dinner with a half-dozen of the players, or to go drinking with them, when maybe they're going to chase girls. This means a lot, because I believe that all reporters should keep a great distance between themselves and the players. It always ought to be an adversary relationship, basically. That's a difficult space to maintain when you're on the road all through a long season. I can remember a trip, when I first started out, when I called room service for my meals for nineteen straight days. It was hard to take, but later I saw it was really an advantage, a strength.

''I've not always been perfectly at ease in a locker room, but I'm comfortable now. It's an earned comfort — it takes a long time. I don't think anybody who hasn't been in a locker room when women are there can believe that it isn't a big deal. Most of the men who have fought so hard to keep women out probably have never seen a locker room with women in it. My presence doesn't change the way the players act or talk. I've begun to see that the pleasure men take in being with each other — playing cards together, being in a bar together — isn't actively anti-female. It isn't against women; it just has nothing to do with them. It seems to come from some point in their lives before they were aware that there *were* women. They have so much fun together. I really have become much more sympathetic to men because of my job.

''I wonder if a lot of the suggestions that men make about women reporters may not have something to do with sexual envy of blacks. I'm sure the black players treat me differently from the way they treat male writers. They don't think I'm a honky — I'm another oppressed minority. They may not have thought this all the way through, but it's there. Male sportswriters all seem to think that the athletes are going to take a shot at us on the road, but it hardly ever happens. In fact, that comes much more from the sportswriters than from the players, and you can tell them I said so.''

Stephanie Salter: (*She grew up in Terre Haute, Indiana, where she was a high-school cheerleader. She went to Purdue and became the editor-in-chief of the undergraduate daily, the* Exponent. *Like Jane Gross and Melissa Ludtke Lincoln, she was a researcher and reporter with* Sports Illustrated. *She became a free-lance writer in 1974, and joined the sports staff of the San Francisco* Examiner *the following year. She covered the Golden State Warriors, of the National Basketball Association, for two seasons. Now she covers the Oakland A's and is a backup writer on the San Francisco Giants, which makes her one of the few women in the country with a regular baseball beat. She has light-brown hair. She talks rapidly, with a wry, half-amused smile. Twenty-nine years old.)*

"I sometimes think the whole sports world exists in order to maintain 77 some code of meaningless courtly manners. I used to have these shouting matches with guards or officials who wanted to keep me out of press boxes, and I was always told I couldn't get in because of the bad language in there. Well, as it happens, I curse a lot — I'm not proud of it, or anything, but it's true — so that always made me laugh. It was hysterical. But the way I talk sort of confirmed something for the men, too — the only kind of woman who wants to come into a press box is the kind who talks dirty. With a lot of sports people, women are either revered or despised. There are good girls — the ones they marry — and there are the other ones, the kind they shack up with on the road. We women writers are a challenge to that simple filing system. They just don't know what to make of us. This isn't the majority attitude with the players anymore, but somehow it carries over and becomes the official sports attitude. It's what the front offices hold on to. The older men in sports almost insist on it, for some reason.

"I'm always amazed at the amount of hostility among the male writers 78 that is directed at the players. Obviously, not all the writers are failed athletes, but there are far too many of them. You hear them asking these smart-aleck questions that are meant to show up the players and prove that the writers know as much about the sport as the players do. It's as if they're fighting over who will be the leader of the pack: Which of us is more virile — me with my pen or you with your bat? At least, we women are free of that.

"I don't think that the presence of women is going to change big-time 79 macho sports in any real way. There are so few of us, and it's all so much bigger than the tiny fists we beat against it. Years ago, I tried to crash the Baseball Writers' annual dinner in New York, and I got thrown out. Now I'm a member of the Baseball Writers, but the invitation to the big New York dinner this year still said it was a stag affair. Men only.

"I'm tired. I don't feel like fighting anymore. The thought of the start of 80 another baseball season is so damned discouraging. I really love baseball, but I don't look forward to standing outside the clubhouse anymore and going through all that crap. Neither the A's nor the Giants are opening their clubhouses this year. When you get these bad feelings, you begin to ask yourself, 'Why *am* I doing this?' I think of myself as a feminist, as somebody who wants to win a cause, but I've begun to wonder about myself. Am I looking for male approval? Am I here because I'm incapable of not trying to please men in some special way? But this is a trap that's sort of been set for me. Maybe I've begun to think there's something wrong with me because so many other people seem to think there is.

"I hate the analogy of women and blacks, but it's there. When you stand outside the clubhouse, you're the perfect symbol of the eternal outsider. I always feel as if my arms were tied to my sides. I have dreams that I'm outside some clubhouse and there are ropes around me. There have been times when I just couldn't do it anymore, because it hurt so much. I had to go away, because they'd made me cry again."

Lawrie Mifflin: *(She graduated from Yale in 1973, worked as a summer trainee at the Philadelphia* Bulletin, *and then attended the Columbia School of Journalism. She was hired by the [New York* Daily] News *as a general-assignment reporter, and then went on the City Hall beat. After two years, she became the first woman reporter in the* News *sports department. She covers the New York Cosmos and the New York Rangers — both of which admit women to their locker rooms. She is married to an artist, Richard Raiselis, but has kept her own name. She is five feet tall, with thick hair, large eyes, and an earnest eager manner. Twenty-seven years old.)*

"I'm pretty strange, because I really believe in all the clichés about sports. I think sports do build character. I believe that sports allow you to channel your aggressions and to use them in a specific, controlled way. Men have always been brought up with that advantage, but women have been taught to hang back, not to sweat too much. If I had my way, I'd rather be a professional athlete than a sportswriter. If I could get paid enough for it, I'd be a professional field-hockey player. I play every Sunday in the fall. I get up at six in the morning and take a train out to the middle of New Jersey and then change to another train and then walk a mile to the field. I play left wing with the Essex team, in the New Jersey women's league. I grew up in Swarthmore, outside Philadelphia. That's always been a great center for women's sports, for some reason. I was the oldest of five children — I have two brothers and two sisters — so the locker room has never been a surprise to me. At Swarthmore High, the girls' field-hockey team was just as important as the boys' football team. The school had *six* competitive hockey teams for the girls. Everybody always called it 'hockey' — the other kind was 'ice hockey.' It wasn't until I was about eighteen, at Yale, that I realized that most people thought that only big ugly girls were supposed to take sports seriously.

"Not enough sportswriters have been trained as journalists. They don't seem to have learned to ask the right questions, and they don't challenge the answers they get. A lot of them grew up knowing all the names and rules and stats in sports, and they seem to think that's enough. There isn't an analogy to this anywhere else in newspaper work.

"I think that to the players all of us reporters are aliens. They tend to 85
lump women into the same group of aliens, and that really disturbs some of
the regular writers. These men are suddenly forced to realize that they're
strangers in the locker room, too, and not part of the team at all. They're
forced to see that they're really much closer to any woman reporter there —
even someone brand-new on the job — than they are to the players, because
they and the women are both in the same business. It almost drives them
crazy. But this is true only of some of the older writers. Most of the younger
men think of us as being the same as they are — of the same ilk. They haven't reached the stage of feeling bitter about sports.

"I've never wanted to be part of the hanging-out side of sports. I never 86
go into the locker room when the Rangers have a practice, because I don't
have a deadline then. Women can't be part of all that, and I don't miss it at
all. My husband has nothing to do with sports. Most of our friends are
painters and sculptors, and we never talk about sports. I think I'd be sort of
depressed about the whole sports scene if I never could get away from it.

"I don't think there's any advantage to being a woman in my business. 87
The real advantage for me is my age. The Rangers are a very young team,
and the players relate to me because we're about the same age. We can be
friends. I've always been able to get along with men in an easy, non-sexual
way. The younger people are, the less they worry about sex differences."

Men and women, sports and sex, tradition and privacy, young people 88
and older people — that parade float has become still more crowded with
symbols and overtones, and still more, I believe, we on the sidewalk should
resist looking for a moral or an easy summary as it creaks past us. I am upset
by the cruelties that men in sports have inflicted on the women who have recently come into their world, hoping to share its pleasures and complexities
and rewards. I pull back instinctively from these cuts and slights, and I suspect that I have hoped to purge myself of my own complicity in them by
writing about the subject. But nothing is easy here, and, like Stephanie
Salter, I must also ask myself why I was so attracted to sports in the first
place, and (in my own case) why I have continued to watch sports and to
write about sports now that I am well past the age when, according to
Jerome Holtzman, I should have left them. I am not persuaded by Maury Allen's arguments about the sexual implications of our adulation of athletes,
but I can't quite say they are a lie. I have always sensed a covert resentment
of the players among men in the front office and in the press box, who
spend their adult lives in pursuit of these gifted, golden creatures. The players are fawned upon and also bullied and patronized, it seems to me, because out there on the field, in the light and the noise, they can actually do
that beautiful thing that all of us once wished so deeply to be able to do. Per-

haps we can now guess also that our mixed envy and hatred of them persists — not just in the stadium but on the road and in their hotels — because they are at some peak of youth and physical power and freedom and sexuality that all the rest of us men have longed for and still long for. Maybe this is what sports are all about.

It seems to me that the people who run sports and who claim to be most concerned about the "sexual privacy" of their athletes in the clubhouse — surely one of the most sexless and joyless surroundings in which men and women can meet — are men who want to keep both sports and sex in some safe, special place where they first locked them up when they were adolescents. The new presence of capable, complicated women in the inner places of sports means that relations between the sexes cannot be relegated just to marriage, or just to hotel rooms, either. When women are not easy to sum up or dismiss, traditional male responses to them suddenly begin to look pathetic. The mass male preening of the locker room and the foul-mouthed aggressiveness of the team bus lose their purpose when grownups fail to pay attention, and most mothers I know would probably just as soon be spared the fussy, hypocritical anxieties that beset front-office elders who wish to preserve the innocence of American children by presenting them with an image of sports as a place of infantile sexual purity. Sex becomes a lot simpler and happier when it is freed from these old obsessions, and in time it may become even more significant than the athletes perceive it to be. If men discover that the company of men does not equal the company of men and women together, they may decide that sports can be a common property, a great dream or pageant or drama to be shared among us all, and that its idealization as a male ritual and religion is part of a national neurosis — a form of infantilism that degrades its players and watchers and feeds childish anxieties and delusions, which we can all begin to outgrow now, at long last.

One missing voice here, it will be noticed, is that of the players. This is a considerable omission. In the past weeks, I did ask a good many baseball players and basketball players and hockey players what they thought about the arrival of women reporters in their locker rooms, and many of them showed an awareness of the conflicting issues involved. But they also expressed strong feelings about their own privacy, their wives' anxieties, and the importance of a clubhouse in maintaining team morale. "That's where you *become* a team," said Vida Blue — who, by the way, favors the admission of women reporters to his own San Francisco Giants clubhouse. Players have a difficult sort of life, all in all, and their customary attitude of irritation or sullen patience or cynicism about the habitual cajoling and bullying and meddling they must put up with at the hands of the front office and the writers and the fans has not been improved by the news that some *court* has now ruled that their own privacy can be taken care of with a robe or a towel. It is my own belief, however, that the players' privacy has already been fatally compromised by the presence of the scrambling, questioning, rumor-hunting male reporters in the clubhouse. At the same time, I think the reporters are demeaned when they are forced to kneel or crane or shove one another for a better position beside the cubicle of some naked, sweating sports hero, or to follow him to the door of the shower room or the training room in hope of the favor of one more muttered quote. I think we should ask the athletes to keep their uniforms on for as long as seems necessary for the press to do its job, and to let everyone in to talk to them. In time, it may be hoped, newspaper readers will diminish their demand that athletes be transformed into mere celebrities; when that happens, we can close the clubhouse altogether and give our attention, as writers and fans, to watching the players when they are at their splendid best, which is on the field.

On a weekend in late February, I went to Madison Square Garden, 91 where I watched New York's two pairs of local professional winter teams have at each other on successive nights. On Saturday, the Knicks beat the Nets by 111 to 107; on Sunday the Rangers upset the powerful Islanders, 3–2. Both games were noisy, exciting affairs, with the doubly partisan crowds in wild voice. I visited the locker rooms after both games, and found many other male reporters there, of course, and a few women. A basketball locker room is a good deal smaller and scruffier than a baseball clubhouse, and the extremely tall undressing or towel-clad or naked or getting-dressed basketball players in the quiet Nets' room and in the somewhat happier Knicks' quarters were — well, close together. Nobody minded, that I could see — or if anyone minded he kept quiet about it. Nobody *looked*, and then, because I was looking to see if anyone was looking, I began to feel embarrassed at being there on such an odd errand. I talked to a few players, and ended up in conversation with Phil Jackson, a bony, bearded six-foot-eight forward and center, who used to play for the Knicks and is now a player-coach with the Nets. He was towelling himself after his shower and chatting with Eric and Melissa Ludtke Lincoln. I told him what I was there for, and Jackson said, ''Nobody thinks about it anymore. Oh, we had some rookies on the Knicks last year who were a little tight about it — a few guys ran into the training room — but we told them to shape up, and they did. I don't know why baseball makes so much of it all. Nobody cares or notices. Nobody looks — except for Melissa here. Melissa is a peeker, a regular Peeping Thomasina.''

He laughed, and we laughed, and he put on his underpants. 92

The next night, in the Rangers' locker room, I talked to Dave Maloney, 93 the team's twenty-two-year-old captain, who is a defenseman. I had heard that hockey players were generally more modest than basketball players, but my impression that night was almost the opposite. Maybe it was because there were more women there — four or five of them, at least, includ-

119

ing a photographer and a member of a TV crew — or maybe it was because there are so many more people on a hockey squad than a basketball squad that the cumulative nakedness seemed both more noticeable and less noticed. I had seen Lawrie Mifflin talking to Maloney about the slambang game we had just watched, and when she moved along to interview another player (she had a preoccupied, near-deadline expression) I introduced myself to Maloney. He had a freshly skinned patch on the bridge of his already battered nose, and he seemed almost terminally exhausted. "Boy, I'm glad I don't have to play eighty games like that one!" he said, in an "o"-accenting Canadian voice.

I asked him what he thought of Lawrie Mifflin.

"Lawrie is — well, I *like* Lawrie," Maloney said. "She shoots straight. She's friendly. When she's in here asking questions it's just two people talking together — not a man and a woman but friends. She's patient, and patient people are better at that job, I think. Lawrie is just like a sister."

I told him that these were almost exactly the words she had used when she talked about her feeling about the Rangers. Then I asked him if he had ever felt anxious about the presence of women in the Ranger locker room.

"I guess I was sort of surprised by it when I first came up, three years ago," Maloney said, "but I got used to it. This is the big city, and you learn to go along with things. But I'll tell you, we never had anything like this back home. I come from a small city in Canada — Kitchener — and it's different there. I thought about it when I first saw Lawrie and the other girls in here, and I realized that the last woman I'd seen in a hockey-team locker room was my mother. I was about seven years old then, and she was in there to lace up my skates."

Afterword: Three years have passed since this story was written, and some alterations are visible on the troubled landscape it describes. The baseball commissioner's office has continued to encourage equal clubhouse access to all accredited reporters, regardless of sex, and there has been no restriction on women reporters at the Championship Series and World Series games. At the same time, a few clubs — among them the Reds, the Indians, the Cubs, and the Expos — continued to ban women from their clubhouses as recently as last summer. This local option appears to depend on the private preference of an incumbent manager or general manager, and has often altered when that job changed hands.

Many of the women quoted in the article have moved along to other journalistic undertakings. Diane K. Shah writes a thrice-weekly sports column for the Los Angeles *Herald-Examiner*. Melissa Ludtke Lincoln is a researcher/reporter with *Time*, whose range of assignments includes medicine and the press. Betty Cuniberti became a Washington feature and cityside correspondent for the Los Angeles *Times* after her own paper, the Washington *Star*, ceased publication last year. B. J. Phillips is a correspondent with the Atlanta bureau of *Time*. Jane Gross is a sportswriter with the New York *Times;* she was on the baseball beat last summer, doing backup coverage on both the Yankees and Mets, as well as other assignments. Stephanie Salter still covers the San Francisco Giants and the Oakland A's for the San Francisco *Examiner*. Lawrie Mifflin is a writer and associate producer with the ABC "Sports-Beat" television show.

"The women who have quit writing sports in the last couple of years 100 have done it of their own accord," Stephanie Salter said not long ago. "It was time for them to move on to something else — maybe something better. There still aren't many women on the baseball beat, but that's because it's such a plum. Most women sportswriters still get stuck with high-school sports or tennis, so things haven't changed all *that* much, I guess. There's been one breakthrough: my membership card in the Baseball Writers Association no longer has a 'Mr.' printed on it. I hope that's not what this whole struggle was for."

B. J. Phillips said, "I did five long years on the sports beat. It was a great 101 ride, but now I want something different. I think I may know too much about sports now. There are a lot more women in the business today than there were when I came along. Almost every little paper in the South seems to have at least one woman writing sports. The biggest change has been in peer respect. So many women have done a good professional job in sports that we're accepted and admired by our colleagues now. That's what it's all about. The athletes never were a problem.

"My last assignment writing sports for *Time* was the Thomas Hearns– 102 Sugar Ray Leonard fight in Las Vegas last summer. I was riding on the press bus there one day and some old troglodyte sportswriter peeked at the press card on my shirt and saw who I worked for. 'Say, what do you do for them, honey?' he said. 'Are you one of their leg-girls?' So it ended for me just the way it started — with an insult."

She laughed. 103

QUESTIONS ON MEANING

1. "Sports," Angell says, "means a lot in this country" (paragraph 13). Does he treat his subject too seriously? How important is the issue he discusses? What do the principals in the controversy say about the importance of the issue?

2. Angell derives the bulk of his essay from interviews. Do his conclusions follow from the information he assembles? Look, for instance, at paragraph 89. Does it logically follow from the facts in the essay? Or is it merely Angell's speculation?

3. Notice the contrasts among the different sports in the athletes' responses to the "threat" of female reporters. What information does Angell provide about these contrasts? Why, for example, are basketball players less concerned about the presence of women in the locker room than are football players?

QUESTIONS ON STRATEGY

1. "Sharing the Beat" begins (paragraphs 1–4) with a discussion of the commissioner of baseball and his response to the challenge of women sportswriters. Sometimes Angell quotes Bowie Kuhn directly, using quotation marks; sometimes he uses indirect quotation. How effective is the latter technique? Do you get the feeling that some of the words not in quotation marks come directly from the advisory memorandum while others are Angell's paraphrase? Which are which? Why doesn't the essay quote the whole memorandum?
2. "The stadium locker rooms became officially heterosexual on September 26th" (paragraph 2). What were the locker rooms before that day? What is Angell's tone in this sentence?
3. What is the tone of the sentence "Bowie Kuhn did not have a very happy time of it in the courts last fall" (paragraph 3)?
4. Look at the last sentence of paragraph 9. Would it have worked to put this sentence at the beginning of the essay? How does Angell arrange his material so that we agree with him when he tells us that "something was going on here"?
5. What is the function of paragraph 13? Notice the division between this paragraph and the following one. What does the new section, beginning with paragraph 14, accomplish in this essay? Why is it separated from the text before it?

EXPLORATIONS

1. "Sharing the Beat" is about the gathering and reporting of sports news. Read a week's worth of sports news in a daily newspaper from a major league city. Pay particular attention to the kinds of information sportswriters derive from locker room interviews. Is this the bulk of their reporting or only a "frill"? Does the news you read on the sports pages "mean a lot"?
2. Angell's reputation as a sportswriter rests securely on his brilliant work as *The New Yorker*'s baseball correspondent. Study his columns — collected in such books as *The Summer Game* and *Five Seasons* — and explain what sports in America mean to Angell.

WRITING TOPICS

1. Consider Angell's use of the interview. Why does he so extensively present the exact words of his interviewees? Would "Sharing the Beat" be as effective, or more effective, if he had instead used only the information derived

from interviews to mount an argument or make a case? Write an essay of your own on this topic using the material Angell's interviews provide, but using no direct quotes.

2. By presenting us with a generous sampling of the remarks he elicited from those involved in the controversy, Angell gives us a kaleidoscope of views without compromising or obscuring his own well-defined personal perspective. Try his technique yourself: Write an essay on a specific problem in which you state your own opinion clearly and strongly but make room for the judgments and even the prejudices of at least three involved, interested, and informed people whom you interview. Make a special effort to incorporate these other points of view into a coherent and balanced essay on a carefully defined subject.

3. Angell's discussion of women's difficulty in sharing the sports beat with male reporters assumes that "sports mean a lot" in contemporary America. With reference to another major issue or controversy that has arisen around sports — the use of drugs by athletes, the high salaries of professional athletes, violence in sports, the training of Olympic athletes in the U.S. and in communist countries — write an essay in which you identify and examine the meaning of sports in our society.

BOOKS AVAILABLE IN PAPERBACK

Five Seasons. New York: Warner Books. *Essays on baseball.*

Late Innings. New York: Ballantine. *Essays on baseball.*

The Summer Game. New York: Popular Library. *Essays on baseball.*

NORMAN
MAILER

*B*ORN IN NEW JERSEY *in 1923, Norman Mailer attended Harvard University, where he began to study engineering. Literature took over. He published* short stories *in* The Harvard Advocate, *of which he was an editor, won* Story Magazine's *college writing contest in 1941, and drafted a novel before he became a private in the 112th Cavalry during World War II. After serving in the Pacific, he wrote* The Naked and the Dead *(1948), which remains the best American novel of that war.*

Norman Mailer's subsequent history includes many novels like The Deer Park *(1955);* The Executioner's Song *(1979), which, although it reports on the murderer Gary Gilmore, won the Pulitzer Prize for fiction; and* Ancient Evenings *(1983). Yet he has written less fiction than nonfiction: His journalism includes* The Presidential Papers *(1963);* Cannibals and Christians *(1966);* The Armies of the Night *(1968), which won both the Pulitzer Prize and the National Book Award; and* Of a Fire on the Moon *(1971),* The Prisoner of Sex *(1971), and* Some Honorable Men *(1976), which assembles earlier essays on political conventions and campaigns. Other books including* Advertisements for Myself *(1959) combine fiction and nonfiction.*

For some critics, the last title might do as a summary of Mailer's career. For Mailer's history is not only his books; and his books are full of his history. Married

*six times, he has needed to produce best sellers to pay alimony and child support for
eight children; the amount and nature of his writing has been affected by his personal
life.*

We take this essay from Of a Fire on the Moon, *Mailer's book about the first
moon shot in July of 1969. America's space program, which lagged at first behind the
Soviet Union's, was about to vault ahead by a great adventure, dreamed about for
centuries: A human being would walk on the surface of the moon.*

*In the book Mailer calls himself Aquarius. It is characteristic of much contempo-
rary nonfiction (see Edward Hoagland, pp. 323–337, and Annie Dillard, pp. 469–
482) to make the author part of the story. In the first chapter Mailer speaks of Mailer:*

> *It was a decade [the sixties] so unbalanced in relation to previous
> American history that Aquarius, who had begun it by stabbing his
> second wife in 1960, was to finish by running in a Democratic Pri-
> mary for Mayor of New York during the hottest May and June he
> could ever recall. In sixty days he must have made three hundred
> speeches, he appeared on more radio and television than he could re-
> member, walked streets, shook hands, sometimes two or three thou-
> sand hands a day, worked fourteen hours a day, often sixteen, went
> on four and five hours sleep, and awoke on many a morning with the
> clear and present certainty that he was going to win. . . .*
> *He came in fourth in a field of five.*

But Of a Fire on the Moon, *despite the author's pseudonymous presence, remains
an account — objective, historical, responsible — of technological adventure in a real
world outside the author's psyche. Mailer has confronted a problem common to the
essayist: how to amalgamate the personal and the objective, to record both the observation and the observer with his possible distortions. In this book alone of his extensive work, Mailer makes use of his early scientific training to write about technology
and shows himself, among his many talents, an excellent clarifier of science for the
layperson. His novelist's gifts of insight and interpretation reveal themselves when
he speaks of the psychology of the astronauts, integrating personality, science, and
social observation. The mixture is considerable, but no ingredient, isolated, could be
complete.*

The Psychology of
Astronauts

Well, let us make an approach to the astronauts. Aquarius sees them for   1
the first time on the fifth of July, eleven days before the launch. They are in a
modern movie theater with orange seats and a dark furrowed ceiling overhead, much like marcelled waves in a head of hair, a plastic ceiling built

doubtless to the plans of one of the best sound engineers in the country. Sound is considerably ahead of smell as a fit province for scientific work, but since the excellence of acoustics in large and small concert chambers seems to bear more relation to old wood and the blessings of monarchs and bishops than to the latest development of the technical art, the sound system in this movie theater (seats 600) is dependably intolerable most of the time. The public address system squeals and squeaks (it is apparently easier to have communication with men one quarter of a million miles away) and one never gets a fair test of the aural accommodations. The walls and overhead are of plastic composition, and so far as one can tell, the tone is a hint sepulchral, then brightened electronically, finally harsh and punishing to that unnamed fine nerve which runs from the anus to the eardrum. As the sound engineers became more developed, the plastic materials provided for their practice by corporations grew acoustically more precise and spiritually more flattering — it was the law of the century. One was forever adjusting to public voices through the subtlest vale of pain.

Still this movie theater was the nearest approach to a diadem in the Manned Spacecraft Center. The theater was part of the visitors' center, where tourists could go through the space museum, a relatively modest affair of satellites, capsules, dioramas, posters and relics, now closed and given over to the installation of monitors and cables for the television networks, even as the gallery to the rear of the theater was now being converted into the Apollo News Center and would consist finally of endless aisles of desks, telephones and typewriters, plus one giant Buddha of a coffee urn. (Coffee is the closest the press ever comes to *satori*.°)

In the theater, perhaps eight rows back of the front seats, was a raised platform on which television cameras and crews were mounted. From the stage they must have looked not unrelated to artillery pieces on the battlement of a fort — in the front row were fifty photographers, which is to say fifty sets of torsos and limbs each squeezed around its own large round glass eye. Little flares of lightning flashed out of bulbs near their heads. The astronauts did not really have to travel to the moon — life from another planet was before them already. In the middle ranks, between the front row and the barricade of television cameras, were seated several hundred newspaper men and women come to Houston for the conference this morning. They were a curious mixture of high competence and near imbecility; some assigned to Space for years seemed to know as much as NASA engineers; others, innocents in for the big play on the moon shot, still were not just certain where laxatives ended and physics began. It was as if research students from the Institute of Advanced Studies at Princeton had been put in with a group

---

satori   State of enlightenment in Zen Buddhism.

of fine young fellows from an Army class in remedial reading. Out of such a bag would questions come to the astronauts. Wait! There will be samples.

The astronauts entered from the wings wearing gas masks, gray snout-   4
nosed covers which projected out from their mouths and gave their profiles the intent tusk-ready slouch of razorback hogs. They were aware of this — it was apparent in the good humor with which they came in. In fact, a joke of some dimensions had been flickering for a few days — the Press had talked of greeting them with white hospital masks. In the attempt to protect the astronauts as much as possible from preflight infection they were being kept in a species of limited quarantine — their contacts with nonessential personnel were restricted. Since journalists fit this category, today's press conference had installed Armstrong, Aldrin and Collins up on the stage in a plastic box about twelve feet wide, ten feet deep and ten feet high. Blowers within this three-walled plastic room blew air from behind them out into the audience: thereby, the breath of the astronauts could enter the theater, but the airborne germs of journalists would not blow back. It made a kind of sense. Of course the cause of the common cold was still unknown, but gross studies of infection would surmise a partial quarantine might be effective partially. However, the instrumentation of this premise was not happy. The astronauts looked a bit absurd in their plastic box, and the few journalists who had actually fleshed their joke by putting on masks caused the astronauts to grin broadly as though to dissociate themselves from the pyramids of precaution they were in fact obeying.

Once they sat down, their manner changed. They were seated behind a   5
walnut-brown desk on a pale blue base which displayed two painted medallions in circles — NASA and Apollo 11. Behind them at the rear of the plastic booth stood an American flag; the Press actually jeered when somebody brought it onstage in advance of the astronauts. Aquarius could not remember a press conference where Old Glory had ever been mocked before, but it had no great significance, suggesting rather a splash of derision at the thought that the show was already sufficiently American enough. In fact, between the steady reporters who worked out of Houston and the astronauts, there was that kind of easy needling humor which is the measure of professional respect to be found among teams and trainers.

So the entrance went well. The astronauts walked with the easy saunter   6
of athletes. They were comfortable in motion. As men being scrutinized by other men they had little to worry about. Still, they did not strut. Like all good professional athletes, they had the modesty of knowing you could be good and still lose. Therefore they looked to enjoy the snouts they were wearing, they waved at reporter friends they recognized, they grinned. A reporter called back to Collins, ''Now, you look good.'' It all had that characteristically American air which suggests that men who are successful in their profession do best to take their honors lightly.

Once they sat down, however, the mood shifted. Now they were there to answer questions about a phenomenon which even ten years ago would have been considered material unfit for serious discussion. Grown men, perfectly normal-looking, were now going to talk about their trip to the moon. It made everyone uncomfortable. For the relation of everyone to each other and to the event was not quite real. It was as if a man had died and been brought back from death. What if on questioning he turned out to be an ordinary fellow? "Well, you see," he might say, "having visited death, I come back with the following conclusions. . . ." What if he had a droning voice? There was something of this in the polite unreality of the questioning. The century was like a youth who made love to the loveliest courtesan in Cathay. Afterward he was asked what he thought and scratched his head and said, "I don't know. Sex is kind of overrated." So now people were going to ask questions of three heroes about their oncoming voyage, which on its face must be in contention for the greatest adventure of man. Yet it all felt as if three young junior executives were announcing their corporation's newest subdivision.

Perhaps for this reason, the quiet gaiety of their entrance had deserted them as they sat behind the desk in the plastic booth. Now it was as if they did not know if they were athletes, test pilots, engineers, corporation executives, some new kind of priest, or sheepish American boys caught in a position of outlandish prominence — my God, how did they ever get into this? It was as if after months in simulators with knowing technicians geared to the same code languages, they were now debouched into the open intellectual void of this theater, obliged to look into the uncomprehending spirits of several hundred media tools (human) all perplexed and worried at their journalistic ability to grasp more than the bare narrative of what was coming up. Yaws° abounded. Vacuums in the magnetism of the mood. Something close to boredom. The astronauts were going to the moon, but everybody was a little frustrated — the Press because the Press did not know how to push into nitty-gritty for the questions, the astronauts because they were not certain how to begin to explain the complexity of their technique. Worse, as if they did not really wish to explain, but were obliged out of duty to the program, even if their privacy was invaded.

So the conference dragged on. While the focus of attention was naturally on Armstrong for commanding the flight, he seemed in the beginning to be the least at ease. He spoke with long pauses, he searched for words. When the words came out, their ordinary content made the wait seem excessive.

Yaws As a technical term, describes the movement of a spacecraft about its vertical axis; Mailer uses it several times metaphorically.

He minted no phrases. "We are here" . . . a pause . . . "to be able to talk about this attempt" . . . a real pause, as if the next experience were ineffable but with patience would yet be captured . . . "because of the success of four previous Apollo command flights" . . . pause, as if to pick up something he had left out . . . "and a number of unmanned flights." A shy smile. "Each of those flights" — he was more wooden than young Robert Taylor, young Don Ameche, young Randolph Scott — "contributed in a great way" . . . deprecatory smile . . . "to this flight." As a speaker he was all but limp — still it did not leave him unremarkable. Certainly the knowledge he was an astronaut restored his stature, yet even if he had been a junior executive accepting an award, Armstrong would have presented a quality which was arresting, for he was extraordinarily remote. He was simply not like other men. He would have been more extraordinary in fact if he had been just a salesman making a modest inept dull little speech, for then one would have been forced to wonder how he had ever gotten his job, how he could sell even one item, how in fact he got out of bed in the morning. Something particularly innocent or subtly sinister was in the gentle remote air. If he had been a young boy selling subscriptions at the door, one grandmother might have warned her granddaughter never to let him in the house; another would have commented, "That boy will go very far." He was apparently in communion with some string in the universe others did not think to play.

Collins and Aldrin followed with their opening remarks, and they had 10 personalities which were more comfortable to grasp. Aldrin, all meat and stone, was a man of solid presentation, dependable as a tractor, but suggesting the strength of a tank, dull, almost ponderous, yet with the hint of unpredictability, as if, eighteen drinks in him, his eyes would turn red, he would arm-wrestle a gorilla or invite you to join in jumping out a third-story window in order to see who could do the better somersault on the follow-through out of the landing. This streak was radium and encased within fifty psychical and institutional caskings of lead, but it was there, Aquarius thought, perhaps a clue in the way he dressed — very dressy for an astronaut — a green luminous silk suit, a white shirt, a green luminous tie. It clashed with the stolid presentation of his language. Aldrin spoke in a deep slow comfortingly nasal tone — a mighty voice box — his face was strong and grim. The movie director in Aquarius would have cast him on the spot for Major in Tank Cavalry. He had big features and light brown hair, almost gold. His eyes took a turn down like samurai eyes, the corners of his lips took a right-angle turn down — it gave him the expression of a serious man at home on a field of carnage, as if he were forever saying, "This is serious stuff, fellows, there's lots of blood around." So Aldrin also looked like the kind of jock who could be headmaster of a prep school. He had all the locker-room heartiness and solemnity of a team man. Although he had been a pole-vaulter at West Point, it would have been easy to mistake him for a shot-putter, a lacrosse player, or a baseball catcher. In football he would have probably been a linebacker. For this last, he was actually not big enough (since the astronauts were required to be no more than five feet eleven inches tall and could hardly be overweight), but he was one of those men who looked larger than his size for his condition was excellent — every discipline of his moves spoke of grim devoted unrelenting support given to all his body-world of muscle. From the back of the neck to the joints of the toes, from the pectorals to the hamstrings, the deltoids to the abdominals, he was a life given over to good physical condition, a form of grace, since the agony of the lungs when straining is not alien to the agony of the soul. Leave it that Aldrin was so strong he had a physical presence which was bigger than his bulk.

He talked like a hardworking drill. He had the reputation of being the best physicist and engineer among the astronauts — he had written a valuable thesis on Orbital Rendezvous Techniques at MIT, but he put no humor into his presentation, he was selling no soap. If you did not read technologese, you might as well forget every last remark for his words did not translate, not unless you were ready to jog along with him on technology road. Here is the way he gave himself to the Press: ''We do have a few items on the Lem side of the house on this particular mission. We'll be picking up where Apollo 10 left off when they did their phasing maneuver. And at this point after departing the Command Module, coming down in the descent orbit, we'll be igniting the descent engine for the first time under a long burn condition when it is not docked with the Command Module. And executing this burn under control of a computer, being directed towards the various targets that are fed into the computer will be new on this flight. Also we'll be making use of the landing radar and its inputs into the computer. Inputs in terms of altitude and velocity updates which will bring us down in the prescribed conditions as we approach the surface of the moon. Of course, the actual control of the touchdown itself will be a rather new item in that it will be testing this man-machine interface to a very sophisticated degree. The touchdown itself will be the ultimate test on the landing gear and the various systems that are in the spacecraft. The environment of one-sixth G will be seen for the first time by crews and spacecraft. We'll also be exposed to thermal conditions that have not been experienced before. The two-man EVA is something that is a first in our program. Sleeping in the Lem on the lunar surface, which we hope to be able to do, will be another new item in that flight.''

He went on to talk of star sightings and the powered ascent from the moon — that moment when, having landed successfully and reconnoitered the moon ground, they would be back in the Lem and ready to ascend — would the motor ignite or did the moon have a curse? Aldrin spoke of this as a "new item," then of rendezvous with the Command Module, which would return them to earth, of "various contingencies that can develop," of "a wider variety of trajectory conditions" — he was talking about not being able to join up, wandering through space, lost forever to life in that short eternity before they expired of hunger and thirst. Small hint of that in these verbal formulations. Even as the Nazis and the Communists had used to speak of mass murder as liquidation, so the astronauts spoke of possible personal disasters as "contingency." The heart of astronaut talk, like the heart of all bureaucratic talk, was a jargon which could be easily converted to computer programming, a language like Fortran or Cobol or Algol. Anti-dread formulations were the center of it, as if words like pills were there to suppress emotional symptoms. Yet Aldrin, powerful as a small bull, deep as his grasp of Celestial Mechanics, gave off in his air of unassailable solemnity some incommunicable speech about the depth of men's souls and that razor's edge between the hero's endeavor and vainglory. Vainglory looked real to him, one might assume, real as true peril — he had the deep gloomy clumsy dignity of a man who had been face to face in some stricken hour with the depths of his own nature, more complex than he had hitherto known.

Collins, in contrast, moved easily; Collins was cool. Collins was the man 13 nearly everybody was glad to see at a party, for he was the living spirit of good and graceful manners. Where Armstrong referred to Wapakoneta, Ohio, as his hometown, and showed a faint but ineradicable suspicion of anyone from a burg larger than his own, where Aldrin protected himself from conversation with the insulations of a suburban boyhood and encapsulement among his incommunicable fields of competency, Collins had been born in a well-set up apartment off the Borghese Gardens in Rome. His father, General James L. Collins, was military attaché (and could conceivably have been having a drink around the corner in the bar at the Hassler to celebrate the birth of his son). Since the year was 1930, Dick Diver could have been getting his going-over from the Fascisti police in the basement of *Tender Is the Night*. No surprise then if Collins had a manner. It was in part the manner of Irish elegance — a man must be caught dead before he takes himself seriously. It was as if Collins were playing a fine woodwind which had the merriment and the sadness (now that the madness was gone) of those American expatriates for whom culture began in the Year One of *The Sun Also Rises*.° Indeed, if Collins was later to grow a mustache on the trip

---

Tender Is the Night, by F. Scott Fitzgerald, and *The Sun Also Rises*, by Ernest Hemingway, both take place in the decadent world of American expatriates in early twentieth century Europe. Dick Diver, the principal character in *Tender Is the Night*, is arrested after a night of carousing.

back, an act which increased his slight but definite resemblance to the young Hemingway, he had a personal style which owed more to Fitzgerald. It was Fitzgerald, after all, who first suggested that you could become the nicest man in the world. So Collins had that friendliness which promises it would be sacrilege to give offense in a social situation. It was apparently as unnatural for him not to make a small joke as it would have been offensive to Aldrin not to take on a matter in its full seriousness. Yet Collins had little opportunity to show his humor. It existed mainly in the fine light smiling presence he bestowed on the interview while the others were asked all the questions. Collins was the only one of the three not landing on the moon. So he would obviously be the one whose remarks would go into the last paragraph, where the layout man would probably lop them off. Therefore nobody had bothered to direct a question to him through all the interview.

Toward the end of the press conference, somebody asked of the astronauts at large, "Two questions. Firstly, what precautions have been taken at your own homes to prevent you from catching germs from your own family? And secondly, is this the last period that you will spend at home here with your families?" The Public Affairs Officer, Brian Duff, was quick to say, "Take a crack at that, Mike."

It could not have been easy to have waited so long for so little. But Collins came up smiling, and said, "My wife and children have signed a statement that they have no germs and — and yes this will be the last weekend that we will be home with our families." It was not much of a joke but the press conference had not been much of a joke either, and the Press brightened, they laughed. Collins, quick not to offend the man who had asked the question, now added, "Seriously, there are no special precautions being taken."

His conversational manner was easy. It was apparent that of the three, he was the only one you could drink with comfortably. Since the ability to drink with your material is as important to a journalist as the heft of his hammer to a carpenter, a sense of dismay passed through the press corps — why hadn't NASA had the simple sense of press relations to put Collins in command? What a joy it could have been to cover this moon landing with a man who gave neat quotes, instead of having to contend with Armstrong, who surrendered words about as happily as a hound allowed meat to be pulled out of his teeth. Collins would have been perfect. In combination with his manner, so obviously at ease with a martini, he had the trim build, the bald forehead, and economical features of a college boxer, or a shortstop, or a quarterback. (In fact he was the best handball player among the astronauts and had been captain of his wrestling team at St. Albans.) He looked like copy, he talked like copy, and Armstrong had the sad lonely mien of a cross-country runner. Of course, since he also had the sly privacy of a man whose thoughts may never be read — what a vast boon was this to the Press! — one could, if picturing Armstrong as an athlete, see him playing end. He might, thus sly and private, be difficult to keep up with on pass patterns.

The story resided, however, with the two men who would land on the moon — it could reside nowhere else — but since Collins with a few smiles and a remark or two had become the favorite, a question and then another came his way at the end of the interview. Finally, the real question came. 17

"Colonel Collins, to people who are not astronauts, you would appear to have the most frustrating job on the mission, not going all the way. How do you feel about that?" The contradiction implicit in being an astronaut was here on this point — it was skewered right here. If they were astronauts, they were men who worked for the team, but no man became an astronaut who was not sufficiently exceptional to suspect at times that he might be the best of all. Nobody wins at handball who is not determined to win. 18

He answered quickly. "I don't feel in the slightest bit frustrated. I'm going 99.9 percent of the way there, and that suits me just fine." Growing up in Rome, Puerto Rico, Baltimore and Washington, Texas and Oklahoma, son of one of the more cultivated purlieus of the military grace, the code would be to keep your cool. The only real guide to aristocracy in American life was to see who could keep his cool under the most searing conditions of unrest, envy, ambition, jealousy and heat. So not a quiver showed. "I couldn't be happier right where I am," he concluded and the voice was not hollow, it did not offer a cousin to a squeak. Still nobody believed him. Somewhere in the room was the leached-out air of a passion submitted to a discipline. For a moment Collins was damnably like an actor who plays a good guy. 19

Armstrong came in quickly. "I'd like to say in that regard that the man in the Command Module" . . . pause . . . "of course by himself" . . . another pause . . . "has a giant-sized job." When Armstrong paused and looked for the next phrase he sometimes made a sound like the open crackling of static on a pilot's voice band with the control tower. One did not have the impression that the static came from him so much as that he had listened to so much static in his life, suffered so much of it, that his flesh, his cells, like it or not, were impregnated with the very cracklings of static. "He has to run Buzz's job and my job" . . . static . . . "along with his own job simultaneously" . . . static . . . "in addition act as relay to the ground" . . . pause and static. . . . "It's at least a three-man job and" — he murmured a few words — "Michael is certainly not lacking for something to do while he's circling around." Then Armstrong flashed a smile. One of his own jokes came. His humor was pleasant and small-town, not without a taste of the tart. "And if he can't think of anything else, he can always look out the window and admire the view." 20

Now came a question from a reporter who was new on the job: "From
your previous experience in the two and a half hours or so that you're atop
the rocket before actual blast-off, is this a period of maximum tension, rather
like being in a dentist's waiting room?"

A temporary inability to understand the question was finally replaced by
this speech. "It's one of the phases that we have a very high confidence in,"
Armstrong answered with his characteristic mixture of modesty and technical arrogance, of apology and tightlipped superiority. "It's nothing new. It's
the thing that's been done before," now static while he searched for the appropriate addition, "and done very well on a number of occasions, and
we're quite sure this girl will go," he said solemnly, pleasantly, lightly, carefully, sadly, sweetly. He was a presence in the room, as much a spirit as a
man. One hardly knew if he were the spirit of the high thermal currents, or
that spirit of neutrality which rises to the top in bureaucratic situations, or
both, both of course — why should Armstrong have a soul less divided than
the unruly world of some billions of men? Indeed contradictions lay subtly
upon him — it was not unlike looking at a bewildering nest of leaves: some
are autumn fallings, some the green of early spring. So Armstrong seemed
of all the astronauts the man nearest to being saintly, yet there was something as hard, small-town and used in his face as the look of a cashier over
pennies. When he stopped to think, six tired parallel lines stood out on his
forehead, and his hair was very straight, small-town hair-colored humorless
straight, his pupils were very small, hardly larger than buckshot, you could
believe he flew seventy-eight combat missions off the *Essex* near Korea. He
was very thin-mouthed, almost as thin and wide a mouth as Joe E. Brown,
yet with no comic spirit, or better, or worse, the spirit of comedy gave orders
to the mouth most of the time. Much like President Nixon or Wernher von
Braun° (whom we are yet to meet) he would smile on command. Then a
very useful smile appeared — the smile of an enterprising small-town boy.
He could be an angel, he could be the town's devil. Who knew? You could
not penetrate the flash of the smile — all of America's bounty was in it.
Readiness to serve, innocence, competence, modesty, sly humor, and then a
lopsided yawing slide of a dumb smile at the gulfs of one's own ignorance,
like oops am I small-town dumb! — that was also in it. Aquarius decided it
was not easy to trust him then — the smile was a vehicle to remove Armstrong from the scene. But when he spoke, all ambition was muzzled. He
spoke with the unendurably slow and triple caution of a responsibility-laden
politician who was being desperately careful to make no error of fact, give

---

Wernher von Braun (1912–1977), German-born rocket expert; developed rockets for
Germany in World War II, then came to America in 1945 and worked with the U.S. space
program.

no needless offense to enemies, and cross no conflicting zones of loyalty among friends. Add the static, and he was no happy public speaker. At communicating he was as tight as a cramped muscle.

Perversely, it became his most impressive quality, as if what was best in 23 the man was most removed from the surface, so valuable that it must be protected by a hundred reservations, a thousand cautions, as if finally he had such huge respect for words that they were like tangible omens and portents, zephyrs and beasts of psychic presence, as if finally something deep, delicate and primitive would restrain him from uttering a single word of fear for fear of materializing his dread. So, once, men had been afraid to utter the name of the Lord, or even to write it in such a way as to suggest the sound, for that might be enough to summon some genie of God's displeasure at so disrupting the heavens. Armstrong of course did not brandish an ego one could perceive on meeting; where Aldrin gave off the stolid confidence of the man who knows that problems can be solved if properly formulated and appropriately attacked (which is to say attacked in good condition!) and where Collins offered the wiry graceful tension of a man who will quietly die to maintain his style, Armstrong could seem more like a modest animal than a man — tracer hints of every forest apprehension from the puma to the deer to the miseries of the hyena seemed to stalk at the edge of that small-town clearing he had cut into his psyche so that he might offer the world a person. But his thoughts seemed to be looking for a way to drift clear of any room like this where he was trapped with psyche-eaters, psyche-gorgers, and the duty of responding to questions heard some hundreds of times.

On the other hand, he was a professional and had learned how to con- 24 tend in a practical way with the necessary language. Indeed, how his choice of language protected him!

"Mr. Armstrong, at the time you are down on the moon, what will be 25 your overriding consideration and what will be your main concern?"

"Well," said Armstrong, "immediately upon touchdown our concern is 26 the integrity of the Lunar Module itself" . . . nnnnnnnhr went the sound of the static. . . . "For the first two hours after touchdown we have a very busy time verifying the integrity of the Lunar Module and all of its systems" . . . nnnnhr. . . . "A great deal of technical discussion . . . between spacecraft and ground during a time period when most people will be wondering, well what does it look like out there? . . . We will be eager to comment" . . . nnnnhr . . . "but reluctant to do so in the face of these more important considerations on which . . . the entire rest of the lunar mission depends."

Aldrin, the formalist, had said just previously, "I think the most critical 27 portion of the EVA will be our ability to anticipate and to interpret things that appear not to be as we expected them to be, because if we don't interpret them correctly then they will become difficult." It was the credo of the rationalist. Phenomena are only possessed of menace when they do not accommodate themselves to language-controls. Or, better, to initial-controls. EVA stood for Extravehicular Activity, that is for action taken outside their vehicle, the Lem. EVA therefore referred to their walk on the moon; but the sound of the letters E, V, A might inspire less perturbation than the frank admission that men would now dare to walk on an ancient and alien terrain where no life breathed and beneath the ground no bodies were dead.

It was, of course, a style of language all the astronauts had learned. There were speeches where you could not tell who was putting the words together — the phrases were impersonal, interlocking. One man could have finished a sentence for another. "Our order of priorities was carefully integrated into the flight plan . . . there is no requirement on the specific objectives that we're meeting on the surface to go great distances from the spacecraft, and to do so would only utilize time that we now have programmed doing things in the specific mission objectives." Sell newspapers with that kind of stuff! The quote could belong to any one of a dozen astronauts. In this case it happened to be not Aldrin but Armstrong.

Only on occasion did the language reveal its inability to blanket all situations. Mainly on personal matters. There came a question from one of the remedial readers. "Tell us very briefly how your families have reacted to the fact that you're taking this historic mission."

"Well," Aldrin deliberated, "I think in my particular case, my family has had five years now to become accustomed to this eventuality, and over six months to face it very closely. I think they look on this as a tremendous challenge for me. They look upon it also as an invasion somewhat of their privacy and removing of my presence away from the family for a considerable period of time." He spoke glumly, probably thinking at this moment neither of his family nor himself — rather whether his ability to anticipate and interpret had been correctly employed in the cathexis-loaded dynamic shift vector area of changed field domestic situations (which translates as: attractive wife and kids playing second fiddle to boss astronaut number two sometimes blow group stack). Aldrin was a man of such powerful potentialities and iron disciplines that the dull weight of appropriately massed jargon was no mean gift to him. He obviously liked it to work. It kept explosives in their package. When his laboriously acquired speech failed to mop up the discharge of a question, he got as glum as a fastidious housewife who cannot keep the shine on her floor.

They could not, of course, restrain the questions which looked for ultimate blood. "James Gunn, BBC. You had mentioned that your flight, like all others, contains very many risks. What, in view of that, will your plans be" — a British courtesy in passing — "in the extremely unlikely event that the Lunar Module does not come up off the lunar surface?"

Armstrong smiled. His detestation of answering questions in public had   32
been given its justification. Journalists would even ask a man to comment on
the emotions of his oncoming death. "Well," said Armstrong, "that's an
unpleasant thing to think about." If, as was quite possible, he had been
closer to death than anyone in the room, and more than once, more than
once, that did not mean the chalice of such findings was there to be fingered
by fifty. "We've chosen not to think about that up to the present time. We
don't think that's at all a likely situation. It's simply a possible one." He
had, however, not answered the question. If he put in twelve and more
hours a day in simulators, if there were weeks when they worked seventy
and eighty hours a week at the abrasive grind of laying in still more hierarchies of numbers and banks of ratio in their heads, well, they were accustomed to hard work. So the grind today of being interviewed in full press
conference, then by the wire services, then by magazine writers and finally
for the television networks, a fourteen-hour day before it would all be done,
and of the worst sort of work for them — objects on display to be chipped at
by some of the worst word-sculptors ever assembled in southeastern Texas
— well, that would still be work they must perform to the best of their duty.
Being an astronaut was a mission. Since the political and power transactions
of the age on which NASA's future was — put no nice word on it — hung,
were not in spirit religious, the astronauts did not emphasize their sense of
vocation. But being an astronaut was a mission and therefore you were
obliged to perform every aspect of your work as well as you could. At a
press conference you answered questions. So Armstrong now finally said in
answer to what they would do if the Lunar Module did not come up off the
lunar surface, "At the present time we're left without recourse should that
occur."

When the conference was done, there was only a small pattering of ap-   33
plause from the Press. The atmosphere had been equal to any other dull
press conference in which a company had unveiled a new and not very special product. Resentment in the Press was subtle but deep. An event of such
dimensions and nothing to show for it. The American cool was becoming a
narcotic. The horror of the Twentieth Century was the size of each new
event, and the paucity of its reverberation.

But what if you're unable to get off the moon?   34
"Unpleasant thing to think about."   35

I I

It was the answer Aquarius thought about after the conference was   36
done, for that was the nearest anyone had come to saying that a man could
get killed in the pits of this venture. And yes, they did think about it. A man

who was in training for six months to go to the moon would be obliged to think about his death. Yet, if to contemplate the failure of the ascent stage of the Lunar Module to rise off the moon was unpleasant for Armstrong to think about, did that derive automatically and simply because it would mean death, or was it, bottomless taint of the unpleasant, a derivation deep out of the incommensurable fact that the moon ground would be the place where his body must rest in death? People who had nearly died from wounds spoke of the near death as offering a sensation that one was rising out of one's body. So had spoken Hemingway long ago, writing in Paris, writing in Spain, probably writing in apartments off the Borghese Gardens near where Collins had been born. Now was there to be a future science of death, or did death (like smell and sound and time — like the theory of the dream) resist all scientists, navigators, nomenclature and charts and reside in the realm of such unanswerables as whether the cause of cancer was a malfunction of the dream? *Did* the souls of the dead choose to rise? Was the thought of expiring on the moon an abyss of unpleasantness because the soul must rest in the tombless vacuums of a torso dead on the moon and therefore not able to voyage toward its star? A vertigo of impressions, but Aquarius had been living at the edge of such thoughts for years. It was possible there was nothing more important in a man's life than the hour and the route and the power of his death, yes, certainly if his death were to launch him into another kind of life. And the astronauts — of this he was convinced — would think this way, or at least would have that vein of imagination in some inviolate and noncommunicatory circuit of their brain; somewhere, far below the language of their communication, they must suspect that the gamble of a trip to the moon and back again, if carried off in all success, might give thrust for some transpostmortal insertion to the stars. Varoom! Last of all over the years had Aquarius learned how to control the rapid acceleration of his brain. Perhaps as a result, he was almost — in these first few days of covering the astronauts in Houston — fond of the banality of their speech and the anodyne of technologese.

But that press conference reserved exclusively for the magazine writers was about to begin — the writers would be working at least half as hard as the astronauts this day — and Aquarius on his way over to the Lunar Receiving Laboratory, where the interview was to be staged (for reasons soon explained) was wondering if the glints and notes of these cosmic, if barely sketched, hypotheses about earth, moon, life, death, the dream and the psychology of astronauts would be offered the ghost of a correlative. Aquarius was contemplating again the little fact that man had not done so very much with Freud's theory of the dream — had the theory of wish fulfillment shown a poor ability "to anticipate and interpret things that appear to be not as we expected them to be"? Did that old Freudian theory of the dream bear the same relation to the veritable dimensions of the dream that a Fourth of July rocket could present to Saturn V?

I I I

Since the astronauts were being guarded against infection, they were 38 seen next behind the protection of a glass wall in the visitors' room at the Lunar Receiving Laboratory. An entire building had been constructed to quarantine them on their return, a species of hospital dormitory, galley and laboratory for the moon rocks. Since for twenty-one days after their return they would not be able to be in the same room with their families, or with the NASA technicians and officials who would debrief them, a chamber like the visitors' room in a prison had been built with a plate-glass partition hermetically sealed from floor to ceiling running down the middle. Dialogue through the glass wall proceeded through microphones.

Now, for the rest of the day, the astronauts would receive the other media layers here: TV, radio, wire service, magazines, etc. Now the magazine 39 writers could sit within a few feet of their subjects, and yet — as if suggesting some undiscovered metaphysical properties of glass — they were obliged at the same time to feel a considerable distance away. Perhaps the full lighting on the astronauts and the relative gloom on the writers' side of the enclosure may have suggested the separation of stage and audience, but probably the effect was due most to the fact that laying-on of hands through that glass, so certainly shatterproof, could never occur, and so there was a dislocation of the sense of space. The astronauts were near enough to sit for a portrait, but — through the glass — they were as far away as history.

There was a new intimacy to the questions however. The setting was of 40 aid, and besides, the magazine writers were in need of more. One of them took up immediately on the question which had bothered Aquarius, but the approach was practical now. How indeed would the astronauts spend their time if they found they could not get off the moon? Would they pray, would they leave messages for their family, or would they send back information on the moon? Such were the alternatives seen by the questioner.

Aldrin had the happy look of a linebacker who is standing right in the 41 center of a hole in the line as the runner tries to come through. "I'd probably spend it working on the availability of the ascent engine."

That brought a laugh, and there would be others to follow, but the 42 twenty or so magazine writers had the leisure to ask their questions out of a small group, and so there was not the itch of the newspaperman to look for a quick lead and therefore ask brutal or leading or tendentious questions. Indeed there was no need to ask any question whatever just so that the journalist and his newspaper could be identified as present at the conference.

(Such identifications give smaller newspapers and their reporters a cumulative status over the years with public relations men.) No, here the magazine writers could take their time, they could pursue a question, even keep after the astronaut. Covertly, the mood of a hunt was on. Since they would have more time to write their pieces, by severer standards would they be judged. So they had to make the astronauts come to life whether the astronauts wished to exhibit themselves or not.

Will you take personal mementos? Armstrong was asked.

"If I had a choice, I guess I'd take more fuel," he said with a smile for the frustration this might cause the questioner.

The magazine writers kept pushing for personal admission, disclosure of emotion, admission of unruly fear — the astronauts looked to give replies as proper and well-insulated as the plate glass which separated them. So Armstrong replied to a question about his intuition by making a short disclaimer, which concluded, "Interpret the problem properly, then attack it." Logical positivism all the way was what he would purvey. Don't make predictions without properly weighted and adequate inventories of knowledge. Surely he trusted his intuitions, the questioner persisted. "It has never been a strong suit," said Armstrong in a mild and honest voice. Obviously, the natural aim of technology was to make intuition obsolescent, and Armstrong was a shining knight of technology. But, in fact, he had to be lying. A man who had never had strong intuitions would never have known enough about the sensation to disclaim its presence in himself.

Would he at least recognize that his endeavor was equal in magnitude to Columbus' adventure?

He disclaimed large reactions, large ideas. "Our concern has been directed mainly to doing the job." He virtually said, "If not me, another." If they would insist on making him a hero, he would be a hero on terms he alone would make clear. There had been only one Columbus — there were ten astronauts at least who could do the job, and hundreds of men to back them up. He was the representative of a collective will.

Sitting in his drab gray-green suit, a suit as close to no color as possible, his shirt pale blue, his tie nondescript dark gray-blue, a blue-green wall behind him (perhaps to hint at empyreans° of sky) his neck seemed subtly separated from his collar, as if — no matter how neatly he was dressed — his clothes felt like a tent to him, like a canvas drop out of which his head protruded through the hole of his collar. They were popping baseballs at him, he was dodging.

"Will you keep a piece of the moon for yourself?" asked a questioner. It was a beautiful question. If he admitted desire, one could ask if the Arm-

---

empyreans The heavens.

strong house would sleep on nights of full moon when the piece of rock bayed silently to its distant mistress, and emanations wandered down the stairs. But Armstrong said stiffly, "At this time, no plans have been made." . . . (Would he ever have the desire to steal a rock, Aquarius asked silently.) "No," Armstrong went on, "that's not a prerogative we have available to us." He could of course have said, "We can't do it," but in trouble he always talked computerese. The use of "we" was discouraged. "A joint exercise has demonstrated" became the substitution. "Other choices" became "peripheral secondary objectives." "Doing our best" was "obtaining maximum advantage possible." "Confidence" became "very high confidence level." "Ability to move" was a "mobility study." "Turn off" was "disable"; "turn on" became "enable." It was as if the more natural forms of English had not been built for the computer: Latin maybe, but not simple Anglo-Saxon. That was too primitive a language — only the general sense could be conveyed by the words: the precise intent was obliged to be defined by the tone of the voice. Computerese preferred to phase out such options. The message had to be locked into a form which could be transmitted by pulse or by lack of pulse, one binary digit at a time, one bit, one bug to be installed in each box. You could not break through computerese.

Through it all, Collins would smile, turn his sensitive presence as eyes to 50 the questioners, ears to the answer. His smile would flicker at the plastic obsidian impenetrability of computerese. "Darn it all," his smile would seem to say to the magazine writers, "if I had to learn how to translate this stuff, I'm sure you fellows can do as well!" Once again, Collins was being asked few questions.

They turned after a while to Aldrin and began to draw some flecks of a 51 true-blooded response. He was, of course, equally impenetrable in the beginning, but after a time he may have made the mistake of essaying a joke. Asked of his reactions to visiting the moon, he proceeded to build a wall of verbal brick, then abruptly with that clumsy odd sobriety, almost engaging, with which he was forever showing his willingness to serve, Aldrin made a remark about having been a boy scout. "I attained the rank of tenderfoot," he said. He gave a discomfited smile. "I hope I don't have a tender foot after walking around the moon." It was so bad a joke that one had to assume it was full of interior reference for him, perhaps some natural male anxiety at the thought of evil moon rays passing into one's private parts. A glum expression sat next to gloom — the damnedest things can happen to a good man.

Then they queried Aldrin on personal mementos. Would he be taking 52 any along?

Well, yes, he admitted reluctantly, he would be taking a little family jew- 53 elry along. He stopped, he looked mulish. It was obvious he didn't want to go on. The primitive value of the objects, their power, their retention of charms, their position in the possible hierarchy of the amulets would be vitiated by describing them. On the other hand, a high quotient of availability-for-miscellaneous-unprogrammed-situations (known in the old days as charity, spontaneity, or generosity of spirit) also ranked high in good astronaut qualifications. So Aldrin gave answers even if he didn't want to.

Well, he admitted, the family jewelry were . . . *rings*. He had two heavy gold rings on two fingers. Yes, he nodded distrustfully, looking for a moment like a chow forced to obey a command he cannot enjoy, yes, on the flight, he would probably still be wearing them.

What else in the way of family jewelry?

But now Aldrin had had enough. "Personal category," he grunted.

A Viennese or German correspondent asked in a heavy accent of Armstrong, "Have you had any der-reams?"

Dreams. Armstrong smiled. He couldn't say he did. The smile was as quick to protect him as the quick tail flick of a long-suffering cow standing among horseflies in a summer meadow's heat, yes, smile-and-flick went Armstrong, "I guess after twenty hours in a simulator, I guess I sometimes have dreams of computers."

Yet as the questions went on, the game was turning. The German might have asked his question about dreams with the happy anticipation that any material provided would offer a feast — the symbols of the dream were pot roast after all and gravied potatoes to the intellectual maw of a nice German head, but the answer, frustrating as nearly all the answers had been, now succeeded in working up a counterpressure. Slowly, unmistakably, the intellectuals and writers on the dark side of the glass were becoming a little weary of the astronauts. Collins' implacable cheerful cool, Aldrin's doughty monk's cloth of squaredom, Armstrong's near-to-facetious smile began to pique their respect. The questions began to have a new tone, an edge, the subtlest quivering suggestion that intellectual contempt was finally a weapon not to be ignored. Were these astronauts not much more than brain-programmed dolts? The contempt was a true pressure. For give an athlete brains, give an aviator brains, give an engineer a small concealed existence as presumptive poet, and whatever is not finished in the work of their ego, whatever is soft in their vanity, will then be exercised by the contempt of an intellectual. The writers were pushing Armstrong now.

Why, why ultimately, they were asking, is it so important to go to the moon? Man to man, they were asking, brain to brain, their leverage derived from the additional position of asking as writer to small-town boy: why is it important?

Armstrong tried to be general. He made a speech in fair computerese about the nation's resources, and the fact that NASA's efforts were now tapped into this root. Well, then, asked a dry voice, are we going to the moon only for economic reasons, only to get out of an expensive hole? No, said Armstrong.

Do you see any philosophical reason why we might be going? the voice 62
went on, as if to imply: are you aware there is philosophy to existence as
well?

Armstrong had now been maneuvered to the point where there was no 63
alternative to offer but a credo, or claim that he was spiritually neuter. That
would have violated too much in him. Yes, he blurted now, as if, damn
them and damn their skills, they had wanted everything else of him this
day, they had had everything else of him, including his full cooperation,
now damn them good, they could have his philosophy too if they could
comprehend it. "I think we're going," he said, and paused, static burning
in the yaws of his pause, "I think we're going to the moon because it's in the
nature of the human being to face challenges." He looked a little defiant, as
if probably they might not know, some critical number of them might never
know what he was talking about, "It's by the nature of his *deep inner soul.*"
The last three words came out as if they had seared his throat by their extor-
tion. How his privacy had been invaded this day. "Yes," he nodded, as if
noting what he had had to give up to writers, "we're required to do these
things just as salmon swim upstream."

I V

That was a fair haul for a working day — Aquarius now had a catch to 64
fry. Yet the day was hardly over for our astronauts. They still had to have
their conversations with the television networks. Since each man would
have his own half hour before the camera, that meant there would be three
interviews for each man, or nine altogether. With breaks and dinner, their
day would continue for another six hours.

Aquarius was invited to audit a filming and chose Armstrong's session 65
with NBC. He had an idea Armstrong would be more comfortable in a TV
interview and he was not wrong. But then Armstrong had indicated his
concern for good television earlier at the full press conference when he had
apologized for the program they would send from the moon. "I don't mean
to sound discouraging but I don't have high hopes that the picture that we
will be able to send back from the surface will be nearly so good as those you
have been looking at from the recent flights from the Command Module.
The camera is somewhat different and is somewhat more restricted in the
kinds of lenses that we can use, and the kinds of lighting we have available
to us. . . . And I suspect that you will be somewhat disappointed at those
pictures. I hope that you'll recognize that it's just one of the problems that
you face in an environment like the lunar surface and it'll be some time before we really get high quality in our lunar surface pictures back on TV link."

It was the one time he had spoken without many pauses, almost as if he 66
were talking already to the TV audience rather than to reporters, almost as if
he just simply believed that Americans were entitled to good television —

one of their inalienable rights. And now, up before the TV cameras, Armstrong looked not at all uncomfortable at the thought of being presented to some forty or fifty million viewers.

Indeed, Aquarius was to see cool pieces and parts of the half hour in thirty-section segments, minute segments and two-minute segments over the next few weeks, particularly during the days of the flight. During many a pause on the trip to the moon, the TV screen would cut to the face of Armstrong, Aldrin or Collins standing or sitting with the blue-green wall of the Lunar Receiving Laboratory behind him. Whether the filmed insertion was to elucidate some remark of the commentators, or merely to fill some frayed space in the ongoing hours of exposition and recapitulation, the effect after having seen ten concrete bits from this interview was to recognize that a new species of commercial was being evolved. NASA was vending space. Armstrong was working directly for his corporate mill. Despite the fact that this future audience of forty million would be listening and studying him, he spoke without long pauses, and seemed oddly enough to be at ease, a salesman with a clear modest mild soft sell. But, then, Aquarius decided, it was not really so very odd. If Armstrong's most recognizable passion was to safeguard his privacy, a desire which approached the force of sanctuary to him, then there was nothing on television he would be likely to reveal or betray. He came, after all, from that heartland of American life which had first induced the particular public personality now bequeathed to all TV viewers as the most viable decorum — that intolerable mixture of bland agreeability and dissolved salt which characterized all performers who appeared in public each day for years and prospered. That view of the world, if designing a face, would have snubbed the nose, faded out the color of the eyes, snugged the lips, slicked the hair and dispensed with the ears for they were protuberances with obscene interior curves — first cousins to the navel.

Armstrong was being interviewed by Frank McGee who turned in a good workmanlike job. McGee, a friendly fellow with a bony face and eyeglasses (whose frames whether tortoiseshell, plastic or pale gold would be remembered afterward as silver wire), had a personality all reminiscent of a country parson, a coach of a rifle team or the friendly investigator from a long-established high-minded insurance company. He was obviously the very ring-tailed hawk of Waspitude.

Their collaboration on the questions and responses had the familiar comfort of piety. Armstrong came near to chatting with him. It was implicit to Network Nugatory that a chatty tone went hand in hand with the pious. So the dullest but most functional, which is to say the most impermeable side of Armstrong was naturally presented. He responded soberly, even chastely to questions about whether he had been elated when chosen — "I have to say that I was" — but quickly added that there could have been many pitfalls during the waiting period (such as intervening flights, which might not succeed) and so he had not indulged any large excitement at any particular period.

He was determinedly modest, going clear out of his way to specify that 70 he was certain the Apollo 12 crew was as competent as his own to make this first trip to the moon, and went on once again to give credit for success to all the Americans who had been working to back them up. "It's their success more than ours," said Armstrong, as if the trip had been completed already, or perhaps this was intended to be the commercial to be employed after touchdown, or lunar ascent, or splashdown. Queried about his private life and the fact that he would lose it after the achievement, he said diffidently, in a voice which would win him twenty million small-town cheers, "I think a private life is possible within the context of such an achievement." Aquarius' mind began to wander — he failed to make notes. Recovering attention at some shift in the mood he realized that Armstrong had finished this interview for he was saying ". . . to take man to another heavenly body . . . we thank all of you for your help and prayers."

There was a hand from the TV crew when the cameras stopped. The 71 trade unions once again were backing patriotic and muscular American effort. "Godspeed and good luck, Neil" one of them actually cried out into the wall of the glass, and Armstrong smiled and waved, and there was more good feeling here than ever at the other conference with Press and magazine. It was apparent the television interview had added little to the store of Aquarius.

But by one detail it had. McGee, referring to a story in *Life* by Dora Jane 72 Hamblin about Armstrong, spoke of a recurring dream the astronaut had had when a boy. In this dream, he was able to hover over the ground if he held his breath.

Aquarius always felt a sense of woe when he found himself subscribing 73 to a new legend. Glut and the incapacity to absorb waste were the evils of the century — the pearls of one's legends were not often founded on real grains of sand. The moment he read the story in *Life*, Aquarius had become infatuated with Armstrong's recurrent dream. It was a beautiful dream — to hold one's breath and to levitate; not to fly and not to fall, but to hover. It was beautiful because it might soon prove to be prophetic, beautiful because it was profound and it was mysterious, beautiful because it was appropriate to a man who would land on the moon. It was therefore a dream on which one might found a new theory of the dream, for any theory incapable of explaining this visitor of the night would have to be inadequate, unless it were ready to declare that levitation, breath, and the moon were not proper provinces of the dream.

Because it was, however, awesome, prophetic, profound, mysterious 74 and appropriate, Aquarius hated to loose the vigors of his imagination onto the meaning of this dream unless he could believe it had actually happened.

It was too perfect to his needs to accept it when he read it. But after studying Armstrong this day, listening to his near-humorous admission that yes, he had had that dream when he was a boy, there was a quietness at the center of his reply which gave balm to the sore of Aquarius' doubt. He knew he had now chosen to believe the dream had occurred.

And this conviction was not without the most direct kind of intellectual intoxication, for it dramatized how much at odds might be the extremes of Armstrong's personality or for that matter the personality of astronauts. From their conscious mind to their unconscious depth, what a spectrum could be covered! Yes, Aquarius thought, astronauts have learned not only to live with opposites, but it was conceivable that the contradictions in their nature were so located in the very impetus of the age that their personality might begin to speak, for better or worse, of some new psychological constitution to man. For it was true — astronauts had come to live with adventures in space so vast one thought of the infinities of a dream, yet their time on the ground was conventional, practical, technical, hardworking, and in the center of the suburban middle class. If they engaged the deepest primitive taboos, they all but parodied the conventional in public manner; they embarked on odysseys whose success or failure was so far from being entirely in their own control that they must be therefore fatalistic, yet the effort was enterprising beyond the limits of the imagination. They were patriots, but they were moonmen. They lived with absolute lack of privacy, their obvious pleasure was to be alone in the sky. They were sufficiently selfless to be prepared to die for their mission, their team, their corporate NASA, their nation; yet they were willy-nilly narcissistic as movie stars. "Sugar, I tried and couldn't make doo-doo," says Lulu Meyers in *The Deer Park*. The heart pressure, the brain waves, the bowel movements of astronauts were of national interest. They were virile men, but they were prodded, probed, tapped into, poked, flexed, tested, subjected to a pharmacology of stimulants, depressants, diuretics, laxatives, retentives, tranquilizers, motion sickness pills, antibiotics, vitamins and food which was designed to control the character of their feces. They were virile, but they were done to, they were done to like no healthy man alive. So again their activity was hazardous, far-flung, bold, demanding of considerable physical strength, yet the work and physical condition called for the ability to live in cramped conditions with passive bodies, the patience to remain mentally alert and physically inactive for days. They lived, it was evident, with no ordinary opposites in their mind and brain. On the one hand to dwell in the very center of technological reality (which is to say that world where every question must have answers and procedures, or technique cannot itself progress) yet to inhabit — if only in one's dreams — that other world where death, metaphysics and the unanswerable questions of eternity must reside, was to suggest natures so divided that they could have been the most miserable and unbalanced of men if they did not contain in their huge contradictions some of the profound and accelerating opposites of the century itself. The century would seek to dominate nature as it had never been dominated, would attack the idea of war, poverty and natural catastrophe as never before. The century would create death, devastation and pollution as never before. Yet the century was now attached to the idea that man must take his conception of life out to the stars. It was the most soul-destroying and apocalyptic of centuries. So in their turn the astronauts had personalities of unequaled banality and apocalyptic dignity. So they suggested in their contradictions the power of the century to live with its own incredible contradictions and yet release some of the untold energies of the earth. A century devoted to the rationality of technique was also a century so irrational as to open in every mind the real possibility of global destruction. It was the first century in history which presented to sane and sober minds the fair chance that the century might not reach the end of its span. It was a world half convinced of the future death of our species yet half aroused by the apocalyptic notion that an exceptional future still lay before us. So it was a century which moved with the most magnificent display of power into directions it could not comprehend. The itch was to accelerate — the metaphysical direction unknown.

Aquarius, aware of the profundity of his natural bent for error, aware of the ineradicably romantic inclination of his mind to believe all those tales and legends he desired to believe, nonetheless came to a conclusion on this hot Saturday evening, July 5, on the southeastern rim of Houston, that Armstrong when a boy had indeed had a recurring dream in which he would hold his breath and rise from the ground and hover, and on this dream Aquarius, who had been reconnoitering for months through many a new thought (new at the very least to him) on the architecture and function and presence of the dream, would build his theory, on Armstrong's dream would Aquarius commit himself. Any notes toward a new psychology could take their departure from here, from this *fact*. And as this evening went on, and he continued to the party at Pete Conrad's house and talked to the future commander of Apollo 12 over the steaks at charcoal grill, and Conrad made his confession of dreaming for years of going to the moon, and now concluded somberly, manfully — one had to be manful when contemplating the cost of desire — "now the moon is nothing but facts to me," Aquarius felt confirmation building in his mood, his happiness and his senses, that this grim tough job of writing for enough money to pay his debts and buy his little plot of time, was going to be possibly, all passions directed, all disciplines flexed, a work whose size might relieve the chore. And as he thought of the little details he had picked up in the biographies of Collins, of Aldrin, of Armstrong, he thought that yes, the invasion of the moon was signal di-

147

rect to commence his new psychology — he would call it, yes, beneath this Texas moon, full near the Fourth of July, he would call it The Psychology of Astronauts, for they were either the end of the old or the first of the new men, and one would have nothing to measure them by until the lines of the new psychology had begun to be drawn.

QUESTIONS ON MEANING

1. Does Mailer present a clear and comprehensive short view of his subject, the psychology of astronauts, touching on all the main points, summarizing the whole topic? How has he defined the subject? What does he suggest its importance is?
2. "The Psychology of Astronauts" is a dense mix of reportage and speculation. It comments on press conferences with the astronauts of the Apollo mission, but Mailer is not content with simple coverage. He reports on what he saw of the astronauts in a very controlled setting, but he also comments on the setting, the other members of the press — covering the coverage, so to speak. He reflects on what he sees and cannot see, probing the event for a clue to its mystery. Look through the essay and try to determine the proportions Mailer keeps: How much of the work is reportage, how much speculation?
3. How does Mailer characterize the astronauts' language? What part does their language play in their psychology? What does it tell Mailer about the mission?
4. Though charmed by Mike Collins, Mailer clearly gives special emphasis to Neil Armstrong. Aside from his role as commander of the mission, what does Mailer find in this particular astronaut that justifies his prominence in the essay?
5. Paragraph 36 develops a link between death, dreams, and dread. How does Mailer make this linkage? How does he develop these ideas throughout the essay? What is the relevance of Armstrong's dream?

QUESTIONS ON STRATEGY

1. Why does Mailer call himself Aquarius? What is the significance of this name? What effect does it have in the essay?
2. In paragraph 75, probing "the personality of astronauts," Mailer describes "the contradictions in their nature." What is his main point about their contradictions? How does he develop the point? Where, and why, does he restate the point?
3. Mailer reflects often on language. How would you characterize his own language? What kind of sentence constructions does Mailer favor? How do these constructions contribute to his tone?

E X P L O R A T I O N S

1. "The Psychology of Astronauts" appears as a chapter near the beginning of Mailer's book *Of a Fire on the Moon*. Some of the important thematic material introduced in this chapter is developed later in the book. Read "The Psychology of Machines" (part 2, chapter 1) and "The Iron of Astronauts" (part 2, chapter 5). How do those chapters develop the themes Mailer introduces in "The Psychology of Astronauts"?

W R I T I N G   T O P I C S

1. Does every highly specialized profession give rise to its own psychology? Using some of Mailer's techniques — language analysis, or close observation, for example — write an essay describing the psychology of waitresses or dentists, auto mechanics or salespeople.
2. Has Aquarius really "learned how to control the rapid acceleration of his brain," as he claims in paragraph 36? Mailer's style has, over the years, attracted criticism for its excessive energy. Look through this essay for places where Mailer's style goes too far. Write an essay on the excesses of Mailer's writing.

B O O K S   A V A I L A B L E   I N   P A P E R B A C K

Advertisements for Myself. New York: G. P. Putnam's Sons. *Stories and essays*.

The Armies of the Night: History as a Novel, the Novel as History. New York: New American Library. *Nonfiction: Personal account of a 1967 antiwar demonstration*.

Cannibals and Christians. New York: Pinnacle Books. *Stories and essays*.

The Deer Park. New York: G. P. Putnam's Sons. *Novel*.

The Executioner's Song. New York: Warner Books. *Novel*.

Marilyn. New York: G. P. Putnam's Sons. *Nonfiction: Biography of American movie actress Marilyn Monroe (1926–1962); illustrated with photographs*.

The Naked and the Dead. New York: Holt, Rinehart & Winston, Owl Books. *Novel*.

Of Women and Their Elegance. New York: Pinnacle Books. *Nonfiction; illustrated with photographs by Milton H. Greene*.

Pieces and Pontifications. 2 vols. Boston: Little, Brown. *Essays*.

The Short Fiction of Norman Mailer. New York: Pinnacle Books.

Why Are We in Vietnam? New York: Holt, Rinehart & Winston, Owl Books. *Novel*.

PAUL
FUSSELL

AFTER MANY YEARS of teaching English at Rutgers University, Paul Fussell (b. 1924) recently moved to a chair in English literature at the University of Pennsylvania. He was an undergraduate at Pomona College in California, where he was born the son of a millionaire. He saw combat in World War II as an infantry officer, was wounded, and returned to do his Ph.D. at Harvard. He wrote two books on eighteenth-century literature and Poetic Meter and Poetic Form *(1965, revised 1979). In* The Great War and Modern Memory *(1975) he investigated the British experience of World War I and especially the books in which that war found its way into literature.* The Great War and Modern Memory *won Fussell the National Book Critics Circle Award and the National Book Award in 1976. He has written many articles and book reviews for magazines, especially for* Harper's *and* The New Republic *(which published ''Notes on Class'' in 1980). These essays are collected in* The Boy Scout Handbook and Other Observations *(1982), on the jacket of which we read that the author ''is working on a study of the behavior of the imagination in the Second World War.''*

Paul Fussell is a historian of society and the imagination whose field of investigation is largely literature. In ''Notes on Class'' he makes ironic commentary on the class structure of our country. Because we lack the rigid social hierarchies of some

European countries, with aristocracies of ancient fortunes and inherited titles, we sometimes pretend that our society is classless. Fussell — *whose book on the subject,* Class: A Guide Through the American Status System, *was published in 1983 — writes about the American class system with wit and sarcasm.*

Notes on Class

If the dirty little secret used to be sex, now it is the facts about social class. 1
No subject today is more likely to offend. Over thirty years ago Dr. Kinsey generated considerable alarm by disclosing that despite appearances one-quarter of the male population had enjoyed at least one homosexual orgasm. A similar alarm can be occasioned today by asserting that despite the much-discussed mechanism of ''social mobility'' and the constant redistribution of income in this country, it is virtually impossible to break out of the social class in which one has been nurtured. Bad news for the ambitious as well as the bogus, but there it is.

Defining class is difficult, as sociologists and anthropologists have 2
learned. The more data we feed into the machines, the less likely it is that significant formulations will emerge. What follows here is based not on interviews, questionnaires, or any kind of quantitative technique but on perhaps a more trustworthy method — perception. Theory may inform us that there are three classes in America, high, middle, and low. Perception will tell us that there are at least nine, which I would designate and arrange like this:

> Top Out-of-Sight
> Upper
> Upper Middle
> —
> Middle
> High-Proletarian
> Mid-Proletarian
> Low-Proletarian
> —
> Destitute
> Bottom Out-of-Sight

In addition, there is a floating class with no permanent location in this hierarchy. We can call it Class X. It consists of well-to-do hippies, ''artists,'' ''writers'' (who write nothing), floating bohemians, politicians out of office, disgraced athletic coaches, residers abroad, rock stars, ''celebrities,'' and the shrewder sort of spies.

The quasi-official division of the population into three economic classes called high-, middle-, and low-income groups rather misses the point, because as a class indicator the amount of money is not as important as the source. Important distinctions at both the top and bottom of the class scale arise less from degree of affluence than from the people or institutions to whom one is beholden for support. For example, the main thing distinguishing the top three classes from each other is the amount of money inherited in relation to the amount currently earned. The Top Out-of-Sight Class (Rockefellers, du Ponts, Mellons, Fords, Whitneys) lives on inherited capital entirely. Its money is like the hats of the Boston ladies who, asked where they got them, answer, "Oh, we *have* our hats." No one whose money, no matter how ample, comes from his own work, like film stars, can be a member of the Top Out-of-Sights, even if the size of his income and the extravagance of his expenditure permit him temporary social access to it.

Since we expect extremes to meet, we are not surprised to find the very lowest class, Bottom Out-of-Sight, similar to the highest in one crucial respect: it is given its money and kept sort of afloat not by its own efforts but by the welfare machinery or the prison system. Members of the Top Out-of-Sight Class sometimes earn some money, as directors or board members of philanthropic or even profitable enterprises, but the amount earned is laughable in relation to the amount already possessed. Membership in the Top Out-of-Sight Class depends on the ability to flourish without working at all, and it is this that suggests a curious brotherhood between those at the top and the bottom of the scale.

It is this also that distinguishes the Upper Class from its betters. It lives on both inherited money and a salary from attractive, if usually slight, work, without which, even if it could survive and even flourish, it would feel bored and a little ashamed. The next class down, the Upper Middle, may possess virtually as much as the two above it. The difference is that it has earned most of it, in law, medicine, oil, real-estate, or even the more honorific forms of trade. The Upper Middles are afflicted with a bourgeois sense of shame, a conviction that to live on the earnings of others, even forebears, is not entirely nice.

The Out-of-Sight Classes at top and bottom have something else in common: they are literally all but invisible (hence their name). The façades of Top Out-of-Sight houses are never seen from the street, and such residences (like Rockefeller's upstate New York premises) are often hidden away deep in the hills, safe from envy and its ultimate attendants, confiscatory taxation and finally expropriation. The Bottom Out-of-Sight Class is equally invisible. When not hidden away in institutions or claustrated in monasteries, lamaseries, or communes, it is hiding from creditors, deceived bail-bondsmen, and merchants intent on repossessing cars and furniture. (This class is visible briefly in one place, in the spring on the streets of New York City, but after this ritual yearly show of itself it disappears again.) When you pass a house with a would-be impressive façade addressing the street, you know it is occupied by a mere member of the Upper or Upper Middle Class. The White House is an example. Its residents, even on those occasions when they are Kennedys, can never be classified as Top Out-of-Sight but only Upper Class. The house is simply too conspicuous, and temporary residence there usually constitutes a come-down for most of its occupants. It is a hopelessly Upper-or Upper-Middle-Class place.

Another feature of both Top and Bottom Out-of-Sight Classes is their 7 anxiety to keep their names out of the papers, and this too suggests that socially the President is always rather vulgar. All the classes in between Top and Bottom Out-of-Sight slaver for personal publicity (monograms on shirts, inscribing one's name on lawn-mowers and power tools, etc.), and it is this lust to be known almost as much as income that distinguishes them from their Top and Bottom neighbors. The High- and Mid-Prole Classes can be recognized immediately by their pride in advertising their physical presence, a way of saying, "Look! We pay our bills and have a known place in the community, and you can find us there any time." Thus hypertrophied house-numbers on the front, or house numbers written "Two Hundred Five" ("Two Hundred and Five" is worse) instead of 205, or flamboyant house or family names blazoned on façades, like "The Willows" or "The Polnickis."

(If you go behind the façade into the house itself, you will find a fairly 8 trustworthy class indicator in the kind of wood visible there. The top three classes invariably go in for hardwoods for doors and panelling; the Middle and High-Prole Classes, pine, either plain or "knotty." The knotty-pine "den" is an absolute stigma of the Middle Class, one never to be overcome or disguised by temporarily affected higher usages. Below knotty pine there is plywood.)

Façade study is a badly neglected anthropological field. As we work 9 down from the (largely white-painted) bank-like façades of the Upper and Upper Middle Classes, we encounter such Middle and Prole conventions as these, which I rank in order of social status:

Middle

1. A potted tree on either side of the front door, and the more pointy and symmetrical the better.
2. A large rectangular picture-window in a split-level "ranch" house, displaying a table-lamp between two side curtains. The cellophane on the lampshade must be visibly inviolate.
3. Two chairs, usually metal with pipe arms, disposed on the front porch as a "conversation group," in stubborn defiance of the traffic thundering past.

High-Prole

4. Religious shrines in the garden, which if small and understated, are slightly higher class than

Mid-Prole

5. Plaster gnomes and flamingos, and blue or lavender shiny spheres supported by fluted cast-concrete pedestals.

Low-Prole

6. Defunct truck tires painted white and enclosing flower beds. (Auto tires are a grade higher.)
7. Flower-bed designs worked in dead light bulbs or the butts of disused beer bottles.

The Desitute have no façades to decorate, and of course the Bottom Out-of-Sights, being invisible, have none either, although both these classes can occasionally help others decorate theirs — painting tires white on an hourly basis, for example, or even watering and fertilizing the potted trees of the Middle Class. Class X also does not decorate its façades, hoping to stay loose and unidentifiable, ready to re-locate and shape-change the moment it sees that its cover has been penetrated.

In this list of façade conventions an important principle emerges. Organic materials have higher status than metal or plastic. We should take warning from Sophie Portnoy's° aluminum venetian blinds, which are also lower than wood because the slats are curved, as if "improved," instead of classically flat. The same principle applies, as *The Preppy Handbook* has shown so effectively, to clothing fabrics, which must be cotton or wool, never Dacron or anything of that prole kind. In the same way, yachts with wood hulls, because they must be repaired or replaced (at high cost) more often, are classier than yachts with fiberglass hulls, no matter how shrewdly merchandised. Plastic hulls are cheaper and more practical, which is precisely why they lack class.

As we move down the scale, income of course decreases, but income is less important to class than other seldom-invoked measurements: for example, the degree to which one's work is supervised by an omnipresent immediate superior. The more free from supervision, the higher the class, which is why a dentist ranks higher than a mechanic working under a foreman in a large auto shop, even if he makes considerably more money than the dentist. The two trades may be thought equally dirty: it is the dentist's freedom from supervision that helps confer class upon him. Likewise, a high-school

---

Sophie Portnoy   A character in Philip Roth's novel *Portnoy's Complaint* (1969).

teacher obliged to file weekly "lesson plans" with a principal or "curriculum co-ordinator" thereby occupies a class position lower than a tenured professor, who reports to no one, even though the high-school teacher may be richer, smarter, and nicer. (Supervisors and Inspectors are titles that go with public schools, post offices, and police departments: the student of class will need to know no more.) It is largely because they must report that even the highest members of the naval and military services lack social status: they all have designated supervisors — even the Chairman of the Joint Chiefs of Staff has to report to the President.

Class is thus defined less by bare income than by constraints and insecurities. It is defined also by habits and attitudes. Take television watching. The Top Out-of-Sight Class doesn't watch at all. It owns the companies and pays others to monitor the thing. It is also entirely devoid of intellectual or even emotional curiosity: it *has* its ideas the way it has its money. The Upper Class does look at television but it prefers Camp offerings, like the films of Jean Harlow or Jon Hall. The Upper Middle Class regards TV as vulgar except for the highminded emissions of National Educational Television, which it watches avidly, especially when, like the Shakespeare series, they are the most incompetently directed and boring. Upper Middles make a point of forbidding children to watch more than an hour a day and worry a lot about violence in society and sugar in cereal. The Middle Class watches, preferring the more "beautiful" kinds of non-body-contact sports like tennis or gymnastics or figure-skating (the music is a redeeming feature here). With High-, Mid-, and Low-Proles we find heavy viewing of the soaps in the daytime and rugged body-contact sports (football, hockey, boxing) in the evening. The lower one is located in the Prole classes the more likely one is to watch "Bowling for Dollars" and "Wonder Woman" and "The Hulk" and when choosing a game show to prefer "Joker's Wild" to "The Family Feud," whose jokes are sometimes incomprehensible. Destitutes and Bottom Out-of-Sights have in common a problem involving choice. Destitutes usually "own" about three color sets, and the problem is which three programs to run at once. Bottom Out-of-Sights exercise no choice at all, the decisions being made for them by correctional or institutional personnel.

The time when the evening meal is consumed defines class better than, say, the presence or absence on the table of ketchup bottles and ashtrays shaped like little toilets enjoining the diners to "Put Your Butts Here." Destitutes and Bottom Out-of-Sights eat dinner at 5:30, for the Prole staff on which they depend must clean up and be out roller-skating or bowling early in the evening. Thus Proles eat at 6:00 or 6:30. The Middles eat at 7:00, the Upper Middles at 7:30 or, if very ambitious, at 8:00. The Uppers and Top Out-of-Sights dine at 8:30 or 9:00 or even later, after nightly protracted "cocktail" sessions lasting usually around two hours. Sometimes they forget to eat at all.

12

13

Similarly, the physical appearance of the various classes defines them
fairly accurately. Among the top four classes thin is good, and the bottom
two classes appear to ape this usage, although down there thin is seldom a
matter of choice. It is the three Prole classes that tend to fat, partly as a result
of their use of convenience foods and plenty of beer. These are the classes
too where anxiety about slipping down a rung causes nervous overeating,
resulting in fat that can be rationalized as advertising the security of steady
wages and the ability to "eat out" often. Even "Going Out for Breakfast" is
not unthinkable for Proles, if we are to believe that they respond to the Mc-
Donald's TV ads as they're supposed to. A recent magazine ad for a diet
book aimed at Proles stigmatizes a number of erroneous assumptions about
body weight, proclaiming with some inelegance that "They're all a crock."
Among such vulgar errors is the proposition that "All Social Classes Are
Equally Overweight." This the ad rejects by noting quite accurately:

> Your weight is an advertisement of your social standing. A
> century ago, corpulence was a sign of success. But no more.
> Today it is the badge of the lower-middle-class, where obesity
> is *four times* more prevalent than it is among the upper-middle
> and middle classes.

It is not just four times more prevalent. It is at least four times more visible,
as any observer can testify who has witnessed Prole women perambulating
shopping malls in their bright, very tight jersey trousers. Not just obesity
but the flaunting of obesity is the Prole sign, as if the object were to give
maximum aesthetic offense to the higher classes and thus achieve a form of
revenge.

Another physical feature with powerful class meaning is the wearing of
plaster casts on legs and ankles by members of the top three classes. These
casts, a sort of white badge of honor, betoken stylish mishaps with frivolous
but costly toys like horses, skis, snowmobiles, and mopeds. They signify a
high level of conspicuous waste in a social world where questions of un-
payable medical bills or missed working days do not apply. But in the matter
of clothes, the Top Out-of-Sight is different from both Upper and Upper
Middle Classes. It prefers to appear in new clothes, whereas the class just
below it prefers old clothes. Likewise, all three Prole classes make much of
new garments, with the highest possible polyester content. The question
does not arise in the same form with Destitutes and Bottom Out-of-Sights.
They wear used clothes, the thrift shop and prison supply room serving as
their Bonwit's and Korvette's.

This American class system is very hard for foreigners to master, partly
because most foreigners imagine that since America was founded by the
British it must retain something of British institutions. But our class system

is more subtle than the British, more a matter of gradations than of blunt divisions, like the binary distinction between a gentleman and a cad. This seems to lack plausibility here. One seldom encounters in the United States the sort of absolute prohibitions which (half-comically, to be sure) one is asked to believe define the gentleman in England. Like these:

> A gentleman never wears brown shoes in the city, or
> A gentleman never wears a green suit, or
> A gentleman never has soup at lunch, or
> A gentleman never uses a comb, or
> A gentleman never smells of anything but tar, or
> "No gentleman can fail to admire Bellini" — W. H. Auden.

In America it seems to matter much less the way you present yourself — green, brown, neat, sloppy, scented — than what your backing is — that is, where your money comes from. What the upper orders display here is no special uniform but the kind of psychological security they derive from knowing that others recognize their freedom from petty anxieties and trivial prohibitions.

"Language most shows a man," Ben Jonson used to say. "Speak, that I 17 may see thee." As all acute conservatives like Jonson know, dictional behavior is a powerful signal of a firm class line. Nancy Mitford so indicated in her hilarious essay of 1955, "The English Aristocracy," based in part on Professor Alan S. C. Ross's more sober study "Linguistic Class-Indicators in Present-Day English." Both Mitford and Ross were interested in only one class demarcation, the one dividing the English Upper Class ("U," in their shorthand) from all below it ("non-U"). Their main finding was that euphemism and genteelism are vulgar. People who are socially secure risk nothing by calling a spade a spade, and indicate their top-dog status by doing so as frequently as possible. Thus the U-word is *rich*, the non-U *wealthy*. What U-speakers call *false teeth* non-U's call *dentures*. The same with *wigs* and *hairpieces, dying* and *passing away* (or *over*).

For Mitford, linguistic assaults from below are sometimes so shocking 18 that the only kind reaction of a U-person is silence. It is "the only possible U-response," she notes, "to many embarrassing modern situations: the ejaculation of 'cheers' before drinking, for example, or 'It was so nice seeing you' after saying goodbye. In silence, too, one must endure the use of the Christian name by comparative strangers. . . ." In America, although there are more classes distinguishable here, a linguistic polarity is as visible as in England. Here U-speech (or our equivalent of it) characterizes some Top Out-of-Sights, Uppers, Upper Middles, and Class X's. All below is a waste land of genteelism and jargon and pretentious mispronunciation, pathetic evidence of the upward social scramble and its hazards. Down below, the ear is bad and no one has been trained to listen. Culture words especially are the downfall of the aspiring. Sometimes it is diphthongs that invite disgrace, as in *be-yóu-ti-ful*. Sometimes the aspirant rushes full-face into disaster by flourishing those secret class indicators, the words *exquisite* and *despicable*, which, like another secret sign, *patina*, he (and of course she as often) stresses on the middle syllable instead of the first. High-class names from cultural history are a frequent cause of betrayal, especially if they are British, like Henry Purcell. In America non-U speakers are fond of usages like ''Between he and I.'' Recalling vaguely that mentioning oneself last, as in ''He and I were there,'' is thought gentlemanly, they apply that principle uniformly, to the entire destruction of the objective case. There's also a problem with *like*. They remember something about the dangers of illiteracy its use invites, and hope to stay out of trouble by always using *as* instead, finally saying things like ''He looks as his father.'' These contortions are common among young (usually insurance or computer) trainees, raised on Leon Uris° and *Playboy*, most of them Mid- or High-Proles pounding on the firmly shut doors of the Middle Class. They are the careful, dark-suited first-generation aspirants to American respectability and (hopefully, as they would put it) power. Together with their deployment of the anomalous nominative case on all occasions goes their preference for jargon (you can hear them going at it on airplanes) like *parameters* and *guidelines* and *bottom lines* and *funding, dialogue, interface,* and *lifestyles*. Their world of language is one containing little more than smokescreens and knowing innovations. ''Do we gift the Johnsons, dear?'' the corporate wife will ask the corporate husband at Christmas time.

Just below these people, down among the Mid- and Low-Proles, the complex sentence gives trouble. It is here that we get sentences beginning with elaborate pseudo-genteel participles like ''Being that it was a cold day, the furnace was on.'' All classes below those peopled by U-speakers find the gerund out of reach and are thus forced to multiply words and say, ''The people in front of him at the theater got mad due to the fact that he talked so much'' instead of ''His talking at the theater annoyed the people in front.'' (But *people* is not really right: *individuals* is the preferred term with non-U speakers. Grander, somehow.) It is also in the domain of the Mid- and Low-Prole that the double negative comes into its own as well as the superstitious avoidance of *lying* because it may be taken to imply telling untruths. People are thus depicted as always *laying* on the beach, the bed, the grass, the sidewalk, and without the slightest suggestion of their performing sexual exhibitions. A similar unconscious inhibition determines that *set* replace *sit* on all occasions, lest low excremental implications be inferred. The ease with

---

Leon Uris Popular American novelist, author of *Exodus* (1958) and *Trinity* (1976).

which *sit* can be interchanged with the impolite word is suggested in a Second World War anecdote told by General Matthew Ridgway. Coming upon an unidentifiable head and shoulders peeping out of a ditch near the German border, he shouted. ''Put up your hands, you son of a bitch!'', to be answered, so he reports, ''Aaah, go sit in your hat.''

All this is evidence of a sad fact. A deep class gulf opens between two 20 current generations: the older one that had some Latin at school or college and was taught rigorous skeptical ''English,'' complete with the diagramming of sentences; and the younger one taught to read by the optimistic look-say method and encouraged to express itself — as the saying goes — so that its sincerity and well of ideas suffer no violation. This new generation is unable to perceive the number of syllables in a word and cannot spell and is baffled by all questions of etymology (it thinks *chauvinism* has something to do with gender aggressions). It cannot write either, for it has never been subjected to tuition in the sort of English sentence structure which resembles the sonata in being not natural but artificial, not innate but mastered. Because of its misspent, victimized youth, this generation is already destined to fill permanently the middle-to-low slots in the corporate society without ever quite understanding what devilish mechanism has prevented it from ascending. The disappearance of Latin as an adjunct to the mastery of English can be measured by the rapid replacement of words like *continuing* by solecisms like *ongoing*. A serious moment in cultural history occurred a few years ago when gasoline trucks changed the warning word on the rear from *Inflammable* to *Flammable*. Public education had apparently produced a population which no longer knew *In-* as an intensifier. That this happened at about the moment when every city was rapidly running up a ''Cultural Center'' might make us laugh, if we don't cry first. In another few generations Latinate words will be found only in learned writing, and the spoken language will have returned to the state it was in before the revival of learning. Words like *intellect* and *curiosity* and *devotion* and *study* will have withered away together with the things they denote.

There's another linguistic class-line, dividing those who persist in honor- 21 ing the nineteenth-century convention that advertising, if not commerce itself, is reprehensible and not at all to be cooperated with, and those proud to think of themselves not as skeptics but as happy consumers, fulfilled when they can image themselves as functioning members of a system by responding to advertisements. For U-persons a word's succeeding in an ad is a compelling reason never to use it. But possessing no other source of idiom and no extra-local means of criticizing it, the subordinate classes are pleased to appropriate the language of advertising for personal use, dropping brand names all the time and saying things like ''They have some lovely fashions in that store.'' In the same way they embrace all sub-professional euphemisms gladly and employ them proudly, adverting without irony to hair

Exercise

To what class would you assign each of the following?

1. A fifty-five-year-old pilot for a feeder airline who cuts his own grass, watches wrestling on TV, and has a knotty-pine den?
2. A small-town podiatrist who says "Have a nice day" and whose wife is getting very fat?
3. A young woman trust officer in a large New York bank who loves to watch Channel 13, WNET, and likes to be taken out to restaurants said to serve "gourmet" food?
4. A periodontist in a rich suburb? Is his class higher than that of an exodontist in a large midwestern city who earns more?
5. A man in a rich Northeastern suburb who, invited to a dinner party on Tuesday night, appears in a quiet suit with a white shirt but at a similar, apparently more formal dinner party on Saturday night shows up in a bright green linen jacket, red trousers, no tie, and no socks?
6. Students of all kinds?

Answers

1. Pilots have roughly the same class as field-grade Army officers, that is, High Prole. Feeder airline pilots have less status than national airline pilots, and those who work for the longest established international airlines like Pan Am and TWA have the highest status of all. The Middle-Class den and the Mid-Prole TV wrestling addiction cancel each other out.
2. At the moment, High Prole. If his wife gets much fatter, he will sink to Mid-Prole.
3. Middle, with hopeless fantasies about being Upper-Middle.
4. The periodontist is Middle. Because he is not a "professional specialist," the exodontist is slightly lower, regardless of where he lives or what he earns.
5. He is from the Upper-Middle Class, but he'd like to be taken for a member of the Upper. The suit on Tuesday night is to give the impression that he's just returned from the city, where he "works." The weekend get-up validates his identity as a suburbanite, devoting his weekend to much-needed unbuttoning and frivolity. The difference between Tuesday and Saturday is supposed to be significant. But I don't trust this man. He pays too much attention to his clothes to be really Upper Class.
6. All students, regardless of age or institution attended, are Mid-Proles, as their large consumption of beer and convenience food suggests. Sometimes they affect the used clothing of the Destitute, but we should not be fooled.

stylists, sanitary engineers, and funeral directors in complicity with the consumer world which cynically casts them as its main victims. They see nothing funny in paying a high price for an article and then, after a solemn pause, receiving part of it back in the form of a "rebate." Trapped in a world wholly defined by the language of consumption and the hype, they harbor restively, defending themselves against actuality by calling habitual drunkards *people with alcohol problems,* madness *mental illness,* drug use *drug abuse,* building lots *homesites,* houses *homes* ("They live in a lovely $250,000 home"), and drinks *beverages.*

Those delighted to employ the vacuous commercial "Have a nice day" 22 and those who wouldn't think of saying it belong manifestly to different classes, no matter how we define them, and it is unthinkable that those classes will ever melt. Calvin Coolidge said that the business of America is business. Now apparently the business of America is having a nice day. Tragedy? Don't need it. Irony? Take it away. Have a nice day. Have a nice day. A visiting Englishman of my acquaintance, a U-speaker if there ever was one, has devised the perfect U-response to "Have a nice day": "Thank you," he says, "but I have other plans." The same ultimate divide separates the two classes who say respectively when introduced, "How do you do?" and "Pleased to meet you." There may be comity between those who think *prestigious* a classy word and those who don't, but it won't survive much strain, like relations between those who think *momentarily* means in a moment (airline captain over loudspeaker: "We'll be taking off momentarily, folks") and those who know it means for a moment. Members of these two classes can sit in adjoining seats on the plane and get along fine (although there's a further division between those who talk to their neighbors in planes and elevators and those who don't), but once the plane has emptied, they will proceed toward different destinations. It's the same with those who conceive that *type* is an adjective ("He's a very classy type person") and those who know it's only a noun or verb.

The pretence that either person can feel at ease in the presence of the 23 other is an essential element of the presiding American fiction. Despite the lowness of the metaphor, the idea of the melting pot is high-minded and noble enough, but empirically it will be found increasingly unconvincing. It is our different language habits as much as anything that make us, as the title of Richard Polenberg's book puts it, *One Nation Divisible.*

Some people invite constant class trouble because they believe the offi- 24 cial American publicity about these matters. The official theory, which experience is constantly disproving, is that one can earn one's way out of his original class. Richard Nixon's behavior indicates dramatically that this is not so. The sign of the Upper Class to which he aspired is total psychological security, expressed in loose carriage, saying what one likes, and imperviousness to what others think. Nixon's vast income from law and politics — his San Clemente property aped the style of the Upper but not the Top Out-of-

Sight Class, for everyone knew where it was, and he wanted them to know — could not alleviate his original awkwardness and meanness of soul or his nervousness about the impression he was making, an affliction allied to his instinct for cunning and duplicity. Hammacher Schlemmer might have had him specifically in mind as the consumer of their recently advertised "Champagne Recork": "This unusual stopper keeps 'bubbly' sprightly, sparkling after uncorking ceremony is over. Gold electro-plated." I suspect that it is some of these same characteristics that make Edward Kennedy often seem so inauthentic a member of the Upper Class. (He's not Top Out-of-Sight because he chooses to augment his inheritance by attractive work.)

What, then, marks the higher classes? Primarily a desire for privacy, if 25 not invisibility, and a powerful if eccentric desire for freedom. It is this instinct for freedom that may persuade us that inquiring into the American class system this way is an enterprise not entirely facetious. Perhaps after all the whole thing has something, just something, to do with ethics and aesthetics. Perhaps a term like *gentleman* still retains some meanings which are not just sartorial and mannerly. Freedom and grace and independence: it would be nice to believe those words still mean something, and it would be interesting if the reality of the class system — and everyone, after all, hopes to rise — should turn out to be a way we pay those notions a due if unwitting respect.

QUESTIONS ON MEANING

1. Fussell rejects the usual class divisions based on economics. How does he determine people's class affiliations? How many different criteria does he use to separate one class from another? Which distinguishing characteristic does he emphasize and develop most heavily?
2. Is Fussell for or against the distinctions on which a class system is based? Or is he a neutral observer of this social phenomenon? How can you tell? Can you detect in him an allegiance to any particular class?
3. At the end of the essay, Fussell indicates three characteristics that a class system might be based on. How do these characteristics relate to the criteria Fussell develops in the rest of the essay? What does Fussell's conclusion tell us about his view of class structures?

QUESTIONS ON STRATEGY

1. Fussell titles his essay "*Notes* on Class." How does his organization of the essay follow from this title? Is the structure of the essay effective? Does it leave you with the feeling that the author didn't take time to finish his task?

2. Fussell concludes that inquiry into the class system is "an enterprise not entirely facetious." Yet his essay seems to be largely facetious, at times even a bit outrageous. Does he intend that we take him seriously? What gives his essay a facetious tone? What gives it a serious tone?
3. Does Fussell generalize broadly, using particular details only for illustration? Or does he make primary use of the specifics? How does he organize his data?

EXPLORATIONS

1. Look at Alison Lurie's essay "Clothing as a Sign System" (pages 202–224). How do her approaches to "reading" people's costumes relate to Fussell's efforts to define and use what he calls "façade conventions" (paragraphs 9 and 10)? Look at the emphasis these authors give to language, not only as an indicator of types of people but also as a model for nonverbal communication. How is attention to language essential to both essays?

WRITING TOPICS

1. Fussell states that all students are Mid-Proles. Write an essay arguing that he is right or wrong. If you disagree with his assessment, state your grounds explicitly. Are his categorical descriptions of the various classes in error, or does he misread the evidence? If you agree, consider the implications of his view. Why does the educational experience determine membership in this class? Do students from all classes suspend their identities to assume this one?
2. "Notes on Class" was originally published in 1980. Write an essay bringing Fussell's categorizations up to date, defining class lines as they manifest themselves today.

BOOKS AVAILABLE IN PAPERBACK

Abroad: British Literary Traveling Between the Wars. New York: Oxford University Press. *Nonfiction: Literary history.*

The Great War and Modern Memory. New York: Oxford University Press. *Nonfiction: Cultural history.*

Poetic Meter and Poetic Form. Rev. ed. New York: Vintage. *Nonfiction: Literary criticism.*

JAMES
BALDWIN

J AMES BALDWIN *was born in 1924 in Harlem, a native son of the American
black ghetto. He was also born a writer, or as near as anybody can be. "I began
plotting novels at about the time I learned to read," he has written. "My first professional triumph . . . occurred at the age of twelve or thereabouts, when a short story I
had written about the Spanish revolution won some sort of prize in an extremely
short-lived church newspaper. I remember the story was censored by the lady editor,
though I don't remember why, and I was outraged."*

*A series of fellowships supported Baldwin when he was young — a Saxton when
he was only twenty-one in 1945, a Rosenwald in 1948, a Guggenheim in 1954, a*
Partisan Review *fellowship in 1956, and support from the Ford Foundation in
1959. His first novel was the autobiographical* Go Tell It on the Mountain *(1953),
followed by the essay collection* Notes of a Native Son *(1955).*

Many novels have followed, and many essays. The Fire Next Time *(1963) was a
crucial document in the struggle for civil rights that occupied the sixties before the
Vietnam War took center stage. Although fiction has been his chief calling, outrage
has led James Baldwin into nonfiction. "One writes out of one thing only — one's
own experience," he says. "Everything depends on how relentlessly one forces from*

this experience the last drop, sweet or bitter, it can possibly give. This is the only real concern of the artist, to recreate out of the disorder of life that order which is art.''

Baldwin's title to this essay refers to Richard Wright's novel Native Son *(1940), which tells the story of a black man raised in Chicago's ghetto who turns to violence to express his outrage. Writing directly out of his experience, Baldwin uses the personal essay, in clear and forceful prose, to move beyond autobiography toward social analysis and urgent moral thought.*

Notes of
a Native Son

On the 29th of July, in 1943, my father died. On the same day, a few   1
hours later, his last child was born. Over a month before this, while all our energies were concentrated in waiting for these events, there had been, in Detroit, one of the bloodiest race riots of the century. A few hours after my father's funeral, while he lay in state in the undertaker's chapel, a race riot broke out in Harlem. On the morning of the 3rd of August, we drove my father to the graveyard through a wilderness of smashed plate glass.

The day of my father's funeral had also been my nineteenth birthday. As   2
we drove him to the graveyard, the spoils of injustice, anarchy, discontent, and hatred were all around us. It seemed to me that God himself had devised, to mark my father's end, the most sustained and brutally dissonant of codas. And it seemed to me, too, that the violence which rose all about us as my father left the world had been devised as a corrective for the pride of his eldest son. I had declined to believe in that apocalypse which had been central to my father's vision; very well, life seemed to be saying, here is something that will certainly pass for an apocalypse until the real thing comes along. I had inclined to be contemptuous of my father for the conditions of his life, for the conditions of our lives. When his life had ended I began to wonder about that life and also, in a new way, to be apprehensive about my own.

I had not known my father very well. We had got on badly, partly be-   3
cause we shared, in our different fashions, the vice of stubborn pride. When he was dead I realized that I had hardly ever spoken to him. When he had been dead a long time I began to wish I had. It seems to be typical of life in America, where opportunities, real and fancied, are thicker than anywhere else on the globe, that the second generation has no time to talk to the first. No one, including my father, seems to have known exactly how old he was,

but his mother had been born during slavery. He was of the first generation of free men. He, along with thousands of other Negroes, came North after 1919 and I was part of that generation which had never seen the landscape of what Negroes sometimes call the Old Country.

He had been born in New Orleans and had been a quite young man there during the time that Louis Armstrong, a boy, was running errands for the dives and honky-tonks of what was always presented to me as one of the most wicked of cities — to this day, whenever I think of New Orleans, I also helplessly think of Sodom and Gomorrah. My father never mentioned Louis Armstrong, except to forbid us to play his records; but there was a picture of him on our wall for a long time. One of my father's strong-willed female relatives had placed it there and forbade my father to take it down. He never did, but he eventually maneuvered her out of the house and when, some years later, she was in trouble and near death, he refused to do anything to help her.

He was, I think, very handsome. I gather this from photographs and from my own memories of him, dressed in his Sunday best and on his way to preach a sermon somewhere, when I was little. Handsome, proud, and ingrown, "like a toe-nail," somebody said. But he looked to me, as I grew older, like pictures I had seen of African tribal chieftains: he really should have been naked, with war-paint on and barbaric mementos, standing among spears. He could be chilling in the pulpit and indescribably cruel in his personal life and he was certainly the most bitter man I have ever met; yet it must be said that there was something else in him, buried in him, which lent him his tremendous power and, even, a rather crushing charm. It had something to do with his blackness, I think — he was very black — with his blackness and his beauty, and with the fact that he knew that he was black but did not know that he was beautiful. He claimed to be proud of his blackness but it had also been the cause of much humiliation and it had fixed bleak boundaries to his life. He was not a young man when we were growing up and he had already suffered many kinds of ruin; in his outrageously demanding and protective way he loved his children, who were black like him and menaced, like him; and all these things sometimes showed in his face when he tried, never to my knowledge with any success, to establish contact with any of us. When he took one of his children on his knee to play, the child always became fretful and began to cry; when he tried to help one of us with our homework the absolutely unabating tension which emanated from him caused our minds and our tongues to become paralyzed, so that he, scarcely knowing why, flew into a rage and the child, not knowing why, was punished. If it ever entered his head to bring a surprise home for his children, it was, almost unfailingly, the wrong surprise and even the big watermelons he often brought home on his back in the summertime led to the most appalling scenes. I do not remember, in all those years, that one of his children was ever glad to see him come home. From what I was able to gather of his early life, it seemed that this inability to establish contact with other people had always marked him and had been one of the things which had driven him out of New Orleans. There was something in him, therefore, groping and tentative, which was never expressed and which was buried with him. One saw it most clearly when he was facing new people and hoping to impress them. But he never did, not for long. We went from church to smaller and more improbable church, he found himself in less and less demand as a minister, and by the time he died none of his friends had come to see him for a long time. He had lived and died in an intolerable bitterness of spirit and it frightened me, as we drove him to the graveyard through those unquiet, ruined streets, to see how powerful and overflowing this bitterness could be and to realize that this bitterness now was mine.

When he died I had been away from home for a little over a year. In that year I had had time to become aware of the meaning of all my father's bitter warnings, had discovered the secret of his proudly pursed lips and rigid carriage: I had discovered the weight of white people in the world. I saw that this had been for my ancestors and now would be for me an awful thing to live with and that the bitterness which had helped to kill my father could also kill me.

He had been ill a long time — in the mind, as we now realized, reliving instances of his fantastic intransigence in the new light of his affliction and endeavoring to feel a sorrow for him which never, quite, came true. We had not known that he was being eaten up by paranoia, and the discovery that his cruelty, to our bodies and our minds, had been one of the symptoms of his illness was not, then, enough to enable us to forgive him. The younger children felt, quite simply, relief that he would not be coming home anymore. My mother's observation that it was he, after all, who had kept them alive all these years meant nothing because the problems of keeping children alive are not real for children. The older children felt, with my father gone, that they could invite their friends to the house without fear that their friends would be insulted or, as had sometimes happened with me, being told that their friends were in league with the devil and intended to rob our family of everything we owned. (I didn't fail to wonder, and it made me hate him, what on earth we owned that anybody else would want.)

His illness was beyond all hope of healing before anyone realized that he was ill. He had always been so strange and had lived, like a prophet, in such unimaginably close communion with the Lord that his long silences which were punctuated by moans and hallelujahs and snatches of old songs while he sat at the living-room window never seemed odd to us. It was not until he refused to eat because, he said, his family was trying to poison him that my mother was forced to accept as a fact what had, until then, been only an unwilling suspicion. When he was committed it was discovered that he had

167

tuberculosis and, as it turned out, the disease of his mind allowed the disease of his body to destroy him. For the doctors could not force him to eat, either, and, though he was fed intravenously, it was clear from the beginning that there was no hope for him.

In my mind's eye I could see him, sitting at the window, locked up in his terrors; hating and fearing every living soul including his children who had betrayed him, too, by reaching towards the world which had despised him. There were nine of us. I began to wonder what it could have felt like for such a man to have had nine children whom he could barely feed. He used to make jokes about our poverty, which never, of course, seemed very funny to us; they could not have seemed very funny to him, either, or else our all too feeble response to them would never have caused such rages. He spent great energy and achieved, to our chagrin, no small amount of success in keeping us away from the people who surrounded us, people who had all-night rent parties to which we listened when we should have been sleeping, people who cursed and drank and flashed razor blades on Lenox Avenue. He could not understand why, if they had so much energy to spare, they could not use it to make their lives better. He treated almost everybody on our block with a most uncharitable asperity and neither they, nor, of course, their children were slow to reciprocate.

The only white people who came to our house were welfare workers and bill collectors. It was almost always my mother who dealt with them, for my father's temper, which was at the mercy of his pride, was never to be trusted. It was clear that he felt their very presence in his home to be a violation: this was conveyed by his carriage, almost ludicrously stiff, and by his voice, harsh and vindictively polite. When I was around nine or ten I wrote a play which was directed by a young, white schoolteacher, a woman, who then took an interest in me, and gave me books to read and, in order to corroborate my theatrical bent, decided to take me to see what she somewhat tactlessly referred to as "real" plays. Theater-going was forbidden in our house, but, with the really cruel intuitiveness of a child, I suspected that the color of this woman's skin would carry the day for me. When, at school, she suggested taking me to the theater, I did not, as I might have done if she had been a Negro, find a way of discouraging her, but agreed that she should pick me up at my house one evening. I then, very cleverly, left all the rest to my mother, who suggested to my father, as I knew she would, that it would not be very nice to let such a kind woman make the trip for nothing. Also, since it was a schoolteacher, I imagine that my mother countered the idea of sin with the idea of "education," which word, even with my father, carried a kind of bitter weight.

Before the teacher came my father took me aside to ask *why* she was coming, what *interest* she could possibly have in our house, in a boy like me. I said I didn't know but I, too, suggested that it had something to do with education. And I understood that my father was waiting for me to say something — I didn't quite know what; perhaps that I wanted his protection against this teacher and her "education." I said none of these things and the teacher came and we went out. It was clear, during the brief interview in our living room, that my father was agreeing very much against his will and that he would have refused permission if he had dared. The fact that he did not dare caused me to despise him: I had no way of knowing that he was facing in that living room a wholly unprecedented and frightening situation.

Later, when my father had been laid off from his job, this woman became 12 very important to us. She was really a very sweet and generous woman and went to a great deal of trouble to be of help to us, particularly during one awful winter. My mother called her by the highest name she knew: she said she was a "christian." My father could scarcely disagree but during the four or five years of our relatively close association he never trusted her and was always trying to surprise in her open, Midwestern face the genuine, cunningly hidden, hideous motivation. In later years, particularly when it began to be clear that this "education" of mine was going to lead me to perdition, he became more explicit and warned me that my white friends in high school were not really my friends and that I would see, when I was older, how white people would do anything to keep a Negro down. Some of them could be nice, he admitted, but none of them were to be trusted and most of them were not even nice. The best thing was to have as little to do with them as possible. I did not feel this way and I was certain, in my innocence, that I never would.

But the year which preceded my father's death had made a great change 13 in my life. I had been living in New Jersey, working in defense plants, working and living among southerners, white and black. I knew about the south, of course, and about how southerners treated Negroes and how they expected them to behave, but it had never entered my mind that anyone would look at me and expect *me* to behave that way. I learned in New Jersey that to be a Negro meant, precisely, that one was never looked at but was simply at the mercy of the reflexes the color of one's skin caused in other people. I acted in New Jersey as I had always acted, that is as though I thought a great deal of myself — I had to *act* that way — with results that were, simply, unbelievable. I had scarcely arrived before I had earned the enmity, which was extraordinarily ingenious, of all my superiors and nearly all my co-workers. In the beginning, to make matters worse, I simply did not know what was happening. I did not know what I had done, and I shortly began to wonder what *anyone* could possibly do, to bring about such unanimous, active, and unbearably vocal hostility. I knew about jim-crow° but I

---

jim-crow From Jim Crow, a black stereotype in a nineteenth-century song; used to refer to racist discrimination, especially that supported by law or custom.

had never experienced it. I went to the same self-service restaurant three times and stood with all the Princeton boys before the counter, waiting for a hamburger and coffee; it was always an extraordinarily long time before anything was set before me; but it was not until the fourth visit that I learned that, in fact, nothing had ever been set before me: I had simply picked something up. Negroes were not served there, I was told, and they had been waiting for me to realize that I was always the only Negro present. Once I was told this, I determined to go there all the time. But now they were ready for me and, though some dreadful scenes were subsequently enacted in that restaurant, I never ate there again.

It was the same story all over New Jersey, in bars, bowling alleys, diners, places to live. I was always being forced to leave, silently, or with mutual imprecations. I very shortly became notorious and children giggled behind me when I passed and their elders whispered or shouted — they really believed that I was mad. And it did begin to work on my mind, of course; I began to be afraid to go anywhere and to compensate for this I went places to which I really should not have gone and where, God knows, I had no desire to be. My reputation in town naturally enhanced my reputation at work and my working day became one long series of acrobatics designed to keep me out of trouble. I cannot say that these acrobatics succeeded. It began to seem that the machinery of the organization I worked for was turning over, day and night, with but one aim: to eject me. I was fired once, and contrived, with the aid of a friend from New York, to get back on the payroll; was fired again, and bounced back again. It took a while to fire me for the third time, but the third time took. There were no loopholes anywhere. There was not even any way of getting back inside the gates.

That year in New Jersey lives in my mind as though it were the year during which, having an unsuspected predilection for it, I first contracted some dread, chronic disease, the unfailing symptom of which is a kind of blind fever, a pounding in the skull and fire in the bowels. Once this disease is contracted, one can never be really carefree again, for the fever, without an instant's warning, can recur at any moment. It can wreck more important things than race relations. There is not a Negro alive who does not have this rage in his blood — one has the choice, merely, of living with it consciously or surrendering to it. As for me, this fever has recurred in me, and does, and will until the day I die.

My last night in New Jersey, a white friend from New York took me to the nearest big town, Trenton, to go to the movies and have a few drinks. As it turned out, he also saved me from, at the very least, a violent whipping. Almost every detail of that night stands out very clearly in my memory. I even remember the name of the movie we saw because its title impressed me as being so patly ironical. It was a movie about the German occupation of France, starring Maureen O'Hara and Charles Laughton and called *This*

Land Is Mine. I remember the name of the diner we walked into when the movie ended: it was the "American Diner." When we walked in the counterman asked what we wanted and I remember answering with the casual sharpness which had become my habit: "We want a hamburger and a cup of coffee, what do you think we want?" I do not know why, after a year of such rebuffs, I so completely failed to anticipate his answer, which was, of course, "We don't serve Negroes here." This reply failed to discompose me, at least for the moment. I made some sardonic comment about the name of the diner and we walked out into the streets.

This was the time of what was called the "brown-out," when the lights 17 in all American cities were very dim. When we re-entered the streets something happened to me which had the force of an optical illusion, or a nightmare. The streets were very crowded and I was facing north. People were moving in every direction but it seemed to me, in that instant, that all of the people I could see, and many more than that, were moving toward me, against me, and that everyone was white. I remember how their faces gleamed. And I felt, like a physical sensation, a *click* at the nape of my neck as though some interior string connecting my head to my body had been cut. I began to walk. I heard my friend call after me, but I ignored him. Heaven only knows what was going on in his mind, but he had the good sense not to touch me — I don't know what would have happened if he had — and to keep me in sight. I don't know what was going on in my mind, either; I certainly had no conscious plan. I wanted to do something to crush these white faces, which were crushing me. I walked for perhaps a block or two until I came to an enormous, glittering, and fashionable restaurant in which I knew not even the intercession of the Virgin would cause me to be served. I pushed through the doors and took the first vacant seat I saw, at a table for two, and waited.

I do not know how long I waited and I rather wonder, until today, what I 18 could possibly have looked like. Whatever I looked like, I frightened the waitress who shortly appeared, and the moment she appeared all of my fury flowed towards her. I hated her for her white face, and for her great, astounded, frightened eyes. I felt that if she found a black man so frightening I would make her fright worth-while.

She did not ask me what I wanted, but repeated, as though she had 19 learned it somewhere, "We don't serve Negroes here." She did not say it with the blunt, derisive hostility to which I had grown so accustomed, but, rather, with a note of apology in her voice, and fear. This made me colder and more murderous than ever. I felt I had to do something with my hands. I wanted her to come close enough for me to get her neck between my hands.

So I pretended not to have understood her, hoping to draw her closer. 20 And she did step a very short step closer, with her pencil poised incongruously over her pad, and repeated the formula: ''. . . don't serve Negroes here.''

Somehow, with the repetition of that phrase, which was already ringing in my head like a thousand bells of a nightmare, I realized that she would never come any closer and that I would have to strike from a distance. There was nothing on the table but an ordinary water-mug half full of water, and I picked this up and hurled it with all my strength at her. She ducked and it missed her and shattered against the mirror behind the bar. And, with that sound, my frozen blood abruptly thawed, I returned from wherever I had been, I *saw*, for the first time, the restaurant, the people with their mouths open, already, as it seemed to me, rising as one man, and I realized what I had done, and where I was, and I was frightened. I rose and began running for the door. A round, potbellied man grabbed me by the nape of the neck just as I reached the doors and began to beat me about the face. I kicked him and got loose and ran into the streets. My friend whispered, *''Run!''* and I ran.

My friend stayed outside the restaurant long enough to misdirect my pursuers and the police, who arrived, he told me, at once. I do not know what I said to him when he came to my room that night. I could not have said much. I felt, in the oddest, most awful way, that I had somehow betrayed him. I lived it over and over and over again, the way one relives an automobile accident after it has happened and one finds oneself alone and safe. I could not get over two facts, both equally difficult for the imagination to grasp, and one was that I could have been murdered. But the other was that I had been ready to commit murder. I saw nothing very clearly but I did see this: that my life, my *real* life, was in danger, and not from anything other people might do but from the hatred I carried in my own heart.

II

I had returned home around the second week in June — in great haste because it seemed that my father's death and my mother's confinement were both but a matter of hours. In the case of my mother, it soon became clear that she had simply made a miscalculation. This had always been her tendency and I don't believe that a single one of us arrived in the world, or has since arrived anywhere else, on time. But none of us dawdled so intolerably about the business of being born as did my baby sister. We sometimes amused ourselves, during those endless, stifling weeks, by picturing the baby sitting within in the safe, warm dark, bitterly regretting the necessity of becoming a part of our chaos and stubbornly putting it off as long as possible. I understood her perfectly and congratulated her on showing such good sense so soon. Death, however, sat as purposefully at my father's bedside as life stirred within my mother's womb and it was harder to understand why he so lingered in that long shadow. It seemed that he had bent, and for a long time, too, all of his energies towards dying. Now death was ready for him but my father held back.

All of Harlem, indeed, seemed to be infected by waiting. I had never before known it to be so violently still. Racial tensions throughout this country were exacerbated during the early years of the war, partly because the labor market brought together hundreds of thousands of ill-prepared people and partly because Negro soldiers, regardless of where they were born, received their military training in the south. What happened in defense plants and army camps had repercussions, naturally, in every Negro ghetto. The situation in Harlem had grown bad enough for clergymen, policemen, educators, politicians, and social workers to assert in one breath that there was no "crime wave" and to offer, in the very next breath, suggestions as to how to combat it. These suggestions always seemed to involve playgrounds, despite the fact that racial skirmishes were occurring in the playgrounds, too. Playground or not, crime wave or not, the Harlem police force had been augmented in March, and the unrest grew — perhaps, in fact, partly as a result of the ghetto's instinctive hatred of policemen. Perhaps the most revealing news item, out of the steady parade of reports of muggings, stabbings, shootings, assaults, gang wars, and accusations of police brutality, is the item concerning six Negro girls who set upon a white girl in the subway because, as they all too accurately put it, she was stepping on their toes. Indeed she was, all over the nation.

I had never before been so aware of policemen, on foot, on horseback, on corners, everywhere, always two by two. Nor had I ever been so aware of small knots of people. They were on stoops and on corners and in doorways, and what was striking about them, I think, was that they did not seem to be talking. Never, when I passed these groups, did the usual sound of a curse or a laugh ring out and neither did there seem to be any hum of gossip. There was certainly, on the other hand, occurring between them communication extraordinarily intense. Another thing that was striking was the unexpected diversity of the people who made up these groups. Usually, for example, one would see a group of sharpies standing on the street corner, jiving the passing chicks; or a group of older men, usually, for some reason, in the vicinity of a barber shop, discussing baseball scores, or the numbers, or making rather chilling observations about women they had known. Women, in a general way, tended to be seen less often together — unless they were church women, or very young girls, or prostitutes met together for an unprofessional instant. But that summer I saw the strangest combinations: large, respectable, churchly matrons standing on the stoops or the corners with their hair tied up, together with a girl in sleazy satin whose face bore the marks of gin and the razor, or heavy-set, abrupt, no-nonsense older men, in company with the most disreputable and fanatical "race" men, or these same "race" men with the sharpies, or these sharpies with the churchly women. Seventh Day Adventists and Methodists and Spiritualists seemed to be hobnobbing with Holyrollers and they were all, alike, entangled with the most flagrant disbelievers; something heavy in their stance seemed to indicate that they had all, incredibly, seen a common vision, and on each face there seemed to be the same strange, bitter shadow.

The churchly women and the matter-of-fact, no-nonsense men had children in the Army. The sleazy girls they talked to had lovers there, the sharpies and the "race" men had friends and brothers there. It would have demanded an unquestioning patriotism, happily as uncommon in this country as it is undesirable, for these people not to have been disturbed by the bitter letters they received, by the newspaper stories they read, not to have been enraged by the posters, then to be found all over New York, which described the Japanese as "yellow-bellied Japs." It was only the "race" men, to be sure, who spoke ceaselessly of being revenged — how this vengeance was to be exacted was not clear — for the indignities and dangers suffered by Negro boys in uniform; but everybody felt a directionless, hopeless bitterness, as well as that panic which can scarcely be suppressed when one knows that a human being one loves is beyond one's reach, and in danger. This helplessness and this gnawing uneasiness does something, at length, to even the toughest mind. Perhaps the best way to sum all this up is to say that the people I knew felt, mainly, a peculiar kind of relief when they knew that their boys were being shipped out of the south, to do battle overseas. It was, perhaps, like feeling that the most dangerous part of a dangerous journey had been passed and that now, even if death should come, it would come with honor and without the complicity of their countrymen. Such a death would be, in short, a fact with which one could hope to live.

It was on the 28th of July, which I believe was a Wednesday, that I visited my father for the first time during his illness and for the last time in his life. The moment I saw him I knew why I put off this visit so long. I had told my mother that I did not want to see him because I hated him. But this was not true. It was only that I *had* hated him and I wanted to hold on to this hatred. I did not want to look on him as a ruin: it was not a ruin I had hated. I imagine that one of the reasons people cling to their hates so stubbornly is because they sense, once hate is gone, that they will be forced to deal with pain.

We traveled out to him, his older sister and myself, to what seemed to be the very end of a very Long Island. It was hot and dusty and we wrangled, my aunt and I, all the way out, over the fact that I had recently begun to smoke and, as she said, to give myself airs. But I knew that she wrangled with me because she could not bear to face the fact of her brother's dying. Neither could I endure the reality of her despair, her unstated bafflement as to what had happened to her brother's life, and her own. So we wrangled and I smoked and from time to time she fell into a heavy reverie. Covertly, I watched her face, which was the face of an old woman; it had fallen in, the eyes were sunken and lightless; soon she would be dying, too.

In my childhood — it had not been so long ago — I had thought her beau- 29 tiful. She had been quick-witted and quick-moving and very generous with all the children and each of her visits had been an event. At one time one of my brothers and myself had thought of running away to live with her. Now she could no longer produce out of her handbag some unexpected and yet familiar delight. She made me feel pity and revulsion and fear. It was awful to realize that she no longer caused me to feel affection. The closer we came to the hospital the more querulous she became and at the same time, natu- rally, grew more dependent on me. Between pity and guilt and fear I began to feel that there was another me trapped in my skull like a jack-in-the-box who might escape my control at any moment and fill the air with screaming.

She began to cry the moment we entered the room and she saw him ly- 30 ing there, all shriveled and still, like a little black monkey. The great, gleam- ing apparatus which fed him and would have compelled him to be still even if he had been able to move brought to mind, not beneficence, but torture; the tubes entering his arm made me think of pictures I had seen when a child, of Gulliver, tied down by the pygmies on that island. My aunt wept and wept, there was a whistling sound in my father's throat; nothing was said, he could not speak. I wanted to take his hand, to say something. But I do not know what I could have said, even if he could have heard me. He was not really in that room with us, he had at last really embarked on his journey; and though my aunt told me that he said he was going to meet Jesus, I did not hear anything except that whistling in his throat. The doctor came back and we left, into that unbearable train again, and home. In the morning came the telegram saying that he was dead. Then the house was suddenly full of relatives, friends, hysteria, and confusion and I quickly left my mother and the children to the care of those impressive women, who, in Negro communities at least, automatically appear at times of bereavement armed with lotions, proverbs, and patience, and an ability to cook. I went downtown. By the time I returned, later the same day, my mother had been carried to the hospital and the baby had been born.

III

For my father's funeral I had nothing black to wear and this posed a nag- 31 ging problem all day long. It was one of those problems, simple, or impos- sible of solution, to which the mind insanely clings in order to avoid the mind's real trouble. I spent most of that day at the downtown apartment of a girl I knew, celebrating my birthday with whiskey and wondering what to wear that night. When planning a birthday celebration one naturally does not expect that it will be up against competition from a funeral and this girl had anticipated taking me out that night, for a big dinner and a night club afterwards. Sometime during the course of that long day we decided that we would go out anyway, when my father's funeral service was over. I imagine *I* decided it, since, as the funeral hour approached, it became clearer and clearer to me that I would not know what to do with myself when it was over. The girl, stifling her very lively concern as to the possible effects of the whiskey on one of my father's chief mourners, concentrated on being conciliatory and practically helpful. She found a black shirt for me somewhere and ironed it and, dressed in the darkest pants and jacket I owned, and slightly drunk, I made my way to my father's funeral.

The chapel was full, but not packed, and very quiet. There were, mainly, my father's relatives, and his children, and here and there I saw faces I had not seen since childhood, the faces of my father's one-time friends. They were very dark and solemn now, seeming somehow to suggest that they had known all along that something like this would happen. Chief among the mourners was my aunt, who had quarreled with my father all his life; by which I do not mean to suggest that her mourning was insincere or that she had not loved him. I suppose that she was one of the few people in the world who had, and their incessant quarreling proved precisely the strength of the tie that bound them. The only other person in the world, as far as I knew, whose relationship to my father rivaled my aunt's in depth was my mother, who was not there.

It seemed to me, of course, that it was a very long funeral. But it was, if anything, a rather shorter funeral than most, nor, since there were no overwhelming, uncontrollable expressions of grief, could it be called — if I dare to use the word — successful. The minister who preached my father's funeral sermon was one of the few my father had still been seeing as he neared his end. He presented to us in his sermon a man whom none of us had ever seen — a man thoughtful, patient, and forbearing, a Christian inspiration to all who knew him, and a model for his children. And no doubt the children, in their disturbed and guilty state, were almost ready to believe this; he had been remote enough to be anything and, anyway, the shock of the incontrovertible, that it was really our father lying up there in that casket, prepared the mind for anything. His sister moaned and this grief-stricken moaning was taken as corroboration. The other faces held a dark, non-committal thoughtfulness. This was not the man they had known, but they had scarcely expected to be confronted with *him*; this was, in a sense deeper than questions of fact, the man they had not known, and the man they had not known may have been the real one. The real man, whoever he had been, had suffered and now he was dead: this was all that was sure and all that mattered now. Every man in the chapel hoped that when his hour came he, too, would be eulogized, which is to say forgiven, and that all of his lapses, greeds, errors, and strayings from the truth would be invested with coherence and looked upon with charity. This was perhaps the last thing human beings could give each other and it was what they demanded, after all, of the Lord. Only the Lord saw the midnight tears, only He was present when one of His children, moaning and wringing hands, paced up and down the room. When one slapped one's child in anger the recoil in the heart reverberated through heaven and became part of the pain of the universe. And when the children were hungry and sullen and distrustful and one watched them, daily, growing wilder, and further away, and running headlong into danger, it was the Lord who knew what the charged heart endured as the strap was laid to the backside; the Lord alone who knew what one *would* have said if one had had, like the Lord, the gift of the living word. It was the Lord who knew of the impossibility every parent in that room faced: how to prepare the child for the day when the child would be despised and how to *create* in the child — by what means? — a stronger antidote to this poison than one had found for oneself. The avenues, side streets, bars, billiard halls, hospitals, police stations, and even the playgrounds of Harlem — not to mention the houses of correction, the jails, and the morgue — testified to the potency of the poison while remaining silent as to the efficacy of whatever antidote, irresistibly raising the question of whether or not such an antidote existed; raising, which was worse, the question of whether or not an antidote was desirable; perhaps poison should be fought with poison. With these several schisms in the mind and with more terrors in the heart than could be named, it was better not to judge the man who had gone down under an impossible burden. It was better to remember: *Thou knowest this man's fall; but thou knowest not his wrassling.*

While the preacher talked and I watched the children — years of changing their diapers, scrubbing them, slapping them, taking them to school, and scolding them had had the perhaps inevitable result of making me love them, though I am not sure I knew this then — my mind was busily breaking out with a rash of disconnected impressions. Snatches of popular songs, indecent jokes, bits of books I had read, movie sequences, faces, voices, political issues — I thought I was going mad; all these impressions suspended, as it were, in the solution of the faint nausea produced in me by the heat and liquor. For a moment I had the impression that my alcoholic breath, inefficiently disguised with chewing gum, filled the entire chapel. Then someone began singing one of my father's favorite songs and, abruptly, I was with him, sitting on his knee, in the hot, enormous, crowded church which was the first church we attended. It was the Abyssinia Baptist Church on 138th Street. We had not gone there long. With this image, a host of others came. I had forgotten, in the rage of my growing up, how proud my father had been of me when I was little. Apparently, I had had a voice and my father had liked to show me off before the members of the church. I had forgotten what he had looked like when he was pleased but now I remembered that he had always been grinning with pleasure when my solos ended. I even remembered certain expressions on his face when he teased my mother — had he loved her? I would never know. And when had it all begun to change? For now it seemed that he had not always been cruel. I remembered being taken for a haircut and scraping my knee on the footrest of the barber's chair and I remembered my father's face as he soothed my crying and applied the stinging iodine. Then I remembered our fights, fights which had been of the worst possible kind because my technique had been silence.

I remembered the one time in all our life together when we had really spoken to each other.

It was on a Sunday and it must have been shortly before I left home. We were walking, just the two of us, in our usual silence, to or from church. I was in high school and had been doing a lot of writing and I was, at about this time, the editor of the high school magazine. But I had also been a Young Minister and had been preaching from the pulpit. Lately, I had been taking fewer engagements and preached as rarely as possible. It was said in the church, quite truthfully, that I was "cooling off."

My father asked me abruptly, "You'd rather write than preach, wouldn't you?"

I was astonished at his question — because it was a real question. I answered, "Yes."

That was all we said. It was awful to remember that that was all we had *ever* said.

The casket now was opened and the mourners were being led up the aisle to look for the last time on the deceased. The assumption was that the family was too overcome with grief to be allowed to make this journey alone and I watched while my aunt was led to the casket and, muffled in black, and shaking, led back to her seat. I disapproved of forcing the children to look on their dead father, considering that the shock of his death, or, more truthfully, the shock of death as a reality, was already a little more than a child could bear, but my judgment in this matter had been overruled and there they were, bewildered and frightened and very small, being led, one by one, to the casket. But there is also something very gallant about children at such moments. It has something to do with their silence and gravity and with the fact that one cannot help them. Their legs, somehow, seem *exposed*, so that it is at once incredible and terribly clear that their legs are all they have to hold them up.

I had not wanted to go to the casket myself and I certainly had not wished to be led there, but there was no way of avoiding either of these forms. One of the deacons led me up and I looked on my father's face. I cannot say that it looked like him at all. His blackness had been equivocated by powder and there was no suggestion in that casket of what his power had or could have been. He was simply an old man dead, and it was hard to believe that he had ever given anyone either joy or pain. Yet, his life filled that room. Further up the avenue his wife was holding his newborn child. Life and death so close together, and love and hatred, and right and wrong, said something to me which I did not want to hear concerning man, concerning the life of man.

After the funeral, while I was downtown desperately celebrating my   42
birthday, a Negro soldier, in the lobby of the Hotel Braddock, got into a fight with a white policeman over a Negro girl. Negro girls, white policemen, in or out of uniform, and Negro males — in or out of uniform — were part of the furniture of the lobby of the Hotel Braddock and this was certainly not the first time such an incident had occurred. It was destined, however, to receive an unprecedented publicity, for the fight between the policeman and the soldier ended with the shooting of the soldier. Rumor, flowing immediately to the streets outside, stated that the soldier had been shot in the back, an instantaneous and revealing invention, and that the soldier had died protecting a Negro woman. The facts were somewhat different — for example, the soldier had not been shot in the back, and was not dead, and the girl seems to have been as dubious a symbol of womanhood as her white counterpart in Georgia usually is, but no one was interested in the facts. They preferred the invention because this invention expressed and corroborated their hates and fears so perfectly. It is just as well to remember that people are always doing this. Perhaps many of those legends, including Christianity, to which the world clings began their conquest of the world with just some such concerted surrender to distortion. The effect, in Harlem, of this particular legend was like the effect of a lit match in a tin of gasoline. The mob gathered before the doors of the Hotel Braddock simply began to swell and to spread in every direction, and Harlem exploded.

The mob did not cross the ghetto lines. It would have been easy, for ex-   43
ample, to have gone over Morningside Park on the west side or to have crossed the Grand Central railroad tracks at 125th Street on the east side, to wreak havoc in white neighborhoods. The mob seems to have been mainly interested in something more potent and real than the white face, that is, in white power, and the principal damage done during the riot of the summer of 1943 was to white business establishments in Harlem. It might have been a far bloodier story, of course, if, at the hour the riot began, these establishments had still been open. From the Hotel Braddock the mob fanned out, east and west along 125th Street, and for the entire length of Lenox, Seventh, and Eighth avenues. Along each of these avenues, and along each major side street — 116th, 125th, 135th, and so on — bars, stores, pawnshops, restaurants, even little luncheonettes had been smashed open and entered and looted — looted, it might be added, with more haste than efficiency. The shelves really looked as though a bomb had struck them. Cans of beans and

soup and dog food, along with toilet paper, corn flakes, sardines, and milk tumbled every which way, and abandoned cash registers and cases of beer leaned crazily out of the splintered windows and were strewn along the avenues. Sheets, blankets, and clothing of every description formed a kind of path, as though people had dropped them while running. I truly had not realized that Harlem *had* so many stores until I saw them all smashed open; the first time the word *wealth* ever entered my mind in relation to Harlem was when I saw it scattered in the streets. But one's first, incongruous impression of plenty was countered immediately by an impression of waste. None of this was doing anybody any good. It would have been better to have left the plate glass as it had been and goods lying in the stores.

It would have been better, but it would also have been intolerable, for Harlem had needed something to smash. To smash something is the ghetto's chronic need. Most of the time it is the members of the ghetto who smash each other, and themselves. But as long as the ghetto walls are standing there will always come a moment when these outlets do not work. That summer, for example, it was not enough to get into a fight on Lenox Avenue, or curse out one's cronies in the barber shops. If ever, indeed, the violence which fills Harlem's churches, pool halls, and bars erupts outward in a more direct fashion, Harlem and its citizens are likely to vanish in an apocalyptic flood. That this is not likely to happen is due to a great many reasons, most hidden and powerful among them the Negro's real relation to the white American. This relation prohibits, simply, anything as uncomplicated and satisfactory as pure hatred. In order really to hate white people, one has to blot so much out of the mind — and the heart — that this hatred itself becomes an exhausting and self-destructive pose. But this does not mean, on the other hand, that love comes easily: the white world is too powerful, too complacent, too ready with gratuitous humiliation, and, above all, too ignorant and too innocent for that. One is absolutely forced to make perpetual qualifications and one's own reactions are always canceling each other out. It is this, really, which has driven so many people mad, both white and black. One is always in the position of having to decide between amputation and gangrene. Amputation is swift but time may prove that the amputation was not necessary—or one may delay the amputation too long. Gangrene is slow, but it is impossible to be sure that one is reading one's symptoms right. The idea of going through life as a cripple is more than one can bear, and equally unbearable is the risk of swelling up slowly, in agony, with poison. And the trouble, finally, is that the risks are real even if the choices do not exist.

"But as for me and my house," my father had said, "we will serve the Lord." I wondered, as we drove him to his resting place, what this line had meant for him. I had heard him preach it many times. I had preached it once myself, proudly giving it an interpretation different from my father's. Now the whole thing came back to me, as though my father and I were on our way to Sunday school and I were memorizing the golden text: *And if it seem evil unto you to serve the Lord, choose you this day whom you will serve; whether the gods which your fathers served that were on the other side of the flood, or the gods of the Amorites, in whose land ye dwell: but as for me and my house, we will serve the Lord.* I suspected in these familiar lines a meaning which had never been there for me before. All of my father's texts and songs, which I had decided were meaningless, were arranged before me at his death like empty bottles, waiting to hold the meaning which life would give them for me. This was his legacy: nothing is ever escaped. That bleakly memorable morning I hated the unbelievable streets and the Negroes and whites who had, equally, made them that way. But I knew that it was folly, as my father would have said, this bitterness was folly. It was necessary to hold on to the things that mattered. The dead man mattered, the new life mattered; blackness and whiteness did not matter; to believe that they did was to acquiesce in one's own destruction. Hatred, which could destroy so much, never failed to destroy the man who hated and this was an immutable law.

It began to seem that one would have to hold in the mind forever two 46 ideas which seemed to be in opposition. The first idea was acceptance, the acceptance, totally without rancor, of life as it is, and men as they are: in the light of this idea, it goes without saying that injustice is a commonplace. But this did not mean that one could be complacent, for the second idea was of equal power: that one must never, in one's own life, accept these injustices as commonplace but must fight them with all one's strength. This fight begins, however, in the heart and it now had been laid to my charge to keep my own heart free of hatred and despair. This intimation made my heart heavy and, now that my father was irrecoverable, I wished that he had been beside me so I could have searched his face for the answers which only the future would give me now.

QUESTIONS ON MEANING

1. For Baldwin, the death of his father came as a life-changing shock: It altered the meaning of the past and it offered unsettling intimations of the future. How are Baldwin and his father alike? How do they differ? What do they discuss "the one time in all our life together when we had really spoken to each other"? How does Baldwin finally feel about his father's death?
2. What is Baldwin's "dread, chronic disease" (paragraph 15)? How does it relate to his father's disease?

3. In the grip of his mental illness, Baldwin's father felt that his children had betrayed him "by reaching towards the world which had despised him" (paragraph 9). What world is it? How does Baldwin show himself reaching toward this world?

4. During the year before his father's death, Baldwin discovered "the weight of white people in this world." What contributed to this discovery? What did his discovery lead him to do? How does he relate this discovery to his understanding of his father?

QUESTIONS ON STRATEGY

1. Like Fussell, Baldwin calls his essay "notes." Are the two essays organized similarly? Which has a looser structure and more informal language? Is one less effective than the other? Why?

2. "Notes of a Native Son" was published in 1955. Usage has changed since then. What does Baldwin mean by *blackness* in paragraphs 5 and 41? How does his meaning differ from the meaning of that word today?

3. Paragraph 24 provides transition from Baldwin's family situation to the crisis in Harlem. When else does Baldwin parallel his family's circumstances and those of society?

4. Baldwin's narrative skill is evident throughout "Notes of a Native Son." Paragraphs 16 through 22 and paragraphs 32 through 41 are self-contained narratives. How do Baldwin's powers of description and his memory and imagination amplify these narratives and connect them to his points in the essay?

EXPLORATIONS

1. One problem facing the autobiographer is his strategy of disclosure: how much he needs to tell, what he should leave out, what he should emphasize. Read Baldwin's novel *Go Tell It on the Mountain*. Compare the fact of this essay with the fiction of the novel. Which seems more candid in its autobiographical disclosure? What does the breadth of the novel tell you about Baldwin's strategy of disclosure in the essay?

WRITING TOPICS

1. In "Notes of a Native Son," Baldwin presents his relationship with his father as the determining influence on his life. Notice how he defines the importance of this relationship, illustrates it, and analyzes it. Use his essay as a model for an essay in which you describe and analyze a determining influence on your own life.

2. Notice the significance of each detail of the narratives beginning with paragraph 16 and 32. Consider how Baldwin prepares us for the irony that he is

denied service in the "American Diner," for example. Write an essay in which you use a short narrative to strengthen an argument or observation.

BOOKS AVAILABLE IN PAPERBACK

Blues for Mister Charlie. New York: Dell. *Play.*

The Fire Next Time. New York: Dell. *Essays.*

Go Tell It on the Mountain: New York: Dell. *Novel.*

Going to Meet the Man. New York: Dell. *Stories.*

If Beale Street Could Talk. New York: New American Library. *Novel.*

Just Above My Head. New York: Dell. *Novel.*

Notes of a Native Son. New York: Bantam. *Essays.*

TRUMAN
CAPOTE

*T*RUMAN CAPOTE *was born in 1924. Like Gore Vidal (see pp. 190–201) he never went to college and began to publish at an early age. He became an office boy at* The New Yorker *magazine when he was seventeen and published his first novel,* Other Voices, Other Rooms, *in 1948, the year he turned twenty-four. An advertising campaign featured a photograph of the young author stretched out glowering on a sofa. A year later he brought out his first collection of short stories,* A Tree of Night *(1949), and he has since published two more novels —* The Grass Harp *(1951) and* Breakfast at Tiffany's *(1958) — and written the screenplay for* Beat the Devil *(1954).*

Capote has devoted himself primarily to nonfiction. ("Everything here is factual," he writes in a preface, "which doesn't mean that it is the truth.") Local Color (1951) was a collection of sketches and impressions, lyrical and slight and gorgeous. With The Muses Are Heard *(1956), which recounts an American musical on tour in the Soviet Union, he met factuality head-on. The best known of his books — he calls it "a nonfiction novel" — is* In Cold Blood *(1965), which details a multiple murder in Kansas, the flight and capture of the murderers, and their execution by hanging.* The Dogs Bark *(1973) collects many of Capote's essays;* Music for Chameleons *(1980) is a subsequent collection.*

"A Ride Through Spain" Capote has called "a lark." With little matter or idea, it lives by the energy of its description and observation. It is narrative, but little happens; it is descriptive, and the description exists for its own sake. "A Ride Through Spain" takes pleasure in making much out of little — a lyrical outburst of delight in language.

A Ride Through Spain

Certainly the train was old. The seats sagged like the jowls of a bulldog, windows were out and strips of adhesive held together those that were left; in the corridor a prowling cat appeared to be hunting mice, and it was not unreasonable to assume his search would be rewarded. 1

Slowly, as though the engine were harnessed to elderly coolies, we crept out of Granada. The southern sky was as white and burning as a desert; there was one cloud, and it drifted like a traveling oasis. 2

We were going to Algeciras, a Spanish seaport facing the coast of Africa. In our compartment there was a middle-aged Australian wearing a soiled linen suit; he had tobacco-colored teeth and his fingernails were unsanitary. Presently he informed us that he was a ship's doctor. It seemed curious, there on the dry, dour plains of Spain, to meet someone connected with the sea. Seated next to him there were two women, a mother and daughter. The mother was an overstuffed, dusty woman with sluggish, disapproving eyes and a faint mustache. The focus for her disapproval fluctuated; first, she eyed me rather strongly because as the sunlight fanned brighter, waves of heat blew through the broken windows and I had removed my jacket — which she considered, perhaps rightly, discourteous. Later on, she took a dislike to the young soldier who also occupied our compartment. The soldier, and the woman's not very discreet daughter, a buxom girl with the scrappy features of a prizefighter, seemed to have agreed to flirt. Whenever the wandering cat appeared at our door, the daughter pretended to be frightened, and the soldier would gallantly shoo the cat into the corridor: this by-play gave them frequent opportunity to touch each other. 3

The young soldier was one of many on the train. With their tasseled caps set at snappy angles, they hung about in the corridors smoking sweet black cigarettes and laughing confidentially. They seemed to be enjoying themselves, which apparently was wrong of them, for whenever an officer appeared the soldiers would stare fixedly out the windows, as though enraptured by the landslides of red rock, the olive fields and stern stone 4 mountains. Their officers were dressed for a parade, many ribbons, much brass; and some wore gleaming, improbable swords strapped to their sides. They did not mix with the soldiers, but sat together in a first-class compartment, looking bored and rather like unemployed actors. It was a blessing, I suppose, that something finally happened to give them a chance at rattling their swords.

The compartment directly ahead was taken over by one family: a delicate, attenuated, exceptionally elegant man with a mourning ribbon sewn around his sleeve, and traveling with him, six thin, summery girls, presumably his daughters. They were beautiful, the father and his children, all of them, and in the same way: hair that had a dark shine, lips the color of pimientos, eyes like sherry. The soldiers would glance into their compartment, then look away. It was as if they had seen straight into the sun.

Whenever the train stopped, the man's two youngest daughters would descend from the carriage and stroll under the shade of parasols. They enjoyed many lengthy promenades, for the train spent the greatest part of our journey standing still. No one appeared to be exasperated by this except myself. Several passengers seemed to have friends at every station with whom they could sit around a fountain and gossip long and lazily. One old woman was met by different little groups in a dozen-odd towns — between these encounters she wept with such abandon that the Australian doctor became alarmed: why no, she said, there was nothing he could do, it was just that seeing all her relatives made her so happy.

At each stop cyclones of barefooted women and somewhat naked children ran beside the train sloshing earthen jars of water and furrily squalling *Agua! Agua!* For two pesetas you could buy a whole basket of dark runny figs, and there were trays of curious white-coated candy doughnuts that looked as though they should be eaten by young girls wearing Communion dresses. Toward noon, having collected a bottle of wine, a loaf of bread, a sausage and a cheese, we were prepared for lunch. Our companions in the compartment were hungry, too. Packages were produced, wine uncorked, and for a while there was a pleasant, almost graceful festiveness. The soldier shared a pomegranate with the girl, the Australian told an amusing story, the witch-eyed mother pulled a paper-wrapped fish from between her bosoms and ate it with a glum relish.

Afterward everyone was sleepy; the doctor went so solidly to sleep that a fly meandered undisturbed over his open-mouthed face. Stillness etherized the whole train; in the next compartment the lovely girls leaned loosely, like six exhausted geraniums; even the cat had ceased to prowl, and lay dreaming in the corridor. We had climbed higher, the train moseyed across a plateau of rough yellow wheat, then between the granite walls of deep ravines where wind, moving down from the mountains, quivered in strange, thorny trees. Once, at a parting in the trees, there was something I'd wanted to see, a castle on a hill, and it sat there like a crown.

It was a landscape for bandits. Earlier in the summer, a young English- 9
man I know (rather, know of) had been motoring through this part of Spain
when, on the lonely side of a mountain, his car was surrounded by swarthy
scoundrels. They robbed him, then tied him to a tree and tickled his throat
with the blade of a knife. I was thinking of this when without preface a spat-
ter of bullet fire strafed the dozy silence.

It was a machine gun. Bullets rained in the trees like the rattle of casta- 10
nets, and the train, with a wounded creak, slowed to a halt. For a moment
there was no sound except the machine gun's cough. Then, "Bandits!" I
said in a loud, dreadful voice.

"*Bandidos!*" screamed the daughter. 11

"*Bandidos!*" echoed her mother, and the terrible word swept through the 12
train like something drummed on a tom-tom. The result was slapstick in a
grim key. We collapsed on the floor, one cringing heap of arms and legs.
Only the mother seemed to keep her head; standing up, she began systematically to stash away her treasures. She stuck a ring into the buns of her hair
and without shame hiked up her skirts and dropped a pearl-studded comb
into her bloomers. Like the cryings of birds at twilight, airy twitterings of
distress came from the charming girls in the next compartment. In the corridor the officers bumped about yapping orders and knocking into each other.

Suddenly, silence. Outside, there was the murmur of wind in leaves, of 13
voices. Just as the weight of the doctor's body was becoming too much for
me, the outer door of our compartment swung open, and a young man
stood there. He did not look clever enough to be a bandit.

"*Hay un médico en el tren?*" he said, smiling. 14

The Australian, removing the pressure of his elbow from my stomach, 15
climbed to his feet. "I'm a doctor," he admitted, dusting himself, "Has
someone been wounded?"

"*Si, Señor.* An old man. He is hurt in the head," said the Spaniard, who 16
was not a bandit: alas, merely another passenger. Settling back in our seats,
we listened, expressionless with embarrassment, to what had happened. It
seemed that for the last several hours an old man had been stealing a ride by
clinging to the rear of the train. Just now he'd lost his hold, and a soldier,
seeing him fall, had starting firing a machine gun as a signal for the engineer
to stop the train.

My only hope was that no one remembered who had first mentioned 17
bandits. They did not seem to. After acquiring a clean shirt of mine which he
intended to use as a bandage, the doctor went off to his patient, and the
mother, turning her back with sour prudery, reclaimed her pearl comb. Her
daughter and the soldier followed after us as we got out of the carriage and
strolled under the trees, where many passengers had gathered to discuss the
incident.

Two soldiers appeared carrying the old man. My shirt was wrapped 18
around his head. They propped him under a tree and all the women clus-

tered about vying with each other to lend him their rosary; someone brought a bottle of wine, which pleased him more. He seemed quite happy, and moaned a great deal. The children who had been on the train circled around him, giggling.

We were in a small wood that smelled of oranges. There was a path, and it led to a shaded promontory; from here, one looked across the valley where sweeping stretches of scorched golden grass shivered as though the earth were trembling. Admiring the valley, and the shadowy changes of light on the hills beyond, the six sisters, escorted by their elegant father, sat with their parasols raised above them like guests at a *fête champêtre.*° The soldiers moved around them in a vague, ambitious manner; they did not quite dare to approach, though one brash, sassy fellow went to the edge of the promontory and called, *"Yo te quiero mucho."*° The words returned with the hollow sub-music of a perfect echo, and the sisters, blushing, looked more deeply into the valley.

A cloud, somber as the rocky hills, had massed in the sky, and the grass below stirred like the sea before a storm. Someone said he thought it would rain. But no one wanted to go: not the injured man, who was well on his way through a second bottle of wine, nor the children who, having discovered the echo, stood happily caroling into the valley. It was like a party, and we all drifted back to the train as though each of us wished to be the last to leave. The old man, with my shirt like a grand turban on his head, was put into a first-class carriage and several eager ladies were left to attend him.

In our compartment, the dark, dusty mother sat just as we had left her. She had not seen fit to join the party. She gave me a long, glittering look. *"Bandidos,"* she said with a surly, unnecessary vigor.

The train moved away so slowly butterflies blew in and out the windows.

QUESTIONS ON MEANING

1. Look over the first three paragraphs. What background information does Capote give us about this particular ride through Spain? Why doesn't he tell us more about his own motives for traveling to Algeciras, or those of the Australian doctor, or of the soldiers? What purpose does the omission of this information serve in the essay?
2. In some of his essays, Capote features himself as an important, generally humorous, character. What is his role in this essay? How does he contribute

---

fête champêtre   An outdoor festival.
"Yo te quiero mucho"   I want you very much.

to the action he describes? How does paragraph 9 lead up to his involvement in the story?

QUESTIONS ON STRATEGY

1. Notice the similes in Capote's opening paragraphs. The seats sag "like the jowls of a bulldog"; the cloud drifts "like a traveling oasis." The images are vivid and effective in themselves, but how does each unify its paragraph?
2. In paragraphs 19 and 20 Capote presents a stretch of pure and simple description. What sort of physical details does he select for emphasis? How do his choice of words and his use of figurative language help this emphasis?

EXPLORATIONS

1. One of Capote's great strengths as a writer is his appreciation of the function of the setting in a narrative. The decrepit train of "A Ride Through Spain" suits his purposes exactly here, as he conveys the innocence and conviviality of travel in a holiday mood. In Capote's famous short story "A Tree of Night," he uses a similar setting for entirely different narrative purposes. Read this story and compare it with "A Ride Through Spain." Describe how Capote varies the details of his description to accommodate the contrasting moods and themes of the two stories.

WRITING TOPICS

1. Write a brief narrative in which you are both an observer and a participant in the action. Try to be as tactful and resourceful as Capote: Restrict your active role in the story as much as possible, but make it count for as much as you can.

BOOKS AVAILABLE IN PAPERBACK

Breakfast at Tiffany's. New York: New American Library. *Novel.*

The Dogs Bark: Public People and Private Places. New York: New American Library. *Essays.*

The Grass Harp and *A Tree of Night and Other Stories.* New York: New American Library. *Short novel and stories.*

In Cold Blood: A True Account of a Multiple Murder and Its Consequences. New York: New American Library. *Nonfiction.*

The Muses Are Heard. New York: Vintage. *Nonfiction: Account of an American musical comedy in the Soviet Union.*

Music for Chameleons: New Writing. New York: New American Library. *Essays.*

Other Voices, Other Rooms. New York: New American Library. *Novel.*

GORE
VIDAL

*G*ORE VIDAL *(b. 1925) never went to college. After graduating from Phillips Exeter Academy in 1945 he entered the Army and served in the Aleutian Islands. He published his first novel,* Williwaw, *in 1946, the year he turned twenty-one. Numerous novels have followed, including* Julian *(1964),* Myra Breckinridge *(1968),* 1876 *(1976),* Kalki *(1978), and* Duluth *(1983), which was his eighteenth. As an essayist he has also kept busy.* Homage to Daniel Shays *(1973) reprinted three earlier collections of essays. Two later collections are* Matters of Fact and Fiction *(1977) and* The Second American Revolution *(1982).*

The twenty-ninth Republican convention in Miami Beach in August 1968 nominated Richard M. Nixon to run for a second term as president. In 1960 Nixon, who had been vice-president for two terms under Dwight D. Eisenhower, had been narrowly defeated by John F. Kennedy. In 1962 Nixon lost his attempt to become governor of California and at a press conference after the defeat told reporters that they would not have a Nixon to kick around anymore. President Lyndon B. Johnson, who succeeded Kennedy after his assassination in 1963, massively defeated the conservative Republican Barry Goldwater in 1964. By the time of the 1968 convention, President Johnson, unpopular because of the Vietnam War, had taken himself out of the running, and Nixon's opponent would be Vice-President Hubert Humphrey, nomi-

nated by the Democrats after the assassination of his major opponent, President Kennedy's younger brother Robert. The same year had seen the assassination of the black American leader Martin Luther King, Jr. In this violent American era, Nixon's main opponents at the Republican convention were the more liberal Nelson Rockefeller, governor of New York, and the conservative governor of California, Ronald Reagan.

Politics and social criticism have boiled at the center of Gore Vidal's work, be it fiction or essay. Grandson of a senator, step-brother of Jacqueline Bouvier Kennedy Onassis, he has twice run for office himself. In 1960 he ran as Democrat-Liberal candidate for the U.S. House of Representatives from the state of New York; in 1982 he entered the Democratic primary in California for a Senate seat. Candidacy provided him another platform from which to speak his piece, though he never came close to winning. His own politics, generally liberal, are innovative and far too eccentric for the American electorate. When he write about Democrats, his sarcasm is at least as considerable as when he writes about Republicans.

Gore Vidal's most effective political action has taken the essay form, as in this exercise in ironic observation.

The Twenty-Ninth Republican Convention

Miami Beach, Florida
August 5–8, 1968

The dark blue curtains part. As delegates cheer, the nominee walks to-   1
ward the lectern, arms loose, shoulders somewhat rigid like a man who. . . .
No, as Henry James once said in quite a different but no less dramatic
context, it cannot be done. What is there to say about Richard M. Nixon that
was not said eight years ago? What is there to say that he himself did not say
at that memorable ''last'' press conference in Los Angeles six years ago? For
some time he has ceased to figure in the conscious regions of the mind, a
permanent resident, one had thought, of that limbo where reside the Stas-
sens° and the Deweys° and all those other ambitious men whose failures
seemed so entirely deserved. But now, thanks to two murders in five years,

---

Stassens Harold E. Stassen (b. 1907), unsuccessful candidate for the Republican presidential nomination in 1948, 1964, and 1968.

Deweys Thomas E. Dewey (1902–1971), Republican candidate for president in 1948,
defeated in an upset victory by Harry S Truman.

Richard Nixon is again a presidential candidate. No second acts to American careers? Nonsense. What is lacking are decent codas. At Miami Beach, we were reminded that no politician can ever be written off this side of Arlington.°

The week before the convention began, various Republican leaders met at the Fontainebleau Hotel to write a platform, knowing that no matter what wisdom this document might contain it would be ignored by the candidate. Nevertheless, to the extent issues ever intrude upon the making of Presidents, the platform hearings do give publicity to different points of view, and that is why Ronald Reagan took time from his busy schedule as Governor of California to fly to Miami Beach in order to warn the platform committee of the dangers of crime in the streets. The Governor also made himself available to the flower of the national and international press who sat restively in a windowless low-ceilinged dining room of the Fontainebleau from two q'clock to two-thirty to "just a short wait, please, the Governor is on his way," interviewing one another and trying to look alert as the television cameras, for want of a candidate, panned from face to face. At last, His Excellency, as Ivy Baker Priest would say, entered the room, flanked by six secret servicemen. As they spread out on either side of him, they cased us narrowly and I knew that simply by looking into my face they could see the imaginary gun in my pocket.

Ronald Reagan is a well-preserved not young man. Close-to, the painted face is webbed with delicate lines while the dyed hair, eyebrows, and eyelashes contrast oddly with the sagging muscle beneath the as yet unlifted chin, soft earnest of wattle-to-be. The effect, in repose, suggests the work of a skillful embalmer. Animated, the face is quite attractive and at a distance youthful; particularly engaging is the crooked smile full of large porcelain-capped teeth. The eyes are interesting: small, narrow, apparently dark, they glitter in the hot light, alert to every move, for this is enemy country — the liberal Eastern press who are so notoriously immune to that warm and folksy performance which Reagan quite deliberately projects over their heads to some legendary constituency at the far end of the tube, some shining Carverville where good Lewis Stone forever lectures Andy Hardy° on the virtues of thrift and the wisdom of the contract system at Metro-Goldwyn-Mayer.

The questions begin. Why don't you announce your candidacy? Are you a candidate? Why do people feel you will take votes away from George Wal-

---

Arlington Arlington National Cemetery.
Lewis Stone . . . Andy Hardy Stone (1879–1953), portrayed Judge James Hardy, father of teenage Andy (played by Mickey Rooney), in the Andy Hardy film series (1937–1947).

lace?° Having answered these questions a hundred times before, the actor does not pause to consider his responses. He picks up each cue promptly, neatly, increasing the general frustration. Only once does the answer-machine jam. "Do you *want* to be President?" The room goes silent. The smile suddenly looks to have been drawn in clay, fit for baking in a Laguna kiln. Then the candidate finds the right button. He pushes it. We are told what an honor it is for any citizen to be considered for the highest office on earth. . . . We stop listening; he stops listening to himself.

"Governor, even though you're not a candidate, you must know that   5 there is a good deal of support for you. . . ." The questioner's irony is suitably heavy. Reagan's lips purse — according to one biographer this is a sign he is displeased; there was a good deal of lip-pursing during the conference not to mention the days to come. "Well," he speaks through pursed lips, "I'd have to be unconscious not to know what was going on but. . . ." As he continues the performance, his speech interlarded with "my lands" (for some reason Right Wingers invariably talk like Little Orphan Annie), I recalled my last glimpse of him, at the Cow Palace in San Francisco four years ago. The Reagans were seated in a box, listening to Eisenhower. While Mrs. Reagan darted angry looks about the hall (displeased at the press?), the star of Death Valley Days° was staring intently at the speaker on the platform. Thus an actor prepares, I thought, and I suspected even then that Reagan would some day find himself up there on the platform. If only because as the age of television progresses, the Reagans will be the rule, not the exception. "Thank you, Governor," said a journalist, and everyone withdrew, leaving Ronald Reagan with his six secret servicemen — one black, a ratio considerably better than that of the convention itself where only two percent could claim Africa as motherland.

Seventy-second Street beach is a gathering place for hustlers of all sexes.   6 With some bewilderment, they watch one of their masters, the Chase Manhattan Bank made flesh — sweating flesh — display his wounds to the sandy and the dull, a Coriolanus but in reverse, one besotted with the vulgar. In shirt-sleeves but firmly knotted tie, Nelson Aldrich Rockefeller stands on a platform crowded with officials and aides (most seriously crowded by the Governor of Florida, Claude Kirk, who wears a bright orange sports jacket and a constant smile for his people, who regard him, the few who know

---

George Wallace (b. 1919), American Independent party presidential candidate in 1968, a conservative Democrat who was governor of Alabama from 1963 to 1966 and would be again from 1971 to 1978; sought the Democratic presidential nomination in 1972 and 1976; in 1972 he was paralyzed from the waist down when he was shot while campaigning.
Death Valley Days A television western in the 1950s and 1960s, narrated in 1965–66 by Reagan.

who he is, with bright loathing). Ordinarily Rockefeller's face is veal-white, as though no blood courses beneath that thick skin. But now, responding to the lowering day, he has turned a delicate conch pink. What is he saying? "Well, let's face it, there's been some disagreement among the pollsters." The upper class tough boy accent (most beautifully achieved by Montgomery Clift in *The Heiress*) proves effective even down here where consonants are disdained and vowels long. Laughter from the audience in clothes, bewildered looks from the hustlers in their bathing suits. "Like, man, who *is* it?"

"But now Harris and Gallup have agreed that I can beat. . . ." Rockefeller quotes at length from those polls which are the oracles of our day, no, the very gods who speak to us of things to come. Over and over again, he says, "Let's face it," a phrase popular twenty years ago, particularly among girls inclined to alcoholism ("the Governor drinks an occasional Dubonnet on the rocks before dinner," where did I read that?). Beside him stands his handsome wife, holding a large straw hat and looking as if she would like to be somewhere else, no loving Nancy Reagan or loyal Pat Nixon she. The convention is full of talk that there has been trouble between them. Apparently . . . one of the pleasures of American political life is that, finally, only personalities matter. Is he a nice man? Is she happy with him? What else should concern a sovereign people?

Rockefeller puts down the polls, takes off his glasses, and starts to attack the Administration. "Look at what they're doing," he says with a fine vehemence. "They're *exhilarating* the war!" But although Rockefeller now sounds like a peace candidate, reprising Bobby Kennedy and Eugene McCarthy,° he has always been devoted to the war in Vietnam and to the principle underlying it: American military intervention wherever "freedom is endangered." Consequently — and consistently — he has never found any defense budget adequate. Two years ago at a dinner in New York, he was more hawk than Johnson as he told us how the Viet Cong were coldbloodedly "shooting little mayors" (the phrase conjured up dead ponies); mournfully, he shook his head, "Why can't they learn to fight fair?" Nevertheless, compared to Nixon and Reagan, Rockefeller is positively Lincolnesque. All of us on 72nd Street Beach liked him, except perhaps the hustlers wanting to score, and we wished him well, knowing that he had absolutely no chance of being nominated.

By adding the third character to tragedy, Sophocles changed the nature of drama. By exalting the chorus and diminishing the actors, television has changed entirely the nature of our continuing history. Watching things as

---

Eugene McCarthy (b. 1916), U.S. senator from Minnesota from 1959 to 1970; opposed U.S. involvement in Vietnam as an unsuccessful candidate for the Democratic presidential nomination in 1968.

they happen, the viewer is part of events in a way new to man. And never is he so much a part of the whole as when things do not happen, for, as Andy Warhol so wisely observed, people will always prefer to look at something rather than nothing; between plain wall and flickering commercial, the eyes will have the second. As hearth and fire were once center to the home or lair so now the television set is the center of modern man's being, all points of the room converge upon its presence and the eye watches even as the mind dozes, much as our ancestors narcotized themselves with fire.

At Miami Beach television was everywhere: in the air, on the streets, in hotel lobbies, on the convention floor. "From gavel to gavel" the networks spared us nothing in the way of empty speeches and mindless interviews, but dull and uninformative as the events themselves were, something rather than nothing was being shown and the eye was diverted while the objects photographed (delegates et al.) reveled in the exposure even though it might be no more than a random shot of a nose being picked or a crotch rearranged. No matter: for that instant the one observed existed for all his countrymen. As a result the delegates were docile beyond belief, stepping this way and that as required by men with wired helmets and handmikes which, like magic wands, could confer for an instant total recognition. 10

The fact that television personalities so notoriously took precedence over the politicians at Miami Beach was noted with sour wonder by journalists who have begun to fear that their rendering of events that all can see into lines of linear type may prove to be as irrelevant an exercise as turning contemporary literature into Greek. The fact that in a hotel lobby it was Eric Sevareid° not John Tower° who collected a crowd was thought to be a sign of the essential light-mindedness of the electorate. Yet Sevareid belongs to the country in a way few politicians ever do. Certainly most people see more of David Brinkley than they do of their own relatives and it is no wonder that they are eager to observe him in the flesh. Only Ronald Reagan among the politicians at Miami exerted the same spell, and for the same reason: he is a bona fide star of the Late Show, equally ubiquitous, equally mythic. 11

Miami Beach is a rich sandbar with a drawbridge, and in no sense part of the main. The televised convention made it even more remote than it is. So locked were we all in what we were doing that Miami's Negro riots on Wednesday went almost unnoticed. There are those who thought that the Republicans deliberately played down the riots, but that is too Machiavellian.° The fact is no one was interested. For those involved in creating that 12

Eric Sevareid   (b. 1912), longtime television correspondent for CBS News.

John Tower   (b. 1925), U.S. Republican senator from Texas, from 1961 to the present.

Machiavellian   Using cunning or deceit in pursuit of political ends; from principles set forth by Niccolò Machiavelli (1469–1527), Italian statesman and political philosopher.

formidable work of television art, the 29th Republican convention, there was only one important task, creating suspense where none was. Everyone pretended that Reagan and Rockefeller could stop Nixon on the first ballot and so persuasive is the medium that by continually acting as if there might be a surprise, all involved came to believe that there would be one.

Even Nixon who should have known better fell victim to the collective delusion. On Tuesday he made his deal with Thurmond°: no candidate for Vice-President displeasing to the South. Yet there was never, we now know, any danger of the Southern delegations switching to Reagan, despite the actor's enormous appeal to them. After all, how could they not love a man who had campaigned for a segregationist Southern politician (Charlton Lyons of Louisiana), who had denounced the income tax as "Marxist," and federal aid to education as "a tool of tyranny," and welfare as an "encouragement to divorce and immorality," and who generally sounded as if he wouldn't mind nuking North Vietnam and maybe China, too? He was their man but Nixon was their leader.

By the time the balloting began on Wednesday night, it was all over. There were of course idle pleasures. Everett Dirksen° prowling from camera to camera, playing the part of a Senator with outrageous pleasure. Strom Thurmond, High Constable of the South, staring coldly at the delegates with stone catfish face. John Lindsay° of New York, slyly separating his elegant persona from any words that he might be called upon to say. The public liked Lindsay but the delegates did not. They regarded him with the same distaste that they regard the city of which he is mayor, that hellhole of niggers and kikes and commies, of dope and vice and smut. . . . So they talk among themselves, until an outsider approaches; then they shift gears swiftly and speak gravely of law and order and how this is a republic not a democracy.

A lady from Vermont read the roll of the States as though each state had somehow grievously offended her. Alabama was plainly a thorn to be plucked, while Alaska was a blot upon the Union. She did achieve a moment of ribald good humor when she asked one state chairman *which* Rockefeller his state was voting for. But long before the Yankee virago had got to Wisconsin it was plain that Nixon was indeed "the one" as the signs had proclaimed, and immediately the Medium began to look in on the hotel

---

Thurmond Strom Thurmond (b. 1902), conservative Republican U.S. senator from South Carolina from 1954 to the present, switched from Democratic to Republican party in 1964.

Everett Dirksen (1896–1969), liberal Republican senator from Illinois from 1951 to his death in 1969.

John Lindsay (b. 1921), mayor of New York City from 1966 to 1974, the first Republican mayor of that city in twenty years; became a Democrat and unsuccessfully campaigned for the Democratic presidential nomination in 1972.

suites, to confront the losers, hoping for tears, and reveal the winner, hoping for . . . well, *what* do you hope for with Nixon?

The technician. Once nominated Nixon gravely explained how he had 16 pulled it off. He talked about the logistics of campaigning. He took us backstage. It was a nice background briefing, but nothing more. No plans for the ghettos, no policy for Asia, just political maneuvering. He did assure us that he would select ''a candidate for Vice President who does not divide this country.'' Apparently he would have a free hand because ''I won the nomination without paying any price or making any deals.'' The next day of course he revealed the nature of his deal with the Southerners and the price he must now pay for their support: Spiro Agnew of Maryland. Despite the howls of the party liberals and the total defection of the blacks. Nixon had probably done the wise thing. He could now give Wallace a run for his money not only in the necessary South but also among the lower white orders in the North who this year are more than ready to give their dusky cousins what the candidate once referred to, in angrier days, as ''the shaft.''

Thursday was the big day. Agnew was proposed, opposed, nominated. 17 A lumbering man who looks like a cross between Lyndon Johnson and Juan Perón, his acceptance speech was thin and ungrammatical; not surprisingly, he favored law and order. Adequate on civil rights when he became governor, Agnew behaved boorishly to the black establishment of Baltimore in the wake of riots last spring. This made him acceptable to Thurmond. Even so, all but the most benighted conservatives are somewhat concerned at Agnew's lack of experience. Should Nixon be elected and die, a man with only one year's experience as governor of a backward border state would become Emperor of the West. Though firm with niggers, how would he be on other issues? No one knows, including the candidate himself whose great virtue, in his own eyes, ''is that I try to be credible — I want to be believed. That's one of the most priceless assets.'' So it is. So it is.

Nixon is now on stage, ready to accept for a second time his party's nom- 18 ination. He is leaner than in the past. In a thickly made-up face, the smile is not unappealing, upper lip slightly hooked over teeth in the Kennedy manner. With his jawline collapsing in a comforting way, the middle-aged Nixon resembles the average voter who, we are told, is forty-seven years old. The candidate swings neatly to left, hands raised, two forefingers of each hand making the victory salute. Arms drop. Slide step to right. Arms again extended above head as hands make salute. Then back to center stage and the lectern. The television camera zooms in on the speech: one can see lines crossed out, words added; the type is large, the speech mercifully short.

Nixon begins. The voice is deep and slightly toneless, without regional 19 accent, like a radio announcer's. We have been told that he wrote his own script. It is possible. Certainly every line was redolent of that strange un-charm characteristic of the man. He spoke of Eisenhower ("one of the greatest Americans of our time — or of any time") who was watching them from his hospital bed. "His heart is with us!" the candidate exclaimed, reminding us inadvertently that that poor organ was hardly the General's strongest contribution to the moral crusade the times require. No matter, "let's win this one for Ike!" (A rousing echo of *Knute Rockne*, a film in which the youthful Ronald Reagan had been most affecting.) Nixon next paid careful tribute to his Republican competitors, to the platform and, finally, to Spiro Agnew "a statesman of the first rank who will be a great campaigner." He then drew a dark picture of today's America, ending with "did we come all this way for this?" Despite the many hours of literary labor, Nixon's style was seldom felicitous; he was particularly afflicted by "thisness": "This I say is the real voice of America. And in this year 1968 this is. . . ." The real voice of America, needless to say, is Republican; "the forgotten Americans — the nonshouters, the nondemonstrators"; in short, the nonprotesting white Protestants, who must, he enjoined, commit themselves to the truth, "to see it like it is, and to tell it like it is," argot just slightly wrong for now but to Nixon "tell it like it is" must sound positively raunchy, the sort of thing had he been classy Jack Kennedy he might have heard at Vegas, sitting around with the Clan and their back-scratchers.

Solemnly Nixon addressed himself to Vietnam. His Administration would "bring to an honorable end the war." How? Well, "after an era of confrontation, the time has come for an era of negotiation." But in case that sounded like dangerous accommodation he quickly reminded us that since the American flag is spit on almost daily around the world, it is now "time we started to act like a great nation." But he did not tell us how a great nation should act. Last January, he said that the war will end only when the Communists are convinced that the U.S. "will use its immense power and is not going to back down." In March he said, "There is no alternative to the continuation of the war in Vietnam." It is of course never easy to determine what if anything Nixon means. When it was revealed that his recent support of public housing was not sincere but simply expedient (his secret remarks to a Southern caucus had been taped), no one was surprised. "He just had to say that," murmur his supporters whenever he contradicts himself, and they admire him for it. After all, his form of hyprocrisy is deeply American: if you can't be good, be careful. Significantly, he was most loudly applauded when he struck this year's favorite Republican note: *Remember the Pueblo.* "The United States has fallen so low that a fourth rate military power like North Korea [can] hijack a United States naval vessel. . . ." Quite forgotten were his conciliatory words of last spring: "If the captured American Intelligence spy ship violated North Korean waters, the United States has no choice but to admit it."

Nixon next praised the courts but then allowed that some of them have gone "too far in weakening the peace forces as against the criminal forces."

Attacks on the judiciary are surefire with Republicans. Witness the old Nixon five years after the Supreme Court's 1954 decision on the integration of schools: "the Administration's position has not been, is not now, and should not be immediate total integration." Like Barry Goldwater he tends to the radical belief that the Supreme Court's decisions "are not, necessarily, the law of the land." Happily, once the present Attorney General is replaced, it will be possible to "open a new front against the filth peddlers and the narcotics peddlers who are corrupting the lives of our children." As for the forty million poor, they can take heart from the example of past generations of Americans who were aided not by government "but because of what people did for themselves." Those small inequities that now exist in the American system can be easily taken care of by "the greatest engine of progress ever developed in the history of man — American private enterprise." The poor man who wants "a piece of the action" (Vegas again) is very apt to get it if the streets are orderly and enough tax cuts are given big business to encourage it to be helpful.

If Nixon's reputation as the litmus-paper man of American politics is deserved, his turning mauve instead of pink makes it plain that the affluent majority intend to do nothing at all in regard to the black and the poor and the aged, except repress with force their demonstrations, subscribing finally not so much to the bland hortatory generalities of the platform and the acceptance speech but to the past statements of the real Nixon who has said (1) "If the conviction rate was doubled in this country, it would do more to eliminate crime in the future than a quadrupling of the funds for any governmental war on poverty." (2) "I am opposed to pensions in any form, as it makes loafing more attractive to [sic] working." (3) To tie health care to social security "would set up a great state program which would inevitably head in the direction of herding the ill and elderly into institutions whether they desire this or not." Echo of those Republicans in 1935 who declared that once Social Security was law "you won't have a name any longer, only a number." Most ominous of all, the candidate of the military-industrial complex has no wish to decrease the military budget. Quite the contrary. As recently as last June he was warning us that "the United States has steadily fallen behind the Soviet Union in the leveling of its spending on research and development of advance systems to safeguard the nation." In short, there is no new Nixon, only the old Nixon experimenting with new campaigning techniques in response, as the Stalinists used to say, to new necessities. Nixon concluded his speech on a note of self-love. Most viewers thought it inappropriate: since no one loves him, why should he? To his credit, he sounded slightly embarrassed as he spoke of the boy from Whittier — a mis-fire but worth a try.

Friday. On the plane to New York. A leading Republican liberal remarks, "Awful as it was, he made a vote-getting speech." He is probably right.

Nixon has said in the past that no Republican can hope to get the Negro vote, so why try for it? Particularly when the principal danger to Nixon's candidacy is George Wallace, in the North as well as South. Nixon is also perfectly aware of a little-known statistic: the entire black vote plus the entire vote of whites under twenty-five is slightly less than one-fourth of the total electorate. Since Nixon has no chance of attracting either category, he has, by selecting Agnew, served notice that he is the candidate of that average forty-seven-year-old voter who tends to dislike and fear the young and the black and the liberal; in fact, the more open Nixon is in his disdain of this one-fourth of a nation, the more pleasing he will seem to the remaining three-fourths who want a change, any change, from Johnson-Humphrey as well as some assurance that the dissident forces at work in American life will be contained. The great technician has worked out a winning combination and, barring the (obligatory?) unexpected, it is quite likely that it will pay off and Richard Milhous Nixon will become the 37th President of the United States.

QUESTIONS ON MEANING

1. Gore Vidal's account of the 1968 Republican convention seems even more brilliant today than when it appeared, and even prescient. By observing the corruptions involved in Nixon's nomination — the crass dealing, the coarse and evasive language, the manipulation of the media — Vidal provided unwitting commentary on Nixon's eventual undoing: the Watergate scandal. Identify the many points Vidal makes about the dishonesty, the hypocrisy, the emptiness of Nixon's politics. Is Nixon unique? How widespread does Vidal believe this corruption is?

2. On one level, this essay is a descriptive report of the twenty-ninth Republican convention. Vidal covers the event as a correspondent. But as he proceeds, a point of view emerges. Clearly, he dislikes Nixon. He claims to like Rockefeller, but he's obviously not a Republican. Define Vidal's point of view. How does he feel about political life in America? What earns his disapproval in the way we elect a president? Summarize his criticisms.

QUESTIONS ON STRATEGY

1. In paragraph 20 how does Vidal make Nixon's dishonesty stand out? Where else does he use a candidate's previous statements to test his campaign positions?

2. Paragraph 3 is a good example of Vidal's irony — deft, even graceful, but very sharp. His purpose in this paragraph seems to be descriptive. But what precisely does he describe? How does he slant the details of his description,

especially the adjectives? How does the reference to MGM fit in with the point Vidal has been making about Reagan's physical appearance?

3. Look through Vidal's account for other references and allusions to Hollywood. What is their purpose in the essay? How do they relate to Vidal's descriptions of goings-on at the convention?

4. Vidal is very witty. His essay is full of quips and barbs, parenthetical asides, and ironic references and allusions. Some are almost wisecracks — calling Rockefeller ''the Chase Manhattan Bank made flesh,'' for example. Does Vidal use these one-liners merely to get a laugh? How do they support or undermine Vidal's argument? What do they imply about Vidal's seriousness?

EXPLORATIONS

1. Both Norman Mailer and Gore Vidal note the influence of the media on the people and the events they cover. Examine ''The Psychology of Astronauts'' and ''The Twenty-Ninth Republican Convention'' as critiques of contemporary journalism in general and of television journalism in particular. How do Mailer and Vidal perceive the media? Whose view seems closer to the truth, more plausible, or better informed?

WRITING TOPICS

1. Follow a major national news story, preferably an election, both on television and in newspapers. Keeping Vidal's points about the packaging of news in mind, describe in an essay the coverage of the story, considering the accuracy, fairness, and usefulness of the reporting.

2. Watch a presidential press conference, observing the president's performance. How is his makeup done? What effect does the lighting have? Is the president effective at dodging troublesome questions? Does he mumble or stumble when surprised? Note details like these, review the report of the press conference in the next day's *New York Times*, and write a critique of the president's public style.

BOOKS AVAILABLE IN PAPERBACK

Burr. New York: Ballantine. *Novel.*

Creation. New York: Ballantine. *Novel.*

1876. New York: Ballantine. *Novel.*

An Evening with Richard Nixon. New York: Vintage. *An ''entertainment'': A dramatic history of the career of the thirty-seventh president, in his own words.*

Homage to Daniel Shays: Collected Essays, 1952–1972. New York: Vintage.

Julian. New York: Vintage. *Novel.*

Matters of Fact and Fiction: Essays, 1973–1976. New York: Vintage.

The Second American Revolution and Other Essays, 1976–1982. New York: Vintage.

Washington, D.C. New York: Ballantine. *Novel.*

ALISON
LURIE

A LISON LURIE (b. 1926) grew up in New York City and graduated from Radcliffe College. *She has worked as a ghostwriter and librarian, raised three
sons, and written six novels, most recently* The War Between the Tates *(1974) and*
Only Children *(1979). She is a professor of English at Cornell University, and she
has been a Fellow of the Guggenheim and Rockefeller Foundations.*

In the series "The Making of a Writer" in the New York Times Book Review,
*Lurie remembered that as a child, certain she would grow up to be an old maid, she
took to writing stories. "With a pencil and a paper, I could revise the world." A few
years later, instead, she found herself married with two small children — and with
two novels that publishers would not touch. She tried giving up writing, substituting a family life of tuna fish casseroles and playground excursions. But not writing
did not satisfy her. She returned to it by way of the essay, making a memoir of a
friend who died young, and then writing her third novel — which publishers touched
and readers read.*

*Alison Lurie's ironic fiction belongs with the work of modern English novelists
like Evelyn Waugh, Nancy Mitford, and Anthony Powell. Her observation has been
accused of wickedness; Gore Vidal called her "the Queen Herod of Modern Fiction."*

When she writes essays — often for the New York Review of Books *— she brings her irony and humor with her. Henry James said that a novelist must be "one of those on whom nothing is lost." In her fiction, and in her observations on the clothes we wear, nothing is lost on Alison Lurie.*

"Clothing as a Sign System" begins her book The Language of Clothes, *which is copiously illustrated. But without illustration, her prose supplies the pictures; and an overriding idea, using analogy as tracks for the train of thought, carries the reader to Alison Lurie's chosen destination.*

Clothing as a Sign System

For thousands of years human beings have communicated with one an- 1
other first in the language of dress. Long before I am near enough to talk to you on the street, in a meeting, or at a party, you announce your sex, age and class to me through what you are wearing — and very possibly give me important information (or misinformation) as to your occupation, origin, personality, opinions, tastes, sexual desires and current mood. I may not be able to put what I observe into words, but I register the information unconsciously; and you simultaneously do the same for me. By the time we meet and converse we have already spoken to each other in an older and more universal tongue.

The statement that clothing is a language, though occasionally made 2
with the air of a man finding a flying saucer in his backyard, is not new. Balzac, in *Daughter of Eve* (1839), observed that for a woman dress is "a continual manifestation of intimate thoughts, a language, a symbol." Today, as semiotics becomes fashionable, sociologists tell us that fashion too is a language of signs, a nonverbal system of communication. The French structuralist Roland Barthes, for instance, in "The Diseases of Costume," speaks of theatrical dress as a kind of writing, of which the basic element is the sign.

None of these theorists, however, have gone on to remark what seems 3
obvious: that if clothing is a language, it must have a vocabulary and a grammar like other languages. Of course, as with human speech, there is not a single language of dress, but many: some (like Dutch and German) closely related and others (like Basque) almost unique. And within every language of clothes there are many different dialects and accents, some almost unintelligible to members of the mainstream culture. Moreover, as with speech, each individual has his own stock of words and employs personal variations of tone and meaning.

The vocabulary of dress includes not only items of clothing, but also hair styles, accessories, jewelry, make-up and body decoration. Theoretically at least this vocabulary is as large as or larger than that of any spoken tongue, since it includes every garment, hair style, and type of body decoration ever invented. In practice, of course, the sartorial resources of an individual may be very restricted. Those of a sharecropper, for instance, may be limited to five or ten "words" from which it is possible to create only a few "sentences" almost bare of decoration and expressing only the most basic concepts. A so-called fashion leader, on the other hand, may have several hundred "words" at his or her disposal, and thus be able to form thousands of different "sentences" that will express a wide range of meanings. Just as the average English-speaking person knows many more words than he or she will ever use in conversation, so all of us are able to understand the meaning of styles we will never wear.

To choose clothes, either in a store or at home, is to define and describe ourselves. Occasionally, of course, practical considerations enter into these choices: considerations of comfort, durability, availability and price. Especially in the case of persons of limited wardrobe, an article may be worn because it is warm or rainproof or handy to cover up a wet bathing suit — in the same way that persons of limited vocabulary use the phrase "you know" or adjectives such as "great" or "fantastic." Yet, just as with spoken language, such choices usually give us some information, even if it is only equivalent to the statement "I don't give a damn what I look like today." And there are limits even here. In this culture, like many others, certain garments are taboo for certain persons. Most men, however cold or wet they might be, would not put on a woman's dress, just as they would not use words and phrases such as "simply marvelous," which in this culture are considered specifically feminine.

Besides containing "words" that are taboo, the language of clothes, like speech, also includes modern and ancient words, words of native and foreign origin, dialect words, colloquialisms, slang and vulgarities. Genuine articles of clothing from the past (or skillful imitations) are used in the same way a writer or speaker might use archaisms: to give an air of culture, erudition or wit. Just as in educated discourse, such "words" are usually employed sparingly, most often one at a time — a single Victorian cameo or a pair of 1940s platform shoes or an Edwardian velvet waistcoat, never a complete costume. A whole outfit composed of archaic items from a single period, rather than projecting elegance and sophistication, will imply that one is on one's way to a masquerade, acting in a play or film or putting oneself on display for advertising purposes. Mixing garments from several different periods of the past, on the other hand, suggests a confused but intriguingly "original" theatrical personality. It is therefore often fashionable in those sections of the art and entertainment industry in which instant celebrities are manufactured and sold.

When using archaic words, it is essential to choose ones that are decently 7
old. The sight of a white plastic Courrèges miniraincoat and boots (in 1963 the height of fashion) at a gallery opening or theater today would produce the same shiver of ridicule and revulsion as the use of words such as "groovy," "Negro," or "self-actualizing."

In *Taste and Fashion*, one of the best books ever written on costume, the 8
late James Laver proposed a timetable to explain such reactions; this has come to be known as Laver's Law. According to him, the same costume will be

Indecent	10 years before its time
Shameless	5 years before its time
Daring	1 year before its time
Smart	
Dowdy	1 year after its time
Hideous	10 years after its time
Ridiculous	20 years after its time
Amusing	30 years after its time
Quaint	50 years after its time
Charming	70 years after its time
Romantic	100 years after its time
Beautiful	150 years after its time

Laver possibly overemphasizes the shock value of incoming fashion, which today may be seen merely as weird or ugly. And of course he is speaking of the complete outfit, or "sentence." The speed with which a single "word" passes in and out of fashion can vary, just as in spoken and written languages.

The appearance of foreign garments in an otherwise indigenous costume 9
is similar in function to the use of foreign words or phrases in standard English speech. This phenomenon, which is common in certain circles, may have several different meanings.

First, of course, it can be a deliberate sign of national origin in someone 10
who otherwise, sartorially or linguistically speaking, has no accent. Often this message is expressed through headgear. The Japanese-American lady in Western dress but with an elaborate Oriental hairdo, or the Oxford-educated Arab who tops his Savile Row suit with a turban, are telling us graphically that they have not been psychologically assimilated; that their ideas and opinions remain those of an Asian. As a result we tend to see the non-European in Western dress with native headgear or hairdo as dignified, even formidable; while the reverse outfit — the Oriental lady in a kimono and a plas-

tic rain hat, or the sheik in native robes and a black bowler — appears comic. Such costumes seem to announce that their wearers, though not physically at ease in our country, have their heads full of half-baked Western ideas. It would perhaps be well for Anglo-American tourists to keep this principle in mind when traveling to exotic places. Very possibly the members of a package tour in Mexican sombreros or Russian bearskin hats look equally ridiculous and weak-minded to the natives of the countries they are visiting.

More often the wearing of a single foreign garment, like the dropping of a foreign word or phrase in conversation, is meant not to advertise foreign origin or allegiance but to indicate sophistication. It can also be a means of advertising wealth. When we see a fancy Swiss watch, we know that its owner either bought it at home for three times the price of a good English or American watch, or else he or she spent even more money traveling to Switzerland.

Casual dress, like casual speech, tends to be loose, relaxed and colorful. It often contains what might be called "slang words": blue jeans, sneakers, baseball caps, aprons, flowered cotton housedresses and the like. These garments could not be worn on a formal occasion without causing disapproval, but in ordinary circumstances they pass without remark. "Vulgar words" in dress, on the other hand, give emphasis and get immediate attention in almost any circumstances, just as they do in speech. Only the skillful can employ them without some loss of face, and even then they must be used in the right way. A torn, unbuttoned shirt, or wildly uncombed hair, can signify strong emotions: passion, grief, rage, despair. They are most effective if people already think of you as being neatly dressed, just as the curses of well-spoken persons count for more than those of the customarily foul-mouthed.

Items of dress that are the sartorial equivalent of forbidden words have more impact when they appear seldom and as if by accident. The Edwardian lady, lifting her heavy floor-length skirt to board a tram, appeared unaware that she was revealing a froth of lacy petticoats and embroidered black stockings. Similarly, today's braless executive woman, leaning over her desk at a conference, may affect not to know that her nipples show through her silk blouse. Perhaps she does not know it consciously; we are here in the ambiguous region of intention vs. interpretation which has given so much trouble to linguists.

In speech, slang terms and vulgarities may eventually become respectable dictionary words; the same thing is true of colloquial and vulgar fashions. Garments or styles that enter the fashionable vocabulary from a colloquial source usually have a longer life span than those that begin as vulgarities. Thigh-high patent leather boots, first worn by the most obvious variety of rentable female as a sign that she was willing to help act out certain male fantasies, shot with relative speed into and out of high fashion; while blue jeans made their way upward much more gradually from work clothes to casual to business and formal wear, and are still engaged in a slow descent.

Though the idea is attractive, it does not seem possible to equate differ- 15 ent articles of clothing with the different parts of speech. A case can be made, however, for considering trimmings and accessories as adjectives or adverbs — modifiers in the sentence that is the total outfit — but it must be remembered that one era's trimmings and accessories are another's essential parts of the costume. At one time shoes were actually fastened with buckles, and the buttons on the sleeves of a suit jacket were used to secure turned-up cuffs. Today such buttons, or the linked brass rods on a pair of Gucci shoes, are purely vestigial and have no useful function. If they are missing, however, the jacket or the shoes are felt to be damaged and unfit for wear.

Accessories, too, may be considered essential to an outfit. In the 1940s 16 and 1950s, for instance, a woman was not properly dressed unless she wore gloves. Emily Post, among many others, made this clear:

> Always wear gloves, of course, in church, and also on the street. A really smart woman wears them outdoors always, even in the country. Always wear gloves in a restaurant, in a theatre, when you go to lunch, or to a formal dinner, or to a dance. . . . A lady never takes off her gloves to shake hands, no matter when or where. . . . On formal occasions she should *put gloves on* to shake hands with a hostess or with her own guests.

If we consider only those accessories and trimmings that are currently 17 optional, however, we may reasonably speak of them as modifiers. It then becomes possible to distinguish an elaborately decorated style of dress from a simple and plain one, whatever the period. As in speech, it is harder to communicate well in a highly decorated style, though when this is done successfully the result may be very impressive. A costume loaded with accessories and trimmings can easily appear cluttered, pretentious or confusing. Very rarely the whole becomes greater than its many parts, and the total effect is luxurious, elegant and often highly sensual.

As writers on costume have often pointed out, the average individual 18 above the poverty line has many more clothes than he needs to cover his body, even allowing for washing and changes of weather. Moreover, we often discard garments that show little or no wear and purchase new ones. What is the reason for this? Some have claimed that it is all the result of brainwashing by commercial interests. But the conspiracy theory of fashion change — the idea that the adoption of new styles is simply the result of a plot by greedy designers and manufacturers and fashion editors — has, I think, less foundation than is generally believed. Certainly the fashion industry might like us to throw away all our clothes each year and buy a whole new wardrobe, but it has never been able to achieve this goal. For one thing, it is not that the public will wear anything suggested to it, nor has it ever been true. Ever since fashion became big business, designers have proposed a bewildering array of styles every season. A few of these have been selected or adapted by manufacturers for mass production, but only a certain proportion of them have caught on.

As James Laver has remarked, modes are but the reflection of the manners of the time; they are the mirror, not the original. Within the limits imposed by economics, clothes are acquired, used and discarded just as words are, because they meet our needs and express our ideas and emotions. All the exhortations of experts on language cannot save outmoded terms of speech or persuade people to use new ones "correctly." In the same way, those garments that reflect what we are or want to be at the moment will be purchased and worn, and those that do not will not, however frantically they may be ballyhooed.

In the past, gifted artists of fashion from Worth to Mary Quant have been able to make inspired guesses about what people will want their clothes to say each year. Today a few designers seem to have retained this ability, but many others have proved to be as hopelessly out of touch as designers in the American auto industry. The classic case is that of the maxiskirt, a style which made women look older and heavier and impeded their movements at a time (1969) when youth, slimness and energy were at the height of their vogue. The maxiskirt was introduced with tremendous fanfare and not a little deception. Magazines and newspapers printed (sometimes perhaps unknowingly) photos of New York and London street scenes populated with hired models in long skirts disguised as passers-by, to give readers in Podunk and Lesser Puddleton the impression that the capitals had capitulated. But these strenuous efforts were in vain: the maxiskirt failed miserably, producing well-deserved financial disaster for its backers.

The fashion industry is no more able to preserve a style that men and women have decided to abandon than to introduce one they do not choose to accept. In America, for instance, huge advertising budgets and the whole-hearted cooperation of magazines such as *Vogue* and *Esquire* have not been able to save the hat, which for centuries was an essential part of everyone's outdoor (and often of their indoor) costume. It survives now mainly as a utilitarian protection against weather, as part of ritual dress (at formal weddings, for example) or as a sign of age or individual eccentricity.

As with speech, the meaning of any costume depends on circumstances. It is not "spoken" in a vacuum, but at a specific place and time, any change in which may alter its meaning. Like the remark "Let's get on with this damn business," the two-piece tan business suit and boldly striped shirt and tie that signify energy and determination in the office will have quite another resonance at a funeral or picnic.

According to Irving Goffman, the concept of "proper dress" is totally 23 dependent on situation. To wear the costume considered "proper" for a situation acts as a sign of involvement in it, and the person whose clothes do not conform to these standards is likely to be more or less subtly excluded from participation. When other signs of deep involvement are present, rules about proper dress may be waived. Persons who have just escaped from a fire or flood are not censured for wearing pajamas or having uncombed hair; someone bursting into a formal social occasion to announce important news is excused for being in jeans and T-shirt.

In language we distinguish between someone who speaks a sentence 24 well — clearly, and with confidence and dignity — and someone who speaks it badly. In dress too, manner is as important as matter, and in judging the meaning of any garment we will automatically consider whether it fits well or is too large or too small; whether it is old or new; and especially whether it is in good condition, slightly rumpled and soiled or crushed and filthy. Cleanliness may not always be next to godliness, but it is usually regarded as a sign of respectability or at least of self-respect. It is also a sign of status, since to be clean and neat always involves the expense of time and money.

In a few circles, of course, disregard for cleanliness has been considered a 25 virtue. Saint Jerome's remark that "the purity of the body and its garments means the impurity of the soul" inspired generations of unwashed and smelly hermits. In the sixties some hippies and mystics scorned overly clean and tidy dress as a sign of compromise with the Establishment and too great an attachment to the things of this world. There is also a more widespread rural and small-town dislike of the person whose clothes are too clean, slick and smooth. He — or, less often, she — is suspected of being untrustworthy, a smoothie or a city slicker.

In general, however, to wear dirty, rumpled or torn clothing is to invite 26 scorn and condescension. This reaction is ancient; indeed it goes back beyond the dawn of humanity. In most species, a strange animal in poor condition — mangy, or with matted and muddy fur — is more likely to be attacked by other animals. In the same way, shabbily dressed people are more apt to be treated shabbily. A man in a clean, well-pressed suit who falls down in a central London or Manhattan street is likely to be helped up sooner than one in filthy tatters.

At certain times and places — a dark night, a deserted alley — dirt and 27 rags, like mumbled or growled speech, may be alarming. In Dickens's *Great Expectations* they are part of the terror the boy Pip feels when he first sees the convict Magwitch in the graveyard: "A fearful man, all in coarse grey, with a great iron on his leg. A man with no hat, and with broken shoes, and with an old rag tied round his head."

A costume not only appears at a specific place and time, it must be "spoken" — that is, worn — by a specific person. Even a simple statement like "I want a drink," or a simple costume — shorts and T-shirt, for example — will have a very different aspect in association with a sixty-year-old man, a sixteen-year-old girl and a six-year-old child. But age and sex are not the only variables to be considered. In judging a costume we will also take into account the physical attributes of the person who is wearing it, assessing him or her in terms of height, weight, posture, racial or ethnic type and facial features and expression. The same outfit will look different on a person whose face and body we consider attractive and on one whom we think ugly. Of course, the idea of "attractiveness" itself is not only subjective, but subject to the historical and geographical vagaries of fashion, as Sir Kenneth Clark° has demonstrated in *The Nude*. In twentieth-century Britain and America, for instance, weight above the norm has been considered unattractive and felt to detract from dignity and status; as Emily Post put it in 1922, "The tendency of fat is to take away from one's gentility; therefore, any one inclined to be fat must be ultra conservative — in order to counteract the effect." The overweight person who does not follow this rule is in danger of appearing vulgar or even revolting. In Conrad's *Lord Jim* the shame of the corrupt Dutch captain is underlined by the fact that, though grossly fat, he wears orange-and-green-striped pajamas in public.

In dress as in language there is a possible range of expression from the most eccentric statement to the most conventional. At one end of the spectrum is the outfit of which the individual parts or "words" are highly incongruent, marking its wearer (if not on stage or involved in some natural disaster) as very peculiar or possibly deranged. Imagine for instance a transparent sequined evening blouse over a dirty Victorian cotton petticoat and black rubber galoshes. (I have observed this getup in real life; it was worn to a lunch party at a famous Irish country house.) If the same costume were worn by a man, or if the usual grammatical order of the sentence were altered — one of the galoshes placed upside down on the head, for example — the effect of insanity would be even greater.

At the opposite end of the spectrum is the costume that is the equivalent of a cliché; it follows some established style in every particular and instantly establishes its wearer as a doctor, a debutante, a hippie or a whore. Such outfits are not uncommon, for as two British sociologists have remarked,

---

Sir Kenneth Clark (1903–1983), British art historian and author of *Civilisation*, a history of Western civilization made into a television series. *The Nude: A Study in Ideal Form* (1956) is an art historical study of the nude form.

"Identification with and active participation in a social group always involves the human body and its adornment and clothing." The more significant any social role is for an individual, the more likely he or she is to dress for it. When two roles conflict, the costume will either reflect the more important one or it will combine them, sometimes with incongruous effects, as in the case of the secretary whose sober, efficient-looking dark suit only partly conceals a tight, bright, low-cut blouse.

The cliché outfit may in some cases become so standardized that it is 31 spoken of as a "uniform": the pin-striped suit, bowler and black umbrella of the London City man, for instance, or the blue jeans and T-shirts of high-school students. Usually, however, these costumes only look like uniforms to outsiders; peers will be aware of significant differences. The London businessman's tie will tell his associates where he went to school; the cut and fabric of his suit will allow them to guess at his income. High-school students, in a single glance, can distinguish new jeans from those that are fashionably worn, functionally or decoratively patched or carelessly ragged; they grasp the fine distinctions of meaning conveyed by straight-leg, flared, boot-cut and peg-top. When two pairs of jeans are identical to the naked eye a label handily affixed to the back pocket gives useful information, identifying the garment as expensive (so-called designer jeans) or discount-department-store. And even within the latter category there are distinctions: in our local junior high school, according to a native informant, "freaks always wear Lees, greasers wear Wranglers, and everyone else wears Levis."

Of course, to the careful observer all these students are only identical be- 32 low the waist; above it they may wear anything from a lumberjack shirt to a lace blouse. Grammatically, this costume seems to be a sign that in their lower or physical natures these persons are alike, however dissimilar they may be socially, intellectually or aesthetically. If this is so, the opposite statement can be imagined — and was actually made by my own college classmates thirty years ago. During the daytime we wore identical baggy sweaters over a wide variety of slacks, plaid kilts, full cotton or straight tweed or slinky jersey skirts, ski pants and Bermuda shorts. "We're all nice coeds from the waist up; we think and talk alike," this costume proclaimed, "but as women we are infinitely various."

The extreme form of conventional dress is the costume totally deter- 33 mined by others: the uniform. No matter what sort of uniform it is — military, civil or religious; the outfit of a general, a postman, a nun, a butler, a football player or a waitress — to put on such livery is to give up one's right to act as an individual — in terms of speech, to be partially or wholly censored. What one does, as well as what one wears, will be determined by external authorities — to a greater or lesser degree, depending upon whether one is, for example, a Trappist monk or a boy scout. The uniform acts as a

211

sign that we should not or need not treat someone as a human being, and that they need not and should not treat us as one. It is no accident that people in uniform, rather than speaking to us honestly and straightforwardly, often repeat mechanical lies. "It was a pleasure having you on board," they say; "I cannot give you that information"; or "The doctor will see you shortly."

Constant wearing of official costume can so transform someone that it becomes difficult or impossible for him or her to react normally. Dr. Grantly, the archdeacon in Anthony Trollope's *The Warden* (1855), is pious and solemn even when alone with his wife: " 'Tis only when he has exchanged that ever-new shovel hat for a tasselled nightcap, and those shining black habiliments for his accustomed *robe de nuit*, that Dr. Grantly talks, and looks, and thinks like an ordinary man."

To take off a uniform is usually a relief, just as it is a relief to abandon official speech; sometimes it is also a sign of defiance. When the schoolgirls in Flannery O'Connor's story "A Temple of the Holy Ghost" come home on holiday, she writes that "They came in the brown convent uniforms they had to wear at Mount St. Scholastica but as soon as they opened their suitcases, they took off the uniforms and put on red skirts and loud blouses. They put on lipstick and their Sunday shoes and walked around in the high heels all over the house."

In certain circumstances, however, putting on a uniform may be a relief, or even an agreeable experience. It can ease the transition from one role to another, as Anthony Powell points out in *Faces in My Time* when he describes joining the British Army in 1939:

> Complete forgetfulness was needed of all that had constituted one's life only a few weeks before. This condition of mind was helped by the anonymity of uniform, something which has to be experienced to be appreciated; in one sense more noticeable off duty in such environments as railway carriages or bars.

It is also true that both physical and psychological disadvantage can be concealed by a uniform, or even canceled out; the robes of a judge or a surgeon may successfully hide a scrawny physique or fears of incompetence, giving him or her both dignity and confidence.

Unlike most civilian clothing, the uniform is often consciously and deliberately symbolic. It identifies its wearer as a member of some group and often locates him or her within a hierarchy; sometimes it gives information about his or her achievements, as do the merit badges of a scout and the battle ribbons of a general. Even when some details of an official costume are not dictated from above, they may by custom come to have a definite meaning. James Laver remarks that in Britain

> until quite recently it was still possible to deduce a clergy-man's religious opinions from his neckwear. If you wore an

ordinary collar with a white tie you were probably Low Church and Evangelical. If you wore any version of the Roman collar you displayed your sympathy with the . . . Oxford Movement.

It is likely that when they were first designed all uniforms made symbolic 38 sense and were as easy to "read" as the outfit of a *Playboy* Bunny today. But official costume tends to freeze the styles of the time in which it was invented, and today the sixteenth-century uniforms of the guards at the Tower of London or the late-Edwardian morning dress of the butler may merely seem old-fashioned to us. Military uniforms, as James Laver points out, were originally intended "to impress and even to terrify the enemy" in hand-to-hand combat (just like the war whoops and battle cries that accompanied them), and warriors accordingly disguised themselves as devils, skeletons and wild beasts. Even after gunpowder made this style of fighting rare, the desire to terrify "survived into modern times in such vestigial forms as the death's head on the hussar's headgear and the bare ribs of the skeleton originally painted on the warrior's body and later transformed into the froggings of his tunic."

The wearing of a uniform by people who are obviously not carrying out 39 the duties it involves has often suggested personal laxity — as in the case of drunken soldiers carousing in the streets. In this century, however, it has been adopted as a form of political protest, and both men and women have appeared at rallies and marches in their Army, Navy, or police uniforms, the implied statement being "I'm a soldier, but I support disarmament/open housing/gay rights," etc. A related development in the 1960s was the American hippie custom of wearing parts of old Army uniforms — Civil War, World War I and World War II. This military garb puzzled many observers, especially when it appeared in anti-Vietnam demonstrations. Others understood the implicit message, which was that the longhaired kid in the Confederate tunic or the Eisenhower jacket was not some kind of coward or sissy; that he was not against all wars — just against the cruel and unnecessary one he was in danger of being drafted into.

Between cliché and madness in the language of dress are all the known 40 varieties of speech: eloquence, wit, information, irony, propaganda, humor, pathos and even (though rarely) true poetry. Just as a gifted writer combines unexpected words and images, risking (and sometimes briefly gaining) the reputation of being deranged, so certain gifted persons have been able to combine odd items of clothing, old and new, native and foreign, into a brilliant eloquence of personal statement. While other people merely follow the style of the age in which they live, these men and women transform contemporary fashion into individual expression. Some of their achievements are celebrated in the history of costume, but here, as in all the arts, there must be many unknown geniuses.

Unfortunately, just as there are more no-talent artists than there are geniuses, there are also many persons who do not dress very well, not because of lack of money but because of innate lack of taste. In some cases their clothes are merely monotonous, suggesting an uninteresting but consistent personality. Others seem to have a knack for combining colors, patterns and styles in a way that — rightly or wrongly — suggests personal awkwardness and disharmony. In Henry James's *The Bostonians* (1886), the bad taste in clothes of the heroine, Verena Tarrant, foreshadows her moral confusion and her bad taste in men. Verena, who has bright-red hair, makes her first public appearance wearing "a light-brown dress, of a shape that struck [Basil Ransom] as fantastic, a yellow petticoat, and a large crimson sash fastened at the side; while round her neck, and falling low upon her flat young chest, she had a double chain of amber beads." And, as if this were not enough, Verena also carried "a large red fan, which she kept constantly in movement."

Like any elaborate nonverbal language, costume is sometimes more eloquent than the native speech of its wearers. Indeed, the more inarticulate someone is verbally, the more important are the statements made by his or her clothes. People who are skilled in verbal discourse, on the other hand, can afford to be somewhat careless or dull in their dress, as in the case of certain teachers and politicians. Even they, of course, are telling us something, but they may not be telling us very much.

Men and women in uniform are not the only ones who wear clothes they have not selected themselves. All of us were first dressed in such garments, and often our late childhood and early adolescence were made stormy by our struggles to choose our own wardrobe — in verbal terms, to speak for ourselves. A few of us did not win this battle, or won only temporarily, and became those men (or, more rarely, women) most of whose clothes are selected by their wives, husbands or mothers.

All of us, however, even as adults, have at some time been the grateful or ungrateful recipients of garments bought by relatives or friends. Such a gift is a mixed blessing, for to wear clothes chosen by someone else is to accept and project their donor's image of you; in a sense, to become a ventriloquist's doll. Sometimes, of course, the gift may be welcome or flattering: the Christmas tie that is just right, the low-cut lace nightgown that encourages a woman of only moderate attractions to think of herself as a glamourpuss. Often, however, the gift is felt as a demand, and one harder to refuse because it comes disguised as a favor. When I was first married I dressed in a style that might be described as Radcliffe Beatnik (black jerseys and bright cotton-print skirts). My mother-in-law, hoping to remodel me into a nice country-club young matron, frequently presented me with tiny-collared, classically styled silk blouses and cashmere sweaters in white, beige or pale green which I never wore and could not give away because they were monogrammed.

To put on someone else's clothes is symbolically to take on their personality. This is true even when one's motives are hostile. In Dickens's *Our Mutual Friend* (1864–65), the teacher Bradley Headstone disguises himself in "rough waterside second-hand clothing" and a "red neckerchief stained black . . . by wear" which are identical with those worn by Rogue Riderhood, so that Riderhood shall be blamed for the murder Headstone is planning to commit. In assuming this costume Headstone literally becomes just such a low, vicious and guilty man as Riderhood.

In this culture the innocent exchange of clothing is most common among teenage girls, who in this way confirm not only their friendship but their identity, just as they do by using the same slang and expressing the same ideas. The custom may persist into adult life, and also occurs between lovers and between husband and wife, though in the latter case the borrowing is usually one-way. The sharing of clothes is always a strong indication of shared tastes, opinions and even personality. Next time you are at a large party, meeting or public event, look around the room and ask yourself if there is anyone present whose clothes you would be willing to wear yourself on that occasion. If so, he or she is apt to be a soul mate.

Perhaps the most difficult aspect of sartorial communication is the fact that any language that is able to convey information can also be used to convey misinformation. You can lie in the language of dress just as you can in English, French or Latin, and this sort of deception has the advantage that one cannot usually be accused of doing it deliberately. The costume that suggests youth or wealth, unlike the statement that one is twenty-nine years old and has a six-figure income, cannot be directly challenged or disproved.

A sartorial lie may be white, like Cinderella's ball gowns; it may be various shades of gray, or it may be downright black, as in the case of the radical-hippie disguise of the FBI informant or the stolen military uniform of the spy. The lie may be voluntary, or it may be involuntary, as when a tomboy is forced into a velvet party dress by her parents. It may even be unconscious, as with the man who innocently wears a leather vest and boots to a bar patronized by homosexuals, or the American lady touring Scotland in a plaid she thought looked awfully pretty in the shop, but to which she has no hereditary right. If a complete grammar of clothing is ever written it will have to deal not only with these forms of dishonesty, but with many others that face linguists and semioticians°: ambiguity, error, self-deception, misinterpretation, irony and framing.

semioticians Philosophers who deal with the functions of signs and symbols in language.

Theatrical dress, or costume in the colloquial sense, is a special case of
sartorial deception, one in which the audience willingly cooperates, recog-
nizing that the clothes the actor wears, like the words he speaks, are not his
own. Sometimes, however, what is only a temporary disguise for an actor
becomes part of the everyday wardrobe of some members of the public.
Popular culture, which has done so much to homogenize our life, has at the
same time, almost paradoxically, helped to preserve and even to invent distinctive dress through a kind of feedback process. It is convenient for producers of films, TV programs and commercials that clothes should instantly
and clearly indicate age, class, regional origin and if possible occupation and
personality. Imagine that a certain costume is assigned to an actor representing a tough, handsome young auto mechanic, by a costume designer who
has seen something like it in a local bar. Actual auto mechanics, viewing the
program and others like it, unconsciously accept this outfit as characteristic;
they are imitated by others who have not even seen the program. Finally the
outfit becomes standard, and thus genuine.

Somewhere between theatrical costume and the uniform is ritual dress,
the special clothing we adopt for the important ceremonies of our life: birth
(the christening robe), college graduation, weddings, funerals and other
portentous occasions that also tend to involve ritual speech.

A more ambiguous sort of disguise is the costume that is deliberately
chosen on the advice of others in order to deceive the beholder. For over a
hundred years books and magazines have been busy translating the correct
language of fashion, telling men and women what they should wear to seem
genteel, rich, sophisticated and attractive to the other sex. Journals addressed to what used to be called "the career girl" advised her how to dress
to attract "the right kind of man" — successful, marriage-minded. Regardless of the current fashion, a discreet femininity was always recommended:
soft fabrics and colors, flowers and ruffles in modest profusion, hair slightly
longer and curlier than that of the other girls in the office. The costume must
be neither too stylish (suggesting expense to the future husband) nor dowdy
(suggesting boredom). Above all, a delicate balance must be struck between
the prim and the seductive, one tending not to attract men and the other to
attract the wrong kind. Times have changed somewhat, and the fashion
pages of magazines such as *Cosmopolitan* now seem to specialize in telling
the career girl what to wear to charm the particular wrong type of man who
reads *Playboy*, while the editorial pages tell her how to cope with the resulting psychic damage.

Two recent paperbacks, *Dress for Success* and *The Woman's Dress for Success Book*, by John T. Molloy, instruct businessmen and women on how to select their clothes so that they will look efficient, authoritative and reliable

even when they are incompetent, weak and shifty. Molloy, who is by no means unintelligent, claims that his "wardrobe engineering" is based on scientific research and opinion polls. Also, in a departure from tradition, he is interested in telling women how to get promoted, not how to get married. The secret, apparently, is to wear an expensive but conventional "skirted suit" in medium gray or navy wool with a modestly cut blouse. No sweaters, no pants, no very bright colors, no cleavage, no long or excessively curly hair.

Anyone interested in scenic variety must hope that Molloy is mistaken; but my own opinion-polling, unfortunately, back him up. A fast-rising lady executive in a local bank reports to me — reluctantly — that "Suits do help separate the women from the girls — provided the women can tolerate the separation, which is another question altogether." 53

We put on clothing for some of the same reasons that we speak: to make living and working easier and more comfortable, to proclaim (or disguise) our identities and to attract erotic attention. James Laver has designated these motives as the Utility Principle, the Hierarchical Principle and the Seduction Principle. Anyone who has recently been to a large party or professional meeting will recall that most of the conversation that was not directed to practical ends ("Where are the drinks?" "Here is the agenda for this afternoon") was principally motivated by the Hierarchical or the Seduction Principle. In the same way, the clothes worn on that occasion, as well as more or less sheltering the nakedness of those present, were chosen to indicate their wearer's place in the world and/or to make him or her look more attractive. 54

The earliest utilitarian clothing was probably makeshift. Faced with extremes of climate — icy winters, drenching rainstorms or the baking heat of the sun — men and women slung or tied the skins of animals around themselves; they fastened broad leaves to their heads as simple rain hats and made crude sandals from strips of hide or bark, as primitive tribes do today. Such protective clothing has a long history, but it has never acquired much prestige. The garment with a purely practical function is the glamourless equivalent of the flat, declarative sentence: "It's raining." "I'm working in the garden." But it is difficult, in costume as in speech, to make a truly simple statement. The pair of plain black rubbers which states that it is raining may also remark, "The streets are wet, and I can't afford to damage my shoes." If the streets are not in fact very wet, the rubbers may also declare silently, "This is a dull, timid, fussy person." 55

Sometimes, regardless of the weather, utility in itself is a minus quality. The more water-repellent a raincoat is, ordinarily, the more it repels admiration — unless it is also fashionably colored or cut, or in some other way evidently expensive. Boots of molded synthetic leather that keep your feet 56 warm and dry are thought to be less aesthetically pleasing than decorated leather ones which soon leak, and thus imply ownership of a car or familiarity with taxis.

Practical clothing usually seems most attractive when it is worn by persons who do not need it and probably never will need it. The spotless starched pinafore that covers a child's party dress or the striped overalls favored by some of today's college students look much more charming than they would on the housemaids and farmers for whom they were first intended.

This transformation of protective clothing into fashionable costume has a long history. As Rachel Kemper points out, the sort of garments that become fashionable most rapidly and most completely are those which were originally designed for warfare, dangerous work or strenuous sports:

> Garments intended to deflect the point of a lance, flying arrows, or solar radiation possess a strange kind of instant chic and are sure to be modified into fashions for both men and women. Contemporary examples abound: the ubiquitous aviator glasses that line the rails of fashionable singles bars, perforated racing gloves that grip the wheels of sedate family cars, impressively complicated scuba divers' watches that will never be immersed in any body of water more challenging than the country-club pool.

Common sense and most historians of costume have assumed that the demands of either utility, status or sex must have been responsible for the invention of clothing. However, as sometimes happens in human affairs, both common sense and the historians were apparently wrong: scholars have recently informed us that the original purpose of clothing was magical. Archaeologists digging up past civilizations and anthropologists studying primitive tribes have come to the conclusion that, as Rachel Kemper puts it, "Paint, ornament, and rudimentary clothing were first employed to attract good animistic powers and to ward off evil." When Charles Darwin visited Tierra del Fuego, a cold, wet, disagreeable land plagued by constant winds, he found the natives naked except for feathers in their hair and symbolic designs painted on their bodies. Modern Australian bushmen, who may spend hours decorating themselves and their relatives with patterns in colored clay, often wear nothing else but an amulet or two.

However skimpy it may be, primitive dress almost everywhere, like primitive speech, is full of magic. A necklace of shark's teeth or a girdle of cowrie shells or feathers serves the same purpose as a prayer or spell, and may magically replace — or more often supplement — a spoken charm. In the first instance a form of *contagious* magic is at work: the shark's teeth are believed to endow their wearer with the qualities of a fierce and successful fisherman. The cowrie shells, on the other hand, work through *sympathetic* magic: since they resemble the female sexual parts, they are thought to increase or preserve fertility.

In civilized society today belief in the supernatural powers of clothing — 61 like belief in prayers, spells and charms — remains widespread, though we denigrate it with the name "superstition." Advertisements announce that improbable and romantic events will follow the application of a particular sort of grease to our faces, hair or bodies; they claim that members of the opposite (or our own) sex will be drawn to us by the smell of a particular soap. Nobody believes those ads, you may say. Maybe not, but we behave as though we did: look in your bathroom cabinet.

The supernatural garments of European folk tales — the seven-league 62 boots, the cloaks of invisibility and the magic rings — are not forgotten, merely transformed, so that today we have the track star who can only win a race in a particular hat or shoes, the plain-clothes cop who feels no one can see him in his raincoat and the wife who takes off her wedding ring before going to a motel with her lover. Amulets also remain very popular: circlets of elephant hair for strength and long life, copper bracelets as a charm against arthritis. In both cases what is operating is a form of magical thinking like that of the Australian aborigine: Elephants are strong and long-lived; if we constantly rub ourselves with their hair we may acquire these qualities. Copper conducts electricity, therefore it will conduct nerve impulses to cramped and unresponsive muscles, either by primitive contagious magic as with the elephant-hair bracelet, or by the modern contagious magic of pseudoscience: the copper "attracting and concentrating free-floating electrons," as a believer explained it to me.

Sympathetic or symbolic magic is also often employed, as when we hang 63 crosses, stars or one of the current symbols of female power and solidarity around our necks, thus silently involving the protection of Jesus, Jehovah or Astarte. Such amulets, of course, may be worn to announce our allegiance to some faith or cause rather than as a charm. Or they may serve both purposes simultaneously — or sequentially. The crucifix concealed below the parochial-school uniform speaks only to God until some devilish human force persuades its wearer to remove his or her clothes; then it acts — or fails to act — as a warning against sin as well as a protective talisman.

Articles of clothing, too, may be treated as if they had mana, the imper- 64 sonal supernatural force that tends to concentrate itself in objects. When I was in college it was common to wear a particular "lucky" sweater, shirt or hat to final examinations, and this practice continues today. Here it is usually contagious magic that is at work: the chosen garment has become lucky by being worn on the occasion of some earlier success, or has been given to its owner by some favored person. The wearing of such magical garments is especially common in sports, where they are often publicly credited with bringing their owners luck. Their loss or abandonment is thought to cause injury as well as defeat. Actors also believe ardently in the magic of clothes, possibly because they are so familiar with the near-magical transforming power of theatrical costume.

Sometimes the lucky garment is believed to be even more fortunate when it is put on backwards or inside out. There may be different explanations of this belief. A student of my acquaintance, whose faded lucky sweat shirt bears the name of her high-school swimming team, suggests that reversing the garment places the printed side against her body, thus allowing the mana to work on her more directly.

Ordinarily, nonmagical clothes may also be worn inside out or reversed for magical reasons. The custom of turning your apron to change your luck after a series of household mishaps is widely known in both Britain and America; I have seen it done myself in upstate New York. Gamblers today sometimes turn their clothes before commencing play, and the practice was even more common in the past. The eighteenth-century British statesman Charles James Fox often sat at the gaming tables all night long with his coat turned inside out and his face blackened to propitiate the goddess of chance. Or perhaps to disguise himself from her; according to folk tradition, the usual explanation for the turning of garments is that it confuses demons. In blackface and with the elegant trimmings of his dress coat hidden, Fox was invisible to Lady Luck; the evil spirits that haunt housewives fail to recognize their intended victims and fly on to torment someone else.

At the other extreme from clothing which brings good luck and success is the garment of ill-omen. The most common and harmless version of this is the dress, suit or shirt which (like some children) seems to attract or even to seek out dirt, grease, protruding nails, falling ketchup and other hazards. Enid Nemy, who has written perceptively about such clothes for *The New York Times*, suggests that they may be lazy: "they'd just as soon rest on a hanger, or in a box — and they revolt when they're hauled into action." Or, she adds, they may be snobs, unwilling to associate with ordinary people. Whatever the cause, such accident-prone garments rarely if ever reform, and once one has been identified it is best to break off relations with it immediately. Otherwise, like accident-prone persons, it is apt to involve you in much inconvenience and possibly actual disaster, turning some important interview or romantic tryst into a scene of farce or humiliation. More sinister, and fortunately more rare, is the garment which seems to attract disasters to you rather than to itself. Ms. Nemy mentions an orange linen dress that apparently took a dislike to its owner, one Margaret Turner of Dover Publications. Orange clothes, as it happens, are likely to arouse hostility in our culture, but this dress seems to have been a special case. "Women friends seemed cattier, men seemed more aloof, and I'd get into bad situations with my boss," Ms. Turner reported. "And that wasn't all. I'd spill coffee, miss train connections, and the car would break down."

Even when our clothes are not invested with this sort of supernatural 68 power, they may have symbolic meanings that tend to increase with age. The man who comes home from work to discover that his wife has thrown out his shabby, stained tweed jacket or his old army pants is often much angrier than the situation seems to call for, and his anger may be mixed with depression and even fear. Not only has he lost a magical garment, he has been forced to see his spouse as in some real sense his enemy — as a person who wishes to deprive him of comfort and protection.

A pleasanter sort of magic occurs in the exchange of garments common 69 among lovers. In the Middle Ages a lady would often give her kerchief or glove to a chosen knight. When he went into battle or fought in a tournament he would place it against his heart or pin it to his helmet. Today, probably because of the taboo against the wearing of female garments by men, the traffic is all one-way. The teenage girl wears her boyfriend's basketball jacket to school; the secretary who has spent the night impulsively and successfully at a friend's apartment goes home next morning with his London Fog raincoat over her disco outfit; and the wife, in a playful and affectionate mood, puts on her husband's red flannel pajama top. Often the woman feels so good and looks so well in the magical borrowed garment that it is never returned.

If the relationship sours, though, the exchange alters its meaning; the 70 good spell becomes a curse. The magical article may be returned, often in poor condition: soiled or wrinkled, or with "accidental" cigarette burns. Or it may be deliberately destroyed: thrown in the trash, or even vindictively cut to shreds. An especially refined form of black magic is to give the garment away to the Salvation Army, in the hope that it will soon be worn by a drunken and incontinent bum — ideally, someplace where your former lover will see and recognize it.

As with the spoken language, communication through dress is easiest 71 and least problematical when only one purpose is being served; when we wear a garment solely to keep warm, to attend a graduation ceremony, to announce our political views, to look sexy or to protect ourselves from bad luck. Unfortunately, just as with speech, our motives in making any statement are apt to be double or multiple. The man who goes to buy a winter coat may simultaneously want it to shelter him from bad weather, look expensive and fashionable, announce that he is sophisticated and rugged, attract a certain sort of sexual partner and magically infect him with the qualities of Robert Redford.

Naturally it is often impossible to satisfy all these requirements and make 72 all these statements at once. Even if they do not contradict one another, the

221

ideal garment of our fantasy may not be available in any of the stores we can get to, and if it is we may not be able to afford it. Therefore, just as with speech, it often happens that we cannot say what we really mean because we don't have the right "words." The woman who complains formulaically that she hasn't got anything to wear is in just this situation. Like a tourist abroad, she may be able to manage all right in shops and on trains, but she cannot go out to dinner, because her vocabulary is so limited that she would misrepresent herself and perhaps attract ridicule.

At present all these difficulties are compounded by contradictory messages about the value of dress in general. The Protestant ethic stressed modestly and simplicity of dress. Cleanliness was next to godliness, but finery and display were of the Devil, and the serious man or woman had no time for such folly. Even today to declare that one never pays much attention to what he or she is wearing is to claim virtue, and usually to receive respect. At the same time, however, we are told by advertisers and fashion experts that we must dress well and use cosmetics to, as they put it, liberate the "natural" beauty within. If we do not "take care of our looks" and "make the best of ourselves," we are scolded by our relatives and pitied by our friends. To juggle these conflicting demands is difficult and often exhausting.

When two or more wishes or demands conflict, a common psychological result is some disorder of expression. Indeed, one of the earliest theorists of dress, the psychologist J. C. Flügel, saw all human clothing as a neurotic symptom. In his view, the irreconcilable emotions are modesty and the desire for attention:

> . . . our attitude towards clothes is *ab initio* "ambivalent," to use the invaluable term which has been introduced into psychology by the psychoanalysists; we are trying to satisfy two contradictory tendencies. . . . In this respect the discovery, or at any rate the use, of clothes, seems, in its psychological aspects, to resemble the process whereby a neurotic symptom is developed.

Flügel is considering only a single opposition; he does not even contemplate the neurotic confusion that can result when three or more motives are in conflict — as they often are. Given this state of things, we should not be surprised to find in the language of clothing the equivalent of many of the psychological disorders of speech. We will hear, or rather see, the repetitive stammer of the man who always wears the same jacket or pair of shoes whatever the climate or occasion; the childish lisp of the woman who clings to the frills and ribbons of her early youth; and those embarrassing lapses of the tongue — or rather of the garment — of which the classical examples are the unzipped fly and the slip that becomes a social error. We will also notice the signs of more temporary inner distress: the too-loud or harsh "voice" that exhausts our eye rather than our ear with glaring colors and clashing patterns, and the drab, colorless equivalent of the inability to speak above a whisper.

Dress is an aspect of human life that arouses strong feelings, some in- 76
tensely pleasant and others very disagreeable. It is no accident that many of our daydreams involve fine raiment; nor that one of the most common and disturbing human nightmares is of finding ourselves in public inappropri-
ately and/or incompletely clothed.

For some people the daily task of choosing a costume is tedious, oppres- 77
sive or even frightening. Occasionally such people tell us that fashion is un-
necessary; that in the ideal world of the future we will all wear some sort of identical jump suit — washable, waterproof, stretchable, temperature-con-
trolled; timeless, ageless and sexless. What a convenience, what a relief it will be, they say, never to worry about how to dress for a job interview, a romantic tryst or a funeral!

Convenient perhaps, but not exactly a relief. Such a utopia would give 78
most of us the same kind of chill we feel when a stadium full of Communist-
bloc athletes in identical sports outfits, shouting slogans in unison, appears on TV. Most people do not want to be told what to wear any more than they want to be told what to say. In Belfast recently four hundred Irish Republi-
can prisoners ''refused to wear any clothes at all, draping themselves day and night in blankets,'' rather than put on prison uniforms. Even the offer of civilian-style dress did not satisfy them; they insisted on wearing their own clothes brought from home, or nothing. Fashion is free speech, and one of the privileges, if not always one of the pleasures, of a free world.

QUESTIONS ON MEANING

1. Lurie unifies her essay by a consistent use of analogy — a rhetorical tech-
   nique by which a similarity between two different things provides the basis for an argument about both. This essay is about clothes and about language. Is it about anything else? Which aspects of the analogy between fashion and language effectively persuade us that Lurie's argument is sound?
2. Lurie often translates into language the statements made or implied by cos-
   tume. In paragraph 55, for example, she argues that a practical garment is the equivalent of a flat, declarative sentence. Plain black rubbers are like the state-
   ment ''It's raining.'' She points out that ''the rubbers may also declare silently, 'This is a dull, timid, fussy person.' '' What effect does the adverb *silently* have? Where do her translations rely on inference and implication?
3. In her consideration of conventional fashion, Lurie discusses the ''cliché out-
   fit'' and the uniform (paragraphs 30–39). How are the two similar? What distinguishes them from each other?

QUESTIONS ON STRATEGY

1. In the first part of her essay, Lurie uses her analogy most directly. Later when she analyzes the meaning of clothing, to wearer and observer, she refers less often to clothes as language. When does she change her strategy? Why does she do it?
2. The concepts of magical clothing (paragraphs 59–66) and malevolent clothing (paragraphs 67–70) have only a tangential bearing on the relation between clothing and words. How do they fit or not fit with the rest of the essay? What other tangents does Lurie introduce in this essay? Do they support or detract from her argument? Why?

EXPLORATIONS

1. Study the window displays in some department stores. Notice how the clothing is presented. How lifelike are the mannequins? How are they posed? To what extent has the window dresser translated the clothes on display? Also study several magazines that carry fashion advertising (*Vogue*, *Glamour*, *Esquire*, *New York Times* Sunday fashion supplements for men and women). How do fashion photographers present the clothing of designers and manufacturers? Can we translate their images? Write an essay on the influence of display and advertising on the language of clothing.
2. When Fussell, in his essay on page 150, puts people into categories according to the clothes they wear, how is he similar to Lurie, and how is he different? Does one author seem more serious than the other? What aspects of their styles account for the differences in their relative seriousness?

WRITING TOPICS

1. Use an analogy like Lurie's to write an essay about some other category of consumer goods. Is there a language of cars? Of bicycles? Of home appliances? Can you translate the pictures hung on the walls, or the wrought-iron railing around the porch? Consider the utility of such objects as well as their implications about status. What does the consumer good reveal about its owner? What does the owner hope to reveal by possessing the good?

BOOK AVAILABLE IN PAPERBACK

The Language of Clothes. New York: Vintage Books. *Nonfiction.*

EDWARD
ABBEY

B ORN IN PENNSYLVANIA in 1927, Edward Abbey took his B.A. at the University of New Mexico and has become an enthusiastic southwesterner; he lives in Wolf Hole, Arizona. Working as park ranger and fire lookout for the National Park Service, he had time to pursue his literary vocation. He has published several novels, including **Black Sun** *(1971) and* **The Monkey Ranch Gang** *(1975), but Abbey is best known for his journals and essays on the natural world.* Desert Solitaire *came out in 1968, followed by many books including* The Journey Home: Some Words in Defense of the American West *(1977) and* Abbey's Road *(1979).*

Almost as prominent as Abbey's love for the desert is his bitterness toward those who exploit and waste the natural world. Filling out a questionnaire for a reference book, he gave his religion as Piute (an American Indian people) and his politics as agrarian anarchist. In ''The Most Beautiful Place on Earth,'' which begins Desert Solitaire, *Abbey concerns himself largely, by means of concrete image and anecdote, with placing himself and therefore his reader in the natural world. His language sets the reader in the desert that Abbey loves. But the reader will also discover, in phrases that form a dark background to bright desert, the other world to which this paradise is alternative: ''the clamor and filth and confusion of the cultural apparatus.''*

The Most Beautiful Place
on Earth

The First Morning

This is the most beautiful place on earth.

There are many such places. Every man, every woman, carries in heart and mind the image of the ideal place, the right place, the one true home, known or unknown, actual or visionary. A houseboat in Kashmir, a view down Atlantic Avenue in Brooklyn, a gray gothic farmhouse two stories high at the end of a red dog road in the Allegheny Mountains, a cabin on the shore of a blue lake in spruce and fir country, a greasy alley near the Hoboken waterfront, or even, possibly, for those of a less demanding sensibility, the world to be seen from a comfortable apartment high in the tender, velvety smog of Manhattan, Chicago, Paris, Tokyo, Rio or Rome — there's no limit to the human capacity for the homing sentiment. Theologians, sky pilots, astronauts have even felt the appeal of home calling to them from up above, in the cold black outback of interstellar space.

For myself I'll take Moab, Utah. I don't mean the town itself, of course, but the country which surrounds it — the canyonlands. The slickrock desert. The red dust and the burnt cliffs and the lonely sky — all that which lies beyond the end of the roads.

The choice became apparent to me this morning when I stepped out of a Park Service housetrailer — my caravan — to watch for the first time in my life the sun come up over the hoodoo stone of Arches National Monument.

I wasn't able to see much of it last night. After driving all day from Albuquerque — 450 miles — I reached Moab after dark in cold, windy, clouded weather. At park headquarters north of town I met the superintendent and the chief ranger, the only permanent employees, except for one maintenance man, in this particular unit of America's national park system. After coffee they gave me a key to the housetrailer and directions on how to reach it; I am required to live and work not at headquarters but at this one-man station some twenty miles back in the interior, on my own. The way I wanted it, naturally, or I'd never have asked for the job.

Leaving the headquarters area and the lights of Moab, I drove twelve miles farther north on the highway until I came to a dirt road on the right, where a small wooden sign pointed the way: Arches National Monument Eight Miles. I left the pavement, turned east into the howling wilderness. Wind roaring out of the northwest, black clouds across the stars — all I could see were clumps of brush and scattered junipers along the roadside. Then another modest signboard:

WARNING: QUICKSAND
DO NOT CROSS WASH
WHEN WATER IS RUNNING

The wash looked perfectly dry in my headlights. I drove down, across, up the other side and on into the night. Glimpses of weird humps of pale rock on either side, like petrified elephants, dinosaurs, stone-age hobgoblins. Now and then something alive scurried across the road: kangaroo mice, a jackrabbit, an animal that looked like a cross between a raccoon and a squirrel — the ringtail cat. Farther on a pair of mule deer started from the brush and bounded obliquely through the beams of my lights, raising puffs of dust which the wind, moving faster than my pickup truck, caught and carried ahead of me out of sight into the dark. The road, narrow and rocky, twisted sharply left and right, dipped in and out of tight ravines, climbing by degrees toward a summit which I would see only in the light of the coming day. 7

Snow was swirling through the air when I crossed the unfenced line and passed the boundary marker of the park. A quarter-mile beyond I found the ranger station — a wide place in the road, an informational display under a lean-to shelter, and fifty yards away the little tin government housetrailer where I would be living for the next six months. 8

A cold night, a cold wind, the snow falling like confetti. In the lights of the trunk I unlocked the housetrailer, got out bedroll and baggage and moved in. By flashlight I found the bed, unrolled my sleeping bag, pulled off my boots and crawled in and went to sleep at once. The last I knew was the shaking of the trailer in the wind and the sound, from inside, of hungry mice scampering around with the good news that their long lean lonesome winter was over — their friend and provider had finally arrived. 9

This morning I awake before sunrise, stick my head out of the sack, peer through a frosty window at a scene dim and vague with flowing mists, dark fantastic shapes looming beyond. An unlikely landscape. 10

I get up, moving about in long underwear and socks, stooping carefully under the low ceiling and lower doorways of the housetrailer, a machine for living built so efficiently and compactly there's hardly room for a man to breathe. An iron lung it is, with windows and venetian blinds. 11

The mice are silent, watching me from their hiding places, but the wind is still blowing and outside the ground is covered with snow. Cold as a tomb, a jail, a cave; I lie down on the dusty floor, on the cold linoleum sprinkled with mouse turds, and light the pilot on the butane heater. Once this thing gets going the place warms up fast, in a dense unhealthy way, with a 12 layer of heat under the ceiling where my head is and nothing but frigid air from the knees down. But we've got all the indispensable conveniences: gas cookstove, gas refrigerator, hot water heater, sink with running water (if the pipes aren't frozen), storage cabinets and shelves, everything within arm's reach of everything else. The gas comes from two steel bottles in a shed outside; the water comes by gravity flow from a tank buried in a hill close by. Quite luxurious for the wilds. There's even a shower stall and a flush toilet with a dead rat in the bowl. Pretty soft. My poor mother raised five children without any of these luxuries and might be doing without them yet if it hadn't been for Hitler, war and general prosperity.

Time to get dressed, get out and have a look at the lay of the land, fix a breakfast. I try to pull on my boots but they're stiff as iron from the cold. I light a burner on the stove and hold the boots upside down above the flame until they are malleable enough to force my feet into. I put on a coat and step outside. Into the center of the world, God's navel, Abbey's country, the red wasteland.

The sun is not yet in sight but signs of the advent are plain to see. Lavender clouds sail like a fleet of ships across the pale green dawn; each cloud, planed flat on the wind, has a base of fiery gold. Southeast, twenty miles by line of sight, stand the peaks of the Sierra La Sal, twelve to thirteen thousand feet above sea level, all covered with snow and rosy in the morning sunlight. The air is dry and clear as well as cold; the last fogbanks left over from last night's storm are scudding away like ghosts, fading into nothing before the wind and the sunrise.

The view is open and perfect in all directions except to the west where the ground rises and the skyline is only a few hundred yards away. Looking toward the mountains I can see the dark gorge of the Colorado River five or six miles away, carved through the sandstone mesa, though nothing of the river itself down inside the gorge. Southward, on the far side of the river, lies the Moab valley between thousand-foot walls of rock, with the town of Moab somewhere on the valley floor, too small to be seen from here. Beyond the Moab valley is more canyon and tableland stretching away to the Blue Mountains fifty miles south. On the north and northwest I see the Roan Cliffs and the Book Cliffs, the two-level face of the Uinta Plateau. Along the foot of those cliffs, maybe thirty miles off, invisible from where I stand, runs U.S. 6–50, a major east-west artery of commerce, traffic, and rubbish, and the main line of the Denver–Rio Grande Railroad. To the east, under the spreading sunrise, are more mesas, more canyons, league on league of red cliff and arid tablelands, extending through purple haze over the bulging curve of the planet to the ranges of Colorado — a sea of desert.

Within this vast perimeter, in the middle ground and foreground of the picture, a rather personal demesne, are the 33,000 acres of Arches National

Monument of which I am now sole inhabitant, usufructuary,° observer and custodian.

What are the Arches? From my place in front of the housetrailer I can see 17 several of the hundred or more of them which have been discovered in the park. These are natural arches, holes in the rock, windows in stone, no two alike, as varied in form as in dimension. They range in size from holes just big enough to walk through to openings large enough to contain the dome of the Capitol building in Washington, D.C. Some resemble jug handles or flying buttresses, others natural bridges but with this technical distinction: a natural bridge spans a watercourse — a natural arch does not. The arches were formed through hundreds of thousands of years by the weathering of the huge sandstone walls, or fins, in which they are found. Not the work of a cosmic hand, nor sculptured by sand-bearing winds, as many people prefer to believe, the arches came into being and continue to come into being through the modest wedging action of rainwater, melting snow, frost, and ice, aided by gravity. In color they shade from off-white through buff, pink, brown and red, tones which also change with the time of day and the moods of the light, the weather, the sky.

Standing there, gaping at this monstrous and inhuman spectacle of rock 18 and cloud and sky and space, I feel a ridiculous greed and possessiveness come over me. I want to know it all, possess it all, embrace the entire scene intimately, deeply, totally, as a man desires a beautiful woman. An insane wish? Perhaps not — at least there's nothing else, no one human, to dispute possession with me.

The snow-covered ground glimmers with a dull blue light, reflecting the 19 sky and the approaching sunrise. Leading away from me the narrow dirt road, an alluring and primitive track into nowhere, meanders down the slope and toward the heart of the labyrinth of naked stone. Near the first group of arches, looming over a bend in the road, is a balanced rock about fifty feet high, mounted on a pedestal of equal height; it looks like a head from Easter Island, a stone god, or a petrified ogre.

Like a god, like an ogre? The personification of the natural is exactly the 20 tendency I wish to suppress in myself, to eliminate for good. I am here not only to evade for a while the clamor and filth and confusion of the cultural apparatus but also to confront, immediately and directly if it's possible, the bare bones of existence, the elemental and fundamental, the bedrock which sustains us. I want to be able to look at and into a juniper tree, a piece of quartz, a vulture, a spider, and see it as it is in itself, devoid of all humanly

---

usufructuary One who has the use and enjoyment of something belonging to another.

ascribed qualities, anti-Kantian,° even the categories of scientific description. To meet God or Medusa face to face, even if it means risking everything human in myself. I dream of a hard and brutal mysticism in which the naked self merges with a nonhuman world and yet somehow survives still intact, individual, separate. Paradox and bedrock.

Well — the sun will be up in a few minutes and I haven't even begun to make coffee. I take more baggage from my pickup, the grub box and cooking gear, go back in the trailer and start breakfast. Simply breathing, in a place like this, arouses the appetite. The orange juice is frozen, the milk slushy with ice. Still chilly enough inside the trailer to turn my breath to vapor. When the first rays of the sun strike the cliffs I fill a mug with steaming coffee and sit in the doorway facing the sunrise, hungry for the warmth.

Suddenly it comes, the flaming globe, blazing on the pinnacles and minarets and balanced rocks, on the canyon walls and through the windows in the sandstone fins. We greet each other, sun and I, across the black void of ninety-three million miles. The snow glitters between us, acres of diamonds almost painful to look at. Within an hour all the snow exposed to the sunlight will be gone and the rock will be damp and steaming. Within minutes, even as I watch, melting snow begins to drip from the branches of a juniper nearby; drops of water streak slowly down the side of the trailerhouse.

I am not alone after all. Three ravens are wheeling near the balanced rock, squawking at each other and at the dawn. I'm sure they're as delighted by the return of the sun as I am and I wish I knew the language. I'd sooner exchange ideas with the birds on earth than learn to carry on intergalactic communications with some obscure race of humanoids on a satellite planet from the world of Betelgeuse.° First things first. The ravens cry out in husky voices, blue-black wings flapping against the golden sky. Over my shoulder comes the sizzle and smell of frying bacon.

That's the way it was this morning.

Solitaire

Still the first day, All Fools' Day, here at the Center. Merle McRae and Floyd Bence — the superintendent and the chief ranger — appear at noon, bringing me five hundred gallons of water in a tank truck and a Park Service pickup truck outfitted with shortwave radio, fire tools, climbing rope, shovel, tow chain, first aid kit, stretcher, axe, etc.; the pickup and its equip-

---

anti-Kantian Immanuel Kant (1724–1804) was a German metaphysician who proposed that external reality was known only as it conformed to the structure of the human mind.

Betelgeuse A large star in the constellation Orion.

ment they will leave with me. I am to use it in patrolling the roads within the park, for assisting tourists in trouble, and for hauling firewood to and garbage from the campgrounds. Once a week I may drive the government vehicle to headquarters and Moab for fuel and supplies.

We fill the water tank buried in the slope above the housetrailer and have 26 lunch together in the sunshine, sitting at a wooden picnic table near my doorway. Merle the super, the boss, is a slender, graceful man of about fifty years, with a fine, grave, expressive face toughened though not hardened by a life spent mostly out-of-doors. He was born and raised on a small ranch in New Mexico, went to the University of Virginia, and has made his living as a cattle rancher, dude rancher, CCC° supervisor (during the Great Depression) and, since 1940, as a ranger in the National Park Service. He gives me an impression of tenderness, generosity and imperturbable good humor, but also complains, gently, of the hypothetical ulcer he expects to acquire from his years of struggle with administrative paper work. Married, he has three children; the oldest boy attends the University of Utah.

Floyd Bence is a tall powerful man around thirty years old, an archeolo- 27 gist by training, married, with two children. Because of his interests and academic background he should be working at some place like Mesa Verde or Chaco Canyon, poking about in dusty ruins, but is happy enough with his present situation so long as he is free to spend at least part of his time outside the office; the two things he dreads most, as a Park Service career man, are promotion to a responsible high-salaried administrative position, and a transfer back East to one of the cannonball parks like Appomattox or Gettysburg or Ticonderoga. Like myself he'd rather go hungry in the West than flourish and fatten in the Siberian East. A violent prejudice, doomed to disappointment. But at the moment, in the sparkling air and brilliant sunlight of the Utah desert, bad news seems far away.

"Well, Ranger Abbey," says Merle, "how do you like it out here in the 28 middle of nowhere?"

I said it was okay by me. 29

They smile. "Kind of lonesome?" Floyd asks. 30

I said it was all right. 31

After lunch we get into the cab of the government pickup, all three of us, 32 and tour the park. Arches National Monument remains at this time what the Park Service calls an undeveloped area, although to me it appears quite adequately developed. The roads, branching out, lead to within easy walking distance of most of the principal arches, none more than two miles beyond the end of a road. The roads are not paved, true, but are easily passable to

---

CCC Civilian Conservation Corps, a government agency established during the Depression to create jobs and to beautify and maintain public spaces.

any automobile except during or immediately after a rainstorm. The trails are well marked, easy to follow; you'd have to make an effort to get lost. There are three small campgrounds, each with tables, fireplaces, garbage cans and pit toilets. (Bring your own water.) We even supply the firewood, in the form of pinyon pine logs and old fence posts of cedar, which it will be my task to find and haul to the campgrounds.

We drive the dirt roads and walk out some of the trails. Everything is lovely and wild, with a virginal sweetness. The arches themselves, strange, impressive, grotesque, form but a small and inessential part of the general beauty of this country. When we think of rock we usually think of stones, broken rock, buried under soil and plant life, but here all is exposed and naked, dominated by the monolithic formations of sandstone which stand above the surface of the ground and extend for miles, sometimes level, sometimes tilted or warped by pressures from below, carved by erosion and weathering into an intricate maze of glens, grottoes, fissures, passageways, and deep narrow canyons.

At first look it all seems like a geologic chaos, but there is method at work here, method of a fanatic order and perseverance: each groove in the rock leads to a natural channel of some kind, every channel to a ditch and gulch and ravine, each larger waterway to a canyon bottom or broad wash leading in turn to the Colorado River and the sea.

As predicted, the snowfall has disappeared by this time and all watercourses in the park are dry except for the one spring-fed perennial stream known as Salt Creek, a glassy flow inches deep that trickles over shoals of quicksand and between mud flats covered with white crusts of alkali. Though it looks potable the water is too saline for human consumption; horses and cattle can drink it but not men. Or so I am informed by Merle and Floyd. I choose to test their belief by experiment. Squatting on the shore of the stream, I dip my cupped hands into the water and sample a little. Pretty bad, neither potable nor palatable. Perhaps, I suggest, a man could learn to drink this water by taking only a little each day, gradually increasing the dosage . . . ?

"You try that," says Merle.

"Yeah," Floyd says, "give us a report at the end of the summer."

Late this afternoon we return to the housetrailer. Floyd lends me a park ranger shirt which he says he doesn't need anymore and which I am to wear in lieu of a uniform, so as to give me an official sort of aspect when meeting the tourists. Then there's this silver badge I'm supposed to pin to the shirt. The badge gives me the authority to arrest malefactors and evildoers, Floyd explains. Or anyone at all, for that matter.

I place Floyd and Merle under arrest at once, urging them to stay and have supper with me. I've got a big pot of pinto beans simmering on the stove. But they won't stay, they have promises to keep and must leave, and soon they're driving off in the water-truck over the rocky road to the highway and Moab. Climbing the rise behind the housetrailer I watch them go, the truck visible for a mile or so before the road winds deeper into the complex of sand dunes, corraded° monoliths and hogback ridges to the west.

Beyond the highway, about ten miles away, rise the talus slopes and vertical red walls of Dead Horse Mesa, a flat-topped uninhabited island in the sky which extends for thirty miles north and south between the convergent canyons of the Green and Colorado rivers. Public domain. Above the mesa the sun hangs behind streaks and streamers of wind-whipped clouds. More storms coming. 40

But for the time being, around my place at least, the air is untroubled, and I become aware for the first time today of the immense silence in which I am lost. Not a silence so much as a great stillness — for there are a few sounds: the creek of some bird in a juniper tree, an eddy of wind which passes and fades like a sigh, the ticking of the watch on my wrist — slight noises which break the sensation of absolute silence but at the same time exaggerate my sense of the surrounding, overwhelming peace. A suspension of time, a continuous present. If I look at the small device strapped to my wrist the numbers, even the sweeping second hand, seem meaningless, almost ridiculous. No travelers, no campers, no wanderers have come to this part of the desert today and for a few moments I feel and realize that I am very much alone. 41

There is nothing to do but return to the trailer, open a can of beer, eat my supper. 42

Afterwards I put on hat and coat and go outside again, sit on the table, and watch the sky and the desert dissolve slowly into mystery under the chemistry of twilight. We need a fire. I range around the trailer, pick up some dead sticks from under the junipers and build a little squaw fire, for company. 43

Dark clouds sailing overhead across the fields of the stars. Stars which are unusually bold and close, with an icy glitter in their light — glints of blue, emerald, gold. Out there, spread before me to the south, east, and north, the arches and cliffs and pinnacles and balanced rocks of sandstone (now entrusted to my care) have lost the rosy glow of sunset and become soft, intangible, in unnamed unnameable shades of violet, colors that seem to radiate from — not overlay — their surfaces. 44

A yellow planet floats on the west, brightest object in the sky. Venus. I listen closely for the call of an owl, a dove, a nighthawk, but can hear only the crackle of my fire, a breath of wind. 45

The fire. The odor of burning juniper is the sweetest fragrance on the face of the earth, in my honest judgment; I doubt if all the smoking censers of Dante's paradise could equal it. One breath of juniper smoke, like the per- 46

---

corraded Eroded.

fume of sagebrush after rain, evokes in magical catalysis, like certain music, the space and light and clarity and piercing strangeness of the American West. Long may it burn.

The little fire wavers, flickers, begins to die. I break another branch of juniper over my knee and add the fragments to the heap of coals. A wisp of bluish smoke goes up and the wood, arid as the rock from which it came, blossoms out in fire.

> Go thou my incense upward from this hearth
> And ask the gods to pardon this clear flame.

I wait and watch, guarding the desert, the arches, the sand and barren rock, the isolated junipers and scattered clumps of sage surrounding me in stillness and simplicity under the starlight.

Again the fire begins to fail. Letting it die, I take my walking stick and go for a stroll down the road into the thickening darkness. I have a flashlight with me but will not use it unless I hear some sign of animal life worthy of investigation. The flashlight, or electrical torch as the English call it, is a useful instrument in certain situations but I can see the road well enough without it. Better, in fact.

There's another disadvantage to the use of the flashlight: like many other mechanical gadgets it tends to separate a man from the world around him. If I switch it on my eyes adapt to it and I can see only the small pool of light which it makes in front of me; I am isolated. Leaving the flashlight in my pocket where it belongs, I remain a part of the environment I walk through and my vision though limited has no sharp or definite boundary.

This peculiar limitation of the machine becomes doubly apparent when I return to the housetrailer. I've decided to write a letter (to myself) before going to bed, and rather than use a candle for light I'm going to crank up the old generator. The generator is a small four-cylinder gasoline engine mounted on a wooden block not far from the trailer. Much too close, I'd say. I open the switch, adjust the choke, engage the crank and heave it around. The engine sputters, gasps, catches fire, gains momentum, winds up into a roar, valves popping, rockers thumping, pistons hissing up and down inside their oiled jackets. Fine: power surges into the wiring, the light bulbs inside the trailer begin to glow, brighten, becoming incandescent. The lights are so bright I can't see a thing and have to shade my eyes as I stumble toward the open door of the trailer. Nor can I hear anything but the clatter of the generator. I am shut off from the natural world and sealed up, encapsulated, in a box of artificial light and tyrannical noise.

Once inside the trailer my senses adjust to the new situation and soon enough, writing the letter, I lose awareness of the lights and the whine of the motor. But I have cut myself off completely from the greater world which surrounds the man-made shell. The desert and the night are pushed back — I can no longer participate in them or observe; I have exchanged a great and unbounded world for a small, comparatively meager one. By choice, certainly; the exchange is temporarily convenient and can be reversed whenever I wish.

Finishing the letter I go outside and close the switch on the generator. 53 The light bulbs dim and disappear, the furious gnashing of pistons whimpers to a halt. Standing by the inert and helpless engine, I hear its last vibrations die like ripples on a pool somewhere far out on the tranquil sea of desert, somewhere beyond Delicate Arch, beyond the Yellow Cat badlands, beyond the shadow line.

I wait. Now the night flows back, the mighty stillness embraces and in- 54 cludes me; I can see the stars again and the world of starlight. I am twenty miles or more from the nearest fellow human, but instead of loneliness I feel loveliness. Loveliness and a quiet exultation.

The Serpents of Paradise

The April mornings are bright, clear and calm. Not until the afternoon 55 does the wind begin to blow, raising dust and sand in funnel-shaped twisters that spin across the desert briefly, like dancers, and then collapse — whirlwinds from which issue no voice or word except the forlorn moan of the elements under stress. After the reconnoitering dust-devils comes the real the serious wind, the voice of the desert rising to a demented howl and blotting out sky and sun behind yellow clouds of dust, sand, confusion, embattled birds, last year's scrub-oak leaves, pollen, the husks of locusts, bark of juniper. . . .

Time of the red eye, the sore and bloody nostril, the sand-pitted wind- 56 shield, if one is foolish enough to drive his car into such a storm. Time to sit indoors and continue that letter which is never finished — while the fine dust forms neat little windrows under the edge of the door and on the windowsills. Yet the springtime winds are as much a part of the canyon country as the silence and the glamorous distances; you learn, after a number of years, to love them also.

The mornings therefore, as I started to say and meant to say, are all the 57 sweeter in the knowledge of what the afternoon is likely to bring. Before beginning the morning chores I like to sit on the sill of my doorway, bare feet planted on the bare ground and a mug of hot coffee in hand, facing the sunrise. The air is gelid, not far above freezing, but the butane heater inside the trailer keeps my back warm, the rising sun warms the front, and the coffee warms the interior.

Perhaps this is the loveliest hour of the day, though it's hard to choose. 58 Much depends on the season. In midsummer the sweetest hour begins at sundown, after the awful heat of the afternoon. But now, in April, we'll take the opposite, that hour beginning with the sunrise. The birds, returning from wherever they go in winter, seem inclined to agree. The pinyon jays are whirling in garrulous, gregarious flocks from one stunted tree to the next and back again, erratic exuberant games without any apparent practical function. A few big ravens hang around and croak harsh clanking statements of smug satisfaction from the rimrock, lifting their greasy wings now and then to probe for lice. I can hear but seldom see the canyon wrens singing their distinctive song from somewhere up on the cliffs: a flutelike descent — never ascent — of the whole-tone scale. Staking out new nesting claims, I understand. Also invisible but invariably present at some indefinable distance are the mourning doves whose plaintive call suggests irresistibly a kind of seeking-out, the attempt by separated souls to restore a lost communion:

Hello . . . they seem to cry, *who . . . are . . . you?*

And the reply from a different quarter. *Hello . . .* (pause) *where . . . are . . . you?*

No doubt this line of analogy must be rejected. It's foolish and unfair to impute to the doves, with serious concerns of their own, an interest in questions more appropriate to their human kin. Yet their song, if not a mating call or a warning, must be what it sounds like, a brooding meditation on space, on solitude. The game.

Other birds, silent, which I have not yet learned to identify, are also lurking in the vicinity, watching me. What the ornithologist terms l.g.b.'s — little gray birds — they flit about from point to point on noiseless wings, their origins obscure.

As mentioned before, I share the housetrailer with a number of mice. I don't know how many but apparently only a few, perhaps a single family. They don't disturb me and are welcome to my crumbs and leavings. Where they came from, how they got into the trailer, how they survived before my arrival (for the trailer had been locked up for six months), these are puzzling matters I am not prepared to resolve. My only reservation concerning the mice is that they do attract rattlesnakes.

I'm sitting on my doorstep early one morning, facing the sun as usual, drinking coffee, when I happen to look down and see almost between my bare feet, only a couple of inches to the rear of my heels, the very thing I had in mind. No mistaking that wedgelike head, that tip of horny segmented tail peeping out of the coils. He's under the doorstep and in the shade where the ground and air remain very cold. In his sluggish condition he's not likely to strike unless I rouse him by some careless move of my own.

There's a revolver inside the trailer, a huge British Webley .45, loaded, but it's out of reach. Even if I had it in my hands I'd hesitate to blast a fellow creature at such close range, shooting between my own legs at a living target flat on solid rock thirty inches away. It would be like murder; and where would I set my coffee? My cherrywood walking stick leans against the trailerhouse wall only a few feet away but I'm afraid that in leaning over for it I might stir up the rattler or spill some hot coffee on his scales.

Other considerations come to mind. Arches National Monument is 66 meant to be among other things a sanctuary for wildlife — for all forms of wildlife. It is my duty as a park ranger to protect, preserve and defend all living things within the park boundaries, making no exceptions. Even if this were not the case I have personal convictions to uphold. Ideals, you might say. I prefer not to kill animals. I'm a humanist; I'd rather kill a *man* than a snake.

What to do. I drink some more coffee and study the dormant reptile at 67 my heels. It is not after all the mighty diamondback, *Crotalus atrox*, I'm confronted with but a smaller species known locally as the horny rattler or more precisely as the Faded Midget. An insulting name for a rattlesnake, which may explain the Faded Midget's alleged bad temper. But the name is apt: he is small and dusty-looking, with a little knob above each eye — the horns. His bite though temporarily disabling would not likely kill a full-grown man in normal health. Even so I don't really want him around. Am I to be compelled to put on boots or shoes every time I wish to step outside? The scorpions, tarantulas, centipedes, and black widows are nuisance enough.

I finish my coffee, lean back and swing my feet up and inside the door- 68 way of the trailer. At once there is a buzzing sound from below and the rattler lifts his head from his coils, eyes brightening, and extends his narrow black tongue to test the air.

After thawing out my boots over the gas flame I pull them on and come 69 back to the doorway. My visitor is still waiting beneath the doorstep, basking in the sun, fully alert. The trailerhouse has two doors. I leave by the other and get a long-handled spade out of the bed of the government pickup. With this tool I scoop the snake into the open. He strikes; I can hear the click of the fangs against steel, see the stain of venom. He wants to stand and fight, but I am patient; I insist on herding him well away from the trailer. On guard, head aloft — that evil slit-eyed weaving head shaped like the ace of spades — tail whirring, the rattler slithers sideways, retreating slowly before me until he reaches the shelter of a sandstone slab. He backs under it.

You better stay there, cousin, I warn him; if I catch you around the trailer 70 again I'll chop your head off.

A week later he comes back. If not him, his twin brother. I spot him one 71 morning under the trailer near the kitchen drain, waiting for a mouse. I have to keep my promise.

This won't do. If there are midget rattlers in the area there may be 72 diamondbacks too — five, six or seven feet long, thick as a man's wrist, dangerous. I don't want *them* camping under my home. It looks as though I'll have to trap the mice.

However, before being forced to take that step I am lucky enough to cap- 73 ture a gopher snake. Burning garbage one morning at the park dump, I see a long slender yellow-brown snake emerge from a mound of old tin cans and plastic picnic plates and take off down the sandy bed of a gulch. There is a burlap sack in the cab of the truck which I carry when plucking Kleenex flowers from the brush and cactus along the road; I grab that and my stick, run after the snake and corner it beneath the exposed roots of a bush. Making sure it's a gopher snake and not something less useful, I open the neck of the sack and with a great deal of coaxing and prodding get the snake into it. The gopher snake, *Drymarchon corais couperi*, or bull snake, has a reputation as the enemy of rattlesnakes, destroying or driving them away whenever encountered.

Hoping to domesticate this sleek, handsome and docile reptile, I release him inside the trailerhouse and keep him there for several days. Should I attempt to feed him? I decide against it — let him eat mice. What little water he may need can also be extracted from the flesh of his prey.

The gopher snake and I get along nicely. During the day he curls up like a cat in the warm corner behind the heater and at night he goes about his business. The mice, singularly quiet for a change, make themselves scarce. The snake is passive, apparently contented, and makes no resistance when I pick him up with my hands and drape him over an arm or around my neck. When I take him outside into the wind and sunshine his favorite place seems to be inside my shirt, where he wraps himself around my waist and rests on my belt. In this position he sometimes sticks his head out between shirt buttons for a survey of the weather, astonishing and delighting any tourists who may happen to be with me at the time. The scales of a snake are dry and smooth, quite pleasant to the touch. Being a cold-blooded creature, of course, he takes his temperature from that of the immediate environment — in this case my body.

We are compatible. From my point of view, friends. After a week of close association I turn him loose on the warm sandstone at my doorstep and leave for a patrol of the park. At noon when I return he is gone. I search everywhere beneath, nearby and inside the trailerhouse, but my companion has disappeared. Has he left the area entirely or is he hiding somewhere close by? At any rate I am troubled no more by rattlesnakes under the door.

The snake story is not yet ended.

In the middle of May, about a month after the gopher snake's disappearance, in the evening of a very hot day, with all the rosy desert cooling like a griddle with the fire turned off, he reappears. This time with a mate.

I'm in the stifling heat of the trailer opening a can of beer, barefooted, about to go outside and relax after a hard day watching cloud formations. I happen to glance out the little window near the refrigerator and see two gopher snakes on my verandah engaged in what seems to be a kind of ritual dance. Like a living caduceus° they wind and unwind about each other in

---

caduceus   A staff with two entwined snakes along it; familiar as the symbol for physicians.

undulant, graceful, perpetual motion, moving slowly across a dome of sandstone. Invisible but tangible as music is the passion which joins them — sexual? combative? both? A shameless *voyeur*, I stare at the lovers, and then to get a closer view run outside and around the trailer to the back. There I get down on hands and knees and creep toward the dancing snakes, not wanting to frighten or disturb them. I crawl to within six feet of them and stop, flat on my belly, watching from the snake's-eye level. Obsessed with their ballet, the serpents seem unaware of my presence.

The two gopher snakes are nearly identical in length and coloring; I cannot be certain that either is actually my former household pet. I cannot even be sure that they are male and female, though their performance resembles so strongly a *pas de deux*° by formal lovers. They intertwine and separate, glide side by side in perfect congruence, turn like mirror images of each other and glide back again, wind and unwind again. This is the basic pattern but there is a variation: at regular intervals the snakes elevate their heads, facing one another, as high as they can go, as if each is trying to outreach or overawe the other. Their heads and bodies rise, higher and higher, then topple together and the rite goes on.

I crawl after them, determined to see the whole thing. Suddenly and simultaneously they discover me, prone on my belly a few feet away. The dance stops. After a moment's pause the two snakes come straight toward me, still in flawless unison, straight toward my face, the forked tongues flickering, their intense wild yellow eyes staring directly into my eyes. For an instant I am paralyzed by wonder; then, stung by a fear too ancient and powerful to overcome I scramble back, rising to my knees. The snakes veer and turn and race away from me in parallel motion, their lean elegant bodies making a soft hissing noise as they slide over the sand and stone. I follow them for a short distance, still plagued by curiosity, before remembering my place and the requirements of common courtesy. For godsake let them go in peace, I tell myself. Wish them luck and (if lovers) innumerable offspring, a life of happily ever after. Not for their sake alone but for your own.

In the long hot days and cool evenings to come I will not see the gopher snakes again. Nevertheless I will feel their presence watching over me like totemic deities, keeping the rattlesnakes far back in the brush where I like them best, cropping off the surplus mouse population, maintaining useful connections with the primeval. Sympathy, mutual aid, symbiosis, continuity.

How can I descend to such anthropomorphism? Easily — but is it, in this case, entirely false? Perhaps not. I am not attributing human motives to my snake and bird acquaintances. I recognize that when and where they serve purposes of mine they do so for beautifully selfish reasons of their own.

---

pas de deux   An expressive dance for two performers, usually male and female, particularly in ballet.

Which is exactly the way it should be. I suggest, however, that it's a foolish, simple-minded rationalism which denies any form of emotion to all animals but man and his dog. This is no more justified than the Moslems are in denying souls to women. It seems to be possible, even probable, that many of the nonhuman undomesticated animals experience emotions unknown to us. What do the coyotes mean when they yodel at the moon? What are the dolphins trying so patiently to tell us? Precisely what did those two enraptured gopher snakes have in mind when they came gliding toward my eyes over the naked sandstone? If I had been as capable of trust as I am susceptible to fear I might have learned something new or some truth so very old we have all forgotten it.

> They do not sweat and whine about their condition,
> They do not lie awake in the dark and weep for their sins. . . .

All men are brothers, we like to say, half-wishing sometimes in secret it were not true. But perhaps it is true. And is the evolutionary line from protozoan to Spinoza° any less certain? That also may be true. We are obliged, therefore, to spread the news, painful and bitter though it may be for some to hear, that all living things on earth are kindred.

QUESTIONS ON MEANING

1. How would you define what Abbey is seeking in the wilderness? Why is it impossible to find it in a city? Paragraphs 50–54 provide some hints. Where else does Abbey make the same point in a different, less direct way?
2. Abbey refers more than once to a letter he is writing to himself. What is the relation between his essay and the letter?
3. Why does Abbey want to suppress the "personification of the natural" (paragraph 20)? Does he succeed in doing so? In paragraphs 22 and 58–61, does his description of sunrise and of birds in song fit with his goal? Why or why not? How does he address the issue of personification of nature later, when he observes the dance of the gopher snakes (paragraphs 79–83)?

QUESTIONS ON STRATEGY

1. Notice how Abbey describes his "personal demesne" in paragraphs 16–18. What is the connotation of *demesne*? Is it appropriate here, in a description of "this monstrous and inhuman spectacle"? Why or why not?

°**Spinoza** (1632–1677), pantheistic philosopher of Portuguese-Jewish descent; equated God with the forces and laws of nature.

2. Consider Abbey's confrontation with the rattlesnake in paragraphs 64–70. He rejects the idea of shooting it: "It would be like murder; and where would I set my coffee?" In paragraph 66 he notes, "I'm a humanist; I'd rather kill a *man* than a snake." What effect do these ironies have in Abbey's anecdote? How do they relate to his concluding statement "all living things on earth are kindred"?

3. Although this essay is written mostly in the present tense, Abbey does not maintain a strict consistency of tense, something every student is warned against in composition courses. Why does Abbey shift tenses (paragraphs 4, 10, 28–32)? Does he do it unconsciously or deliberately? Is it effective or unnecessary? Why?

EXPLORATIONS

1. Compare Abbey's desire "to confront, immediately and directly if possible, the bare bones of existence, the elemental and fundamental, the bedrock which sustains us" and Walker Percy's objectives in "The Loss of the Creature." Consider the two authors' tone, approach to their subject, effectiveness, and plausibility.

WRITING TOPICS

1. If you have ever kept a journal, and can lay your hands on it, revise a portion which recounts daily life using Abbey as your model.

2. Stay alone, or as nearly alone as you can, for one day; write an account of your ideas and sensations during solitude, using Abbey as your model.

3. Abbey's essay is divided into three distinct but interrelated parts. Each can be read separately, but together they form a whole. Review Abbey's essay, studying each section and considering how he makes them work together to form that coherent whole. Write an autobiographical essay of your own based on Abbey's example.

BOOKS AVAILABLE IN PAPERBACK

Abbey's Road. New York: Dutton. *Essays.*

Black Sun. New York: Avon. *Novel.*

The Brave Cowboy. New York: Avon. *Novel.*

Desert Solitaire. New York: Simon & Schuster, Touchstone Books. *Nonfiction: Personal history.*

Down the River. New York: Dutton. *Nonfiction: Personal history.*

Fire on the Mountain. New York: Avon. *Novel.*

Good News. New York: Dutton. *Novel.*

The Journey Home: Some Words in Defense of the American West. New York: Dutton. *Nonfiction: Personal history.*

The Monkey-Wrench Gang. New York: Avon. *Novel.*

RICHARD
SELZER

*R*ICHARD SELZER (b. 1928) grew up in Troy, New York, where his father was
a family physician. Selzer took his B.S. from Union College in nearby
Schenectady and his M.D. from Albany Medical College. He became a surgeon and
since 1960 has taught at Yale University and lived in New Haven, where he conducts
a private practice in general surgery. His essays and short stories have appeared in
Harper's, Esquire, Redbook, Mademoiselle, American Review, and An-
taeus. His first book was a collection of short stories, Rituals of Surgery (1974), followed by books of essays: Mortal Lessons (1977), Confessions of a Knife (1979),
and Letters to a Young Doctor (1982).

With Selzer, as with several contemporary essayists, it is sometimes difficult to
distinguish fiction from nonfiction; he uses vivid narrative devices to make points of
information. Few such essayists write about science. Of all contemporary prose-writ-
ing scientists, Selzer is most decorative or belletristic, but his subject remains the profession and priesthood of surgery. In "Letter to a Young Surgeon," from his most
recent essay collection, he writes out of recollection and personal experience, offering
advice to someone who will undergo the training he remembers so vividly. His recommendations are practical, and his prose allows him wide reference and allusion — to
etymology, to literature, and by analogy to other professions. Above all, his advice
features reflection on a craft that is also an art, a glory, and a state of mind.

Letter to
a Young Surgeon

At this, the start of your surgical internship, it is well that you be told 1
how to behave in an operating room. You cannot observe decorum unless
you first know what decorum is. Say that you have already changed into a
scrub suit, donned cap, mask and shoe covers. You have scrubbed your
hands and been helped into your gown and gloves. Now stand out of the
way. Eventually, your presence will be noticed by the surgeon, who will
motion you to take up a position at the table. Surgery is not one of the polite
arts, as are Quilting and Illuminating Manuscripts. Decorum in the operating room does not include doffing your cap in the presence of nurses. Even
the old-time surgeons knew this and operated without removing their hats.

The first rule of conversation in the operating room is silence. It is a rule 2
to be broken freely by the Master, for he is engaged in the art of teaching.
The forceful passage of bacteria through a face mask during speech increases
the contamination of the wound and therefore the possibility of infection in
that wound. It is a risk that must be taken. By the surgeon, wittingly, and by
the patient, unbeknownst. Say what you will about a person's keeping control over his own destiny, there are some things that cannot be helped. Being made use of for teaching purposes in the operating room is one of them.
It is an inevitable, admirable and noble circumstance. Besides, I have pla-
cated Fate too long to believe that She would bring on wound infection as
the complication of such a high enterprise.

Observe the least movement of the surgeon's hands. See how he holds 3
out his hand to receive the scalpel. See how the handle of it rides between
his thumb and fingertips. The scalpel is the subtlest of the instruments,
transmitting the nervous current in the surgeon's arm to the body of the patient. Too timidly applied, and it turns flabby, lifeless; too much pressure
and it turns vicious. See how the surgeon applies the blade to the skin —
holding it straight in its saddle lest he undercut and one edge of the incision
be thinner than the other edge. The application of knife to flesh proclaims
the master and exposes the novice. See the surgeon advancing his hand
blindly into the abdomen as though it were a hollow in a tree. He is wary,
yet needing to know. Will it be something soft and dead? Or a sudden pain
in his bitten finger!

The point of the knife is called the *tang*, from the Latin word for *touch*. 4
The sharp curving edge is the *belly* of the blade. The tang is for assassins, the
belly for surgeons. Enough! You will not hold this knife for a long time. Do
not be impatient for it. Nor reckon the time. Ripen only. Over the course of

your training you will be given ever more elaborate tasks to perform. But for now, you must watch and wait. Excessive ego, arrogance and self-concern in an intern are out of place, as they preclude love for the patient on the table. There is no room for clever disobedience here. For the knife is like fire. The small child yearns to do what his father does, and he steals matches from the man's pocket. The fire he lights in his hiding place is beautiful to him; he toasts marshmallows in it. But he is just as likely to be burned. And reverence for the teacher is essential to the accumulation of knowledge. Even a bad surgeon will teach if only by the opportunity to see what not to do.

You will quickly come to detect the difference between a true surgeon and a mere product of the system. Democracy is not the best of all social philosophies in the selection of doctors for training in surgery. Anyone who so desires, and who is able to excel academically and who is willing to undergo the harsh training, can become a surgeon whether or not he is fit for the craft either manually or by temperament. If we continue to award licenses to the incompetent and the ill-suited, we shall be like those countries where work is given over not to those who can do it best, but to those who need it. That offers irritation enough in train stations; think of the result in airplane cockpits or operating rooms. Ponder long and hard upon this point. The mere decision to be a surgeon will not magically confer upon you the dexterity, compassion and calmness to do it.

Even on your first day in the operating room, you must look ahead to your last. An old surgeon who has lost his touch is like an old lion whose claws have become blunted, but not the desire to use them. Knowing when to quit and retire from the consuming passion of your life is instinctive. It takes courage to do it. But do it you must. No consideration of money, power, fame or fear of boredom may give you the slightest pause in laying down your scalpel when the first flagging of energy, bravery or confidence appears. To withdraw gracefully is to withdraw in a state of grace. To persist is to fumble your way to injury and ignominy.

Do not be dismayed by the letting of blood, for it is blood that animates this work, distinguishes it from its father, Anatomy. Red is the color in which the interior of the body is painted. If an operation be thought of as a painting in progress, and blood red the color of the brush, it must be suitably restrained and attract no undue attention; yet any insufficiency of it will increase the perishability of the canvas. Surgeons are of differing stripes. There are those who are slow and methodical, obsessive beyond all reason. These tortoises operate in a field as bloodless as a cadaver. Every speck of tissue in its proper place, every nerve traced out and brushed clean so that a Japanese artist could render it down to the dendrites. Should the contents of a single capillary be inadvertently shed, the whole procedure comes to a halt while Mr. Clean irrigates and suctions and mops and clamps and ties until once again the operative field looks like Holland at tulip time. Such a surgeon tells time not by the clock but by the calendar. For this, he is ideally equipped with an iron urinary bladder which he has disciplined to contract no more than once a day. To the drop-in observer, the work of such a surgeon is faultless. He gasps in admiration at the still life on the table. Should the same observer leave and return three hours later, nothing will have changed. Only a few more millimeters of perfection.

Then there are the swashbucklers who crash through the underbrush waving a machete, letting tube and ovary fall where they may. This surgeon is equipped with gills so that he can breathe under blood. You do not set foot in his room without a slicker and boots. Seasoned nurses quake at the sight of those arms, elbow-deep and *working*. It is said that one such surgeon entertained the other guests at a department Christmas party by splenectomizing a cat in thirty seconds from skin to skin. 8

Then there are the rest of us who are neither too timid nor too brash. We are just right. And now I shall tell you a secret. To be a good surgeon does not require immense technical facility. Compared to a violinist it is nothing. The Japanese artist, for one, is skillful at double brushing, by which technique he lays on color with one brush and shades it off with another, both brushes being held at the same time and in the same hand, albeit with different fingers. Come to think of it, a surgeon, like a Japanese artist, ought to begin his training at the age of three, learning to hold four or five instruments at a time in the hand while suturing with a needle and thread held in the teeth. By the age of five he would be able to dismantle and reconstruct an entire human body from calvarium to calcaneus unassisted and in the time it would take one of us to recite the Hippocratic Oath. A more obvious advantage of this baby surgeon would be his size. In times of difficulty he could be lowered whole into the abdomen. There, he could swim about, repair the works, then give three tugs on a rope and . . . Presto! Another gallbladder bites the dust. 9

In the absence of any such prodigies, each of you who is full-grown must learn to exist in two states — Littleness and Bigness. In your littleness you descend for hours each day through a cleft in the body into a tiny space that is both your workshop and your temple. Your attention in Lilliput is total and undistracted. Every artery is a river to be forded or dammed, each organ a mountain to be skirted or moved. At last, the work having been done, you ascend. You blink and look about at the vast space peopled by giants and massive furniture. Take a deep breath . . . and you are Big. Such instantaneous hypertrophy is the process by which a surgeon reenters the outside world. Any breakdown in this resonance between the sizes causes the surgeon to live in a Renaissance painting where the depth perception is so bad. 10

Nor ought it to offend you that, a tumor having been successfully removed, and the danger to the patient having been circumvented, the very 11 team of surgeons that only moments before had been a model of discipline and deportment comes loose at the seams and begins to wobble. Jokes are told, there is laughter, a hectic gaiety prevails. This is in no way to be taken as a sign of irreverence or callousness. When the men of the Kalahari return from the hunt with a haunch of zebra, the first thing everybody does is break out in a dance. It is a rite of thanksgiving. There will be food. They have made it safely home.

Man is the only animal capable of tying a square knot. During the course of an operation you may be asked by the surgeon to tie a knot. As drawing and coloring are the language of art, incising, suturing and knot tying are the grammar of surgery. A facility in knot tying is gained only by tying ten thousand of them. When the operation is completed, take home with you a package of leftover sutures. Light a fire in the fireplace and sit with your lover on a rug in front of the fire. Invite her to hold up her index finger, gently crooked in a gesture of beckoning. Using her finger as a strut, tie one of the threads about it in a square knot. Do this one hundred times. Now make a hundred grannies. Only then may you permit yourself to make love to her. This method of learning will not only enable you to master the art of knot tying, both grannies and square, it will bind you, however insecurely, to the one you love.

To do surgery without a sense of awe is to be a dandy — all style and no purpose. No part of the operation is too lowly, too menial. Even when suturing the skin at the end of a major abdominal procedure, you must operate with piety, as though you were embellishing a holy reliquary. The suturing of the skin usually falls to the lot of the beginning surgeon, the sights of the Assistant Residents and Residents having been firmly set upon more biliary, more gastric glories. In surgery, the love of inconsiderable things must govern your life — ingrown toenails, thrombosed hemorrhoids, warts. Never disdain the common ordinary ailment in favor of the exotic or rare. To the patient every one of his ailments is unique. One is not to be amused or captivated by disease. Only to a woodpecker is a wormy tree more fascinating than one uninhabited. There is only absorption in your patient's plight. To this purpose, willingly accept the smells and extrusions of the sick. To be spattered with the phlegm, vomitus and blood of suffering is to be badged with the highest office.

The sutured skin is all of his operation that the patient will see. It is your signature left upon his body for the rest of his life. For the patient, it is the emblem of his suffering, a reminder of his mortality. Years later, he will idly run his fingers along the length of the scar, and he will hush and remember. The good surgeon knows this. And so he does not overlap the edges of the skin, makes no dog-ears at the corners. He does not tie the sutures too tightly lest there be a row of permanent crosshatches. (It is not your purpose to construct a ladder upon which a touring louse could climb from pubis to navel and back.) The good surgeon does not pinch the skin with forceps. He leaves the proper distance between the sutures. He removes the sutures at the earliest possible date, and he uses sutures of the finest thread. All these things he does and does not do out of reverence for his craft and love for his patient. The surgeon who does otherwise ought to keep his hands in his pockets. At the end of the operation, cholecystectomy, say, the surgeon may ask you to slit open the gallbladder so that everyone in the room might examine the stones. Perform even this cutting with reverence as though the organ were still within the patient's body. You cut, and notice how the amber bile runs out, leaving a residue of stones. Faceted, shiny, they glisten. Almost at once, these wrested dewy stones surrender their warmth and moisture; they grow drab and dull. The descent from jewel to pebble takes place before your eyes.

Deep down, I keep the vanity that surgery is the red flower that blooms 15 among the leaves and thorns that are the rest of Medicine. It is Surgery that, long after it has passed into obsolescence, will be remembered as the glory of Medicine. Then men shall gather in mead halls and sing of that ancient time when surgeons, like gods, walked among the human race. Go ahead. Revel in your Specialty; it is your divinity.

It is quest and dream as well. 16

The incision has been made. One expects mauve doves and colored 17 moths to cloud out of the belly in celebration of the longed-for coming. Soon the surgeon is greeted by the eager blood kneeling and offering its services. Tongues of it lap at his feet; flames and plumes hold themselves aloft to light his way. And he follows this guide that flows just ahead of him through rifts, along the edges of cliffs, picking and winding, leaping across chasms, at last finding itself and pooling to wait for him. But the blood cannot wait a moment too long lest it become a blob of coagulum, something annulled by its own puddling. The surgeon rides the patient, as though he were riding a burro down into a canyon. This body is beautiful to him, and he to it — he whom the patient encloses in the fist of his flesh. For months, ever since the first wild mitosis, the organs had huddled like shipwrecks. When would he come? Will he never come? And suddenly, into the sick cellar — fingers of light! The body lies stupefied at the moment of encounter. The cool air stirs the buried flesh. Even the torpid intestine shifts its slow coils to make way.

Now the surgeon must take care. The fatal glissade, once begun, is not to 18 be stopped. Does this world, too, he wonders, roll within the precincts of mercy? The questing dreamer leans into the patient to catch the subtlest sounds. He hears the harmonies of their two bloods, his and the patient's. They sing of death and the beauty of the rose. He hears the playing together of their two breaths. If Pythagoras is right, there is no silence in the universe. Even the stars make music as they move.

Only do not succumb to self-love. I know a surgeon who, having left the room, is certain, beyond peradventure of doubt, that his disembodied radiance lingers on. And there are surgeons of such aristocratic posture that one refrains only with difficulty from slipping them into the nobility. As though they had risen from Mister to Doctor to Professor, then on to Baron, Count, Archduke, then further, to Apostle, Saint. I could go further.

Such arrogance can carry over to the work itself. There was a surgeon in New Haven, Dr. Truffle, who had a penchant for long midline incisions — from sternum to pubis — no matter the need for exposure. Somewhere along the way, this surgeon had become annoyed by the presence of the navel, which, he decided, interrupted the pure line of his slice. Day in, day out, it must be gone around, either to the right or to the left. Soon, what was at first an annoyance became a hated impediment that must be got rid of. Mere circumvention was not enough. And so, one day, having arrived at the midpoint of his downstroke, this surgeon paused to cut out the navel with a neat ellipse of skin before continuing on down to the pubis. Such an elliptical incision when sutured at the close of the operation forms the continuous straight line without which this surgeon could not live. Once having cut out a navel (the first incidental umbilectomy, I suppose, was the hardest) and seeing the simple undeviate line of his closure, he vowed never again to leave a navel behind. Since he was otherwise a good surgeon, and very successful, it was not long before there were thousands of New Haveners walking around minus their belly buttons. Not that this interfered with any but the most uncommon of activities, but to those of us who examined them postoperatively, these abdomens had a blind, bland look. Years later I would happen upon one of these bellies and know at once the author of the incision upon it. Ah, I would say, Dr. Truffle has been here.

It is so difficult for a surgeon to remain "unconscious," retaining the clarity of vision of childhood, to know and be secure in his ability, yet be unaware of his talents. It is almost impossible. There are all too many people around him paying obeisance, pandering, catering, beaming, lusting. Yet he must try.

It is not enough to love your work. Love of work is a kind of self-indulgence. You must go beyond that. Better to perform endlessly, repetitiously, faithfully, the simplest acts, like trimming the toenails of an old man. By so doing, you will not say *Here I Am,* but *Here It Is.* You will not announce your love but will store it up in the bodies of your patients to carry with them wherever they go.

Many times over, you will hear otherwise sensible people say, "You have golden hands," or, "Thanks to you and God, I have recovered." (Notice the order in which the credit is given.) Such ill-directed praise has no significance. It is the patient's disguised expression of relief at having come through, avoided death. It is a private utterance, having nothing to do with you. Still, such words are enough to turn a surgeon's head, if any more turning were needed.

Avoid these blandishments at all cost. You are in service to your patients,   24
and a servant should know his place. The world is topsy-turvy in which a master worships his servant. You are a kindly, firm, experienced servant, but a servant still. If any patient of mine were to attempt to bathe my feet, I'd kick over his basin, suspecting that he possessed not so much a genuine sentiment as a conventional one. It is beneath your dignity to serve as an object of veneration or as the foil in an act of contrition. To any such effusion a simple "Thank you" will do. The rest is pride, and everyone knoweth before *what* that goeth.

Alexander the Great had a slave whose sole responsibility was to whis-   25
per "Remember, you are mortal" when he grew too arrogant. Perhaps every surgeon should be assigned such a deflator. The surgeon is the mere instrument which the patient takes in his hand to heal himself. An operation, then, is a time of revelation, both physical and spiritual, when, for a little while, the secrets of the body are set forth to be seen, to be touched, and the surgeon himself is laid open to Grace.

An operation is a reenactment of the story of Jonah and the Whale. In   26
surgery, the patient is the whale who swallows up the surgeon. Unlike Jonah, however, the surgeon does not cry out *non serviam*, but willingly descends into the sick body in order to cut out of it the part that threatens to kill it. In an operation where the patient is restored to health, the surgeon is spewed out of the whale's body, and both he and his patient are healed. In an operation where the patient dies on the table, the surgeon, although he is rescued from the whale and the sea of blood, is not fully healed, but will bear the scars of his sojourn in the belly of the patient for the rest of his life.

QUESTIONS ON MEANING

1. Paragraphs 13 and 14 concern the surgeon's "love of inconsiderable things." What sorts of things is Selzer referring to? Are they inconsiderable to everyone? How does Selzer bring out their significance?
2. In paragraph 26 Selzer characterizes a successful operation as one in which both surgeon and patient are healed. How does he mean this? Of what is the surgeon healed? Is this the sort of "healing work" that Wendell Berry writes about in "The Making of a Marginal Farm"?

QUESTIONS ON STRATEGY

1. Selzer uses many examples, both brief and extended, to support his many points of advice. Almost every paragraph provides a new and different ex-

ample or simile. Why are his examples effective? Where are they most effective? Are there any places where they are not effective?

2. In paragraphs 19–24 Selzer develops his last piece of advice to the young intern: "Only do not succumb to self-love." How many different arguments does he present against self-love? Why does he use an extended example in paragraph 20 and only brief examples in the other paragraphs in this passage?

3. Does Selzer's comment "Revel in your Specialty; it is your divinity" (paragraph 15) contradict his injunction against self-love in paragraph 19? How does he balance these two ideas throughout the essay?

4. The essay ends with two paragraphs containing very different examples. What is the relation between the two? Is paragraph 25 an effective transition, or is it superfluous? Why?

5. Why does the story of Jonah and the whale make an effective conclusion?

6. The essay is addressed to a young surgeon, but is Selzer writing for another audience as well? What are the messages directed to his different audiences? What might their different reactions be?

EXPLORATIONS

1. Though they write from different perspectives, one as participant and the other as observer, and for different audiences, both Richard Selzer and Tom Wolfe try to describe the "right stuff" required for the performance of highly technical and specialized tasks, both involving the risk of life. Write an essay explaining their similarities in emphasis and approach. Consider particularly their handling of religious feeling.

WRITING TOPICS

1. Write an essay in which you adapt Selzer's perspective to Wolfe's subject: Write a letter from an experienced astronaut to an aspiring testpilot. Using Wolfe's details about the stern tests awaiting the young candidate, introduce him or her to the secrets of the profession.

BOOKS AVAILABLE IN PAPERBACK

Letters to a Young Doctor. New York: Simon & Schuster. *Essays.*

Mortal Lessons: Notes on the Art of Surgery. New York: Simon & Schuster, Touchstone Books. *Essays.*

ADRIENNE
RICH

*W*HEN ADRIENNE RICH (b. 1929) was a junior in college, the poet W. H. Auden selected her first book of poems, A Change of World, for the Yale Series of Younger Poets Award. It was published in 1951 as she graduated from Radcliffe College, and a year later she became a Guggenheim Fellow. After six further books of poems, including Diving into the Wreck, which won the National Book Award in 1974, she published her Poems Selected and New 1950–74 (1975). More recent books of poetry are The Dream of a Common Language (1978) and A Wild Patience Has Taken Me This Far (1981).

Rich's first prose book was Of Woman Born: Motherhood as Experience and Institution (1976). "Women and Honor" comes from her collection On Lies, Secrets, and Silence (1979). At the time of her remarkable early success, she was widely praised as a talented young writer and sometimes criticized as conventional or even complacent. In a long and gradual change, she has become a spokeswoman for the principled anger of feminist outrage. No one of her talented generation of American writers has taken so decisively a radical direction.

The form of "Women and Honor" is as radical as the thinking. Subtitled "Some Notes on Lying" and first delivered as a lecture, this essay uses brevity of statement, aphorism, and suggestion of the fragmentary to underscore its urgency. Rich leaves the blank spaces between paragraphs for her readers to fill in.

Women and Honor: Some Notes on Lying

(These notes are concerned with relationships between and among women. When "personal relationship" is referred to, I mean a relationship between two women. It will be clear in what follows when I am talking about women's relationships with men.)

The old, male idea of honor. A man's "word" sufficed — to other men — without guarantee.

"Our Land Free, Our Men Honest, Our Women Fruitful" — a popular colonial toast in America.

Male honor also having something to do with killing: *I could not love thee, Dear, so much / Lov'd I not Honour more* ("To Lucasta, On Going to the Wars"). Male honor as something needing to be avenged: hence, the duel.

Women's honor, something altogether else: virginity, chastity, fidelity to a husband. Honesty in women has not been considered important. We have been depicted as generically whimsical, deceitful, subtle, vacillating. And we have been rewarded for lying.

Men have been expected to tell the truth about facts, not about feelings. They have not been expected to talk about feelings at all.

Yet even about facts they have continually lied.

We assume that politicians are without honor. We read their statements trying to crack the code. The scandals of their politics: not that men in high places lie, only that they do so with such indifference, so endlessly, still expecting to be believed. We are accustomed to the contempt inherent in the political lie.

———

To discover that one has been lied to in a personal relationship, however, leads one to feel a little crazy.

———

Lying is done with words, and also with silence.

The woman who tells lies in her personal relationships may or may not plan or invent her lying. She may not even think of what she is doing in a calculated way.

A subject is raised which the liar wishes buried. She has to go down- 11
stairs, her parking meter will have run out. Or, there is a telephone call she
ought to have made an hour ago.

She is asked, point-blank, a question which may lead into painful talk: 12
"How do you feel about what is happening between us?" Instead of trying
to describe her feelings in their ambiguity and confusion, she asks, "How
do *you* feel?" The other, because she is trying to establish a ground of openness and trust, begins describing her own feelings. Thus the liar learns more
than she tells.

And she may also tell herself a lie: that she is concerned with the other's 13
feelings, not with her own.

But the liar is concerned with her own feelings. 14

The liar lives in fear of losing control. She cannot even desire a relation- 15
ship without manipulation, since to be vulnerable to another person means
for her the loss of control.

The liar has many friends, and leads an existence of great loneliness. 16

———

The liar often suffers from amnesia. Amnesia is the silence of the uncon- 17
scious.

To lie habitually, as a way of life, is to lose contact with the unconscious. 18
It is like taking sleeping pills, which confer sleep but blot out dreaming. The
unconscious wants truth. It ceases to speak to those who want something
else more than truth.

In speaking of lies, we come inevitably to the subject of truth. There is 19
nothing simple or easy about this idea. There is no "the truth," "a truth" —
truth is not one thing, or even a system. It is an increasing complexity. The
pattern of the carpet is a surface. When we look closely, or when we become
weavers, we learn of the tiny multiple threads unseen in the overall pattern,
the knots on the underside of the carpet.

This is why the effort to speak honestly is so important. Lies are usually 20
attempts to make everything simpler — for the liar — than it really is, or
ought to be.

In lying to others we end up lying to ourselves. We deny the importance 21
of an event, or a person, and thus deprive ourselves of a part of our lives. Or
we use one piece of the past or present to screen out another. Thus we lose
faith with our own lives.

The unconscious wants truth, as the body does. The complexity and fe- 22
cundity of dreams come from the complexity and fecundity of the uncon-

scious struggling to fulfill that desire. The complexity and fecundity of poetry come from the same struggle.

An honorable human relationship — that is, one in which two people have the right to use the word "love" — is a process, delicate, violent, often terrifying to both persons involved, a process of refining the truths they can tell each other.

It is important to do this because it breaks down human self-delusion and isolation.

It is important to do this because in so doing we do justice to our own complexity.

It is important to do this because we can count on so few people to go that hard way with us.

I come back to the questions of women's honor. Truthfulness has not been considered important for women, as long as we have remained physically faithful to a man, or chaste.

We have been expected to lie with our bodies: to bleach, redden, unkink or curl our hair, pluck eyebrows, shave armpits, wear padding in various places or lace ourselves, take little steps, glaze finger and toe nails, wear clothes that emphasized our helplessness.

We have been required to tell different lies at different times, depending on what the men of the time needed to hear. The Victorian wife or the white southern lady, who were expected to have no sensuality, to "lie still"; the twentieth-century "free" woman who is expected to fake orgasms.

We have had the truth of our bodies withheld from us or distorted; we have been kept in ignorance of our most intimate places. Our instincts have been punished: clitoridectomies for "lustful" nuns or for "difficult" wives. It has been difficult, too, to know the lies of our complicity from the lies we believed.

The lie of the "happy marriage," of domesticity — we have been complicit, have acted out the fiction of a well-lived life, until the day we testify in court of rapes, beatings, psychic cruelties, public and private humiliations.

Patriarchal lying has manipulated women both through falsehood and through silence. Facts we needed have been withheld from us. False witness has been borne against us.

And so we must take seriously the question of truthfulness between women, truthfulness among women. As we cease to lie with our bodies, as we cease to take on faith what men have said about us, is a truly womanly idea of honor in the making?

———————

Women have been forced to lie, for survival, to men. How to unlearn this 34 among other women?

"Women have always lied to each other." 35
"Women have always whispered the truth to each other." 36
Both of these axioms are true. 37

"Women have always been divided against each other." 38
"Women have always been in secret collusion." 39
Both of these axioms are true. 40

In the struggle for survival we tell lies. To bosses, to prison guards, the 41 police, men who have power over us, who legally own us and our children, lovers who need us as proof of their manhood.

There is a danger run by all powerless people: that we forget we are ly- 42 ing, or that lying becomes a weapon we carry over into relationships with people who do not have power over us.

———————

I want to reiterate that when we talk about women and honor, or women 43 and lying, we speak within the context of male lying, the lies of the power-ful, the lie as false source of power.

Women have to think whether we want, in our relationships with each 44 other, the kind of power that can be obtained through lying.

Women have been driven mad, "gaslighted," for centuries by the refuta- 45 tion of our experience and our instincts in a culture which validates only male experience. The truth of our bodies and our minds has been mystified to us. We therefore have a primary obligation to each other: not to under-mine each others' sense of reality for the sake of expediency; not to gaslight each other.

Women have often felt insane when cleaving to the truth of our experi- 46 ence. Our future depends on the sanity of each of us, and we have a pro-found stake, beyond the personal, in the project of describing our reality as candidly and fully as we can to each other.

———————

There are phrases which help us not to admit we are lying: "my pri- 47 vacy," "nobody's business but my own." The choices that underlie these phrases may indeed be justified; but we ought to think about the full mean-ing and consequences of such language.

Women's love for women has been represented almost entirely through silence and lies. The institution of heterosexuality has forced the lesbian to dissemble, or be labeled a pervert, a criminal, a sick or dangerous woman, etc., etc. The lesbian, then, has often been forced to lie, like the prostitute or the married women.

Does a life "in the closet" — lying, perhaps of necessity, about ourselves to bosses, landlords, clients, colleagues, family, because the law and public opinion are founded on a lie — does this, can it, spread into private life, so that lying (described as *discretion*) becomes an easy way to avoid conflict or complication? can it become a strategy so ingrained that it is used even with close friends and lovers?

Heterosexuality as an institution has also drowned in silence the erotic feelings between women. I myself lived half a lifetime in the lie of that denial. That silence makes us all, to some degree, into liars.

When a woman tells the truth she is creating the possibility for more truth around her.

———

The liar leads an existence of unutterable loneliness.

The liar is afraid.

But we are all afraid: without fear we become manic, hubristic, self-destructive. What is this particular fear that possesses the liar?

She is afraid that her own truths are not good enough.

She is afraid, not so much of prison guards or bosses, but of something unnamed within her.

The liar fears the void.

The void is not something created by patriarchy, or racism, or capitalism. It will not fade away with any of them. It is part of every woman.

"The dark core," Virginia Woolf named it, writing of her mother. The dark core. It is beyond personality; beyond who loves us or hates us.

We begin out of the void, out of darkness and emptiness. It is part of the cycle understood by the old pagan religions, that materialism denies. Out of death, rebirth; out of nothing, something.

The void is the creatrix, the matrix. It is not mere hollowness and anarchy. But in women it has been identified with lovelessness, barrenness, sterility. We have been urged to fill our "emptiness" with children. We are not supposed to go down into the darkness of the core.

Yet, if we can risk it, the something born of that nothing is the beginning   62
of our truth.

The liar in her terror wants to fill up the void, with anything. Her lies are   63
a denial of her fear; a way of maintaining control.

———————

Why do we feel slightly crazy when we realize we have been lied to in a   64
relationship?

We take so much of the universe on trust. You tell me: ''In 1950 I lived on   65
the north side of Beacon Street in Somerville.'' You tell me: ''She and I were
lovers, but for months now we have only been good friends.'' You tell me:
''It is seventy degrees outside and the sun is shining.'' Because I love you,
because there is not even a question of lying between us, I take these accounts of the universe on trust: your address twenty-five years ago, your relationship with someone I know only by sight, this morning's weather. I
fling unconscious tendrils of belief, like slender green threads, across statements such as these, statements made so unequivocally, which have no tone
or shadow of tentativeness. I build them into the mosaic of my world. I allow my universe to change in minute, significant ways, on the basis of
things you have said to me, of my trust in you.

I also have faith that you are telling me things it is important I should   66
know; that you do not conceal facts from me in an effort to spare me, or
yourself, pain.

Or, at the very least, that you will say, ''There are things I am not telling   67
you.''

When we discover that someone we trusted can be trusted no longer, it   68
forces us to reexamine the universe, to question the whole instinct and concept of trust. For awhile, we are thrust back onto some bleak, jutting ledge,
in a dark pierced by sheets of fire, swept by sheets of rain, in a world before
kinship, or naming, or tenderness exist; we are brought close to formless-
ness.

———————

The liar may resist confrontation, denying that she lied. Or she may use   69
other language: forgetfulness, privacy, the protection of someone else. Or,
she may bravely declare herself a coward. This allows her to go on lying,
since that is what cowards do. She does not say, *I was afraid*, since this
would open the question of other ways of handling her fear. It would open
the question of what is actually feared.

She may say, *I didn't want to cause pain*. What she really did not want is to   70
have to deal with the other's pain. The lie is a short-cut through another's
personality.

Truthfulness, honor, is not something which springs ablaze of itself; it has to be created between people.

This is true in political situations. The quality and depth of the politics evolving from a group depends in very large part on their understanding of honor.

Much of what is narrowly termed "politics" seems to rest on a longing for certainty even at the cost of honesty, for an analysis which, once given, need not be reexamined. Such is the deadendedness — for women — of Marxism in our time.

Truthfulness anywhere means a heightened complexity. But it is a movement into evolution. Women are only beginning to uncover our own truths; many of us would be grateful for some rest in that struggle, would be glad just to lie down with the sherds we have painfully unearthed, and be satisfied with those. Often I feel this like an exhaustion in my own body.

The politics worth having, the relationships worth having, demand that we delve still deeper.

The possibilities that exist between two people, or among a group of people, are a kind of alchemy. They are the most interesting thing in life. The liar is someone who keeps losing sight of these possibilities.

When relationships are determined by manipulation, by the need for control, they may possess a dreary, bickering kind of drama, but they cease to be interesting. They are repetitious; the shock of human possibilities has ceased to reverberate through them.

When someone tells me a piece of the truth which has been withheld from me, and which I needed in order to see my life more clearly, it may bring acute pain, but it can also flood me with a cold, sea-sharp wash of relief. Often such truths come by accident, or from strangers.

It isn't that to have an honorable relationship with you, I have to understand everything, or tell you everything at once, or that I can know, beforehand, everything I need to tell you.

It means that most of the time I am eager, longing for the possibility of telling you. That these possibilities may seem frightening, but not destructive, to me. That I feel strong enough to hear your tentative and groping words. That we both know we are trying, all the time, to extend the possibilities of truth between us.

The possibility of life between us.

QUESTIONS ON MEANING

1. In her parenthetical introductory note, Rich distinguishes between women's ''personal relationships'' and their relationships with men. Is Rich saying that ''personal relationships'' between men and women are impossible? Where does she return to this distinction? What is its importance to the essay? By ''personal relationships'' between women, is Rich referring only to sexual relationships or does she also include nonsexual relationships between women?

2. How does Rich lead us up to the statement in paragraph 57? What is the importance of this statement to the sequence of paragraphs 52–63? What is ''the void''?

3. Rich says that women have been forced to lie in response to the pressures and expectations of a patriarchal culture. What are some manifestations of these lies? What problems does this lying pose for women's relationships with women?

QUESTIONS ON STRATEGY

1. How does this essay differ in form from the other essays in this book? How does it differ even from a loosely structured essay like Paul Fussell's ''Notes on Class''? Is Rich's material organized systematically or is it random? Is her method of organization appropriate to the sort of information she presents?

2. Rich generalizes widely about the experience of women. Does omission of illustrative examples mean that she lacks evidence for her assertions? What kind of evidence does she give? Is her argument persuasive? If not, would examples make it more persuasive?

3. What audience do you think Rich had in mind for this essay? Cite evidence from the text to support your conclusion.

EXPLORATIONS

1. Both Adrienne Rich and Diane Johnson are contemporary feminists. Compare Rich's essay with Diane Johnson's ''Rape'' (pp. 338–348) for tone, strategy, and meaning.

2. In the eighteenth century, Mary Wollstonecraft published *A Vindication of the Rights of Woman*. As a way of appreciating how feminism has changed since its beginnings, and of reassessing Rich's argument and style, read chapter 2, ''The Prevailing Opinion of a Sexual Character Discussed,'' or chapter 9, ''Of the Pernicious Effects Which Arise from the Unnatural Distinctions Established in Society,'' in Wollstonecraft's book. What issues does Wollstonecraft present? What is her tone? How does she differ in these particulars from Rich? How does Rich emulate Wollstonecraft?

WRITING TOPICS

1. Write an essay illustrating Rich's axiom "In lying to others we end up lying to ourselves" in paragraph 21. Draw on specific details from your personal history or from a chapter in the history of the United States.

BOOKS AVAILABLE IN PAPERBACK

Adrienne Rich's Poetry: Texts of the Poems, The Poet on Her Work, Reviews, and Criticism. Selected and edited by Barbara Charlesworth Gelpi and Albert Gelpi. New York: Norton. *A Norton Critical Edition.*

A Change of World. New Haven: Yale University Press. *Poems.*

Diving into the Wreck: Poems, 1971–1972. New York: Norton.

The Dream of a Common Language: Poems, 1974–1977. New York: Norton.

Leaflets: Poems, 1965–1968. New York: Norton.

Of Woman Born: Motherhood as Experience and Institution. New York: Bantam. *Nonfiction: Social history and personal history.*

On Lies, Secrets, and Silence: Selected Prose, 1966–1978. New York: Norton. *Essays.*

Poems: Selected and New, 1950–1974. New York: Norton.

A Wild Patience Has Taken Me This Far: Poems, 1978–1981. New York: Norton.

Will to Change: Poems. New York: Norton.

JEREMY
BERNSTEIN

*J*EREMY BERNSTEIN *was born in Rochester, New York, in 1929, son of a rabbi. Although he really wanted to be a jazz trumpeter, after graduating from Harvard in 1951 he took his M.A. and Ph.D. in physics at Harvard and then spent time at the Institute for Advanced Study in Princeton and at the National Science Foundation. He taught physics for five years at New York University and now teaches at Stevens Institute of Technology, Hoboken, New Jersey.*

But Jeremy Bernstein has also spent twenty years on the staff of The New Yorker *magazine, writing mostly about physics, computers, and other topics in physical science. He moves as comfortably among sentences and paragraphs as among equations. He has written many books, beginning with* The Analytical Engine: Computers — Past, Present, and Future *(1964, revised 1981). His* Einstein *came out in 1973, and he has published collections of his scientific essays for general magazines. This essay comes from* Experiencing Science *(1978). His most recent collection is* Science Observed *(1982), subtitled "Essays Out of My Mind."*

Writing this essay on calculators, Bernstein finds an appropriate beginning in personal anecdote, then typically carries his reader into technological exposition by an informal transition: "I bring all of this up because. . . ." His fluid and anecdotal style incorporates an interview with Arthur Clarke, stories about innovative mathe-

*maticians, and reference to scientific history and to a Beethoven symphony. Every-
thing serves Bernstein's purpose: to explain difficult scientific concepts to the interested but uninformed reader.*

Calculators:
Self-Replications

In the spring of 1955, I completed my Ph.D. thesis for the Harvard Physics Department. I had done a theoretical problem, my principal memory of
which is that it required the computation of seventy-five numerical integrals.
An integral, for the nonspecialist, is simply the area under a given curve.
Each integral took me something like two days to compute; and the seventy-
five, nearly six months. Some elementary integrals could be looked up in
books, but mine could not. I had to calculate them myself. The mind boggles
now at how I once spent six months of my life — and not unhappily: Sisyphus,° as Camus° pointed out, was basically a happy man.

Just as I was finishing this task, there appeared on the scene a whiz kid
from Cal Tech. He was about to begin a post-doctoral appointment at MIT,
and it turned out, much to my amazement, that he had done essentially the
same problem with two notable differences: (1) His basic theory was better,
and (2) he had cultivated a group at MIT that had built one of the first electronic computers — a vacuum-tube affair — and, though a dinosaur by
present standards, it enabled him to calculate each of his integrals in about
two minutes. I decided that in the future I had two choices: I had either to
learn to deal with electronic computers, or to avoid numerical integrals. In
the past twenty years, I have, by and large, chosen the latter alternative.

I bring all of this up because a number of morals can be drawn about man
and the machines he has created. In science, theory and experiment interre-
late but, generally speaking, an experimenter begins from some sort of theoretical premise. For example, in high-energy physics, these premises can
take such a simple qualitative form as: If the laws of nature were symmetric
between particle and antiparticle, then the neutral-pi meson could decay
only into an even number of light quanta. Don't worry if that terminology is

---

Sisyphus   In Greek mythology, the king of Corinth who was condemned to roll a
heavy rock up a hill in Hades only to have it roll down again as it neared the top.

Camus   Albert Camus (1913–1960), French existentialist novelist, essayist, and playwright whose book *The Myth of Sisyphus* (1955) dealt with irrationality, absurdity, and suicide.

unfamiliar. The point is that this is a statement that could be — indeed *was* — made without aid of any computer. Even in the case of theoretical statements involving numerical work done by computer, the theoretical structure is always developed by a physicist and not the computer. Computers do not create theories of physics. And no paper in theoretical physics, at least until now, has required the use of a computer to be understood.

In a typical modern high-energy experiment, millions of events occur — 4 photographed tracks in a bubble chamber, or photographed spark discharges, for example. Experimenters make extensive use of computers in recording and analyzing these events. It is not uncommon for an experimenter to prepare a plot on which each point itself represents a million events. Obviously, this kind of data processing must be done by computer. But for the results to be comprehensible, they must be fitted by some sort of curve that arises from a humanly created theory. The chain is human to human, with the machine somewhere in between. It is sometimes said that the computer is to this process as the microscope is to vision. I think this analogy is flawed. Forty-eight people staring at a glass of water with the unaided eye will not see the microbes swimming around in it, while one person with a microscope will see them. The microscope has revealed something that was, in principle, invisible to the human eye. On the other hand, there is nothing the computer does in this chain that could not be done by enough human brain power. Although it took me six months, I did finally do the numerical integrals.

Recently I had the opportunity of discussing this matter with Arthur 5 Clarke, whose fictional computer HAL — invented in collaboration with Stanley Kubrick for *2001*° — could do about *anything*. Indeed, HAL could do too *much* of anything. Clarke made the point that electronic computers can now do computation that would require the whole human race working together to accomplish without them (perhaps a more estimable activity than many others the race often engages in). Furthermore, the speed of the individual operations on the computer is something totally beyond human capability; its basic calculations can be completed in the millionths of a second or less. Still, in the man-machine-man process, the machine in the middle can, at least in principle — and, at least, at present — be replaced by humans. Clarke once wrote a story entitled "Into the Comet," in which a spaceship's computer fails and, lacking the proper orbit, the ship heads for disaster. A crewman, of Japanese origin, teaches the entire crew to make abacuses with wires and beads and the ship is saved.

2001 *2001: A Space Odyssey* (1968), the first modern, large-scale science fiction film, pitting humans against their machines on a space voyage. Directed by Stanley Kubrick, screenplay by the science fiction writer Arthur C. Clarke.

The computer has quantitatively enlarged the sort of calculations and experiments an individual scientist can take on in his lifetime, but, as far as I can tell, it has, on its own, created nothing. In this respect, I am reminded of my one and only encounter with the great Hungarian-born American mathematician John von Neumann. It was von Neumann who developed the theory of stored programming — that is, the capacity of a computer to modify its own instructions as a computation unfolds. He delivered a series of lectures at Harvard while I was an undergraduate there, and I was enormously impressed. After one lecture, I found myself in Harvard Square alongside the great man himself as he hurried by to find the subway. I thought, correctly as it turned out, that this would be the only chance I would ever have to ask him a question. I seized the occasion. "Professor von Neumann," I asked, "will the computer ever replace the human mathematician?" "Sonny, don't worry about it." Literally, that is what he answered.

All this having been said, it must be added that the computer has injected something into modern scientific thinking beyond mere technology. For the first time, I believe, it has presented us with a machine-tooled model — still primitive — of ourselves. I recently read in a history of computers (*The Computer from Pascal to von Neumann*, by Herman Goldstine) that in his early papers on the logical design of computers, von Neumann took his notation from two physiologists, Warren S. McCulloch and Walter Pitts, who were trying to make a mathematical model of the human nervous system. Von Neumann was trying to create what might be described as an electronic nervous system. Now, clearly it would be a fatal mistake to try to construct a model of the nervous system by working from the outside in. That is to say, if one takes as primary data products of the nervous system such as Einstein's theory of relativity, Beethoven's Ninth Symphony, and Van Gogh's *Starry Night* and, from these, attempts to deduce the construction of the apparatus that produced them, one is not likely to get very far. It would be like trying to deduce the structure of the elementary particles of subnuclear physics by contemplating Mount Everest. The idea, rather, is to put together a vast array of very primitive objects and to see what such an array working in concert can produce. The fundamental components of the McCulloch-Pitts model, described in their celebrated paper entitled "A Logical Calculus of the Ideas Imminent in Nervous Activity," were "neurons" connected by wires that could transmit electrical pulses. (In the human brain there are about ten billion neurons — organic molecules about a hundred-thousandth of a centimeter in diameter — wired together by axons, or fibers, that can be several feet long.) For purpose of the analysis, a neuron acts as a relay station for electrical pulses. If such a station receives a sufficiently strong impulse, it will "fire," or emit a pulse. If these neurons are wired together, in units, things can be arranged so that it takes the activation of, for example, a pair of neurons to fire a third one and so on. That event in this so-called logic circuit might be described, in the language of formal logic, as *A plus B implies C*. Now, it has been known since the pioneering work of Bertrand Russell and Alfred North Whitehead° that even the most complicated mathematical statements can be broken down to a collection of such primitive logical propositions. Hence, McCulloch and Pitts were emboldened to conclude: "Anything that can be exhaustively and unambiguously described, anything that can be completely and unambiguously put into words is, *ipso facto,*° realizable by a suitable finite neural network." In other words, neural networks can carry out the processes of mathematical logic.

Von Neumann was deeply impressed by this analysis, since the comput- 8 ing machines he was designing were essentially neural networks with electronic devices — vacuum tubes in the original, and now archaic, versions of the machines — playing the role of the organic neurons. These machines, therefore, could in principle do anything that a McCulloch-Pitts model could do. Being the kind of genius that he was, von Neumann did not leave the analysis there. He built on the work of a remarkable young British mathematician, Alan Mathison Turing, whose work remains largely unknown, except to specialists. Yet it may turn out that, when a future historian of automation looks back at the really revolutionary implications of the so-called computer revolution, these will have much more to do with the as yet unrealized abstract ideas of Alan Turing, as generalized by von Neumann, than all of the new airline reservation systems, and the like, put together.

Alan Turing, whose life is described in a moving book written by his 9 mother in 1959, died five years earlier at the age of 42, perhaps by suicide. From 1936 through 1938, he studied at Princeton, where his work came to the attention of von Neumann. (Some of the work was done independently by the American logician Emil L. Post, but apparently von Neumann was not aware of it.) Von Neumann offered him a position as his assistant at the Institute for Advanced Study. Turing declined it, preferring to return to King's College, in Cambridge, England, where he was a Fellow. He later worked on the construction of the first British computers.

Turing invented what is now known as the Turing machine, which is ac- 10 tually not a real machine at all but rather, an abstract construct — an idea — for an apparatus that could be instructed to make mathematical calculations. There are various ways of describing the basic idea. But as Mark Kac, a professor of mathematics at Rockefeller University, has put it, the Turing machine has an infinitely long tape divided into identical-sized squares, each one of which either is blank or contains a slash. Over the tape, there is a

Bertrand Russell and Alfred North Whitehead English mathematicians and philosophers (Russell, 1872–1970; Whitehead, 1861–1947) who together wrote *Principia Mathematica* (1910), a study of the structure of mathematical and logical thinking.

ipso facto By the very nature of the case.

movable arrow. The machine can be given four basic directions, denoted: L, R, * and /. The L means move the arrow one step to the left; R, one step right; * means erase the slash; / means print slash.

The machine may be programmed to carry out a sequence of operations (see Figure 1). Assume for the sake of the discussion that a given Turing machine had four slashes on an infinitely long tape, one each in Squares 10, 11, 12, and 13. To get it to double those four — in other words, to get it to multiply 4 X 2 — one would first move the pointer to Square 9, and then issue a sequence of instructions, bearing in mind that at each step the machine has to be given two alternative courses of action: (1) R (that is, move the pointer one square to the right): if blank repeat Step 1 (that is, move another square to the right), or if not blank erase / and go to Step 2; (2) L: if blank print / and go to Step 3, or if not blank reprint / and repeat Step 2; (3) L: if blank print / and go to Step 4, or if not blank reprint / and repeat Step 3; (4) R: if blank leave blank and go to Step 1, or if not blank reprint / and repeat Step 4. Now this entire sequence is repeated four times, after which the answer appears as a series of eight slashes, in Squares 5 through 12. (Unfortunately, for the pointer and the machine's imaginary fuel supply, there is no way in this early Turing program to stop the pointer; after completion of the fourth series, it keeps encountering blank squares, leaving them blank and moving one space to the right — on to eternity!)

All this may seem a bit primitive, but Turing went on to prove a most remarkable theorem: that it is possible to construct a general-purpose machine — he called it a universal machine — on whose tape one can write any number of programs, or codes made of slashes and blanks, and that the universal machine would read these instructions and carry them out. This universal machine can carry out any set of operations that any given Turing machine is able to carry out. It is the abstract embodiment of all Turing machines. (In Turing's time, it was believed that a universal machine would have to be enormous and have to be given millions of instructions, but now the theory has been greatly simplified. Professor Marvin Minsky of MIT holds the record for building the smallest universal machine — it has twenty-eight instructions.) In Professor Kac's words: "The Turing machine owes its fundamental importance to the remarkable theorem that all *concrete* mathematical calculations can be programmed on it. . . . In other words, every concretely stated computational task will be performed by the machine when it is provided with an appropriate, finite set of instructions." (Turing also showed that problems exist for which no program can be devised in principle. These are the computing machine analogues of the undecidable propositions of the mathematics of Gödel.° The machine is, in this respect, no better or worse off than the human mathematician.)

Gödel Kurt Gödel (b. 1906), Austrian-born mathematician. Gödel's proof (1931) showed that there is no logical basis for any logical system in mathematics.

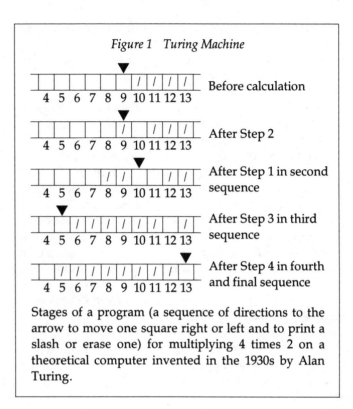

Figure 1 Turing Machine

Before calculation

After Step 2

After Step 1 in second sequence

After Step 3 in third sequence

After Step 4 in fourth and final sequence

Stages of a program (a sequence of directions to the arrow to move one square right or left and to print a slash or erase one) for multiplying 4 times 2 on a theoretical computer invented in the 1930s by Alan Turing.

Now for the great leap forward. Von Neumann asked himself whether 13 programs could be devised that would instruct the Turing machine to reproduce itself. It had always been supposed that machines were used to produce objects that are less complicated than the machines themselves, that only biological reproduction transmitted total complexity or, indeed, through mutation, increased the complexity. A machine tool, for example, by itself cannot make a machine tool. One must adjoin to it a set of instructions, and these usually take the form of a human operator. Hence, the complete system is the machine tool plus the human operator. Clearly, this system will, under normal circumstances, produce a machine tool minus the human operator — hence vastly less complex.

Von Neumann discussed these matters in the Vanuxem lectures at 14 Princeton in 1953, and since then these talks have acquired an almost legendary character. They were never fully recorded, however, though fragments appeared in a book entitled *The Computer and the Brain,* and they were discussed in 1955 in an article in *Scientific American* by John G. Kemeny, now president of Dartmouth.

When we discuss self-replicating machines we must be clear about the 15 ground rules. In Kemeny's words: "What do we mean by reproduction? If we mean the creation of an object like the original out of nothing, then no machine can reproduce, but neither can a human being. . . . The characteristic feature of the reproduction of life is that the living organism can create a new organism like itself out of inert matter surrounding it.

"If we agree that machines are not alive, and if we insist that the creation of life is an essential feature of reproduction, then we have begged the question. A machine cannot reproduce. So we must reformulate the problem in a way that won't make machine reproduction logically impossible. We must omit the word 'living.' We shall ask that the machine create a new organism like itself out of simple parts contained in the environment."

Von Neumann showed, as early as 1948, that any self-replicating apparatus must necessarily contain the following elements. There must be the raw materials. In his abstract example, these are just squares of paper — "cells" — waiting around to be organized. Then we need the program that supplies instructions. There must be a "factory" — an automaton that follows the instructions and takes the waiting cells and puts them together according to a program. Since we want to end up with a machine that, like the original, contains a blueprint of itself, we must have a duplicator, a sort of Xerox machine that takes any instruction and makes a copy. Finally, we must have a supervisor. Each time the supervisor receives an instruction, it has it copied and then gives it to the factory to be acted on. Hence, once the thing gets going it will duplicate itself, and, indeed, von Neumann produced an abstract model containing some 200,000 cells which theoretically did just this.

Those who have had some education in modern genetic theory may have heard bells going off, or had the sense of *déjà vu*, upon reading the above description. It could apply as well, in abstract outline, to biological reproduction. We are, by now, so used to the idea of computer analogies to biological systems that they may appear obvious. One must keep in mind that they were not obvious at all; indeed, they are only a few decades old. Von Neumann's analysis was five years ahead of the discovery of the double-helix structure of DNA, and preceded by several more years the full unfolding of what is called the "central dogma" of genetic replication. In a Vanuxem lecture in 1970, Freeman Dyson of the Institute for Advanced Study made a sort of glossary translation from von Neumann's machine to its biological counterpart. The "factory" is the ribosomes; the copying machine is the enzymes RNA and DNA polymerase; the supervisor is the repressor and depressor control molecules; and the plan itself is the RNA and DNA. Von Neumann was there first.

His early training in Budapest was as a chemical engineer, and he never lost his feeling for engineering practicalities. He was not content to think purely in the abstract. Hence, he raised the following question: Real automata, including biological ones, are subject to error. There is a risk of failure in each of the basic operations — a wire can come loose. How can one design a system that will be reliable even if the basic operations are not completely reliable? The secret was *redundancy*. Suppose, to take an example from Goldstine, one has three identical machines, each of which makes a long calculation in which each machine makes, on the average, 100 errors. The way to improve reliability is to connect the machines, and require them to agree on one step before they go on to the next. If the system were set up so that once two machines agreed they could set the third at the agreed value and then proceed, then it turns out that the chance of error would be reduced from 1 in 100 to 1 in 33 million! Von Neumann concluded that the central nervous system must be organized redundantly to make it function at a suitable error level. This conclusion also appears to be correct. Von Neumann realized, too, that if the universal Turing machine could be made to reproduce itself, it could evolve. If the program was changed, say, by "mutation," and this change was such that the machine could still reproduce, it would produce an altered offspring.

In Freeman Dyson's words, "Von Neumann believed that the possibility of a universal automaton was ultimately responsible for the possibility of indefinitely continued biological evolution. In evolving from simpler to more complex organisms, you do not have to redesign the basic biochemical machinery as you go along. You have only to modify and extend the genetic instructions. . . . Everything we have learned about evolution since 1948 tends to confirm that von Neumann was right."

Where does all of this leave us? The point I have been trying to make is that, as far as I can see, the most profound impact of the computer on society may not be as much in what it can do in practice, impressive though this is, as in what the machine *is* in theory — and has less to do with its capacity as calculator than with its capacity for self-replication.

Recently, I discussed these matters with Professor Minsky, who is one of the foremost authorities on machine intelligence. He told me that von Neumann's complex arguments have now been greatly simplified by his successors. Abstract models of self-reproducing machines have been devised that are extremely simple. Moreover, real computing machines have elements in their design that are beginning to resemble self-replication. One uses a computer to program the design of a computer, and this design is given to a computer that supervises the actual physical construction of the new computer. One must supply from the outside the actual silicon chips on which the circuitry is printed, so, in this sense, the process is not really self-contained. Minsky says most people now agree that a truly self-replicating automaton would have to be the size of a factory (one of whose functions would be the manufacture of silicon chips). It now seems conceivable — in principle, at least, the logic is there — that perhaps with the addition of some primitive biological components (who knows what!), the process can be further developed to the stage where self-producing automatons can be made that are compact and, acting in concert, can do just about anything. In his Vanuxem lecture, Dyson gives several examples of what colonies of these machines might accomplish, for good or evil, if let loose on earth or in outer space — such as bringing vegetation, light, and heat to Mars. With a little thought the reader can supply his own examples. For some reason, as admiring as I am of the logic of automatons, I find the prospect chilling.

I suspect — and this is also emphasized in Dyson's lecture — that for self-reproducing machines to do anything interesting they must have a very high level of interorganization. As Dyson put it: "The fully developed colony must be as well-coordinated as the cells of a bird. There must be automata with specialized functions corresponding to muscle, liver, and nerve cell. There must be high-quality sense organs and a central battery of computers performing the functions of a brain," which may mutate and proliferate. In time, we may no longer recognize them. In this respect, Sara Turing quotes a letter, in her book about her son, that she received from the wife of one of Turing's closest colleagues, M. H. A. Newman. Mrs. Newman wrote: "I remember sitting in our garden at Bowdon about 1949 while Alan and my husband discussed the machine and its future activities. I couldn't take part in the discussion and it was one of many that had passed over my head, but suddenly my ear picked up a remark which sent a shiver down my back. Alan said reflectively, 'I suppose, when it gets to that stage, we shan't know how it does it.' "

QUESTIONS ON MEANING

1. Bernstein begins with an anecdote about his dissertation. What point emerges in the first two paragraphs? How do these paragraphs introduce the essay's main themes?
2. Bernstein feels that computers cannot replace all of a human being's functions. What can a computer do that a human cannot, and what can a human do that a computer cannot? What are the similarities and differences between a self-replicating computer and a reproductive human?
3. What does Bernstein identify as the computer's really new contribution to scientific thinking? How does he feel about this contribution? Does he appear to have taken von Neumann's advice (in paragraph 6)?

QUESTIONS ON STRATEGY

1. To define von Neumann's genius, Bernstein compares von Neumann's work to that of biologists before and after him (beginning in paragraph 7). What are some of the relationships he establishes? How do they help clarify the contributions of von Neumann?

2. Bernstein pays close attention to the career of Alan Turing. How does his discussion of Turing's work help him establish von Neumann's importance? What else does Bernstein's emphasis on Turing accomplish?

EXPLORATIONS

1. Bernstein refers to Arthur Clarke's science fiction treatment of the computer. See *2001: A Space Odyssey* (or read Clarke's screenplay for the film, available in paperback) and consider how effectively Clarke provides a dramatic analogue to the kind of moral concerns Bernstein discusses in "Calculators: Self-Replications."

WRITING TOPICS

1. Bernstein's essay relies on a combination of personal anecdote, research, and interview for material. How much does Bernstein emphasize the results of his research? Write an essay in which you supplement what you know about a well-defined subject — perhaps a specialized one such as a sport, an academic discipline, or a technical skill — with what you can learn from interviewing an expert or with additional information and anecdotes from your own experience.

2. Bernstein's essay was written more than ten years ago. Read some current popular or scientific literature (weekly news magazines, the *New York Times Magazine, Omni, Science 84, Scientific American*), particularly related to artificial or machine intelligence, to determine whether any of Bernstein's speculations in paragraphs 22 and 23 have been realized. Write an essay about any such developments or about aspects of such technological advances that support Bernstein's and Mrs. Newman's "shivers" of apprehension.

BOOKS AVAILABLE IN PAPERBACK

The Analytical Engine: Computers — Past, Present, and Future. Rev. ed. New York: Morrow. *Nonfiction: Technological history.*

Ascent: Of the Invention of Mountain Climbing and Its Practice. Lincoln: University of Nebraska Press. *Essays.*

Einstein. New York: Penguin. *Nonfiction: Biography of Albert Einstein (1879–1955).*

Science Observed. New York: Basic Books. *Essays.*

MICHAEL J.
ARLEN

*M*ICHAEL J. ARLEN *was born in 1930 in England but grew up in the United States. His father was the author Michael Arlen, an Armenian exile, who wrote an enormously popular novel of the 1920s,* The Green Hat, *which became a Greta Garbo film. An early book by the son is* Exiles *(1970), a moving reminiscence of his father and mother. Another is* Passage to Ararat *(1975), which recounts Michael J. Arlen's exploration of his Armenian heritage.*

But this author is best known for his television criticism, which appears regularly in The New Yorker. *Several books collect these columns, including* The View from Highway 1 *(1976), from which we take this essay, and most recently* The Camera Age *(1981). In* Thirty Seconds *(1980) he wrote a devastating two-hundred-page narrative of the talent, energy, money, and intelligence that combined to produce a thirty-second television commercial for American Telephone & Telegraph.*

Most newspaper television critics write criticism as ephemeral as the product they criticize. Arlen himself usually covers the programming of the moment, so that his material dates as quickly as milk; but his incisive intelligence and his deft prose style reach below the surface of the day to provide disquieting views of the culture that malnourishes us. In ''The Cold, Bright Charms of Immortality'' we find Arlen speculating on the subject of death — as old as humankind's questioning — by narrowing his attention to a screen perhaps nineteen inches diagonal, which provides his observing wisdom with details to question, criticize, and integrate.

The Cold, Bright Charms of Immortality

In the modern world, death breaks into our lives suddenly — as it were, by surprise — even though it remains a fact that most men and women in this country still die in their beds of what used to be called old age. A death occurs in the family! Long-distance telephone calls criss-cross through the night. The survivors — uneasy with a sense of uniqueness, their separate grief imprisoned in their separate civilities — stand about in suits and overcoats while tiny explosions detonate inside their heads, and then start for home.

The Sioux, I'm told, placed their dead on platforms up in the branches of trees along the Platte River — companionable treefuls of dead Sioux. The Crow made sure to show their grief by cutting off part of a finger. The Arapaho acknowledged death's imminence by singing a song to it; an abandoned warrior, dying, would brace himself against a rock and sing the Death Song until he died. Generally, nowadays, we do things differently.

An uncle of mine died a few weeks ago — a kind and modest man whom I much cared about; he was seventy-three at the time of his heart attack, which, as my sister insisted, had come "out of nowhere." His dying naturally made me think of death — at first, in the usual manner, whereby for a while after the death of a close friend or relative harsh winds of mortality gust with a sudden, temporary significance through the heads of those remaining. Then, perhaps because he had been such a calm, methodical, gently purposive man, and there had been something calm, methodical, and — yes — gently purposive about his death and the manner of its arrival, I found myself feeling the moment quite differently. For an instant, death itself seemed almost like a modest, commonplace event — perhaps like what it was. In his fine book *The Lives of a Cell*, Dr. Lewis Thomas has written: "There are three billion of us on the earth, and all three billion must be dead, on a schedule, within this lifetime." Just then, from inside one's modern, individual isolation, one could nearly sense the dim, communal, ordinary idea of a mortality that was beyond us, and that human beings sometimes reached for — without attaining. And so afterward, mindful of the invisible community, I thought of television, and wondered what — were I to watch it steadily for a while — I might find that this pervasive communicator was telling us, or not telling us, about our mass, ongoing, connective activity; about death.

I picked a finite period of one week to study, and therein I watched, with reasonable fidelity, ten or twelve hours each day. I wrote down only references to death or dying, as follows:

Friday: On *The Edge of Night,* there were two references to the earlier murder of a young woman named Taffy Simms. On *Days of Our Lives,* Bob said, "Phyllis, you almost died." From the NBC local news: "A mine disaster in northern France has claimed forty-one lives." And "Eighteen persons were killed in Brazil this morning as a train crashed into a bus." And "Fifteen died today in Portugal when two passenger trains collided outside a railroad station in Lisbon." And "Eighteen people were reported strangled in the Ethiopian city of Asmara. This brings the total number of deaths by strangulation to forty-five." The death of Jack Benny was reported, accompanied by a photograph of Benny during his early days on radio, when he worked for NBC, and prominently displaying the NBC microphone. There was a film from Darwin, Australia, that briefly showed a dead victim of the Darwin cyclone being carried away on a stretcher, and also presented an interview with a survivor. "What happened to your wife?" the reporter asked. "My wife was killed," the survivor said. The CBS network news mentioned the forty-one mine-explosion deaths in France, and the fifteen Portuguese who had been killed this morning in a train crash "just outside Lisbon's main railroad station." There was an item about Jack Benny: "Benny Kubelsky, better known as Jack Benny, died in his home today of cancer. For half a century, Jack Benny made people laugh by laughing at himself." On *Kolchak,* a score of people were murdered by a vampire. In the movie *The Last Run,* a man fell to his death; another man was shot and then burned up in a car; two men were killed in a gunfight. On *Police Woman,* the dead body of a man was found in a car trunk, and four men were killed in a gunfight.

Saturday: There were no deaths in any of the entertainment programs. From the NBC network news: "In recent months, more than twenty thousand people have died of starvation" in Bangladesh. And "Doctors have said that more tests will be needed to determine the cause of the fall last evening which resulted in the death of columnist Amy Vanderbilt. Miss Vanderbilt was an authority and author of several books on etiquette." In an ABC documentary, *Crashes: The Illusion of Safety,* there were references to numerous plane crashes, in which a total of forty-eight hundred people had died. On the NBC late news, there was an item about a retired policeman who had been shot and killed. And "There still appears to be some mystery surrounding the death of columnist Amy Vanderbilt. Police have indicated the possibility of suicide, although her husband has said he knows of nothing to indicate that motivation."

Sunday: On *World of Survival*, a reef crab was killed by an octopus. "A 7
very sad day for the crab," said the announcer. From the CBS local news:
"Pakistani authorities have estimated that over three hundred people have
been killed in an earthquake in northern Pakistan." And "Nicaraguan guerrillas killed three guards yesterday." And "Three persons were killed in a
four-car accident at the corner of Barlow and a Hundred and Thirty-ninth
Street." CBS News (whose parent company, CBS, had hired Benny away
from NBC) provided an hour-long *Tribute to Jack Benny*. There were brief
scenes of Hollywood celebrities arriving in cars. "This was the day of his
[Jack Benny's] funeral, and all of Hollywood was there," said correspondent
Charles Kuralt. A 1967 CBS tape showed the late Ed Sullivan. "It's true that
Jack Benny spoke his first words on the air on an Ed Sullivan radio show,"
said Mr. Kuralt. Benny's former CBS announcer, Don Wilson, said, "Jack,
above all, was a great human being . . . Jack was a very normal person . . .
He never went to a psychiatrist — he never had to." There was a tape of
Benny's recent appearance with Dinah Shore on CBS's *Dinah!* "One of the
last times he made us laugh was just this fall, when the premiere of the new
Dinah Shore program had a walk-on guest," said Charles Kuralt. Milton
Berle said, "We've lost an institution . . . It's like the sinking of the Statue of
Liberty." CBS board chairman, William Paley, was interviewed and spoke
of Benny's "professionalism that was unique and outstanding." There was
a tape of Benny doing a skit with his violin. "The violin is stilled," said Mr.
Kuralt. On *Kojak*, an old man was shot to death by gangsters, and two men
were killed in a gunfight. On *Columbo*, one woman was strangled to death,
and another woman was drowned in her bathtub.

Monday: On *The Edge of Night*, there were two references to the murder 8
of Taffy Simms. In a Popeye cartoon, a bully was pushed off a tall building
and fell into an open coffin, which was hammered closed. From the ABC local news: "A sniper, armed with a rifle, has killed three people in the town
of Olean, New York." And "The dead are still being counted at the scene of
the massive earthquake in northern Pakistan." From the ABC network
news: "Authorities in northwest Pakistan say the death toll from an earthquake there has reached four thousand seven hundred, and is likely to go
higher." On *Gunsmoke*, two men were killed in a gunfight. On *Born Free*, a
man was killed by a leopard. In *Frankenstein: The True Story*, seven corpses
were disinterred.

Tuesday: From the CBS local news: "Twelve fishermen are feared 9
drowned after two boats capsized in heavy seas" off the coast of southern
Italy. And "An Israeli patrol reportedly shot and killed three guerrillas as
they were spotted crossing the border." On *Hawaii Five-O*, a man was murdered with a hara-kiri knife, and another man was shot and killed in a gunfight. On *Barnaby Jones*, a man was killed in a gunfight.

Wednesday: From the NBC local and network news: "Twenty-three per- 10
sons were feared dead as a busload of holiday skiers plunged into a lake near

the town of Omachi, north of Tokyo." And "Two policemen were killed this afternoon in an auto accident as they were driving in response to an emergency call." On *Cannon*, one man was killed in an overturned car, and another man was shot to death by a rifle. On *The Manhunter*, one man was killed by being pushed out of a tall building, and another man was killed by a pistol shot.

Thursday: On *The Edge of Night*, a character referred to "the tragic death of Taffy Simms." Three bandits were blown up by dynamite in a Popeye cartoon. From the ABC local news: "Word from the National Safety Council is that this year's Christmas holiday death toll is down by 20 percent." From the ABC network news: "Four Arab civilians were killed by Israelis in a raid across the border early this morning." On *Ironside*, a judge shot to death a man who was trying to kill him. On *Harry O*, an unknown man was shot to death; a woman was beaten to death; another man was shot to death, and the man who shot him was killed. From the ABC late news: "Fire killed a two-year-old girl and injured several members of her family. Indications are that the victim, Carmen Allen, had been playing with matches."

It's hard to know what a "survey" of this kind proves, beyond the obvious, which in this case is that we are a violent people — seemingly entranced by violence — and have no serious regard for death. Also, I'm not at all sure what can be conveyed in prose of the experience of watching television for its acknowledgments of death. Twelve hours or so of television for seven days adds up to roughly eighty-four hours of more or less continuous broadcasting — the equivalent of around a half million words. How to convey the *absence* of death — real death — from this daily torrent of supposedly realistic narrative and imagery?

On the whole, a study of death on television turns up few surface surprises. After all, it should be no surprise by now that half of American network prime-time entertainment programming seems to be crime-oriented, and employs death by murder or in gunfights casually and routinely, as a simple plot device. (In fact, in most detective programs nowadays — as if they were following a prescribed ritual — there is usually a key murder of an unknown but significant figure within the first five minutes; there is sometimes a throwaway murder of a secondary character in the middle; and there is invariably a gunfight, which kills off one or two secondary or unknown characters, within the last five minutes.) Nor, in the area of news reporting, should it be much of a surprise that the detached and captionlike quality of the networks' regular news coverage is generally carried over into their accounts of death in the nation and across the world. Thus, snippets of information about the death of Brazilians in a bus crash or of Frenchmen in a mine disaster are blithely transmitted between snippets of information about factory layoffs in Detroit or gold speculation in London.

Perhaps, in the end, the surprise is that one is so little surprised. We ac- 14
cept the fact that death is mentioned so rarely on television — and usually in
such a relentlessly offhand and stylized manner — because we apparently
accept the idea that, as a nation, we have no wish to confront death, or deal
with it, except by euphemism and avoidance. Doubtless, to a considerable extent this is true. It doesn't seem to be true of most of the rest of the world,
especially of the poorer and less advanced countries, where — despite enormous populations, and the contrary expectations of many Western military
experts — people appear to care hugely about human life and death, but perhaps it is more true of technologically progressive countries, or, at any rate,
it is becoming true. Still, even here in America — with our Forest Lawns°
and pet cemeteries — our proverbial avoidance of or uncaringness about
death often seems illusory or skin-deep. In private lives, for example, there
are surely myriad explosions of grief, incomprehension, and deep human
response taking place literally all the time in the isolation of families where
death occurs. And in public America — though the surface appears impervi-
ous to death — it was, ironically, television that, some time ago, on the occasions of the deaths of the two Kennedy brothers and Dr. Martin Luther
King, helped the American people break through their apparent fear of
death and death's imagery, and assisted in creating a nearly national rite of
passage.

To be sure, the deaths of the two Kennedys and of Dr. King were extraor- 15
dinary events — touched not only by public and private loss but also by high
drama and by a kind of national guilt. (That is, if we had been more aware
and sensible of death, we might have been less bland in letting these three
notable, high-profile men walk prematurely into theirs.) One might, then,
say that television respects death only in the famous. But this misses the
point. First, if it were generally true that television (or our public society) respected death only in the famous, that would be at worst a commponplace
of life; art alone, which can draw a Sancho Panza as vividly as a knight of La
Mancha,° seems consistently to skirt class differences. But, for the most
part, even when television attempts to deal with the death of famous persons what it commonly does is to attend briskly and meretriciously to the *fa-
mousness* of the departed, and to leave the death, and everything that humanly has to do with death, at arm's length. Thus, at the death of Jack
Benny — a man who had clearly been much liked in his lifetime, and whose
dying had doubtless produced many true feelings of loss and change — the
texture of his leaving us was somehow cleaned up for television. No grief
appeared on camera. The chairman of the CBS "family" spoke about "pro-

---

Forest Lawns   A series of luxurious cemeteries in California.
    Sancho Panza . . . knight of La Mancha   Sancho Panza is the bumbling servant of
Don Quixote, the "man of La Mancha," in Cervantes's *Don Quixote.*

fessionalism." Taped highlights were shown of a man who had existed ten or twenty years before. As for the death of the less famous Miss Vanderbilt, her accident popped in and out of the news for a day and a half not as the real death of a real woman but as hoked-up "mystery."

The point seems to be that television — this great communicating force — has settled into a role of largely ignoring the reality of death. It does this in part by simply not mentioning it, as if, despite the fact that folktales since ancient times have been filled with the reality of human death, it had lately become — for our "mass audience" — an irrelevant subject. And it does this, perhaps inadvertently, by asserting that the whole reality of death is violence. In entertainment programs, for example, a woman is matter-of-factly drowned in a bathtub; two unknown men are killed in a gun battle; a character — possessed of no past, present, or future — is shot to death by fleeing burglars. In almost no instances of fictional death on television do the dead victims, or their deaths, have any depth or meaning — or, sometimes, even identity — for the audience. (Indeed, one could state it almost as an axiom that no one in a popular television drama who has a fully developed character ever dies.) And when death occurs it arrives invariably through violence, though it is usually a casual, spurious, stage violence, unconnected to personality or feeling, either among the characters or in the audience — a ubiquitous, toy violence. On the news programs, where deaths are regularly announced, these, too, are generally the result of violence or catastrophe, are similarly anonymous, and take place in the unconnected remoteness either of a brief factual caption or of a distant, meaningless locale. In a sense, one might say that the standard news broadcasts, with their nightly accounts of the deaths of fifteen identity-less Portuguese in a train crash, or of a dozen persona-less Italian fishermen in a shipwreck, come close to representing the actual scattered randomness of death as it occurs on this planet. But, once again, these real deaths are treated as if they had no meaning — except as the statistical by-product of some disaster. Death is usually reported to us in the sterility of numbers — "body counts" — and on the few occasions when a person has been found who is humanly connected to real death (as with the two-sentence interview of the man who had lost his wife in Darwin), the cameras, or editors, move gingerly in their treatment of the situation, compressing or squeezing out the humanity and skipping quickly on.

The matter of violence on television has been much discussed recently, though its connection with death seems mainly to be a specious and distorting one. Certainly there has been a plenitude of violent action in commercial broadcasting, and, quite plausibly, there have been a number of surveys, studies, and pronouncements dealing with the subject. Critics, on the whole, have said that there is too much violence on the airwaves, and that violent entertainment tends to breed violent citizens. Telefilm producers have replied that the citizens were violent to begin with, and that everyone knows that detective or Western programs are only fiction, and that, besides, the audience loves a good gunfight. Probably this is a situation in which both sides are to some degree right. Clearly, there is an oversupply of violence, and, also clearly, the majority of the viewers don't take the stuff very seriously. The trouble is that death is not the same as violence. Death is not inseparable from violence. It's true that crimes of violence have increased in this country in recent years, as it's true that the reporting and communicating of crimes of violence have increased in recent years, but in most of its occurrences in the world and in America death is (how else to say it?) *itself:* supremely ordinary, supremely deep. Each week, across the seven continents of the earth, roughly a million human beings die, and most of them die from a classic confluence of age and state of health and the vagaries of life. In other words, to shy away from death because it has been glibly associated with violence — and with stage violence, at that — is like throwing out *King Lear* along with the proverbial bathwater of trivial detective stories. For example, I've read approving comments lately from consumer groups and certain network executives on the decline in the ''level of violence'' on children's programs, and, basically, this is bound to be an improvement. On the other hand, in the entire week of television that I watched I never once saw death appear in human form on a children's program (I discount *Popeye*, which seems in this regard no worse and no better than *Hawaii Five-O*). There is a time in childhood when we first become aware of death — when we try to open our eyes to it, have bad dreams, and ask strange, tactless questions. It seems regrettable, at the least — especially considering the frequent presence of death in the great children's stories — that our television fathers and families just won't talk about death to young people.

But it's not only children in our society who are isolated from death by our communications organizations. Virtually all the rest of us have been left to shift for ourselves in dealing with this great, commonplace matter — have been made enemies of death, terrified and stricken by its seeming uniqueness, frozen at gravesides into our separate overcoats. One has heard it said that everyone must deal with death on his own, and perhaps that's true in terms of the physical act of one human being's dying. But for much of history both the dying and the survivors (soon to be the dying) have devised systems — tribal custom or religion — whereby it was possible to place death where it belonged, as part of the continuous, collective cycle of human life. In our era, television has pushed its way into the void left by the fading presence of religion and tribal authority. Television is, if not a formal system, at any rate a huge, cool authority, and also a kind of family, and juggling act, and troupe of players — and priesthood. Indeed, once, with the Kennedy deaths and the death of Martin Luther King, it showed what it could do in incorporating into the community not just a particular or famous death but *death.* Since then, however, it has been mainly silent on the subject. We do not die, apparently, except in numbers, or in Rangoon, or with blank faces in a gunfight. The institution of television often claims to be a mirror reflecting our society, and often many of us are agreeable to thinking that this is so. Perhaps it's more and more worth realizing that it is a mirror that reflects only a part of us. Our deaths, at least — that mass collective act — are not yet part of the reflection.

QUESTIONS ON MEANING

1. Why do Arlen's various feelings about his uncle's death lead him to a study of death as portrayed on television? Why should Arlen think of television directly after meditating on "the dim, communal, ordinary idea of a mortality that was beyond us"? What is the connection for him?
2. What is Arlen's answer to critics who claim that there is too much death, particularly violent death, on television? What kind of television coverage of death might Arlen approve? What examples does he give of television's successful acknowledgement of death?
3. In paragraph 3 Arlen says that "death itself seemed almost like a modest, commonplace event — perhaps like what it was." Could the effect of television coverage of death be to make death seem like a "commonplace event"? What is the difference between Arlen's feeling and the feelings generated by television coverage?

QUESTIONS ON STRATEGY

1. What is the purpose of paragraph 2?
2. Arlen devotes about one-third of his essay to a list of references to death on television. Why does he choose this cataloguing technique? What purposes does it serve? How does he prevent us from becoming bored as we read the list? Does he arrange the items in striking or amusing ways? Which examples stand out? Why?

EXPLORATIONS

1. "In our era," Arlen writes, "television has pushed its way into the void left by the fading presence of religion and tribal authority" (paragraph 18). If this idea sounds familiar to you, perhaps you have encountered it in the work of Marshall McLuhan or in the many discussions among media critics that McLuhan's theories stimulated. Explore and explain the connections between Arlen's ideas about the "tribal" nature of television and McLuhan's ideas as presented in his *Understanding Media,* particularly chapter 1, an introduction to his ideas, and chapter 31, on television.

WRITING TOPICS

1. Do commercial movies and contemporary novels deal any more authentically with the issue of death than television does? Argue yes or no in an essay, citing specific examples.
2. The rites, customs, and traditions of a tribal culture are the result of a long evolutionary process stretching over many generations. Television has been in existence only for about fifty years — two generations. Write an essay in which you challenge some of Arlen's arguments, calling into question his assumptions about television's place in our lives.

BOOKS AVAILABLE IN PAPERBACK

The Camera Age: Essays on Television. New York: Penguin.

Living-Room War. New York: Penguin. *Essays on television.*

Passage to Ararat and *Exiles.* New York: Penguin. *Nonfiction: Account of a journey to Armenia, and biography of the author's father (Armenian-born British novelist Michael Arlen, 1895–1956) and mother.*

Thirty Seconds. New York: Penguin. *Nonfiction: Account of the making of a television commercial.*

TOM

WOLFE

*T*OM WOLFE *(b. 1931), known as a master of the new journalism, is not to be confused with the novelist Thomas Wolfe (1900–1938), who wrote* Look Homeward, Angel. *The contemporary Tom Wolfe is famous not for fiction but for essays that encroach upon fiction's territory.*

He was born in Virginia, attended Washington and Lee University, and received a Ph.D. in American Studies from Yale. Instead of turning professor, Wolfe became journalist, first as a reporter — he was Latin American correspondent for the Washington Post *— and then as a feature writer for magazines. The first examples of his hyperventilated prose style appeared in* Esquire *and in the* New York Herald Tribune's Sunday *magazine, called* New York. *He continued to write for* New York *when it survived the death of the newspaper, and for* Harper's *magazine as well.*

Also a cartoonist and artist, Wolfe has published a collection of drawings and exhibited his graphic work in one-man shows. His books began with The Kandy-Kolored Tangerine-Flake Streamline Baby *(1968), in which he examined facets of popular culture.* The Electric Kool-Aid Acid Test *(1968) told of Ken Kesey's Merry Pranksters, dropouts, speed-freaks, and acid-heads of the 1960s. The* Pump House Gang *(1968) explored the California surfing culture, and* Radical Chic and Mau-mauing the Flak Catchers *(1970) discussed fashions in politics. Fashions in* art and architecture occupied The Painted Word *(1975) and* From Bauhaus to Our House *(1981). In 1982 he published* The Purple Decade, *which collected essays from his earlier books.*

Wolfe is sometimes credited with inventing the new journalism; just as widely, critics deny him the credit or deny that this journalism is new. Surely Tom Wolfe's style is his own, and certain features are idiosyncratic — his frequent use of ellipses, his careening sentences and sentence fragments, his energetic use of slang, idiom, and professional jargon. Perhaps his major innovation has been the subjectivity of his reportage, his frequent attempts to enter the minds of his subjects as if they were characters in a novel and he the novelist who invented them.

The Right Stuff (1979) won the American Book Award for general nonfiction in 1980. We reprint the chapter that gives the book its title. In writing about the military test pilots who became the astronauts of the American space program, men accustomed to trying out experimental aircraft, Wolfe writes a calmer prose than in his earlier work; maybe the subject matter provides its own breathlessness.

Whatever we decide about Wolfe's originality, we cannot deny his success. He has a genius for inventing phrases that quickly seem inevitable. Among his other gifts to the language, Tom Wolfe has contributed "radical chic," "the me-decade," and, most recently, "the right stuff."

The Right Stuff

What an extraordinary grim stretch that had been . . . and yet thereafter 1 Pete and Jane would keep running into pilots from other Navy bases, from the Air Force, from the Marines, who had been through their own extraordinary grim stretches. There was an Air Force pilot named Mike Collins, a nephew of former Army Chief of Staff J. Lawton Collins. Mike Collins had undergone eleven weeks of combat training at Nellis Air Force Base, near Las Vegas, and in that eleven weeks twenty-two of his fellow trainees had died in accidents, which was an extraordinary rate of two per week. Then there was a test pilot, Bill Bridgeman. In 1952, when Bridgeman was flying at Edwards Air Force Base, sixty-two Air Force pilots died in the course of thirty-six weeks of training, an extraordinary rate of 1.7 per week. Those figures were for fighter-pilot trainees only; they did not include the test pilots, Bridgeman's own confreres, who were dying quite regularly enough.

Extraordinary, to be sure; except that every veteran of flying small high- 2 performance jets seemed to have experienced these bad strings.

In time, the Navy would compile statistics showing that for a career 3 Navy pilot, i.e., one who intended to keep flying for twenty years as Conrad did, there was a 23 percent probability that he would die in an aircraft accident. This did not even include combat deaths, since the military did not classify death in combat as accidental. Furthermore, there was a better than even chance, a 56 percent probability, to be exact, that at some point a career Navy pilot would have to eject from his aircraft and attempt to come down by parachute. In the era of jet fighters, ejection meant being exploded out of the cockpit by a nitroglycerine charge, like a human cannonball. The ejection itself was so hazardous — men lost knees, arms, and their lives on the rim of the cockpit or had the skin torn off their faces when they hit the ''wall'' of air outside — that many pilots chose to wrestle their aircraft to the ground rather than try it . . . and died that way instead.

The statistics were not secret, but neither were they widely known, having been eased into print rather obliquely in a medical journal. No pilot, and certainly no pilot's wife, had any need of the statistics in order to know the truth, however. The funerals took care of that in the most dramatic way possible. Sometimes, when the young wife of a fighter pilot would have a little reunion with the girls she went to school with, an odd fact would dawn on her: *they* have not been going to funerals. And then Jane Conrad would look at Pete . . . Princeton, Class of 1953 . . . Pete had already worn his great dark sepulchral bridge coat more than most boys of the Class of '53 had worn their tuxedos. How many of those happy young men had buried more than a dozen friends, comrades, and co-workers? (Lost through violent death in the execution of everyday duties.) At the time, the 1950's, students from Princeton took great pride in going into what they considered highly competitive, aggressive pursuits, jobs on Wall Street, on Madison Avenue, and at magazines such as *Time* and *Newsweek*. There was much fashionably brutish talk of what ''dog-eat-dog'' and ''cutthroat'' competition they found there; but in the rare instances when one of these young men died on the job, it was likely to be from choking on a chunk of Chateaubriand, while otherwise blissfully boiled, in an expense-account restaurant in Manhattan. How many would have gone to work, or stayed at work, on cutthroat Madison Avenue if there had been a 23 percent chance, nearly one chance in four, of dying from it? Gentlemen, we're having this little problem with chronic violent death. . . .

And yet was there any basic way in which Pete (or Wally Schirra or Jim Lovell or any of the rest of them) was different from other college boys his age? There didn't seem to be, other than his love of flying. Pete's father was a Philadelphia stockbroker who in Pete's earliest years had a house in the Main Line suburbs, a limousine, and a chauffeur. The Depression eliminated the terrific brokerage business, the house, the car, and the servants; and by and by his parents were divorced and his father moved to Florida. Perhaps because his father had been an observation balloonist in the First World War — an adventurous business, since the balloons were prized targets of enemy aircraft — Pete was fascinated by flying. He went to Princeton on the Holloway Plan, a scholarship program left over from the Second World War in which a student trained with midshipmen from the Naval Academy during the summers and graduated with a commission in the Regular Navy. So Pete graduated, received his commission, married Jane, and headed off to Pensacola, Florida, for flight training.

Then came the difference, looking back on it. 6

A young man might go into military flight training believing that he was 7 entering some sort of technical school in which he was simply going to acquire a certain set of skills. Instead, he found himself all at once enclosed in a fraternity. And in this fraternity, even though it was military, men were not rated by their outward rank as ensigns, lieutenants, commanders, or whatever. No, herein the world was divided into those who had it and those who did not. This quality, this *it*, was never named, however, nor was it talked about in any way.

As to just what this ineffable quality was . . . well, it obviously involved 8 bravery. But it was not bravery in the simple sense of being willing to risk your life. The idea seemed to be that any fool could do that, if that was all that was required, just as any fool could throw away his life in the process. No, the idea here (in the all-enclosing fraternity) seemed to be that a man should have the ability to go up in a hurtling piece of machinery and put his hide on the line and then have the moxie, the reflexes, the experience, the coolness, to pull it back in the last yawning moment — and then to go up again *the next day*, and the next day, and every next day, even if the series should prove infinite — and, ultimately, in its best expression, do so in a cause that means something to thousands, to a people, a nation, to humanity, to God. Nor was there *a test* to show whether or not a pilot had this righteous quality. There was, instead, a seemingly infinite series of tests. A career in flying was like climbing one of those ancient Babylonian pyramids made up of a dizzy progression of steps and ledges, a ziggurat, a pyramid extraordinarily high and steep; and the idea was to prove at every foot of the way up that pyramid that you were one of the elected and anointed ones who had *the right stuff* and could move higher and higher and even — ultimately, God willing, one day — that you might be able to join that special few at the very top, that elite who had the capacity to bring tears to men's eyes, the very Brotherhood of the Right Stuff itself.

None of this was to be mentioned, and yet it was acted out in a way that 9 a young man could not fail to understand. When a new flight (i.e., a class) of trainees arrived at Pensacola, they were brought into an auditorium for a little lecture. An officer would tell them: "Take a look at the man on either side of you." Quite a few actually swiveled their heads this way and that, in the interest of appearing diligent. Then the officer would say: "One of the three of you is not going to make it!'' — meaning, not get his wings. That was the opening theme, the *motif* of primary training. We already know that one-third of you do not have the right stuff — it only remains to find out who.

Furthermore, that was the way it turned out. At every level in one's progress up that staggeringly high pyramid, the world was once more divided into those men who had the right stuff to continue the climb and those who had to be *left behind* in the most obvious way. Some were eliminated in the course of the opening classroom work, as either not smart enough or not hardworking enough, and were left behind. Then came the basic flight instruction, in single-engine, propeller-driven trainers, and a few more — even though the military tried to make this stage easy — were washed out and left behind. Then came more demanding levels, one after the other, formation flying, instrument flying, jet training, all-weather flying, gunnery, and at each level more were washed out and left behind. By this point easily a third of the original candidates had been, indeed, eliminated . . . from the ranks of those who might prove to have the right stuff.

In the Navy, in addition to the stages that Air Force trainees went through, the neophyte always had waiting for him, out in the ocean, a certain grim gray slab; namely, the deck of an aircraft carrier; and with it perhaps the most difficult routine in military flying, carrier landings. He was shown films about it, he heard lectures about it, and he knew that carrier landings were hazardous. He first practiced touching down on the shape of a flight deck painted on an airfield. He was instructed to touch down and gun right off. This was safe enough — the shape didn't move, at least — but it could do terrible things to, let us say, the gyroscope of the soul. *That shape!* — *it's so damned small!* And more candidates were washed out and left behind. Then came the day, without warning, when those who remained were sent out over the ocean for the first of many days of reckoning with the slab. The first day was always a clear day with little wind and a calm sea. The carrier was so steady that it seemed, from up there in the air, to be resting on pilings, and the candidate usually made his first carrier landing successfully, with relief and even *élan*. Many young candidates looked like terrific aviators up to that very point — and it was not until they were actually standing on the carrier deck that they first began to wonder if they had the proper stuff, after all. In the training film the flight deck was a grand piece of gray geometry, perilous, to be sure, but an amazing abstract shape as one looks down upon it on the screen. And yet once the newcomer's two feet were on it . . . *Geometry* — my God, man, this is a . . . skillet! It *heaved*, it moved up and down underneath his feet, it pitched up, it pitched down, it rolled to port (this great beast *rolled!*) and it rolled to starboard, as the ship moved into the wind and, therefore, into the waves, and the wind kept sweeping across, sixty feet up in the air out in the open sea, and there were no railings whatsoever. This was a *skillet!* — a frying pan! — a short-order grill! — not gray but black, smeared with skid marks from one end to the other and glistening with pools of hydraulic fluid and the occasional jet-fuel slick, all of it still hot, sticky, greasy, runny, virulent from God knows what traumas — still ablaze! — consumed in detonations, explosions, flames, combustion, roars, shrieks, whines, blasts, horrible shudders, fracturing impacts, as little men in screaming red and yellow and purple and green shirts with black Mickey Mouse helmets over their ears skittered about on the surface as if for their very lives (you've said it now!), hooking fighter planes onto the catapult shuttles so that they can explode their afterburners and be slung off the deck in a red-mad fury with a *kaboom!* that pounds through the entire deck — a procedure that seems absolutely controlled, orderly, sublime, however, compared to what he is about to watch as aircraft return to the ship for what is known in the engineering stoicisms of the military as "recovery and arrest." To say that an F-4 was coming back onto this heaving barbecue from out of the sky at a speed of 135 knots . . . that might have been the truth in the training lecture, but it did not begin to get across the idea of what the newcomer saw from the deck itself, because it created the notion that perhaps the plane was gliding in. On the deck one knew differently! As the aircraft came closer and the carrier heaved on into the waves and the plane's speed did not diminish and the deck did not grow steady — indeed, it pitched up and down five or ten feet per greasy heave — one experienced a neural alarm that no lecture could have prepared him for: This is not an *airplane* coming toward me, it is a brick with some poor sonofabitch riding it (*someone much like myself!*) and it is not *gliding*, it is *falling*, a fifty-thousand-pound brick, headed not for a stripe on the deck but for *me* — and with a horrible *smash!* it hits the skillet, and with a blur of momentum as big as a freight train's it hurtles toward the far end of the deck — another blinding storm! — another roar as the pilot pushes the throttle up to full military power and another smear of rubber screams out over the skillet — and this is nominal!° — quite okay! — for a wire stretched across the deck has grabbed the hook on the end of the plane as it hit the deck tail down, and the smash was the rest of the fifteen-ton brute slamming onto the deck, as it tripped up, so that it is now straining against the wire at full throttle, in case it hadn't held and the plane had "boltered" off the end of the deck and had to struggle up into the air again. And already the Mickey Mouse helmets are running toward the fiery monster. . . .

And the candidate, looking on, begins to *feel* that great heaving sun-blaz- 12 ing deathboard of a deck wallowing in his own vestibular system — and suddenly he finds himself backed up against his own limits. He ends up going to the flight surgeon with so-called conversion symptoms. Overnight he develops blurred vision or numbness in his hands and feet or sinusitis so severe that he cannot tolerate changes in altitude. On one level the symptom is

---

nominal   Commonly used in aeronautics to mean according to plan.

real. He really cannot see too well or use his fingers or stand the pain. But somewhere in his subconscious he knows it is a plea and a beg-off; he shows not the slightest concern (the flight surgeon notes) that the condition might be permanent and affect him in whatever life awaits him outside the arena of the right stuff.

Those who remained, those who qualified for carrier duty — and even more so those who later on qualified for *night* carrier duty — began to feel a bit like Gideon's warriors. *So many have been left behind!* The young warriors were now treated to a deathly sweet and quite unmentionable sight. They could gaze at length upon the crushed and wilted pariahs who had washed out. They could inspect those who did not have that righteous stuff.

The military did not have very merciful instincts. Rather than packing up these poor souls and sending them home, the Navy, like the Air Force and the Marines, would try to make use of them in some other role, such as flight controller. So the washout has to keep taking classes with the rest of his group, even though he can no longer touch an airplane. He sits there in the classes staring at sheets of paper with cataracts of sheer human mortification over his eyes while the rest steal looks at him . . . this man reduced to an ant, this untouchable, this poor sonofabitch. And in what test had he been found wanting? Why, it seemed to be nothing less than *manhood* itself. Naturally, this was never mentioned, either. Yet there it was. *Manliness, manhood, manly courage* . . . there was something ancient, primordial, irresistible about the challenge of this stuff, no matter what a sophisticated and rational age one might think he lived in.

Perhaps because it could not be talked about, the subject began to take on superstitious and even mystical outlines. A man either had it or he didn't! There was no such thing as having *most* of it. Moreover, it could blow at any seam. One day a man would be ascending the pyramid at a terrific clip, and the next — bingo! — he would reach his own limits in the most unexpected way. Conrad and Schirra met an Air Force pilot who had had a great pal at Tyndall Air Force Base in Florida. This man had been the budding ace of the training class; he had flown the hottest fighter-style trainer, the T-38, like a dream; and then he began the routine step of being checked out in the T-33. The T-33 was not nearly as hot an aircraft as the T-38; it was essentially the old P-80 jet fighter. It had an exceedingly small cockpit. The pilot could barely move his shoulders. It was the sort of airplane of which everybody said, "You don't get into it, you *wear* it." Once inside a T-33 cockpit this man, this budding ace, developed claustrophobia of the most paralyzing sort. He tried everything to overcome it. He even went to a psychiatrist which was a serious mistake for a military officer if his superiors learned of it. But nothing worked. He was shifted over to flying jet transports, such as the C-135. Very demanding and necessary aircraft they were, too, and he was still spoken of as an excellent pilot. But as everyone knew —

and, again, it was never explained in so many words — only those who were assigned to fighter squadrons, the ''fighter jocks,'' as they called each other with a self-satisfied irony, remained in the true fraternity. Those assigned to transports were not humiliated like washouts — *somebody* had to fly those planes — nevertheless, they, too, had been *left behind* for lack of the right stuff.

Or a man could go for a routine physical one fine day, feeling like a mil- 16 lion dollars, and be grounded for *fallen arches*. It happened! — just like that! (And try raising them.) Or for breaking his wrist and losing only *part* of its mobility. Or for a minor deterioration of eyesight, or for any of hundreds of reasons that would make no difference to a man in an ordinary occupation. As a result all fighter jocks began looking upon doctors as their natural enemies. Going to see a flight surgeon was a no-gain proposition; a pilot could only hold his own or lose in the doctor's office. To be grounded for a medical reason was no humiliation, looked at objectively. But it was a humiliation, nonetheless! — for it meant you no longer had that indefinable, unutterable, integral stuff. (It could blow at *any* seam.)

All the hot young fighter jocks began trying to test the limits themselves 17 in a superstitious way. They were like believing Presbyterians of a century before who used to probe their own experience to see if they were truly among *the elect*. When a fighter pilot was in training, whether in the Navy or the Air Force, his superiors were continually spelling out strict rules for him, about the use of the aircraft and conduct in the sky. They repeatedly forbade so-called hot-dog stunts, such as outside loops, buzzing, flat-hatting, hedgehopping and flying under bridges. But somehow one got the message that the man who truly *had* it could ignore those rules — not that he should make a point of it, but that he *could* — and that after all there was only one way to find out — and that in some strange unofficial way, peeking through his fingers, his instructor halfway expected him to challenge all the limits. They would give a lecture about how a pilot should never fly without a good solid breakfast — eggs, bacon, toast, and so forth — because if he tried to fly with his blood-sugar level too low, it could impair his alertness. Naturally, the next day every hot dog in the unit would get up and have a breakfast consisting of one cup of black coffee and take off and go up into a vertical climb until the weight of the ship exactly canceled out the upward pull of the engine and his air speed was zero, and he would hang there for one thick adrenal instant — and then fall like a rock, until one of three things happened: he keeled over nose first and regained his aerodynamics and all was well, he went into a spin and fought his way out of it, or he went into a spin and had to eject or crunch it, which was always supremely possible.

Likewise, ''hassling'' — mock dogfighting — was strictly forbidden, and 18 so naturally young fighter jocks could hardly wait to go up in, say, a pair of F-100s and start the duel by making a pass at each other at 800 miles an hour, the winner being the pilot who could slip in behind the other one and get locked in on his tail ("wax his tail"), and it was not uncommon for some eager jock to try too tight an outside turn and have his engine flame out, whereupon, unable to restart it, he has to eject . . . and he shakes his fist at the victor as he floats down by parachute and his half-a-million-dollar aircraft goes *kaboom!* on the palmetto grass or the desert floor, and he starts thinking about how he can get together with the other guy back at the base in time for the two of them to get their stories straight before the investigation: "I don't know what happened, sir. I was pulling up after a target run, and it just flamed out on me." Hassling was forbidden, and hassling that led to the destruction of an aircraft was a serious court-martial offense, and the man's superiors knew that the engine hadn't *just flamed out*, but every unofficial impulse on the base seemed to be saying: "Hell, we wouldn't give you a nickel for a pilot who hasn't done some crazy rat-racing like that. It's all part of the right stuff."

The other side of this impulse showed up in the reluctance of the young jocks to admit it when they had maneuvered themselves into a bad corner they couldn't get out of. There were two reasons why a fighter pilot hated to declare an emergency. First, it triggered a complex and very public chain of events at the field: all other incoming flights were held up, including many of one's comrades who were probably low on fuel; the fire trucks came trundling out to the runway like yellow toys (as seen from way up there), the better to illustrate one's hapless state; and the bureaucracy began to crank up the paper monster for the investigation that always followed. And second, to declare an emergency, one first had to reach that conclusion in his own mind, which to the young pilot was the same as saying: "A minute ago I still *had* it — now I need your help!" To have a bunch of young fighter pilots up in the air thinking this way used to drive flight controllers crazy. They would see a ship beginning to drift off the radar, and they couldn't rouse the pilot on the microphone for anything other than a few meaningless mumbles, and they would know he was probably out there with engine failure at a low altitude, trying to reignite by lowering his auxiliary generator rig, which had a little propeller that was supposed to spin in the slipstream like a child's pinwheel.

"Whiskey Kilo Two Eight, do you want to declare an emergency?"

This would rouse him! — to say: "Negative, negative, Whiskey Kilo Two Eight is not declaring an emergency."

Kaboom. Believers in the right stuff would rather crash and burn.

One fine day, after he had joined a fighter squadron, it would dawn on the young pilot exactly how the losers in the great fraternal competition were now being left behind. Which is to say, not by instructors or other superiors or by failures at prescribed levels of competence, but by death. At this point the essence of the enterprise would begin to dawn on him. Slowly, step by step, the ante had been raised until he was now involved in what was surely the grimmest and grandest gamble of manhood. Being a fighter pilot — for that matter, simply taking off in a single-engine jet fighter of the Century series, such as an F-102, or any of the military's other marvelous bricks with fins on them — presented a man, on a perfectly sunny day, with more ways to get himself killed than his wife and children could imagine in their wildest fears. If he was barreling down the runway at two hundred miles an hour, completing the takeoff run, and the board started lighting up red, should he (a) abort the takeoff (and try to wrestle with the monster, which was gorged with jet fuel, out in the sand beyond the end of the runway) or (b) eject (and hope that the goddamned human cannonball trick works at zero altitude and he doesn't shatter an elbow or a kneecap on the way out) or (c) continue the takeoff and deal with the problem aloft (knowing full well that the ship may be on fire and therefore seconds away from exploding)? He would have one second to sort out the options and act, and this kind of little workaday decision came up all the time. Occasionally a man would look coldly at the binary problem he was now confronting every day — Right Stuff/Death — and decide it wasn't worth it and voluntarily shift over to transports or reconnaissance or whatever. And his comrades would wonder, for a day or so, what evil virus had invaded his soul . . . as they left him behind. More often, however, the reverse would happen. Some college graduate would enter Navy aviation through the Reserves, simply as an alternative to the Army draft, fully intending to return to civilian life, to some waiting profession or family business; would become involved in the obsessive business of ascending the ziggurat pyramid of flying; and, at the end of his enlistment, would astound everyone back home and very likely himself as well by signing up for another one. What on earth got into him? He couldn't explain it. After all, the very words for it had been amputated. A Navy study showed that two-thirds of the fighter pilots who were rated in the top rungs of their groups — i.e., the hottest young pilots — reenlisted when the time came, and practically all were college graduates. By this point, a young fighter jock was like the preacher in *Moby Dick* who climbs up into the pulpit on a rope ladder and then pulls the ladder up behind him; except the pilot could not use the words necessary to express the vital lessons. Civilian life, and even home and hearth, now seemed not only far away but far *below*, back down many levels of the pyramid of the right stuff.

A fighter pilot soon found he wanted to associate only with other fighter 24 pilots. Who else could understand the nature of the little proposition (right stuff/death) they were all dealing with? And what other subject could compare with it? It was riveting! To talk about it in so many words was forbidden, of course. The very words *death, danger, bravery, fear* were not to be uttered except in the occasional specific instance or for ironic effect. Nevertheless, the subject could be adumbrated in *code* or *by example*. Hence the endless evenings of pilots huddled together talking about flying. On these long and drunken evenings (the bane of their family life) certain theorems would be propounded and demonstrated — and all by *code* and *example*. One theorem was: There are no *accidents* and no fatal flaws in the machines; there are only pilots with the wrong stuff. (I.e., blind Fate can't kill me.) When Bud Jennings crashed and burned in the swamps at Jacksonville, the other pilots in Pete Conrad's squadron said: *How could he have been so stupid?* It turned out that Jennings had gone up in the SNJ with his cockpit canopy opened in a way that was expressly forbidden in the manual, and carbon monoxide had been sucked in from the exhaust, and he passed out and crashed. All agreed that Bud Jennings was a good guy and a good pilot, but his epitaph on the ziggurat was: *How could he have been so stupid?* This seemed shocking at first, but by the time Conrad had reached the end of that bad string at Pax River, he was capable of his own corollary to the theorem: viz., no single factor ever killed a pilot; there was always a chain of mistakes. But what about Ted Whelan, who fell like a rock from 8,100 feet when his parachute failed? Well, the parachute was merely part of the chain: first, someone should have caught the structural defect that resulted in the hydraulic leak that triggered the emergency; second, Whelan did not check out his seat-parachute rig, and the drogue failed to separate the main parachute from the seat; but even after those two mistakes, Whelan had fifteen or twenty seconds, as he fell, to disengage himself from the seat and open the parachute manually. Why just stare at the scenery coming up to smack you in the face! And everyone nodded. (He failed — but I wouldn't have!) Once the theorem and the corollary were understood, the Navy's statistics about one in every four Navy aviators dying meant nothing. The figures were averages, and averages applied to those with average stuff.

A riveting subject, especially if it were one's own hide that was on the line. Every evening at bases all over America, there were military pilots huddled in officers clubs eagerly cutting the right stuff up in coded slices so they could talk about it. What more compelling topic of conversation was there in the world? In the Air Force there were even pilots who would ask the tower for priority landing clearance so that they could make the beer call on time, at 4 P.M. sharp, at the Officers Club. They would come right out and state the reason. The drunken rambles began at four and sometimes went on for ten or twelve hours. Such conversations! They diced that righteous stuff up into little bits, bowed ironically to it, stumbled blindfolded around it, groped, lurched, belched, staggered, bawled, sang, roared, and feinted at it with self-deprecating humor. Nevertheless! — they never mentioned it by name. No, they used the approved codes, such as: "Like a jerk I got myself into a hell of a corner today." They told of how they "lucked out of it." To get across the extreme peril of his exploit, one would use certain oblique cues. He would say, "I looked over at Robinson" — who would be known to the listeners as a non-com who sometimes rode backseat to read radar — "and he wasn't talking any more, he was just staring at the radar, like this, giving it that *zombie* look. Then I *knew* I was in trouble!" Beautiful! Just right! For it would also be known to the listeners that the non-coms advised one another: "*Never* fly with a lieutenant. *Avoid* captains and majors. Hell, man, do yourself a favor: don't fly with anybody below colonel." Which in turn said: "Those young bucks shoot dice with death!" And yet once in the air the non-com had his own standards. He was determined to remain as outwardly cool as the pilot, so that when the pilot did something that truly petrified him, he would say nothing; instead, he would turn silent, catatonic, like a zombie. Perfect! *Zombie.* There you had it, compressed into a single word all of the foregoing. I'm a hell of a pilot! I shoot dice with death! And now all you fellows know it! And I haven't spoken of that unspoken stuff even once!

The talking and drinking began at the beer call, and then the boys would 26 break for dinner and come back afterward and get more wasted and more garrulous or else more quietly fried, drinking good cheap PX booze until 2 A.M. The night was young! Why not get the cars and go out for a little proficiency run? It seemed that every fighter jock thought himself an ace driver, and he would do anything to obtain a hot car, especially a sports car, and the drunker he was, the more convinced he would be about his driving skills, as if the right stuff, being indivisible, carried over into any enterprise whatsoever, under any conditions. A little proficiency run, boys! (There's only one way to find out!) And they would roar off in close formation from, say, Nellis Air Force Base, down Route 15, into Las Vegas, barreling down the highway, rat-racing, sometimes four abreast, jockeying for position, piling into the most listless curve in the desert flats as if they were trying to root each other out of the groove at the Rebel 500 — and then bursting into downtown Las Vegas with a rude fraternal roar like the Hell's Angels — and the natives chalked it up to youth and drink and the bad element that the Air Force attracted. They knew nothing about the right stuff, of course.

More fighter pilots died in automobiles than in airplanes. Fortunately, 27 there was always some kindly soul up the chain to certify the papers "line of duty," so that the widow could get a better break on the insurance. That was okay and only proper because somehow the system itself had long ago said *Skol!* and *Quite right!* to the military cycle of Flying & Drinking and Drinking & Driving, as if there were no other way. Every young fighter jock knew the feeling of getting two or three hours' sleep and then waking up at 5:30 A.M. and having a few cups of coffee, a few cigarettes, and then carting his poor quivering liver out to the field for another day of flying. There were those who arrived not merely hungover but still drunk, slapping oxygen tank cones over their faces and trying to burn the alcohol out of their systems, and then going up, remarking later: "I don't *advise* it, you understand, but it *can* be done." (Provided you have the right stuff, you miserable pudknocker.)

Air Force and Navy airfields were usually on barren or marginal stretches of land and would have looked especially bleak and Low Rent to an ordinary individual in the chilly light of dawn. But to a young pilot there was an inexplicable bliss to coming out to the flight line while the sun was just beginning to cook up behind the rim of the horizon, so that the whole field was still in shadow and the ridges in the distance were in silhouette and the flight line was a monochrome of Exhaust Fume Blue, and every little red light on top of the water towers or power stanchions looked dull, shriveled, congealed, and the runway lights, which were still on, looked faded, and even the landing lights on a fighter that had just landed and was taxiing in were no longer dazzling, as they would be at night, and looked instead like shriveled gobs of candlepower out there — and yet it was beautiful, exhilarating! — for he was revved up with adrenalin, anxious to take off before the day broke, to burst up into the sunlight over the ridges before all those thousands of comatose souls down there, still dead to the world, snug in home and hearth, even came to their senses. To take off in an F-100F at dawn and cut on the afterburner and hurtle twenty-five thousand feet up into the sky in thirty seconds, so suddenly that you felt not like a bird but like a trajectory, yet with full control, full control of *four tons* of thrust, all of which flowed from your will and through your fingertips, with the huge engine right beneath you, so close that it was as if you were riding it bareback, until all at once you were supersonic, an event registered on earth by a tremendous cracking boom that shook windows, but up here only by the fact that you now felt utterly free of the earth — to describe it, even to wife, child, near ones and dear ones, seemed impossible. So the pilot kept it to himself, along with an even more indescribable . . . an even more sinfully inconfessable . . . feeling of superiority, appropriate to him and to his kind, lone bearers of the right stuff.

From *up here* at dawn the pilot looked down upon poor hopeless Las Vegas (or Yuma, Corpus Christi, Meridian, San Bernardino, or Dayton) and began to wonder: How can all of them down there, those poor souls who will soon be waking up and trudging out of their minute rectangles and inching along their little noodle highways toward whatever slots and grooves make up their everyday lives — how could they live like that, with such earnestness, if they had the faintest idea of what it was like up here in this righteous zone?

But of course! Not only the washed-out, grounded, and dead pilots had been left behind — but also all of those millions of sleepwalking souls who never even attempted the great gamble. The entire world below . . . *left behind*. Only at this point can one begin to understand just how big, how titanic, the ego of the military pilot could be. The world was used to enormous egos in artists, actors, entertainers of all sorts, in politicians, sports figures, and even journalists, because they had such familiar and convenient ways to show them off. But that slim young man over there in uniform, with the enormous watch on his wrist and the withdrawn look on his face, that young officer who is so shy that he can't even open his mouth unless the subject is flying — that young pilot — well, my friends, his ego is even *bigger!* — so big, it's *breathtaking!* Even in the 1950's it was difficult for civilians to comprehend such a thing, but *all* military officers and many enlisted men tended to feel superior to civilians. It was really quite ironic, given the fact that for a good thirty years the rising business classes in the cities had been steering their sons away from the military, as if from a bad smell, and the officer corps had never been held in lower esteem. Well, career officers returned the contempt in trumps. They looked upon themselves as men who lived by higher standards of behavior than civilians, as men who were the bearers and protectors of the most important values of American life, who maintained a sense of discipline while civilians abandoned themselves to hedonism, who maintained a sense of honor while civilians lived by opportunism and greed. Opportunism and greed: there you had your much-vaunted corporate business world. Khrushchev was right about one thing: when it came time to hang the capitalist West, an American businessman would sell him the rope. When the showdown came — and the showdowns always came — not all the wealth in the world or all the sophisticated nuclear weapons and radar and missile systems it could buy would take the place of those who had the uncritical willingness to face danger, those who, in short, had the right stuff.

In fact, the feeling was so righteous, so exalted, it could become religious. Civilians seldom understood this, either. There was no one to teach them. It was no longer the fashion for serious writers to describe the glories of war. Instead, they dwelt upon its horrors, often with cynicism or disgust. It was left to the occasional pilot with a literary flair to provide a glimpse of the pilot's self-conception in its heavenly or spiritual aspect. When a pilot named Robert Scott flew his P-43 over Mount Everest, quite a feat at the time, he brought his hand up and snapped a salute to his fallen adversary. He thought he had *defeated* the mountain, surmounting all the forces of nature that had made it formidable. And why not? "God is my co-pilot," he said — that became the title of his book — and he meant it. So did the most gifted of all the pilot authors, the Frenchman Antoine de Saint-Exupéry. As he gazed down upon the world . . . from up there . . . during transcontinental flights, the good Saint-Ex saw civilization as a series of tiny fragile patches clinging to the otherwise barren rock of Earth. He felt like a lonely sentinel, a protector of those vulnerable little oases, ready to lay down his life in their behalf, if necessary; a saint, in short, true to his name, flying up here at the right hand of God. The good Saint-Ex! And he was not the only one. He was merely the one who put it into words most beautifully and anointed himself before the altar of the right stuff.

QUESTIONS ON MEANING

1. What is the right stuff?
2. What sort of man does the rigorous fighter-pilot training produce? How does Wolfe feel about the men who have the right stuff? How do they feel about themselves? Does he share their attitude?

QUESTIONS ON STRATEGY

1. In this early chapter from his book about the astronauts, Wolfe is primarily interested in defining the right stuff. He introduces this key phrase in paragraphs 8 and 9. Why doesn't he simply state the term and quickly define it? How does he go about defining it? What purpose does his technique serve?
2. Paragraph 4 uses the rhetorical device of comparison and contrast. What is being compared? What larger comparison is implied? Consider how Wolfe manages the paragraph. Are his details matters of fact? Does he invent or improvise to fill out the comparison?
3. In paragraph 8 Wolfe compares a fighter pilot's career to "climbing one of those ancient Babylonian pyramids made up of a dizzy progression of steps and ledges, a ziggurat, a pyramid extraordinarily high and steep." He returns to this simile from time to time. What associations does Wolfe suggest with this comparison? Does he bring up these associations in other ways?
4. Wolfe's writing almost adheres to a formula involving the repetition of his key phrase. In paragraphs 9 through 22, how often does Wolfe use this formula? How does he vary his emphasis? What effect does this technique have?
5. How does Wolfe's use of punctuation affect his tone?

EXPLORATIONS

1. Wolfe observes that those who have the right stuff experience a feeling "so righteous, so exalted, it could become religious" (paragraph 31). In "The Psychology of Astronauts," Norman Mailer concludes that the astronauts "must suspect that the gamble of a trip to the moon and back again, if carried off in all success, might give thrust for some transpostmortal insertion to the stars." What sort of religious feeling are these writers talking about in their essays? What is the importance of death to that religious feeling?

WRITING TOPICS

1. The astronauts whom Norman Mailer writes about in ''The Psychology of
Astronauts'' are products of the rigorous training Tom Wolfe describes.
Drawing on the essays by Wolfe and Mailer, develop a critical view of the
Apollo mission's place in the American consciousness. How did the nation
respond to the astronauts and their mission? What imaginative needs of the
American people did the moon shot fulfill? What expectations did it arouse?
Write an essay evaluating the success of the Apollo mission as an event in
the national psyche.

BOOKS AVAILABLE IN PAPERBACK

The Electric Kool-Aid Acid Test. New York: Bantam. *Nonfiction: A journey through the 1960s drug culture with novelist Ken Kesey.*

From Bauhaus to Our House. New York: Pocket Books. *Nonfiction: Architectural history and criticism.*

In Our Time. New York: Farrar, Straus & Giroux, Noonday Press. *Essays.*

The Kandy-Kolored Tangerine-Flake Streamline Baby. New York: Bantam. *Essays.*

Mauve Gloves & Madmen, Clutter & Vine. New York: Bantam. *Essays.*

The Painted Word. New York: Bantam. *Nonfiction: Art history and criticism.*

The Pumphouse Gang. New York: Bantam. *Essays.*

The Purple Decades: A Reader. New York: Farrar, Straus & Giroux, Noonday Press. *Essays.*

The Right Stuff. New York: Bantam. *Nonfiction: History of Project Mercury and America's first astronauts.*

JOHN
M^CPHEE

*J*OHN McPHEE *was born (1931) in Princeton, New Jersey, where he took his B.A. at the University and where he lives. He attended Cambridge University in England, wrote for television, worked on the staff of* Time, *and now writes regularly for* The New Yorker *magazine. His first book was a profile of the Princeton University basketball player Bill Bradley, later a Rhodes scholar at Oxford, then a forward for the New York Knickerbockers, and now U.S. senator from New Jersey. McPhee has written about the headmaster of a prep school, a desolate section of New Jersey, tennis, geology, Alaska, the Scottish Highlands, physics, and whitewater canoeing. His wide-ranging nonfiction books begin with* A Sense of Where You Are *(1965) and continue through many titles to his profile of the state of Alaska,* Coming into the Country *(1977) and recently two books about geology,* Basin and Range *(1981) and* In Suspect Terrain *(1983).*

His work appeals to readers not because of his authority about a subject — like Lewis Thomas's in medicine and biology or John Kenneth Galbraith's in economics — but because readers trust him to collect ten thousand items of detail (who could have imagined there was so much to know about oranges?) and to assemble this information into shapely paragraphs and impeccable sentences. Give him the materials of an improbable subject — oranges, pinball, birch bark canoes — and McPhee's carpentry will fashion a palace of pleasurable prose.

Oranges

The custom of drinking orange juice with breakfast is not very wide-   1
spread, taking the world as a whole, and it is thought by many peoples to be
a distinctly American habit. But many Danes drink it regularly with breakfast, and so do Hondurans, Filipinos, Jamaicans, and the wealthier citizens
of Trinidad and Tobago. The day is started with orange juice in the Colom-
bian Andes, and, to some extent, in Kuwait. Bolivians don't touch it at
breakfast time, but they drink it steadily for the rest of the day. The "play
lunch," or morning tea, that Australian children carry with them to school is
usually an orange, peeled spirally halfway down, with the peel replaced
around the fruit. The child unwinds the peel and holds the orange as if it
were an ice-cream cone. People in Nepal almost never peel oranges, preferring to eat them in cut quarters, the way American athletes do. The sour oranges of Afghanistan customarily appear as seasoning agents on Afghan
dinner tables. Squeezed over Afghan food, they cut the grease. The Sha-
mouti Orange, of Israel, is seedless and sweet, has a thick skin, and grows in
Hadera, Gaza, Tiberias, Jericho, the Jordan Valley, and Jaffa; it is exported
from Jaffa, and for that reason is known universally beyond Israel as the
Jaffa Orange. The Jaffa Orange is the variety that British people consider superior to all others, possibly because Richard the Lionhearted spent the winter of 1191–92 in the citrus groves of Jaffa. Citrus trees are spread across the
North African coast from Alexandria to Tangier, the city whose name was
given to tangerines. Oranges tend to become less tart the closer they are
grown to the equator, and in Brazil there is one kind of orange that has virtually no acid in it at all. In the principal towns of Trinidad and Tobago, oranges are sold on street corners. The vender cuts them in half and sprinkles
salt on them. In Jamaica, people halve oranges, get down on their hands and
knees, and clean floors with one half in each hand. Jamaican mechanics use
oranges to clear away grease and oil. The blood orange of Spain, its flesh
streaked with red, is prized throughout Europe. Blood oranges grow well in
Florida, but they frighten American women. Spain has about thirty-five million orange trees, grows six billion oranges a year, and exports more oranges
than any other country, including the United States. In the Campania region
of Italy, land is scarce; on a typical small patch, set on a steep slope, orange
trees are interspersed with olive and walnut trees, grapes are trained to

cover trellises overhead, and as many as five different vegetables are grown on the ground below. The over-all effect is that a greengrocer's shop is springing out of the hillside. Italy produces more than four billion oranges a year, but most of its citrus industry is scattered in gardens of one or two acres. A Frenchman sits at the dinner table, and, as the finishing flourish of the meal, slowly and gently disrobes an orange. In France, peeling the fruit is not yet considered an inconvenience. French preferences run to the blood oranges and the Thomson Navels of Spain, and to the thick-skinned, bland *Maltaises*, which the French import not from Malta but from Tunisia. France itself only grows about four hundred thousand oranges each year, almost wholly in the Department of the *Alpes Maritimes*. Sometimes, Europeans eat oranges with knives and forks. On occasion, they serve a dessert orange that has previously been peeled with such extraordinary care that strips of the peel arc outward like the petals of a flower from the separated and reassembled segments in the center. The Swiss sometimes serve oranges under a smothering of sugar and whipped cream; on a hot day in a Swiss garden, orange juice with ice is a luxurious drink. Norwegian children like to remove the top of an orange, make a little hole, push a lump of sugar into it, and then suck out the juice. English children make orange-peel teeth and wedge them over their gums on Halloween. Irish children take oranges to the movies, where they eat them while they watch the show, tossing the peels at each other and at the people on the screen. In Reykjavik, Iceland, in greenhouses that are heated by volcanic springs, orange trees yearly bear fruit. In the New York Botanical Garden, six mature orange trees are growing in the soil of the Bronx. Their trunks are six inches in diameter, and they bear well every year. The oranges are for viewing and are not supposed to be picked. When people walk past them, however, they sometimes find them irresistible.

The first known reference to oranges occurs in the second book of the *Five Classics*, which appeared in China around 500 B.C. and is generally regarded as having been edited by Confucius. The main course of the migration of the fruit — from its origins near the South China Sea, down into the Malay Archipelago, then on four thousand miles of ocean current to the east coast of Africa, across the desert by caravan and into the Mediterranean basin, then over the Atlantic to the American continents — closely and sometimes exactly kept pace with the major journeys of civilization. There were no oranges in the Western Hemisphere before Columbus himself introduced them. It was Pizarro who took them to Peru. The seeds the Spaniards carried came from trees that had entered Spain as a result of the rise of Islam. The development of orange botany owes something to Vasco da Gama and even more to Alexander the Great; oranges had symbolic importance in the paintings of Renaissance masters; in other times, at least two overwhelming invasions of the Italian peninsula were inspired by the visions of paradise that oranges engendered in northern minds. Oranges were once the fruit of the gods, to whom they were the golden apples of the Hesperides, which were stolen by Hercules. Then, in successive declensions, oranges became the fruit of emperors and kings, of the upper prelacy, of the aristocracy, and, by the eighteenth century, of the rich bourgeoisie. Another hundred years went by before they came within reach of the middle classes, and not until early in this century did they at last become a fruit of the community.

Just after the Second World War, three scientists working in central Florida surprised themselves with a simple idea that resulted in the development of commercial orange-juice concentrate. A couple of dozen enormous factories sprang out of the hammocks, and Florida, which can be counted on in most seasons to produce about a quarter of all the oranges grown in the world, was soon putting most of them through the process that results in small, trim cans, about two inches in diameter and four inches high, containing orange juice that has been boiled to high viscosity in a vacuum, separated into several component parts, reassembled, flavored, and then frozen solid. People in the United States used to consume more fresh oranges than all other fresh fruits combined, but in less than twenty years the per-capita consumption has gone down seventy-five per cent, as appearances of actual oranges in most of the United States have become steadily less frequent. Fresh, whole, round, orange oranges are hardly extinct, of course, but they have seen better days since they left the garden of the Hesperides. 3

Fresh oranges have become, in a way, old-fashioned. The frozen product made from them is pure and sweet, with a laboratory-controlled balance between its acids and its sugars; its color and its flavor components are as uniform as science can make them, and a consumer opening the six-ounce can is confident that the drink he is about to reconstitute will taste almost exactly like the juice that he took out of the last can he bought. Fresh orange juice, on the other hand, is probably less consistent in flavor than any other natural or fermented drink, with the possible exception of wine. 4

The taste and aroma of oranges differ by type, season, county, state, and country, and even as a result of the position of the individual orange in the framework of the tree on which it grew. Ground fruit — the orange that one can reach and pick from the ground — is not as sweet as fruit that grows high on the tree. Outside fruit is sweeter than inside fruit. Oranges grown on the south side of a tree are sweeter than oranges grown on the east or west sides, and oranges grown on the north side are the least sweet of the lot. The quantity of juice in an orange, and even the amount of Vitamin C it contains, will follow the same pattern of variation. Beyond this, there are differentiations of quality inside a single orange. Individual segments vary from one another in their content of acid and sugar. But that is cutting it 5 pretty fine. Orange men, the ones who actually work in the groves, don't discriminate to that extent. When they eat an orange, they snap out the long, thin blades of their fruit knives and peel it down, halfway, from the blossom end, which is always sweeter and juicier than the stem end. They eat the blossom half and throw the rest of the orange away.

An orange grown in Florida usually has a thin and tightly fitting skin, and it is also heavy with juice. Californians say that if you want to eat a Florida orange you have to get into a bathtub first. California oranges are light in weight and have thick skins that break easily and come off in hunks. The flesh inside is marvelously sweet, and the segments almost separate themselves. In Florida, it is said that you can run over a California orange with a ten-ton truck and not even wet the pavement. The differences from which these hyperboles arise will prevail in the two states even if the type of orange is the same. In arid climates, like California's, oranges develop a thick albedo, which is the white part of the skin. Florida is one of the two or three most rained-upon states in the United States. California uses the Colorado River and similarly impressive sources to irrigate its oranges, but of course irrigation can only do so much. The annual difference in rainfall between the Florida and California orange-growing areas is one million one hundred and forty thousand gallons per acre. For years, California was the leading orange state, but Florida surpassed California in 1942, and grows three times as many oranges now. California oranges, for their part, can safely be called three times as beautiful.

The color of an orange has no absolute correlation with the maturity of the flesh and juice inside. An orange can be as sweet and ripe as it will ever be and still glisten like an emerald in the tree. Cold — coolness, rather — is what makes an orange orange. In some parts of the world, the weather never gets cold enough to change the color; in Thailand, for example, an orange is a green fruit, and traveling Thais often blink with wonder at the sight of oranges the color of flame. The ideal nighttime temperature in an orange grove is forty degrees. Some of the most beautiful oranges in the world are grown in Bermuda, where the temperature, night after night, falls consistently to that level. Andrew Marvell's poem wherein the "remote Bermudas ride in the ocean's bosom unespied" was written in the sixteen-fifties, and contains a description, from hearsay, of Bermuda's remarkable oranges, set against their dark foliage like "golden lamps in a green night." Cool air comes down every night into the San Joaquin Valley in California, which is formed by the Coast Range to the west and the Sierra Nevadas to the east. The tops of the Sierras are usually covered with snow, and before dawn the temperature in the valley edges down to the frost point. In such cosmetic surroundings, it is no wonder that growers have heavily implanted the San Joaquin Valley with the Washington Navel Orange, which is the most beautiful orange grown in any quantity in the United States, and is certainly as attractive to the eye as any orange grown in the world. Its color will go to a deep, flaring cadmium orange, and its surface has a suggestion of coarseness, which complements its perfect ellipsoid shape.

Among orange groups, the navel orange is an old one. In his *Hesperides,* 8 *or Four Books on the Culture and Use of the Golden Apples,* Giovanni Battista Ferrari, a Sienese Jesuit priest of the seventeenth century, described it, saying: "This orange imitates to some extent the fertility of the tree which bears it, in that it struggles, though unsuccessfully, to reproduce the fruit upon itself." It is thus a kind of monster. Just beneath the navel-like opening in the blossom end of each navel orange, there is a small and, more or less, fetal orange, usually having five or six pithy segments. The navel strain that we know now originated in Bahia, Brazil, probably as a bud sport, or mutation, of the Brazilian Selecta Orange. In 1870, an American Presbyterian missionary in Bahia was impressed by the seedlessness and rich flavor of this unusual orange with an umbilicus at its blossom end, and sent twelve nursery-size trees to the United States Department of Agriculture in Washington. The department propagated the trees and sent the progeny to anyone who cared to give them a try. In 1873, Mrs. Luther C. Tibbets, of Riverside, California, wrote for a pair of trees, got them, and planted them in her yard. Mrs. Tibbets' trees caught the attention of her neighbors and, eventually, of the world. From them have descended virtually every navel orange grown anywhere on earth today, including the Carter, the Golden Nugget, the Surprise, the Golden Buckeye, the Robertson, and the Thomson. The patriarchal one should by rights be called the Bahia, but merely because of its brief residence in the District of Columbia it has been known for ninety-six years as the Washington Navel Orange.

In the United States, in a typical year, around twenty-five billion oranges 9 are grown. These include, among others, Maltese Ovals, Pope Summers, Nonpareils, Rubys, Sanford Bloods, Early Oblongs, Magnum Bonums, St. Michaels, Mediterranean Sweets, Lamb Summers, Lue Gim Gongs, Drake Stars, Whites, Whittakers, Weldons, Starks, Osceolas, Majorcas, Homosassas, Enterprises, Arcadias, Circassians, Centennials, Fosters, Dillars, Bessies, and Boones, but not — in all of these cases — in any appreciable quantity. Actually, one variety alone constitutes fully half of the total crop. Originally known in California as the Rivers Late Orange and in Florida as the Hart's Tardiff, it was imported into the United States early in the eighteen-seventies in unlabeled packages from the Thomas Rivers Nursery, of Sawbridgeworth, Hertfordshire. The easygoing Mr. Rivers had not only left off the name of the orange trees; he also failed to note where he had found them. They grew to be big, vigorous trees that bore remarkable quantities of almost seedless fruit containing lots of juice, which had a racy tartness in delicious proportion to its ample sugars. As supposedly different varieties, the trees were already beginning to prosper when an orange grower from Spain, traveling in California, felt suddenly at home in a grove of the so-called Rivers Lates. "That," said the Spanish grower, clearing up all mysteries with one unequivocal remark, "is the Late Orange of Valencia."

Out of the bewildering catalogue of orange varieties and strains, the Valencia has emerged in this century as something close to a universal orange. It is more widely and extensively planted than any other. From Florida and California and Central and South America to South Africa and Australia, Valencias grow in abundance in nearly all the orange centers of the world except Valencia. Having given the world the most remunerative orange yet known, Spain now specializes in its celebrated strains of bloods and navels. Only two per cent of the Spanish crop are Valencias, and perhaps only half of that comes from the groves of Valencia itself; much of the remainder grows in old, untended groves near Seville, where cattle wander through and munch oranges on the trees, on either bank of the Guadalquivir.

The Valencia is a spring and summer orange, and the Washington Navel ripens in the fall and winter. The two varieties overlap twice with perfect timing in California — where, together, they are almost all of the total crop — and the orange industry there never stops. In Florida, the Valencia harvest begins in late March and ends in June, and for about four months there is no picking. Florida grows few navel oranges, somewhat to the state's embarrassment. Florida growers tried hard enough, some seventy or eighty years ago, but the Washington Navel, in the language of pomology, proved to be too shy a bearer there. Instead, to meet the fall and winter markets, Florida growers have a number of locally developed early varieties to choose from, and in the main they seem to prefer three: the Pineapple Orange, the Parson Brown, and the Hamlin.

The Pineapple developed in the eighteen-seventies and was so named because its full, heavy aroma gave packinghouse employees the feeling that they were working in Hawaii rather than in Florida. The Pineapple is fairly seedy, usually containing about a dozen seeds, but it is rich in flavor, loaded with juice, and pretty to look at, with its smooth-textured, bright-orange skin and its slightly elongated shape. The skin is weak, though, and highly subject to decay. Most oranges, with appropriate care, will live about a month after they are picked. Pineapple Oranges don't have anything like that kind of stamina. (The Temple Orange and the Murcott Honey Orange, which are not actually oranges, ripen at the same time that Pineapples do. They are natural hybrids, almost certainly tangors — half orange, half tangerine — and they are so sweet that people on diets sometimes eat them before dinner in order to throttle their appetites. Oranges float, but these have so much sugar in them that if you drop one into a bucket of water it will go straight to the bottom. Murcotts were named for Charles Murcott Smith, one of the first men to propagate them. Advertisements have, from time to time, claimed that Temple Oranges were native to the Orient and sacred to a little-known sect of the Buddhist faith, and the seeds from which Florida's trees eventually sprang were stolen from a temple against the resistance of guardian priests. Temple Oranges are in fact named for William Chase Temple, who, long ago, was general manager of the Florida Citrus Exchange.)

Parson Nathan L. Brown was a Florida clergyman who grew oranges to 13 supplement his income; the seedy, pebble-skinned orange that now carries his name was discovered in his grove about a hundred years ago. It tends to have pale-yellow flesh and pale-yellow juice, for, in general, the color of orange juice is light among early-season oranges, deeper in mid-season varieties, and deeper still in late ones.

The seedless, smooth-skinned Hamlin, also named for a Florida grove 14 owner, ripens in October, ordinarily about two weeks ahead of the Parson Brown.

Both Hamlins and Parson Browns, when they are harvested, are usually 15 as green as grass. They have to be ripe, because an orange will not continue to ripen after it has been picked. Many other fruits — apples and pears, for example — go on ripening for weeks after they leave the tree. Their flesh contains a great deal of starch, and as they go on breathing (all fruit breathes until it dies, and should be eaten before it is dead), they gradually convert the starch to sugar. When oranges breathe, there is no starch within them to be converted. Whatever sugars, acids, and flavor essences they have were necessarily acquired on the tree. Hence, an advertisement for "tree-ripened" oranges is essentially a canard. There is no other way to ripen oranges. It is against the law to market oranges that are not tree-ripened — that is to say, oranges that are not ripe. Women see a patch or even a hint of green on an orange in a store and they seem to feel that they are making a knowledgeable decision when they avoid it. Some take home a can of concentrated orange juice instead. A good part, if not all, of the juice inside the can may have come from perfectly ripe, bright-green oranges.

Some oranges that become orange while they are still unripe may turn 16 green again as they ripen. When cool nights finally come to Florida, around the first of the year, the Valencia crop is fully developed in size and shape, but it is still three months away from ripeness. Sliced through the middle at that time, a Valencia looks something like a partitioned cupful of rice, and its taste is overpoweringly acid. But in the winter coolness, the exterior surface turns to bright orange, and the Valencia appears to be perfect for picking. Warm nights return, however, during the time of the Valencia harvest. On the trees in late spring, the Valencias turn green again, growing sweeter each day and greener each night.

QUESTIONS ON MEANING

1. McPhee engages his readers principally by informing them. "The Literature of Fact," the name of the course he teaches at Princeton, defines the genre in which he writes. But the primacy of fact does not prevent the expression of opinion. Where in this essay does McPhee express opinion? Is there a line of argument in the essay?

2. We ordinarily think of oranges as a natural phenomenon, fruit that grew on trees long before humans discovered the possibility of eating it. McPhee presents the orange in an altogether different light — as a product of human ingenuity. Cite specific information from the essay about the influence of individual men and women on the evolution of this fruit.

QUESTIONS ON STRATEGY

1. This essay appeared as a chapter in McPhee's book *Oranges*. It might have been written as an encyclopedia entry or a publicity release of the Florida Citrus Commission. What makes McPhee's essay rise above the often dry prose of an encyclopedia entry or the commercial style of a publicity release? What aspects of McPhee's style of presentation generate interest while setting forth an abundance of facts?

EXPLORATIONS

1. A primary strength of the book *Oranges* is its organization. After arresting our attention in this opening chapter with a dazzling profusion of facts about a subject we think of as familiar, McPhee goes on in the rest of his book to tell us a great deal more. He keeps us reading by following the cycle of orange cultivation and harvest. Read *Oranges* with a particular attention to the ways in which McPhee subordinates his store of information about every aspect of his subject to a sustained emphasis on the life cycles of the commercial orange.

WRITING TOPICS

1. Look up *orange* in the *Encyclopaedia Britannica*; you will find many facts McPhee doesn't mention in this essay. Bearing in mind the abundance of facts in McPhee's sentences, accumulate enough interesting bits of information to compose a sequence of paragraphs or one long paragraph in his style. Choose your data with a view toward the coherence and interest of what you write.

2. Look up another topic, comparable to McPhee's, in an encyclopedia: apples, potatoes, wheat. For an exercise, write a long paragraph modelled on McPhee's style in which you amalgamate sundry facts in graceful sentences.

BOOKS AVAILABLE IN PAPERBACK

Basin and Range. New York: Farrar, Straus & Giroux, Noonday Press. *Nonfiction: Account of a geologist at work.*

Coming into the Country. New York: Bantam. *Nonfiction: Account of a journey through the Alaskan wilderness.*

The Deltoid Pumpkinseed. New York: Farrar, Straus & Giroux, Noonday Press. *Nonfiction: Account of attempt to develop an unusual aircraft.*

Giving Good Weight. New York: Farrar, Straus & Giroux, Noonday Press. *Essays.*

The John McPhee Reader. Edited by William L. Howarth. New York: Farrar, Straus & Giroux, Noonday Press. *Essays.*

Levels of the Game. New York: Farrar, Straus & Giroux, Noonday Press. *Nonfiction: Account of a tennis match between Arthur Ashe and Clark Graebner.*

Oranges. New York: Farrar, Straus & Giroux, Noonday Press. *Nonfiction: Everything about oranges.*

Pieces of the Frame. New York: Farrar, Straus & Giroux, Noonday Press. *Essays.*

The Pine Barrens. New York: Farrar, Straus & Giroux, Noonday Press. *Nonfiction: Natural history of the pine barrens of southern New Jersey.*

A Sense of Where You Are: A Profile of William Warren Bradley. 2nd ed. New York: Farrar, Straus & Giroux, Noonday Press. *Nonfiction: Account of the college basketball player (now a U.S. senator) at work.*

JOHN
UPDIKE

*J*OHN UPDIKE *(b. 1932) grew up in Pennsylvania, where his father taught high school mathematics. Updike went to Harvard University, spent a year in Oxford on a fellowship, and then worked for three years on the staff of* The New Yorker *magazine. In 1957 he settled in Massachusetts to write full time.*

Best known for his fiction, he has published many novels and collections of short stories. His fictional prose is often lyric, and yet he remains a realist. Some of his best-known novels are Rabbit, Run *(1960),* The Centaur *(1963),* Couples *(1968),* Rabbit Redux *(1971),* The Coup *(1978), and* Rabbit Is Rich *(1981). He has also written several books of poems, is frequently anthologized as a poet, and is author of three essay collections; like football players who run, pass, and kick, he is a triple threat.* Assorted Prose *(1965) and* Picked-Up Pieces *(1976) reprinted book reviews from* The New Yorker *and a variety of articles. In 1983 his third collection of essays,* Hugging the Shore, *gathered almost nine hundred pages of literary criticism, largely from* The New Yorker. *Reviewers have come to realize that John Updike is not only a major novelist of our time but also a major critic. William H. Pritchard, writing in* The Hudson Review, *says that John Updike's work as a whole "in substantial intelligent creation will eventually be seen as second to none in our time."*

Although he is not known for his sportswriting, Updike's notes on Ted Williams's last baseball game, first published in The New Yorker, *have found their place in collections of the best baseball prose. Wednesday, September 28, 1960, the young novelist entered Fenway Park to watch possibly the greatest hitter of all time take his final at-bats before retiring. It took Updike five days to write this small article, a "lyric little bandbox" of an essay that sums up forever the fan's view of a great athlete on the field.*

Many years later a sportswriter asked Ted Williams — grizzled, a bit plump, slow, still grumpy, still graceful as a trout — what he thought of "Hub Fans Bid Kid Adieu." The Splendid Splinter never lacked consciousness of his historical position. After a pause, he summed it up. "It has the mystique," he said.

Hub Fans Bid Kid Adieu

Fenway Park, in Boston, is a lyric little bandbox of a ballpark. Everything 1
is painted green and seems in curiously sharp focus, like the inside of an old-fashioned peeping-type Easter egg. It was built in 1912 and rebuilt in 1934, and offers, as do most Boston artifacts, a compromise between Man's Euclidean° determinations and Nature's beguiling irregularities. Its right field is one of the deepest in the American League, while its left field is the shortest; the high left-field wall, three hundred and fifteen feet from home plate along the foul line, virtually thrusts its surface at right-handed hitters. On the afternoon of Wednesday, September 28th, 1960, as I took a seat behind third base, a uniformed groundkeeper was treading the top of this wall, picking batting-practice home runs out of the screen, like a mushroom gatherer seen in Wordsworthian perspective on the verge of a cliff. The day was overcast, chill, and uninspirational. The Boston team was the worst in twenty-seven seasons. A jangling medley of incompetent youth and aging competence, the Red Sox were finishing in seventh place only because the Kansas City Athletics had locked them out of the cellar. They were scheduled to play the Baltimore Orioles, a much nimbler blend of May and December, who had been dumped from pennant contention a week before by the insatiable Yankees. I, and 10,453 others, had shown up primarily because this was the Red Sox's last home game of the season, and therefore the last time in all eternity that their regular left fielder, known to the headlines as TED, KID, SPLINTER, THUMPER, TW, and, most cloyingly, MISTER WON-

---

Euclidian   Relating to the geometry of Euclid; geometrical.

DERFUL, would play in Boston. "WHAT WILL WE DO WITHOUT TED? HUB FANS ASK" ran the headline on a newspaper being read by a bulb-nosed cigar smoker a few rows away. Williams' retirement had been announced, doubted (he had been threatening retirement for years), confirmed by Tom Yawkey, the Red Sox owner, and at last widely accepted as the sad but probable truth. He was forty-two and had redeemed his abysmal season of 1959 with a — considering his advanced age — fine one. He had been giving away his gloves and bats and had grudgingly consented to a sentimental ceremony today. This was not necessarily his last game; the Red Sox were scheduled to travel to New York and wind up the season with three games there.

I arrived early. The Orioles were hitting fungos° on the field. The day before, they had spitefully smothered the Red Sox, 17–4, and neither their faces nor their drab gray visiting-team uniforms seemed very gracious. I wondered who had invited them to the party. Between our heads and the lowering clouds a frenzied organ was thundering through, with an appositeness perhaps accidental, "You *maaaade* me love you, I didn't wanna do it, I didn't wanna do it. . . ."

The affair between Boston and Ted Williams was no mere summer romance; it was a marriage composed of spats, mutual disappointments, and, toward the end, a mellowing hoard of shared memories. It fell into three stages, which may be termed Youth, Maturity, and Age; or Thesis, Antithesis, and Synthesis; or Jason, Achilles, and Nestor.°

First, there was the by now legendary epoch when the young bridegroom came out of the West and announced "All I want out of life is that when I walk down the street folks will say 'There goes the greatest hitter who ever lived.'" The dowagers of local journalism attempted to give elementary deportment lessons to this child who spake as a god, and to their horror were themselves rebuked. Thus began the long exchange of backbiting, bat-flipping, booing, and spitting that has distinguished Williams' public relations. The spitting incidents of 1957 and 1958 and the similar dockside courtesies that Williams has now and then extended to the grandstand should be judged against this background: the left-field stands at Fenway for twenty years have held a large number of customers who have bought their way in primarily for the privilege of showering abuse on Williams. Greatness necessarily attracts debunkers, but in Williams' case the hostility has been systematic and unappeasable. His basic offense against the fans

---

fungos Fly balls hit for fielding practice.
Jason, Achilles, and Nestor Jason, a youthful Greek hero noted for his quest of the Golden Fleece; Achilles, Greek warrior who fought at Troy; Nestor, in his old age, a counselor to the Greeks at Troy.

has been to wish that they weren't there. Seeking a perfectionist's vacuum, he has quixotically desired to sever the game from the ground of paid spectatorship and publicity that supports it. Hence his refusal to tip his cap to the crowd or turn the other cheek to newsmen. It has been a costly theory — it has probably cost him, among other evidences of good will, two Most Valuable Player awards, which are voted by reporters — but he has held to it. While his critics, oral and literary, remained beyond the reach of his discipline, the opposing pitchers were accessible, and he spanked them to the tune of .406 in 1941. He slumped to .356 in 1942 and went off to war.

In 1946, Williams returned from three years as a Marine pilot to the second of his baseball avatars, that of Achilles, the hero of incomparable prowess and beauty who nevertheless was to be found sulking in his tent while the Trojans (mostly Yankees) fought through to the ships. Yawkey, a timber and mining maharajah, had surrounded his central jewel with many gems of slightly lesser water, such as Bobby Doerr, Dom DiMaggio, Rudy York, Birdie Tebbetts, and Johnny Pesky. Throughout the late forties, the Red Sox were the best paper team in baseball, yet they had little three-dimensional to show for it, and if this was a tragedy, Williams was Hamlet. A succinct review of the indictment — and a fair sample of appreciative sports-page prose — appeared the very day of Williams' valedictory, in a column by Huck Finnegan in the Boston *American* (no sentimentalist, Huck):

> Williams' career, in contrast [to Babe Ruth's], has been a series of failures except for his averages. He flopped in the only World Series he ever played in (1946) when he batted only .200. He flopped in the playoff game with Cleveland in 1948. He flopped in the final game of the 1949 season with the pennant hinging on the outcome (Yanks 5, Sox 3). He flopped in 1950 when he returned to the lineup after a two-month absence and ruined the morale of a club that seemed pennant-bound under Steve O'Neill. It has always been Williams' records first, the team second, and the Sox non-winning record is proof enough of that.

There are answers to all this, of course. The fatal weakness of the great Sox slugging teams was not-quite-good-enough pitching rather than Williams' failure to hit a home run every time he came to bat. Again, Williams' depressing effect on his teammates has never been proved. Despite ample coaching to the contrary, most insisted that they *liked* him. He has been generous with advice to any player who asked for it. In an increasingly combative baseball atmosphere, he continued to duck beanballs docilely. With umpires he was gracious to a fault. This courtesy itself annoyed his critics, whom there was no pleasing. And against the ten crucial games (the seven World Series games with the St. Louis Cardinals, the 1948 playoff with the Cleveland Indians, and the two-game series with the Yankees at the end of the 1949 season, when one victory would have given the Red Sox the pennant) that make up the Achilles' heel of Williams' record, a mass of statistics can be set showing that day in and day out he was no slouch in the clutch. The correspondence columns of the Boston papers now and then suffer a sharp flurry of arithmetic on this score; indeed, for Williams to have distributed all his hits so they did nobody else any good would constitute a feat of placement unparalleled in the annals of selfishness.

Whatever residue of truth remains of the Finnegan charge those of us who love Williams must transmute as best we can, in our own personal crucibles. My personal memories of Williams began when I was a boy in Pennsylvania, with two last-place teams in Philadelphia to keep me company. For me, "W'ms, 1f" was a figment of the box scores who always seemed to be going 3-for-5. He radiated, from afar, the hard blue glow of high purpose. I remember listening over the radio to the All-Star Game of 1946, in which Williams hit two singles and two home runs, the second one off a Rip Sewell "blooper" pitch; it was like hitting a balloon out of the park. I remember watching one of his home runs from the bleachers of Shibe Park; it went over the first baseman's head and rose methodically along a straight line and was still rising when it cleared the fence. The trajectory seemed qualitatively different from anything anyone else might hit. For me, Williams is the classic ballplayer of the game on a hot August weekday, before a small crowd, when the only thing at stake is the tissue-thin difference between a thing done well and a thing done ill. Baseball is a game of the long season, of relentless and gradual averaging-out. Irrelevance — since the reference point of most individual contests is remote and statistical — always threatens its interest, which can be maintained not by the occasional heroics that sportswriters feed upon but by players who always *care;* who care, that is to say, about themselves and their art. Insofar as the clutch hitter is not a sportswriter's myth, he is a vulgarity, like a writer who writes only for money. It may be that, compared to such managers' dreams as the manifestly classy Joe DiMaggio and the always helpful Stan Musial, Williams was an icy star. But of all team sports, baseball, with its graceful intermittences of action, its immense and tranquil field sparsely settled with posed men in white, its dispassionate mathematics, seems to be best suited to accommodate, and be ornamented by, a loner. It is an essentially lonely game. No other player visible to my generation concentrated within himself so much of the sport's poignance, so assiduously refined his natural skills, so constantly brought to the plate that intensity of competence that crowds the throat with joy.

By the time I went to college, near Boston, the lesser stars Yawkey had assembled around Williams had faded, and his rigorous pride of craftsmanship had become itself a kind of heroism. This brittle and temperamental player developed an unexpected quality of persistence. He was always coming back — back from Korea, back from a broken collarbone, a shattered elbow, a bruised heel, back from drastic bouts of flu and ptomaine poisoning. Hardly a season went by without some enfeebling mishap, yet he always came back, and always looked like himself. The delicate mechanism of timing and power seemed sealed, shockproof, in some case deep within his frame. In addition to injuries, there was a heavily publicized divorce, and the usual storms with the press, and the Williams Shift — the maneuver, custom-built by Lou Boudreau of the Cleveland Indians, whereby three infielders were concentrated on the right side of the infield. Williams could easily have learned to punch singles through the vacancy on his left and fattened his average hugely. This was what Ty Cobb,° the Einstein of average, told him to do. But the game had changed since Cobb; Williams believed that his value to the club and to the league was as a slugger, so he went on pulling the ball, trying to blast it through three men, and paid the price of perhaps fifteen points of lifetime average. Like Ruth before him, he bought the occasional home run at the cost of many directed singles — a calculated sacrifice certainly not, in the case of a hitter as average-minded as Williams, entirely selfish.

After a prime so harassed and hobbled, Williams was granted by the relenting fates a golden twilight. He became at the end of his career perhaps the best *old* hitter of the century. The dividing line falls between the 1956 and the 1957 seasons. In September of the first year, he and Mickey Mantle were contending for the batting championship. Both were hitting around .350, and there was no one else near them. The season ended with a three-game series between the Yankees and the Sox, and, living in New York then, I went up to the Stadium. Williams was slightly shy of the four hundred at-bats needed to qualify; the fear was expressed that the Yankee pitchers would walk him to protect Mantle. Instead, they pitched to him. It was wise. He looked terrible at the plate, tired and discouraged and unconvincing. He never looked very good to me in the Stadium. The final outcome in 1956 was Mantle .353, Williams .345.

The next year, I moved from New York to New England and it made all the difference. For in September of 1957, in the same situation, the story was reversed. Mantle finally hit .365; it was the best season of his career. But Williams, though sick and old, had run away from him. A bout of flu had laid him low in September. He emerged from his cave in the Hotel Somerset haggard but irresistible; he hit four successive pinch-hit home runs. "I feel terrible," he confessed, "but every time I take a swing at the ball it goes out of the park." He ended the season with thirty-eight home runs and an average of .388, the highest in either league since his own .406, and, coming

9

10

Ty Cobb Baseball star with the Detroit Tigers from 1905 to 1928; holds the lifetime batting average record at .367.

from a decrepit man of thirty-nine, an even more supernal figure. With eight or so of the "leg hits" that a younger man would have beaten out, it would have been .400. And the next year, Williams, who in 1949 and 1953 had lost batting championships by decimal whiskers to George Kell and Mickey Vernon, sneaked in behind his teammate Pete Runnels and filched his sixth title, a bargain at .328.

In 1959, it seemed all over. The dinosaur thrashed around in the .200 swamp for the first half of the season, and was even benched ("rested," Manager Mike Higgins tactfully said). Old foes like the late Bill Cunningham began to offer batting tips. Cunningham thought Williams was jiggling his elbows; in truth, Williams' neck was so stiff he could hardly turn his head to look at the pitcher. When he swung, it looked like a Calder mobile with one thread cut; it reminded you that since 1954 Williams' shoulders had been wired together. A solicitous pall settled over the sports pages. In the two decades since Williams had come to Boston, his status had imperceptibly shifted from that of a naughty prodigy to that of a municipal monument. As his shadow in the record books lengthened, the Red Sox teams around him declined, and the entire American League seemed to be losing life and color to the National. The inconsistency of the new super-stars — Mantle, Colavito, and Kaline — served to make Williams appear all the more singular. And off the field, his private philanthrophy — in particular, his zealous chairmanship of the Jimmy Fund, a charity for children with cancer — gave him a civic presence matched only by that of Richard Cardinal Cushing. In religion, Williams appears to be a humanist, and a selective one at that, but he and the abrasive-voiced Cardinal, when their good works intersect and they appear in the public eye together, make a handsome pair of seraphim.

Humiliated by his '59 season, Williams determined, once more, to come back. I, as a specimen Williams partisan, was both glad and fearful. All baseball fans believe in miracles; the question is, how *many* do you believe in? He looked like a ghost in spring training. Manager Jurges warned us ahead of time that if Williams didn't come through he would be benched, just like anybody else. As it turned out, it was Jurges who was benched. Williams entered the 1960 season needing eight home runs to have a lifetime total of 500; after one time at bat in Washington, he needed seven. For a stretch, he was hitting a home run every second game that he played. He passed Lou Gehrig's lifetime total, and finished with 521, thirteen behind Jimmy Foxx, who alone stands between Williams and Babe Ruth's unapproachable 714. The summer was a statistician's picnic. His two-thousandth walk came and went, his eighteen-hundredth run batted in, his sixteenth All-Star Game. At one point, he hit a home run off a pitcher, Don Lee, off whose father, Thornton Lee, he had hit a home run a generation before. The only comparable season for a forty-two-year-old man was Ty Cobb's in 1928. Cobb batted .323 and hit one homer. Williams batted .316 but hit twenty-nine homers.

In sum, though generally conceded to be the greatest hitter of his era, he 13
did not establish himself as "the greatest hitter who ever lived." Cobb, for
average, and Ruth, for power, remain supreme. Cobb, Rogers Hornsby, Joe
Jackson, and Lefty O'Doul, among players since 1900, have higher lifetime
averages than Williams' .344. Unlike Foxx, Gehrig, Hack Wilson, Hank
Greenberg, and Ralph Kiner, Williams never came close to matching Babe
Ruth's season home-run total of sixty. In the list of major-league batting records, not one is held by Williams. He is second in walks drawn, third in
home runs, fifth in lifetime average, sixth in runs batted in, eighth in runs
scored and in total bases, fourteenth in doubles, and thirtieth in hits. But if
we allow him merely average seasons for the four-plus seasons he lost to
two wars, and add another season for the months he lost to injuries, we get
a man who in all the power totals would be second, and not a very distant
second, to Ruth. And if we further allow that these years would have been
not merely average but prime years, if we allow for all the months when Williams was playing in sub-par condition, if we permit his early and later years
in baseball to be some sort of index of what the middle years could have
been, if we give him a right-field fence that is not, like Fenway's, one of the
most distant in the league, and if — the least excusable "if" — we imagine
him condescending to outsmart the Williams Shift, we can defensibly assemble, like a colossus induced from the sizable fragments that do remain, a
statistical figure not incommensurate with his grandiose ambition. From the
statistics that are on the books, a good case can be made that in the *combination* of power and average Williams is first; nobody else ranks so high in both
categories. Finally, there is the witness of the eyes; men whose memories go
back to Shoeless Joe Jackson — another unlucky natural — rank him and
Williams together as the best-looking hitters they have seen. It was for our
last look that ten thousand of us had come.

Two girls, one of them with pert buckteeth and eyes as black as vest but- 14
tons, the other with white skin and flesh-colored hair, like an underdevel-
oped photograph of a redhead, came and sat on my right. On my other side
was one of those frowning chestless young-old men who can frequently be
seen, often wearing sailor hats, attending ball games alone. He did not once
open his program but instead tapped it, rolled up, on his knee as he gave the
game his disconsolate attention. A young lady, with freckles and a depressed, dainty nose that by an optical illusion seemed to thrust her lips forward for a kiss, sauntered down into the box seat right behind the roof of the
Oriole dugout. She wore a blue coat with a Northeastern University emblem
sewed to it. The girls beside me took it into their heads that this was Williams' daughter. She looked too old to me, and why would she be sitting behind the visitors' dugout? On the other hand, from the way she sat there,
staring at the sky and French-inhaling, she clearly was *somebody*. Other fans
came and eclipsed her from view. The crowd looked less like a weekday

315

ballpark crowd than like the folks you might find in Yellowstone National Park, or emerging from automobiles at the top of scenic Mount Mansfield. There were a lot of competitively well-dressed couples of tourist age, and not a few babes in arms. A row of five seats in front of me was abruptly filled with a woman and four children, the youngest of them two years old, if that. Someday, presumably, he could tell his grandchildren that he saw Williams play. Along with these tots and second-honeymooners, there were Harvard freshmen, giving off that peculiar nervous glow created when a sufficient quantity of insouciance is saturated with enough insecurity; thick-necked Army officers with brass on their shoulders and steel in their stares; pepperings of priests; perfumed bouquets of Roxbury Fabian fans; shiny salesmen from Albany and Fall River; and those gray, hoarse men — taxi drivers, slaughterers, and bartenders — who will continue to click through the turnstiles long after everyone else has deserted to television and tramporamas. Behind me, two young male voices blossomed, cracking a joke about God's five proofs that Thomas Aquinas exists — typical Boston College levity.

The batting cage was trundled away. The Orioles fluttered to the sidelines. Diagonally across the field, by the Red Sox dugout, a cluster of men in overcoats were festering like maggots. I could see a splinter of white uniform, and Williams' head, held at a self-deprecating and evasive tilt. Williams' conversational stance is that of a six-foot-three-inch man under a six-foot ceiling. He moved away to the patter of flash bulbs, and began playing catch with a young Negro outfielder named Willie Tasby. His arm, never very powerful, had grown lax with the years, and his throwing motion was a kind of muscular drawl. To catch the ball, he flicked his glove hand onto his left shoulder (he batted left but threw right, as every schoolboy ought to know) and let the ball plop into it comically. This catch session with Tasby was the only time all afternoon I saw him grin.

A tight little flock of human sparrows who, from the lambent and pampered pink of their faces, could only have been Boston politicians moved toward the plate. The loudspeakers mammothly coughed as someone huffed on the microphone. The ceremonies began. Curt Gowdy, the Red Sox radio and television announcer, who sounds like everybody's brother-in-law, delivered a brief sermon, taking the two words "pride" and "champion" as his text. It began, "Twenty-one years ago, a skinny kid from San Diego, California . . ." and ended, "I don't think we'll ever see another like him." Robert Tibolt, chairman of the board of the Greater Boston Chamber of Commerce, presented Williams with a big Paul Revere silver bowl. Harry Carlson, a member of the sports committee of the Boston Chamber, gave him a plaque, whose inscription he did not read in its entirety, out of deference to Williams' distaste for this sort of fuss. Mayor Collins, seated in a wheelchair, presented the Jimmy Fund with a thousand-dollar check.

Then the occasion himself stooped to the microphone, and his voice sounded, after the others, very Californian; it seemed to be coming, excellently amplified, from a great distance, adolescently young and as smooth as a butternut. His thanks for the gifts had not died from our ears before he glided, as if helplessly, into "In spite of all the terrible things that have been said about me by the knights of the keyboard up there. . . ." He glanced up at the press rows suspended behind home plate. The crowd tittered, appalled. A frightful vision flashed upon me, of the press gallery pelting Williams with erasers, of Williams clambering up the foul screen to slug journalists, of a riot, of Mayor Collins being crushed. ". . . And they *were* terrible things," Williams insisted, with level melancholy, into the mike. "I'd like to forget them, but I can't." He paused, swallowed his memories, and went on, "I want to say that my years in Boston have been the greatest thing in my life." The crowd, like an immense sail going limp in a change of wind, sighed with relief. Taking all the parts himself, Williams then acted out a vivacious little morality drama in which an imaginary tempter came to him at the beginning of his career and said, "Ted, you can play anywhere you like." Leaping nimbly into the role of his younger self (who in biographical actuality had yearned to be a Yankee), Williams gallantly chose Boston over all the other cities, and told us that Tom Yawkey was the greatest owner in baseball and we were the greatest fans. We applauded ourselves lustily. The umpire came out and dusted the plate. The voice of doom announced over the loudspeakers that after Williams' retirement his uniform number, 9, would be permanently retired — the first time the Red Sox had so honored a player. We cheered. The national anthem was played. We cheered. The game began.

Williams was third in the batting order, so he came up in the bottom of 18 the first inning, and Steve Barber, a young pitcher born two months before Williams began playing in the major leagues, offered him four pitches, at all of which he disdained to swing, since none of them were within the strike zone. This demonstrated simultaneously that Williams' eyes were razor-sharp and that Barber's control wasn't. Shortly, the bases were full, with Williams on second. "Oh, I hope he gets held up at third! That would be wonderful," the girl beside me moaned, and, sure enough, the man at bat walked and Williams was delivered into our foreground. He struck the pose of Donatello's David, the third-base bag being Goliath's head. Fiddling with his cap, swapping small talk with the Oriole third baseman (who seemed delighted to have him drop in), swinging his arms with a sort of prancing nervousness, he looked fine — flexible, hard, and not unbecomingly substantial through the middle. The long neck, the small head, the knickers whose cuffs were worn down near his ankles — all these clichés of sports cartoon iconography were rendered in the flesh.

With each pitch, Williams danced down the baseline, waving his arms 19 and stirring dust, ponderous but menacing, like an attacking goose. It occurred to about a dozen humorists at once to shout "Steal home! Go, go!"

Williams' speed afoot was never legendary. Lou Clinton, a young Sox out-
fielder, hit a fairly deep fly to center field. Williams tagged up and ran home.
As he slid across the plate, the ball, thrown with unusual heft by Jackie
Brandt, the Oriole center fielder, hit him on the back.

"Boy, he was really loafing, wasn't he?" one of the collegiate voices behind me said.

"It's cold," the other voice explained. "He doesn't play well when it's
cold. He likes heat. He's a hedonist."

The run that Williams scored was the second and last of the inning. Gus
Triandos, of the Orioles, quickly evened the score by plunking a home run
over the handy left-field wall. Williams, who had had this wall at his back for
twenty years, played the ball flawlessly. He didn't budge. He just stood still,
in the center of the little patch of grass that his patient footsteps had worn
brown, and, limp with lack of interest, watched the ball pass overhead. It
was not a very interesting game. Mike Higgins, the Red Sox manager, with
nothing to lose, had restricted his major-league players to the left-field line
— along with Williams, Frank Malzone, a first-rate third baseman, played
the game — and had peopled the rest of the terrain with unpredictable
youngsters fresh, or not so fresh, off the farms. Other than Williams' recurrent appearances at the plate, the *maladresse*° of the Sox infield was the sole
focus of suspense; the second baseman turned every grounder into a juggling act, while the shortstop did a breathtaking impersonation of an open
window. With this sort of assistance, the Orioles wheeled their way into a
4–2 lead. They had early replaced Barber with another young pitcher, Jack
Fisher. Fortunately (as it turned out), Fisher is no cutie; he is willing to burn
the ball through the strike zone, and inning after inning this tactic punctured
Higgins' string of test balloons.

Whenever Williams appeared at the plate — pounding the dirt from his
cleats, gouging a pit in the batter's box with his left foot, wringing resin out
of the bat handle with his vehement grip, switching the stick at the pitcher
with an electric ferocity — it was like having a familiar Leonardo appear in a
shuffle of *Saturday Evening Post* covers. This man, you realized — and here,
perhaps, was the difference, greater than the difference in gifts — really desired to hit the ball. In the third inning, he hoisted a high fly to deep center.
In the fifth, we thought he had it; he smacked the ball hard and high into the
heart of his power zone, but the deep right field in Fenway and the heavy air
and a casual east wind defeated him. The ball died. Al Pilarcik leaned his
back against the big "380" painted on the right-field wall and caught it. On
another day, in another park, it would have been gone. (After the game,
Williams said, "I didn't think I could hit one any harder than that. The conditions weren't good.")

---

maladresse Ineptness, clumsiness.

The afternoon grew so glowering that in the sixth inning the arc lights 24
were turned on — always a wan sight in the daytime, like the burning headlights of a funeral procession. Aided by the gloom, Fisher was slicing
through the Sox rookies, and Williams did not come to bat in the seventh.
He was second up in the eighth. This was almost certainly his last time to
come to the plate in Fenway Park, and instead of merely cheering, as we had
at his three previous appearances, we stood, all of us, and applauded. I had
never before heard pure applause in a ballpark. No calling, no whistling,
just an ocean of handclaps, minute after minute, burst after burst, crowding
and running together in continuous succession like the pushes of surf at the
edge of the sand. It was a sombre and considered tumult. There was not a
boo in it. It seemed to renew itself out of a shifting set of memories as the
Kid, the Marine, the veteran of feuds and failures and injuries, the friend of
children, and the enduring old pro evolved down the bright tunnel of
twenty-two summers toward this moment. At last, the umpire signalled for
Fisher to pitch; with the other players, he had been frozen in position. Only
Williams had moved during the ovation, switching his bat impatiently, ignoring everything except his cherished task. Fisher wound up, and the applause sank into a hush.

Understand that we were a crowd of rational people. We knew that a 25
home run cannot be produced at will; the right pitch must be perfectly met
and luck must ride with the ball. Three innings before, we had seen a brave
effort fail. The air was soggy, the season was exhausted. Nevertheless, there
will always lurk, around the corner in a pocket of our knowledge of the
odds, an indefensible hope, and this was one of the times, which you now
and then find in sports, when a density of expectation hangs in the air and
plucks an event out of the future.

Fisher, after his unsettling wait, was low with the first pitch. He put the 26
second one over, and Williams swung mightily and missed. The crowd
grunted, seeing that classic swing, so long and smooth and quick, exposed.
Firsher threw the third time, Williams swung again, and there it was. The
ball climbed on a diagonal line into the vast volume of air over center field.
From my angle, behind third base, the ball seemed less an object in flight
than the tip of the towering, motionless construct, like the Eiffel Tower or
the Tappan Zee Bridge. It was in the books while it was still in the sky.
Brandt ran back to the deepest corner of the outfield grass, the ball descended beyond his reach and struck in the crotch where the bullpen met
the wall, bounced chunkily, and vanished.

Like a feather caught in a vortex, Williams ran around the square of bases 27
at the center of our beseeching screaming. He ran as he always ran out home
runs — hurriedly, unsmiling, head down, as if our praise were a storm of
rain to get out of. He didn't tip his cap. Though we thumped, wept, and
chanted ''We want Ted'' for minutes after he hid in the dugout, he did not
come back. Our noise for some seconds passed beyond excitement into a

kind of immense open anguish, a wailing, a cry to be saved. But immortality is nontransferable. The papers said that the other players, and even the umpires on the field, begged him to come out and acknowledge us in some way, but he refused. Gods do not answer letters.

Every true story has an anticlimax. The men on the field refused to disappear, as would have seemed decent, in the smoke of Williams' miracle. Fisher continued to pitch, and escaped further harm. At the end of the inning, Higgins sent Williams out to his left-field position, then instantly replaced him with Carrol Hardy, so we had a long last look at Williams as he ran out there and then back, his uniform jogging, his eyes steadfast on the ground. It was nice, and we were grateful, but it left a funny taste.

One of the scholasticists behind me said, "Let's go. We've seen everything. I don't want to spoil it." This seemed a sound aesthetic decision. Williams' last word had been so exquisitely chosen, such a perfect fusion of expectation, intention, and execution, that already it felt a little unreal in my head, and I wanted to get out before the castle collapsed. But the game, though played by clumsy midgets under the feeble glow of the arc lights, began to tug at my attention, and I loitered in the runway until it was over. Williams' homer had, quite incidentally, made the score 4–3. In the bottom of the ninth inning, with one out, Marlin Coughtry, the second-base juggler, singled. Vic Wertz, pitch-hitting, doubled off the left-field wall, Coughtry advancing to third. Pumpsie Green walked, to load the bases. Willie Tasby hit a double-play ball to the third baseman, but in making the pivot throw Billy Klaus, an ex–Red Sox infielder, reverted to form and threw the ball past the first baseman and into the Red Sox dugout. The Sox won, 5–4. On the car radio as I drove home I heard that Williams, his own man to the end, had decided not to accompany the team to New York. He had met the little death that awaits athletes. He had quit.

QUESTIONS ON MEANING

1. What sort of hero was Ted Williams? Why is it necessary for Updike to present so many facts in support of his argument that Williams was a great ball player?
2. Consider all the details Updike presents about Wednesday, September 28, 1960, in Fenway Park. How do his details create an appropriate setting for the miracle of Williams's last at-bat?
3. Updike writes his essay along two distinct lines: He reports the events of the day in Fenway Park (paragraphs 1 and 2 and paragraphs 14–29) and in between he presents an argument for Ted Williams's ambition to be "the greatest hitter who ever lived." How does Updike's argument serve his re-

portage? How does he make the transition from reporting to analysis in paragraphs 2 and 3 and from analysis to reporting in paragraphs 13 and 14?

4. Is Updike's argument for Williams balanced? What is his opinion of Williams? Why doesn't he simply conclude that Williams was not the greatest hitter of all time and leave it at that?

QUESTIONS ON STRATEGY

1. How does Updike set the scene in paragraphs 1 and 2 and again in paragraphs 14–17? What kind of mood does he create? Why does he describe the crowd in such detail?
2. Paragraph 3 compares the relation between Ted Williams and the hometown fans to a marriage; paragraph 4 continues the comparison. How does Updike use the analogy in the rest of the essay?
3. Where and how does Updike make the transition from scene setting to reporting? Why does he emphasize newspaper headlines? Notice the last sentence in paragraph 1. Why is this apparently minor piece of information situated so prominently?

EXPLORATIONS

1. Updike presents an array of facts to support his argument that Williams was "perhaps the best *old* hitter of the century." Compare Updike's handling of factual material with McPhee's (pages 298–307).

WRITING TOPICS

1. One way to appropriate an author's techniques for your own purposes is to write a parody. Ernest Thayer's poem "Casey at the Bat" provides a parallel to Updike's description of Ted Williams coming up to bat for the last time. Write a report of Casey's last at-bat in Updike's style.
2. It's possible that you have witnessed a great moment of vindication such as Updike describes. If you have, write an essay in which you describe the setting and define the achievement as carefully as Updike has in "Hub Fans Bid Kid Adieu."

BOOKS AVAILABLE IN PAPERBACK

Bech: A Book. New York: Vintage. *Stories.*

Bech Is Back. New York: Fawcett Crest. *Stories.*

The Centaur. New York: Fawcett Crest. *Novel.*

The Coup. New York: Fawcett Crest. *Novel.*

Couples. New York: Fawcett Crest. *Novel.*

A Month of Sundays. New York: Fawcett Crest. *Novel.*

Museums and Women, and Other Stories. New York: Vintage.

Picked-Up Pieces. New York: Fawcett Crest. *Essays.*

Pigeon Feathers and Other Stories. New York: Fawcett Crest.

Rabbit is Rich. New York: Fawcett Crest. *Novel.*

Rabbit Redux. New York: Fawcett Crest. *Novel.*

Rabbit, Run. New York: Fawcett Crest. *Novel.*

Too Far to Go: The Maples Stories. New York: Fawcett Crest.

EDWARD
HOAGLAND

EDWARD HOAGLAND (b. 1932) published his first novel two years after graduating from college. He spent a decade writing novels and short stories and more recently has concentrated on essays for Harper's, the Atlantic, and other magazines, editorials for the New York Times, and books of travel. His book-length journal of time spent in British Columbia is called Notes from the Century Before (1965). African Calliope (1979) is subtitled "A Journey to the Sudan," and there are four essay collections — The Courage of Turtles (1971), Walking the Dead Diamond River (1973), Red Wolves and Black Bears (1976), Tugman's Passage (1982) — as well as The Edward Hoagland Reader (1979), edited by Geoffrey Wolff.

Hoagland worked with a traveling circus when he was young and later used the experience in a novel. Mostly he has worked as a writer. He returns to particular themes or topics: New York tugboats, tugboat captains, tugboat crews; animals; and life in the woods. As you might expect, he divides his time as well as his prose between Manhattan, where he lives with his family during the school year, and a small town in remote northern Vermont, where the Hoagland family spends its summers. Reading this author's essays, one flips back and forth between the wilderness of the north country and the wilderness of city streets.

Another repeated subject is the wilderness of men and women. If Hoagland alter-
nates contrasting neighborhoods, his mind — like most active minds — also moves
from pole to pole. Many people think their best by means of internal dialogue, mount-
ing an inner debate between opposing forces. In ''Women and Men,'' such an inner
dialogue forms the essay, and the reader follows the tug and pull of a subject as di-
verse, and as unified, as the two sexes.

Women and Men

One reason the effects wrought by the Women's Movement remain clouded in uncertainty is that its goals have been divided between matters of simple justice and matters of androgyny.° The simple part is that any fair-minded person who walks into a bank and sees that all the tellers are women and all the officers are men is going to cast a vote for women's rights. This might not have been the case a dozen years ago — nor is it now in back-woods America — any more than other principles of social justice that we re-gard as elementary have always been considered so. But powerful inertial forces opposing change in the United States have a way of abruptly caving in; and nowadays most people who learn that women are discriminated against in questions of jobs, salary, access to education, or property rights are going to react the same. That battle, however painful, has been uncom-plicated and, except for what amounts to a mopping-up operation, seems to have been won.

What is utterly unknown, unwon, is the extent of the changes in sexual-ity itself that are under way. Some women activists wanted men to cease to exist. Others wanted women to become like men. Others wanted women to become like men and men to become like women, in the old sense — while still others wanted everybody to become the same, somewhere in between.

The mainstream of the Movement took an attitude on the subject too am-biguous to put into words. It both did and didn't wish for punitive as well as substantive change. It both did and didn't advocate equality between the sexes in complex, potentially anguished areas like child custody and ali-mony law and military service. It both did and didn't look forward comfort-ably to a bisexual world.

Usually, one need only see one's mother, if she is over sixty, to recognize that an immense, recent inequity existed between what the two sexes could

---

androgyny   A combining of both male and female characteristics.

do in the span of their lives. And yet a lot of confusion arose because of the comparison the Movement drew between this struggle and the civil rights movement of ten or fifteen years before. Linking them was an effective tactic for adding momentum, righteousness, and rage to the new cause, and plenty of people actually came to believe that middle-class white women in suburban America were a trod-upon underclass that had suffered injuries equatable to the mean and savage constrictions that had been imposed upon American blacks. To say that such a notion is absurd is not to belittle the wrong done to that row of underpaid bank tellers, who could work for twenty years with never a chance to advance themselves. But the result has been that any solution sounded so easy. If women were essentially identical with men, another institutionalized outrage could be set right, another long-suffering ''minority'' could be integrated into the vast, egalitarian mega-class through what by now has become quite standard methods of corrective laws and pressure politics. If women and men could be compared with rival ethnic constituencies, the imbalance between them could be construed as having originated only through prejudice, not biological imperatives. If men and women have no more need for each other *as* men and women than black people have for Caucasians as Caucasians — if they could now merely blend together — then legal remedies would be able to deal with the difficulties quite handily.

This is not to suggest our customs are not due for a profound overhaul. 5 Apart from the issue of what is right, there are enough new imperatives arising from technology to have seen to that. But it will be an overhaul reaching to the wellsprings of how we express our love and lead our lives and how children are raised. Two by two, we've gone into Noah's Ark — or wherever we wanted to go — and to have gone always in twos implies some innate difference between the parties who have joined hands. Otherwise it could have been done as well in ones or threes or fours.

Surely, also, not just considerations of unit efficiency created this ar- 6 rangement for raising a family. There must have been a feeling that life was thinner when lived either homosexually or in harem style — that a partner picked from Column A went best with one from Column B, and that the pairing probably thereafter should be adhered to. Where feminism has argued that Columns B and A should be equal by custom and before the law, it is not at all the same as saying there aren't and never should have been two columns. In primitive cultures, polygyny or polyandry did sometimes ensure that the most vigorous members of a tribe had the most mates and descendants. But ''serial polygamy'' in the form of divorce, as we now have it, does not necessarily do that, because modern-day divorce, even though accepted as a social alternative, is seldom such a sign of vigor, balance, and initiative as in those cultures the acquisition of several wives or husbands used to be.

My own reaction has been to agree, slowly, sometimes too begrudgingly, with most of the proposals for social equity the Movement made. But always I was astonished at how easy the proponents have thought the whole thing was going to be, once the Neanderthals arrayed against them had been overcome. It was as if two races from different continents that had been adventitiously brought into bitter conflict were to exchange declarations of understanding in order to have peace.

In lovemaking, "These are my nipples, but there are *your* nipples," said the representative from Atlantis, working diligently as a political act to awaken them to the same level of sensitivity as hers. "This your penis," she continued. "But *this* penis, which is called a clitoris, is *my* penis." And, indeed, although a penis corresponds not to the clitoris but to the vagina or uterus in its central importance to a man, for the moment it seemed she was right. That her hips were large was an embarrassment, even an affront, to her.

Not long ago (to take a literary example), Ernest Hemingway and other writers of the hairy-chested school were receiving such a chivvying for their roosterly preoccupations that an alarmist might have wondered whether some precious part of our admiration for bigger figures — like Homer's Achilles and Shakespeare's Henry V, and real-life heroes, such as Garibaldi — might also go by the boards. But women have generally taken such men to their hearts, just as other men do. Such a whole-hog, sustained assault against old-fashioned masculinity was never in the cards. Instead, the scope to emulate traditional heroes is being lost; and this, more than any sectarian animosity, will be what changes literature — people may not remember what Homer was talking about.

A crowded, tight, computerized world with regimentation that begins with a prenatal forecast of gender and extends to the grave must be more "feminine" in its field of action, regardless of the success or failure of any concerted effort to dismantle "masculinity," as it has been known. Masculinity must have more range, more space to operate in, because of the implication it carries that force may be used. Fistfights, pig slaughtering, river-swimming, home-brewed liquor, a hunting rifle in the closet, a mufflerless jalopy smoking from the tail pipe, or a no-prisoners-are-taken policy in a corporate boardroom set-to: these are "male." On the other hand, it would be reasonable to assume that a woman who is a sales manager in a cutthroat business and jogs four miles every evening for relaxation can read *The Iliad* as vividly as anybody who happens to possess male genitalia.

There will be people more taken with the sensibility of Jane Austen, and people who prefer Herman Melville, without reference to their own gender, sex as such having come to matter much less. We will have statistical improvements in every Olympic sport, ever-superior performances on the cello and at figure skating, while fame, as lately, continues to be quick, neuter, and bankable, emphasizing not only self-promotion, but a homogenized celebrity, so that new faces can be substituted easily. It is already impossible to paddle a canoe anywhere that hasn't got a zip code, and our admirable competitions in the marathon are not run in wild, open country, where they might convey the authority of an ancient marathon, but as though under glass, through the middle of Boston and New York City, as glorified folk festivals.

It's admirable that so many people can run twenty-six miles, now when they no longer need to, and that upwards of two million New Yorkers are willing to leave their telephones long enough to watch them. And of course the argument that liberty has diminished with all of this shrinking of operational territory and (as it seems to me) options of temperament — with the decline in regional distinctions, individual responsibility, and sexual definition, and the swing toward an egalitarianism of the lowest common denominator, by which, for example, a prospective President must run for office for many years full time — can be stood on its head. There is evidence, on the contrary, of an unprecedented freedom. With so many "subcultures," the pleasure of variety is everywhere. More people may be living in different ways than was imaginable before. Even for a macho man, no doubt, another brand of liberty is in the offing whenever, blindly feeling around, he manages to locate it. 12

Plenty of women in their twenties and thirties do evince a rare exuberance; one meets older women who sharply envy them the era they have been born into. And if, accordingly, many men of twenty-eight or thirty-three tend to display a peculiar muteness, it is not that they have special cause for complaint but that they are "not themselves," in the apt phrase — which is exactly what the feminist revolution has demanded. Very young men, bearing expectations better rooted in the chameleon realm of androgyny, appear to be more cheerful. And middle-aged men, although perhaps caught in the familiar hodgepodge of mid-life misdoubts and ironies like middle-aged women, nevertheless may confess to having had the best of both worlds. As young men, they were prepared to rule the roost like Chanticleer, but now they watch the parade of change with quite a sympathetic interest, such as older men feel for younger women anyway, which often outweighs the sort of fatherly favoritism that they otherwise might direct toward younger men. 13

The women most vocal in Women's Lib haven't wished to concede the intricate interdependence that has existed between women and men, because to acknowledge such a complication would be to grant that unpredictable and agonizing problems might arise. Still, as a codicil to their prognostications, they have added the encouragement that men also are going to be liberated from unnecessary or discomforting constraints. One can see, in fact, that women, being franker and more approachable, have made the ritual of 14

327

courtship a good deal easier, softening the old charade men had to go through in trying to win over a leery but conniving adversary with small lies and legerdemain. And when they work, it is a considerable convenience to the former "breadwinner." Even in high-strung professions like the law or public relations, women are by no means unanimous in advocating that men be unmanned and women masculinized until everybody starts from a hermaphrodite position, there to allow the personality to bend as it will. If young women are happier, so much the better for everybody; and on the tender question of who raises the children, possibly television raises them now anyway.

Technology is more leveling than feminism, as is the density in which we live, and our fat standard of living, combined with its recent shrinkage. (That is, we are left with less room to stretch out in a show of either masculine or feminine fervor — only the fat.) Not all the married women muscling into the commercial arena to earn a living really want to; and no military provision remains for young men to test themselves without the risk of a push-button war. Nor can young men afford the gasoline to drive from Atlanta to Seattle and back, the way they used to do as a substitute for going to war. After one gets through being glad that boys no longer have to prove that they are brave and strong, one begins to wonder whether an offbeat soul who wanted to could find a rip in the protective padding of bureaucratic regulation that surrounds us in order to accomplish such a coup.

We have to trust that people won't obliterate themselves in their inventions. Genetically, we are nearly identical to mankind fifty thousand years ago; and some of us delight in the continuity represented by this, while others may be appalled. But we count on each other — that the other fellow won't cross the highway divider in his car and knock us dead, won't molest our children on the way to school, won't accuse us of committing a crime we didn't do. In political, civil, and money matters we depend on one another, just as in the arts there could be no drama, music, painting, poetry if there were no community of response. Clasping a lover, feeling a heartbeat, one doesn't immediately know whose blood it is — and there is a triumph in this. Maybe eventually, in the same way, people won't care what biological equipment a lover has. And yet the pleasure of lovemaking derives from two people repeatedly trying to position themselves as opportunely as they can for insemination to occur. They can murmur nothings in the meantime, or vary the approach by trying to climb headfirst inside each other for a prenatal interlude. But the final sensation is basically just such as will best serve to help us replicate ourselves.

The differences between the sexes used to be exaggerated to create a worse imbalance in rights and duties, but this was not only so that men could amass more power of the purse and of the sweets of life; it was also because a woman needed to mother six or eight children if two or three of them were to reach adulthood. In 1800 American women bore an average of seven children apiece, in the process of settling the continent. From their very bellies they produced a family; and one of the dislocations of feminism has been not to allow for the complexity of the War between the Sexes, as that half-humorous battle used to be called. Like the conflict between the generations, it had at its core real dissimilarities, as well as opportunism and bullying. Each sex belittled the other's pretensions and anatomical protuberances, and agreed to certain bitter trade-offs, which, though not fairly balanced, appeared yet more inequitable when looked at from one side or the other — the husband's unofficial permission to stray from fidelity, versus the wife's to "take him to the cleaners" and keep the children in a divorce. But even in a man's world, women exercised substantial veto power. They helped determine who had children and who did not, who slept well and who endured insomnia, who was relatively contented and long-lived and who scarcely contrived to get his bags unpacked. "Behind every good man," the saying went, though recently there has been a commotion about how weak and shaky men are, as if this were a revelation, not the original discovery of "Nursing," that first bastion of the female professional.

Women, waiting out the sexual urgencies of men, have insisted upon 18 some show of strength or nervous energy in a partner, as well as love and kindness, and all the lavish emblems of success and a commitment to the way of the world — but more fragile, nonconformist virtues, too, lest these be lost. The man as suitor buys flowers as a token of his earning power and in appreciation of the lady's finer tastes, yet in the tableau that they go through he must also smell the flowers appreciatively and admire them himself. He must moon with her by moonlight, as well as make big bucks under the bright light of the sun.

From their urge for permanence, women have generally avoided love af- 19 fairs outside their own social class. The built-in passion for the female body that men are saddled with has created a constant dilemma for them: Did the gentleman want the lady in particular that he was with, or just an all-night squeeze? Was his love so abiding that it would transfer to the child that she might have by him? Did he "need" his ladylove enough, did he pay enough attention to her to stick by her through the task of feeding, as well as conceiving, babies? Was he conventional enough to make a go of things — yet, at the same time (and passion tested him for this), could he weather sleepless nights, did he have a sense of joy and fun, did he come back after a rebuff or when the woman whom he said he loved didn't look her best? And she, too — could she do without sleep? Was she clever or beautiful enough even in periods of discouragement to persuade another person to try to have more babies with her or at least continue to put food on the table for the earlier ones, instead of setting out to look for other ladies to make more babies with?

Though one knows women who enjoy playing with a man's body with the same utilitarian satisfaction that a man would feel in making free with theirs — women with grown children who cast a roving eye, women undergoing the trauma of divorce with the same frenetic sexual reaction that many men have felt, adventurous younger women who have set themselves a cut-off date of thirty or so, when they hope to turn "serious" — at least up until now, most women are far from being as casual about sex as a man. Nevertheless, besides the wish for steadiness, many have had a taste for what was reckless and randy in a man, looking especially for physical vigor or daring, or looked particularly to "trade up," with respect to social class. Many a woman has preferred the man who set his hat at a tilt and touched her leg without first asking if he could — except that the pain of that choice was that he might not go slow afterwards. For practical reasons, she has needed to choose one partner and try to hold him to fidelity, whereas, in theory — with his body tooled to father not just two or three children but hundreds — he could mate again and again. And so she has delayed expressing her preference, cultivating her good looks, waiting for him to choose her first, then prove his loyalty.

Some men have their heartstrings tied to their children and suffer an awful wrench if they lose them in a divorce. Still, they have that opposing imperative — to plant more offspring, not only among their contemporaries but in the next generation, and with ladies of the Left and Right, ladies who blow the trumpet and ladies who play the harp. This tension between the sexes enriches as well as afflicts us, having envolved by a primeval path. And though once in a while a Movement figure has warned the lesbian or radical wings against indulging in an open hatred of men — cautioning, for instance, that the occasional crime of rape should not be interpreted as a whole-cloth hatred of all women by all men — there has been too little recognition that the angry ebullience, the crowing and the snapping back and forth between the sexes, is not just connected with the issues of the moment but is an age-old torque.

No one is so fragile as a woman, but no one is as fragile as a man. A lady, in sitting on my lap, becomes my child, but when she unbuttons her blouse, I become her child. A balance is struck, yet not a flattening balance of the kind that would make men and women the same. Her strengths make me feel strong, as do her weaknesses, and she says mine operate similarly. If this were not the case, our lovemaking would become only a business of rubbing two sticks together and our affections would level out to a primitive state. A revolution moving toward bisexuality under the umbrella of civil rights for women will be profound indeed, but because so much of sex is simulated anyway, no one can predict how drastically sex is likely to change.

In sex and love, contradictions abound. The responsive woman who moistens almost visibly when she perceives a comely professional man wearing the flush of conquest — put somebody in her path who *isn't* a comer, whose ribs she can feel, and she will sometimes bend above him, opening to his needs until she feels his ribs grow tallowy. If two men love her, they may hate each other or may become the best of friends. Although it's sexy if she is gentle, it can also be sexy if she's ungentle; and though most women don't want a kinky lover, a little stitching of kinkiness in him will prolong and spice their pleasure. The oldest riddle is that the same woman who draws men and glances wholesale, as though she had been brought into being expressly for procreation, is often mediocre as a mother. Yet that woman with the passion-peach complexion who might not wish to mother children — how deliciously she mothers men! The less in need they really are, the better. She turns apricot. We see the uneasy long legs, the breasts like brandy snifters (though modestly covered), the tumbling hair; and yet alongside these importunings, perhaps in the straight neck, sits an aloof boy.

It's no coincidence that boys could play Shakespeare's female roles 24 rather convincingly, because part of what attracts a man to a woman is a swirl of emanations from her that resembles "boyishness"; and vice versa. The juice of sex is the consent of two adults to go to bed together, but counter to that, they both do look for secret semblances — plump Momma, and so on. Probably the biggest discovery of a young man's sexual awakening is that whatever he wants to do is not so far removed from what his girlfriend wants. So this could be called a species of androgyny, as is so much of the more complicated playacting, the chameleon coloration, of sex later on. It's an androgyny we are familiar with, however, an androgyny like that of Henry V himself, as Shakespeare imagined him in a play that is entirely predicated upon the fact that the hero king actually existed as a warrior, wooer, ruler, lover. Utterly masculine, Henry was androgynous because playful. But remove him as a sounding board, and you would have an art without echoes, history as archaeology — what was it *like* when there were men and women?

Sex draws us back into society from self-absorption. The ocean beach, 25 the lights along the skyline, soon lose their romance if we have no company to enjoy them with. And our breadth of sympathy for other people is expanded if there is even a distant possibility that we might become sexual partners with them. A friend of mine, now married to a district attorney, had as her last lover a man under indictment for draft evasion. Another friend is married to a golf pro and dresses in the height of Miami sports fashion, but was first married to a professional woodsman and rattlesnake hunter. Men's hearts, too, have always gone out to the proverbial waitress and the proverbial duchess in quick succession, noticing their various vulnerabilities all the more because they are of the opposite sex. The $60,000-a-year executive, whose cough is unexpectedly deep-voiced in the morning, but whose soft excesses of flesh almost seem to "ask" for cancer because they are appendices without a function now, first had to struggle out of the posh suburbs, where her husband's salary had put her, in order to struggle back in.

Nor has the endless priapism° of men much function lately; and the recent increased stress on sado-masochism — the agony attached to sexual fantasy — may be the result. Sex both as a tranquilizer and as the apple of contemporary existence may be nearly as necessary nowadays as the old sex of procreation was, though the tension it assuages is partly of its own making. Endless priapism, but no resolution. From a practical standpoint, it might seem absurd that men still wear two balls and women two breasts, as if they had need for them; yet — though it comes to nothing — people probably enjoy more bouts of sex than ever before. At least, the practice has spread more democratically through society, and is continued later in life, although big breasts as an ideal would seem to parody the actualities of the situation.

We struggle to complete ourselves — male with female, chatterbox with suppressed personality, blond-haired soul who hugs the exotic personage whose hair is black. And the extraordinary mating leap we make is possible only because there is a gap to leap. If acrimony alone were the upshot of the barriers that separate the sexes, their collapse would not be missed. But, under unisex, will we leap at all? And when the sex organs have been reduced to instruments of light pleasure, will the ecstasy of climax — losing even its present tenuous connection with childbearing — keep only its imitation of death at the end?

Anybody who remembers the persecution homosexuals suffered until recently will be in favor of some degree of androgyny. Yet nobody knows, and few people wish to think about, the significance of homosexuality in the new order of things. Is it a manifestation of neurosis, or not? Are rights to be accorded homosexuals that are appropriate to a religious-political minority, or to a "handicapped" minority? How will the limits of their normalcy be defined — up to and including marriage and the right to adopt children? The infant science of psychology is asked to decide whether an unabashedly homosexual grade-school teacher will influence the budding sexuality of his (her) students. Will the thinness — if it is a thinness — of homosexual life spread everywhere with bisexuality? And is androgyny or bisexuality any different from a dozen other forms of homogenization that are under way in the lives we live?

Perhaps, nevertheless, sexual intercourse will remain a deep, not light, pleasure, of profound significance, whatever the pretext for it may be. Perhaps, indeed, the Reagan and Moral Majority electoral landslide is not merely a sort of "Ghost Dance" of American cultural conservatism (as I tend to believe), but a genuine reversal of direction. Or on the contrary, androg-

---

priapism   A preoccupation with virility.

yny may be an irresistible phenomenon, not to be opposed by "Ghost Dance" political movements or wistful traditionalists of a less hidebound stripe, such as me — a natural means of birth control, in other words, for a society gradually growing old.

Sex has always been "dehumanizing," as the saying goes — for Samson, 30 and occasionally for everybody else. Yet part of why we emphasize it so perfervidly in an age when nature outdoors is dwindling is just that it *is* dehumanizing — animal, "natural." Better than baseball or jogging, it lifts us out of our envelopes of propriety. What a relief it would be in other corners of one's life to do exactly what one does in a romance — lean one's lovesick head against the lady's shoulder and ask indulgence and understanding. To tremble, sleepless from picturing somebody else, and then be able to lay one's face against that person's back and breasts — this is luxury, just as is the "animal" rassling and thrashing.

But the flip side of our mating leap is the inconstancy that often charac 31 terizes friendship between the sexes. We will confess the scary cancer operation, the close brush with a nervous breakdown, while touching hands during that first all-night conversation. Splurging every dearest detail of a childhood spent on the Arkansas River, a Bronze Star won under zany circumstances on the Mekong River, we want the other person to know the very best and worst of us. Yet, a month later, in mutual exasperation, we claim we never want to see each other again. Although at any other time we are disgusted by other people's body by-products, we had tried to swallow each other's tongue. Neglecting our friends (an offense for which we will now probably try to make the lover pay), we had poured out our hearts — the young lawyer for Westinghouse who still harbors a faint, secret ambition to become Secretary of State, the young advertising copywriter who labors over her diary at night in hopes of blossoming like Virginia Woolf, now absolutely try to cut the rope. Teenagers like to say, "I'll never speak to you again," a more explicitly frightening threat in such a social stage of life as theirs.

Of course the criticism usually made of homosexual affairs is that *they* are 32 too fragile or short-lived. But the passionate fragility of a homosexual love affair does not really correspond to the all-or-nothing commitment of two people who are preparing to raise children together. It is instead, in this respect, a make-believe, a dead-end. Heterosexuals break off so sharply because they are looking for a partner in a twenty-year task. They must preserve an edge of total involvement for the love to come. Better a fresh start. Tear free suddenly and get away intact.

Life is surely still somewhat at risk, still full of opportunities to rely on 33 oneself, with the fanning out that people do, in lives "laid back" or intense. The change toward serial or temporary marriages amounts to a new mode of isolation, spiritual more than physical, and the lady who began by listening to you as attentively as a geisha on your first evening together ends the affair by lighting up a cigarillo, as she gruffly tells you that you and she are through.

The right to a legal abortion is central to feminist demands, and, by its nature, cannot be guaranteed by applying the concept of "equal access." Plenty of women who recognize that the current rightward-moving pendulum in politics offers no serious threat to their recently won civic and professional mobility feel on occasion, though, an atavistic panic that above their rib cage they are forever hostage to what lies below; that only with the option of abortion can they be as free as a man. And their claim seems reasonable to me — a tragic but necessary trade-off that contemporary life requires. I'm offended not by the idea, only by the flippancy and brutality with which it is sometimes propounded.

At heart, their proposition is that it takes two people — a woman as well as a man — to have children; that the woman is not simply a vessel for an embryo that, designedly or inadvertently, has been planted by a man. Both man and woman must be at risk and in favor of what is happening. But the question that immediately follows is whether the principle is to work both ways — if the man as well as the woman is part of the equation and ought to be involved right through. Do single women, going beyond their power to terminate a pregnancy with or without the consent of the father, also have a moral right to initiate a pregnancy with an anonymously or carelessly donated vial of sperm, and then possibly flip out the fetus three months later, if they change their mind, their whim for self-fulfillment having meanwhile turned elsewhere? Some lesbians, in particular, welcome this additional freedom, but to my way of thinking, the welfare or the "rights," of the unborn may be more at hazard here than in the controversy over abortion itself, by which the unborn run the risk of never being born at all. In an imperfect world, many children are going to grow up without the benefit of two parents representing the two sexes, but they need not start out with fewer than two.

"Happiness is androgynous," as a heterosexual friend of mine was saying the other day. It must be so, because whenever one does see a grin of utter glee, or feel the same transfiguring smile of pleasure stretching one's own face, there is nothing "male" or "female" about the sensation. In real happiness, the lines of the face that distinguish us from one another by gender are erased; we become of the same race. But in attaining these epiphanies, we often need to leap the gap — one sex toward the other — for the sake of just this rich delight of compromising with one another.

"Strangely, laughter seems to me like the sexual act, which is perhaps the laughter of two bodies," says V. S. Pritchett. However, among feminists who neither wish to participate in the age-old, lifelong, gingerly, and rather exciting process of accommodation nor to become lesbians, there is a third course.

Oriana Fallaci's novel, *A Man*, revives a singularly innovative way of 38 dealing with the continuing appeal of macho men: pick 'em wild and pick 'em doomed. Her brave Green revolutionary, Alexander Panagoulis, is so far-out, frenetic, heroic, and self-destructive that it would be impossible for him ever to "tie her down." She can have her splendid romance without troubling to try to leap the gap because, in due course, he can only die, young and violently, freeing her from the necessity of making any compromising commitment to him, as well as from the likelihood that she will ever fall in love again. Who, after all, in raw maleness, could ever measure up to him? Nor need she wear a widow's weeds in a darkened drawing room, as women who loved mourning used to; she can roam the world as entrepreneur and parajournalist. And to be inseminated by such a hero would be ideal. In lovemaking, she has handled his war wounds and torture scars. He then departs the scene; and the lady, if she has a mind to, can marry her obliging, tidy-minded business manager for help in raising the twice-blest child.

As a program, it might prove popular, if enough heroes were at hand. It 39 resembles the "hammer date" that Lenny Bruce° liked to talk about in his monologues. A young stud wanted to screw, but he didn't want to have to hang around afterwards talking endlessly to his woman in return for her favors. So he got into bed with her, had his fuck, hit her over the head with the hammer, and went home.

This is an exaggeration. I meet women who wore jackboots and helped 40 bust down the barriers at all-male saloons a decade ago, and who announce plaintively, ironically, to anybody listening that they "want to sue for peace," that they are marriageable, that with an amniocentesis it isn't yet too late for them to have a baby. Other women say they never *did* wear jackboots, that their opinions, if known, would be unfashionable among their sophisticated friends. And, of course, since even men in macho garb in fact are also greatly tamed (in backwoods America, too, if one puts one's ear close to the ground), conditions at the moment hint at a truce.

QUESTIONS ON MEANING

1. In the first sentence Hoagland identifies the two goals, as he sees them, of the Women's Movement — justice and androgyny. Which of these goals engages most of his attention in the essay? What role does the other goal have? Does he just drop it or does it have some relation to his primary subject?

Lenny Bruce (1926–1966), comedian during the 1950s and early 1960s whose vehicle was social satire that often included off-color humor.

2. Hoagland draws a multifaceted definition of *androgyny* throughout the essay. What are some of the facets of his definition? What is his opinion about the desirability of achieving an androgynous society? What aspects of androgyny does he most approve of and disapprove of?

3. Paragraphs 9 and 10 are concerned with a loss in scope for the model of "old-fashioned masculinity." What does Hoagland mean by this? How does Hoagland detach this phenomenon from the consequences of the women's movement? Why does it suit his argument to do so? How does paragraph 11 extend his argument?

4. Paragraphs 23 and 24 concern the contradictions inherent in male-female interdependence. How do these contradictions relate to the "leap" Hoagland deals with, among other things, in paragraphs 27–37? What is the significance of this leap?

5. Paragraphs 38–40 present Hoagland's conclusion: What is it? Does his final perspective surprise you?

QUESTIONS ON STRATEGY

1. Hoagland writes with quick leaps of insight from paragraph to paragraph. How does paragraph 8, for example, fit with paragraphs 7 and 9? Does it provide a transition? Is it a digression? What is the point of Hoagland's shift from the androgyny of Shakespeare's hero in paragraph 24 to the idea he uses to open paragraph 25? Give other examples of Hoagland's leaps and explain why they are effective or ineffective.

2. Paragraph 15 contains a witty contrast between fat and muscle. How does this imagery convey his attitude toward our standard of living? How does it relate to "the protective padding of bureaucratic regulation" in the last sentence of the paragraph? In paragraph 23 Hoagland vividly evokes the sensuous appeal of a woman who "mothers men." How does his imagery serve his argument here? What other purpose does it have in this paragraph?

EXPLORATIONS

1. In paragraphs 14–21 Hoagland surveys "the intricate interdependence that has existed between women and men." He touches on several themes considered by Adrienne Rich in "Women and Honor: Some Notes on Lying" (pages 251–260): the "lies and legerdemain" of relations between the sexes, the indirection and uncertainty of courtship, the issue of rape. Review both essays for what they have to say about the history of relations between men and women. Which essay seems more persuasive? Does either seem more honest, or more disinterested, than the other? Does Rich's or Hoagland's view come closest to your own? Why?

WRITING TOPICS

1. Hoagland entertains a subject both perennial and topical, on which he finds himself divided, on which his mind conducts an internal dialogue. Find a subject on which your own mind conducts a dialogue: liberalism and con-

servatism in politics, amateurism and professionalism in collegiate athletics, ethnic identity and the American melting pot. Write an essay using Hoagland as a model of fairness and intensity.

2. Like Michael J. Arlen in ''The Cold, Bright Charms of Immortality'' (pages 272–281), Hoagland is concerned with contemporary attitudes toward one of the irreducible human problems. Both take a critical look at the way mass culture addresses fundamental questions, like life against death or women and men. If you sympathize sufficiently with Hoagland's view of the sexes, apply his doubts about the current state of things to Arlen's special beat — television. Take a sample of television's attitudes towards the divisions between men and women. Catalog your findings, as Arlen does, and write an essay on television's contributions to the debate about women's liberation.

BOOKS AVAILABLE IN PAPERBACK

African Calliope: A Journey to the Sudan. New York: Penguin. *Nonfiction: Personal history.*

The Edward Hoagland Reader. Edited and with an introduction by Geoffrey Wolff. New York: Vintage. *Essays.*

Notes from the Century Before: A Journal from British Columbia. San Francisco: North Point Press. *Nonfiction: Personal history.*

Red Wolves and Black Bears. New York: Penguin. *Essays.*

The Tugman's Passage. New York: Penguin. *Novel.*

DIANE
JOHNSON

D IANE JOHNSON (b. 1934) took her B.A. at the University of Utah and her
Ph.D. at the University of California at Los Angeles. She now lives in Berkeley, teaches at the University of California at Davis, and writes novels, biographies,
and essays. The latest of her five novels are The Shadow Knows (1974) and Lying
Low (1978), and she recently published a biography of mystery writer Dashiell
Hammett. Her essays, mostly book reviews enlarged by generality, appear in the
New York Review of Books *and the* New York Times Book Review. *"Rape"*
comes from her essay collection Terrorists and Novelists (1982), a title that expresses not only Diane Johnson's range but also her desire to connect extremes of social reality and the printed page.

Johnson's prose, as in "Rape," creates reasonable discourse about subjects to
which reason is seldom applied. Sometimes we belittle the word intellectual, assuming that intellect is useful in evading or denying the emotional facts of life. Sometimes
we are right. But Johnson's intellect does its proper task, in a lucid progress of good
sentences that sort unpleasant matters into discernible units, subject to the clarification of mind.

Rape

No other subject, it seems, is regarded so differently by men and women 1
as rape. Women deeply dread and resent it to an extent that men apparently
cannot recognize; it is perhaps the ultimate and essential complaint that
women have to make against men. Of course men may recognize that it is
wrong to use physical force against another person, and that rape laws are
not prosecuted fairly and so on, but at a certain point they are apt to say,
"But what was she doing there at that hour anyway?" or "Luckily he didn't
really hurt her," and serious discussion ceases.

Women sense — indeed, are carefully taught to feel — that the institution 2
of rape is mysteriously protected by an armor of folklore, Bible tales, legal
precedents, specious psychological theories. Most of all it seems protected
by a rooted and implacable male belief that women want to be raped —
which most women, conscientiously examining their motives, maintain they
do not — or deserve to be raped, for violation of certain customs governing
dress or behavior, a strange proposition to which women are more likely to
accede.

While women can all imagine themselves as rape victims, most men 3
know they are not rapists. So incidents that would be resented on personal
grounds if happening to their "own" women do not have even the intrinsic
interest for them of arguments on principle against military intervention in
the political destiny of foreign nations, as in Vietnam, where the "rape" of
that country was referred to in the peace movement and meant defoliation
of crops. But unlike the interest in the political destiny of Vietnam, which
greatly diminished when the danger to American males, via the draft, was
eliminated, rape is an abiding concern to women.

Even if they don't think about it very much, most have incorporated into 4
their lives routine precautions along lines prescribed by the general culture.
From a woman's earliest days she is attended by injunctions about strangers, and warnings about dark streets, locks, escorts, and provocative behavior. She internalizes the lessons contained therein, that to break certain
rules is to invite or deserve rape. Her fears, if not entirely conscious, are at
least readily accessible, and are continually activated by a vast body of exemplary literature, both traditional and in the daily paper. To test this, ask
yourself, if you are a woman, or ask any woman what she knows about
Richard Speck, the Boston Strangler, and "that thing that happened over on
_____ Street last week," and you will find that she has considerable rape literature by heart.

It seems important, in attempting to assess the value or seriousness of 5
Susan Brownmiller's polemic on rape (*Against Our Will*), to understand that
there are really two audiences for it, one that will know much of what she

has to say already, and another that is ill-equipped by training or sympathy to understand it at all. This likely accounts for a certain unevenness of tone, veering from indignation to the composed deployment of statistics in the manner of a public debater. It is not surprising that women began in the past few years by addressing their complaints abut rape to one another, not to men, and one infers that the subject is still thought to be of concern only to women. It remains to be seen what if any rhetorical strategies will prove to be of value in enlisting the concern of men.

That rape is aggressive, hostile, and intended to exact female submission, and that it is the extreme expression of underlying shared masculine attitudes, is, I think, most women's intuition of the subject, even women who have not been raped but who have tacitly accepted that this is how men are. Women who have in fact been raped (more than 255,000 each year) are certain of it after the indifference, disbelief, and brutality of police, doctors, judges, jurors, and their own families. That the actual rapists, making examples of a few women, in effect frighten and control all women seems obvious, even inarguable.

What is left to be explained, though neither Brownmiller nor Jean Mac-Kellar, in another recent book on rape (*Rape: The Bait and the Trap*), can satisfactorily explain it, is what this primal drama of domination and punishment is about, exactly. Both books communicate an impression of an escalating conflict, with the increasing collective force of female anger and indignation about rape not only effecting some changes in judiciary and police procedures, and even, perhaps, in popular attitudes, but also effecting an increase in anxiety about the subject, exemplified by the obligatory rape scenes in current movies and best sellers. Perhaps it is even female anger that is effecting an increase in rape itself, as if, whatever is at stake in this ancient hostility, it is now the rapist who has his back to the wall.

It is not too extreme to say that Brownmiller's book is exceedingly distressing, partly because it is exceedingly discouraging; it is a history of the failure of legal schemes and social sciences to improve society, at least society as viewed from a female perspective; it is the history of the failure of the social sciences even to address themselves to the peculiar mystery of male aggression toward those weaker than themselves. This failure seems in turn to demonstrate the powerlessness of human institutions before the force of patently untrue and sinister myths, whose ability to reflect, but also to determine, human behavior seems invincible. The disobedient Eve, the compliant Leda,° the lying wife of Potiphar° are still the keys to popular assumptions about women.

Leda Impregnated by Zeus, who came to her in the form of a swan.

Wife of Potiphar In Genesis, wife of a wealthy Egyptian. She tries to seduce Joseph and, when she fails, accuses him of trying to seduce her.

But Brownmiller's book is also distressing in another way that wicked   9
myths and scary stories are distressing, that is, because they are meant to
be. Here in one handy volume is every admonitory rape story you were ever
told, horrifying in the way that propaganda is horrifying and also titillating
just in the way that publishers hope a book will be titillating. Brownmiller is
trapped in the fallacy of imitative form, and by the duplicitous powers of literature itself to contain within it its own contradictions, so that the exemplary anecdotes from Red Riding Hood to Kitty Genovese to the Tralala
scene in *Last Exit to Brooklyn* must appeal at some level to the instincts they
illustrate and deprecate. The book may be criticized for an emotional tone
that is apparently impossible to exclude from an effective work on a subject
so inaccessible to rational analysis. Because rape is an important topic of a
potentially sensational and prurient nature, it is too bad that the book is not
a model of surpassing tact and delicacy, unassailable learning and scientific
methodology. Instead it is probably the book that was needed on this subject at this time, and may in fact succeed where reticence has failed to legiti-
mate the fundamental grievance of women against men.

Much of the book is devoted to an attempt to locate in history the reasons   10
for rape, but inquiry here is fruitless because though history turns up evidence, it offers little explanation. One learns merely that rape has been with
us from earliest times, that it is associated variously with military policy,
with ideas of property and possession (to rape someone's wife was interpreted as the theft of something from him), with interracial struggles and
complicated tribal and class polarities of all kinds (masters and slaves, cowboys and Indians), with intrasexual power struggles, as in the rape of young
or weak men in prison by gangs of stronger ones, and within families, by
male relatives of young girls or children.

None of these patterns is, except in one respect, wholly consistent with   11
the others, but viewed together they induce a kind of dispirited resignation
to natural law, from which are derived the supposed constants of human nature, maybe including rape. The respect in which violations of conquered
women in Bangladash and of Indian (or white) women in pioneer America,
or of men in prison, are alike is that they all dramatize some authority conflict. In war between groups of males, women are incidental victims and
prizes, but in the back of the car the dispute arises between a man and a
woman on her own behalf. The point at issue seems to be ''maistrye,'' as the
Wife of Bath° knew; and the deepest lessons of our culture have inculcated
in both sexes the idea that he is going to prevail. This in turn ensures that he
usually does, but the central question of why it is necessary to have male
mastery remains unanswered, and perhaps unasked. Meantime, the lesson

---

Wife of Bath   A bawdy character in Chaucer's *Canterbury Tales.*

of history seems to elevate the right of the male to exact obedience and inflict punishment to the status of immutable law.

Anthropology seems to support this, too, despite Brownmiller's attempts to find a primitive tribe (the obligingly rape-free Arapesh) to prove otherwise. Rather inconsistently, she conjectures that the origin of monogamy lies in the female's primordial fear of rape and consequent willingness to attach herself to some male as his exclusive property. If this is so, it would be the only instance in which the female will has succeeded in dictating social arrangements. In any case, alternate and better hypotheses exist for the origin of the family, generally that it developed for the protection of the young. The insouciance of Brownmiller's generalizations invites cavil and risks discrediting her book, and with it her subject. Granting that a primitive tribe can be found to illustrate any social model whatever, one would like to know just what all the anthropological evidence about rape is. If rape is the primordial norm; if, as Lévi-Strauss° says, women were the first currency; if male humans in a state of nature run mad raping, unlike chimpanzees, who we are told do not, is rape in fact aberrant? Perhaps it is only abhorrent.

It seems evident that whatever the facts of our nature, it is our culture that leads women in some degree to collaborate in their own rape, an aspect of the matter that men seem determined to claim absolves *them* from responsibility. Perhaps this is implicit in the assumptions about male power they are heir to. But every woman also inherits assumptions about female submission. In even the simplest fairy tale, the vaguely sexual content of the punishment needs no elaboration: every woman darkly knows what really happened to Red Riding Hood in the woods — and to Grandmother, too, for that matter. Most women do not go into the woods alone, but the main point is that the form of the prohibition as it is expressed in most stories is not "Do not go into the woods lest you be raped," but "Obey me by not going into the woods or you *will* be raped."

Thus the idea of sexual punishment for disobedience is learned very early, and is accepted. Who has done this to you, Desdemona?° "Nobody; I myself; farewell," says Desdemona meekly as she dies. Everyone feels that Carmen,° that prick-tease, is "getting what she deserves," poor Lucrece's° suicide is felt to be both noble and tactful, maybe Anna Karenina's° too. So if

---

Lévi-Strauss   Claude Lévi-Strauss (b. 1908), French anthropologist.

Desdemona   In Shakespeare's play *Othello*, wife of the title character. She is murdered by him when he mistakenly believes that she was unfaithful to him.

Carmen   In the French tale and the opera by George Bizet, Carmen is a seductive Spanish gypsy who is stabbed by her jilted lover.

Lucrece   In Roman legend, Lucrece stabs herself after telling her father and husband that she has been raped.

Anna Karenina   Anna Karenina, in Tolsoy's novel, commits adultery.

a woman is raped, she feels, besides outrage, deep guilt and a need to find out what she has done "wrong" to account for it, even if her sin is only one of omission; for example, concerned citizens in Palo Alto were told a few days ago that "Sometimes women are raped because of carelessness."

To the extent that a woman can convince a jury that she was neither care- 15
less nor seductive, her attacker may be found guilty and she may be absolved from guilt, but more often in rape trials something is found in her behavior to "account" for her fate. The point is that whatever the circumstances of a rape, social attitudes and legal processes at the present time make the victim guilty of her own rape. Even the most innocent victim is likely to be told by her mother, "I told you never to walk home alone," and this is sometimes the attitude of an entire population, as in Bangladesh, where thousands of raped wives were repudiated by their husbands.

The unfortunate rape victim is in some ways worse off the more "femi- 16
nine," the better socialized, she is, for she will have accepted normal social strictures: do not play rough, do not make noise or hit. Then she will be judged at the trial of her attacker on the extent to which she has struggled, hit, bitten (though she would not be expected to resist an armed robber). Not to struggle is to appear to want to be raped. In the courtroom men pretend not to understand the extent to which cultural inhibitions prevent women from resisting male force, even moral force, though in the parking lot they seem to understand it very well.

In the practical world, who are the rapists, who are the raped, what is to 17
be done? It is here that Brownmiller's account is most interesting and most disturbing. Both Brownmiller and MacKellar agree on the statistical particulars: the rape victim is most likely a teen-aged black girl but she may be a woman of any age, and she will know her attacker to some extent in about half of the cases. The rapist is the same sort of person as other violent offenders: young, uneducated, unemployed, likely black or from another deprived subculture; the rapist is *not* the shy, hard-up loner living with his mother, victim of odd obsessions; a quarter of all rapes are done in gangs or pairs.

The sociology of rapists has some difficult political implications, as 18
Brownmiller, to judge from the care with which she approaches it, is well aware. She traces the complicated history of American liberalism and Southern racism which has led to the present pass, in which people who have traditionally fought for human freedom seem committed to obstructing freedom for women. Historically, she reminds us, the old left, and the Communist Party in particular,

> understood rape as a political act of subjugation only when the
> victim was black and the offender was white. White-on-white
> rape was merely "criminal" and had no part in their Marxist

canon. Black-on-black rape was ignored. And black-on-white rape, about which the rest of the country was phobic, was discussed in the oddly reversed world of the Jefferson School as if it never existed except as a spurious charge that "the state" employed to persecute black men.

Meantime, circumstances have changed; folk bigotry, like folk wisdom, turns out to contain a half-truth, or grain of prescience; and the black man has taken to raping. Now

> the incidence of actual rape combined with the looming spectre of the black man as rapist to which the black man in the name of his manhood now contributes, must be understood as a control mechanism against the freedom, mobility and aspirations of all women, white and black. The crossroads of racism and sexism had to be a violent meeting place. There is no use pretending it doesn't exist.

It is at this crossroads that the problem appears most complex and most insoluble. Not only rapists, but also people more suavely disguised as right-thinking, like the ACLU and others associated with the civil-rights movement, still feel that protection of black men's rights is more important than injustice to women, whether white or black. Black men and white women are in effect pitted against one another in such a way as to impede the progress of both groups, and in particular to conceal and perpetuate the specific victimization of black women. Various studies report that blacks do up to 90 percent of rapes, and their victims are 80 to 90 percent black women, who now must endure from men of their own race what they historically had to endure from whites. A black girl from the ages of ten to fifteen is twelve times more likely than others to be a victim of this crime.

In this situation, which will win in the long run, sexism or racism? Who are the natural antagonists? It seems likely, on the evidence, that sexism, being older, will prevail.

The MacKellar/Amir book, a short, practical manual about rape, something to be used perhaps by jurors or counselors, gives a picture of the crime and of the rapist which is essentially the same as Brownmiller's. But MacKellar's advice, when compared with Brownmiller's, is seen to be overlaid by a kind of naive social optimism. What can women do? They can avoid hitch-hiking; they can be better in bed: "if women were less inhibited with their men the sense of depravity that their prudishness inspires might be reduced," as if it were frustrated middle-class husbands who were out raping; authorities can search out those "many youngsters warped by a brutish home life [who] can still be recuperated for a reasonably good adult life if given therapy in time"; "Education. Education helps to reduce rape."

Maybe. But does any evidence exist to suggest that any of this would really help? Brownmiller has found none, but I suppose she would agree with

MacKellar that for America's violent subcultures we must employ "the classical remedies of assimilating the people in these subcultures, economically and socially, in opportunities for education, jobs, and decent housing," and change the fundamental values of American society. "As long as aggressive, exploitive behavior remains the norm, it can be expected that individuals will make these errors and that the weaker members of society will be the victim."

Until aggressive, exploitive behavior is not the norm, a few practical 23
measures are being suggested. The LEAA study, MacKellar, and Brownmiller are all in favor of prosecuting rape cases and of punishing rapists. Brownmiller feels the punishment should suit the crime, that it should be made similar to penalties for aggravated assault, which it resembles. MacKellar feels that the penalty should fit the criminal: "a nineteen-year-old unemployed black with a fourth-grade education and no father, whose uptight, superreligious mother has, after a quarrel, kicked him out of the home, should not be judged by the same standard nor receive the same kind of sentence as a white middle-aged used-car salesman, twice divorced, who rapes a girl he picks up at a newsstand during an out-of-town convention." She does not, by the way, say who should get the stiffer sentence, and I can think of arguments either way.

Both agree that corroboration requirements and courtroom questions 24
about a victim's prior sexual history should be eliminated, and in this the government-sponsored study for the Law Enforcement Assistance Administration (*Rape and Its Victims*) also agrees. At present the established view holds that whether or not a raped girl is a virgin or is promiscuous is germane to the issue of whether a forced act of sexual intercourse has occurred in a given case. This reflects the ancient idea that by violating male standards of female chastity, a woman forfeits her right to say no.

The LEAA study found that prosecutors' offices in general were doing 25
little to urge the revision of outdated legal codes, and that the legal system is in fact impeding reform. It observes (in a nice trenchant style that makes better reading than most government reports) that

> since rapists have no lobby, the major opposition to reform
> measures can be expected from public defenders, the defense
> bar in general, and groups, such as the American Civil Liber-
> ties Union, that are vigilant with respect to the rights of crimi-
> nal defendants.

The conclusion one cannot help coming to is that whatever is to be done 26
about rape will have to be done by women primarily. Brownmiller feels that law enforcement must include 50 percent women. She finds it significant that whereas male law-enforcement authorities report 15 or 20 percent of rape complaints to be "unfounded," among the ones they actually bother to write down, women investigators find only 2 percent of such reports to be

unfounded, exactly the number of unfounded reports of other violent crimes. Apparently the goal of male-female law enforcement is not without its difficulties; women police officers in Washington, D.C., recently have complained that their male patrol-car partners are attempting to force them to have sexual intercourse. Since these women are armed with service revolvers, we may soon see an escalation of what appears to be the Oldest Conflict.

MacKellar and the LEAA report both favor some sort of rape sentencing by degree, as in murder, with rape by a stranger constituting first-degree rape, and third degree taking cognizance of situations in which the victim may be judged to have shared responsibility for initiating the situation that led to the rape — for instance, hitchhiking. This is a compromise that would be unacceptable to feminist groups who feel that a woman is no more responsible for a rape under those circumstances than a man would be thought to be who was assaulted in the same situation.

It is likely that the concept of penalty by degree, with its concession to history, will prevail here, but one sees the objection on principle. While men continue to believe that men have a right to assert their authority over women by sexual and other means, rape will continue, and this in turn suggests two more measures. One is control of pornography, which Brownmiller argues is the means by which the rape ethic is promulgated. In spite of objections about censorship and about the lack of evidence that pornography and violence are related, Brownmiller's argument here is a serious one. She also feels that women should learn self-defense, if only to give them increased self-confidence and awareness of their bodies. But it is easy to see that this is yet another way in which the female might be made to take responsibility for being raped. If a woman learns karate and is raped anyway, the question will become, why hadn't she learned it better?

Surely the definition of civilization is a state of things where the strong refrain from exercising their advantages over the weak. If men can be made to see that the abolition of sexual force is necessary in the long-term interest of making a civilization, then they may cooperate in implementing whatever measures turn out to be of any use. For the short term, one imagines, the general effect of female activism about rape will be to polarize men and women even more than nature has required. The cooperation of state authorities, if any, may ensue from their perception of rape, especially black-on-white rape, as a challenge to white male authority (as in the South). This in turn may produce an unlikely and ominous coalition of cops and feminists, and the generally severer prosecution and sentencing which we see as the current response to other forms of violent crime. But do we know that rapists will emerge from the prisons — themselves centers of homosexual rape — any less inclined to do it again?

Meantime, one feels a certain distaste for the congratulatory mood sur- 30
rounding proposed law-enforcement reforms devoted entirely to making
the crime less miserable for the victim while denying or concealing the complicity of so many men in its perpetuation. This implies a state of things worthy of a society described by Swift.°

QUESTIONS ON MEANING

1. "Rape" is a book review as well as an essay in its own right. What are Johnson's opinions about the books she reviews? What is her larger argument
   about rape? How does her attitude toward the books relate to her larger argument? How does she use the books to make her own points?
2. As Johnson asserts, rape is a universal phenomenon. But consider the facts
   presented in paragraphs 17–20. Does Johnson explain how or why "the extreme expression of underlying shared masculine attitudes" has become restricted almost exclusively to blacks? How does her conclusion in paragraph
   20 relate to this problem?
3. Diane Johnson writes about rape as a "primal drama," an "ancient hostility." What perspective is implied by these terms? Is this perspective shared
   to any degree by the writers whose books Johnson discusses?

QUESTIONS ON STRATEGY

1. Aside from the books under review, Johnson quotes, paraphrases, and generalizes about a number of divergent views about rape. Do any of them represent her own views? How does Johnson indicate her detachment from
   many of these views? Why does she include prejudices, false assumptions,
   and other doubtful statements?

EXPLORATIONS

1. In paragraph 13 Johnson argues that "our culture . . . leads women in some
   degree to collaborate in their own rape." Her example is the fairy tale "Little
   Red Riding Hood." Think about the fairy tale. Was Red Riding Hood told
   not to go into the woods alone? Who rescued her? From whom? Look up the
   Grimm version of the story, titled in some translations "Little Red-Cap."
   Does it seem to be a rape allegory? How might it lead women to collaborate
   in their own rape?

Swift   Jonathan Swift (1667–1745), English author best known for *Gulliver's Travels*,
which satirically depicted the political and social structure of the day.

WRITING TOPICS

1. In *Endless Rapture: Rape, Romance, and the Female Imagination* (1983), Helen Hazen writes:

> We have no evidence to prove or disprove that women want to be raped. We do have reports of individual attitudes. Most women state that they do not want to be raped, and it is probably safe to accept their word at face value. But the world of the imagination is a different matter, and there is plentiful evidence that both rape and a broader spectrum of seemingly unpleasant impositions are forced onto women by themselves for the sheer sake of enjoyment. This imposition occurs regularly in both the simplest and most sophisticated of women's fiction, and I believe that there are logical explanations for it that have nothing to do with a pathological society. Rather, the explanation is that a rape fantasy is quite healthy.

Hazen's primary subject is the romance genre of fiction. Her main point is that the plots of these immensely popular books primarily provide a healthy rape fantasy. Write an essay supporting or refuting Hazen's point.

BOOKS AVAILABLE IN PAPERBACK

Lying Low. New York: Vintage. *Novel.*

The Shadow Knows. New York: Vintage. *Novel.*

WENDELL
BERRY

WENDELL BERRY (b. 1934) was born and attended college in Kentucky, then taught in New York and California for several years before returning for good to his native soil. Over many years he farmed and wrote while he commuted to teach at the University of Kentucky. In 1977 he quit his professorship to devote himself entirely to writing and farming.

Berry has published eight books of poetry, the latest The Wheel (1982). He has written three novels, of which A Place on Earth (1967) was revised and reissued in 1983. Many readers who admire his poems and novels find his essays the best of his writing. North Point Press recently issued and re-issued many volumes by Berry, including the books listed above and Recollected Essays, 1965–1980 (1981), from which we take "The Making of a Marginal Farm." This book includes selections from his Sierra Club book The Unsettling of America (1977) and four earlier essay collections. In 1981 Berry also published a book of shorter pieces about agriculture, The Gift of Good Land, and in 1983 his essays on language and literature, Standing by Words.

To his essays, like "The Making of a Marginal Farm," Berry brings the images of a lyric poet and the narrative line of a novelist. Reading him we feel his attachment *to land, we see the landscape he sees, we feel the Kentucky wind; we are caught up in the desire that thrust him into years of farm work. At the same time we become aware of ideas, values attached to particulars and deriving from them, that form a system of beliefs both general and widely applicable.*

The Making
of a Marginal Farm

One day in the summer of 1956, leaving home for school, I stopped on the side of the road directly above the house where I now live. From there you could see a mile or so across the Kentucky River Valley, and perhaps six miles along the length of it. The valley was a green trough full of sunlight, blue in its distances. I often stopped here in my comings and goings, just to look, for it was all familiar to me from before the time my memory began: woodlands and pastures on the hillsides; fields and croplands, wooded slew-edges and hollows in the bottoms; and through the midst of it the tree-lined river passing down from its headwaters near the Virginia line toward its mouth at Carrollton on the Ohio.

Standing there, I was looking at land where one of my great-great-great-grandfathers settled in 1803, and at the scene of some of the happiest times of my own life, where in my growing-up years I camped, hunted, fished, boated, swam, and wandered — where, in short, I did whatever escaping I felt called upon to do. It was a place where I had happily been, and where I always wanted to be. And I remember gesturing toward the valley that day and saying to the friend who was with me: "That's all I need."

I meant it. It was an honest enough response to my recognition of its beauty, the abundance of its lives and possibilities, and of my own love for it and interest in it. And in the sense that I continue to recognize all that, and feel that what I most need is here, I can still say the same thing.

And yet I am aware that I must necessarily mean differently — or at least a great deal more — when I say it now. Then I was speaking mostly from affection, and did not know, by half, what I was talking about. I was speaking of a place that in some ways I knew and in some ways cared for, but did not live in. The differences between knowing a place and living in it, between cherishing a place and living responsibly in it, had not begun to occur to me. But they are critical differences, and understanding them has been perhaps the chief necessity of my experience since then.

I married in the following summer, and in the next seven years lived in a 5
number of distant places. But, largely because I continued to feel that what I
needed was here, I could never bring myself to want to live in any other
place. And so we returned to live in Kentucky in the summer of 1964, and
that autumn bought the house whose roof my friend and I had looked down
on eight years before, and with it "twelve acres more or less." Thus I began
a profound change in my life. Before, I had lived according to expectation
rooted in ambition. Now I began to live according to a kind of destiny rooted
in my origins and in my life. One should not speak too confidently of one's
"destiny"; I use the word to refer to causes that lie deeper in history and
character than mere intention or desire. In buying the little place known as
Lanes Landing, it seems to me, I began to obey the deeper causes.

We had returned so that I could take a job at the University of Kentucky 6
in Lexington. And we expected to live pretty much the usual academic life: I
would teach and write; my "subject matter" would be, as it had been, the
few square miles in Henry County where I grew up. We bought the tiny
farm at Lanes Landing, thinking that we would use it as a "summer place,"
and on that understanding I began, with the help of two carpenter friends,
to make some necessary repairs on the house. I no longer remember exactly
how it was decided, but that work had hardly begun when it became a full-
scale overhaul.

By so little our minds had been changed: this was not going to be a house 7
to visit, but a house to live in. It was as though, having put our hand to the
plow, we not only did not look back, but could not. We renewed the old
house, equipped it with plumbing, bathroom, and oil furnace, and moved in
on July 4, 1965.

Once the house was whole again, we came under the influence of the 8
"twelve acres more or less." This acreage included a steep hillside pasture,
two small pastures by the river, and a "garden spot" of less than half an
acre. We had, besides the house, a small barn in bad shape, a good large
building that once had been a general store, and a small garage also in usable
condition. This was hardly a farm by modern standards, but it was land that
could be used, and it was unthinkable that we would not use it. The land
was not good enough to afford the possibility of a cash income, but it would
allow us to grow our food — or most of it. And that is what we set out to do.

In the early spring of 1965 I had planted a small orchard; the next spring 9
we planted our first garden. Within the following six or seven years we reclaimed the pastures, converted the garage into a henhouse, rebuilt the
barn, greatly improved the garden soil, planted berry bushes, acquired a
milk cow — and were producing, except for hay and grain for our animals,
nearly everything that we ate: fruit, vegetables, eggs, meat, milk, cream,
and butter. We built an outbuilding with a meat room and a food-storage
cellar. Because we did not want to pollute our land and water with sewage,

and in the process waste nutrients that should be returned to the soil, we built a composting privy. And so we began to attempt a life that, in addition to whatever else it was, would be responsibly agricultural. We used no chemical fertilizers. Except for a little rotenone, we used no insecticides. As our land and our food became healthier, so did we. And our food was of better quality than any that we could have bought.

We were not, of course, living an idyll. What we had done could not have been accomplished without difficulty and a great deal of work. And we had made some mistakes and false starts. But there was great satisfaction, too, in restoring the neglected land, and in feeding ourselves from it.

Meanwhile, the forty-acre place adjoining ours on the downriver side had been sold to a "developer," who planned to divide it into lots for "second homes." This project was probably doomed by the steepness of the ground and the difficulty of access, but a lot of bulldozing — and a lot of damage — was done before it was given up. In the fall of 1972, the place was offered for sale and we were able to buy it.

We now began to deal with larger agricultural problems. Some of this new land was usable; some would have to be left in trees. There were perhaps fifteen acres of hillside that could be reclaimed for pasture, and about two and a half acres of excellent bottomland on which we would grow alfalfa for hay. But it was a mess, all of it badly neglected, and a considerable portion of it badly abused by the developer's bulldozers. The hillsides were covered with thicket growth; the bottom was shoulder high in weeds; the diversion ditches had to be restored; a bulldozed gash meant for "building sites" had to be mended; the barn needed a new foundation, and the cistern a new top; there were no fences. What we had bought was less a farm than a reclamation project — which has now, with a later purchase, grown to seventy-five acres.

While we had only the small place, I had got along very well with a Gravely "walking tractor" that I owned, and an old Farmall A that I occasionally borrowed from my Uncle Jimmy. But now that we had increased our acreage, it was clear that I could not continue to depend on a borrowed tractor. For a while I assumed that I would buy a tractor of my own. But because our land was steep, and there was already talk of a fuel shortage — and because I liked the idea — I finally decided to buy a team of horses instead. By the spring of 1973, after a lot of inquiring and looking, I had found and bought a team of five-year-old sorrel mares. And — again by the generosity of my Uncle Jimmy, who has never thrown any good thing away — I had enough equipment to make a start.

Though I had worked horses and mules during the time I was growing up, I had never worked over ground so steep and problematical as this, and it had been twenty years since I had worked a team over ground of any kind.

Getting started again, I anticipated every new task with uneasiness, and sometimes with dread. But to my relief and delight, the team and I did all that needed to be done that year, getting better as we went along. And over the years since then, with that team and others, my son and I have carried on our farming the way it was carried on in my boyhood, doing everything with our horses except baling the hay. And we have done work in places and in weather in which a tractor would have been useless. Experience has shown us — or re-shown us — that horses are not only a satisfactory and economical means of power, especially on such small places as ours, but are probably *necessary* to the most conservative use of steep land. Our farm, in fact, is surrounded by potentially excellent hillsides that were maintained in pasture until tractors replaced the teams.

Another change in our economy (and our lives) was accomplished in the 15 fall of 1973 with the purchase of our first wood-burning stove. Again the petroleum shortage was on our minds, but we also knew that from the pasture-clearing we had ahead of us we would have an abundance of wood that otherwise would go to waste — and when that was gone we would still have our permanent wood lots. We thus expanded our subsistence income to include heating fuel, and since then have used our furnace only as a "backup system" in the coldest weather and in our absences from home. The horses also contribute significantly to the work of fuel-gathering; they will go easily into difficult places and over soft ground or snow where a truck or a tractor could not move.

As we have continued to live on and from our place, we have slowly be- 16 gun its restoration and healing. Most of the scars have now been mended and grassed over, most of the washes stopped, most of the buildings made sound; many loads of rocks have been hauled out of the fields and used to pave entrances or fill hollows; we have done perhaps half of the necessary fencing. A great deal of work is still left to do, and some of it — the rebuilding of fertility in the depleted hillsides — will take longer than we will live. But in doing these things we have begun a restoration and a healing in ourselves.

I should say plainly that this has not been a "paying proposition." As a 17 reclamation project, it has been costly both in money and in effort. It seems at least possible that, in any other place, I might have had little interest in doing any such thing. The reason I have been interested in doing it here, I think, is that I have felt implicated in the history, the uses, and the attitudes that have depleted such places as ours and made them "marginal."

I had not worked long on our "twelve acres more or less" before I saw 18 that such places were explained almost as much by their human history as by their nature. I saw that they were not "marginal" because they ever were unfit for human use, but because in both culture and character *we* had been unfit to use them. Originally, even such steep slopes as these along the lower Kentucky River Valley were deep-soiled and abundantly fertile; "jumper" plows and generations of carelessness impoverished them. Where yellow clay is at the surface now, five feet of good soil may be gone. I once wrote that on some of the nearby uplands one walks as if "knee-deep" in the absence of the original soil. On these steeper slopes, I now know, that absence is shoulder-deep.

That is a loss that is horrifying as soon as it is imagined. It happened easily, by ignorance, indifference, "a little folding of the hands to sleep." It cannot be remedied in human time; to build five feet of soil takes perhaps fifty or sixty thousand years. This loss, once imagined, is potent with despair. If a people in adding a hundred and fifty years to itself subtracts fifty thousand from its land, what is there to hope?

And so our reclamation project has been, for me, less a matter of idealism or morality than a kind of self-preservation. A destructive history, once it is understood as such, is a nearly insupportable burden. Understanding it is a disease of understanding, depleting the sense of efficacy and paralyzing effort, unless it finds healing work. For me that work has been partly of the mind, in what I have written, but that seems to have depended inescapably on work of the body and of the ground. In order to affirm the values most native and necessary to me — indeed, to affirm my own life as a thing decent in possibility — I needed to know in my own experience that this place did not have to be abused in the past, and that it can be kindly and conservingly used now.

With certain reservations that must be strictly borne in mind, our work here has begun to offer some of the needed proofs.

Bountiful as the vanished original soil of the hillsides may have been, what remains is good. It responds well — sometimes astonishingly well — to good treatment. It never should have been plowed (some of it never should have been cleared), and it never should be plowed again. But it can be put in pasture without plowing, and it will support an excellent grass sod that will in turn protect it from erosion, if properly managed and not overgrazed.

Land so steep as this cannot be preserved in row crop cultivation. To subject it to such an expectation is simply to ruin it, as its history shows. Our rule, generally, has been to plow no steep ground, to maintain in pasture only such slopes as can be safely mowed with a horse-drawn mower, and to leave the rest in trees. We have increased the numbers of livestock on our pastures gradually, and have carefully rotated the animals from field to field, in order to avoid overgrazing. Under this use and care, our hillsides have mended and they produce more and better pasturage every year.

As a child I always intended to be a farmer. As a young man, I gave up that intention, assuming that I could not farm and do the other things I wanted to do. And then I became a farmer almost unintentionally and by a kind of necessity. That wayward and necessary becoming — along with my marriage, which has been intimately a part of it — is the major event of my life. It has changed me profoundly from the man and the writer I would otherwise have been.

There was a time, after I had left home and before I came back, when this 25 place was my "subject matter." I meant that too, I think, on the day in 1956 when I told my friend, "That's all I need." I was regarding it, in a way too easy for a writer, as a mirror in which I saw myself. There was obviously a sort of narcissism in that — and an inevitable superficiality, for only the surface can reflect.

In coming home and settling on this place, I began to *live* in my subject, 26 and to learn that living in one's subject is not at all the same as "having" a subject. To live in the place that is one's subject is to pass through the surface. The simplifications of distance and mere observation are thus destroyed. The obsessively regarded reflection is broken and dissolved. One sees that the mirror was a blinder; one can now begin to see where one is. One's relation to one's subject ceases to be merely emotional or esthetical, or even merely critical, and becomes problematical, practical, and responsible as well. Because it must. It is like marrying your sweetheart.

Though our farm has not been an economic success, as such success is 27 usually reckoned, it is nevertheless beginning to make a kind of economic sense that is consoling and hopeful. Now that the largest expenses of purchase and repair are behind us, our income from the place is beginning to run ahead of expenses. As income I am counting the value of shelter, subsistence, heating fuel, and money earned by the sale of livestock. As expenses I am counting maintenance, newly purchased equipment, extra livestock feed, newly purchased animals, reclamation work, fencing materials, taxes, and insurance.

If our land had been in better shape when we bought it, our expenses 28 would obviously be much smaller. As it is, once we have completed its restoration, our farm will provide us a home, produce our subsistence, keep us warm in winter, and earn a modest cash income. The significance of this becomes apparent when one considers that most of this land is "unfarmable" by the standards of conventional agriculture, and that most of it was producing nothing at the time we bought it.

And so, contrary to some people's opinion, it *is* possible for a family to 29 live on such "marginal" land, to take a bountiful subsistence and some cash income from it, and, in doing so, to improve both the land and themselves. (I believe, however, that, at least in the present economy, this should not be attempted without a source of income other than the farm. It is now extremely difficult to pay for the best of farmland by farming it, and even "marginal" land has become unreasonably expensive. To attempt to make a living from such land is to impose a severe strain on land and people alike.)

I said earlier that the success of our work here is subject to reservations. There are only two of these, but both are serious.

The first is that land like ours — and there are many acres of such land in this country — can be conserved in use only by competent knowledge, by a great deal more work than is required by leveler land, by a devotion more particular and disciplined than patriotism, and by ceaseless watchfulness and care. All these are cultural values and resources, never sufficiently abundant in this country, and now almost obliterated by the contrary values of the so-called "affluent society."

One of my own mistakes will suggest the difficulty. In 1974 I dug a small pond on a wooded hillside that I wanted to pasture occasionally. The excavation for that pond — as I should have anticipated, for I had better reason than I used — caused the hillside to slump both above and below. After six years the slope has not stabilized, and more expense and trouble will be required to stabilize it. A small hillside farm will not survive many mistakes of that order. Nor will a modest income.

The true remedy for mistakes is to keep from making them. It is not in the piecemeal technological solutions that our society now offers, but in a change of cultural (and economic) values that will encourage in the whole population the necessary respect, restraint, and care. Even more important, it is in the possibility of settled families and local communities, in which the knowledge of proper means and methods, proper moderations and restraints, can be handed down, and so accumulate in place and stay alive; the experience of one generation is not adequate to inform and control its actions. Such possibilities are not now in sight in this country.

The second reservation is that we live at the lower end of the Kentucky River watershed, which has long been intensively used, and is increasingly abused. Strip mining, logging, extractive farming, and the digging, draining, roofing, and paving that go with industrial and urban "development," all have seriously depleted the capacity of the watershed to retain water. This means not only that floods are higher and more frequent than they would be if the watershed were healthy, but that the floods subside too quickly, the watershed being far less a sponge, now, than it is a roof. The floodwater drops suddenly out of the river, leaving the steep banks soggy, heavy, and soft. As a result, great strips and blocks of land crack loose and slump, or they give way entirely and disappear into the river in what people here call "slips."

The flood of December 1978, which was unusually high, also went down extremely fast, falling from banktop almost to pool stage within a couple of days. In the aftermath of this rapid "drawdown," we lost a block of bottomland an acre square. This slip, which is still crumbling, severely damaged our place, and may eventually undermine two buildings. The same flood started a slip in another place, which threatens a third building. We have yet another building situated on a huge (but, so far, very gradual) slide that starts at the river and, aggravated by two state highway cuts, goes almost to the hilltop. And we have serious river bank erosion the whole length of our place.

What this means is that, no matter how successfully we may control erosion on our hillsides, our land remains susceptible to a more serious cause of erosion that we cannot control. Our river bank stands literally at the cutting edge of our nation's consumptive economy. This, I think, is true of many "marginal" places — it is true, in fact, of many places that are not marginal. In its consciousness, ours is an upland society; the ruin of watersheds, and what that involves and means, is little considered. And so the land is heavily taxed to subsidize an "affluence" that consists, in reality, of health and goods stolen from the unborn. 36

Living at the lower end of the Kentucky River watershed is what is now known as "an educational experience" — and not an easy one. A lot of information comes with it that is severely damaging to the reputation of our people and our time. From where I live and work, I never have to look far to see that the earth does indeed pass away. But however that is taught, and however bitterly learned, it is something that should be known, and there is a certain good strength in knowing it. To spend one's life farming a piece of the earth so passing is, as many would say, a hard lot. But it is, in an ancient sense, the human lot. What saves it is to love the farming. 37

QUESTIONS ON MEANING

1. Berry says "I became a farmer almost unintentionally" but also says he had "always intended to be a farmer" (paragraph 24). How does that contrast relate to the contrast in paragraph 5 between "expectation rooted in ambition" and "destiny rooted in . . . origins"? How does Berry develop the contrasts? How do they help Berry account for his vocation as a farmer?
2. What is the "disease of understanding" Berry talks about in paragraph 20? He speaks of the "healing work" of farming in several contexts. In what different ways is farming healing?
3. What is the difference to Berry between "knowing a place and living in it" and between "living in one's subject" and " 'having' a subject"?
4. Berry tries to teach us something of what he has learned from living on the land. How do his strategies and objectives as a farmer on marginal soil tell us what he thinks of his native land in the broad sense — of America, its history and culture? In paragraph 9, Berry uses the word *responsibly*. To whom is he responsible? Can you discover an ethic of responsibility in this essay as a whole?

QUESTIONS ON STRATEGY

1. In paragraph 14, Berry uses the word *conservative*. How does he mean this word? What are its connotations?
2. Notice how Berry manages the tone of his prose voice in paragraphs 17–19. How does he build toward the climactic intensity of paragraph 19? Which of his words and phrases contribute to the mood of this sequence? How would you define or describe this mood?

EXPLORATIONS

1. Nature in the wild state is Edward Abbey's subject (pages 225–241). Nature under cultivation is Wendell Berry's. Yet both of their essays tell the same fundamental story of a man finding himself, and a place for himself, in a natural setting. This is an old story, in several senses, but it is typical of American literature. Abbey and Berry are among the heirs of Emerson and Thoreau, whose essays, also strongly autobiographical, explored similar moral and imaginative terrain. Read Emerson's "On Nature" and Thoreau's chapter "The Bean-Field" in *Walden* for background on Abbey and Berry. What seems new or different in the twentieth-century effort to "confront, immediately and directly if it's possible, the bare bones of existence, the elemental and fundamental, the bedrock which sustains us"?

WRITING TOPICS

1. Write an essay in which you define your own attitude toward the difficulty perceived by Berry and Abbey, and perhaps Walker Percy (pages 74–91), in coming to terms with the essentials of life in a highly developed culture. Do the constraints of contemporary society make certain experiences impossible? Do you think that the strategies of these writers are likely to restore possibilities for a closer understanding of and connection with nature?
2. One of Berry's tactics in "The Making of a Marginal Farm" is to establish in the first four paragraphs what he has learned as an adult about the things he believed as a youth. Write an essay on any subject using this approach as an introduction.

BOOKS AVAILABLE IN PAPERBACK

A Continuous Harmony: Essays Cultural and Agricultural. New York: Harcourt Brace Jovanovich, Harvest Books.

The Country of Marriage. New York: Harcourt Brace Jovanovich, Harvest Books. *Poems.*

Farming: A Hand Book. New York: Harcourt Brace Jovanovich, Harvest Books. *Poems.*

The Gift of Good Land: Further Essays Cultural and Agricultural. San Francisco: North Point Press.

The Memory of Old Jack. New York: Harcourt Brace Jovanovich, Harvest Books. *Novel.*

A Place on Earth. Rev. ed. San Francisco: North Point Press. *Novel.*

Recollected Essays, 1965–1980. San Francisco: North Point Press.

The Wheel. San Francisco: North Point Press. *Poems.*

JOAN
DIDION

*J*OAN DIDION *is a fifth-generation Californian, born in 1934 in Sacramento,*
who took her B.A. at Berkeley and lives in Los Angeles. Between college and mar-
riage to the writer John Gregory Dunne, she lived in New York for seven years,
where she worked as an editor for Vogue *and wrote essays for the* National Review
and the Saturday Evening Post. *In California, Didion and Dunne separately write*
novels and magazine articles and collaborate on screenplays. Didion's novels are Run
River *(1963),* Play It as It Lays *(1970), and* A Book of Common Prayer *(1977);*
her books of essays are Slouching Towards Bethlehem *(1968) and* The White Album *(1979). Her most recent publication is* Salvador *(1983), an essay deriving from*
a visit to Central America in 1982.

Joan Didion is one of our best nonfiction writers. She describes the alien, simple
California she grew up in and the southern California where she now lives — a land-
scape of drive-ins and orange groves, ocean and freeway, the Manson murders and
ordinary, domestic, adulterous homicide. She has done witness to the turmoils of the
decades, especially the sixties — drugs, Vietnam, and personal breakdown. Expertly
sensitive and inventive with language, she is most talented in the representation of
hysteria. While her book about El Salvador mentions politics, it is essentially the rec-
ord of a sensibility, sensitive to fear, exposed to an atmosphere that engenders it:
"Terror is the given of the place."

Much of Didion's journalism derives from interviews. She has written of herself: "My only advantage as a reporter is that I am so physically small, so temperamentally unobtrusive, and so neurotically inarticulate that people tend to forget that my presence runs counter to their best interests. And it always does. That is one last thing to remember: writers are always selling somebody out.*"*

"Some Dreamers of the Golden Dream" comes from Slouching Towards Bethlehem *and originally appeared in the* Saturday Evening Post *in 1966. It is a model of the essay as narrative, and if we did not know that Didion was a novelist we would suspect her of novelistic tendencies. Compounded of interviews and research, it reads like fiction and thus exemplifies the new journalism. Like the best novelists, however, Didion is not only an expert storyteller; by choosing and juxtaposing details, she judges as well as she reports. Although she is reticent in overt criticism of her subjects, her implicit moral vision remains devastating.*

Some Dreamers
of the Golden Dream

This is a story about love and death in the golden land, and begins with   1
the country. The San Bernardino Valley lies only an hour east of Los Angeles by the San Bernardino Freeway but is in certain ways an alien place: not the coastal California of the subtropical twilights and the soft westerlies off the Pacific but a harsher California, haunted by the Mojave just beyond the mountains, devastated by the hot dry Santa Ana wind that comes down through the passes at 100 miles an hour and whines through the eucalyptus windbreaks and works on the nerves. October is the bad month for the wind, the month when breathing is difficult and the hills blaze up spontaneously. There has been no rain since April. Every voice seems a scream. It is the season of suicide and divorce and prickly dread, wherever the wind blows.

The Mormons settled this ominous country, and then they abandoned it,   2
but by the time they left the first orange tree had been planted and for the next hundred years the San Bernardino Valley would draw a kind of people who imagined they might live among the talismanic fruit and prosper in the dry air, people who brought with them Midwestern ways of building and cooking and praying and who tried to graft those ways upon the land. The graft took in curious ways. This is the California where it is possible to live and die without ever eating an artichoke, without ever meeting a Catholic or a Jew. This is the California where it is easy to Dial-A-Devotion, but hard to buy a book. This is the country in which a belief in the literal interpreta-

tion of Genesis has slipped imperceptibly into a belief in the literal interpretation of *Double Indemnity*,° the country of the teased hair and the Capris and the girls for whom all life's promise comes down to a waltz-length white wedding dress and the birth of a Kimberly or a Sherry or a Debbi and a Tijuana divorce and a return to hairdressers' school. "We were just crazy kids," they say without regret, and look to the future. The future always looks good in the golden land, because no one remembers the past. Here is where the hot wind blows and the old ways do not seem relevant, where the divorce rate is double the national average and where one person in every thirty-eight lives in a trailer. Here is the last stop for all those who come from somewhere else, for all those who drifted away from the cold and the past and the old ways. Here is where they are trying to find a new life style, trying to find it in the only places they know to look: the movies and the newspapers. The case of Lucille Marie Maxwell Miller is a tabloid monument to that new life style.

Imagine Banyan Street first, because Banyan is where it happened. The way to Banyan is to drive west from San Bernardino out Foothill Boulevard, Route 66: past the Santa Fe switching yards, the Forty Winks Motel. Past the motel that is nineteen stucco tepees: "SLEEP IN A WIGWAM — GET MORE FOR YOUR WAMPUM." Past Fontana Drag City and the Fontana Church of the Nazarene and the Pit Stop A Go-Go; past Kaiser Steel, through Cucamonga, out to the Kapu Kai Restaurant-Bar and Coffee Shop, at the corner of Route 66 and Carnelian Avenue. Up Carnelian Avenue from the Kapu Kai, which means "Forbidden Seas," the subdivision flags whip in the harsh wind. "HALF-ACRE RANCHES! SNACK BARS! TRAVERTINE ENTRIES! $95 DOWN." It is the trail of an intention gone haywire, the flotsam of the New California. But after a while the signs thin out on Carnelian Avenue, and the houses are no longer the bright pastels of the Springtime Home owners but the faded bungalows of the people who grow a few grapes and keep a few chickens out here, and then the hill gets steeper and the road climbs and even the bungalows are few, and here — desolate, roughly surfaced, lined with eucalyptus and lemon groves — is Banyan Street.

Like so much of this country, Banyan suggests something curious and unnatural. The lemon groves are sunken, down a three- or four-foot retaining wall, so that one looks directly into their dense foliage, too lush, unsettlingly glossy, the greenery of nightmare; the fallen eucalyptus bark is too dusty, a place for snakes to breed. The stones look not like natural stones but like the rubble of some unmentioned upheaval. There are smudge pots, and a closed cistern. To one side of Banyan there is the flat valley, and to the other the

---

Double Indemnity A 1944 mystery movie, from the book by James M. Cain, in which an insurance salesman is coerced into a plot to murder a man, for which the widow could collect double indemnity, that is, a double insurance payment for "accidental" death.

San Bernardino Mountains, a dark mass looming too high, too fast, nine, ten, eleven thousand feet, right there above the lemon groves. At midnight on Banyan Street there is no light at all, and no sound except the wind in the eucalyptus and a muffled barking of dogs. There may be a kennel somewhere, or the dogs may be coyotes.

Banyan Street was the route Lucille Miller took home from the twenty-   5
four-hour Mayfair Market on the night of October 7, 1964, a night when the moon was dark and the wind was blowing and she was out of milk, and Banyan Street was where, at about 12:30 A.M., her 1964 Volkswagen came to a sudden stop, caught fire, and began to burn. For an hour and fifteen minutes Lucille Miller ran up and down Banyan calling for help, but no cars passed and no help came. At three o'clock that morning, when the fire had been put out and the California Highway Patrol officers were completing their report, Lucille Miller was still sobbing and incoherent, for her husband had been asleep in the Volkswagen. "What will I tell the children, when there's nothing left, nothing left in the casket," she cried to the friend called to comfort her. "How can I tell them there's nothing left?"

In fact there was something left, and a week later it lay in the Draper   6
Mortuary Chapel in a closed bronze coffin blanketed with pink carnations. Some 200 mourners heard Elder Robert E. Denton of the Seventh-Day Adventist Church of Ontario speak of "the temper of fury that has broken out among us." For Gordon Miller, he said, there would be "no more death, no more heartaches, no more misunderstandings." Elder Ansel Bristol mentioned the "peculiar" grief of the hour. Elder Fred Jensen asked "what shall it profit a man, if he shall gain the whole world, and lose his own soul?" A light rain fell, a blessing in a dry season, and a female vocalist sang "Safe in the Arms of Jesus." A tape recording of the service was made for the widow, who was being held without bail in the San Bernardino County Jail on a charge of first-degree murder.

Of course she came from somewhere else, came off the prairie in search   7
of something she had seen in a movie or heard on the radio, for this is a Southern California story. She was born on January 17, 1930, in Winnipeg, Manitoba, the only child of Gordon and Lily Maxwell, both schoolteachers and both dedicated to the Seventh-Day Adventist Church, whose members observe the Sabbath on Saturday, believe in an apocalyptic Second Coming, have a strong missionary tendency, and, if they are strict, do not smoke, drink, eat meat, use makeup, or wear jewelry, including weddings rings. By the time Lucille Maxwell enrolled at Walla Walla College in College Place, Washington, the Adventist school where her parents then taught, she was an eighteen-year-old possessed of unremarkable good looks and remarkable high spirits. "Lucille wanted to see the world," her father would say in retrospect, "and I guess she found out."

The high spirits did not seem to lend themselves to an extended course of study at Walla Walla College, and in the spring of 1949 Lucille Maxwell met and married Gordon ("Cork") Miller, a twenty-four-old graduate of Walla Walla and of the University of Oregon dental school, then stationed at Fort Lewis as a medical officer. "Maybe you could say it was love at first sight," Mr. Maxwell recalls. "Before they were ever formally introduced, he sent Lucille a dozen and a half roses with a card that said even if she didn't come out on a date with him, he hoped she'd find the roses pretty anyway." The Maxwells remember their daughter as a "radiant" bride.

Unhappy marriages so resemble one another that we do not need to know too much about the course of this one. There may or may not have been trouble on Guam, where Cork and Lucille Miller lived while he finished his Army duty. There may or may not have been problems in the small Oregon town where he first set up private practice. There appears to have been some disappointment about their move to California: Cork Miller had told friends that he wanted to become a doctor, that he was unhappy as a dentist and planned to enter the Seventh-Day Adventist College of Medical Evangelists at Loma Linda, a few miles south of San Bernardino. Instead he bought a dental practice in the west end of San Bernardino County, and the family settled there, in a modest house on the kind of street where there are always tricycles and revolving credit and dreams about bigger houses, better streets. That was 1957. By the summer of 1964 they had achieved the bigger house on the better street and the familiar accouterments of a family on its way up: the $30,000 a year, the three children for the Christmas card, the picture window, the family room, the newspaper photographs that showed "Mrs. Gordon Miller, Ontario Heart Fund Chairman. . . ." They were paying the familiar price for it. And they had reached the familiar season of divorce.

It might have been anyone's bad summer, anyone's siege of heat and nerves and migraine and money worries, but this one began particularly early and particularly badly. On April 24 an old friend, Elaine Hayton, died suddenly; Lucille Miller had seen her only the night before. During the month of May, Cork Miller was hospitalized briefly with a bleeding ulcer, and his usual reserve deepened into depression. He told his accountant that he was "sick of looking at open mouths," and threatened suicide. By July 8, the conventional tensions of love and money had reached the conventional impasse in the new house on the acre lot at 8488 Bella Vista, and Lucille Miller filed for divorce. Within a month, however, the Millers seemed reconciled. They saw a marriage counselor. They talked about a fourth child. It seemed that the marriage had reached the traditional truce, the point at which so many resign themselves to cutting both their losses and their hopes.

But the Millers' season of trouble was not to end that easily. October 7 began as a commonplace enough day, one of those days that sets the teeth on edge with its tedium, its small frustrations. The temperature reached 102° in San Bernardino that afternoon, and the Miller children were home from school because of Teachers' Institute. There was ironing to be dropped off. There was a trip to pick up a prescription for Nembutal,° a trip to a self-service dry cleaner. In the early evening, an unpleasant accident with the Volkswagen: Cork Miller hit and killed a German shepherd, and afterward said that his head felt "like it had a Mack truck on it." It was something he often said. As of that evening Cork Miller was $63,479 in debt, including the $29,637 mortgage on the new house, a debt load which seemed oppressive to him. He was a man who wore his responsibilities uneasily, and complained of migraine headaches almost constantly.

He ate alone that night, from a TV tray in the living room. Later the Millers watched John Forsythe and Senta Berger in *See How They Run*, and when the movie ended, about eleven, Cork Miller suggested that they go out for milk. He wanted some hot chocolate. He took a blanket and pillow from the couch and climbed into the passenger seat of the Volkswagen. Lucille Miller remembers reaching over to lock his door as she backed down the driveway. By the time she left the Mayfair Market, and long before they reached Banyan Street, Cork Miller appeared to be asleep. 12

There is some confusion in Lucille Miller's mind about what happened between 12:30 A.M., when the fire broke out, and 1:50 A.M., when it was reported. She says that she was driving east on Banyan Street at about 35 m.p.h. when she felt the Volkswagen pull sharply to the right. The next thing she knew the car was on the embankment, quite near the edge of the retaining wall, and flames were shooting up behind her. She does not remember jumping out. She does remember prying up a stone with which she broke the window next to her husband, and then scrambling down the retaining wall to try to find a stick. "I don't know how I was going to push him out," she says. "I just thought if I had a stick, I'd push him out." She could not, and after a while she ran to the intersection of Banyan and Carnelian Avenue. There are no houses at that corner, and almost no traffic. After one car had passed without stopping, Lucille Miller ran back down Banyan toward the burning Volkswagen. She did not stop, but she slowed down, and in the flames, she could see her husband. He was, she said, "just black." 13

At the first house up Sapphire Avenue, half a mile from the Volkswagen, Lucille Miller finally found help. There Mrs. Robert Swenson called the sheriff, and then, at Lucille Miller's request, she called Harold Lance, the Millers' lawyer and their close friend. When Harold Lance arrived he took Lucille Miller home to his wife, Joan. Twice Harold Lance and Lucille Miller returned to Banyan Street and talked to the Highway Patrol officers. A third 14

Nembutal A barbiturate drug used as a sedative.

time Harold Lance returned alone, and when he came back he said to Lucille Miller, "O.K. . . . you don't talk any more."

When Lucille Miller was arrested the next afternoon, Sandy Slagle was with her. Sandy Slagle was the intense, relentlessly loyal medical student who used to baby-sit for the Millers, and had been living as a member of the family since she graduated from high school in 1959. The Millers took her away from a difficult home situation, and she thinks of Lucille Miller not only as "more or less a mother or a sister" but as "the most wonderful character" she has ever known. On the night of the accident, Sandy Slagle was in her dormitory at Loma Linda University, but Lucille Miller called her early in the morning and asked her to come home. The doctor was there when Sandy Slagle arrived, giving Lucille Miller an injection of Nembutal. "She was crying as she was going under," Sandy Slagle recalls. "Over and over she'd say, 'Sandy, all the hours I spent trying to save him and now what are they trying to *do* to me?' "

At 1:30 that afternoon, Sergeant William Paterson and Detectives Charles Callahan and Joseph Karr of the Central Homicide Division arrived at 8488 Bella Vista. "One of them appeared at the bedroom door," Sandy Slagle remembers, "and said to Lucille, 'You've got ten minutes to get dressed or we'll take you as you are.' She was in her nightgown, you know, so I tried to get her dressed."

Sandy Slagle tells the story now as if by rote, and her eyes do not waver. "So I had her panties and bra on her and they opened the door again, so I got some Capris on her, you know, and a scarf." Her voice drops. "And then they just took her."

The arrest took place just twelve hours after the first report that there had been an accident on Banyan Street, a rapidity which would later prompt Lucille Miller's attorney to say that the entire case was an instance of trying to justify a reckless arrest. Actually what first caused the detectives who arrived on Banyan Street toward dawn that morning to give the accident more than routine attention were certain apparent physical inconsistencies. While Lucille Miller had said that she was driving about 35 m.p.h. when the car swerved to a stop, an examination of the cooling Volkswagen showed that it was in low gear, and that the parking rather than the driving lights were on. The front wheels, moreover, did not seem to be in exactly the position that Lucille Miller's description of the accident would suggest, and the right rear wheel was dug in deep, as if it had been spun in place. It seemed curious to the detectives, too, that a sudden stop from 35 m.p.h. — the same jolt which was presumed to have knocked over a gasoline can in the back seat and somehow started the fire — should have left two milk cartons upright on the back floorboard, and the remains of a Polaroid camera box lying apparently undisturbed on the back seat.

No one, however, could be expected to give a precise account of what did and did not happen in a moment of terror, and none of these inconsistencies seemed in themselves incontrovertible evidence of criminal intent. But they did interest the Sheriff's Office, as did Gordon Miller's apparent unconsciousness at the time of the accident, and the length of time it had taken Lucille Miller to get help. Something, moreover, struck the investigators as wrong about Harold Lance's attitude when he came back to Banyan Street the third time and found the investigation by no means over. "The way Lance was acting," the prosecuting attorney said later, "they thought maybe they'd hit a nerve."

And so it was that on the morning of October 8, even before the doctor 20 had come to give Lucille Miller an injection to calm her, the San Bernardino County Sheriff's Office was trying to construct another version of what might have happened between 12:30 and 1:50 A.M. The hypothesis they would eventually present was based on the somewhat tortuous premise that Lucille Miller had undertaken a plan which failed: a plan to stop the car on the lonely road, spread gasoline over her presumably drugged husband, and, with a stick on the accelerator, gently "walk" the Volkswagen over the embankment, where it would tumble four feet down the retaining wall into the lemon grove and almost certainly explode. If this happened, Lucille Miller might then have somehow negotiated the two miles up Carnelian to Bella Vista in time to be home when the accident was discovered. This plan went awry, according to the Sheriff's Office hypothesis, when the car would not go over the rise of the embankment. Lucille Miller might have panicked then — after she had killed the engine the third or fourth time, say, out there on the dark road with the gasoline already spread and the dogs baying and the wind blowing and the unspeakable apprehension that a pair of headlights would suddenly light up Banyan Street and expose her there — and set the fire herself.

Although this version accounted for some of the physical evidence — the 21 car in low because it had been started from a dead stop, the parking lights on because she could not do what needed doing without some light, a rear wheel spun in repeated attempts to get the car over the embankment, the milk cartons upright because there had been no sudden stop — it did not seem on its own any more or less credible than Lucille Miller's own story. Moreover, some of the physical evidence did seem to support her story: a nail in a front tire, a nine-pound rock found in the car, presumably the one with which she had broken the window in an attempt to save her husband. Within a few days an autopsy had established that Gordon Miller was alive when he burned, which did not particularly help the State's case, and that he had enough Nembutal and Sandoptal in his blood to put the average person to sleep, which did: on the other hand Gordon Miller habitually took both Nembutal and Fiorinal (a common headache prescription which contains Sandoptal), and had been ill besides.

It was a spotty case, and to make it work at all the State was going to 22 have to find a motive. There was talk of unhappiness, talk of another man.

That kind of motive, during the next few weeks, was what they set out to establish. They set out to find it in accountants' ledgers and double-indemnity clauses and motel registers, set out to determine what might move a woman who believed in all the promises of the middle class — a woman who had been chairman of the Heart Fund and who always knew a reasonable little dressmaker and who had come out of the bleak wild of prairie fundamentalism to find what she imagined to be the good life — what should drive such a woman to sit on a street called Bella Vista and look out her new picture window into the empty California sun and calculate how to burn her husband alive in a Volkswagen. They found the wedge they wanted closer at hand than they might have at first expected, for, as testimony would reveal later at the trial, it seemed that in December of 1963 Lucille Miller had begun an affair with the husband of one of her friends, a man whose daughter called her "Auntie Lucille," a man who might have seemed to have the gift for people and money and the good life that Cork Miller so noticeably lacked. The man was Arthwell Hayton, a well-known San Bernardino attorney and at one time a member of the district attorney's staff.

In some ways it was the conventional clandestine affair in a place like San Bernardino, a place where little is bright or graceful, where it is routine to misplace the future and easy to start looking for it in bed. Over the seven weeks that it would take to try Lucille Miller for murder, Assistant District Attorney Don A. Turner and defense attorney Edward P. Foley would between them unfold a curiously predictable story. There were the falsified motel registrations. There were the lunch dates, the afternoon drives in Arthwell Hayton's red Cadillac convertible. There were the interminable discussions of the wronged partners. There were the confidantes ("I knew everything," Sandy Slagle would insist fiercely later. "I knew every time, places, everything") and there were the words remembered from bad magazine stories ("Don't kiss me, it will trigger things," Lucille Miller remembered telling Arthwell Hayton in the parking lot of Harold's Club in Fontana after lunch one day) and there were the notes, the sweet exchanges: "Hi Sweetie Pie! You are my cup of tea!! Happy Birthday — you don't look a day over 29!! Your baby, Arthwell."

And, toward the end, there was the acrimony. It was April 24, 1964, when Arthwell Hayton's wife, Elaine, died suddenly, and nothing good happened after that. Arthwell Hayton had taken his cruiser, *Captain's Lady*, over to Catalina that weekend; he called home at nine o'clock Friday night, but did not talk to his wife because Lucille Miller answered the telephone and said that Elaine was showering. The next morning the Haytons' daughter found her mother in bed, dead. The newspapers reported the death as accidental, perhaps the result of an allergy to hair spray. When Arthwell Hayton flew home from Catalina that weekend, Lucille Miller met him at the airport, but the finish had already been written.

It was in the breakup that the affair ceased to be in the conventional   25
mode and began to resemble instead the novels of James M. Cain, the movies of the late 1930's, all the dreams in which violence and threats and blackmail are made to seem commonplaces of middle-class life. What was most
startling about the case that the State of California was preparing against Lucille Miller was something that had nothing to do with law at all, something
that never appeared in the eight-column afternoon headlines but was always
there between them: the revelation that the dream was teaching the dreamers how to live. Here is Lucille Miller talking to her lover sometime in the
early summer of 1964, after he had indicated that, on the advice of his minister, he did not intend to see her any more: "First, I'm going to go to that
dear pastor of yours and tell him a few things. . . . When I do tell him that,
you won't be in the Redlands Church any more. . . . Look, Sonny Boy, if
you think your reputation is going to be ruined, your life won't be worth
two cents." Here is Arthwell Hayton, to Lucille Miller: "I'll go to Sheriff
Frank Bland and tell him some things that I know about you until you'll
wish you'd never heard of Arthwell Hayton." For an affair between a Sev-
enty-Day Adventist dentist's wife and a Seventh-Day Adventist personal-
injury lawyer, it seems a curious kind of dialogue.

"Boy, I could get that little boy coming and going," Lucille Miller later   26
confided to Erwin Sprengle, a Riverside contractor who was a business partner of Arthwell Hayton's and a friend to both the lovers. (Friend or no, on
this occasion he happened to have an induction coil attached to his telephone in order to tape Lucille Miller's call.) "And he hasn't got one thing on
me that he can prove. I mean, I've got concrete — he has nothing concrete."
In the same taped conversation with Erwin Sprengle, Lucille Miller mentioned a tape that she herself had surreptitiously made, months before, in
Arthwell Hayton's car.

"I said to him, I said 'Arthwell, I just feel like I'm being used.' . . . He   27
started sucking his thumb and said 'I love you. . . . This isn't something that
happened yesterday. I'd marry you tomorrow if I could. I don't love Elaine.'
He'd love to hear that played back, wouldn't he?"

"Yeah," drawled Sprengle's voice on the tape. "That would be just a lit-   28
tle incriminating, wouldn't it?"

"Just a *little* incriminating," Lucille Miller agreed. "It really *is*."   29

Later on the tape, Sprengle asked where Cork Miller was.   30

"He took the children down to the church."   31

"You didn't go?"   32

"No."   33

"You're naughty."   34

It was all, moreover, in the name of "love"; everyone involved placed a   35
magical faith in the efficacy of the very word. There was the significance that
Lucille Miller saw in Arthwell's saying that he "loved" her, that he did not
"love" Elaine. There was Arthwell insisting, later, at the trial, that he had

never said it, that he may have "whispered sweet nothings in her ear" (as her defense hinted that he had whispered in many ears), but he did not remember bestowing upon her the special seal, saying the word, declaring "love." There was the summer evening when Lucille Miller and Sandy Slagle followed Arthwell Hayton down to his new boat in its mooring at Newport Beach and untied the lines with Arthwell aboard, Arthwell and a girl with whom he later testified he was drinking hot chocolate and watching television. "I did that on purpose," Lucille Miller told Erwin Sprengle later, "to save myself from letting my heart do something crazy."

January 11, 1965, was a bright warm day in Southern California, the kind of day when Catalina floats on the Pacific horizon and the air smells of orange blossoms and it is a long way from the bleak and difficult East, a long way from the cold, a long way from the past. A woman in Hollywood staged an all-night sit-in on the hood of her car to prevent repossession by a finance company. A seventy-year-old pensioner drove his station wagon at five miles an hour past three Gardena poker parlors and emptied three pistols and a twelve-gauge shotgun through their windows, wounding twenty-nine people. "Many young women become prostitutes just to have enough money to play cards," he explained in a note. Mrs. Nick Adams said that she was "not surprised" to hear her husband announce his divorce plans on the Les Crane Show, and, farther north, a sixteen-year-old jumped off the Golden Gate Bridge and lived.

And, in the San Bernardino County Courthouse, the Miller trial opened. The crowds were so bad that the glass courtroom doors were shattered in the crush, and from then on identification disks were issued to the first forty-three spectators in line. The line began forming at 6 A.M., and college girls camped at the courthouse all night, with stores of graham crackers and No-Cal.

All they were doing was picking a jury, those first few days, but the sensational nature of the case had already suggested itself. Early in December there had been an abortive first trial, a trial at which no evidence was ever presented because on the day the jury was seated the San Bernardino *Sun-Telegram* ran an "inside" story quoting Assistant District Attorney Don Turner, the prosecutor, as saying, "We are looking into the circumstances of Mrs. Hayton's death. In view of the current trial concerning the death of Dr. Miller, I do not feel I should comment on Mrs. Hayton's death." It seemed that there had been barbiturates in Elaine Hayton's blood, and there had seemed some irregularity about the way she was dressed on that morning when she was found under the covers, dead. Any doubts about the death at the time, however, had never gotten as far as the Sheriff's Office. "I guess somebody didn't want to rock the boat," Turner said later. "These were prominent people."

Although all of that had not been in the *Sun-Telegram*'s story, an immedi- 39
ate mistrial had been declared. Almost as immediately, there had been another development: Arthwell Hayton had asked newspapermen to an 11
A.M. Sunday morning press conference in his office. There had been television cameras, and flash bulbs popping. "As you gentlemen may know,"
Hayton had said, striking a note of stiff bonhomie, "there are very often
women who become amorous toward their doctor or lawyer. This does not
mean on the physician's or lawyer's part that there is any romance toward
the patient or client."

"Would you deny that you were having an affair with Mrs. Miller?" a re- 40
porter had asked.

"I would deny that there was any romance on my part whatsoever." 41

It was a distinction he would maintain through all the wearing weeks to 42
come.

So they had come to see Arthwell, these crowds who now milled be- 43
neath the dusty palms outside the courthouse, and they had also come to
see Lucille, who appeared as a slight, intermittently pretty woman, already
pale from lack of sun, a woman who would turn thirty-five before the trial
was over and whose tendency toward haggardness was beginning to show,
a meticulous woman who insisted, against her lawyer's advice, on coming
to court with her hair piled high and lacquered. "I would've been happy if
she'd come in with it hanging loose, but Lucille wouldn't do that," her lawyer said. He was Edward P. Foley, a small, emotional Irish Catholic who
several times wept in the courtroom. "She has a great honesty, this
woman," he added, "but this honesty about her appearance always worked
against her."

By the time the trial opened, Lucille Miller's appearance included mater- 44
nity clothes, for an official examination on December 18 had revealed that
she was then three and a half months pregnant, a fact which made picking a
jury even more difficult than usual, for Turner was asking the death penalty.
"It's unfortunate but there it is," he would say of the pregnancy to each ju-
ror in turn, and finally twelve were seated, seven of them women, the
youngest forty-one, an assembly of the very peers — housewives, a machin-
ist, a truck driver, a grocery-store manager, a filing clerk — above whom Lucille Miller had wanted so badly to rise.

That was the sin, more than the adultery, which tended to reinforce the 45
one for which she was being tried. It was implicit in both the defense and the
prosecution that Lucille Miller was an erring woman, a woman who perhaps
wanted too much. But to the prosecution she was not merely a woman who
would want a new house and want to go to parties and run up high telephone bills ($1,152 in ten months), but a woman who would go so far as to
murder her husband for his $80,000 in insurance, making it appear an acci-
dent in order to collect another $40,000 in double indemnity and straight ac-

371

cident policies. To Turner she was a woman who did not want simply her freedom and a reasonable alimony (she could have had that, the defense contended, by going through with her divorce suit), but wanted everything, a woman motivated by "love and greed." She was a "manipulator." She was a "user of people."

To Edward Foley, on the other hand, she was an impulsive woman who "couldn't control her foolish little heart." Where Turner skirted the pregnancy, Foley dwelt upon it, even calling the dead man's mother down from Washington to testify that her son had told her they were going to have another baby because Lucille felt that it would "do much to weld our home again in the pleasant relations that we used to have." Where the prosecution saw a "calculator," the defense saw a "blabbermouth," and in fact Lucille Miller did emerge as an ingenuous conversationalist. Just as, before her husband's death, she had confided in her friends about her love affair, so she chatted about it after his death, with the arresting sergeant. "Of course Cork lived with it for years, you know," her voice was heard to tell Sergeant Paterson on a tape made the morning after her arrest. "After Elaine died, he pushed the panic button one night and just asked me right out, and that, I think, was when he really — the first time he really faced it." When the sergeant asked why she had agreed to talk to him, against the specific instructions of her lawyers, Lucille Miller said airily, "Oh, I've always been basically quite an honest person. . . . I mean I can put a hat in the cupboard and say it cost ten dollars less, but basically I've always kind of just lived my life the way I wanted to, and if you don't like it you can take off."

The prosecution hinted at men other than Arthwell, and even, over Foley's objections, managed to name one. The defense called Miller suicidal. The prosecution produced experts who said that the Volkswagen fire could not have been accidental. Foley produced witnesses who said that it could have been. Lucille's father, now a junior-high-school teacher in Oregon, quoted Isaiah to reporters: "*Every tongue that shall rise against thee in judgment thou shalt condemn.*" "Lucille did wrong, her affair," her mother said judiciously. "With her it was love. But with some I guess it's just passion." There was Debbie, the Millers' fourteen-year-old, testifying in a steady voice about how she and her mother had gone to a supermarket to buy the gasoline can the week before the accident. There was Sandy Slagle, in the courtroom every day, declaring that on at least one occasion Lucille Miller had prevented her husband not only from committing suicide but from committing suicide in such a way that it would appear an accident and ensure the double-indemnity payment. There was Wenche Berg, the pretty twenty-seven-year-old Norwegian governess to Arthwell Hayton's children, testifying that Arthwell had instructed her not to allow Lucille Miller to see or talk to the children.

Two months dragged by, and the headlines never stopped. Southern 48
California's crime reporters were headquartered in San Bernardino for the
duration: Howard Hertel from the *Times,* Jim Bennett and Eddy Jo Bernal
from the *Herald-Examiner.* Two months in which the Miller trial was pushed
off the *Examiner's* front page only by the Academy Award nominations and
Stan Laurel's death. And finally, on March 2, after Turner had reiterated
that it was a case of "love and greed," and Foley had protested that his client was being tried for adultery, the case went to the jury.

They brought in the verdict, guilty of murder in the first degree, at 4:50 49
P.M. on March 5. "She didn't do it," Debbie Miller cried, jumping up from
the spectators' section. "She didn't *do* it."Sandy Slagle collapsed in her seat
and began to scream. "Sandy, for God's sake please *don't,*" Lucille Miller
said in a voice that carried across the courtroom, and Sandy Slagle was momentarily subdued. But as the jurors left the courtroom she screamed again:
"You're murderers. . . . Every last one of you is a *murderer.*" Sheriff's depu-
ties moved in then, each wearing a string tie that read "1965 SHERIFF'S RO-
DEO," and Lucille Miller's father, that sad-faced junior-high-school teacher
who believed in the word of Christ and the dangers of wanting to see the
world, blew her a kiss off his fingertips.

The California Institution for Women at Frontera, where Lucille Miller is 50
now, lies down where Euclid Avenue turns into country road, not too many
miles from where she once lived and shopped and organized the Heart Fund
Ball. Cattle graze across the road, and Rainbirds sprinkle the alfalfa. Frontera
has a softball field and tennis courts and looks as if it might be a California
junior college, except that the trees are not yet high enough to conceal the
concertina wire around the top of the Cyclone fence. On visitors' day there
are big cars in the parking area, big Buicks and Pontiacs that belong to
grandparents and sisters and fathers (not many of them belong to husbands), and some of them have bumper stickers that say "SUPPORT YOUR LO-
CAL POLICE."

A lot of California murderesses live here, a lot of girls who somehow mis- 51
understood the promise. Don Turner put Sandra Garner here (and her husband in the gas chamber at San Quentin) after the 1959 desert killings
known to crime reporters as "the soda-pop murders." Carole Tregoff is
here, and has been ever since she was convicted of conspiring to murder Dr.
Finch's wife in West Covina, which is not too far from San Bernardino.
Carole Tregoff is in fact a nurse's aide in the prison hospital, and might have
attended Lucille Miller had her baby been born at Frontera; Lucille Miller
chose instead to have it outside, and paid for the guard who stood outside
the delivery room in St. Bernardine's Hospital. Debbie Miller came to take
the baby home from the hospital, in a white dress with pink ribbons, and

Debbie was allowed to choose a name. She named the baby Kimi Kai. The children live with Harold and Joan Lance now, because Lucille Miller will probably spend ten years at Frontera. Don Turner waived his original request for the death penalty (it was generally agreed that he had demanded it only, in Edward Foley's words, "to get anybody with the slightest trace of human kindness in their veins off the jury"), and settled for life imprisonment with the possibility of parole. Lucille Miller does not like it at Frontera, and has had trouble adjusting. "She's going to have to learn humility," Turner says. "She's going to have to use her ability to charm, to manipulate."

The new house is empty now, the house on the street with the sign that says

PRIVATE ROAD
BELLA VISTA
DEAD END

The Millers never did get it landscaped, and weeds grow up around the fieldstone siding. The television aerial has toppled on the roof, and a trash can is stuffed with the debris of family life: a cheap suitcase, a child's game called "Lie Detector." There is a sign on what would have been the lawn, and the sign reads "ESTATE SALE." Edward Foley is trying to get Lucille Miller's case appealed, but there have been delays. "A trial always comes down to a matter of sympathy," Foley says wearily now. "I couldn't create sympathy for her." Everyone is a little weary now, weary and resigned, everyone except Sandy Slagle, whose bitterness is still raw. She lives in an apartment near the medical school in Loma Linda, and studies reports of the case in *True Police Cases* and *Office Detective Stories*. "I'd much rather we not talk about the Hayton business too much," she tells visitors, and she keeps a tape recorder running. "I'd rather talk about Lucille and what a wonderful person she is and how her rights were violated." Harold Lance does not talk to visitors at all. "We don't want to give away what we can sell," he explains pleasantly; an attempt was made to sell Lucille Miller's personal story to *Life*, but *Life* did not want to buy it. In the district attorney's offices they are prosecuting other murders now, and do not see why the Miller trial attracted so much attention. "It wasn't a very interesting murder as murders go," Don Turner says laconically. Elaine Hayton's death is no longer under investigation. "We know everything we want to know," Turner says.

Arthwell Hayton's office is directly below Edward Foley's. Some people 5 around San Bernardino say that Arthwell Hayton suffered; others say that he did not suffer at all. Perhaps he did not, for time past is not believed to have any bearing upon time present or future, out in the golden land where every day the world is born anew. In any case, on October 17, 1965, Arthwell Hayton married again, married his children's pretty governess,

Wenche Berg, at a service in the Chapel of the Roses at a retirement village near Riverside. Later the newlyweds were feted at a reception for seventy-five in the dining room of Rose Garden Village. The bridegroom was in black tie, with a white carnation in his buttonhole. The bride wore a long white *peau de soie* dress and carried a shower bouquet of sweetheart roses with stephanotis streamers. A coronet of seed pearls held her illusion veil.

QUESTIONS ON MEANING

1. "Some Dreamers of the Golden Dream" describes a "new life style" in a specific part of California. How does Didion set the scene for her subject in the opening paragraphs? How does she characterize the class of people she describes? What details does she furnish about their lives?
2. Though this essay is in large part a narrative about a particular crime, it is also a moral essay. Didion has a definite point of view about what she reports, one that encompasses more than the specifics of Lucille Miller's crime and punishment. What is her view? What larger issues emerge from her treatment of this story?
3. Didion introduces "a belief in the literal interpretation of *Double Indemnity*" in paragraph 2. Where in this story does reality imitate art? Where might the reality of this story find its way back into art?

QUESTIONS ON STRATEGY

1. Didion first presents the story of Cork Miller's death from Lucille Miller's point of view (paragraphs 5-6 and 11-17), then from the authorities' point of view (paragraphs 18-22). How does she handle the transition between the two? How do we know what she thinks of the evidence?
2. When Didion calls the case of Lucille Miller "a tabloid monument" to a new kind of life style (paragraph 2), she tells us something important about her approach to the story. What details of her phrasing, tone, and attitude reflect the tabloid journalist's preference for sensationalism, sentimentality, and cliché? Why does Didion use this emphasis in her story?
3. "Some Dreamers of the Golden Dream" concerns extreme situations — adultery, murder, blackmail, scandal. Yet Didion describes the elements of her story as "conventional," "routine," and "curiously predictable." What effect does this emphasis on the banality of her subject have?

EXPLORATIONS

1. Throughout her essay, Joan Didion refers to the style of Hollywood melo-dramas in the 1930s and 1940s. Movies in this *film noir* tradition emphasized the dark side of middle-class life, taking adultery, greed, and murder as

themes and presenting them from an entirely cynical point of view. *Double Indemnity* and *The Postman Always Rings Twice*, two specimens of the genre, are based on novels by James M. Cain. See one of the films or read one of Cain's books, and evaluate its important to Joan Didion. How does her essay reflect these works? How does the life depicted in "Some Dreamers of the Golden Dream" imitate the art of the American cinema?

WRITING TOPICS

1. Read another of Didion's essays — "Slouching Towards Bethlehem" is a good choice — and write a study of her style and temperament as a chronicler of American life. Be specific about how these essays reveal their author. Define a thesis about her work — for example, "Joan Didion uses dialogue as her major resource in presenting characters" — and give examples to prove your point.

2. Using Didion's first three paragraphs as a model, apply her techniques of observation and description to an essay of your own in which you present a particular setting in terms of its history. Choose a subject that offers a density of reference comparable to Didion's.

BOOKS AVAILABLE IN PAPERBACK

A Book of Common Prayer. New York: Washington Square Press. *Novel.*

Play It as It Lays. New York: Washington Square Press. *Novel.*

Run River. New York: Washington Square Press. *Novel.*

Salvador. New York: Washington Square Press. *Nonfiction.*

Slouching Towards Bethlehem. New York: Washington Square Press. *Essays.*

The White Album. New York: Washington Square Press. *Essays.*

CALVIN
TRILLIN

*C*ALVIN TRILLIN *was born in 1935 in Kansas City, Missouri. He attended Yale University and worked as a reporter for* Time *magazine from 1960 to 1963, when he joined the staff of* The New Yorker. *His novel* Floater *(1980) describes a hero who works for a magazine that sounds very much like* Time. *For* The New Yorker *he has gone traveling; some of his reportage is collected in* U.S. Journal *(1971). He writes a column for the* Nation, *more or less political, from which he has collected* Uncivil Liberties *(1982). But for most readers, the essential Calvin Trillin is the man who celebrates eating, whom Craig Claiborne — former food editor of the* New York Times *and author of cookbooks — calls the "Homer, Dante, and Shakespeare of American food." His finger-lickin' essays, mostly from* The New Yorker, *have been served up in three courses:* American Fried *(1974),* Alice, Let's Eat *(1978), and* Third Helpings *(1983).*

The essay that follows is the second chapter of American Fried, *a book that begins: "The best restaurants in the world are, of course, in Kansas City." If Trillin is accurately dubbed the "Shakespeare of American food," he might also be called the overeater's Woody Allen. Whether he addresses himself to cheeseburgers or presidential press conferences, he remains the funniest straight-faced comedian of the contem-*

porary American essay. His prose style compounds, in balanced sentences, continual disparities of soft drinks and revered deceased Chief Executives.

The Best Restaurants
in the World

I know a radical from Texas who holds the stock market in contempt but refuses to give up his seven shares of Dr. Pepper. He says that Dr. Pepper, like the late President Eisenhower, is above politics. I have personally acted as a courier in bringing desperately craved burnt-almond chocolate ice cream from Will Wright's in Los Angeles to a friend who survived a Beverly Hills childhood and now lives in New York — living like a Spanish Civil War refugee who hates the regime but would give his arm for a decent bowl of gazpacho. I have also, in the dark of night, slipped into a sophisticated apartment in upper Manhattan and left an unmarked paper bag containing a powdered substance called Ranch Dressing — available, my client believes, only in certain supermarkets in the state of Oklahoma. I once knew someone from Alabama who, in moments of melancholy or stress or drunkenness, would gain strength merely by staring up at some imaginary storekeeper and saying, in the accent of an Alabama road-gang worker on his five-minute morning break, "Jes gimme an R.C. and a moon pah."

Because I happened to grow up in Kansas City and now live in New York, there may be, I realize, a temptation to confuse my assessment of Kansas City restaurants with the hallucinations people all over the country suffer when gripped by the fever of Hometown Food Nostalgia. I am aware of the theory held by Bill Vaughan, the humor columnist of the Kansas City *Star*, that millions of pounds of hometown goodies are constantly crisscrossing the country by U.S. mail in search of desperate expatriates — a theory he developed, I believe, while standing in the post office line in Kansas City holding a package of Wolferman's buns that he was about to send off to his son in Virginia. I do not have to be told that there is a tendency among a lot of otherwise sensible adults to believe that the best hamburgers in the world are served in the hamburger stands of their childhood. A friend of mine named William Edgett Smith, after all, a man of good judgment in most matters, clings to the bizarre notion that the best hamburgers in the world are served at Bob's Big Boy — Glendale, California, branch — rather than at Winstead's Drive-in in Kansas City. He has, over the years, stubbornly rejected my acute analysis of the Big Boy as a gimmick burger with a redundant middle bun, a run-of-the-mill triple-decker that is not easily distinguishable from a Howard Johnson's 3-D.

"It has a sesame seed bun," Smith would say, as we sat in some mid-   3
town Manhattan bar eating second-rate cheeseburgers at a dollar seventy-five a throw — two expatriates from the land of serious hamburger-eaters.

"Don't talk to me about seeds on buns," I'd say to Smith. "I had a Big   4
Boy in Phoenix and it is not in any way a class burger."

"Phoenix is not Glendale," Smith would say, full of blind stubbornness.   5

Smith has never been to Winstead's, although he often flies to California   6
to visit his family (in Glendale, it goes without saying) and I have reminded
him that he could lay over in Kansas City for a couple of hours for little extra
fare. He has never been able to understand the monumental purity of the
Winstead's hamburger — no seeds planted on the buns, no strong sauce
that might keep the exquisite flavor of the meat from dominating, no showy
meat-thickness that is the downfall of most hamburgers. Winstead's has
concentrated so hard on hamburgers that for a number of years it served just
about nothing else. Its policy is stated plainly on the menu I have framed on
the kitchen wall for inspiration: "We grind U.S. Graded Choice Steak daily
for the sandwich and broil on a greaseless grill." That is the only claim Winstead's makes, except "Your drinks are served in sterilized glasses."

I can end any suspicion of hometown bias on my part by recounting the   7
kind of conversation I used to have with my wife, Alice, an Easterner, before
I took her back to Kansas City to meet my family and get her something decent to eat. Imagine that we are sitting at some glossy road stop on the Long
Island Expressway, pausing for a bite to eat on our way to a fashionable traffic jam:

> ME: Anybody who served a milkshake like this in Kansas   8
> City would be put in jail.
>
> ALICE: You promised not to indulge in any of that home-   9
> town nostalgia while I'm eating. You know it gives me indigestion.
>
> ME: What nostalgia? Facts are facts. The kind of milkshake   10
> that I personally consumed six hundred gallons of at the
> Country Club Dairy is an historical fact in three flavors. Your
> indigestion is not from listening to my fair-minded remarks on
> the food of a particular American city. It's from drinking that
> gray skim milk this bandit is trying to pass off as a milkshake.
>
> ALICE: I suppose it wasn't you who told me that anybody   11
> who didn't think the best hamburger place in the world was in
> his hometown is a sissy.
>
> ME: But don't you see that one of those places actually *is*   12
> the best hamburger place in the world? Somebody has to be
> telling the truth, and it happens to be me.

Alice has now been to Kansas City many times. If she is asked where the best hamburgers in the world are served, she will unhesitatingly answer, from the results of her own extensive quality testing, that they are served at Winstead's. By the time our first child was three, she had already been to Winstead's a few times, and as an assessor of hamburgers, she is, I'm proud to say, her father's daughter. Once, I asked her what I could bring her from a trip to Kansas City. "Bring me a hamburger," she said. I did. I now realize what kind of satisfaction it must have given my father when I, at about the age of ten, finally agreed with him that *Gunga Din* was the greatest movie ever made.

I once went to Kansas City for the express purpose of making a grand tour of its great restaurants. Almost by coincidence, I found myself on the same plane with Fats Goldberg, the New York pizza baron, who grew up in Kansas City and was going back to visit his family and get something decent to eat. Fats, whose real name is Larry, got his nickname when he weighed about three hundred pounds. Some years ago, he got thin, and he has managed to remain at less than one hundred sixty ever since by subjecting himself to a horrifyingly rigid eating schedule. In New York, Fats eats virtually the same thing every day of his life. But he knows that even a man with his legendary will power — a man who can spend every evening of the week in a Goldberg's Pizzeria without tasting — could never diet in Kansas City, so he lets himself go a couple of times a year while he is within the city limits. For Fats, Kansas City is the DMZ.° He currently holds the world's record for getting from the airport to Winstead's.

Fats seemed a bit nervous about what we would find at Winstead's. For as long as I can remember, everyone in Kansas City has been saying that Winstead's is going downhill. Even in New York, where there has always been obsessive discussion of Winstead's among people from Kansas City, the Cassandras° in our ranks have often talked as if the next double-with-everything-and-grilled-onions I order at Winstead's will come out tasting like something a drugstore counterman has produced by peeling some morbid-looking patty from waxed paper and tossing it on some grease-caked grill — a prophecy that has always proved absolutely false. I can hardly blame a Kansas City emigré for being pessimistic. We have all received letters about Winstead's decline for years — in the way people who grew up in other parts of the country receive letters telling them that the fresh trout they used to love to eat now tastes like turpentine because of the lumber mill upstream or

---

DMZ   In military parlance, demilitarized zone, a specified area in which no fighting is allowed.

Cassandras   In Greek mythology, Cassandra is a prophetess whose fate is always to predict disaster and never to be believed.

that their favorite picnic meadow has become a trailer park. When Winstead's began serving French-fried potatoes several years ago, there was talk of defection in New York. The price of purity is purists. The French fries did turn out to be unspectacular — a lesson, I thought, that craftsmen should stick to their craft. The going-downhill talk was strong a few years later when Winstead's introduced something called an eggburger. My sister has actually eaten an eggburger — she has always had rather exotic tastes — but I found the idea so embarrassing that I avoided William Edgett Smith for days, until I realized he had no way of knowing about it. Fats told me on the plane that there had been a lot of going-downhill talk since Winstead's sold out to a larger company. He seemed personally hurt by the rumors.

"How can people talk that way?" he said, as we were about to land in 16 Kansas City.

"Don't let it bother you, Fats," I said. "People in Paris are probably al- 17 ways going around saying the Louvre doesn't have any decent pictures any more. It's human nature for the locals to badmouth the nearest national monument."

"You'll go to Zarda's Dairy for the banana split, of course," Fats said, 18 apparently trying to cheer himself up by pitching in with some advice for the grand tour. "Also the Toddle House for hash browns. Then you'll have to go to Kresge's for a chili dog."

"Hold it, Fats," I said. "Get control of yourself." He was beginning to 19 look wild. "I'm not sure a grand tour would include Kresge's chili dogs. Naturally, I'll try to get to the Toddle House for the hash browns; they're renowned."

I gave Fats a ride from the airport. As we started out, I told him I was 20 supposed to meet my sister and my grandfather at Mario's — a place that had opened a few years before featuring a special sandwich my sister wanted me to try. Mario cuts off the end of a small Italian loaf, gouges out the bread in the middle, puts in meatballs or sausages and cheese, closes everything in by turning around the end he had cut off and using it as a plug, and bakes the whole thing. He says the patent is applied for.

"Mario's!" Fats said. "What Mario's? When I come into town, I go to 21 Winstead's from the airport."

"My grandfather is waiting, Fats," I said. "He's eighty-eight years old. 22 My sister will scream at me if we're late."

"We could go by the North Kansas City Winstead's branch from here, 23 get a couple to go, and eat them on the *way* to whatzisname's," Fats said. He looked desperate. I realized he had been looking forward to a Winstead's hamburger since his last trip to Kansas City five or six months before — five or six months he had endured without eating anything worth talking about.

That is how Fats and I came to start the grand tour riding toward Mario's 24 clutching Winstead's hamburgers that we would release only long enough to snatch up our Winstead's Frosty Malts ("The Drink You Eat With a Spoon"), and discussing the quality of the top-meat, no-gimmick burger that Winstead's continued to put out. By the time we approached Mario's, I felt that nothing could spoil my day, even if my sister screamed at me for being late.

"There's LaMar's Do-Nuts," Fats said, pulling the steering wheel. "They do a sugar doughnut that's dynamite."

"But my grandfather . . ." I said.

"Just pull over for a second," Fats said. "We'll split a couple."

I can now recount a conversation I would like to have had with the "freelance food and travel writer" who, according to the Kansas City *Star*, spent a few days in town and then called Mario's sandwich "the single best thing I've ever had to eat in Kansas City." I mean no disrespect to Mario, whose sandwich might be good enough to be the single best thing in a lot of cities. I hope he gets his patent.

> ME: I guess if that's the best thing you've ever had to eat in Kansas City you must have got lost trying to find Winstead's. Also, I'm surprised at the implication that a fancy free-lance food and travel writer like you was not allowed into Arthur Bryant's Barbecue, which is only the single best restaurant in the world.
>
> FREE-LANCE FOOD AND TRAVEL WRITER: I happen to like Italian food. It's very Continental.
>
> ME: There are no Italians in Kansas City. It's one of the town's few weaknesses.
>
> FLFTW: Of course there are Italians in Kansas City. There's a huge Italian neighborhood on the northeast side.
>
> ME: In my high school we had one guy we called Guinea Gessler, but he kept insisting he was Swiss. I finally decided he really *was* Swiss. Anyway, he's not running any restaurants. He's in the finance business.
>
> FLFTW: Your high school is not the whole city. I can show you statistics.
>
> ME: Don't tell me about this town, buddy. I was born here.

"Actually, there probably *are* a lot of good restaurants there, because of the stockyards," New Yorkers say — swollen with condescension — when I inform them that the best restaurants in the world are in Kansas City. But, as a matter of fact, there are *not* a lot of good steak restaurants in Kansas City; American restaurants do not automatically take advantage of proximity to the ingredients, as anyone who has ever tried to find a fresh piece of fish on the Florida Coast does not need to told. The best steak restaurant in the world, Jess & Jim's, does happen to be in Kansas City, but it gets its meat from the stockyards in St. Joe, fifty miles away. The most expensive steak on the menu is Jess & Jim's Kansas City Strip Sirloin. When I arrived on the first evening of my tour, it was selling for $6.50, including salad and the best cottage-fried potatoes in the tri-state area. They are probably also the best cottage-fried potatoes in the world, but I don't have wide enough experience in eating cottage fries to make a definitive judgment.

Jess & Jim's is a sort of roadhouse, decorated simply with bowling trophies and illuminated beer signs. But if the proprietor saw one of his waitresses emerge from the kitchen with a steak that was no better than the kind you pay twelve dollars for in New York — in one of those steak houses that also charge for the parsley and the fork and a couple of dollars extra if you want ice in your water — he would probably close up forever from the shame of it all. I thought I might be unable to manage a Jess & Jim's strip sirloin. Normally, I'm not a ferocious steak-eater — a condition I trace to my memories of constant field trips to the stockyards when I was in grade school. (I distinctly remember having gone to the stockyards so many days in a row that I finally said, "Please, teacher, can we have some arithmetic?" But my sister, who went to the same school at the same time, says we never went to the stockyards — which just goes to show how a person's memory can play tricks on her.) As it turned out, I was able to finish my entire Jess & Jim's Kansas City Strip Sirloin — even though I had felt rather full when I sat down at the table. I had eaten a rather large lunch at Winstead's, Mario's and the doughnut place. I had spent the intervening hours listening to my sister tell me about a place on Independence Avenue where the taxi drivers eat breakfast and a place called Laura's Fudge Shop, where you can buy peanut-butter fudge if you're that kind of person, and a place that serves spaghetti in a bucket. My sister has always been interested in that sort of thing — spaghetti in a bucket, chicken in a basket, pig in a blanket. She's really not an eater; she's a container freak.

It has long been acknowledged that the single best restaurant in the world is Arthur Bryant's Barbecue at Eighteenth and Brooklyn in Kansas City — known to practically everybody in town as Charlie Bryant's, after Arthur's brother, who left the business in 1946. The day after my Jess & Jim's Kansas City Strip Sirloin had been consumed, I went to Bryant's with Marvin Rich, an eater I know in Kansas City who practices law on the side. Marvin happens to number among his clients the company that bought Winstead's — the equivalent, in our circle, of a Bronx stickballer having grown up to find himself house counsel to the Yankees. Marvin eats a lot of everything — on the way to Bryant's, for instance, he brought me up-to-date on the local chili-parlor situation with great precision — but I have always thought of him as a barbecue specialist. He even attempts his own barbecue at home — dispatching his wife to buy hickory logs, picking out his own meat, and covering up any mistakes with Arthur Bryant's barbecue sauce, which he keeps in a huge jug in his garage in defiance of the local fire ordinances.

Bryant's specializes in barbecued spareribs and barbecued beef — the beef sliced from briskets of steer that have been cooked over a hickory fire for thirteen hours. When I'm away from Kansas City and depressed, I try to envision someone walking up to the counterman at Bryant's and ordering a beef sandwich to go — for me. The counterman tosses a couple of pieces of bread onto the counter, grabs a half-pound of beef from the pile next to him, slaps it onto the bread, brushes on some sauce in almost the same motion, and then wraps it all up in two thicknesses of butcher paper in a futile attempt to keep the customer's hand dry as he carries off his prize. When I'm *in* Kansas City and depressed, I go to Bryant's. I get a platter full of beef and ham and short ribs. Then I get a plate full of what are undoubtedly the best French-fried potatoes in the world ("I get fresh potatoes and I cook them in pure lard," Arthur Bryant has said. "Pure lard is expensive. But if you want to do a job, you do a job.") Then I get a frozen mug full of cold beer — cold enough so that ice has begun to form on the surface. But all of those are really side dishes to me. The main course at Bryant's, as far as I'm concerned, is something that is given away free — the burned edges of the brisket. The counterman just pushes them over to the side as he slices the beef, and anyone who wants them helps himself. I dream of those burned edges. Sometimes, when I'm in some awful, overpriced restaurant in some strange town — all of my restaurant-finding techniques having failed, so that I'm left to choke down something that costs seven dollars and tastes like a medium-rare sponge — a blank look comes over my face: I have just realized that at that very moment someone in Kansas City is being given those burned edges *free*.

Marvin and I had lunch with a young lawyer in his firm. (I could tell he was a comer: He had spotted a hamburger place at Seventy-fifth and Troost that Marvin thought nobody knew about.) We had a long discussion about a breakfast place called Joe's. "I would have to say that the hash browns at Joe's are the equivalent of the Toddle browns," Marvin said judiciously. "On the other hand, the cream pie at the Toddle House far surpasses Joe's cream pie." I reassured Marvin that I wouldn't think of leaving town without having lunch at Snead's Bar-B-Q. Snead's cuts the burned edges off the brisket with a little more meat attached and puts them on the menu as "brownies." They do the same thing with ham. A mixed plate of ham and beef brownies makes a stupendous meal — particularly in conjunction with a coleslaw that is so superior to the soured confetti they serve in the East that Alice, who has been under the impression that she didn't like coleslaw, was forced to admit that she had never really tasted the true article until she showed up, at an advanced age, at Snead's. Marvin, a man who has never been able to rise above a deep and irrational prejudice against chicken, said nothing about Stroud's, although he must have been aware of local reports that the pan-fried chicken there had so moved the New York gourmet Roy Andries de Groot that he could only respond to his dinner by stopping at the cash register and giving Mrs. Stroud a kiss on the forehead.

After an hour or so of eating, the young lawyer went back to the office 41 ("He's a nice guy," Marvin said, "but I think that theory of his about the banana-cream pie at the airport coffee shop is way off base"), and Marvin and I had a talk with Arthur Bryant himself, who is still pretty affable, even after being called Charlie for twenty-five years. When we mentioned that we had been customers since the early Fifties, it occurred to me that when we first started going to Bryant's it must have been the only integrated restaurant in town. It has always been run by black people, and white people have never been able to stay away. Bryant said that was true. In fact, he said, when mixed groups of soldiers came through Kansas City in those days, they were sent to Bryant's to eat. A vision flashed through my mind:

A white soldier and a black soldier become friends at Fort Riley, Kansas. 42 "We'll stick together when we get to Kansas City," the white soldier says. "We're buddies." They arrive in Kansas City, prepared to go with the rest of the platoon to one of the overpriced and under-seasoned restaurants that line the downtown streets. But the lady at the U.S.O. tells them they'll have to go to "a little place in colored town." They troop toward Bryant's — the white soldier wondering, as the neighborhood grows less and less like the kind of neighborhood he associates with good restaurants, if what his father told him about not paying any attention to the color of a man's skin was such good advice after all. When they get to Bryant's — a storefront with five huge, dusty jugs of barbecue sauce sitting in the window as the only decoration — the white soldier flirts for a moment with the idea of deserting his friend. But they had promised to stick together. He stiffens his resolve, and walks into Bryant's with his friend. He is in THE SINGLE BEST RESTAURANT IN THE WORLD. All of the other guys in the platoon are at some all-white cafeteria eating tasteless mashed potatoes. For perhaps the only time in the history of the Republic, virtue has been rewarded.

Bryant told us that he and his brother learned everything they knew 43 about barbecue from a man named Henry Perry, who originated barbecue in Kansas City. "He was the greatest barbecue man in the world," Bryant said, "but he was a mean outfit." Perry used to enjoy watching his customers take their first bite of a sauce that he made too hot for any human being to eat without eight or ten years of working up to it. What Bryant said about Henry Perry, the master, only corroborated my theory that a good barbecue man is likely to tend toward the sullen — a theory I had felt wilting a bit in the face of Bryant's friendliness. (A man who tends briskets over a hickory fire all night, I figure, is bound to stir up some dark thoughts by morning.) I'm certain, at least, of my theory that a good barbecue man — or a good cook of any kind, for that matter — is not likely to be a promoter or a back-slapper. Once, while my wife and I were waiting to try out the fried clams at a small diner on the Atlantic Coast, I asked the proprietor if he had any lemon. "No, but I'll just make a note of that and I'll have some by next time you come in," he said, turning on his best smile as he made the note. "You have to keep on your toes in this kind of business." We looked around and noticed, for the first time, a flashy new paint job and a wall plaque signifying some kind of good-citizen award. "Watch it," my wife whispered to me, "we're in for a stinker." We were. The redecoration job must have included reinforcing the tables so they would be able to support the weight of the fried clams.

When Arthur Bryant took over the place that had originally been called Perry's #2, he calmed the sauce down, since the sight that made him happiest was not a customer screaming but a customer returning. He eventually introduced French fries, although the barbecued sweet potatoes that Perry used to serve do not sound as if they were the source of a lot of customer complaints. Arthur Bryant is proud that he was the one who built up the business. But he still uses Perry's basic recipe for the sauce ("Twice a year I make me up about twenty-five hundred gallons of it") and Perry's method of barbecuing, and he acknowledges his debt to the master. "It's all Perry," he says. "Everything I'm doing is his." He keeps jugs of barbecue sauce in the window because that was Henry Perry's trademark. I immediately thought of a conversation I would like to have with the mayor and the city council of Kansas City one of these days:

ME: Have you ever heard of Henry Perry?

MAYOR AND CITY COUNCIL (In unison): Is that Commodore Perry?

ME: No, that is Henry Perry, who brought barbecue to Kansas City from Mississippi and therefore is the man who should be recognized as the one towering figure of our culture.

MAYOR AND CITY COUNCIL: Well, we believe that all of our citizens, regardless of their color or national origin —

ME: What I can't understand is why this town is full of statues of the farmers who came out to steal land from the Indians and full of statues of the businessmen who stole the land from the farmers but doesn't even have a three-dollar plaque somewhere for Henry Perry.

MAYOR AND CITY COUNCIL: Well, we certainly think —

ME: As you politicians are always saying, we have *got* to re-order our priorities.

Some time after my grand tour of Kansas City restaurants, I managed to 52
get to the Glendale, California, branch of Bob's for a Big Boy. Since I had to
be in Los Angeles anyway, I decided to take the opportunity to end the debate with Smith once and for all, and also to check out a place called Cassell's Patio, which some people in Los Angeles have claimed has the best
hamburger in the world. (Mr. Cassell ostentatiously grinds his beef right in
front of one's very eyes, but then he uses too much of it for each hamburger
patty. I suspect that Cassell's hamburger probably is the best one available
in Los Angeles, but among Kansas City specialists it would be considered a
very crude burger indeed.)

"The game is just about up, Smith," I informed William Edgett Smith 53
before I left for California. "You won't be able to get away with any of that
'Phoenix is not Glendale' stuff any more."

"Be sure to go to the original branch, across from Bob's international 54
headquarters on Colorado," Smith said.

The Big Boy at Bob's on Colorado Avenue tasted like the Big Boy at Bob's 55
in Phoenix — only slightly superior, in other words, to a McDonald's Big
Mac anywhere. I was not surprised. Smith knows nothing about food. He
once dragged us to a kind of Women's Lib restaurant he had thought was
glorious, and it only required one course for anyone except Smith to realize
that the point of the restaurant was to demonstrate, at enormous damage to
the customers, that women are not necessarily good cooks. I have been at
family-style dinners in Szechuan Chinese restaurants with Smith when his
persistence about including Lobster Cantonese in the order has forced the
rest of us to threaten him with exile to a table of his own. I long ago decided
that the one perceptive remark he ever made about food — the observation
that it is C. C. Brown's in Hollywood rather than Will Wright's that has the
best hot fudge sundae in Southern California — was a fluke, an eyes-shut
home run by a .200 hitter.

"It's all over, Smith," I said to him when I returned to New York. "I had 56
one and I can tell you that Glendale is Phoenix."

"You went to the original, you're sure, on Colorado?" Smith asked. 57

"Right across from Bob's international headquarters," I said. 58

"And you did ask for extra sliced tomatoes?" he said. 59

I paused for a long time, trying to remain calm. "You didn't say anything 60
about extra sliced tomatoes," I said.

"But the whole taste is dependent on extra sliced tomatoes," he said. 61
"The waitress would have been happy to bring you some. Bob prides himself on their friendliness."

"You realize, of course," I said, "that it's only a matter of time before I 62
get back to Glendale and ask for extra sliced tomatoes and call this shameless bluff."

"I'm surprised you didn't ask for sliced tomatoes," Smith said. "It's the sliced tomatoes that really set it off."

QUESTIONS ON MEANING

1. "The Best Restaurants in the World" tells us at least as much about Trillin himself as about Kansas City cuisine. What do restaurants mean to Calvin Trillin? What does he value in a good hamburger, despise in a poor one? What virtues does he celebrate in the preparation of food in general, and what vices does he condemn?
2. Calvin Trillin obviously knows a great deal about restaurants and seems confident that his preferences have some authority. How confident is he? How seriously does he take his expertise?

QUESTIONS ON STRATEGY

1. Trillin features his discussions with friends and family. What does he accomplish by this strategy? How does it affect his point of view? How does it aid Trillin's emphasis?
2. Paragraph 38 begins: "It has long been acknowledged that the single best restaurant in the world is Arthur Bryant's Barbecue." Why does Trillin use the passive voice here? What question does Trillin deliberately leave hanging? How do these tactics fit with his overall strategy?

EXPLORATIONS

1. What makes us laugh? How do we understand, behind Trillin's dead pan, that he mocks and makes comedy of himself? Compare comic prose by Woody Allen and James Thurber. How do their styles of humor differ?

WRITING TOPICS

1. Review Alison Lurie's "Clothing as a Sign System" (pages 202–224). Though Calvin Trillin doesn't attempt a systematic reading of American cuisine in his essay, as Lurie does with fashion in hers, both write as critics of the way people provide themselves with one of life's necessities. Consider their approaches and write in Trillin's style about fashion or in Lurie's about food.
2. Within the limits of his facetiousness, Trillin makes many interesting observations about American life. Look through his essay for the most effective of these, and observe the relations between his points and the jokes, exaggerations, and outright lies that surround them. Then write an essay on any subject in which you try to give weight to your humor, or to lend wit to your seriousness, by writing in Trillin's style.

BOOKS AVAILABLE IN PAPERBACK

Alice, Let's Eat: Further Adventures of a Happy Eater. New York: Vintage. *Essays on food and eating.*

American Fried: Adventures of a Happy Eater. New York: Vintage. *Essays on food and eating.*

Uncivil Liberties. New York: Doubleday, Anchor Books. *Essays.*

FRANCES
FITZGERALD

*F*RANCES FITZGERALD (b. 1940) comes from a notable family. Her maternal
Peabody ancestors include a great-grandfather who founded the Groton School,
an uncle who was governor of Massachusetts, and a series of remarkable women —
poets, abolitionists, sculptors, playwrights, professors, deans, painters, and writers
through a hundred and fifty years of New England history. Her mother (divorced
and remarried) is Marietta Peabody Tree: prominent Democrat, a director of Pan
American Airways and CBS, and the first woman ambassador from the United
States to the United Nations. FitzGerald's half-sister, Penelope Tree, apparently re-
belled against this intellectual tradition: For a while, ten or fifteen years ago, she was
America's most eminent fashion model; now she is a writer. Considering Frances
FitzGerald's politics, her father's career seems equally relevant: Desmond FitzGerald
abandoned Wall Street brokering for spying and became deputy director of the CIA.
While the daughter was indicting American policy in Vietnam, the father was in
charge of a plot to assassinate Fidel Castro with a hypodermic needle disguised as a
ballpoint pen. Daughter's pen proved mightier than father's pen-sword.

FitzGerald graduated from Radcliffe College in 1962. She wrote profiles for the
New York Herald Tribune *Sunday magazine and pursued informal studies in Chi-*

nese and Vietnamese history. By 1966 she was reporting from Vietnam. Her Fire in the Lake *(1972), the book that collected her writing on Vietnam, won a Pulitzer Prize, a National Book Award, and the Bancroft Prize for History. She has also reported on Cuba, Northern Ireland, and the Middle East in* The New Yorker, *the* Atlantic, Harper's, Esquire, *and the* New York Review of Books.

America Revised *(1979) originated as a series of articles in* The New Yorker *on the high school textbook industry and on the changing views of our country that that industry reflects and promotes. These paragraphs combine information and argument. Much information derives from library work, the author consulting variant editions of textbooks for comparison and contrast; other material comes from the journalists' tool of the interview. Strong opinion arises from hard fact. Frances FitzGerald is scrupulous and delicate in her construction, using speculation to introduce a subject, research and interview to document it, and then facts to construct a conclusion.*

Power over the Past

To the uninitiated, the very thought of what goes on in a textbook house   1
must inspire a good deal of vertigo. Way up in some office building sit people — ordinary mortals with red and blue pencils — deciding all the issues of American history, not to mention those of literature and biology. What shall we think of the Vietnam War? Of the American Revolution? What is the nature of American society and what are its values? The responsibility of these people seems awesome, for, as is not true of trade publishers,° the audiences for their products are huge, impressionable, and captive. Children have to read textbooks; they usually have to read all of each textbook and are rarely asked to criticize it for style or point of view. A textbook is there, much like Mt. Everest awaiting George Mallory, and it leaves no alternative. The textbook editors, therefore, must appear to be the arbiters of American values, and the publishing companies the Ministries of Truth° for children. With such power over the past and the future, textbook people — or so the uninitiated assume — should all be philosophers. Oddly, however, few people in the textbook business seem to reflect on their role as truth givers. And most of them are reluctant to discuss the content of their books. Occasionally, a young editor full of injured idealism will ''leak'' a piece of information

---

trade publishers   Publisher of books for the general public — fiction and nonfiction.
Ministries of Truth   From George Orwell's novel *1984*, which describes a totalitarian society in which the Ministry of Truth falsifies records to suit state policy.

about house policy. In one publishing house, a young woman pulled me inside her office conspiratorially to show me a newspaper article attacking a literary anthology that her company had published a few years before. The article expressed outrage about the profanity of the book, pointing to the use of the word "damn" in one short story. "Don't tell anyone I showed you this, or I'll lose my job," the young woman whispered. She went on to say that she had had to revise the anthology — a task that consisted of removing the offending selection and finding stories by two American women and a Puerto Rican man to replace three short stories by Anglo-Saxon men.

"Isn't that a bit arbitrary?" I asked.

"Oh, yes," she said. "But, you see, we're under such great pressure. We'd never sell the book without a Hispanic-American."

The reticence of the textbook people derives, one soon discovers, from the essential ambiguity of their position. On one hand, they are running what amount to Ministries of Truth for children, and, on the other, they are simply trying to make money in one of the freest of free enterprises in the United States, where companies often go under. The market sets limits to the publishers' truth-giving powers. These limits are invisible to outsiders, and they shift like sandbars over time, but the textbook people have a fairly good sense of where they are likely to run aground — and for the rest they feel their way along. Under the circumstances, there is no point in discussing final, or even intermediate, principles, since these would merely upset the navigation. It takes someone used to operating under the norms of trade publishing to demonstrate where principles conflict with market realities.

Robert Bernstein, the president of Random House, runs a large book-publishing complex. In 1974, the head of Pantheon, a Random House division, showed Bernstein the manuscript of what Bernstein thought was an excellent new ninth-grade history of Mississippi. The product of a collaboration between students and faculty of Tougaloo and Millsaps Colleges, the book, unlike the old textbook in use in Mississippi schools, discussed racial conflict frankly and pointed out the contributions that black people had made to the state. The manuscript had been turned down by several textbook houses, but Bernstein — against the advice of some of his own textbook people — backed its publication as a textbook. Pantheon published it as both a trade book and a textbook, under the title *Mississippi: Conflict and Change*. Most of the books never left the warehouse, because the one customer for them, the Mississippi State Textbook Purchasing Board, refused to approve the text for use in state schools at state expense, even though the one textbook in use had gone largely unchanged for ten years and the board was authorized to approve as many as five state histories. As an activist in civil-rights and civil-liberties causes, Bernstein was outraged. So were the authors of the book, and so were some parents, students, and local school officials in Mississippi, and they retained the N.A.A.C.P. Legal Defense and

Educational Fund to file suit against the Mississippi State Textbook Purchasing Board on the ground that its one approved history deprecated black Mississippians and championed white supremacy. "This business is shockingly political," Bernstein told me. "Especially in the South it's shocking."

Shocking as it might be, though, Random House did not join the Legal 6 Defense Fund in bringing suit. Historically, textbook houses do not bring such actions, and rarely, if ever, do they protest when their books are banned by school authorities or burned by outraged citizens. Unlike many trade publishers in similar circumstances (and unlike Pantheon in this case), they acquiesce, give way to pressure, and often cut out the offending passages. In the fall of 1974, a group of parents and other citizens in Kanawha County, West Virginia, demonstrated and finally shut down schools throughout the county in protest against some books newly acquired for classroom use or for the school libraries. Among the objects of their wrath were a number of stories by black writers (the protesters claimed that these were critical of whites), an anti-war poem, and a Mark Twain satire on the Book of Genesis. The incident made national news for weeks and created a good deal of consternation among publishers, teachers, and civil-liberties groups. The Teacher Rights Division of the National Education Association studied the controversy and concluded, not surprisingly, that it was basically a cultural conflict between liberal values and the fundamentalist beliefs of the community. No national organization found anything objectionable in the books, and yet at least one publishing house revised its literary anthology to meet Kanawha County standards.

Trade-book publishers tend to look upon such incidents as First Amend- 7 ment issues, and to see the acquiescence of textbook publishers as pure cowardice — as a betrayal of civil-liberties principles for commercial ends. But there is a sense in which they are wrong. For it is one thing to defend the right to publish a book and quite another to insist that schools must use the book. Why should the editors of Random House, Rand McNally, or Ginn & Company act as the arbiters of the classroom? Who are they to insist that children read Langston Hughes instead of Henry Wadsworth Longfellow, or works by three Anglo-Saxon men instead of works by two American women and one Hispanic-American man? A group like the National Education Association or the Legal Defense Fund can bring a case against a school board for censorship. But textbook publishers are only the servants of the schools, the providers of what they require. And yet textbook publishers rarely make this argument, since, taken to its logical conclusion, it implies that they have — and should have — no standards; that truth is a market commodity, determined by what will sell. Naturally, the publishers do not want to make this admission; hence the swampiness of their public statements, and their strangely unfocussed anxiety when they're asked about their editorial decisions.

To look further into the question of textbook selection and rejection is to see that there is some matter of principle involved. In most countries, national authorities — academies or Ministries of Education — more or less dictate educational policy and the content of textbooks. But the American educational system has always been highly decentralized, and resistant to national authority of any sort. From the publishers' point of view, the educational system is a market, but from the point of view of the schools it is a rough kind of democracy. If a state or a school district wants a certain kind of textbook — a certain kind of truth — should it not have it? The truth is everywhere political, and this system is in principle no less reasonable and no more oppressive of the individual than the alternative of a national authority. In fact, it might be argued that it is less oppressive — that, given the size of the United States, the texts reflect the values and attitudes of society at large much more accurately than they would without decentralization. At least to some degree, they reflect the society itself.

The texts represent the society imperfectly, because the democracy of the educational system is not perfect. In the first place, texts are chosen by adults, and not by the children who must read them. An alternative system is difficult to conceive, but the fact remains that the texts do not represent children. In the second place, not all adults, or even all teachers, have a voice in the selection of schoolbooks. The system of selection is far from uniform across the country, and depends upon a variety of institutions analogous to the Electoral College or to the Senate as it was conceived by the Founding Fathers. About half of the states, for instance, have some form of state-level control over the selection of elementary-school textbooks; slightly fewer states have that control over the choice of secondary-school textbooks. In most of these states, a board of education, a superintendent of schools, or a special textbook committee reviews all texts submitted by the publishers and lists or adopts a certain number of them in each category for use in the public schools. The practices of these review boards vary widely, as does their membership. Some boards, for instance, can by law adopt only a few books in each category, and in practice they may, as the one in Mississippi did, adopt only one. Others simply weed out a few books they judge substandard and leave the real power of decision to the schools. In the so-called non-adoption states, the school districts usually have committees to examine the texts, and the practices of the committees differ more than those of the state boards. The system is, in fact, so complicated nationwide that publishers employ people to spend most of their time figuring out how it works.

The theory behind the practice of state- or districtwide adoptions is that some educational authority should stand between the world of commerce and the hard-pressed teachers to insure that the books meet certain educational standards. The standards are not, however, entirely academic. The guidelines for most state boards include dicta on the subject matter of the

books and on the attitudes they display. The 1976 guidelines of the State Instructional Materials Councils for Florida, for instance, note, "Instructional
materials should accurately portray man's place in ecological systems, including the necessity for the protection of our environment and conservation of our natural resources. [They] should encourage thrift and humane
treatment of people and should not contain any material reflecting unfairly
upon persons because of their race, color, creed, national origin, ancestry,
sex, or occupation." The State of Oregon has traditionally prohibited its
schools from using texts that speak slightingly of the Founding Fathers. In
some cases, the unwritten criteria of state boards are more specific and more
important to the selection of books; in certain instances, they contradict the
written guidelines.

Then, too, the whole system is less than democratic, because it is biassed 11
toward the large adoption units — the large adoption states and the big-city
school districts — and particularly biassed toward the ones that make a narrow selection of books. For example, the recommendation of a social-studies
book by the Texas State Textbook Committee can make a difference of hundreds of thousands of dollars to a publisher. Consequently, that committee
has traditionally had a strong influence on the content of texts. In certain periods, the committee has made it worthwhile for publishers to print a special
Lone Star edition of American history, for use in Texas alone. Much more
important, it has from time to time exercised veto power over the content of
texts used nationwide. For example, in 1961 a right-wing fringe group called
Texans for America intimidated the committee, and it pressed several publishers to make substantial changes in their American-history and geography texts. Macmillan, for one, deleted a passage saying that the Second
World War might have been averted if the United States had joined the
League of Nations. The Silver Burdett Company took out two passages concerning the need for the United States to maintain friendly relations with
other countries and the possibility that some countries would occasionally
disagree with us and substituted passages saying that some countries were
less free than the United States. Various publishers deleted references to
Pete Seeger, Langston Hughes, and several other offenders against the sensibilities of Texans for America. Not only the largest states but combinations
of smaller ones have often exerted an influence disproportionate to the size
of their school populations. The fact that most of the former Confederate
states have state-level adoptions has meant that until recently conservative
white school boards have imposed their racial prejudices not only on the
children in their states but on children throughout the nation.

In sum, the system of adoptions has a significant impact on the way 12
Americans are taught their own history. Because of the Texas State Textbook
Committee, New England children, whose ancestors heartily disapproved
of the Mexican War, have grown up with heroic tales of Davy Crockett and

Sam Houston. Because of actions taken by the Detroit school board and the Newark Textbook Council in the early sixties, textbooks began for the first time to treat the United States as a multiracial society.

The school establishment is not the only group that shapes American history in the textbooks. It is often private-interest groups or citizens' organizations that bring about the most important political changes in the texts. The voices of these outside pressure groups have risen and fallen almost rhythmically in the course of the past fifty years. Sometimes there seems to be a great deal of public interest in textbooks, sometimes very little. What is noteworthy is that until 1960 the voices were pretty much alike; after that, they became much more varied, and the public debate over texts altered dramatically.

The history of public protests against textbooks goes back at least to the middle of the nineteenth century, but these protests grew in size and intensity with the establishment of universal secondary education, in the twentieth. The first important outbreak of them occurred in the years following the First World War. In that period, the mayor of Chicago and the Hearst newspapers, using adjectives such as "unpatriotic" and "un-American," created an uproar over what they said was the pro-British bias of certain texts. (According to Henry Steel Commager,° one of the objects of their rage was an account of the battle of Bunker Hill in a text by Andrew C. McLaughlin. That being a simpler era in the history of textbook publishing, McLaughlin himself answered the charges. According to Commager, he volunteered to change a sentence that read, "Three times the British returned courageously to the attack" to one reading, "Three times the cowardly British returned to the attack.") Simultaneously, the Daughters of the American Revolution attacked some of the texts for not putting enough stress on American military history. The Ku Klux Klan got into the act by complaining of pro-Jewish and pro-Catholic sentiments. Then a number of fundamentalist groups protested against the teaching of evolutionary theory, and eventually succeeded in purging some biology texts of references to evolution. Finally, and with no publicity at all, several utilities associations, including the National Electric Light Association, the American Gas Association, and the American Railway Association, put pressure on the publishers and school officials to doctor the texts in their favor. They got results until their efforts were discovered by the Federal Trade Commission. This wave of right-wing indignation receded as the Depression hit, and for the next ten years such groups remained silent. During the thirties, the peace was broken only by the Wom-

---

Henry Steele Commager (b. 1902), American historian, prolific author of trade books and textbooks.

en's Christian Temperance Union and the liquor interests, whose debate seems to have ended in a draw.

Then, in 1939, there erupted the most furious of all textbook controversies to date, the subject of which was a series on American civilization by Dr. Harold Rugg. A professor at Columbia University Teachers College, Dr. Rugg had written his series (intended for pupils in elementary and junior high school) in the twenties and had begun publishing it in 1930. His aim in writing it had been to bring some realism into the schoolbook description of American society, and to a great extent he succeeded. In one volume, *An Introduction to Problems of American Culture,* he discussed unemployment, the problems faced by new immigrants, class structure, consumerism, and the speedup of life in an industrial society. These questions had never before been dealt with extensively in any school text, and the frankness of his approach remains startling even today. Rugg is probably still the only text writer who has advocated national economic planning and who has used the word ''Socialist'' on the first page of a book. His series does not, however, advocate Socialism. The books are full of pieties about the need for American children to become ''tolerant, understanding and cooperating citizens.'' The series sold very well in the thirties. It was used in school systems containing nearly half of all American children, and for almost a decade there were no complaints about it. In 1939, a chorus of protests suddenly broke out. The first was from the Advertising Federation of America, which was offended by Rugg's disparaging remarks about advertising; then the National Association of Manufacturers, the American Legion, and a columnist for the Hearst press joined in, calling the series Socialist or Communist propaganda. The charges caught on and spread to community groups across the country. Dr. Rugg went on an extensive lecture tour to defend the series, during which he announced publicly that he was neither a Communist nor a Socialist. But in vain. A number of school boards banned the books, and others simply took them out of circulation. In 1938, the Rugg books sold 289,000 copies; in 1944, they sold only 21,000 copies; not long afterward, they disappeared from the market altogether.

During the forties, business associations and right-wing citizens' groups attacked a number of other liberal textbooks and maintained a high level of pressure on the publishers. By 1950 or so, the merely conservative groups had been so successful that they had nothing more to complain about: the texts had become reflections of the National Association of Manufacturers viewpoint. This surrender by the publishers did not, however, end the war; it merely moved the battle lines farther to the right. In the mid-fifties, the anti-fluoridation lobby went on the offensive, followed a few years later by the John Birch Society, which — quite imaginatively — blamed the textbooks for the North Koreans' success in ''brainwashing'' a handful of American prisoners of war. The textbook publishers took this seriously, for by that time they were so sensitive to right-wing pressure that they were checking their books before publication with a member of the Indiana State Textbook Commission named Ada White. Mrs. White believed, among other things, that Robin Hood was a Communist, and she urged that books that told the Robin Hood story be banned from Indiana schools. The publishers were no less mindful of the Texas State House of Representatives, which — in a state that already required a loyalty oath from all textbook writers — approved a resolution urging that "the American history courses in the public schools emphasize in the textbooks our glowing and throbbing history of hearts and souls inspired by wonderful American principles and traditions."

The mid-sixties must have been a bewildering period for the textbook companies. In the space of a year or two, the political wind veered a hundred and eighty degrees. For the first time in publishing history, large-scale protests came from the left and from non-white people, and for the first time such protests were listened to. The turnaround began with a decision made by the Detroit Board of Education. In 1962, the local branch of the N.A.A.C.P. charged that one history text, published by Laidlaw Brothers, depicted slavery in a favorable light, and called on the Detroit board to withdraw it from the city school system. The N.A.A.C.P. and other civil-rights organizations had denounced racial prejudice in the textbooks a number of times in prior years with no real effect. This time, however, the Detroit board withdrew the text, and subsequently began to examine for racial bias all the history texts used in the school system. The Newark Textbook Council soon followed suit. The movement then spread to other big-city school systems and was taken up by organizations representing other racial and ethnic minority groups — Mexican-Americans, Puerto Ricans, American Indians, Asian-Americans, Armenian-Americans, and so on — all of whom claimed, with justice, to have been ignored or abused by the textbooks. Within a few years, a dozen organizations, from the B'nai B'rith's Anti-Defamation League to a new Council on Interracial Books, were studying texts for racial, ethnic, and religious bias and making recommendations for a new generation of texts. What began as a series of discreet protests against individual books became a general proposition: all texts had treated the United States as a white, middle-class society when it was in fact multiracial and multicultural. And this proposition, never so much as suggested before 1962, had by the late sixties come to be a truism for the educational establishment.

The causes of this sudden upsurge of protest and the equally sudden change of perspective among educators are easy to understand in retrospect. As a result of the migrations from South to North during and after the Second World War, black Americans had become by the sixties a strong minority of the population in many Northern cities. In Detroit and Newark, they had become a majority. At the same time, the civil-rights movement had begun to focus national attention on the ugly facts of racial discrimination and prejudice in all areas of American life. A need for a change in the depiction of blacks and other minorities in textbooks, on television, and in advertising was merely one of the themes of the civil-rights movement, but it was the one that was the easiest to deal with. White Americans could resist racial integration in employment, in housing, and in the schools, but no one could deny the minorities at least a token place in the picture of American society. There was no principle to support a counter-argument, and, more important, no reason to make one. An alteration in the symbols could be made without any change in the reality.

The abrupt reversal of perspective in the schools created some panic in the textbook houses. Three or four years — the time it usually takes to produce a new basic text — seemed like an aeon relative to the change in consciousness. A single year was enough to outdate any given picture of America, and nobody could know what the next change would be. (On the evidence of one elementary-school social-studies text, the panic must have reached an all-time high at Noble & Noble. As late as 1964, *New York: Past and Present* made only fleeting reference to blacks. Two years later, another Noble & Noble book, *The New York Story*, included five chapters on blacks.) No sooner had the editors begun to paste in pictures of Ralph Bunche° and write reports on the civil-rights movement than along came the women's movement, sending them quite literally back to the drawing board — this time to change their representation of half the human species.

Only in the mid-seventies did the rate of change slow and the positions harden enough for the publishers to write guidelines for authors and editors on the treatment of racial and other minorities in the textbooks. These guidelines — which have since been published and thus set fast, at least for a while — give instructions on such things as the percentage of illustrations to be devoted to the various groups, and ways to avoid stereotyping in text or pictures. The most interesting thing about them is the rather substantial modifications they make in the English language. The Holt, Rinehart & Winston guidelines on gender, for instance, include such strictures as "Avoid 'the founding fathers,' use 'the founders.'" (Holt also says, "Men are to be shown participating in a variety of domestic chores, such as cooking, sewing, housework, child-rearing, etc. Care should be taken to avoid implying that they are inept at these activities.") Houghton Mifflin advises its editors to make sparing use of quoted material with male references, such as "These are the times that try men's souls"; it has discouraged the use of

---

Ralph Bunche   (1904–1971) Black U.S. diplomat and educator; winner of Nobel Peace Prize in 1950.

"the fatherland" and female pronouns referring to boats. To avoid ethnic stereotyping, its guidelines warn against the overuse of names like "Mary" and "John" and the use of only one ethnic name in lists of arbitrarily chosen names. Macmillan, for its part, urges its editors not to transform ordinary words into negative concepts by adding "black" to them, as in "black market," and it gives "native Americans" as an alternative term for American Indians. There is, as the editors recognize, a certain arbitrariness about these decisions on usage. Allyn & Bacon, for instance, subscribes to "native Americans" but not to "Hispanic-Americans." "We won't use the term Hispanic-Americans," one editor told me, "unless, of course, that becomes the way to go."

As the sixties ended, the publishers may have thought they had found some peace. But it was not to be. Just as soon as their guidelines were issued and pictures of female mechanics and native-American chairpersons began to appear in the books, the reaction set in. The demonstrations in Kanawha County were followed by a spate of smaller-scale protests in communities across the country. Then the John Birch Society emerged from a decade of near-silence to direct or help along (it was difficult to tell which) demonstrations in Washington against one of the new federally funded social-studies programs. Some of the protesters were merely registering conservative objections to what they saw as the excesses of the sixties; others went further, and attacked the whole drive for racial equality and women's rights.

More than automobile manufacturers or toothpaste executives, textbook publishers see themselves as beleaguered, even persecuted, people. And there is some justice in this view, for textbooks have become the lightning rods of American society. In the past, public protest over textbooks occurred only in times of rapid political or social change. Now a great number of organizations and informal groups take an interest in the content of texts. In addition to the racial and ethnic organizations, many of which disagree on what constitutes a "fair and accurate representation" of any given group, a multitude of educational and civil-rights groups have research departments devoted exclusively to the analysis of textbooks. Many of these departments — on the right and on the left — have with experience become sophisticated both in their analyses of text materials and in their methods of approaching publishers, school boards, and the federal bureaucracy. The public battle over texts is thus more intense and more complicated than it has ever been before. At the same time, the publishers have become much more sensitive to the market. Having availed themselves of many of the new market-research techniques, they can now register not just the great upheavals in society but also the slight tremors. They find this a mixed blessing. On the one hand, there are fewer surprises; on the other hand, they have had to become horrendously self-conscious. Does this math text have enough Polish-sounding people buying oranges? Does that third-grade reader show a woman fireperson? What will play in New York that will not offend the sensibilities of Peoria? As the publishers well know, it is impossible to satisfy everyone — or anyone for a long period.

There is perhaps only one group left in the country which does not 23 bother the publishers — or anyway not very often — and that is the academic community. True, scholars do help "develop" textbooks, and occasionally they are permitted to have a significant role in determining their content. In the nineteen-sixties, the federal government was spending large sums for the development of new teaching materials, and groups of scholars selected by the learned societies developed a new generation of textbooks in the natural and social sciences. (The history texts, however, were not affected, for the American Historical Association did not take part.) But most scholars do not take secondary-school (or even college) textbooks seriously — not even when they have a hand in writing them. They do not make a practice of reading textbooks in their field, and no academic journal reviews textbooks on a regular basis. One consequence is that new scholarship trickles down extremely slowly into the school texts; as it proceeds, usually by way of the college texts, the elapsed time between the moment an idea or an approach gains currency in the academic community and the moment it reaches the school texts may be fifteen years or more. Another consequence is that there is no real check on the intellectual quality — or even the factual accuracy — of school textbooks. The result is that on the scale of publishing priorities the pursuit of truth appears somewhere near the bottom.

In a perfectly democratic, or custom-designed, world, every teacher 24 would be allowed to choose his or her own history textbook — which is to say that the publishing houses would publish books in a variety large enough to suit all tastes. But this has somehow never happened, in spite of all the structural changes the textbook business has undergone in the United States over the past hundred years. The late nineteenth century ought to have been the period for a great diversity of books, because scores of publishers were competing then in a burgeoning school market. At the time, however, the content of texts was the least of a publisher's worries, for — particularly in the West, where the competition was the most intense — the sale of books depended largely on which company could most successfully bribe or otherwise corrupt the whiskey dealers, preachers, and political-party hacks who sat on the school boards. This degree of free enterprise proved uneconomical in the long run. In the eighteen-nineties, three of the major companies banded together to form the American Book Company, which acquired a seventy-five to eighty-per-cent monopoly of the textbook market. Yet this streamlining of the industry did not make for a wider selection of books. Indeed, when the American Book Company acquired a total monopoly in geography publishing, it produced no new books in that field for many years. Competition was eventually reestablished, and there was some greater variety in the texts until the ideological freeze of the Cold War. In recent years, the industry has been a model of American free enterprise: four hundred companies (forty of them major ones) have competed fiercely, but with a fairly high degree of probity, to sell more or less the same product to the same people.

In the mid-sixties, there were high hopes in the publishing industry that this situation would change. Sitting at the feet of Marshall McLuhan, the publishers decided that the era of mass production was over — along with the era of literacy and linear reasoning — and that they should at once prepare to deliver instant all-around audiovisual programming with individualized feedback for every child. The era of software had come — the era of total communication and perfect customization. Not only — or even principally — the textbook publishers but a lot of high-rolling communications-industry executives dreamed of equipping every classroom in America with television sets, video cameras, holography sets, and computer terminals. As a first step toward this post-industrial future, the executives built conglomerates designed to put all kinds of software components and communications capability under one roof. Xerox acquired Ginn & Company; RCA bought Random House; CBS acquired Holt, Rinehart & Winston; Raytheon bought D. C. Heath; and Time Inc. acquired Little, Brown and Company and Silver Burdett and, with General Electric, formed the General Learning Corporation.

The problem was that all the new theories about education, information, and business in the future rested on the availability of large-scale government funding, a growing student population, and a ballooning economy. And none of these conditions held for very long. As soon as the costs of the Vietnam War came home, the schools drastically curtailed their multimedia programs, the government cut back funding of research projects to develop new teaching methods and materials, and the conglomerates began to look like no more than the sum of their parts. And then, with great speed, fashion changed, and educational theory turned conservative. Parents and school boards complained that children couldn't read or write anymore — that what they needed was textbook drill. Publishers, up to their ears in machinery, began to look on textbooks as the basic winter coat. While they continued to produce some of the cheapest of the new materials — such things as magazines and filmstrips — they put their money back into books: both the hardbacks and a new generation of paperbacks, which allowed teachers a choice of supplementary material. "It began to dawn on them," one trade-book editor says, "that the book is finally the most efficient retrieval system we possess."

The big basic history textbook thus seems here to say, at least for a bit, and to stay just about what it has always been in this century — a kind of lowest common denominator of American tastes. The books of the seventies are somewhat more diverse than those of the fifties, but still they differ from one another not much more than one year's crop of Detroit sedans. This is hardly surprising, since, like cars, textbooks are expensive to design and relatively cheap to duplicate. The development of a new eleventh-grade history text can cost five hundred thousand dollars (more this year, perhaps), with an additional hundred thousand in marketing costs. Since the public schools across the country now spend less than one percent of their budgets on buying books (textbook publishing is only a seven-hundred-million-dollar-a-year business), publishers cannot afford to have more than one or two basic histories on the market at the same time. Consequently, all of them try to compete for the center of the market, designing their books not to please anyone in particular but to be acceptable to as many people as possible. The word "controversial" is as deeply feared by textbook publishers as it is coveted by trade-book publishers. What a textbook reflects is thus a compromise, an America sculpted and sanded down by the pressures of diverse constituents and interest groups.

QUESTIONS ON MEANING

1. What different groups in society influence textbook publishers? How has that influence changed over the past sixty years? What effect do various interest groups have on the content of history textbooks? How does FitzGerald account for the increase in public protests over the content of high school textbooks?
2. Does the free enterprise system in textbook publishing result in a diversity of textbooks and a democratic representation of American society? Why or why not?

QUESTIONS ON STRATEGY

1. Why does FitzGerald refer to textbook publishers as "Ministries of Truth" for young people (paragraphs 1 and 4)? How does this analogy fit in with her overall view of the textbook publishing industry?
2. Paragraphs 14–21 survey the history of public protests against textbooks. In paragraph 18 FitzGerald analyzes a change on the part of the "educational establishment." How does this paragraph function in the whole sequence? In paragraph 21, how does FitzGerald manage the transition to her discussion of the present state of things?

EXPLORATIONS

1. One way to assess FitzGerald's argument is to test it against the evidence of textbooks you can examine in the light of her essay. Do college texts alter as rapidly as high school texts? Examine two or three sequent editions of an

American history text used in college. Look up controversial subjects, and note any changes you discover from edition to edition. Can you find politically motivated changes in any English texts? What kinds of changes can you find? Are there indications that this textbook responded to pressures mentioned in FitzGerald's article?

2. As a class project, prepare a discussion along the following lines: About half of the participants might investigate the process by which textbooks are selected in their home towns, or in their home states. The other half could look into the problem of censorship, the tendency to ban certain textbooks, or other books, from school libraries. What kinds of books attract this sort of attention? Should parents be allowed to control what their children read?

WRITING TOPICS

1. "In a perfectly democratic, or custom-designed, world, every teacher would be allowed to choose his or her own history textbook." Does this seem ideal to you? Write an essay defining how you think textbooks should be chosen for high-school students, and defend your conclusion.

BOOKS AVAILABLE IN PAPERBACK

America Revised: History Schoolbooks in the Twentieth Century. New York: Vintage. *Nonfiction: Social and educational history.*

Fire in the Lake: The Vietnamese and the Americans in Vietnam. New York: Vintage. *Nonfiction: History.*

MAXINE HONG
KINGSTON

*M*AXINE HONG KINGSTON *was born in California in 1940, the eldest of six children in a Chinese immigrant family. English is her second language, and only recently has she begun to dream in it. She grew up in the town of Stockton, in the San Joaquin Valley, where her family ran a laundry. Stockton's small Chinese population, most of whom came from a village called Sun Woi, regularly gathered at the laundry to tell stories. What the young child remembered became material for the adult writer.*

Kingston graduated from the University of California at Berkeley in 1962 and taught high school in California and Hawaii, where she has lived for many years. She has published poetry, stories, and articles in a variety of magazines — the New York Times Magazine, New West, Ms., The New Yorker, Iowa Review *— and has received extensive honors for her two books of reminiscence. This essay is the first chapter of* The Woman Warrior: Memoirs of a Girlhood Among Ghosts *(1975), which won the National Book Critics Award for Nonfiction. She followed it with* China Men *(1980), which received the American Book Award. From stories that an eldest child heard from her mother, and from the nostalgic ambience of a laundry in Stockton, Maxine Hong Kingston assembles narrative and reminiscence* *that embodies the collision and amalgamation of two cultures — the same combination that produced the author herself.*

Writing as a member of a minority, Kingston has encountered a familiar problem: Some Chinese-Americans complain that she is unrepresentative of her cultural sources. She has replied: "When people criticize my work by saying that it does not reflect their experience, I hear an assumption that one of us — in this case, me — is expected to speak for all the rest. I don't think that is a good expectation. Each one of us has a unique voice, and no one else will see things exactly the way I do, or write about them the way I do." With her eye for particulars, with her intense feeling for family and for her family's alien America, she makes with her unique voice a special human reality.

No Name Woman

"You must not tell anyone," my mother said, "what I am about to tell you. In China your father had a sister who killed herself. She jumped into the family well. We say that your father has all brothers because it is as if she had never been born.

"In 1924 just a few days after our village celebrated seventeen hurry-up weddings — to make sure that every young man who went 'out on the road' would responsibly come home — your father and his brothers and your grandfather and his brothers and your aunt's new husband sailed for America, the Gold Mountain. It was your grandfather's last trip. Those lucky enough to get contracts waved good-bye from the decks. They fed and guarded the stowaways and helped them off in Cuba, New York, Bali, Hawaii. 'We'll meet in California next year,' they said. All of them sent money home.

"I remember looking at your aunt one day when she and I were dressing; I had not noticed before that she had such a protruding melon of a stomach. But I did not think, 'She's pregnant,' until she began to look like other pregnant women, her skirt pulling and the white tops of her black pants showing. She could not have been pregnant, you see, because her husband had been gone for years. No one said anything. We did not discuss it. In early summer she was ready to have the child, long after the time when it could have been possible.

"The village had also been counting. On the night the baby was to be born the villagers raided our house. Some were crying. Like a great saw, teeth strung with lights, files of people walked zigzag across our land, tearing the rice. Their lanterns doubled in the disturbed black water, which drained away through the broken bunds. As the villagers closed in, we could see that some of them, probably men and women we knew well, wore white masks. The people with long hair hung it over their faces. Women with short hair made it stand up on end. Some had tied white bands around their foreheads, arms, and legs.

"At first they threw mud and rocks at the house. Then they threw eggs 5 and began slaughtering our stock. We could hear the animals scream their deaths — the roosters, the pigs, a last great roar from the ox. Familiar wild heads flared in our night windows; the villagers encircled us. Some of the faces stopped to peer at us, their eyes rushing like searchlights. The hands flattened against the panes, framed heads, and left red prints.

"The villagers broke in the front and the back doors at the same time, 6 even though we had not locked the doors against them. Their knives dripped with the blood of our animals. They smeared blood on the doors and walls. One woman swung a chicken, whose throat she had slit, splattering blood in red arcs about her. We stood together in the middle of our house, in the family hall with the pictures and tables of the ancestors around us, and looked straight ahead.

"At that time the house had only two wings. When the men came back, 7 we would build two more to enclose our courtyard and a third one to begin a second courtyard. The villagers pushed through both wings, even your grandparents' rooms, to find your aunt's, which was also mine until the men returned. From this room a new wing for one of the younger families would grow. They ripped up her clothes and shoes and broke her combs, grinding them underfoot. They tore her work from the loom. They scattered the cooking fire and rolled the new weaving in it. We could hear them in the kitchen breaking our bowls and banging the pots. They overturned the great waist-high earthenware jugs; duck eggs, pickled fruits, vegetables burst out and mixed in acrid torrents. The old woman from the next field swept a broom through the air and loosed the spirits-of-the-broom over our heads. 'Pig.' 'Ghost.' 'Pig,' they sobbed and scolded while they ruined our house.

"When they left, they took sugar and oranges to bless themselves. They 8 cut pieces from the dead animals. Some of them took bowls that were not broken and clothes that were not torn. Afterward we swept up the rice and sewed it back up into sacks. But the smells from the spilled preserves lasted. Your aunt gave birth in the pigsty that night. The next morning when I went for the water, I found her and the baby plugging up the family well.

"Don't let your father know that I told you. He denies her. Now that you 9 have started to menstruate, what happened to her could happen to you. Don't humiliate us. You wouldn't like to be forgotten as if you had never been born. The villagers are watchful."

Whenever she had to warn us about life, my mother told stories that ran 10 like this one, a story to grow up on. She tested our strength to establish realities. Those in the emigrant generations who could not reassert brute survival died young and far from home. Those of us in the first American generations have had to figure out how the invisible world the emigrants built around our childhoods fit in solid America.

The emigrants confused the gods by diverting their curses, misleading them with crooked streets and false names. They must try to confuse their offspring as well, who, I suppose, threaten them in similar ways — always trying to get things straight, always trying to name the unspeakable. The Chinese I know hide their names; sojourners take new names when their lives change and guard their real names with silence.

Chinese-Americans, when you try to understand what things in you are Chinese, how do you separate what is peculiar to childhood, to poverty, insanities, one family, your mother who marked your growing with stories, from what is Chinese? What is Chinese tradition and what is the movies?

If I want to learn what clothes my aunt wore, whether flashy or ordinary, I would have to begin, "Remember Father's drowned-in-the-well sister?" I cannot ask that. My mother has told me once and for all the useful parts. She will add nothing unless powered by Necessity, a riverbank that guides her life. She plants vegetable gardens rather than lawns; she carries the odd-shaped tomatoes home from the fields and eats food left for the gods.

Whenever we did frivolous things, we used up energy; we flew high kites. We children came up off the ground over the melting cones our parents brought home from work and the American movie on New Year's Day — *Oh, You Beautiful Doll* with Betty Grable one year, and *She Wore A Yellow Ribbon* with John Wayne another year. After the one carnival ride each, we paid in guilt; our tired father counted his change on the dark walk home.

Adultery is extravagance. Could people who hatch their own chicks and eat the embryos and the heads for delicacies and boil the feet in vinegar for party food, leaving only the gravel, eating even the gizzard lining — could such people engender a prodigal aunt? To be a woman, to have a daughter in starvation time was a waste enough. My aunt could not have been the lone romantic who gave up everything for sex. Women in the old China did not choose. Some man had commanded her to lie with him and be his secret evil. I wonder whether he masked himself when he joined the raid on her family.

Perhaps she encountered him in the fields or on the mountain where the daughters-in-law collected fuel. Or perhaps he first noticed her in the marketplace. He was not a stranger because the village housed no strangers. She had to have dealings with him other than sex. Perhaps he worked an adjoining field, or he sold her the cloth for the dress she sewed and wore. His demand must have surprised, then terrified her. She obeyed him; she always did as she was told.

When the family found a young man in the next village to be her husband, she stood tractably beside the best rooster, his proxy, and promised before they met that she would be his forever. She was lucky that he was her age and she would be the first wife, an advantage secure now. The night she first saw him, he had sex with her. Then he left for America. She had almost forgotten what he looked like. When she tried to envision him, she only saw the black and white face in the group photograph the men had had taken before leaving.

The other man was not, after all, much different from her husband. They 18 both gave orders: she followed. "If you tell your family, I'll beat you. I'll kill you. Be here again next week." No one talked sex, ever. And she might have separated the rapes from the rest of living if only she did not have to buy her oil from him or gather wood in the same forest. I want her fear to have lasted just as long as rape lasted so that the fear could have been contained. No drawn-out fear. But women at sex hazarded birth and hence lifetimes. The fear did not stop but permeated everywhere. She told the man, "I think I'm pregnant." He organized the raid against her.

On nights when my mother and father talked about their life back home, 19 sometimes they mentioned an "outcast table" whose business they still seemed to be settling, their voices tight. In a commensal tradition, where food is precious, the powerful older people made wrongdoers eat alone. Instead of letting them start separate new lives like the Japanese, who could become samurais and geishas, the Chinese family, faces averted but eyes glowering sideways, hung on to the offenders and fed them leftovers. My aunt must have lived in the same house as my parents and eaten at an outcast table. My mother spoke about the raid as if she had seen it, when she and my aunt, a daughter-in-law to a different household, should not have been living together at all. Daughters-in-law lived with their husbands' parents, not their own; a synonym for marriage in Chinese is "taking a daughter-in-law." Her husband's parents could have sold her, mortgaged her, stoned her. But they had sent her back to her own mother and father, a mysterious act hinting at disgraces not told me. Perhaps they had thrown her out to deflect the avengers.

She was the only daughter; her four brothers went with her father, hus- 20 band, and uncles "out on the road" and for some years became western men. When the goods were divided among the family, three of the brothers took land, and the youngest, my father, chose an education. After my grandparents gave their daughter away to her husband's family, they had dispensed all the adventure and all the property. They expected her alone to keep the traditional ways, which her brothers, now among the barbarians, could fumble without detection. The heavy, deep-rooted women were to maintain the past against the flood, safe for returning. But the rare urge west had fixed upon our family, and so my aunt crossed boundaries not delineated in space.

The work of preservation demands that the feelings playing about in 21 one's guts not be turned into action. Just watch their passing like cherry blossoms. But perhaps my aunt, my forerunner, caught in a slow life, let dreams grow and fade and after some months or years went toward what persisted. Fear at the enormities of the forbidden kept her desires delicate, wire and bone. She looked at a man because she liked the way the hair was tucked behind his ears, or she liked the question-mark line of a long torso curving at the shoulder and straight at the hip. For warm eyes or a soft voice or a slow walk — that's all — a few hairs, a line, a brightness, a sound, a pace, she gave up family. She offered us up for a charm that vanished with tiredness, a pigtail that didn't toss when the wind died. Why, the wrong lighting could erase the dearest thing about him.

It could very well have been, however, that my aunt did not take subtle enjoyment of her friend, but, a wild woman, kept rollicking company. Imagining her free with sex doesn't fit, though. I don't know any women like that, or men either. Unless I see her life branching into mine, she gives me no ancestral help.

To sustain her being in love, she often worked at herself in the mirror, guessing at the colors and shapes that would interest him, changing them frequently in order to hit on the right combination. She wanted him to look back.

On a farm near the sea, a woman who tended her appearance reaped a reputation for eccentricity. All the married women blunt-cut their hair in flaps about their ears or pulled it back in tight buns. No nonsense. Neither style blew easily into heart-catching tangles. And at their weddings they displayed themselves in their long hair for the last time. "It brushed the backs of my knees," my mother tells me. "It was braided, and even so, it brushed the backs of my knees."

At the mirror my aunt combed individuality into her bob. A bun could have been contrived to escape into black streamers blowing in the wind or in quiet wisps about her face, but only the older women in our picture album wear buns. She brushed her hair back from her forehead, tucking the flaps behind her ears. She looped a piece of thread, knotted into a circle between her index fingers and thumbs, and ran the double strand across her forehead. When she closed her fingers as if she were making a pair of shadow geese bite, the string twisted together catching the little hairs. Then she pulled the thread away from her skin, ripping the hairs out neatly, her eyes watering from the needles of pain. Opening her fingers, she cleaned the thread, then rolled it along her hairline and the tops of her eyebrows. My mother did the same to me and my sisters and herself. I used to believe that the expression "caught by the short hairs" meant a captive held with a depilatory string. It especially hurt at the temples, but my mother said we were lucky we didn't have to have our feet bound when we were seven. Sisters used to sit on their beds and cry together, she said, as their mothers or their slave removed the bandages for a few minutes each night and let the blood gush back into their veins. I hope that the man my aunt loved appreciated a smooth brow, that he wasn't just a tits-and-ass man.

Once my aunt found a freckle on her chin, at a spot that the almanac said 26 predestined her for unhappiness. She dug it out with a hot needle and washed the wound with peroxide.

More attention to her looks than these pullings of hairs and pickings at 27 spots would have caused gossip among the villagers. They owned work clothes and good clothes, and they wore good clothes for feasting the new seasons. But since a woman combing her hair hexes beginnings, my aunt rarely found an occasion to look her best. Women looked like great sea snails — the corded wood, babies, and laundry they carried were the whorls on their backs. The Chinese did not admire a bent back; goddesses and warriors stood straight. Still there must have been a marvelous freeing of beauty when a worker laid down her burden and stretched and arched.

Such commonplace loveliness, however, was not enough for my aunt. 28 She dreamed of a lover for the fifteen days of New Year's, the time for families to exchange visits, money, and food. She plied her secret comb. And sure enough she cursed the year, the family, the village, and herself.

Even as her hair lured her imminent lover, many other men looked at 29 her. Uncles, cousins, nephews, brothers would have looked, too, had they been home between journeys. Perhaps they had already been restraining their curiosity, and they left, fearful that their glances, like a field of nesting birds, might be startled and caught. Poverty hurt, and that was their first reason for leaving. But another, final reason for leaving the crowded house was the never-said.

She may have been unusually beloved, the precious only daughter, 30 spoiled and mirror gazing because of the affection the family lavished on her. When her husband left, they welcomed the chance to take her back from the in-laws; she could live like the little daughter for just a while longer. There are stories that my grandfather was different from other people, "crazy ever since the little Jap bayoneted him in the head." He used to put his naked penis on the dinner table, laughing. And one day he brought home a baby girl, wrapped up inside his brown western-style greatcoat. He had traded one of his sons, probably my father, the youngest, for her. My grandmother made him trade back. When he finally got a daughter of his own, he doted on her. They must have all loved her, except perhaps my father, the only brother who never went back to China, having once been traded for a girl.

Brothers and sisters, newly men and women, had to efface their sexual 31 color and present plain miens. Disturbing hair and eyes, a smile like no other, threatened the ideal of five generations living under one roof. To focus blurs, people shouted face to face and yelled from room to room. The immigrants I know have loud voices, unmodulated to American tones even after years away from the village where they called their friendships out across the fields. I have not been able to stop my mother's screams in public libraries or over telephones. Walking erect (knees straight, toes pointed forward, not pigeon-toed, which is Chinese-feminine) and speaking in an inaudible voice, I have tried to turn myself American-feminine. Chinese communication was loud, public. Only sick people had to whisper. But at the dinner table, where the family members came nearest one another, no one could talk, not the outcasts nor any eaters. Every word that falls from the mouth is a coin lost. Silently they gave and accepted food with both hands. A preoccupied child who took his bowl with one hand got a sideways glare. A complete moment of total attention is due everyone alike. Children and lovers have no singularity here, but my aunt used a secret voice, a separate attentiveness.

She kept the man's name to herself throughout her labor and dying; she did not accuse him that he be punished with her. To save her inseminator's name she gave silent birth.

He may have been somebody in her own household, but intercourse with a man outside the family would have been no less abhorrent. All the village were kinsmen, and the titles shouted in loud country voices never let kinship be forgotten. Any man within visiting distance would have been neutralized as a lover — "brother," "younger brother," "older brother" — one hundred and fifteen relationship titles. Parents researched birth charts probably not so much to assure good fortune as to circumvent incest in a population that has but one hundred surnames. Everybody has eight million relatives. How useless then sexual mannerisms, how dangerous.

As if it came from an atavism deeper than fear, I used to add "brother" silently to boys' names. It hexed the boys, who would or would not ask me to dance, and made them less scary and as familiar and deserving of benevolence as girls.

But, of course, I hexed myself also — no dates. I should have stood up, both arms waving, and shouted out across libraries, "Hey you! Love me back." I had no idea, though, how to make attraction selective, how to control its direction and magnitude. If I made myself American-pretty so that the five or six Chinese boys in the class fell in love with me, everyone else — the Caucasian, Negro, and Japanese boys — would too. Sisterliness, dignified and honorable, made much more sense.

Attraction eludes control so stubbornly that whole societies designed to organize relationships among people cannot keep order, not even when they bind people to one another from childhood and raise them together. Among the very poor and the wealthy, brothers married their adopted sisters, like doves. Our family allowed some romance, paying adult brides' prices and providing dowries so that their sons and daughters could marry strangers. Marriage promises to turn strangers into friendly relatives — a nation of siblings.

In the village structure, spirits shimmered among the live creatures, bal- 37
anced and held in equilibrium by time and land. But one human being flaring up into violence could open up a black hole, a maelstrom that pulled in
the sky. The frightened villagers, who depended on one another to maintain
the real, went to my aunt to show her a personal, physical representation of
the break she had made in the "roundness." Misallying couples snapped off
the future, which was to be embodied in true offspring. The villagers punished her for acting as if she could have a private life, secret and apart from
them.

If my aunt had betrayed the family at a time of large grain yields and 38
peace, when many boys were born, and wings were being built on many
houses, perhaps she might have escaped such severe punishment. But the
men — hungry, greedy, tired of planting in dry soil, cuckolded — had had to
leave the village in order to send food-money home. There were ghost
plagues, bandit plagues, wars with the Japanese, floods. My Chinese
brother and sister had died of an unknown sickness. Adultery, perhaps only
a mistake during good times, became a crime when the village needed food.

The round moon cakes and round doorways, the round tables of gradu- 39
ated size that fit one roundness into another, round windows and rice bowls
— these talismans had lost their power to warn this family of the law: a family must be whole, faithfully keeping the descent line by having sons to feed
the old and the dead, who in turn look after the family. The villagers came to
show my aunt and her lover-in-hiding a broken house. The villagers were
speeding up the circling of events because she was too shortsighted to see
that her infidelity had already harmed the village, that waves of consequences would return unpredictably, sometimes in disguise, as now, to hurt
her. This roundness had to be made coin-sized so that she would see its circumference: punish her at the birth of her baby. Awaken her to the inexora-
ble. People who refused fatalism because they could invest small resources
insisted on culpability. Deny accidents and wrest fault from the stars.

After the villagers left, their lanterns now scattering in various directions 40
toward home, the family broke their silence and cursed her. "Aiaa, we're
going to die. Death is coming. Death is coming. Look what you've done.
You've killed us. Ghost! Dead ghost! Ghost! You've never been born." She
ran out into the fields, far enough from the house so that she could no
longer hear their voices, and pressed herself against the earth, her own land
no more. When she felt the birth coming, she thought that she had been
hurt. Her body seized together. "They've hurt me too much," she thought.
"This is gall, and it will kill me." With forehead and knees against the earth,
her body convulsed and then relaxed. She turned on her back, lay on the
ground. The black well of sky and stars went out and out and out forever;
her body and her complexity seemed to disappear. She was one of the stars,
a bright dot in blackness, without home, without a companion, in eternal
cold and silence. An agoraphobia rose in her, speeding higher and higher,

bigger and bigger; she would not be able to contain it; there would be no end to fear.

Flayed, unprotected against space, she felt pain return, focusing her body. This pain chilled her — a cold, steady kind of surface pain. Inside, spasmodically, the other pain, the pain of the child, heated her. For hours she lay on the ground, alternately body and space. Sometimes a vision of normal comfort obliterated reality: she saw the family in the evening gambling at the dinner table, the young people massaging their elders' backs. She saw them congratulating one another, high joy on the mornings the rice shoots came up. When these pictures burst, the stars drew yet further apart. Black space opened.

She got to her feet to fight better and remembered that old-fashioned women gave birth in their pigsties to fool the jealous, pain-dealing gods, who do not snatch piglets. Before the next spasms could stop her, she ran to the pigsty, each step a rushing out into emptiness. She climbed over the fence and knelt in the dirt. It was good to have a fence enclosing her, a tribal person alone.

Laboring, this woman who had carried her child as a foreign growth that sickened her every day, expelled it at last. She reached down to touch the hot, wet, moving mass, surely smaller than anything human, and could feel that it was human after all — fingers, toes, nails, nose. She pulled it up on to her belly, and it lay curled there, butt in the air, feet precisely tucked one under the other. She opened her loose shirt and buttoned the child inside. After resting, it squirmed and thrashed and she pushed it up to her breast. It turned its head this way and that until it found her nipple. There, it made little snuffling noises. She clenched her teeth at its preciousness, lovely as a young calf, a piglet, a little dog.

She may have gone to the pigsty as a last act of responsibility: she would protect this child as she had protected its father. It would look after her soul, leaving supplies on her grave. But how would this tiny child without family find her grave when there would be no marker for her anywhere, neither in the earth nor the family hall? No one would give her a family hall name. She had taken the child with her into the wastes. At its birth the two of them had felt the same raw pain of separation, a wound that only the family pressing tight could close. A child with no descent line would not soften her life but only trail after her, ghostlike, begging her to give it purpose. At dawn the villagers on their way to the fields would stand around the fence and look.

Full of milk, the little ghost slept. When it awoke, she hardened her breasts against the milk that crying loosens. Toward morning she picked up the baby and walked to the well.

Carrying the baby to the well shows loving. Otherwise abandon it. Turn its face into the mud. Mothers who love their children take them along. It was probably a girl; there is some hope of forgiveness for boys.

"Don't tell anyone you had an aunt. Your father does not want to hear   47
her name. She has never been born." I have believed that sex was unspeakable and words so strong and fathers so frail that "aunt" would do my father mysterious harm. I have thought that my family, having settled among immigrants who had also been their neighbors in the ancestral land, needed to clean their name, and a wrong word would incite the kinspeople even here. But there is more to this silence: they want me to participate in her punishment. And I have.

In the twenty years since I heard this story I have not asked for details   48
nor said my aunt's name; I do not know it. People who can comfort the dead can also chase after them to hurt them further — a reverse ancestor worship. The real punishment was not the raid swiftly inflicted by the villagers, but the family's deliberately forgetting her. Her betrayal so maddened them, they saw to it that she should suffer forever, even after death. Always hungry, always needing, she would have to beg food from other ghosts, snatch and steal it from those whose living descendants give them gifts. She would have to fight the ghosts massed at crossroads for the buns a few thoughtful citizens leave to decoy her away from village and home so that the ancestral spirits could feast unharassed. At peace, they could act like gods, not ghosts, their descent lines providing them with paper suits and dresses, spirit money, paper houses, paper automobiles, chicken, meat, and rice into eternity — essences delivered up in smoke and flames, steam and incense rising from each rice bowl. In an attempt to make the Chinese care for people outside the family, Chairman Mao encourages us now to give our paper replicas to the spirits of outstanding soldiers and workers, no matter whose ancestors they may be. My aunt remains forever hungry. Goods are not distributed evenly among the dead.

My aunt haunts me — her ghost drawn to me because now, after fifty   49
years of neglect, I alone devote pages of paper to her, though not origamied into houses and clothes. I do not think she always means me well. I am telling on her, and she was a spite suicide, drowning herself in the drinking water. The Chinese are always very frightened of the drowned one, whose weeping ghost, wet hair hanging and skin bloated, waits silently by the water to pull down a substitute.

QUESTIONS ON MEANING

1. Kingston tells the story of her aunt as though she had known her, as though she had been there at her aunt's disgrace. Where did she get her information? What could she have known for fact and what does she create from imagination?

2. In what ways does Kingston's aunt deviate from traditional behavior, even before her pregnancy? Why does Kingston call her aunt "my forerunner" in paragraph 21? In what sense did her aunt define a path for her? What does the author's last name suggest to you about these questions?
3. In paragraph 47, Kingston says she participates in her aunt's punishment. How does she participate? In the way expected of her?

QUESTIONS ON STRATEGY

1. How does Kingston interweave a story, exciting and disturbing as narration, with her interpretation of that story?
2. Paragraphs 48 and 49 make a beautiful equation between the ritual burning of paper sculptures in honor of ancestors and Maxine Hong Kingston's writing about her aunt. How does her concluding image work to reveal her intentions in writing this essay?

EXPLORATIONS

1. How do relations between one generation and the next differ in the ghetto from such relations in middle-class suburban life? What can you discover in James Baldwin's "Notes of a Native Son" (pages 164–183) and "No Name Woman" to indicate that Baldwin and Kingston are in some ways looking back at ghetto life from a new, relatively liberated point of view?

WRITING TOPICS

1. Many American families from various ethnic backgrounds have undergone the experience of assimilation within the past few generations. If you can, interview a member of your family who remembers tales of a period of transition, either from personal experience or from the anecdotes of an earlier generation. Write an essay on the process of cultural assimilation, using details from your interview.
2. Write an essay about some family story you heard as a child that served as a "story to grow up on" (paragraph 10).

BOOKS AVAILABLE IN PAPERBACK

China Men. New York: Vintage. *Nonfiction: Personal history.*

The Woman Warrior: Memoirs of a Girlhood Among Ghosts. New York: Vintage. *Nonfiction: Personal history.*

STEPHEN JAY
GOULD

S TEPHEN JAY GOULD *(b. 1941), whose essays delight and instruct the non-
scientist in the byways of natural history, dedicated* Ever Since Darwin
*(1977) to his father, "who took me to see the tyrannosaurus when I was five."
Maybe the child's visit to a museum formed the whole life.*

*Gould is a paleontologist who teaches geology, biology, and history of science at
Harvard University. After graduating from Antioch College in 1963, he took his
Ph.D. at Columbia University. He is an evolutionist. He writes that his essays
"range broadly from planetary and geological to social and political history, but they
are united . . . by the common thread of evolutionary theory — Darwin's version."
Author of a long book called* Ontogeny and Phylogeny *(1977) and of* The Mismeasure of Man *(1981), which attacks methods of quantifying intelligence, he has
collected three volumes of brief scientific essays mostly from his column, "This View
of Life," in* Natural History *magazine.* Ever Since Darwin *was the first collection,
and he followed it with* The Panda's Thumb *(1980) and* Hen's Teeth and
Horse's Toes *(1983). Among other honors he has won a National Book Award and
become a MacArthur Prize Fellow.*

Writing in the New York Times Book Review *about three great scientific essayists (T. H. Huxley, J. B. S. Haldane, and P. B. Medawar), Gould listed the qualities he admired in terms that we can apply to Gould himself: "All write about the simplest things and draw from them a universe of implications. . . . All maintain an unflinching commitment to rationality amid the soft attractions of an uncritical mysticism. . . . All demonstrate a deep commitment to the demystification of science by cutting through jargon; they show by example rather than exhortation that the most complex concepts can be rendered intelligible to everyone."*

In one of Gould's essays he writes, "I have never been able to raise much personal enthusiasm for disembodied theory. Thus, when I wish to explore the explanatory power of evolutionary theory . . . , I write about apparent oddities resolved by Darwin's view — dwarf male anglerfishes parasitically united with females, wasps that paralyze insects to provide a living feast for their larvae, young birds that kill their siblings by simply pushing them outside a ring of guano." Although Gould may choose these "oddities" for their explanatory function, the reader glimpses in his writing, alongside the enthusiastic explainer, a five-year-old who looks with joy and wonder at the immense skeleton of a dinosaur.

Were Dinosaurs Dumb?

When Muhammad Ali flunked his army intelligence test, he quipped (with a wit that belied his performance on the exam): "I only said I was the greatest; I never said I was the smartest." In our metaphors and fairy tales, size and power are almost always balanced by a want of intelligence. Cunning is the refuge of the little guy. Think of Br'er Rabbit and Br'er Bear; David smiting Goliath with a slingshot; Jack chopping down the beanstalk. Slow wit is the tragic flaw of a giant.

The discovery of dinosaurs in the nineteenth century provided, or so it appeared, a quintessential case for the negative correlation of size and smarts. With their pea brains and giant bodies, dinosaurs became a symbol of lumbering stupidity. Their extinction seemed only to confirm their flawed design.

Dinosaurs were not even granted the usual solace of a giant — great physical prowess. God maintained a discreet silence about the brains of behemoth, but he certainly marveled at its strength: "Lo, now, his strength is in his loins, and his force is in the navel of his belly. He moveth his tail like a cedar. . . . His bones are as strong pieces of brass; his bones are like bars of iron [Job 40:16–18]." Dinosaurs, on the other hand, have usually been reconstructed as slow and clumsy. In the standard illustration, *Brontosaurus* wades in a murky pond because he cannot hold up his own weight on land.

Popularizations for grade school curricula provide a good illustration of   4
prevailing orthodoxy. I still have my third grade copy (1948 edition) of Bertha Morris Parker's *Animals of Yesterday*, stolen, I am forced to suppose, from P.S. 26, Queens (sorry Mrs. McInerney). In it, boy (teleported back to the Jurassic) meets brontosaur:

> It is huge, and you can tell from the size of its head that it must
> be stupid. . . . This giant animal moves about very slowly as it
> eats. No wonder it moves slowly! Its huge feet are very heavy,
> and its great tail is not easy to pull around. You are not surprised that the thunder lizard likes to stay in the water so that
> the water will help it hold up its huge body. . . . Giant dinosaurs were once the lords of the earth. Why did they disappear? You can probably guess part of the answer — their
> bodies were too large for their brains. If their bodies had been
> smaller, and their brains larger, they might have lived on.

Dinosaurs have been making a strong comeback of late, in this age of   5
"I'm OK, you're OK." Most paleontologists are now willing to view them
as energetic, active, and capable animals. The *Brontosaurus* that wallowed in
its pond a generation ago is now running the land, while pairs of males have
been seen twining their necks about each other in elaborate sexual combat
for access to females (much like the neck wrestling of giraffes). Modern anatomical reconstructions indicate strength and agility, and many paleontologists now believe that dinosaurs were warmblooded.

The idea of warmblooded dinosaurs has captured the public imagination   6
and received a torrent of press coverage. Yet another vindication of dinosaurian capability has received very little attention, although I regard it as
equally significant. I refer to the issue of stupidity and its correlation with
size. The revisionist interpretation, which I support in this column, does not
enshrine dinosaurs as paragons of intellect, but it does maintain that they
were not small brained after all. They had the "right-sized" brains for reptiles of their body size.

I don't wish to deny that the flattened, minuscule head of largebodied   7
Stegosaurus houses little brain from our subjective, top-heavy perspective,
but I do wish to assert that we should not expect more of the beast. First of
all, large animals have relatively smaller brains than related, small animals.
The correlation of brain size with body size among kindred animals (all reptiles, all mammals, for example) is remarkably regular. As we move from
small to large animals, from mice to elephants or small lizards to Komodo
dragons, brain size increases, but not so fast as body size. In other words,
bodies grow faster than brains, and large animals have low ratios of brain
weight to body weight. In fact, brains grow only about two-thirds as fast as
bodies. Since we have no reason to believe that large animals are consistently stupider than their smaller relatives, we must conclude that large ani-

mals require relatively less brain to do as well as smaller animals. If we do not recognize this relationship, we are likely to underestimate the mental power of very large animals, dinosaurs in particular.

Second, the relationship between brain and body size is not identical in all groups of vertebrates. All share the same rate of relative decrease in brain size, but small mammals have much larger brains than small reptiles of the same body weight. This discrepancy is maintained at all larger body weights, since brain size increases at the same rate in both groups — two-thirds as fast as body size.

Put these two facts together — all large animals have relatively small brains, and reptiles have much smaller brains than mammals at any common body weight — and what should we expect from a normal, large reptile? The answer, of course, is a brain of very modest size. No living reptile even approaches a middle-sized dinosaur in bulk, so we have no modern standard to serve as a model for dinosaurs.

Fortunately, our imperfect fossil record has, for once, not severely disappointed us in providing data about fossil brains. Superbly preserved skulls have been found for many species of dinosaurs, and cranial capacities can be measured. (Since brains do not fill craniums in reptiles, some creative, although not unreasonable, manipulation must be applied to estimate brain size from the hole within a skull.) With these data, we have a clear test for the conventional hypothesis of dinosaurian stupidity. We should agree, at the outset, that a reptilian standard is the only proper one — it is surely irrelevant that dinosaurs had smaller brains than people or whales. We have abundant data on the relationship of brain and body size in modern reptiles. Since we know that brains increase two-thirds as fast as bodies as we move from small to large living species, we can extrapolate this rate to dinosaurian sizes and ask whether dinosaur brains match what we would expect of living reptiles if they grew so large.

Harry Jerison studied the brain sizes of ten dinosaurs and found that they fell right on the extrapolated reptilian curve. Dinosaurs did not have small brains; they maintained just the right-sized brains for reptiles of their dimensions. So much for Ms. Parker's explanation of their demise.

Jerison made no attempt to distinguish among various kinds of dinosaurs; ten species distributed over six major groups scarcely provide a proper basis for comparison. Recently, James A. Hopson of the University of Chicago gathered more data and made a remarkable and satisfying discovery.

Hopson needed a common scale for all dinosaurs. He therefore compared each dinosaur brain with the average reptilian brain we would expect at its body weight. If the dinosaur falls on the standard reptilian curve, its brain receives a value of 1.0 (called an encephalization quotient, or EQ — the ratio of actual brain to expected brain for a standard reptile of the same body weight). Dinosaurs lying above the curve (more brain than expected in a standard reptile of the same body weight) receive values in excess of 1.0, while those below the curve measure less than 1.0.

Hopson found that the major groups of dinosaurs can be ranked by in- 14 creasing values of average EQ. This ranking corresponds perfectly with inferred speed, agility and behavioral complexity in feeding (or avoiding the prospect of becoming a meal). The giant sauropods, *Brontosaurus* and its allies, have the lowest EQ's — 0.20 to 0.35. They must have moved fairly slowly and without great maneuverability. They probably escaped predation by virtue of their bulk alone, much as elephants do today. The armored ankylosaurs and stegosaurs come next with EQ's of 0.52 to 0.56. These animals, with their heavy armor, probably relied largely upon passive defense, but the clubbed tail of ankylosaurs and the spiked tail of stegosaurs imply some active fighting and increased behavioral complexity.

The ceratopsians rank next at about 0.7 to 0.9. Hopson remarks: "The 15 larger ceratopsians, with their great horned heads, relied on active defensive strategies and presumably required somewhat greater agility than the tail-weaponed forms, both in fending off predators and in intraspecific combat bouts. The smaller ceratopsians, lacking true horns, would have relied on sensory acuity and speed to escape from predators." The ornithopods (duckbills and their allies) were the brainiest herbivores, with EQ's from 0.85 to 1.5. They relied upon "acute senses and relatively fast speeds" to elude carnivores. Flight seems to require more acuity and agility than standing defense. Among ceratopsians, small, hornless, and presumably fleeing *Protoceratops* had a higher EQ than great three-horned *Triceratops*.

Carnivores have higher EQ's than herbivores, as in modern vertebrates. 16 Catching a rapidly moving or stoutly fighting prey demands a good deal more upstairs than plucking the right kind of plant. The giant theropods (*Tyrannosaurus* and its allies) vary from 1.0 to nearly 2.0. Atop the heap, quite appropriately at its small size, rests the little coelurosaur *Stenonychosaurus* with an EQ well above 5.0. Its actively moving quarry, small mammals and birds perhaps, probably posed a greater challenge in discovery and capture than *Triceratops* afforded *Tyrannosaurus*.

I do not wish to make a naive claim that brain size equals intelligence or, 17 in this case, behavioral range and agility (I don't know what intelligence means in humans, much less in a group of extinct reptiles). Variation in brain size within a species has precious little to do with brain power (humans do equally well with 900 or 2,500 cubic centimeters of brain). But comparison across species, when the differences are large, seems reasonable. I do not regard it as irrelevant to our achievements that we so greatly exceed koala bears — much as I love them — in EQ. The sensible ordering among dinosaurs also indicates that even so coarse a measure as brain size counts for something.

If behavioral complexity is one consequence of mental power, then we might expect to uncover among dinosaurs some signs of social behavior that demand coordination, cohesiveness, and recognition. Indeed we do, and it cannot be accidental that these signs were overlooked when dinosaurs labored under the burden of a falsely imposed obtuseness. Multiple trackways have been uncovered, with evidence for more than twenty animals traveling together in parallel movement. Did some dinosaurs live in herds? At the Davenport Ranch sauropod trackway, small footprints lie in the center and larger ones at the periphery. Could it be that some dinosaurs traveled much as some advanced herbivorous mammals do today, with large adults at the borders sheltering juveniles in the center?

In addition, the very structures that seemed most bizarre and useless to older paleontologists — the elaborate crests of hadrosaurs, the frills and horns of ceratopsians, and the nine inches of solid bone above the brain of *Pachycephalosaurus* — now appear to gain a coordinated explanation as devices for sexual display and combat. Pachycephalosaurs may have engaged in head-butting contests much as mountain sheep do today. The crests of some hadrosaurs are well designed as resonating chambers; did they engage in bellowing matches? The ceratopsian horn and frill may have acted as sword and shield in the battle for mates. Since such behavior is not only intrinsically complex, but also implies an elaborate social system, we would scarcely expect to find it in a group of animals barely muddling through at a moronic level.

But the best illustration of dinosaurian capability may well be the fact most often cited against them — their demise. Extinction, for most people, carries many of the connotations attributed to sex not so long ago — a rather disreputable business, frequent in occurrence, but not to anyone's credit, and certainly not to be discussed in proper circles. But, like sex, extinction is an ineluctable part of life. It is the ultimate fate of all species, not the lot of unfortunate and ill-designed creatures. It is no sign of failure.

The remarkable thing about dinosaurs is not that they became extinct, but that they dominated the earth for so long. Dinosaurs held sway for 100 million years while mammals, all the while, lived as small animals in the interstices of their world. After 70 million years on top, we mammals have an excellent track record and good prospects for the future, but we have yet to display the staying power of dinosaurs.

People, on this criterion, are scarcely worth mentioning — 5 million years perhaps since *Australopithecus*, a mere 50,000 for our own species, *Homo sapiens*. Try the ultimate test within our system of values: Do you know anyone who would wager a substantial sum, even at favorable odds, on the proposition that *Homo sapiens* will last longer than *Brontosaurus*?

QUESTIONS ON MEANING

1. Gould's primary intention in this essay is to refute some popular assumptions about "the negative correlation of size and smarts," especially with reference to dinosaurs. Paragraph 2 establishes the two false assumptions Gould will attack. What are they? Which of the two common errors receives more of his attention? Why?
2. What is the importance of Hopson's EQ measure (paragraphs 13 and 14) in Gould's argument? Does it allow Gould to concede something to a point of view he attacks?
3. Paragraphs 18 and 19 analyze the fossil record of dinosaur life for evidence of social behavior demanding "coordination, cohesiveness, and recognition." Is this part of Gould's argument convincing?

QUESTIONS ON STRATEGY

1. Stephen Jay Gould is a specialist in paleontology who writes for a general audience on subjects related to his field. What tricks of phrasing or turns of wit, what references and asides, what touches of style indicate how he defines his audience?
2. In paragraph 6 Gould refers to himself as a revisionist. What tactics does he employ as he goes about revising prevailing thought in his essay? Where does he address the issues as a specialist, and where as a generalist? How much of his revision depends on accommodation rather than attack? Does he try to prove all his points? Do some remain simple assertions? Find specific examples of his various tactics.
3. Paragraph 7 introduces an important fact: "As we move from small to large animals" within related groups, "brains grow only about two-thirds as fast as bodies." How often is this information repeated in the next three paragraphs? Why?

EXPLORATIONS

1. Like John Kenneth Galbraith, Stephen Jay Gould is a Harvard professor with strong academic credentials in his specialty who writes for popular audiences. Both "The Technostructure" (pages 24–34) and "Were Dinosaurs Dumb?" use the same primary organizing strategy: debunking common assumptions. Look through both essays and find specific examples of the ways in which the authors strive to correct their readers' mistaken assumptions without making readers resent them. What measures do these authors take to make themselves pleasant? Do they try for the common touch in any obvious way? Do they flatter their readers, or otherwise assuage them? Look for details like Galbraith's toaster or Gould's apology to Mrs. McInerney. How do these and other devices work in their attacks on public errors?

WRITING TOPICS

1. Using the conclusions you reach in the Explorations questions, write an essay about the role of tact required of an expert writing for the public.
2. Is the fat, lumbering, largely passive dinosaur stereotype that Gould discredits the only popular image of the species? Can you visualize the tyrannosaurus in *King Kong* or *Fantasia*? Do these and other examples of the popular view of dinosaurs fit Gould's stereotype? Is the general view of the negative correlation of size and intellect as simple as Gould makes it seem? Write an essay addressing these questions.

BOOKS AVAILABLE IN PAPERBACK

Ever Since Darwin: Reflections in Natural History. New York: Norton. *Essays.*

The Mismeasure of Man. New York: Norton. *Nonfiction: Study of IQ testing and the controversy surrounding it.*

The Panda's Thumb: More Reflections in Natural History. New York: Norton. *Essays.*

JONATHAN
SCHELL

*J*ONATHAN SCHELL *was born (1943) in New York, where he now lives and*
writes for The New Yorker. *He is often mentioned as a possible successor to Wil-*
liam Shawn, editor of The New Yorker, *when Shawn retires.*

Schell attended Harvard University and the University of California at Berkeley;
he did graduate work in Japan in Far Eastern history. Visiting Vietnam, he accompa-
nied American soldiers in a helicopter raid against the Viet Cong that resulted in the
destruction of a small village. His story of this action appeared first in The New
Yorker *and then as* The Village of Ben Suc *(1967), an early book on the Vietnam*
War. In The Time of Illusion *(1976) he wrote about politics in America from 1969*
through President Nixon's resignation in 1974.

Most recently he has written The Fate of the Earth *(1982), his examination of*
the prospects for nuclear war. When it was first serialized in The New Yorker, *the*
book had an immediate influence on the movement for a nuclear freeze. ''A Republic
of Insects and Grass'' comes from the opening section of The Fate of the Earth.
Here it is Schell's self-appointed task to think about the unthinkable, to employ
mind-numbing numbers without numbing the mind, to cite statistics almost impos-
sible to imagine, yet through images and analogies to bring them into the reader's
terrified comprehension.

A Republic
of Insects and Grass

The "strategic" forces of the Soviet Union — those that can deliver nuclear warheads to the United States — are so far capable of carrying seven thousand warheads with an estimated maximum yield of more than seventeen thousand megatons of explosive power, and, barring unexpected developments in arms-control talks, the number of warheads is expected to rise in the coming years. The actual megatonnage of the Soviet strategic forces is not known, and, for a number of reasons, including the fact that smaller warheads can be delivered more accurately, it is very likely that the actual megatonnage is lower than the maximum possible; however, it is reasonable to suppose that the actual megatonnage is as much as two-thirds of the maximum, which would be about eleven and a half thousand megatons. If we assume that in a first strike the Soviets held back about a thousand megatons (itself an immense force), then the attack would amount to about ten thousand megatons, or the equivalent of eight hundred thousand Hiroshima bombs. American strategic forces comprise about nine thousand warheads with a yield of some three thousand five hundred megatons. The total yield of these American forces was made comparatively low for strategic reasons. American planners discovered that smaller warheads can be delivered more accurately than larger ones, and are therefore more useful for attacking strategic forces on the other side. And, in fact, American missiles are substantially more accurate than Soviet ones. However, in the last year or so, in spite of this advantage in numbers of warheads and in accuracy, American leaders have come to believe that the American forces are inadequate, and, again barring unexpected developments in arms-control talks, both the yield of the American arsenal and the number of warheads in it are likely to rise dramatically. (Neither the United States nor the Soviet Union reveals the total explosive yield of its own forces. The public is left to turn to private organizations, which, by making use of hundreds of pieces of information that *have* been released by the two governments, piece together an over-all picture. The figures I have used to estimate the maximum capacities of the two sides are taken for the most part from tables provided in the latest edition of "The Military Balance," a standard yearly reference work on the strength of military forces around the world, which is published by a research institute in London called the International Institute for Strategic Studies.) The territory of the United States, including Alaska and Hawaii, is three million six hundred and fifteen thousand one hundred and twenty-two square miles. It contains approximately two hundred and twenty-five million people, of

426

whom sixty per cent, or about a hundred and thirty-five million, live in various urban centers with a total area of only eighteen thousand square miles. I asked Dr. Kendall, who has done considerable research on the consequences of nuclear attacks, to sketch out in rough terms what the actual distribution of bombs might be in a ten-thousand-megaton Soviet attack in the early nineteen-eighties on all targets in the United States, military and civilian.

"Without serious distortion," he said, "we can begin by imagining that we would be dealing with ten thousand weapons of one megaton each, although in fact the yields would, of course, vary considerably. Let us also make the assumption, based on common knowledge of weapons design, that on average the yield would be one-half fission and one-half fusion. This proportion is important, because it is the fission products — a virtual museum of about three hundred radioactive isotopes, decaying at different rates — that give off radioactivity in fallout. Fusion can add to the total in ground bursts by radioactivation of ground material by neutrons, but the quantity added is comparatively small. Targets can be divided into two categories — hard and soft. Hard targets, of which there are about a thousand in the United States, are mostly missile silos. The majority of them can be destroyed only by huge, blunt overpressures, ranging anywhere from many hundreds to a few thousand pounds per square inch, and we can expect that two weapons might be devoted to each one to assure destruction. That would use up two thousand megatons. Because other strategic military targets — such as Strategic Air Command bases — are near centers of population, an attack on them as well, perhaps using another couple of hundred megatons, could cause a total of more than twenty million casualties, according to studies by the Arms Control and Disarmament Agency. If the nearly eight thousand weapons remaining were then devoted to the cities and towns of the United States in order of population, every community down to the level of fifteen hundred inhabitants would be hit with a megaton bomb — which is, of course, many, many times what would be necessary to annihilate a town that size. For obvious reasons, industry is highly correlated with population density, so an attack on the one necessarily hits the other, especially when an attack of this magnitude is considered. Ten thousand targets would include everything worth hitting in the country and much more; it would simply *be* the United States. The targeters would run out of targets and victims long before they ran out of bombs. If you imagine that the bombs were distributed according to population, then, allowing for the fact that the attack on the military installations would have already killed about twenty million people, you would have about forty megatons to devote to each remaining million people in the country. For the seven and a half million people in New York City, that would come to three hundred megatons. Bearing in mind what one megaton can do, you can see that this

2

would be preposterous overkill. In practice, one might expect the New York metropolitan area to be hit with some dozens of one-megaton weapons.''

In the first moments of a ten-thousand-megaton attack on the United States, I learned from Dr. Kendall and from other sources, flashes of white light would suddenly illumine large areas of the country as thousands of suns, each one brighter than the sun itself, blossomed over cities, suburbs, and towns. In those same moments, when the first wave of missiles arrived, the vast majority of the people in the regions first targeted would be irradiated, crushed, or burned to death. The thermal pulses could subject more than six hundred thousand square miles, or one-sixth of the total land mass of the nation, to a minimum level of forty calories per centimetre squared — a level of heat that chars human beings. (At Hiroshima, charred remains in the rough shape of human beings were a common sight.) Tens of millions of people would go up in smoke. As the attack proceeded, as much as three-quarters of the country could be subjected to incendiary levels of heat, and so, wherever there was inflammable material, could be set ablaze. In the ten seconds or so after each bomb hit, as blast waves swept outward from thousands of ground zeros, the physical plant of the United States would be swept away like leaves in a gust of wind. The six hundred thousand square miles already scorched by the forty or more calories of heat per centimetre squared would now be hit by blast waves of a minimum of five pounds per square inch, and virtually all the habitations, places of work, and other man-made things there — substantially the whole human construct in the United States — would be vaporized, blasted, or otherwise pulverized out of existence. Then, as clouds of dust rose from the earth, and mushroom clouds spread overhead, often linking to form vast canopies, day would turn to night. (These clouds could blanket as much as a third of the nation.) Shortly, fires would spring up in the debris of the cities and in every forest dry enough to burn. These fires would simply burn down the United States. When one pictures a full-scale attack on the United States, or on any other country, therefore, the picture of a single city being flattened by a single bomb — an image firmly engraved in the public imagination, probably because of the bombings of Hiroshima and Nagasaki — must give way to a picture of substantial sections of the country being turned by a sort of nuclear carpet-bombing into immense infernal regions, literally tens of thousands of square miles in area, from which escape is impossible. In Hiroshima and Nagasaki, those who had not been killed or injured so severely that they could not move were able to flee to the undevastated world around them, where they found help, but in any city where three or four bombs had been used — not to mention fifty, or a hundred — flight from one blast would only be flight toward another, and no one could escape alive. Within these regions, each of three of the immediate effects of nuclear weapons — initial radiation, thermal pulse, and blast wave — would alone be enough to kill most people:

the initial nuclear radiation would subject tens of thousands of square miles to lethal doses; the blast waves, coming from all sides, would nowhere fall below the overpressure necessary to destroy almost all buildings; and the thermal pulses, also coming from all sides, would always be great enough to kill exposed people and, in addition, to set on fire everything that would burn. The ease with which virtually the whole population of the country could be trapped in these zones of universal death is suggested by the fact that the sixty per cent of the population that lives in an area of eighteen thousand square miles could be annihilated with only three hundred one-megaton bombs — the number necessary to cover the area with a maximum of five pounds per square inch of overpressure and forty calories per centimetre squared of heat. That would leave nine thousand seven hundred megatons, or ninety-seven per cent of the megatonnage in the attacking force, available for other targets. (It is hard to imagine what a targeter would do with all his bombs in these circumstances. Above several thousand megatons, it would almost become a matter of trying to hunt down individual people with nuclear warheads.)

The statistics on the initial nuclear radiation, the thermal pulses, and the 4 blast waves in a nuclear holocaust can be presented in any number of ways, but all of them would be only variations on a simple theme — the annihilation of the United States and its people. Yet while the immediate nuclear effects are great enough in a ten-thousand-megaton attack to destroy the country many times over, they are not the most powerfully lethal of the local effects of nuclear weapons. The killing power of the local fallout is far greater. Therefore, if the Soviet Union was bent on producing the maximum overkill — if, that is, its surviving leaders, whether out of calculation, rage, or madness, decided to eliminate the United States not merely as a political and social entity but as a biological one — they would burst their bombs on the ground rather than in the air. Although the scope of severe blast damage would then be reduced, the blast waves, fireballs, and thermal pulses would still be far more than enough to destroy the country, and, in addition, provided only that the bombs were dispersed widely enough, lethal fallout would spread throughout the nation. The amount of radiation delivered by the fallout from a ground burst of a given size is still uncertain — not least because, as Glasstone notes, there has never been a "true land surface burst" of a bomb with a yield of over one kiloton. (The Bikini burst was in part over the ocean.) Many factors make for uncertainty. To mention just a few: the relative amounts of the fallout that rises into the stratosphere and the fallout that descends to the ground near the blast are dependent on, among other things, the yield of the weapon, and, in any case, can be only guessed at; the composition of the fallout will vary with the composition of the material on the ground that is sucked up into the mushroom cloud; prediction of the distribution of fallout by winds of various speeds at various altitudes depends on a choice of several "models"; and the calculation of the arrival time of the fallout — an important calculation, since fallout cannot harm living things until it lands near them — is subject to similar speculative doubts. However, calculations on the basis of figures for a one-megaton ground burst which are given in the Office of Technology Assessment's report show that ten thousand megatons would yield one-week doses around the country averaging more than ten thousand rems. In actuality, of course, the bombs would almost certainly not be evenly spaced around the country but, rather, would be concentrated in populated areas and in missile fields; and the likelihood is that in most places where people lived or worked the doses would be many times the average, commonly reaching several tens of thousands of rems for the first week, while in remote areas they would be less, or, conceivably, even nonexistent. (The United States contains large tracts of empty desert, and to target them would be virtually meaningless from any point of view.)

These figures provide a context for judging the question of civil defense. With overwhelming immediate local effects striking the vast majority of the population, and with one-week doses of radiation then rising into the tens of thousands of rems, evacuation and shelters are a vain hope. Needless to say, in these circumstances evacuation before an attack would be an exercise in transporting people from one death to another. In some depictions of a holocaust, various rescue operations are described, with unafflicted survivors bringing food, clothes, and medical care to the afflicted, and the afflicted making their way to thriving, untouched communities, where churches, school auditoriums, and the like would have been set up for their care — as often happens after a bad snowstorm, say. Obviously, none of this could come about. In the first place, in a full-scale attack there would in all likelihood be no surviving communities, and, in the second place, everyone who failed to seal himself off from the outside environment for as long as several months would soon die of radiation sickness. Hence, in the months after a holocaust there would be no activity of any sort, as, in a reversal of the normal state of things, the dead would lie on the surface and the living, if there were any, would be buried underground.

To this description of radiation levels around the country, an addition remains to be made. This is the fact that attacks on the seventy-six nuclear power plants in the United States would produce fallout whose radiation had much greater longevity than that of the weapons alone. The physicist Dr. Kosta Tsipis, of M.I.T., and one of his students, Steven Fetter, recently published an article in Scientific American called "Catastrophic Releases of Radioactivity," in which they calculate the damage from a one-megaton thermonuclear ground burst on a one-gigawatt nuclear power plant. In such a ground burst, the facility's radioactive contents would be vaporized along with everything nearby, and the remains would be carried up into the mushroom cloud, from which they would descend to the earth with the rest of the fallout. But whereas the fission products of the weapon were newly made, and contained many isotopes that would decay to insignificant levels very swiftly, the fission products in a reactor would be a collection of longer-lived isotopes (and this applies even more strongly to the spent fuel in the reactor's holding pond), since the short-lived ones would, for the most part, have had enough time to reduce themselves to harmless levels. The intense but comparatively short-lived radiation from the weapon would kill people in the first few weeks and months, but the long-lived radiation that was produced both by the weapon and by the power plant could prevent anyone from living on a vast area of land for decades after it fell. For example, after a year an area of some seventeen hundred square miles downwind of a power plant on which a one-megaton bomb had been ground-burst (again assuming a fifteen-mile-an-hour wind) would still be delivering more than fifty rems per year to anyone who tried to live there, and that is two hundred and fifty times the "safe" dose established by the E.P.A. The bomb by itself would produce this effect over an area of only twenty-six square miles. (In addition to offering an enemy a way of redoubling the effectiveness of his attacks in a full-scale holocaust, reactors provide targets of unparalleled danger in possible terrorist nuclear attacks. In an earlier paper, Tsipis and Fetter observe that "the destruction of a reactor with a nuclear weapon, even of relatively small yield, such as a crude terrorist nuclear device, would represent a national catastrophe of lasting consequences." It can be put down as one further alarming oddity of life in a nuclear world that in building nuclear power plants nations have opened themselves to catastrophic devastation and long-term contamination of their territories by enemies who manage to get hold of only a few nuclear weapons.)

If, in a nuclear holocaust, anyone hid himself deep enough under the earth and stayed there long enough to survive, he would emerge into a dying natural environment. The vulnerability of the environment is the last word in the argument against the usefulness of shelters: there is no hole big enough to hide all of nature in. Radioactivity penetrates the environment in many ways. The two most important components of radiation from fallout are gamma rays, which are electromagnetic radiation of the highest intensity, and beta particles, which are electrons fired at high speed from decaying nuclei. Gamma rays subject organisms to penetrating whole-body doses, and are responsible for most of the ill effects of radiation from fallout. Beta particles, which are less penetrating than gamma rays, act at short range, doing harm when they collect on the skin, or on the surface of a leaf. They are harmful to plants on whose foliage the fallout descends — producing "beta burn" — and to grazing animals, which can suffer burns as well as gastrointestinal damage from eating the foliage. Two of the most harmful radioactive isotopes present in fallout are strontium-90 (with a half-life of twenty-eight years) and cesium-137 (with a half-life of thirty years). They are taken up into the food chain through the roots of plants or through direct ingestion by animals, and contaminate the environment from within. Strontium-90 happens to resemble calcium in its chemical composition, and therefore finds its way into the human diet through dairy products and is eventually deposited by the body in the bones, where it is thought to cause bone cancer. (Every person in the world now has in his bones a measurable deposit of strontium-90 traceable to the fallout from atmospheric nuclear testing.)

Over the years, agencies and departments of the government have sponsored numerous research projects in which a large variety of plants and animals were irradiated in order to ascertain the lethal or sterilizing dose for each. These findings permit the prediction of many gross ecological consequences of a nuclear attack. According to "Survival of Food Crops and Livestock in the Event of Nuclear War," the proceedings of the 1970 symposium at Brookhaven National Laboratory, the lethal doses for most mammals lie between a few hundred rads and a thousand rads of gamma radiation; a rad — for "roentgen absorbed dose" — is a roentgen of radiation that has been absorbed by an organism, and is roughly equal to a rem. For example, the lethal doses of gamma radiation for animals in pasture, where fallout would be descending on them directly and they would be eating fallout that had fallen on the grass, and would thus suffer from doses of beta radiation as well, would be one hundred and eighty rads for cattle; two hundred and forty rads for sheep; five hundred and fifty rads for swine; three hundred and fifty rads for horses; and eight hundred rads for poultry. In a ten-thousand-megaton attack, which would create levels of radiation around the country averaging more than ten thousand rads, most of the mammals of the United States would be killed off. The lethal doses for birds are in roughly the same range as those for mammals, and birds, too, would be killed off. Fish are killed at doses of between one thousand one hundred rads and about five thousand six hundred rads, but their fate is less predictable. On the one hand, water is a shield from radiation, and would afford some protection; on the other hand, fallout might concentrate in bodies of water as it ran off the land. (Because radiation causes no pain, animals, wandering at will through the environment, would not avoid it.) The one class of animals containing a number of species quite likely to survive, at least in the short run, is the insect class, for which in most known cases the lethal doses lie between about two thousand rads and about a hundred thousand rads. Insects, therefore, would be destroyed selectively. Unfortunately for the rest of the environment, many of the phytophagous species — insects that feed directly on vegetation — which "include some of the most ravaging species on earth" (according to Dr. Vernon M. Stern, an entomologist at the University of California at Riverside, writing in "Survival of Food Crops"), have very high tolerances, and so could be expected to survive disproportionately, and then to multiply greatly in the aftermath of an attack. The demise of their natural predators the birds would enhance their success.

Plants in general have a higher tolerance to radioactivity than animals do. Nevertheless, according to Dr. George M. Woodwell, who supervised the irradiation with gamma rays, over several years, of a small forest at Brookhaven Laboratory, a gamma-ray dose of ten thousand rads "would devastate most vegetation" in the United States, and, as in the case of the pastured animals, when one figures in the beta radiation that would also be delivered by fallout the estimates for the lethal doses of gamma rays must be reduced — in this case, cut in half. As a general rule, Dr. Woodwell and his colleagues at Brookhaven discovered, large plants are more vulnerable to radiation than small ones. Trees are among the first to die, grasses among the last. The most sensitive trees are pines and the other conifers, for which lethal doses are in roughly the same range as those for mammals. Any survivors coming out of their shelters a few months after the attack would find that all the pine trees that were still standing were already dead. The lethal doses for most deciduous trees range from about two thousand rads of gamma-ray radiation to about ten thousand rads, with the lethal doses for eighty per cent of deciduous species falling between two thousand and eight thousand rads. Since the addition of the beta-ray burden could lower these lethal doses for gamma rays by as much as fifty per cent, the actual lethal doses in gamma rays for these trees during an attack could be from one thousand to four thousand rads, and in a full-scale attack they would die. Then, after the trees had died, forest fires would break out around the United States. (Because as much as three-quarters of the country could be subjected to incendiary levels of the thermal pulses, the sheer scorching of the land could have killed off a substantial part of the plant life in the country in the first few seconds after the detonations, before radioactive poisoning set in.) Lethal doses for grasses on which tests have been done range between six thousand and thirty-three thousand rads, and a good deal of grass would therefore survive, except where the attacks had been heaviest. Most crops, on the other hand, are killed by doses below five thousands rads, and would be eliminated. (The lethal dose for spring barley seedlings, for example, is one thousand nine hundred and ninety rads, and that for spring wheat seedlings is three thousand and ninety rads.)

When vegetation is killed off, the land on which it grew is degraded. And as the land eroded after an attack life in lakes, rivers, and estuaries, already hard hit by radiation directly, would be further damaged by minerals flowing into the watercourses, causing eutrophication — a process in which an oversupply of nutrients in the water encourages the growth of algae and microscopic organisms, which, in turn, deplete the oxygen content of the water. When the soil loses its nutrients, it loses its ability to "sustain a mature community" (in Dr. Woodwell's words), and "gross simplification" of the environment occurs, in which "hardy species," such as moss and grass, replace vulnerable ones, such as trees; and "succession" — the process by which ecosystems recover lost diversity — is then "delayed or even arrested." In sum, a full-scale nuclear attack on the United States would devastate the natural environment on a scale unknown since early geological times, when, in response to natural catastrophes whose nature has not been determined, sudden mass extinctions of species and whole ecosystems occurred all over the earth. How far this "gross simplification" of the environment would go once virtually all animal life and the greater part of plant life had been destroyed and what patterns the surviving remnants of life would arrange themselves into over the long run are imponderables; but it appears that at the outset the United States would be a republic of insects and grass.

QUESTIONS ON MEANING

1. Schell's paragraphs are dense with statistical information and close analysis, but they are well defined in themselves and in relation to each other. In one sentence each, define the subject of each of the first six paragraphs.
2. What is the relation between the first part of Schell's argument (paragraphs 1–6) and the second (paragraphs 7–10), in which he introduces the title phrase? Why does he emphasize the "gross simplification" of the environment in a nuclear war?
3. What is the significance of Schell's note in paragraph 10 that environmental disaster on a nuclear scale is not without precedent in natural history?

QUESTIONS ON STRATEGY

1. The aim of this essay is both descriptive and persuasive. How does Schell accomplish this double objective?

EXPLORATIONS

1. Susan Sontag in "The Imagination of Disaster" surveys the field of science fiction movies and finds some of their implications disturbing. Their "depiction of urban disaster on a colossally magnified scale" appeals to certain "primitive gratifications," she believes, and can tend to "normalize what is psychologically unbearable, thereby inuring us to it." Read her essay, reprinted in *Against Interpretation*. Compare her ideas, and her way of presenting them, to Schell's. Using ideas and examples from Sontag, compose a paragraph for Schell's argument in Schell's style.

WRITING TOPICS

1. Schell writes in opposition to the spread of nuclear weapons. Has he taken the right tack? Do nuclear weapons continue to spread because people don't generally appreciate how dangerous they are? If enough people get sufficiently alarmed, will the problem be on its way to a solution? Or is there another reason, more fundamental than Schell imagines, for the persistence of this danger? Write an essay describing what such a reason might be.

2. Aside from their tremendous destructive potential, one of the worst effects of nuclear weapons may well be the anxiety, conscious and unconscious, that they cause in those aware of their dangers. Schell works hard to arouse these anxieties. Write an essay arguing that he is part of the problem or that he is part of the solution.

BOOKS AVAILABLE IN PAPERBACK

The Fate of the Earth. New York: Avon. *Nonfiction: Study of the nuclear predicament.*

The Time of Illusion. New York: Vintage. *Nonfiction: Study of the contradictions in the presidency of Richard Nixon, offering an unorthodox theory to explain them.*

ALICE
WALKER

ALICE WALKER was born in Georgia in 1944, the youngest of eight children in a sharecropping family. She attended Spelman College in Atlanta, then transferred to Sarah Lawrence College in New York City, from which she graduated. She has taught at Jackson State College and Tougalo College in Mississippi and at Wellesley College. Now, after many years in New York, she lives in San Francisco and teaches at the University of California at Berkeley. Her mother still lives in Georgia, where Alice Walker travels from California to visit her.

Alice Walker has received a grant from the National Endowment and a fellowship from the Radcliffe Institute. She has published a biography of Langston Hughes for young people, three books of poems, two collections of short stories, and three novels. Her most recent novel, The Color Purple, *won the Pulitzer Prize and the American Book Award in 1983.*

She has most recently collected her essays in a volume called In Search of Our Mothers' Gardens *(1983). The following essay from that collection shows the author's many-sided literary capability: imagery like a poet's, narrative like a novelist's. The stew pot of the essay welcomes many ingredients. For Alice Walker, a black woman, the most important source is her relationship with her mother, as she be-*

lieves it is for other black women writers. When Walker is interviewed — the recent success of The Color Purple *has brought Alice Walker's name to the forefront of literary attention -- she returns often to the subject of mothers. In an article in* Ms. *magazine she recalls three gifts that her mother gave her despite poverty (her mother worked all day in affluent kitchens and earned less than twenty dollars a week): a sewing machine, so that the young daughter could make her own dresses for school; at high school graduation a suitcase for going away; and — not the least important for the young author — a typewriter.*

In Search of
Our Mothers' Gardens

I described her own nature and temperament. Told how they needed
a larger life for their expression. . . . I pointed out that in lieu of proper
channels, her emotions had overflowed into paths that dissipated
them. I talked, beautifully I thought, about an art that would be born,
an art that would open the way for women the likes of her. I asked her
to hope, and build up an inner life against the coming of that day. . . .
I sang, with a strange quiver in my voice, a promise song.

                – "AVEY," JEAN TOOMER, *CANE*
            The poet speaking to a prostitute who falls
            asleep while he's talking

When the poet Jean Toomer walked through the South in the early twen-   1
ties, he discovered a curious thing: black women whose spirituality was so
intense, so deep, so *unconscious*, they were themselves unaware of the richness they held. They stumbled blindly through their lives: creatures so
abused and mutilated in body, so dimmed and confused by pain, that they
considered themselves unworthy even of hope. In the selfless abstractions
their bodies became to the men who used them, they became more than
"sexual objects," more even than mere women: they became "Saints." Instead of being perceived as whole persons, their bodies became shrines:
what was thought to be their minds became temples suitable for worship.
These crazy Saints stared out at the world, wildly, like lunatics — or quietly,
like suicides; and the "God" that was in their gaze was as mute as a great
stone.

Who were these Saints? These crazy, loony, pitiful women?   2

Some of them, without a doubt, were our mothers and grandmothers.   3

In the still heat of the post-Reconstruction South, this is how they   4
seemed to Jean Toomer: exquisite butterflies trapped in an evil honey, toil-

ing away their lives in an era, a century, that did not acknowledge them, except as "the *mule* of the world." They dreamed dreams that no one knew — not even themselves, in any coherent fashion — and saw visions no one could understand. They wandered or sat about the countryside crooning lullabies to ghosts, and drawing the mother of Christ in charcoal on courthouse walls.

They forced their minds to desert their bodies and their striving spirits sought to rise, like frail whirlwinds from the hard red clay. And when those frail whirlwinds fell, in scattered particles, upon the ground, no one mourned. Instead, men lit candles to celebrate the emptiness that remained, as people do who enter a beautiful but vacant space to resurrect a God.

Our mothers and grandmothers, some of them: moving to music not yet written. And they waited.

They waited for a day when the unknown thing that was in them would be made known; but guessed, somehow in their darkness, that on the day of their revelation they would be long dead. Therefore to Toomer they walked, and even ran, in slow motion. For they were going nowhere immediate, and the future was not yet within their grasp. And men took our mothers and grandmothers, "but got no pleasure from it." So complex was their passion and their calm.

To Toomer, they lay vacant and fallow as autumn fields, with harvest time never in sight: and he saw them enter loveless marriages, without joy; and become prostitutes, without resistance; and become mothers of children, without fulfillment.

For these grandmothers and mothers of ours were not Saints, but Artists; driven to a numb and bleeding madness by the springs of creativity in them for which there was no release. They were Creators, who lived lives of spiritual waste, because they were so rich in spirituality — which is the basis of Art — that the strain of enduring their unused and unwanted talent drove them insane. Throwing away this spirituality was their pathetic attempt to lighten the soul to a weight their work-worn, sexually abused bodies could bear.

What did it mean for a black woman to be an artist in our grandmothers' time? In our great-grandmothers' day? It is a question with an answer cruel enough to stop the blood.

Did you have a genius of a great-great-grandmother who died under some ignorant and depraved white overseer's lash? Or was she required to bake biscuits for a lazy backwater tramp, when she cried out in her soul to paint watercolors of sunsets, or the rain falling on the green and peaceful pasturelands? Or was her body broken and forced to bear children (who were more often than not sold away from her) — eight, ten, fifteen, twenty children — when her one joy was the thought of modeling heroic figures of rebellion, in stone or clay?

How was the creativity of the black woman kept alive, year after year and   12
century after century, when for most of the years black people have been in
America, it was a punishable crime for a black person to read or write? And
the freedom to paint, to sculpt, to expand the mind with action did not exist.
Consider, if you can bear to imagine it, what might have been the result if
singing, too, had been forbidden by law. Listen to the voices of Bessie
Smith, Billie Holiday, Nina Simone, Roberta Flack, and Aretha Franklin,
among others, and imagine those voices muzzled for life. Then you may begin to comprehend the lives of our "crazy," "Sainted" mothers and grandmothers. The agony of the lives of women who might have been Poets, Novelists, Essayists, and Short-Story Writers (over a period of centuries), who
died with their real gifts stifled within them.

And, if this were the end of the story, we would have cause to cry out in   13
my paraphrase of Okot p'Bitek's great poem:

> O, my clanswomen
> Let us all cry together!
> Come,
> Let us mourn the death of our mother,
> The death of a Queen
> The ash that was produced
> By a great fire!
> O, this homestead is utterly dead
> Close the gates
> With *lacari* thorns,
> For our mother
> The creator of the Stool is lost!
> And all the young men
> Have perished in the wilderness!

But this is not the end of the story, for all the young women — our moth-   14
ers and grandmothers, *ourselves* — have not perished in the wilderness. And
if we ask ourselves why, and search for and find the answer, we will know
beyond all efforts to erase it from our minds, just exactly who, and of what,
we black American women are.

One example, perhaps the most pathetic, most misunderstood one, can   15
provide a backdrop for our mothers' work: Phillis Wheatley, a slave in the
1700s.

Virginia Woolf, in her book *A Room of One's Own*, wrote that in order for   16
a woman to write fiction she must have two things, certainly: a room of her
own (with key and lock) and enough money to support herself.

What then are we to make of Phillis Wheatley, a slave, who owned not   17
even herself? This sickly, frail black girl who required a servant of her own at
times — her health was so precarious — and who, had she been white,

would have been easily considered the intellectual superior of all the women and most of the men in the society of her day.

Virginia Woolf wrote further, speaking of course not of our Phillis, that "any woman born with a great gift in the sixteenth century [insert "eighteenth century," insert "black woman," insert "born or made a slave"] would certainly have gone crazed, shot herself, or ended her days in some lonely cottage outside the village, half witch, half wizard [insert "Saint"], feared and mocked at. For it needs little skill and psychology to be sure that a highly gifted girl who had tried to use her gift of poetry would have been so thwarted and hindered by contrary instincts [add "chains, guns, the lash, the ownership of one's body by someone else, submission to an alien religion"], that she must have lost her health and sanity to a certainty."

The key words, as they relate to Phillis, are "contrary instincts." For when we read the poetry of Phillis Wheatley — as when we read the novels of Nella Larsen or the oddly false-sounding autobiography of that freest of all black women writers, Zora Hurston — evidence of "contrary instincts" is everywhere. Her loyalties were completely divided, as was, without question, her mind.

But how could this be otherwise? Captured at seven, a slave of wealthy, doting whites who instilled in her the "savagery" of the Africa they "rescued" her from . . . one wonders if she was even able to remember her homeland as she had known it, or as it really was.

Yet, because she did try to use her gift for poetry in a world that made her a slave, she was "so thwarted and hindered by . . . contrary instincts, that she . . . lost her health. . . ." In the last years of her brief life, burdened not only with the need to express her gift but also with a penniless, friendless "freedom" and several small children for whom she was forced to do strenuous work to feed, she lost her health, certainly. Suffering from malnutrition and neglect and who knows what mental agonies, Phillis Wheatley died.

So torn by "contrary instincts" was black, kidnapped, enslaved Phillis that her description of "the Goddess" — as she poetically called the Liberty she did not have — is ironically, cruelly humorous. And, in fact, has held Phillis up to ridicule for more than a century. It is usually read prior to hanging Phillis's memory as that of a fool. She wrote:

> The Goddess comes, she moves divinely fair,
> Olive and laurel binds her *golden* hair.
> Wherever shines this native of the skies,
> Unnumber'd charms and recent graces rise. [My italics]

It is obvious that Phillis, the slave, combed the "Goddess's" hair every morning; prior, perhaps, to bringing in the milk, or fixing her mistress's lunch. She took her imagery from the one thing she saw elevated above all others.

With the benefit of hindsight we ask, "How could she?" 24

But at last, Phillis, we understand. No more snickering when your stiff, 25 struggling, ambivalent lines are forced on us. We know now that you were not an idiot or a traitor; only a sickly little black girl, snatched from your home and country and made a slave; a woman who still struggled to sing the song that was your gift, although in a land of barbarians who praised you for your bewildered tongue. It is not so much what you sang, as that you kept alive, in so many of our ancestors, *the notion of song*.

Black women are called, in the folklore that so aptly identifies one's 26 status in society, "the *mule* of the world," because we have been handed the burdens that everyone else — *everyone* else — refused to carry. We have also been called "Matriarchs," "Superwomen," and "Mean and Evil Bitches." Not to mention "Castraters" and "Sapphire's Mama." When we have pleaded for understanding, our character has been distorted; when we have asked for simple caring, we have been handed empty inspirational appellations, then stuck in the farthest corner. When we have asked for love, we have been given children. In short, even our plainer gifts, our labors of fidelity and love, have been knocked down our throats. To be an artist and a black woman, even today, lowers our status in many respects, rather than raises it: and yet, artists we will be.

Therefore we must fearlessly pull out of ourselves and look at and iden- 27 tify with our lives the living creativity some of our great-grandmothers were not allowed to know. I stress *some* of them because it is well known that the majority of our great-grandmothers knew, even without "knowing" it, the reality of their spirituality, even if they didn't recognize it beyond what happened in the singing at church — and they never had any intention of giving it up.

How they did it — those millions of black women who were not Phillis 28 Wheatley, or Lucy Terry or Frances Harper or Zora Hurston or Nella Larsen or Bessie Smith; or Elizabeth Catlett, or Katherine Dunham, either — brings me to the title of this essay, "In Search of Our Mothers' Gardens," which is a personal account that is yet shared, in its theme and its meaning, by all of us. I found, while thinking about the far-reaching world of the creative black woman, that often the truest answer to a question that really matters can be found very close.

In the late 1920s my mother ran away from home to marry my father. 29 Marriage, if not running away, was expected of seventeen-year-old girls. By the time she was twenty, she had two children and was pregnant with a third. Five children later, I was born. And this is how I came to know my mother: she seemed a large, soft, loving-eyed woman who was rarely impatient in our home. Her quick, violent temper was on view only a few times a year, when she battled with the white landlord who had the misfortune to suggest to her that her children did not need to go to school.

She made all the clothes we wore, even my brothers' overalls. She made all the towels and sheets we used. She spent the summers canning vegetables and fruits. She spent the winter evenings making quilts enough to cover all our beds.

During the "working" day, she labored beside — not behind — my father in the fields. Her day began before sunup, and did not end until late at night. There was never a moment for her to sit down, undisturbed, to unravel her own private thoughts; never a time free from interruption — by work or the noisy inquiries of her many children. And yet, it is to my mother — and all our mothers who were not famous — that I went in search of the secret of what has fed that muzzled and often mutilated, but vibrant, creative spirit that the black woman has inherited, and that pops out in wild and unlikely places to this day.

But when, you will ask, did my overworked mother have time to know or care about feeding the creative spirit?

The answer is so simple that many of us have spent years discovering it. We have constantly looked high, when we should have looked high — and low.

For example: in the Smithsonian Institution in Washington, D.C., there hangs a quilt unlike any other in the world. In fanciful, inspired, and yet simple and identifiable figures, it portrays the story of the Crucifixion. It is considered rare, beyond price. Though it follows no known pattern of quiltmaking, and though it is made of bits and pieces of worthless rags, it is obviously the work of a person of powerful imagination and deep spiritual feeling. Below this quilt I saw a note that says it was made by "an anonymous Black woman in Alabama, a hundred years ago."

If we could locate this "anonymous" black woman from Alabama, she would turn out to be one of our grandmothers — an artist who left her mark in the only materials she could afford, and in the only medium her position in society allowed her to use.

As Virginia Woolf wrote further, in *A Room of One's Own*:

> Yet genius of a sort must have existed among women as it must have existed among the working class. [Change this to "slaves" and "the wives and daughters of sharecroppers."] Now and again an Emily Brontë or a Robert Burns [change this to "a Zora Hurston or a Richard Wright"] blazes out and proves its presence. But certainly it never got itself on to pa-

per. When, however, one reads of a witch being ducked, of a woman possessed by devils [or "Sainthood"], of a wise woman selling herbs [our root workers], or even a very remarkable man who had a mother, then I think we are on the track of a lost novelist, a suppressed poet, or some mute and inglorious Jane Austen. . . . Indeed, I would venture to guess that Anon, who wrote so many poems without signing them, was often a woman. . . .

37 And so our mothers and grandmothers have, more often than not anonymously, handed on the creative spark, the seed of the flower they themselves never hoped to see: or like a sealed letter they could not plainly read.

38 And so it is, certainly, with my own mother. Unlike "Ma" Rainey's songs, which retained their creator's name even while blasting forth from Bessie Smith's mouth, no song or poem will bear my mother's name. Yet so many of the stories that I write, that we all write, are my mother's stories. Only recently did I fully realize this: that through years of listening to my mother's stories of her life, I have absorbed not only the stories themselves, but something of the manner in which she spoke, something of the urgency that involves the knowledge that her stories — like her life — must be recorded. It is probably for this reason that so much of what I have written is about characters whose counterparts in real life are so much older than I am.

39 But the telling of these stories, which came from my mother's lips as naturally as breathing, was not the only way my mother showed herself as an artist. For stories, too, were subject to being distracted, to dying without conclusion. Dinners must be started, and cotton must be gathered before the big rains. The artist that was and is my mother showed itself to me only after many years. This is what I finally noticed:

40 Like Mem, a character in *The Third Life of Grange Copeland*, my mother adorned with flowers whatever shabby house we were forced to live in. And not just your typical straggly country stand of zinnias, either. She planted ambitious gardens — and still does — with over fifty different varieties of plants that bloom profusely from early March until late November. Before she left home for the fields, she watered her flowers, chopped up the grass, and laid out new beds. When she returned from the fields she might divide clumps of bulbs, dig a cold pit, uproot and replant roses, or prune branches from her taller bushes or trees — until night came and it was too dark to see.

41 Whatever she planted grew as if by magic, and her fame as a grower of flowers spread over three counties. Because of her creativity with her flowers, even my memories of poverty are seen through a screen of blooms — sunflowers, petunias, roses, dahlias, forsythia, spirea, delphiniums, verbena . . . and on and on.

42 And I remember people coming to my mother's yard to be given cuttings from her flowers; I hear again the praise showered on her because whatever

rocky soil she landed on, she turned into a garden. A garden so brilliant with colors, so original in its design, so magnificent with life and creativity, that to this day people drive by our house in Georgia — perfect strangers and imperfect strangers — and ask to stand or walk among my mother's art.

I notice that it is only when my mother is working in her flowers that she is radiant, almost to the point of being invisible — except as Creator: hand and eye. She is involved in work her soul must have. Ordering the universe in the image of her personal conception of Beauty.

Her face, as she prepares the Art that is her gift, is a legacy of respect she leaves to me, for all that illuminates and cherishes life. She has handed down respect for the possibilities — and the will to grasp them.

For her, so hindered and intruded upon in so many ways, being an artist has still been a daily part of her life. This ability to hold on, even in very simple ways, is work black women have done for a very long time.

This poem is not enough, but it is something, for the woman who literally covered the holes in our walls with sunflowers:

> They were women then
> My mama's generation
> Husky of voice — Stout of
> Step
> With fists as well as
> Hands
> How they battered down
> Doors
> And ironed
> Starched white
> Shirts
> How they led
> Armies
> Headragged Generals
> Across mined
> Fields
> Booby-trapped
> Kitchens
> To discover books
> Desks
> A place for us
> How they knew what we
> *Must* know
> Without knowing a page
> Of it
> Themselves.

Guided by my heritage of a love of beauty and a respect for strength — in search of my mother's garden, I found my own.

And perhaps in Africa over two hundred years ago, there was just such a   48
mother; perhaps she painted vivid and daring decorations in oranges and
yellows and greens on the walls of her hut; perhaps she sang — in a voice
like Roberta Flack's — *sweetly* over the compounds of her village; perhaps
she wove the most stunning mats or told the most ingenious stories of all the
village storytellers. Perhaps she was herself a poet — though only her
daughter's name is signed to the poems that we know.

Perhaps Phillis Wheatley's mother was also an artist.   49

Perhaps in more than Phillis Wheatley's biological life is her mother's   50
signature made clear.

QUESTIONS ON MEANING

1. Why does Walker begin by quoting Jean Toomer? Is he implicated when she
states that rather than "being perceived as whole persons" by men, black
women were generally exploited physically — "their bodies became
shrines"? How does this introduction help Alice Walker define her own interest in the lives of the mothers and grandmothers of today's black women?
2. How does Walker define the creativity of southern black women? What does
she give as evidence of the creative souls that lay beneath the frustrations
and limitations of the lives of women in earlier generations?

QUESTIONS ON STRATEGY

1. Paragraphs 11–14 assert that although generations of black women "died
with their real gifts stifled within them . . . this is not the end of the story."
How does this sequence mark a turning point in Walker's essay? How does
she use it to further define her point of view?
2. In paragraphs 16–18 and 36 Walker refers to Virginia Woolf's polemic *A
Room of One's Own*. How does she use this material to strengthen her argument about black women? What are the differences in emphasis between
Walker and Woolf? How does Walker acknowledge these differences?

EXPLORATIONS

1. James Baldwin's "Notes of a Native Son" describes and analyzes the alienation and suffering of the black people who migrated to northern cities. "In
Search of Our Mothers' Gardens" presents another side of the black experience in America, concentrating on the oppressions and limitations of rural
southern life. Both focus on the relations between their authors' lives in the
arts and the frustrations of their parents. What can these essays teach you
about the place of a creative vocation in the history of a black family's life?

Have Baldwin and Walker vindicated their parents by becoming successful writers?

WRITING TOPICS

1. Is Alice Walker realistic in her expectations about human creativity? Not many plantation owners wrote novels or poetry, painted, or composed music. Few people do, whatever their circumstances. What happens to the creativity of people in general? Write an essay about thwarted creativity. Write about a parent or grandparent or someone you know well. Or write about yourself.

BOOKS AVAILABLE IN PAPERBACK

The Color Purple. New York: Washington Square Press. *Novel.*

Good Night, Willie Lee, I'll See You in the Morning. New York: Dial. *Poems.*

In Love and Trouble: Stories of Black Women. New York: Harcourt Brace Jovanovich, Harvest Books.

Meridian. New York: Washington Square Press. *Novel.*

Once: Poems. New York: Harcourt Brace Jovanovich, Harvest Books.

Revolutionary Petunias and Other Poems. New York: Harcourt Brace Jovanovich, Harvest Books.

The Third Life of Grange Copeland. New York: Harcourt Brace Jovanovich, Harvest Books. *Novel.*

You Can't Keep a Good Woman Down. New York: Harcourt Brace Jovanovich, Harvest Books. *Stories.*

RICHARD
RODRIGUEZ

R ICHARD RODRIGUEZ was born in 1944 in San Francisco, the son of Mexi-
can immigrants. The family moved to Sacramento, where Rodriguez grew up
speaking Spanish until he attended a Catholic school at the age of six. He delivered
newspapers as a boy and worked as a gardener in the summer. He attended a Chris-
tian Brothers high school on a scholarship, then Stanford University for his B.A.,
and he did graduate work at Columbia University, the Warburg Institute in London,
and the University of California at Berkeley. He took his Ph.D. in English Renais-
sance literature. He now lives in San Francisco and works as a lecturer and educa-
tional consultant as well as a free-lance writer.

As an assimilated second-generation American, Rodriguez in his reminiscences
— Hunger of Memory (1982) — argues against affirmative action and bilingual ed-
ucation. ''The Achievement of Desire'' is a chapter from Hunger of Memory, a
personal narrative of Richard Rodriguez's education away from his heritage, ''sepa-
rating me from the life I enjoyed before becoming a student.'' Unlike many members
of American ethnic minorities, Rodriguez largely celebrates this separation. His work
has been admired and denounced. While he tells his experiences of schooling, in a lu-

cid progress of autobiographical exposition, he continually comments on his own story and reaches out for understanding by cross-cultural analogy to a book by an Englishman, separated as a "scholarship boy" from his working-class origins.

The Achievement
of Desire

I stand in the ghetto classroom — "the guest speaker" — attempting to lecture on the mystery of the sounds of our words to rows of diffident students. "Don't you hear it? Listen! The music of our words. *'Sumer is i-cumen in*. . . .' And songs on the car radio. We need Aretha Franklin's voice to fill plain words with music — her life." In the face of their empty stares, I try to create an enthusiasm. But the girls in the back row turn to watch some boy passing outside. There are flutters of smiles, waves. And someone's mouth elongates heavy, silent words through the barrier of glass. Silent words — the lips straining to shape each voiceless syllable: *"Meet meee late errr."* By the door, the instructor smiles at me, apparently hoping that I will be able to spark some enthusiasm in the class. But only one student seems to be listening. A girl, maybe fourteen. In this gray room her eyes shine with ambition. She keeps nodding and nodding at all that I say; she even takes notes. And each time I ask a question, she jerks up and down in her desk like a marionette, while her hand waves over the bowed heads of her classmates. It is myself (as a boy) I see as she faces me now (a man in my thirties).

The boy who first entered a classroom barely able to speak English, twenty years later concluded his studies in the stately quiet of the reading room in the British Museum. Thus with one sentence I can summarize my academic career. It will be harder to summarize what sort of life connects the boy to the man.

With every award, each graduation from one level of education to the next, people I'd meet would congratulate me. Their refrain always the same: "Your parents must be very proud." Sometimes then they'd ask me how I managed it — my "success." (How?) After a while, I had several quick answers to give in reply. I'd admit, for one thing, that I went to an excellent grammar school. (My earliest teachers, the nuns, made my success their ambition.) And my brother and both my sisters were very good students. (They often brought home the shiny school tropies I came to want.) And my mother and father always encouraged me. (At every graduation they were behind the stunning flash of the camera when I turned to look at the crowd.)

As important as these factors were, however, they account inadequately 4
for my academic advance. Nor do they suggest what an odd success I managed. For although I was a very good student, I was also a very bad student. I was a "scholarship boy," a certain kind of scholarship boy. Always successful, I was always unconfident. Exhilarated by my progress. Sad. I became the prized student — anxious and eager to learn. Too eager, too anxious — an imitative and unoriginal pupil. My brother and two sisters enjoyed the advantages I did, and they grew to be as successful as I, but none of them ever seemed so anxious about their schooling. A second-grade student, I was the one who came home and corrected the "simple" grammatical mistakes of our parents. ("Two negatives make a positive.") Proudly I announced — to my family's startled silence — that a teacher had said I was losing all trace of a Spanish accent. I was oddly annoyed when I was unable to get parental help with a homework assignment. The night my father tried to help me with an arithmetic exercise, he kept reading the instructions, each time more deliberately, until I pried the textbook out of his hands, saying, "I'll try to figure it out some more by myself."

When I reached the third grade, I outgrew such behavior. I became more 5
tactful, careful to keep separate the two very different worlds of my day. But then, with ever-increasing intensity, I devoted myself to my studies. I became bookish, puzzling to all my family. Ambition set me apart. When my brother saw me struggling home with stacks of library books, he would laugh, shouting: "Hey, Four Eyes!" My father opened a closet one day and was startled to find me inside, reading a novel. My mother would find me reading when I was supposed to be asleep or helping around the house or playing outside. In a voice angry or worried or just curious, she'd ask: "What do you see in your books?" It became the family's joke. When I was called and wouldn't reply, someone would say I must be hiding under my bed with a book.

(How did I manage my success?) 6

What I am about to say to you has taken me more than twenty years to 7
admit: *A primary reason for my success in the classroom was that I couldn't forget that schooling was changing me and separating me from the life I enjoyed before becoming a student.* That simple realization! For years I never spoke to anyone about it. Never mentioned a thing to my family or my teachers or classmates. From a very early age, I understood enough, just enough about my classroom experiences to keep what I knew repressed, hidden beneath layers of embarrassment. Not until my last months as a graduate student, nearly thirty years old, was it possible for me to think much about the reasons for my academic success. Only then. At the end of my schooling, I needed to determine how far I had moved from my past. The adult finally confronted, and now must publicly say, what the child shuddered from knowing and could never admit to himself or to those many faces that smiled at his every success. ("Your parents must be very proud. . . .")

I

At the end, in the British Museum (too distracted to finish my dissertation) for weeks I read, speed-read, books by modern educational theorists, only to find infrequent and slight mention of students like me. (Much more is written about the more typical case, the lower-class student who barely is helped by his schooling.) Then one day, leafing through Richard Hoggart's *The Uses of Literacy*, I found, in his description of the scholarship boy, myself. For the first time I realized that there were other students like me, and so I was able to frame the meaning of my academic success, its consequent price — the loss.

Hoggart's description is distinguished, at least initially, by deep understanding. What he grasps very well is that the scholarship boy must move between environments, his home and the classroom, which are at cultural extremes, opposed. With his family, the boy has the intense pleasure of intimacy, the family's consolation in feeling public alienation. Lavish emotions texture home life. *Then*, at school, the instruction bids him to trust lonely reason primarily. Immediate needs set the pace of his parents' lives. From his mother and father the boy learns to trust spontaneity and nonrational ways of knowing. *Then*, at school, there is mental calm. Teachers emphasize the value of a reflectiveness that opens a space between thinking and immediate action.

Years of schooling must pass before the boy will be able to sketch the cultural differences in his day as abstractly as this. But he senses those differences early. Perhaps as early as the night he brings home an assignment from school and finds the house too noisy for study.

> He has to be more and more alone, if he is going to "get on." He will have, probably unconsciously, to oppose the ethos of the hearth, the intense gregariousness of the working-class family group. Since everything centres upon the living-room, there is unlikely to be a room of his own; the bedrooms are cold and inhospitable, and to warm them or the front room, if there is one, would not only be expensive, but would require an imaginative leap — out of the tradition — which most families are not capable of making. There is a corner of the living-room table. On the other side Mother is ironing, the wireless is on, someone is singing a snatch of song or Father says intermittently whatever comes into his head. The boy has to cut himself off mentally, so as to do his homework, as well as he can.*

---

*All quotations in this chapter are from Richard Hoggart, *The Uses of Literacy* (London: Chatto and Windus, 1957), chapter 10. [author's note]

The next day, the lesson is as apparent at school. There are even rows of desks. Discussion is ordered. The boy must rehearse his thoughts and raise his hand before speaking out in a loud voice to an audience of classmates. And there is time enough, and silence, to think about ideas (big ideas) never considered at home by his parents.

Not for the working-class child alone is adjustment to the classroom diffi- 11 cult. Good schooling requires that any student alter early childhood habits. But the working-class child is usually least prepared for the change. And, unlike many middle-class children, he goes home and sees in his parents a way of life not only different but starkly opposed to that of the classroom. (He enters the house and hears his parents talking in ways his teachers discourage.)

Without extraordinary determination and the great assistance of others 12 — at home and at school — there is little chance for success. Typically most working-class children are barely changed by the classroom. The exception succeeds. The relative few become scholarship students. Of these, Richard Hoggart estimates, most manage a fairly graceful transition. Somehow they learn to live in the two very different worlds of their day. There are some others, however, those Hoggart pejoratively terms "scholarship boys," for whom success comes with special anxiety. Scholarship boy: good student, troubled son. The child is "moderately endowed," intellectually mediocre, Hoggart supposes — though it may be more pertinent to note the special qualities of temperament in the child. High-strung child. Brooding. Sensitive. Haunted by the knowledge that one *chooses* to become a student. (Education is not an inevitable or natural step in growing up.) Here is a child who cannot forget that his academic success distances him from a life he loved, even from his own memory of himself.

Initially, he wavers, balances allegiance. ("The boy is himself [until he 13 reaches, say, the upper forms] very much of *both* the worlds of home and school. He is enormously obedient to the dictates of the world of school, but emotionally still strongly wants to continue as part of the family circle.") Gradually, necessarily, the balance is lost. The boy needs to spend more and more time studying, each night enclosing himself in the silence permitted and required by intense concentration. He takes his first step toward academic success, away from his family.

From the very first days, through the years following, it will be with his 14 parents — the figures of lost authority, the persons toward whom he feels deepest love — that the change will be most powerfully measured. A separation will unravel between them. Advancing in his studies, the boy notices that his mother and father have not changed as much as he. Rather, when he sees them, they often remind him of the person he once was and the life he earlier shared with them. He realizes what some Romantics also know when they praise the working class for the capacity for human closeness, qualities of passion and spontaneity, that the rest of us experience in like measure only in the earliest part of our youth. For the Romantic, this doesn't make working-class life childish. Working-class life challenges precisely because it is an *adult* way of life.

The scholarship boy reaches a different conclusion. He cannot afford to admire his parents. (How could he and still pursue such a contrary life?) He permits himself embarrassment at their lack of education. And to evade nostalgia for the life he has lost, he concentrates on the benefits education will bestow upon him. He becomes especially ambitious. Without the support of old certainties and consolations, almost mechanically, he assumes the procedures and doctrines of the classroom. The kind of allegiance the young student might have given his mother and father only days earlier, he transfers to the teacher, the new figure of authority. "[The scholarship boy] tends to make a father-figure of his form-master," Hoggart observes.

But Hoggart's calm prose only makes me recall the urgency with which I came to idolize my grammar school teachers. I began by imitating their accents, using their diction, trusting their every direction. The very first facts they dispensed, I grasped with awe. Any book they told me to read, I read — then waited for them to tell me which books I enjoyed. Their every casual opinion I came to adopt and to trumpet when I returned home. I stayed after school "to help" — to get my teacher's undivided attention. It was the nun's encouragement that mattered most to me. (She understood exactly what — my parents never seemed to appraise so well — all my achievements entailed.) Memory gently caressed each word of praise bestowed in the classroom so that compliments teachers paid me years ago come quickly to mind even today.

The enthusiasm I felt in second-grade classes I flaunted before both my parents. The docile, obedient student came home a shrill and precocious son who insisted on correcting and teaching his parents with the remark: "My teacher told us. . . ."

I intended to hurt my mother and father. I was still angry at them for having encouraged me toward classroom English. But gradually this anger was exhausted, replaced by guilt as school grew more and more attractive to me. I grew increasingly successful, a talkative student. My hand was raised in the classroom; I yearned to answer any question. At home, life was less noisy than it had been. (I spoke to classmates and teachers more often each day than to family members.) Quiet at home, I sat with my papers for hours each night. I never forgot that schooling had irretrievably changed my family's life. That knowledge, however, did not weaken ambition. Instead, it strengthened resolve. Those times I remembered the loss of my past with regret, I quickly reminded myself of all the things my teachers could give me. (They could make me an educated man.) I tightened my grip on pencil and books. I evaded nostalgia. Tried hard to forget. But one does not forget by trying to forget. One only remembers. I remembered too well that education had changed my family's life. I would not have become a scholarship boy had I not so often remembered.

Once she was sure that her children knew English, my mother would tell 19
us, "You should keep up your Spanish." Voices playfully groaned in response. "¡Pochos!" my mother would tease. I listened silently.

After a while, I grew more calm at home. I developed tact. A fourth- 20
grade student, I was no longer the show-off in front of my parents. I became a conventionally dutiful son, politely affectionate, cheerful enough, even — for reasons beyond choosing — my father's favorite. And much about my family life was easy then, comfortable, happy in the rhythm of our living together: hearing my father getting ready for work; eating the breakfast my mother had made me; looking up from a novel to hear my brother or one of my sisters playing with friends in the backyard; in winter, coming upon the house all lighted up after dark.

But withheld from my mother and father was any mention of what most 21
mattered to me: the extraordinary experience of first-learning. Late afternoon: In the midst of preparing dinner, my mother would come up behind me while I was trying to read. Her head just over mine, her breath warmly scented with food. "What are you reading?" Or, "Tell me all about your new courses." I would barely respond, "Just the usual things, nothing special." (A half smile, then silence. Her head moving back in the silence. Silence! Instead of the flood of intimate sounds that had once flowed smoothly between us, there was this silence.) After dinner, I would rush to a bedroom with papers and books. As often as possible, I resisted parental pleas to "save lights" by coming to the kitchen to work. I kept so much, so often, to myself. Sad. Enthusiastic. Troubled by the excitement of coming upon new ideas. Eager. Fascinated by the promising texture of a brand-new book. I hoarded the pleasures of learning. Alone for hours. Enthralled. Nervous. I rarely looked away from my books — or back on my memories. Nights when relatives visited and the front rooms were warmed by Spanish sounds, I slipped quietly out of the house.

It mattered that education was changing me. It never ceased to matter. 22
My brother and sisters would giggle at our mother's mispronounced words. They'd correct her gently. My mother laughed girlishly one night, trying not to pronounce *sheep* as *ship*. From a distance I listened sullenly. From that distance, pretending not to notice on another occasion, I saw my father looking at the title pages of my library books. That was the scene on my mind when I walked home with a fourth-grade companion and heard him say that his parents read to him every night. (A strange-sounding book — *Winnie the Pooh*.) Immediately, I wanted to know, "What is it like?" My companion, however, thought I wanted to know about the plot of the book. Another day, my mother surprised me by asking for a "nice" book to read. "Some-

thing not too hard you think I might like." Carefully I chose one, Willa Cather's *My Ántonia*. But when, several weeks later, I happened to see it next to her bed unread except for the first few pages, I was furious and suddenly wanted to cry. I grabbed up the book and took it back to my room and placed it in its place, alphabetically on my shelf.

"Your parents must be very proud of you." People began to say that to me about the time I was in sixth grade. To answer affirmatively, I'd smile. Shyly I'd smile, never betraying my sense of the irony: I was not proud of my mother and father. I was embarrassed by their lack of education. It was not that I ever thought they were stupid, though stupidly I took for granted their enormous native intelligence. Simply, what mattered to me was that they were not like my teachers.

But, "Why didn't you tell us about the award?" my mother demanded, her frown weakened by pride. At the grammar school ceremony several weeks after, her eyes were brighter than the trophy I'd won. Pushing back the hair from my forehead, she whispered that I had "shown" the *gringos*. A few minutes later, I heard my father speak to my teacher and felt ashamed of his labored, accented words. Then guilty for the shame. I felt such contrary feelings. (There is no simple road-map through the heart of the scholarship boy.) My teacher was so soft-spoken and her words were edged sharp and clean. I admired her until it seemed to me that she spoke too carefully. Sensing that she was condescending to them, I became nervous. Resentful. Protective. I tried to move my parents away. "You both must be very proud of Richard," the nun said. They responded quickly. (They were proud.) "We are proud of all our children." Then this afterthought: "They sure didn't get their brains from us." They all laughed. I smiled.

Tightening the irony into a knot was the knowledge that my parents were always behind me. They made success possible. They evened the path. They sent their children to parochial schools because the nuns "teach better." They paid a tuition they couldn't afford. They spoke English to us.

For their children my parents wanted chances they never had — an easier way. It saddened my mother to learn that some relatives forced their children to start working right after high school. To *her* children she would say, "Get all the education you can." In schooling she recognized the key to job advancement. And with the remark she remembered her past.

As a girl new to America my mother had been awarded a high school diploma by teachers too careless or busy to notice that she hardly spoke English. On her own, she determined to learn how to type. That skill got her jobs typing envelopes in letter shops, and it encouraged in her an optimism about the possibility of advancement. (Each morning when her sisters put on uniforms, she chose a bright-colored dress.) The years of young womanhood passed, and her typing speed increased. She also became an excellent speller of words she mispronounced. ''And I've never been to college,'' she'd say, smiling, when her children asked her to spell words they were too lazy to look up in a dictionary.

Typing, however, was dead-end work. Finally frustrating. When her 28 youngest child started high school, my mother got a full-time office job once again. (Her paycheck combined with my father's to make us — in fact — what we had already become in our imagination of ourselves — middle class.) She worked then for the (California) state government in numbered civil service positions secured by examinations. The old ambition of her youth was rekindled. During the lunch hour, she consulted bulletin boards for announcements of openings. One day she saw mention of something called an ''anti-poverty agency.'' A typing job. A glamorous job, part of the governor's staff. ''A knowledge of Spanish required.'' Without hesitation she applied and became nervous only when the job was suddenly hers.

''Everyone comes to work all dressed up,'' she reported at night. And 29 didn't need to say more than that her co-workers wouldn't let her answer the phones. She was only a typist, after all, albeit a very fast typist. And an excellent speller. One morning there was a letter to be sent to a Washington cabinet officer. On the dictating tape, a voice referred to urban guerrillas. My mother typed (the wrong word, correctly): ''gorillas.'' The mistake horrified the anti-poverty bureaucrats who shortly after arranged to have her returned to her previous position. She would go no further. So she willed her ambition to her children. ''Get all the education you can; with an education you can do anything.'' (With a good education *she* could have done anything.)

When I was in high school, I admitted to my mother that I planned to be- 30 come a teacher someday. That seemed to please her. But I never tried to explain that it was not the occupation of teaching I yearned for as much as it was something more elusive: I wanted to *be* like my teachers, to possess their knowledge, to assume their authority, their confidence, even to assume a teacher's persona.

In contrast to my mother, my father never verbally encouraged his chil- 31 dren's academic success. Nor did he often praise us. My mother had to remind him to ''say something'' to one of his children who scored some academic success. But whereas my mother saw in education the opportunity for job advancement, my father recognized that education provided an even more startling possibility: It could enable a person to escape from a life of mere labor.

In Mexico, orphaned when he was eight, my father left school to work as 32 an ''apprentice'' for an uncle. Twelve years later, he left Mexico in frustration and arrived in America. He had great expectations then of becoming an engineer. (''Work for my hands and my head.'') He knew a Catholic priest who promised to get him money enough to study full time for a high school diploma. But the promises came to nothing. Instead there was a dark succession of warehouse, cannery, and factory jobs. After work he went to night school along with my mother. A year, two passed. Nothing much changed, except that fatigue worked its way into the bone; then everything changed. He didn't talk anymore of becoming an engineer. He stayed outside on the steps of the school while my mother went inside to learn typing and shorthand.

By the time I was born, my father worked at "clean " jobs. For a time he was a janitor at a fancy department store. ("Easy work; the machines do it all.") Later he became a dental technician. ("Simple.") But by then he was pessimistic about the ultimate meaning of work and the possibility of ever escaping its claims. In some of my earliest memories of him, my father already seems aged by fatigue. (He has never really grown old like my mother.) From boyhood to manhood, I have remembered him in a single image: seated, asleep on the sofa, his head thrown back in a hideous corpselike grin, the evening newspaper spread out before him. "But look at all you've accomplished," his best friend said to him once. My father said nothing. Only smiled.

It was my father who laughed when I claimed to be tired by reading and writing. It was he who teased me for having soft hands. (He seemed to sense that some great achievement of leisure was implied by my papers and books.) It was my father who became angry while watching on television some woman at the Miss America contest tell the announcer that she was going to college. ("Majoring in fine arts.") "College!" he snarled. He despised the trivialization of higher education, the inflated grades and cheapened diplomas, the half education that so often passed as mass education in my generation.

It was my father again who wondered why I didn't display my awards on the wall of my bedroom. He said he liked to go to doctors' offices and see their certificates and degrees on the wall. ("Nice.") My citations from school got left in closets at home. The gleaming figure astride one of my trophies was broken, wingless, after hitting the ground. My medals were placed in a jar of loose change. And when I lost my high school diploma, my father found it as it was about to be thrown out with the trash. Without telling me, he put it away with his own things for safekeeping.

These memories slammed together at the instant of hearing that refrain familiar to all scholarship students: "Your parents must be very proud. . . ." Yes, my parents were proud. I knew it. But my parents regarded my progress with more than mere pride. They endured my early precocious behavior — but with what private anger and humiliation? As their children got older and would come home to challenge ideas both of them held, they argued before submitting to the force of logic or superior factual evidence with the disclaimer, ''It's what we were taught in our time to believe.'' These discussions ended abruptly, though my mother remembered them on other occasions when she complained that our ''big ideas'' were going to our heads. More acute was her complaint that the family wasn't close anymore, like some others she knew. Why weren't we close, ''more in the Mexican style''? Everyone is so private, she added. And she mimicked the yes and no answers she got in reply to her questions. Why didn't we talk more? (My father never asked.) I never said.

I was the first in my family who asked to leave home when it came time 37 to go to college. I had been admitted to Stanford, one hundred miles away. My departure would only make physically apparent the separation that had occurred long before. But it was going too far. In the months preceding my leaving, I heard the question my mother never asked except indirectly. In the hot kitchen, tired at the end of her workday, she demanded to know, ''Why aren't the colleges here in Sacramento good enough for you? They are for your brother and sister.'' In the middle of a car ride, not turning to face me, she wondered, ''Why do you need to go so far away?'' Late at night, ironing, she said with disgust, ''Why do you have to put us through this big expense? You know your scholarship will never cover it all.'' But when September came there was a rush to get everything ready. In a bedroom that last night I packed the big brown valise, and my mother sat nearby sewing initials onto the clothes I would take. And she said no more about my leaving.

Months later, two weeks of Christmas vacation: The first hours home 38 were the hardest. (''What's new?'') My parents and I sat in the kitchen for a conversation. (But, lacking the same words to develop our sentences and to shape our interests, what was there to say? What could I tell them of the term paper I had just finished on the ''universality of Shakespeare's appeal''?) I mentioned only small, obvious things: my dormitory life; weekend trips I had taken; random events. They responded with news of their own. (One was almost grateful for a family crisis about which there was much to discuss.) We tried to make our conversation seem like more than an interview.

I I

From an early age I knew that my mother and father could read and write 39 both Spanish and English. I had observed my father making his way through what, I now suppose, must have been income tax forms. On other occasions I waited apprehensively while my mother read onion-paper letters airmailed from Mexico with news of a relative's illness or death. For both my parents, however, reading was something done out of necessity and as quickly as possible. Never did I see either of them read an entire book. Nor did I see them read for pleasure. Their reading consisted of work manuals, prayer books, newspaper, recipes.

Richard Hoggart imagines how, at home,

> . . . [The scholarship boy] sees strewn around, and reads regularly himself, magazines which are never mentioned at school, which seem not to belong to the world to which the school introduces him; at school he hears about and reads books never mentioned at home. When he brings those books into the house they do not take their place with other books which the family are reading, for often there are none or almost none; his books look, rather, like strange tools.

In our house each school year would begin with my mother's careful instruction: "Don't write in your books so we can sell them at the end of the year." The remark was echoed in public by my teachers, but only in part: "Boys and girls, don't write in your books. You must learn to treat them with great care and respect."

OPEN THE DOORS OF YOUR MIND WITH BOOKS, read the red and white poster over the nun's desk in early September. It soon was apparent to me that reading was the classroom's central activity. Each course had its own book. And the information gathered from a book was unquestioned. READ TO LEARN, the sign on the wall advised in December. I privately wondered: What was the connection between reading and learning? Did one learn something only by reading it? Was an idea only an idea if it could be written down? In June, CONSIDER BOOKS YOUR BEST FRIENDS. Friends? Reading was, at best, only a chore. I needed to look up whole paragraphs of words in a dictionary. Lines of type were dizzying, the eye having to move slowly across the page, then down, and across. . . . The sentences of the first books I read were coolly impersonal. Toned hard. What most bothered me, however, was the isolation reading required. To console myself for the loneliness I'd feel when I read, I tried reading in a very soft voice. Until: "Who is doing all that talking to his neighbor?" Shortly after, remedial reading classes were arranged for me with a very old nun.

At the end of each school day, for nearly six months, I would meet with her in the tiny room that served as the school's library but was actually only a storeroom for used textbooks and a vast collection of *National Geographics*. Everything about our sessions pleased me: the smallness of the room; the noise of the janitor's broom hitting the edge of the long hallway outside the door; the green of the sun, lighting the wall; and the old woman's face blurred white with a beard. Most of the time we took turns. I began with my elementary text. Sentences of astonishing simplicity seemed to me lifeless and drab: "The boys ran from the rain . . . She wanted to sing . . . The kite rose in the blue." Then the old nun would read from her favorite books, usually biographies of early American presidents. Playfully she ran through complex sentences, calling the words alive with her voice, making it seem that the author somehow was speaking directly to me. I smiled just to listen to her. I sat there and sensed for the very first time some possibility of fellowship between a reader and a writer, a communication, never *intimate* like that I heard spoken words at home convey, but one nonetheless *personal*.

One day the nun concluded a session by asking me why I was so reluc- 43
tant to read by myself. I tried to explain; said something about the way written words made me feel all alone — almost, I wanted to add but didn't, as when I spoke to myself in a room just emptied of furniture. She studied my face as I spoke; she seemed to be watching more than listening. In an uneventful voice she replied that I had nothing to fear. Didn't I realize that reading would open up whole new worlds? A book could open doors for me. It could introduce me to people and show me places I never imagined existed. She gestured toward the bookshelves. (Bare-breasted African women danced, and the shiny hubcaps of automobiles on the back covers of the *Geographic* gleamed in my mind.) I listened with respect. But her words were not very influential. I was thinking then of another consequence of literacy, one I was too shy to admit but nonetheless trusted. Books were going to make me "educated." *That* confidence enabled me, several months later, to overcome my fear of the silence.

In fourth grade I embarked upon a grandiose reading program. "Give 44
me the names of important books," I would say to startled teachers. They soon found out that I had in mind "adult books." I ignored their suggestion of anything I suspected was written for children. (Not until I was in college, as a result, did I read *Huckleberry Finn* or *Alice's Adventures in Wonderland*.) Instead, I read *The Scarlet Letter* and Franklin's *Autobiography*. And whatever I read I read for extra credit. Each time I finished a book, I reported the achievement to a teacher and basked in the praise my effort earned. Despite my best efforts, however, there seemed to be more and more books I needed to read. At the library I would literally tremble as I came upon whole shelves of books I hadn't read. So I read and I read and I read: *Great Expectations*; all the short stories of Kipling; *The Babe Ruth Story*; the entire first volume of the *Encyclopaedia Britannica* (A–ANSTEY); the *Iliad*; *Moby Dick*; *Gone with the Wind*; *The Good Earth*; *Ramona*; *Forever Amber*; *The Lives of the Saints*; *Crime and Punishment*; *The Pearl*. . . . Librarians who initially frowned when I checked out the maximum ten books at a time started saving books they thought I might like. Teachers would say to the rest of the class, "I only wish the rest of you took reading as seriously as Richard obviously does."

But at home I would hear my mother wondering, "What do you see in 45
your books?" (Was reading a hobby like her knitting? Was so much reading

even healthy for a boy? Was it the sign of "brains"? Or was it just a convenient excuse for not helping about the house on Saturday mornings?) Always, "What do you see . . . ?"

What *did* I see in my books? I had the idea that they were crucial for my academic success, though I couldn't have said exactly how or why. In the sixth grade I simply concluded that what gave a book its value was some major idea or theme it contained. If that core essence could be mined and memorized, I would become learned like my teachers. I decided to record in a notebook the themes of the books that I read. After reading *Robinson Crusoe*, I wrote that its theme was "the value of learning to live by oneself." When I completed *Wuthering Heights*, I noted the danger of "letting emotions get out of control." Rereading these brief moralistic appraisals usually left me disheartened. I couldn't believe that they were really the source of reading's value. But for many more years, they constituted the only means I had of describing to myself the educational value of books.

In spite of my earnestness, I found reading a pleasurable activity. I came to enjoy the lonely good company of books. Early on weekday mornings, I'd read in my bed. I'd feel a mysterious comfort then, reading in the dawn quiet — the blue-gray silence interrupted by the occasional churning of the refrigerator motor a few rooms away or the more distant sounds of a city bus beginning its run. On weekends I'd go to the public library to read, surrounded by old men and women. Of, if the weather was fine, I would take my books to the park and read in the shade of a tree. A warm summer evening was my favorite reading time. Neighbors would leave for vacation and I would water their lawns. I would sit through the twilight on the front porches or in backyards, reading to the cool, whirling sounds of the sprinklers.

I also had favorite writers. But often those writers I enjoyed most I was least able to value. When I read William Saroyan's *The Human Comedy*, I was immediately pleased by the narrator's warmth and the charm of his story. But as quickly I became suspicious. A book so enjoyable to read couldn't be very "important." Another summer I determined to read all the novels of Dickens. Reading his fat novels, I loved the feeling I got — after the first hundred pages — of being at home in a fictional world where I knew the names of the characters and cared about what was going to happen to them. And it bothered me that I was forced away at the conclusion, when the fiction closed tight, like a fortune-teller's fist — the futures of all the major characters neatly resolved. I never knew how to take such feelings seriously, however. Nor did I suspect that these experiences could be part of a novel's meaning. Still, there were pleasures to sustain me after I'd finish my books. Carrying a volume back to the library, I would be pleased by its weight. I'd run my fingers along the edge of the pages and marvel at the breadth of my achievement. Around my room, growing stacks of paperback books reenforced my assurance.

I entered high school having read hundreds of books. My habit of read- 49 ing made me a confident speaker and writer of English. Reading also enabled me to sense something of the shape, the major concerns, of Western thought. (I was able to say something about Dante and Descartes and Engels and James Baldwin in my high school term papers.) In these various ways, books brought me academic success as I hoped that they would. But I was not a good reader. Merely bookish, I lacked a point of view when I read. Rather, I read in order to acquire a point of view. I vacuumed books for epigrams, scraps of information, ideas, themes — anything to fill the hollow within me and make me feel educated. When one of my teachers suggested to his drowsy tenth-grade English class that a person could not have a ''complicated idea'' until he had read at least two thousand books, I heard the remark without detecting either its irony or its very complicated truth. I merely determined to compile a list of all the books I had ever read. Harsh with myself, I included only once a title I might have read several times. (How, after all, could one read a book more than once?) And I included only those books over a hundred pages in length. (Could anything shorter be a book?)

There was yet another high school list I compiled. One day I came across 50 a newspaper article about the retirement of an English professor at a nearby state college. The article was accompanied by a list of the ''hundred most important books of Western Civilization.'' ''More than anything else in my life,'' the professor told the reporter with finality, ''these books have made me all that I am.'' That was the kind of remark I couldn't ignore. I clipped out the list and kept it for the several months it took me to read all of the titles. Most books, of course, I barely understood. While reading Plato's *Republic*, for instance, I needed to keep looking at the book jacket comments to remind myself what the text was about. Nevertheless, with the special patience and superstition of a scholarship boy, I looked at every word of the text. And by the time I reached the last word, relieved, I convinced myself that I had read *The Republic*. In a ceremony of great pride, I solemnly crossed Plato off my list.

I I I

The scholarship boy pleases most when he is young — the working-class 51 child struggling for academic success. To his teachers, he offers great satisfaction; his success is their proudest achievement. Many other persons offer to help him. A businessman learns the boy's story and promises to underwrite part of the cost of his college education. A woman leaves him her entire library of several hundred books when she moves. His progress is featured in a newspaper article. Many people seem happy for him. They marvel. "How did you manage so fast?" From all sides, there is lavish praise and encouragement.

In his grammar school classroom, however, the boy already makes students around him uneasy. They scorn his desire to succeed. They scorn him for constantly wanting the teacher's attention and praise. "Kiss Ass," they call him when his hand swings up in response to every question he hears. Later, when he makes it to college, no one will mock him aloud. But he detects annoyance on the faces of some students and even some teachers who watch him. It puzzles him often. In college, then in graduate school, he behaves much as he always has. If anything is different about him it is that he dares to anticipate the successful conclusion of his studies. At last he feels that he belongs in the classroom, and this is exactly the source of the dissatisfaction he causes. To many persons around him, he appears too much the academic. There may be some things about him that recall his beginnings — his shabby clothes; his persistent poverty; or his dark skin (in those cases when it symbolizes his parents' disadvantaged condition) — but they only make clear how far he has moved from his past. He has used education to remake himself.

It bothers his fellow academics to face this. They will not say why exactly. (They sneer.) But their expectations become obvious when they are disappointed. They expect — they want — a student less changed by his schooling. If the scholarship boy, from a past so distant from the classroom, could remain in some basic way unchanged, he would be able to prove that it is possible for anyone to become educated without basically changing from the person one was.

Here is no fabulous hero, no idealized scholar-worker. The scholarship boy does not straddle, cannot reconcile, the two great opposing cultures of his life. His success is unromantic and plain. He sits in the classroom and offers those sitting beside him no calming reassurance about their own lives. He sits in the seminar room — a man with brown skin, the son of working-class Mexican immigrant parents. (Addressing the professor at the head of the table, his voice catches with nervousness.) There is no trace of his parents' accent in his speech. Instead he approximates the accents of teachers and classmates. Coming from *him* those sounds seem suddenly odd. Odd too is the effect produced when *he* uses academic jargon — bubbles at the tip of his tongue: "*Topos* . . . negative capability . . . vegetation imagery in Shakespearean comedy." He lifts an opinion from Coleridge, takes something else from Frye or Empson or Leavis. He even repeats exactly his professor's earlier comment. All his ideas are clearly borrowed. He seems to have no thought of his own. He chatters while his listeners smile — their look one of disdain.

When he is older and thus when so little of the person he was survives, 55
the scholarship boy makes only too apparent his profound lack of *self*-confidence. This is the conventional assessment that even Richard Hoggart repeats:

> [The scholarship boy] tends to over-stress the importance of
> examinations, of the piling-up of knowledge and of received
> opinions. He discovers a technique of apparent learning, of
> the acquiring of facts rather than of the handling and use of
> facts. He learns how to receive a purely literate education, one
> using only a small part of the personality and challenging only
> a limited area of his being. He begins to see life as a ladder, as
> a permanent examination with some praise and some further
> exhortation at each stage. He becomes an expert imbiber and
> doler-out; his competence will vary, but will rarely be accom-
> panied by genuine enthusiasms. He rarely feels the reality of
> knowledge, of other men's thoughts and imaginings, on his
> own pulses. . . . He has something of the blinkered pony
> about him. . . .

But this is criticism more accurate than fair. The scholarship boy is a very
bad student. He is the great mimic; a collector of thoughts, not a thinker; the
very last person in class who ever feels obliged to have an opinion of his
own. In large part, however, the reason he is such a bad student is because
he realizes more often and more acutely than most other students — than
Hoggart himself — that education requires radical self-reformation. As a
very young boy, regarding his parents, as he struggles with an early homework assignment, he knows this too well. That is why he lacks self-assur-
ance. He does not forget that the classroom is responsible for remaking him.
He relies on his teacher, depends on all that he hears in the classroom and
reads in his books. He becomes in every obvious way the worst student, a
dummy mouthing the opinions of others. But he would not be so bad — nor
would he become so successful, a *scholarship* boy — if he did not accurately
perceive that the best synonym for primary "education" is "imitation."

Those who would take seriously the boy's success — and his failure — 56
would be forced to realize how great is the change any academic undergoes,
how far one must move from one's past. It is easiest to ignore such considerations. So little is said about the scholarship boy in pages and pages of educational literature. Nothing is said of the silence that comes to separate the
boy from his parents. Instead, one hears proposals for increasing the self-es-
teem of students and encouraging early intellectual independence. Paragraphs glitter with a constellation of terms like *creativity* and *originality*. (Ignored altogether is the function of imitation in a student's life.) Radical
educationalists meanwhile complain that ghetto schools "oppress" stu-

dents by trying to mold them, stifling native characteristics. The truer critique would be just the reverse: not that schools change ghetto students too much, but that while they might promote the occasional scholarship student, they change most students barely at all.

From the story of the scholarship boy there is no specific pedagogy to glean. There is, however, a much larger lesson. His story makes clear that education is a long, unglamorous, even demeaning process — *a nurturing never natural to the person one was before one entered a classroom.* At once different from most other students, the scholarship boy is also the archetypal "good student." He exaggerates the difficulty of being a student, but his exaggeration reveals a general predicament. Others are changed by their schooling as much as he. They too must re-form themselves. They must develop the skill of memory long before they become truly critical thinkers. And when they read Plato for the first several times, it will be with awe more than deep comprehension.

The impact of schooling on the scholarship boy is only more apparent to the boy himself and to others. Finally, although he may be laughable — a blinkered pony — the boy will not let his critics forget their own change. He ends up too much like them. When he speaks, they hear themselves echoed. In his pedantry, they trace their own. His ambitions are theirs. If his failure were singular, they might readily pity him. But he is more troubling than that. They would not scorn him if this were not so.

I V

Like me, Hoggart's imagined scholarship boy spends most of his years in the classroom afraid to long for his past. Only at the very end of his schooling does the boy-man become nostalgic. In this sudden change of heart, Richard Hoggart notes:

> He longs for the membership he lost, "he pines for some Nameless Eden where he never was." The nostalgia is the stronger and the more ambiguous because he is really "in quest of his own absconded self yet scared to find it." He both wants to go back and yet thinks he has gone beyond his class, feels himself weighted with knowledge of his own and their situation, which hereafter forbids him the simpler pleasures of his father and mother. . . .

According to Hoggart, the scholarship boy grows nostalgic because he remains the uncertain scholar, bright enough to have moved from his past, yet unable to feel easy, a part of a community of academics.

This analysis, however, only partially suggests what happened to me in my last year as a graduate student. When I traveled to London to write a dissertation on English Renaissance literature, I was finally confident of membership in a "community of scholars." But the pleasure that confidence gave me faded rapidly. After only two or three months in the reading room of the British Museum, it became clear that I had joined a lonely community. Around me each day were dour faces eclipsed by large piles of books. There were the regulars, like the old couple who arrived every morning, each holding a loop of the shopping bag which contained all their notes. And there was the historian who chattered madly to herself. ("Oh dear! Oh! Now, what's this? What? Oh, my!") There were also the faces of young men and women worn by long study. And everywhere eyes turned away the moment our glance accidentally met. Some persons I sat beside day after day, yet we passed silently at the end of the day, strangers. Still, we were united by a common respect for the written word and for scholarship. We did form a union, though one in which we remained distant from one another.

More profound and unsettling was the bond I recognized with those 61 writers whose books I consulted. Whenever I opened a text that hadn't been used for years, I realized that my special interests and skills united me to a mere handful of academics. We formed an exclusive — eccentric! — society, separated from others who would never care or be able to share our concerns. (The pages I turned were stiff like layers of dead skin.) I began to wonder: Who, beside my dissertation director and a few faculty members, would ever read what I wrote? And: Was my dissertation much more than an act of social withdrawal? These questions went unanswered in the silence of the Museum reading room. They remained to trouble me after I'd leave the library each afternoon and feel myself shy — unsteady, speaking simple sentences at the grocer's or the butcher's on my way back to my bed-sitter.

Meanwhile my file cards accumulated. A professional, I knew exactly 62 how to search a book for pertinent information. I could quickly assess and summarize the usability of the many books I consulted. But whenever I started to write, I knew too much (and not enough) to be able to write anything but sentences that were overly cautious, timid, strained brittle under the heavy weight of footnotes and qualifications. I seemed unable to dare a passionate statement. I felt drawn by professionalism to the edge of sterility, capable of no more than pedantic, lifeless, unassailable prose.

Then nostalgia began. 63

After years spent unwilling to admit its attractions, I gestured nostalgi- 64 cally toward the past. I yearned for that time when I had not been so alone. I became impatient with books. I wanted experience more immediate. I feared the library's silence. I silently scorned the gray, timid faces around me. I grew to hate the growing pages of my dissertation on genre and Renaissance literature. (In my mind I heard relatives laughing as they tried to make sense of its title.) I wanted something — I couldn't say exactly what. I told myself that I wanted a more passionate life. And a life less thoughtful. And above all, I wanted to be less alone. One day I heard some Spanish academics whispering back and forth to each other, and their sounds seemed ghostly voices recalling my life. Yearning became preoccupation then. Boyhood memories beckoned, flooded my mind. (Laughing intimate voices. Bounding up the front steps of the porch. A sudden embrace inside the door.)

For weeks after, I turned to books by educational experts. I needed to learn how far I had moved from my past — to determine how fast I would be able to recover something of it once again. But I found little. Only a chapter in a book by Richard Hoggart. . . . I left the reading room and the circle of faces.

I came home. After the year in England, I spent three summer months living with my mother and father, relieved by how easy it was to be home. It no longer seemed very important to me that we had little to say. I felt easy sitting and eating and walking with them. I watched them, nevertheless, looking for evidence of those elastic, sturdy strands that bind generations in a web of inheritance. I thought as I watched my mother one night: Of course a friend had been right when she told me that I gestured and laughed just like my mother. Another time I saw for myself: My father's eyes were much like my own, constantly watchful.

But after the early relief, this return, came suspicion, nagging until I realized that I had not neatly sidestepped the impact of schooling. My desire to do so was precisely the measure of how much I remained an academic. *Negatively* (for that is how this idea first occurred to me): My need to think so much and so abstractly about my parents and our relationship was in itself an indication of my long education. My father and mother did not pass their time thinking about the cultural meanings of their experience. It was I who described their daily lives with airy ideas. And yet, *positively*: The ability to consider experience so abstractly allowed me to shape into desire what would otherwise have remained indefinite, meaningless longing in the British Museum. If, because of my schooling, I had grown culturally separated from my parents, my education finally had given me ways of speaking and caring about that fact.

My best teachers in college and graduate school, years before, had tried to prepare me for this conclusion, I think, when they discussed texts of aristocratic pastoral literature. Faithfully, I wrote down all that they said. I memorized it: ''The praise of the unlettered by the highly educated is one of the primary themes of 'elitist' literature.'' But, ''the importance of the praise given the unsolitary, richly passionate and spontaneous life is that it simultaneously reflects the value of a reflective life.'' I heard it all. But there was no way for any of it to mean very much to me. I was a scholarship boy at the time, busily laddering my way up the rungs of education. To pass an examination, I copied down exactly what my teachers told me. It would require many more years of schooling (an inevitable miseducation) in which I came to trust the silence of reading and the habit of abstracting from immediate experience — moving away from a life of closeness and immediacy I remembered with my parents, growing older — before I turned unafraid to desire the past, and thereby achieved what had eluded me for so long — the end of education.

QUESTIONS ON MEANING

1. In paragraph 7 Rodriguez asserts his early awareness that *"schooling was changing me and separating me from the life I enjoyed before becoming a student."* How does he make this awareness central to his overall argument? Trace his development of this insight throughout his essay.
2. Paragraphs 41–43 describe Rodriguez's resistance to reading in grade school. Did his resistance follow from his parents' reading habits (paragraphs 39 and 40)? What enabled Rodriguez to overcome his resistance?
3. Rodriguez outlines his early reading in paragraphs 46–50. What did he see in books? What sorts of naiveté or insufficiency does Rodriguez criticize in his reading? Do you recognize similar shortcomings in your own early reading experiences?
4. Rodriguez devotes several paragraphs (51–58) to the scholarship student who uses his education "to remake himself." What obstacles does such a student face? How did Rodriguez overcome some of those obstacles?

QUESTIONS ON STRATEGY

1. Richard Rodriguez asserts that students like himself do "not straddle, cannot reconcile, the two great opposing cultures" of their lives (paragraph 54). How does the sequence of paragraphs 59–65 develop this point?
2. How was the British Museum a catalyst for Rodriguez's final insight in the essay? What is the irony in Rodriguez's conclusion? How do his final paragraphs illuminate his title?
3. Rodriguez makes more use of the parenthesis than any other essayist in this collection. What is the effect, in the essay as a whole, of this strategy? Cite examples when you answer. Are there cases where you would prefer that parentheses not be used? Are there other means for accomplishing the same ends?

EXPLORATIONS

1. Rodriguez's ideas on bilingual education and affirmative action are controversial. Look at his book *Hunger of Memory* and at some of the criticism of it. Do you agree with his views?

WRITING TOPICS

1. Write an essay about the role of your own education in separating you from your childhood. Try to define as specifically as possible how your schooling led you out of your family identity. Have you made a return to that identity, as Rodriguez did?

BOOK AVAILABLE IN PAPERBACK

Hunger of Memory. New York: Bantam. *Nonfiction: Personal history.*

ANNIE
DILLARD

ANNIE DILLARD (b. 1945) grew up in Pittsburgh and attended Hollins College in Virginia, where she completed her B.A. and M.A. She has taught at Western Washington University and at Wesleyan University in Connecticut. But she has worked mostly as a writer. A book of poems, Tickets for a Prayer Wheel, appeared in 1974. In the same year she published Pilgrim at Tinker Creek, her first prose — an example of the ecstatic natural observation that makes up her best work. The book won a Pulitzer Prize. In 1977 she published Holy the Firm and early in 1982 a work of literary theory called Living by Fiction. Later in the same year she collected her essays into Teaching a Stone to Talk.

Book reviewers often deride miscellaneous collections of work from periodicals, as if a book that preserves magazine pieces must be ephemeral. Annie Dillard writes a note at the front of Teaching a Stone to Talk, to make sure that no one misunderstands her own attitude toward this work: "this is not a collection of occasional pieces, such as a writer brings out to supplement his real work; instead, this is my real work. . . ."

The ellipsis at the quotation's end omits Annie Dillard's last words: "such as it is." Such as it is, Annie Dillard's real work reaches a level of imagination we usually

469

associate not with the essay but with poetry and fiction. Her mind combines qualities not often found together: an almost insatiable curiosity about details of the natural world, science, and thought together with a spiritual appetite, a visionary's or mystic's seeking through religious study and meditation. Combining these qualities, she becomes a major writer of American prose.

In an interview Annie Dillard talks about her difficulty in writing. Every time she tries, she says, "There's just some prohibitive and fatal flaw in the structure. And that's where most people quit. You just have to hang on." Handing essays back to a class of students not long ago, she said, "I hand back these miserable things — that's O.K. I knew they'd be miserable. . . . The assignment was to write a brilliant essay. The assignment is always to write a brilliant essay." It is the assignment she gave herself, and fulfilled, when she wrote "Total Eclipse," from Teaching a Stone to Talk. Dillard's curiosity, observation, narrative, description, and vision conclude this volume with a model of the modern essay.

Total Eclipse

It had been like dying, that sliding down the mountain pass. It had been like the death of someone, irrational, that sliding down the mountain pass and into the region of dread. It was like slipping into fever, or falling down that hole in sleep from which you wake yourself whimpering. We had crossed the mountains that day, and now we were in a strange place — a hotel in central Washington, in a town near Yakima. The eclipse we had traveled here to see would occur early in the next morning.

I lay in bed. My husband, Gary, was reading beside me. I lay in bed and looked at the painting on the hotel room wall. It was a print of a detailed and lifelike painting of a smiling clown's head, made out of vegetables. It was a painting of the sort which you do not intend to look at, and which, alas, you never forget. Some tasteless fate presses it upon you; it becomes part of the complex interior junk you carry with you wherever you go. Two years have passed since the total eclipse of which I write. During those years I have forgotten, I assume, a great many things I wanted to remember — but I have not forgotten that clown painting or its lunatic setting in the old hotel.

The clown was bald. Actually, he wore a clown's tight rubber wig, painted white; this stretched over the top of his skull, which was a cabbage. His hair was bunches of baby carrots. Inset in his white clown makeup, and in his cabbage skull, were his small and laughing human eyes. The clown's glance was like the glance of Rembrandt in some of the self-portraits: lively, knowing, deep, and loving. The crinkled shadows around his eyes were string beans. His eyebrows were parsley. Each of his ears was a broad bean. His thin, joyful lips were red chili peppers; between his lips were wet rows of human teeth and a suggestion of a real tongue. The clown print was framed in gilt and glassed.

To put ourselves in the path of the total eclipse, that day we had driven 4 five hours inland from the Washington coast, where we lived. When we tried to cross the Cascades range, an avalanche had blocked the pass.

A slope's worth of snow blocked the road; traffic backed up. Had the av- 5 alanche buried any cars that morning? We could not learn. This highway was the only winter road over the mountains. We waited as highway crews bulldozed a passage through the avalanche. With two-by-fours and walls of plywood, they erected a one-way, roofed tunnel through the avalanche. We drove through the avalanche tunnel, crossed the pass, and descended several thousand feet into central Washington and the broad Yakima valley, about which we knew only that it was orchard country. As we lost altitude, the snows disappeared; our ears popped; the trees changed, and in the trees were strange birds. I watched the landscape innocently, like a fool, like a diver in the rapture of the deep who plays on the bottom while his air runs out.

The hotel lobby was a dark, derelict room, narrow as a corridor, and 6 seemingly without air. We waited on a couch while the manager vanished upstairs to do something unknown to our room. Beside us on an overstuffed chair, absolutely motionless, was a platinum-blond woman in her forties wearing a black silk dress and a strand of pearls. Her long legs were crossed; she supported her head on her fist. At the dim far end of the room, their backs toward us, sat six bald old men in their shirtsleeves, around a loud television. Two of them seemed asleep. They were drunks. "Number six!" cried the man on television, "Number six!"

On the broad lobby desk, lighted and bubbling, was a ten-gallon aquar- 7 ium containing one large fish; the fish tilted up and down in its water. Against the long opposite wall sang a live canary in its cage. Beneath the cage, among spilled millet seeds on the carpet, were a decorated child's sand bucket and matching sand shovel.

Now the alarm was set for six. I lay awake remembering an article I had 8 read downstairs in the lobby, in an engineering magazine. The article was about gold mining.

In South Africa, in India, and in South Dakota, the gold mines extend so 9 deeply into the earth's crust that they are hot. The rock walls burn the miners' hands. The companies have to air-condition the mines; if the air conditioners break, the miners die. The elevators in the mine shafts run very slowly, down, and up, so the miners' ears will not pop in their skulls. When the miners return to the surface, their faces are deathly pale.

Early the next morning we checked out. It was February 26, 1979, a Monday morning. We would drive out of town, find a hilltop, watch the eclipse, and then drive back over the mountains and home to the coast. How familiar things are here; how adept we are; how smoothly and professionally we check out! I had forgotten the clown's smiling head and the hotel lobby as if they had never existed. Gary put the car in gear and off we went, as off we have gone to a hundred other adventures.

It was dawn when we found a highway out of town and drove into the unfamiliar countryside. By the growing light we could see a band of cirrostratus clouds in the sky. Later the rising sun would clear these clouds before the eclipse began. We drove at random until we came to a range of unfenced hills. We pulled off the highway, bundled up, and climbed one of these hills.

I I

The hill was five hundred feet high. Long winter-killed grass covered it, as high as our knees. We climbed and rested, sweating in the cold; we passed clumps of bundled people on the hillside who were setting up telescopes and fiddling with cameras. The top of the hill stuck up in the middle of the sky. We tightened our scarves and looked around.

East of us rose another hill like ours. Between the hills, far below, was the highway which threaded south into the valley. This was the Yakima valley; I had never seen it before. It is justly famous for its beauty, like every planted valley. It extended south into the horizon, a distant dream of a valley, a Shangri-la. All its hundreds of low, golden slopes bore orchards. Among the orchards were towns, and roads, and plowed and fallow fields. Through the valley wandered a thin, shining river; from the river extended fine, frozen irrigation ditches. Distance blurred and blued the sight, so that the whole valley looked like a thickness or sediment at the bottom of the sky. Directly behind us was more sky, and empty lowlands blued by distance, and Mount Adams. Mount Adams was an enormous, snow-covered volcanic cone rising flat, like so much scenery.

Now the sun was up. We could not see it; but the sky behind the band of clouds was yellow, and, far down the valley, some hillside orchards had lighted up. More people were parking near the highway and climbing the hills. It was the West. All of us rugged individualists were wearing knit caps and blue nylon parkas. People were climbing the nearby hills and setting up shop in clumps among the dead grasses. It looked as though we had all gathered on hilltops to pray for the world on its last day. It looked as though we had all crawled out of spaceships and were preparing to assault the valley below. It looked as though we were scattered on hilltops at dawn to sacrifice virgins, make rain, set stone stelae in a ring. There was no place out of the wind. The straw grasses banged our legs.

Up in the sky where we stood the air was lusterless yellow. To the west 15 the sky was blue. Now the sun cleared the clouds. We cast rough shadows on the blowing grass; freezing, we waved our arms. Near the sun, the sky was bright and colorless. There was nothing to see.

It began with no ado. It was odd that such a well-advertised public event 16 should have no starting gun, no overture, no introductory speaker. I should have known right then that I was out of my depth. Without pause or preamble, silent as orbits, a piece of the sun went away. We looked at it through welders' goggles. A piece of the sun was missing; in its place we saw empty sky.

I had seen a partial eclipse in 1970. A partial eclipse is very interesting. It 17 bears almost no relation to a total eclipse. Seeing a partial eclipse bears the same relation to seeing a total eclipse as kissing a man does to marrying him, or as flying in an airplane does to falling out of an airplane. Although the one experience precedes the other, it in no way prepares you for it. During a partial eclipse the sky does not darken — not even when 94 percent of the sun is hidden. Nor does the sun, seen colorless through protective devices, seem terribly strange. We have all seen a sliver of light in the sky; we have all seen the crescent moon by day. However, during a partial eclipse the air does indeed get cold, precisely as if someone were standing between you and the fire. And blackbirds do fly back to their roosts. I had seen a partial eclipse before, and here was another.

What you see in an eclipse is entirely different from what you know. It is 18 especially different for those of us whose grasp of astronomy is so frail that, given a flashlight, a grapefruit, two oranges, and fifteen years, we still could not figure out which way to set the clocks for Daylight Saving Time. Usually it is a bit of a trick to keep your knowledge from blinding you. But during an eclipse it is easy. What you see is much more convincing than any wild-eyed theory you may know.

You may read that the moon has something to do with eclipses. I have 19 never seen the moon yet. You do not see the moon. So near the sun, it is as completely invisible as the stars are by day. What you see before your eyes is the sun going through phases. It gets narrower and narrower, as the waning moon does, and, like the ordinary moon, it travels alone in the simple sky. The sky is of course background. It does not appear to eat the sun; it is far behind the sun. The sun simply shaves away; gradually, you see less sun and more sky.

The sky's blue was deepening, but there was no darkness. The sun was a 20 wide crescent, like a segment of tangerine. The wind freshened and blew steadily over the hill. The eastern hill across the highway grew dusky and sharp. The towns and orchards in the valley to the south were dissolving into the blue light. Only the thin river held a trickle of sun.

Now the sky to the west deepened to indigo, a color never seen. A dark sky usually loses color. This was a saturated, deep indigo, up in the air. Stuck up into that unworldly sky was the cone of Mount Adams, and the alpenglow was upon it. The alpenglow is that red light of sunset which holds out on snowy mountaintops long after the valleys and tablelands are dimmed. "Look at Mount Adams," I said, and that was the last sane moment I remember.

I turned back to the sun. It was going. The sun was going, and the world was wrong. The grasses were wrong; they were platinum. Their every detail of stem, head, and blade shone lightless and artificially distinct as an art photographer's platinum print. This color has never been seen on earth. The hues were metallic; their finish was matte. The hillside was a nineteenth-century tinted photograph from which the tints had faded. All the people you see in the photograph, distinct and detailed as their faces look, are now dead. The sky was navy blue. My hands were silver. All the distant hills' grasses were finespun metal which the wind laid down. I was watching a faded color print of a movie filmed in the Middle Ages; I was standing in it, by some mistake. I was standing in a movie of hillside grasses filmed in the Middle Ages. I missed my own century, the people I knew, and the real light of day.

I looked at Gary. He was in the film. Everything was lost. He was a platinum print, a dead artist's version of life. I saw on his skull the darkness of night mixed with the colors of day. My mind was going out; my eyes were receding the way galaxies recede to the rim of space. Gary was light-years away, gesturing inside a circle of darkness, down the wrong end of a telescope. He smiled as if he saw me; the stringy crinkles around his eyes moved. The sight of him, familiar and wrong, was something I was remembering from centuries hence, from the other side of death: yes, *that* is the way he used to look, when we were living. When it was our generation's turn to be alive. I could not hear him; the wind was too loud. Behind him the sun was going. We had all started down a chute of time. At first it was pleasant; now there was no stopping it. Gary was chuting away across space, moving and talking and catching my eye, chuting down the long corridor of separation. The skin on his face moved like thin bronze plating that would peel.

The grass at our feet was wild barley. It was the wild einkorn wheat which grew on the hilly flanks of the Zagros Mountains, above the Euphrates valley, above the valley of the river we called *River*. We harvested the grass with stone sickles, I remember. We found the grasses on the hillsides;

we built our shelter beside them and cut them down. That is how he used to look then, that one, moving and living and catching my eye, with the sky so dark behind him, and the wind blowing. God save our life.

From all the hills came screams. A piece of sky beside the crescent sun 25 was detaching. It was a loosened circle of evening sky, suddenly lighted from the back. It was an abrupt black body out of nowhere; it was a flat disk; it was almost over the sun. That is when there were screams. At once this disk of sky slid over the sun like a lid. The sky snapped over the sun like a lens cover. The hatch in the brain slammed. Abruptly it was dark night, on the land and in the sky. In the night sky was a tiny ring of light. The hole where the sun belongs is very small. A thin ring of light marked its place. There was no sound. The eyes dried, the arteries drained, the lungs hushed. There was no world. We were the world's dead people rotating and orbiting around and around, embedded in the planet's crust, while the earth rolled down. Our minds were light-years distant, forgetful of almost everything. Only an extraordinary act of will could recall to us our former, living selves and our contexts in matter and time. We had, it seems, loved the planet and loved our lives, but could no longer remember the way of them. We got the light wrong. In the sky was something that should not be there. In the black sky was a ring of light. It was a thin ring, an old, thin silver wedding band, an old, worn ring. It was an old wedding band in the sky, or a morsel of bone. There were stars. It was all over.

I I I

It is now that the temptation is strongest to leave these regions. We have 26 seen enough; let's go. Why burn our hands any more than we have to? But two years have passed; the price of gold has risen. I return to the same buried alluvial beds and pick through the strata again.

I saw, early in the morning, the sun diminish against a backdrop of sky. I 27 saw a circular piece of that sky appear, suddenly detached, blackened, and backlighted; from nowhere it came and overlapped the sun. It did not look like the moon. It was enormous and black. If I had not read that it was the moon, I could have seen the sight a hundred times and never thought of the moon once. (If, however, I had not read that it was the moon — if, like most of the world's people throughout time, I had simply glanced up and seen this thing — then I doubtless would not have speculated much, but would have, like Emperor Louis of Bavaria in 840, simply died of fright on the spot.) It did not look like a dragon, although it looked more like a dragon than the moon. It looked like a lens cover, or the lid of a pot. It materialized out of thin air — black, and flat, and sliding, outlined in flame.

Seeing this black body was like seeing a mushroom cloud. The heart screeched. The meaning of the sight overwhelmed its fascination. It obliterated meaning itself. If you were to glance out one day and see a row of mushroom clouds rising on the horizon, you would know at once that what you were seeing, remarkable as it was, was intrinsically not worth remarking. No use running to tell anyone. Significant as it was, it did not matter a whit. For what is significance? It is significance for people. No people, no significance. This is all I have to tell you.

In the deeps are the violence and terror of which psychology has warned us. But if you ride these monsters deeper down, if you drop with them farther over the world's rim, you find what our sciences cannot locate or name, the substrate, the ocean or matrix or ether which buoys the rest, which gives goodness its power for good, and evil its power for evil, the unified field: our complex and inexplicable caring for each other, and for our life together here. This is given. It is not learned.

The world which lay under darkness and stillness following the closing of the lid was not the world we know. The event was over. Its devastation lay around about us. The clamoring mind and heart stilled, almost indifferent, certainly disembodied, frail, and exhausted. The hills were hushed, obliterated. Up in the sky, like a crater from some distant cataclysm, was a hollow ring.

You have seen photographs of the sun taken during a total eclipse. The corona fills the print. All of those photographs were taken through telescopes. The lenses of telescopes and cameras can no more cover the breadth and scale of the visual array than language can cover the breadth and simultaneity of internal experience. Lenses enlarge the sight, omit its context, and make of it a pretty and sensible picture, like something on a Christmas card. I assure you, if you send any shepherds a Christmas card on which is printed a three-by-three photograph of the angel of the Lord, the glory of the Lord, and a multitude of the heavenly host, they will not be sore afraid. More fearsome things can come in envelopes. More moving photographs than those of the sun's corona can appear in magazines. But I pray you will never see anything more awful in the sky.

You see the wide world swaddled in darkness; you see a vast breadth of hilly land, and an enormous, distant, blackened valley; you see towns' lights, a river's path, and blurred portions of your hat and scarf; you see your husband's face looking like an early black-and-white film; and you see a sprawl of black sky and blue sky together, with unfamiliar stars in it, some barely visible bands of cloud, and over there, a small white ring. The ring is as small as one goose in a flock of migrating geese — if you happen to notice a flock of migrating geese. It is one 360th part of the visible sky. The sun we see is less than half the diameter of a dime held at arm's length.

The Crab Nebula, in the constellation Taurus, looks, through binoculars, 33 like a smoke ring. It is a star in the process of exploding. Light from its explosion first reached the earth in 1054; it was a supernova then, and so bright it shone in the daytime. Now it is not so bright, but it is still exploding. It expands at the rate of seventy million miles a day. It is interesting to look through binoculars at something expanding seventy million miles a day. It does not budge. Its apparent size does not increase. Photographs of the Crab Nebula taken fifteen years ago seem identical to photographs of it taken yesterday. Some lichens are similar. Botanists have measured some ordinary lichens twice, at fifty-year intervals, without detecting any growth at all. And yet their cells divide; they live.

The small ring of light was like these things — like a ridiculous lichen up 34 in the sky, like a perfectly still explosion 4,200 light-years away: it was interesting, and lovely, and in witless motion, and it had nothing to do with anything.

It had nothing to do with anything. The sun was too small, and too cold, 35 and too far away, to keep the world alive. The white ring was not enough. It was feeble and worthless. It was as useless as a memory; it was as off kilter and hollow and wretched as a memory.

When you try your hardest to recall someone's face, or the look of a 36 place, you see in your mind's eye some vague and terrible sight such as this. It is dark; it is insubstantial; it is all wrong.

The white ring and the saturated darkness made the earth and the sky 37 look as they must look in the memories of the careless dead. What I saw, what I seemed to be standing in, was all the wrecked light that the memories of the dead could shed upon the living world. We had all died in our boots on the hilltops of Yakima, and were alone in eternity. Empty space stoppered our eyes and mouths; we cared for nothing. We remembered our living days wrong. With great effort we had remembered some sort of circular light in the sky — but only the outline. Oh, and then the orchard trees withered, the ground froze, the glaciers slid down the valleys and overlapped the towns. If there had ever been people on earth, nobody knew it. The dead had forgotten those they had loved. The dead were parted one from the other and could no longer remember the faces and lands they had loved in the light. They seemed to stand on darkened hilltops, looking down.

I V

We teach our children one thing only, as we were taught: to wake up. 38 We teach our children to look alive there, to join by words and activities the life of human culture on the planet's crust. As adults we are almost all adept at waking up. We have so mastered the transition we have forgotten we ever learned it. Yet it is a transition we make a hundred times a day, as, like so many will-less dolphins, we plunge and surface, lapse and emerge. We live half our waking lives and all of our sleeping lives in some private, useless, and insensible waters we never mention or recall. Useless, I say. Valueless, I might add — until someone hauls their wealth up to the surface and into the wide-awake city, in a form that people can use.

I do not know how we got to the restaurant. Like Roethke, "I take my waking slow." Gradually I seemed more or less alive, and already forgetful. It was now almost nine in the morning. It was the day of a solar eclipse in central Washington, and a fine adventure for everyone. The sky was clear; there was a fresh breeze out of the north.

The restaurant was a roadside place with tables and booths. The other eclipse-watchers were there. From our booth we could see their cars' California license plates, their University of Washington parking stickers. Inside the restaurant we were all eating eggs or waffles; people were fairly shouting and exchanging enthusiasms, like fans after a World Series game. Did you see . . . ? Did you see . . . ? Then somebody said something which knocked me for a loop.

A college student, a boy in a blue parka who carried a Hasselblad, said to us, "Did you see that little white ring? It looked like a Life Saver. It looked like a Life Saver up in the sky."

And so it did. The boy spoke well. He was a walking alarm clock. I myself had at that time no access to such a word. He could write a sentence, and I could not. I grabbed that Life Saver and rode it to the surface. And I had to laugh. I had been dumbstruck on the Euphrates River, I had been dead and gone and grieving, all over the sight of something which, if you could claw your way up to that level, you would grant looked very much like a Life Saver. It was good to be back among people so clever; it was good to have all the world's words at the mind's disposal, so the mind could begin its task. All those things for which we have no words are lost. The mind — the culture — has two little tools, grammar and lexicon: a decorated sand bucket and a matching shovel. With these we bluster about the continents and do all the world's work. With these we try to save our very lives.

There are a few more things to tell from this level, the level of the restaurant. One is the old joke about breakfast. "It can never be satisfied, the mind, never." Wallace Stevens wrote that, and in the long run he was right. The mind wants to live forever, or to learn a very good reason why not. The mind wants the world to return its love, or its awareness; the mind wants to know all the world, and all eternity, and God. The mind's sidekick, however, will settle for two eggs over easy.

The dear, stupid body is as easily satisfied as a spaniel. And, incredibly, the simple spaniel can lure the brawling mind to its dish. It is everlastingly funny that the proud, metaphysically ambitious, clamoring mind will hush if you give it an egg.

Further: while the mind reels in deep space, while the mind grieves or 45 fears or exults, the workaday senses, in ignorance or idiocy, like so many computer terminals printing out market prices while the world blows up, still transcribe their little data and transmit them to the warehouse in the skull. Later, under the tranquilizing influence of fried eggs, the mind can sort through this data. The restaurant was a halfway house, a decompression chamber. There I remembered a few things more.

The deepest, and most terrifying, was this: I have said that I heard 46 screams. (I have since read that screaming, with hysteria, is a common reaction even to expected total eclipses.) People on all the hillsides, including, I think, myself, screamed when the black body of the moon detached from the sky and rolled over the sun. But something else was happening at that same instant, and it was this, I believe, which made us scream.

The second before the sun went out we saw a wall of dark shadow come 47 speeding at us. We no sooner saw it than it was upon us, like thunder. It roared up the valley. It slammed our hill and knocked us out. It was the monstrous swift shadow cone of the moon. I have since read that this wave of shadow moves 1,800 miles an hour. Language can give no sense of this sort of speed — 1,800 miles an hour. It was 195 miles wide. No end was in sight — you saw only the edge. It rolled at you across the land at 1,800 miles an hour, hauling darkness like plague behind it. Seeing it, and knowing it was coming straight for you, was like feeling a slug of anesthetic shoot up your arm. If you think very fast, you may have time to think, "Soon it will hit my brain." You can feel the deadness race up your arm; you can feel the appalling, inhuman speed of your own blood. We saw the wall of shadow coming, and screamed before it hit.

This was the universe about which we have read so much and never be- 48 fore felt: the universe as a clockwork of loose spheres flung at stupefying, unauthorized speeds. How could anything moving so fast not crash, not veer from its orbit amok like a car out of control on a turn?

Less than two minutes later, when the sun emerged, the trailing edge of 49 the shadow cone sped away. It coursed down our hill and raced eastward over the plain, faster than the eye could believe; it swept over the plain and dropped over the planet's rim in a twinkling. It had clobbered us, and now it roared away. We blinked in the light. It was as though an enormous, loping god in the sky had reached down and slapped the earth's face.

Something else, something more ordinary, came back to me along about 50 the third cup of coffee. During the moments of totality, it was so dark that drivers on the highway below turned on their cars' headlights. We could see the highway's route as a strand of lights. It was bumper-to-bumper down there. It was eight-fifteen in the morning, Monday morning, and people were driving into Yakima to work. That it was as dark as night, and eerie as hell, an hour after dawn, apparently meant that in order to *see* to drive to work, people had to use their headlights. Four or five cars pulled off the road. The rest, in a line at least five miles long, drove to town. The highway ran between hills; the people could not have seen any of the eclipsed sun at all. Yakima will have another total eclipse in 2086. Perhaps, in 2086, businesses will give their employees an hour off.

From the restaurant we drove back to the coast. The highway crossing the Cascades range was open. We drove over the mountain like old pros. We joined our places on the planet's thin crust; it held. For the time being, we were home free.

Early that morning at six, when we had checked out, the six bald men were sitting on folding chairs in the dim hotel lobby. The television was on. Most of them were awake. You might drown in your own spittle, God knows, at any time; you might wake up dead in a small hotel, a cabbage head watching TV while snows pile up in the passes, watching TV while the chili peppers smile and the moon passes over the sun and nothing changes and nothing is learned because you have lost your bucket and shovel and no longer care. What if you regain the surface and open your sack and find, instead of treasure, a beast which jumps at you? Or you may not come back at all. The winches may jam, the scaffolding buckle, the air conditioning collapse. You may glance up one day and see by your headlamp the canary keeled over in its cage. You may reach into a cranny for pearls and touch a moray eel. You yank on your rope; it is too late.

Apparently people share a sense of these hazards, for when the total eclipse ended, an odd thing happened.

When the sun appeared as a blinding bead on the ring's side, the eclipse was over. The black lens cover appeared again, backlighted, and slid away. At once the yellow light made the sky blue again; the black lid dissolved and vanished. The real world began there. I remember now: we all hurried away. We were born and bored at a stroke. We rushed down the hill. We found our car; we saw the other people streaming down the hillsides; we joined the highway traffic and drove away.

We never looked back. It was a general vamoose, and an odd one, for when we left the hill, the sun was still partially eclipsed — a sight rare enough, and one which, in itself, we would probably have driven five hours to see. But enough is enough. One turns at last even from glory itself with a sigh of relief. From the depths of mystery, and even from the heights of splendor, we bounce back and hurry for the latitudes of home.

QUESTIONS ON MEANING

1. What does Annie Dillard learn from the experience of watching a total eclipse? How does this knowledge affect the telling of the story? Find specific instances where the feelings resulting from the experience inform the way she narrates the experience.
2. In paragraph 38 Dillard distinguishes between our waking lives and our sleeping lives, where we live in some "private, useless, and insensible waters we never mention or recall." Why "useless"? Think of "Total Eclipse" as an example of wealth hauled "up to the surface and into the wide-awake city, in a form that people can use" (paragraph 38); how can people "use" Dillard's wealth?
3. In paragraph 14, what is the tone of this sentence: "All of us rugged individualists were wearing knit caps and blue nylon parkas"? What does this tone imply about those watching the eclipse? The paragraph continues with a series of associations; what is the point of these images?
4. What is Dillard talking about in paragraph 24? What notions about individual life arise from this paragraph?

QUESTIONS ON STRATEGY

1. Make sure that you understand the time scheme of this essay. To what time does each paragraph refer?
2. Dillard's essay is divided into four sections. What does each section contain, and why is it a unit?
3. Look carefully at the details in paragraph 9. What do these details have to do with the rest of the essay? Find traces of this paragraph throughout the essay.
4. Why does paragraph 50 belong where it does, rather than in its proper place in the narrative sequence?
5. The word *blind* is often a cliché: "Egad, Sir? Are you *blind?*" In paragraph 18, Annie Dillard writes, "Usually it is a bit of a trick to keep your knowledge from blinding you. But during an eclipse it is easy." What keeps the metaphor from being a cliché?

EXPLORATIONS

1. Read some other essays by Annie Dillard — "Heaven and Earth in Jest" and "Seeing" from *Pilgrim at Tinker Creek*, for example. Compare Dillard's work with Edward Abbey's (pages 225–241) or Wendell Berry's (pages 349–359).

WRITING TOPICS

1. In paragraph 2, Dillard refers to "the complex interior junk you carry with you wherever you go." Out of your own memories, find an example of your

own "complex interior junk." Describe it carefully, and speculate on why "you carry [it] with you wherever you go."

2. Remember a journey of your own, on which you traveled, observed something, and returned home. Using Annie Dillard's essay as a model, write about your own trip, avoiding the actual sequence of events, substituting instead an expressive organization.

BOOKS AVAILABLE IN PAPERBACK

Holy the Firm. New York: Harper & Row. *Essays.*

Living by Fiction. New York: Harper Colophon. *Nonfiction: Literary criticism.*

Pilgrim at Tinker Creek. New York: Bantam. *Nonfiction: Personal history.*

Teaching a Stone to Talk. New York: Harper & Row. *Essays.*

Rhetorical Index

Analogy

Argument and Persuasion

Cause and Effect

Comparison and Contrast

Definition

Narration

Process Analysis

To the Student

We regularly revise the books we publish in order to make them better. To do this well we need to know what instructors and students think of the previous edition. At some point your instructor will be asked to comment on *The Contemporary Essay*; now we would like to hear from you.

Please take a few minutes to complete this questionnaire and send it to Bedford Books of St. Martin's Press, 165 Marlborough Street, Boston, Massachusetts 02116. We promise to listen to what you have to say. Thanks.

School_____

School Location (city, state)_____

Course title_____

Instructor's name_____

Please rate the selections.

	DEFINITELY KEEP	KEEP	DROP	NOT ASSIGNED
Cowley, "The View from 80"	——	——	——	——
White, "The Ring of Time"	——	——	——	——
Galbraith, "The Technostructure"	——	——	——	——
Welty, "The Little Store"	——	——	——	——
Tuchman, "History as Mirror"	——	——	——	——
Thomas, "Medical Lessons from History"	——	——	——	——
Percy, "The Loss of the Creature"	——	——	——	——
Angell, "Sharing the Beat"	——	——	——	——
Mailer, "The Psychology of Astronauts"	——	——	——	——
Fussell, "Notes on Class"	——	——	——	——
Baldwin, "Notes of a Native Son"	——	——	——	——
Capote, "A Ride Through Spain"	——	——	——	——
Vidal, "The Twenty-Ninth Republican Convention"	——	——	——	——
Lurie, "Clothing as a Sign System"	——	——	——	——
Abbey, "The Most Beautiful Place on Earth"	——	——	——	——
Selzer, "Letter to a Young Surgeon"	——	——	——	——
Rich, "Women and Honor"	——	——	——	——
Bernstein, "Calculators"	——	——	——	——

	DEFINITELY KEEP	KEEP	DROP	NOT ASSIGN
Arlen, "The Cold Bright Charms of Immortality"	___	___	___	___
Wolfe, "The Right Stuff"	___	___	___	___
McPhee, "Oranges"	___	___	___	___
Updike, "Hub Fans Bid Kid Adieu"	___	___	___	___
Hoagland, "Women and Men"	___	___	___	___
Johnson, "Rape"	___	___	___	___
Berry, "The Making of a Marginal Farm"	___	___	___	___
Didion, "Some Dreamers of the Golden Dream"	___	___	___	___
Trillin, "The Best Restaurants in the World"	___	___	___	___
FitzGerald, "Power over the Past"	___	___	___	___
Kingston, "No Name Woman"	___	___	___	___
Gould, "Were Dinosaurs Dumb?"	___	___	___	___
Schell, "A Republic of Insects and Grass"	___	___	___	___
Walker, "In Search of Our Mothers' Gardens"	___	___	___	___
Rodriguez, "The Achievement of Desire"	___	___	___	___
Dillard, "Total Eclipse"	___	___	___	___

Any general comments or suggestions?_____

_____

_____

_____

_____

Name_____

Mailing Address_____

_____

Date_____